A DARKNESS AT SETHANON

RAYMOND E. FEIST was born and raised in southern California. He was educated at the University of California, San Diego, where he graduated with honours in Communication Arts. He is the author of nine bestselling and critically acclaimed series: *The Riftwar Saga*, *The Empire Trilogy* (with Janny Wurts), *Krondor's Sons*, *The Serpentwar Saga*, *The Riftwar Legacy*, *Legends of the Riftwar*, *Conclave of the Shadows*, *Darkwar Saga*, *Demonwar Saga* and *Chaoswar Saga*.

Peter Franklin ~~Jones~~ White ?
Covent garden Royal Ballett.
1950 - 1960s - 80s ?

BY THE SAME AUTHOR

RAYMOND E. FEIST

A Darkness at Sethanon

HARPER
Voyager

Harper*Voyager*
An imprint of HarperCollins*Publishers*
1 London Bridge Street
London SE1 9GF

www.harpervoyagerbooks.com

Previously published in paperback by Grafton Books 1987
Reprinted ten times
And by HarperCollins Science Fiction & Fantasy 1993
Reprinted ten times
And by *Voyager* 1997
Reprinted thirty-seven times
And by Harper*Voyager* 2006, 2009

First Published in Great Britian
By Grafton Books 1986

This paperback edition 2013
10

A catalogue record for this book is available from the British Library

ISBN: 978-0-00-750911-9

Set in Janson Text by Palimpsest Book Production Limited, Falkirk, Stirlingshire

Printed and bound by
CPI Group (UK) Ltd, Croydon, CR0 4YY

MIX
Paper from
responsible sources
FSC **FSC C007454**
www.fsc.org

This book is dedicated to my mother,
Barbara A. Feist,
who never doubted for a moment

Acknowledgements

As this book marks the end of *The Riftwar Saga*, the three-book cycle begun with *Magician* and continued through *Silverthorn*, I feel it necessary to again offer heartfelt thanks to those people who in one way or another contributed to whatever quality and success my books have achieved:

The original architects of Midkemia: April and Stephen Abrams; Steve Barrett; Anita and Jon Everson; Dave Guinasso; Conan LaMotte; Tim LaSelle; Ethan Munson; Bob Potter; Rich Spahl; Alan Springer; Lori and Jeff Velten.

Those many others who joined us on Fridays over the years, adding their own touches to the marvellous thing which is the world of Midkemia.

My friends at Grafton Books, past and current.

Harold Matson, my agent, who gave me my first break.

Abner Stein, my agent in Great Britain.

And Janny Wurts, a gifted writer and artist, for showing me how to get more out of my characters when I thought I already knew all there was to know about them.

Each has contributed in his or her own unique way to the three novels that make up *The Riftwar Saga*. The books would have been much poorer by the absence of even one of them.

RAYMOND E. FEIST
San Diego, California

A DARKNESS AT SETHANON

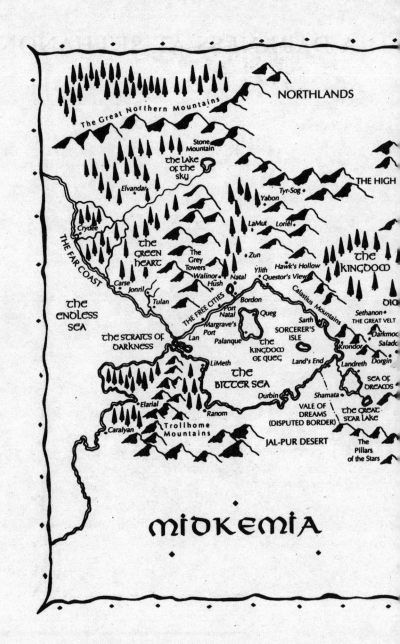

MIDKEMIA

Our Story So Far . . .

*A*FTER THE *RIFTWAR* AGAINST THE *TSURANI, ALIEN INVADERS FROM*
the world of Kelewan, peace reigned in the Kingdom of the Isles for
nearly a year. King Lyam and his brothers, Prince Arutha and Duke Martin,
toured the eastern cities and neighbouring kingdoms, then returned to Lyam's
capital at Rillanon. The Princess Carline, their sister, gave an ultimatum
to her lover, Laurie the minstrel: wed her or leave the palace. Arutha and
Princess Anita became engaged, and plans were made for their wedding in
Krondor, Arutha's city.

When Arutha finally returned to Krondor, late one night, Jimmy the
Hand, a boy thief, stumbled across and foiled a Nighthawk, an assassin,
whose target was Arutha. It was a standing order among the Mockers that
all news of the Nighthawks be reported at once. Jimmy became confused
about where his loyalty lay, with the Mockers – the Guild of Thieves – or
with Arutha, whom he had known the year before. Before he could decide,
Jimmy was set up for murder by Laughing Jack, an officer in the Mockers,
proof Jack was in league with the Nighthawks. During the ambush, Jimmy

was wounded and Laughing Jack killed. Jimmy then decided to warn Arutha.

Warned of the plot, Arutha, Laurie and Jimmy trapped two assassins and imprisoned them in the palace. Arutha discovered the Nighthawks were somehow connected to the temple of the Death Goddess, Lims-Kragma. He ordered the High Priestess to attend him, but by the time she arrived one of the assassins had died and the other was dying. She sought to discover how her temple had been infiltrated by the Nighthawks. Upon dying, one of the captured Nighthawks was revealed as a magically disguised moredhel, a dark elf. The now dead creature rose up, called upon his master, Murmandamus, and attacked the High Priestess and Arutha. Only the magic intervention of Arutha's adviser Father Nathan balked the otherwise unkillable creature.

When the High Priestess and Father Nathan recovered from their ordeal, they warned Arutha that dark and alien powers sought his death. Arutha was troubled over the safety of his brother the King and the others who would be attending Arutha's forthcoming wedding, especially his beloved Anita. Deciding upon a quick solution rather than further magic investigation, Arutha empowered Jimmy to arrange a meeting for him with the Upright Man, the mysterious head of the Mockers.

In darkness, Arutha met one who claimed to speak with the voice of the Upright Man, though it was never made clear to the Prince if the speaker was himself the leader of the thieves. They came to an understanding on the need to rid the city of the Nighthawks and, in the bargain, Jimmy was given into Arutha's service as a squire of the Prince's court. Jimmy had broken oath with the Mockers and his career as a thief was over.

Later the Upright Man sent word of the location of the Nighthawks. Arutha and a company of trusted soldiers raided the Nighthawks' headquarters, the basement of the most expensive brothel in the city. Every assassin was killed or committed suicide. The finding of the body of Golden Dase, a thief and false friend to Jimmy, revealed that the Nighthawks had indeed infiltrated the Mockers. Then the dead assassins rose up, again by some dark power, and only by burning the entire building were they destroyed.

At the palace, Arutha decided the immediate danger was over, and life returned to a semblance of normalcy. The King, the Ambassador from Great Kesh, and other dignitaries arrived at the palace, and Jimmy caught a glimpse of Laughing Jack in the crowd. Jimmy was shocked, for he had been certain the false thief had died.

Arutha alerted his most trusted advisers of the danger and learned strange things were occurring in the north. It was decided there was a connection between those events and the assassins. Jimmy arrived with the news that the palace was honeycombed with secret passages and his fear that he had seen Jack. Arutha decided upon a course of caution, taking care to guard the palace, but determined to proceed with the wedding.

The wedding became a gathering point for all those who had been separated since the Riftwar: in addition to the royal party, Pug the magician came from Stardock, site of the Academy of Magicians. He was a onetime resident of Crydee, home to the King and his family. Kulgan, his old teacher, attended along with Vandros, Duke of Yabon, and Kasumi, the former Tsurani commander, now Earl of LaMut. With King Lyam came Father Tully, another of Arutha's boyhood teachers, now an adviser to the King.

Just before the wedding, Jimmy discovered that a window had been tampered with and Laughing Jack was secreted in a cupola overlooking the hall. Jack overpowered the boy and bound him. When the wedding started, Jimmy managed to foil Jack's attempt at killing Arutha by wiggling forward and kicking Jack. They both fell, but were saved by Pug's magic. But after he had been cut loose, Jimmy discovered Jack's crossbow bolt had struck Anita.

After examining the wounded Anita, Father Nathan, in conference with Father Tully, announced that the bolt had been poisoned and the Princess was dying. Jack was questioned and revealed the truth behind the Nighthawks. He had been saved from death by a strange power named Murmandamus, in return for attempting to kill Arutha. All he knew of the poison was that it was called Silverthorn. With that he died. As Anita neared death, Kulgan the magician remembered that a large library existed at the Ishapian abbey at Sarth, a town up the coast of the Bitter Sea. Pug and Father Nathan used their magic to suspend Anita in time until a cure could be found.

Arutha vowed to travel to Sarth, and after an elaborate ruse to confuse *possible spies, Arutha, Laurie, Jimmy, Martin and Gardan, Captain of the Prince's Royal Household Guard, journeyed north. In the forest south of Sarth, they were attacked by black-armoured moredhel riders, under the command of a moredhel recognized by Laurie as a chieftain from the Yabon mountain clans. Pursuing Arutha's party to the abbey at Sarth, the moredhel were repulsed by the magic of Brother Dominic, an Ishapian monk. The agents of Murmandamus attacked twice more at the Abbey, almost bringing about the death of Brother Micah, revealed to be the former Duke of Krondor, Lord Dulanic. Father John, the Abbot, explained to Arutha that there was a prophecy regarding the return to power of the moredhel, once the 'Lord of the West' was dead. One of Murmandamus's agents had called Arutha that, so it seemed the moredhel believed that the prophecy might be approaching fruition. At Sarth, Arutha also discovered that 'Silverthorn' was a corruption of an elven word, so he decided to journey on to Elvandar and the court of the Elf Queen. Gardan and Dominic were ordered by Arutha and the Abbot to travel to Stardock, to carry the latest news to Pug and the other magicians there.*

In Ylith, they encountered Roald, a mercenary and boyhood friend of Laurie, and Baru, a Hadati hillman from northern Yabon. Baru was seeking the strange moredhel chieftain, called Murad, wishing to avenge Murad's destruction of Baru's village. Both agreed to continue on with Arutha.

At Stardock, Dominic and Gardan were attacked by flying elemental creatures, servants of Murmandamus, and were saved by Pug. Dominic met the magician Kulgan and Katala, Pug's wife, as well as William, Pug's son, and Fantus the firedrake. Pug listened to what they reported and asked the other magic users at Stardock for help. A blind seer, Rogen, had a vision of some dread power behind Murmandamus, which then attacked the old man across time and against probability, in defiance of all Pug understood of magic. A mute girl, Gamina, Rogen's ward, shared the vision, and her mental screaming overwhelmed Pug and his companions. Rogen survived the ordeal, and Gamina used her telepathic ability to recreate the vision for Pug and the others. They saw a city's destruction, and the terrible thing in the vision spoke in an ancient Tsurani tongue. Pug and the others who spoke the language were stunned at hearing this nearly forgotten temple language of Kelewan.

4

In Elvandar, Arutha and his company met the gwali, gentle apelike creatures who were visiting the elves. The elves told of strange encounters with moredhel trackers near the northern borders of the elven forests. Arutha explained his mission and was told of Silverthorn by Tathar, adviser to Queen Aglaranna and Tomas, the Prince Consort and inheritor of the ancient power of the Valheru – the Dragon Lords. Silverthorn grew in one place, on the shores of the Black Lake, Moraelin, a place of dark powers. Tathar warned Arutha that it would be a dangerous journey, but Arutha vowed to continue.

At Stardock, Pug determined that what menaced the Kingdom was of Tsurani origin. Somehow Kelewan and Midkemia again seemed to have their fates intertwined. The only possible source of knowledge about this threat would be the Assembly of Magicians upon Kelewan, thought to be forever closed off to them. Pug revealed to Kulgan and the others that he had found a means of returning to Kelewan. Over their objections, he decided to go back to see what he might do to gain knowledge. Once it was decided, both Meecham the forester, Kulgan's companion for years, and Dominic forced Pug to take them along. Pug established a rift between the two worlds and the three passed through. Back in the Empire of Tsuranuanni, Pug and his friends spoke first with Netoha, Pug's old estate manager, then with Kamatsu, Lord of the Shinzawai, Kasumi's father. The Empire was in turmoil, on the verge of an open break between Warlord and Emperor, but Kamatsu vowed to carry Pug's warning of this alien terror to the High Council, for Pug was convinced that should Midkemia fall, Kelewan would follow. Pug was met by his old friend Hochopepa, a fellow magician, a Great One of the Empire. Hochopepa agreed to plead Pug's cause before the Assembly, for Pug had been named traitor to the Empire and was under sentence of death. But before he could depart, they were assaulted magically and captured by the Warlord's men.

Arutha and his party reached the Black Lake, Moraelin, avoiding a number of moredhel patrols and sentries. Galain the elf was sent by Tomas to carry news of another possible entrance to Moraelin. He told Arutha he would accompany them to the edge of the 'Tracks of the Hopeless', the canyon surrounding the plateau where Moraelin lay. Arutha and his company made *their way to the Black Lake and discovered a strange black building, which they took to be a Valheru edifice. The search for Silverthorn was fruitless, and Arutha and the others spent the night in a cave below the surface of the plateau, where they decided they must enter the building.*

Pug and his companions awoke in a cell and found their magic blocked by an enchantment. Pug was questioned by the Warlord and his two magician aides, the brothers Ergoran and Elgahar, about his purpose in returning to the Empire. The Warlord was convinced it had to do with political opposition to his plans to take control of the Empire from the Emperor. Neither he nor Ergoran believed Pug's story of a strange power of Tsurani origin menacing Midkemia. Elgahar later came to Pug's cell to discuss the matter further, and said he would consider Pug's warning. Before he left, he whispered a speculation to Pug, which Pug agreed was possible. Hochopepa asked Pug what that speculation was, but Pug refused to discuss it. Later, Pug, Meecham, and Dominic were put to torture. After Dominic entered a trance to block the pain, and Meecham was rendered senseless, Pug was tortured. The pain and his resistance to the magic blocking his own caused Pug to succeed in using Magic of the Lesser Path, something thought impossible heretofore. He freed himself and his companions as the Emperor arrived with the Lord of the Shinzawai. The Warlord was executed for treason and Pug was granted permission to conduct research in the Assembly. Elgahar was instrumental in freeing Pug and, when asked why, revealed the speculation he shared with Pug. Both believed the Enemy, the ancient terror that drove the nations to Kelewan at the time of the Chaos Wars, had returned. At the Assembly, Pug discovered a reference to strange beings living in the polar ice, the Watchers. He parted company with his friends and left to seek the Watchers, while Hochopepa, Elgahar, Dominic and Meecham returned to Midkemia and the academy.

While hiding, Jimmy overheard some conversation between a moredhel and two human renegades, which gave him a clue something was not right about the black building. Jimmy convinced Arutha he should explore alone, as he was less likely to fall prey to any trap or ambush. Jimmy entered the strange black building and discovered what looked to be Silverthorn, but too many things about the place rang false. Jimmy returned to the cave with news that the building was one giant trap. Further exploration revealed the cave to be part of a large underground Valheru abode, nearly unrecognizable after ages of erosion. Jimmy then determined that Silverthorn must be under water, as the elves had stated it grew close to the edge of the water and the rainfall that year had been heavy. That night they found the plant and began their flight. Jimmy was injured and the party slowed. They eluded the moredhel sentries but were forced to kill one, alerting Murad, who led the force set to capture Arutha. Near the edge of the elven forests, the exhausted party was forced to halt. Galain ran ahead, seeking his kinsmen Calin and the other elven warriors. The first band of moredhel overtook Arutha and was beaten back, but then Murad arrived with his larger force, including Black Slayers. Baru challenged Murad to single combat, and the strange honour code of the moredhel forced him to accept. Baru killed Murad, cutting his heart out to end the risk of his returning from the dead. Baru was cut down by a moredhel before he could return to his companions, and the battle was rejoined. As the Prince's party was nearly overwhelmed, the elves arrived and drove off the moredhel. Baru was found to be barely alive, and the elves carried the Prince and his party to the safety of Elvandar. The dead Black Slayers returned to life and pursued the elves to the edge of Elvandar, where Tomas arrived with the Spellweavers and destroyed the Black Slayers. At a celebration that night, Arutha learned that Baru would live after a long convalescence. Arutha and Martin considered the end of their quest, both knowing the battle was only a part of a larger conflict, whose final outcome had not been decided.

Pug reached the northern edges of the Empire and, leaving his Tsurani guards, set off across the Thūn-held tundra. The strange centaur-like creatures, who called themselves the Lasura, sent an old warrior to converse with Pug. The creature revealed the existence of dwellers in the ice and ran off declaring Pug mad. Pug at last reached the glacier, where he was met by a cowled being. The Watcher who greeted Pug took him down below the icecap to where a fabulous, magic forest existed. It was called Elvardein and was twin to Elvandar. Pug discovered the Watchers to be elves, the long-vanished eldar, or elder elves. Pug was to stay with them a year and learn arts beyond those he already had at his command.

Arutha reached Krondor safely with the cure for Anita. She was revived, and plans were made to finish the wedding. Carline insisted Laurie and she also get married at once, and for the time being, the palace at Krondor was the scene of joy and happiness.

Peace returned to the Kingdom of the Isles, for almost a year . . .

BOOK IV

Macros Redux

Lo! Death has reared himself a throne
In a strange city.

POE, *The City in the Sea*, st 1

Darkwind

*T*HE WIND CAME FROM NOWHERE.

Ringing into existence with the reverberation of a hammer striking doom, it carried the heat of a forge that fashioned hot war and searing death. It came into being in the heart of a lost land, emerging from some strange place between that which is and that which seeks to be. It blew from the south, when snakes walked upright and spoke ancient words. Angry, it stank of ancient evil, echoing with long forgotten prophecies. In a frenzy the wind spun, swirling out of the void, as if seeking a course, then it seemed to pause, then it blew northward.

The old nurse hummed a simple tune, one handed down from mother to daughter for generations, while she sewed. She paused to glance up from her needlework. Her two small charges lay sleeping, tiny faces serene while they dreamed their tiny dreams. Occasionally fingers would flex or lips would purse in sucking motions, then one or the other would return to quiescence. They were beautiful babies and would grow to be handsome lads, of this the nurse was certain. As men they would have only vague memories of the woman who sat with them this night, but for now they belonged as much to her as their mother, who sat with her husband presiding over a state dinner. Then through the window a strange wind came, chilling her despite its heat. It carried a hint of alien and distorted dissonance in its sound, an evil tune barely perceived. The nurse shivered and looked toward the boys. They became restless, as if ready to wake crying. The nurse hurried to the window and closed the shutters, blocking out the strange and disquieting night air. For a moment it seemed all time held its breath, then, as if with a slight sigh, the breeze died away and the night was calm again. The nurse tightened her shawl about her shoulders and the babies stirred fitfully for another moment, before lapsing into a deep and quiet sleep.

In another room nearby, a young man worked over a list, struggling to put aside personal likes and dislikes as he decided who was to serve at a minor function the next day. It was a task he hated, but he did it well. Then the wind made the window curtains blow inward. Without thinking, the youngster was half out of his chair in a crouch, a dirk seeming to fly from his boot top to his hand, as a street-born sense of wariness signalled danger. Poised to fight, he stood with heart pounding for a long moment, as certain of a death struggle as he had ever been in his conflict-torn life. Seeing no one there, the young man slowly relaxed. The moment was lost. He shook his head in perplexity. An odd disquiet settled in the pit of his stomach as he slowly crossed to the window. For long, slowly passing minutes he gazed toward the north, into the night, where he knew the great mountains lay, and beyond, where an enemy of dark aspect waited. The young man's eyes narrowed as he stared into the gloom, as if seeking to catch a glimpse of some danger lurking out there. Then as the last of the rage and fear fled, he returned to his task. But throughout the balance of the night he occasionally turned to look out the window.

* * *

Out in the city a group of revellers made their way through the streets, seeking another inn and more merry companions. The wind blew past them and they halted a moment, exchanging glances. One, a seasoned mercenary, began to walk again, then halted, considering something. With a sudden loss of interest in celebration, he bade his companions good night and returned to the palace where he had guested for almost a year.

The wind blew out to sea where a ship raced toward its home port after a long patrol. The captain, a tall old man with a scarred face and a white eye, paused as he was touched by the freshening wind. He was about to call for the sheets to be shortened when a strange chill passed through him. He looked over to his first mate, a pock-faced man who had been at his side for years. They exchanged glances, then the wind passed. The captain paused, gave the order to send men aloft, and, after another silent moment, shouted for extra lanterns to be lit against the suddenly oppressive gloom.

Farther to the north, the wind blew through the streets of a city, creating angry little dust swirls that danced a mad caper across the cobbles, skittering along like demented jesters. Within this city men from another world lived beside men born there. In the soldiers' commons of the garrison, a man from that other world wrestled one raised within a mile of where the match was taking place, with heavy wagering among those who watched. Each man had taken one fall and the third would decide the winner. The wind suddenly struck and the two opponents paused, looking about. Dust stung eyes and several seasoned veterans suppressed shudders. Without words the two opponents quit the match, and those who had placed wagers picked up their bets without protest. Silently those in the commons returned to their quarters, the festive mood of the contest having fled before the bitter wind.

The wind swept northward until it struck a forest where little apelike beings, gentle and shy, huddled in the branches, seeking a warmth that only close physical contact can provide. Below, on the floor of the forest, a man sat in meditative pose. His legs were crossed and he rested the backs of his wrists upon his knees, thumbs and fore-fingers forming circles that represent the Wheel of Life to which all creatures are bound. His eyes snapped open at the first caress of the darkling wind and he regarded the being who sat facing him. An old elf, showing but the faint signs of age native to his race, contemplated the human for a moment, seeing the unspoken question. He nodded his head slightly. The human picked up the two weapons that lay at his side. The long sword and half-sword he placed in his belt sash, and with only a gesture of farewell he was off, moving through the trees of the forest as he began his journey to the sea. There he would seek out another man, one who was also counted friend to the elves, and prepare for the final confrontation that would soon begin. As the warrior made his way toward the ocean the leaves rustled in the branches over his head.

In another forest, leaves also trembled, in sympathy with those troubled by the passing darkwind. Across an enormous gulf of stars, around a greenish yellow sun spun a hot planet. Upon that world, below the cap of ice at the north pole, lay a forest twin to that left behind by the travelling warrior. Deep within that second forest sat a circle of beings steeped in timeless lore. They wove magic. A soft, warm glow of light formed a sphere about them, as each sat upon the bare earth, richly coloured robes unblemished by stain of soil. All eyes were closed, but each saw what he or she needed to see. One, ancient beyond the memory of the others, sat above the circle, suspended in the air by the strength of the spell they all wove together. His white hair hung below his shoulders, held back by a simple wire of copper set with a single jade stone upon his forehead. His palms were held up and forward, and his eyes were fixed upon another, a black-robed human, who floated opposite him. That other rode the currents of arcane energy forming a matrix about him, sending his consciousness along those lines, mastering this alien magic. The black-robed one sat in mirror pose, his hands held palm out, but his eyes were closed as he learned. He mentally caressed the fabric of this ancient elven sorcery and felt the intertwined energies of every living thing in this forest, taken and lightly turned, never forced, toward the needs of the community. Thus the Spellweavers used their powers: gently, but persistently, spinning the fibre of these ever present natural energies into a thread of magic that could be used. He touched the magic with his mind and he knew. He knew his powers were growing beyond human understanding, becoming godlike in comparison to what he had once thought were the limits of his talents. He had mastered much in the passing year, yet he knew there was much more to learn. Still, with his tutoring he now had the means to find other sources of knowledge. The secrets known to few but the greatest masters – to pass between worlds by strength of will, to move through time, and even to cheat death – he now understood were possible. And with that understanding, he knew he would someday discover the means of mastering those secrets. If he was granted enough time. And time was at a premium. The leaves of the trees echoed the rustle of the distant darkwind. The man in black set dark eyes upon the ancient being floating before him, as both withdrew their minds from the matrix. Speaking by strength of mind, the man in black said, *So soon, Acaila?*

The other smiled, and pale blue eyes shone forth with a light of their own, a light which when first seen had startled the man in black. Now he knew that light came from a deep power beyond any he had known in any mortal save one. But this was a different power, not the astonishing might of that other but the soothing, healing power of life, love, and serenity. This being was truly one with all around him. To gaze into the glowing eyes was to be made whole, and his smile was a comfort to see. But the thoughts that crossed the distance between the two as they gently floated earthward were troubled. *It has been a year. It would have served us all had we more time, but time passes as it will, and it may be that you are ready.* Then with a texture of thought the black-robed man had come to understand was humour, he added aloud, 'But ready or unready, it is time.'

The others rose as one and for a silent moment the black-clad one felt their minds join with his, in a final farewell. They were sending him back to where a struggle was under way, a struggle in which he was to play a vital part. But they were sending him with much more than he had possessed when he had come to them. He felt the last contact, and said, 'Thank you. I will return to where I can travel quickly home.' Without further words he closed his eyes and vanished. Those in the circle were silent a moment, then each turned to undertake whatever task awaited him or her. In the branches the leaves remained restless and the echo of the darkwind was slow in fading.

The darkwind blew until it reached a ridge trail above a distant vale, where a band of men crouched in hiding. For a brief moment they faced the south, as if seeking the source of this oddly disquieting wind, then they returned to observing the plains below. The two closest to the edge had ridden long and hard in response to a report by an out-riding patrol. Below, an army gathered under banners of ill-aspect. The leader, a greying tall man with a black patch over his right eye hunkered down below the ridge. 'It's as bad as we feared,' he said in hushed tones.

The other man, not as tall but stouter, scratched at a grey-shot black beard as he squatted beside his companion. 'No, it's worse,' he whispered. 'By the number of campfires, there's one hell of a storm brewing down there.'

The man with the eye-patch sat silently for a long moment, then said, 'Well, we've somehow gained a year. I expected them to hit us last summer. It is well we prepared, for now they'll surely come.' He moved in a crouch as he returned to where a tall, blond man held his horse. 'Are you coming?'

The second man said, 'No, I think I'll watch for a while. By seeing how many arrive and at what rate, I may hazard a good guess at how many he's bringing.'

The first man mounted. The blond man said, 'What matter? When he comes, he'll bring all he has.'

'I just don't like surprises, I suppose.'

'How long?' asked the leader.

'Two, three days at most, then it will get too crowded hereabouts.'

'They're certain to have patrols out. Two days at the most.' With a grim smile, he said, 'You're not much as company goes, but after two years I've grown used to having you around. Be careful.'

The second man flashed a broad grin. 'That cuts two ways. You've stung them enough for the last two years they'd love to throw a net over you. It wouldn't do to have them show up at the city gates with your head on a battle pike.'

The blond man said, 'That will not happen.' His open smile was in contrast to his tone, one of determination the other two knew well.

'Well, just see it doesn't. Now, get along.'

The company moved out, with one rider staying behind to accompany the stout man in his watch. After a long minute of observing he muttered softly, 'What are you up to this time, you misbegotten son of a motherless whoremonger? Just what are you going to throw at us this summer, Murmandamus?'

CHAPTER ONE

Festival

J IMMY RACED DOWN THE HALL.

The last few months had been a time of growth for Jimmy. He would be counted sixteen years old the next Midsummer's Day, though no one knew his real age. Sixteen seemed a likely guess, although he might be closer to seventeen or even eighteen years old. Always athletic, he had begun to broaden in the shoulders and had gained nearly a head of height since coming to court. He now looked more the man than the boy.

But some things never changed, and Jimmy's sense of responsibility remained one of them. While he could be counted upon for important tasks, his disregard of the trivial once again threatened to turn the Prince of Kondor's Court into chaos. Duty prescribed that he, as Senior Squire of the Prince's court, be first at assembly, and as usual, he was likely to be last. Somehow punctuality seemed to elude him. He arrived either late or early, but rarely on time.

Squire Locklear stood at the door to the minor hall used as the squires' assembly point, waving frantically for Jimmy to hurry. Of all the squires, only Locklear had become a friend to the Prince's squire since Jimmy returned with Arutha from the quest for Silverthorn. Despite Jimmy's first, accurate judgment that Locklear was a child in many ways, the youngest son of the Baron of Land's End had displayed a certain taste for the reckless that had both surprised and pleased his friend. No matter how chancy a scheme Jimmy plotted, Locklear usually agreed. When delivered up to trouble as a result of Jimmy's gambles with the patience of the court officials, Locklear took his punishment with good grace, counting it the fair price of being caught.

Jimmy sped into the room, sliding across the smooth marble floor as he sought to halt himself. Two dozen green-and-brown-clad squires formed a neat pair of lines in the hall. He looked around, noting everyone was where they were supposed to be. He assumed his own appointed place at the instant that Master of Ceremonies Brian deLacy entered.

When given the rank of Senior Squire, Jimmy had thought it would be all privilege and no responsibility. He had been quickly disabused of that notion. An integral part of the court, albeit a minor one, he was, when he failed his duty, confronted by the single most important fact known to all bureaucrats of any nation or epoch: those above were not interested in excuses, only in results. Jimmy lived and died with every mistake made by the squires. So far, it had not been a good year for Jimmy.

With measured steps and rustling red and black robes of office, the tall, dignified Master of Ceremonies crossed to stand behind Jimmy, technically his first assistant after the Steward of the Royal Household, but most often his biggest problem. Flanking Master deLacy were two purple-and-yellow-uniformed court pages, commoners' sons who would grow up to be servants in the palace, unlike the squires who would some day be among the rulers of the Western Realm. Master deLacy absently tapped his iron-shod staff of office on the floor and said, 'Just beat me in again, did you, Squire James?'

Keeping a straight face, despite the stifled laughter coming from some of the boys in the back ranks, Jimmy said, 'Everyone is accounted for, Master deLacy. Squire Jerome is in his quarters, excused for injury.'

With weary resignation in his voice, deLacy said, 'Yes, I heard of your little disagreement on the playing field yesterday. I think we'll not dwell on your constant difficulties with Jerome. I've had another note from his father. I think in future I'll simply pass these notes to you.' Jimmy tried to look innocent and failed. 'Now, before I go over the day's assignments, I feel it appropriate to point out one fact: you are expected, at all times, to behave as young gentlemen. Toward this cause, I think it also appropriate to discourage a newly emerging trend, namely, wagering upon the outcome of barrel-ball matches played on Sixthday. Do I make myself clear?' The question seemed to be addressed to the assembled squires, but deLacy's hand fell upon Jimmy's shoulder at that moment. 'From this day forward, no more wagering, unless it's something honourable, such as horses, of course. Make no mistake, that is an order.'

All the squires muttered acknowledgement. Jimmy nodded solemnly, secretly relieved he had already placed the bet on that afternoon's match. So much interest among the staff and minor nobility had arisen over this game that Jimmy had been frantically trying to discover a way he could charge admission. There might be a high price to pay should Master deLacy discover Jimmy had already bet on the match, but Jimmy felt honour had been satisfied. DeLacy had said nothing about existing wagers.

Master deLacy quickly went over the schedule prepared the night before by Jimmy. Whatever complaint the Master of Ceremonies might have with his Senior Squire, he had none with the boy's work. Whatever task Jimmy undertook he did well; getting him to undertake the task was usually the problem. When the morning duty was assigned, deLacy said, 'At fifteen minutes before the second hour after noon, assemble on the palace steps, for at two hours after noon, Prince Arutha and his court will arrive for the Presentation. As soon as the ceremony is complete you are excused duty for the rest of the day, so those of you with families here will be free to stay with them. However, two of you will be required to stand ready with the Prince's family and guests. I've selected Squires Locklear and James to serve that duty. You two will go at once to Earl Volney's office and put yourselves at his disposal. That will be all.'

Jimmy stood frozen in chagrined silence for a long moment while deLacy left and the company of Squires broke up. Locklear ambled over to stand before Jimmy and said with a shrug, 'Well, aren't we the lucky ones? Everyone else gets to run around and eat, drink, and' – he threw a sidelong glance at Jimmy and grinned – 'kiss girls. And we've got to stick close to Their Highnesses.'

'I'll kill him,' said Jimmy, venting his displeasure.

Locklear shook his head. 'Jerome?'

'Who else?' Jimmy motioned for his friend to fall in as he walked away from the hall. 'He told deLacy about the betting. He's paying me back for that black eye I gave him yesterday.'

Locklear sighed in resignation. 'We don't stand a chance of beating Thom and Jason and the other apprentices today, with us both not playing.' Locklear and Jimmy were the two best athletes in the company of squires. Nearly as quick as Jimmy, Locklear was second only to him among the squires in swordsmanship. Together they were the two best ball handlers in the palace, and with both out of the match, it was a near certain victory for the apprentices. 'How much did you bet?'

'All of it,' answered Jimmy. Locklear winced. The squires had been pooling their silver and gold for months in anticipation of this match. 'Well, how was I to know deLacy would pull this business? Besides, with all those losses we've had, I got five-to-two odds in favour of the apprentices.' He had spent months developing a losing trend in the squires' game, setting up this big wager. He considered. 'We may not be out of it yet. I'll think of something.'

Changing the subject, Locklear said, 'You just cut it a little fine today. What held you up this time?'

Jimmy grinned, his features losing their dark aspect. 'I was talking to Marianna.' Then his features returned to an expression of disgust. 'She was going to meet me after the game, but now we'll be with the Prince and Princess.' Accompanying his growth since last summer, another change in Jimmy had been his discovery of girls. Suddenly their company and good opinion of him were vital. Given his upbringing and knowledge, especially compared to those of the other squires in court, Jimmy was worldly beyond his years. The former thief had been making his presence known among the younger serving girls of the palace for several months. Marianna was simply the most recent to catch his fancy and be swept off her feet by the clever, witty and handsome young squire. Jimmy's curly brown hair, ready grin, and flashing dark eyes had caused him to become an object of concern for more than one girl's parents among the palace staff.

Locklear attempted to look uninterested, a pose that was quickly eroding as he himself became more often the focus of the palace girls' attention. He was getting taller by the week, it seemed, almost as tall as Jimmy now. His wavy, blond-streaked brown hair and cornflower-blue eyes framed by almost feminine lashes, his handsome smile, and his friendly, easy manner had all made him popular with the younger girls of the palace. He hadn't grown quite comfortable with the idea of girls yet, as at home he had only brothers, but being around Jimmy had already convinced him there was more to girls than he had thought back at Land's End. 'Well,' Locklear said, picking up the pace of their walking, 'if deLacy doesn't find a reason to chuck you out of service, or Jerome doesn't have you beaten by town roughs, some jealous kitchen boy or angry father's likely to comb your hair with a cleaver. But none of them will have a prayer if we're late to the chancery – because Earl Volney will have our heads on pikes. Come on.'

With a laugh and an elbow to the ribs, Locklear was off, with Jimmy a step behind as they ran down the halls. One old servant looked up from his dusting to watch the boys racing along and for a moment reflected on the magic of youth. Then, resigned to the effects of time's passage, he returned to the duties at hand.

* * *

The crowd cheered as the heralds began their march down the steps of the palace. They cheered, in part, because they would now be addressed by their Prince who, while somewhat aloof, was well respected and counted evenhanded with justice. They cheered, in part, because they would see the Princess whom they loved. She was a symbol of continuation of an old line, a link from the past to the future. But most of all they cheered because they were among the lucky citizens not of the nobility who would be allowed to eat from the Prince's larder and to drink from his wine cellar.

The Festival of Presentation was conducted thirty days following the birth of any member of the royal family. How it began remained a mystery, but it was commonly held that the ancient rulers of the city-state of Rillanon were required to show the people, of every rank and station, that the heirs to the throne were born without flaw. Now it was a welcome holiday to the people, for it was as if an extra Midsummer's festival had been granted.

Those guilty of misdemeanours were pardoned; matters of honour were considered resolved and duelling was forbidden for a week and a day following the Presentation; all debts owing since the last Presentation – Princess Anita's nineteen years ago – were forgiven; and for the afternoon and evening, rank was put aside as commoner and noble ate from the same table.

As Jimmy took his place behind the heralds, he realized that someone always had to work. Someone had to prepare all the food being served today, and someone had to clean up tonight. And he had to stand ready to serve Arutha and Anita should they require it. Sighing to himself, he considered again the responsibilities that seemed to find him no matter where he hid.

Locklear hummed softly to himself while the heralds continued to take up position, followed by members of Arutha's Household Guard. The arrival of Gardan, Knight-Marshal of Krondor, and Earl Volney, acting Principate Chancellor, indicated the ceremonies were about to begin.

The grey-haired soldier, his black face set in an amused expression, nodded to the portly Chancellor, then signalled to Master deLacy to begin. The Master of Ceremonies' staff struck the ground and the trumpeters and drummers sounded ruffles and flourishes. The crowd hushed as the Master of Ceremonies struck the ground again, and a herald cried, 'Hearken to me! Hearken to me! His Highness, Arutha conDoin, Prince of Krondor, Lord of the Western Realm, Heir to the throne of Rillanon.' The crowd cheered, though it was more for form than out of any genuine enthusiasm. Arutha was the sort of man who inspired deep respect and admiration, not affection, in the populace.

A tall, rangy, dark-haired man entered, dressed in muted brown clothing of fine weave, his shoulders covered with the red mantle of his office. He paused, his brown eyes narrow, while the herald announced the Princess. When the slender, red-headed Princess of Krondor joined her husband, the merry glint in her green eyes caused him to smile, and the crowd began to cheer in earnest. Here was their beloved Anita, daughter of Arutha's predecessor, Erland.

While the actual ceremony would be quickly over, the introduction of nobles took a great deal longer. A cadre of palace nobles and guests was entitled to public presentation. The first pair of these was announced. 'Their Graces, the Duke and Duchess of Salador.'

A handsome, blond man offered his arm to a dark-haired woman. Laurie, former minstrel and traveller, now Duke of Salador and husband to Princess Carline, escorted his beautiful wife to her brother's side. They had arrived in Krondor a week before, to see their nephews, and would stay another week.

On and on droned the herald as other members of the nobility were introduced and, finally, visiting dignitaries, including the Keshian Ambassador. Lord Hazara-Khan entered with only four bodyguards, forgoing the usual Keshian pomp. The Ambassador was dressed in the style of the desert men of the Jal-Pur: cloth head cover that left only the eyes exposed, long robe of indigo over white tunic and trousers tucked into calf-high black boots. The bodyguards were garbed from head to toe in black.

Then deLacy stepped forward and called, 'Let the populace approach.' Several hundred men and women of varying rank, from the poorest beggar to the richest commoner, gathered below the steps of the palace.

Arutha spoke the ritual words of the Presentation. 'Today is the three hundred tenth day of the second year of the reign of our Lord King, Lyam the First. Today we present our sons.'

DeLacy struck his staff upon the ground and the herald cried out, 'Their Royal Highnesses, the Princes Borric and Erland.' The crowd erupted into a near-frenzy of shouts and cheers as the twin sons of Arutha and Anita, born a month before, were publicly presented for the first time. The nurse selected to care for the boys came forward and gave her charges over to their mother and father. Arutha took Borric, named for his father, while Anita took her own father's namesake. Both babies endured the public showing with good grace, though Erland showed signs of becoming fussy. The crowd continued to cheer, even after Arutha and Anita had returned their sons to the care of the nurse. Arutha graced those gathered below the steps with another rare smile. 'My sons are well and strong, they are born without flaw. They are fit to rule. Do you accept them as sons of the royal house?' The crowd shouted its approbation. Anita reflected her husband's smile. Arutha waved to the crowd. 'Our thanks, good people. Until the feasting, I bid you all good day.'

The ceremony was over. Jimmy hurried to Arutha's side, as was his duty, while Locklear moved to Anita's side. Locklear was formally a junior squire, but he was so often given duty with the Princess that he was commonly considered her personal squire. Jimmy suspected deLacy of wanting to keep himself and Locklear together so watching them would be that much easier. The Prince threw Jimmy a distracted half-smile as he watched his wife and sister fuss over the twins. The Keshian Ambassador had removed his traditional face covering and was smiling at the sight. His four bodyguards hovered close.

'Your Highnesses,' said the Keshian, 'are thrice blessed. Healthy babies are a gift of the gods. And they are sons. And two of them.'

Arutha basked in the glow of his wife, who looked radiant as she regarded her sons in the nurse's arms. 'I thank you, my Lord Hazara-Khan. It is an unexpected benefit having you with us this year.'

'The weather in Durbin is beastly this year,' he said absently as he began to make faces at little Borric. He suddenly remembered his station and more formally said, 'Besides, your Highness, we have a minor matter to finish discussing regarding the new border here in the West.'

Arutha laughed. 'With you, my dear Abdur, minor details become major concerns. I have little love for the prospect of facing you across the negotiating table again. Still, I'll pass along any suggestions you make to His Majesty.'

The Keshian bowed and said, 'I wait upon Your Highness's pleasure.'

Arutha seemed to notice the guards. 'I don't see your sons or Lord Daoud-Khan in attendance.'

'They conduct the business I would normally oversee among my people in the Jal-Pur.'

'These?' said Arutha, indicating the four bodyguards. Each was dressed entirely in jet, even to the scabbards of their scimitars, and while their costuming was similar to that of the desert men, it was different from anything Arutha had seen of Keshians.

'These are izmalis, Highness. They serve as personal protection, nothing more.'

Arutha chose to say nothing as the knot of people around the babies seemed about to break up. The izmalis were famous as body-guards, the finest protection available to the nobility of the Empire of Great Kesh, but rumour had it they were also highly trained spies and, occasionally, assassins. Their abilities were nearly legendary. They were reputed to be everything just short of ghosts in their ability to come and go undetected. Arutha disliked having men only one step away from assassins within his walls, but Abdur was entitled to his personal retinue, and Arutha judged it unlikely the Keshian Ambassador would bring anyone into Krondor who might be dangerous to the Kingdom. Besides himself, Arutha added silently.

'We shall also need to speak of the latest request from Queg regarding docking rights in Kingdom ports,' said Lord Hazara-Khan.

Arutha looked openly amazed. Then his expression changed to one of irritation. 'I suppose a passing fisherman or sailor just mentioned it to you as you disembarked at the harbour?'

'Highness, Kesh has friends in many places,' answered the Ambassador with an ingratiating smile.

'Well, it will certainly do no good to comment on Kesh's Imperial Intelligence Corps, for we both know that' – Hazara-Khan joined in and they both spoke in unison – 'no such group exists.'

Abdur Rachman Memo Hazara-Khan bowed and said, 'With Your Highness's kind permission?'

Arutha bowed slightly as the Keshian made his farewell, then turned to Jimmy. 'What? You two scoundrels drew duty today?'

Jimmy shrugged, indicating it wasn't his idea. Arutha noticed his wife instructing the nurse to return the twins to their nursery. 'Well, you must have done something to warrant deLacy's displeasure. Still, we can't have you missing all the fun. I understand there's supposed to be a particularly good barrel-ball game later this afternoon.'

Jimmy feigned surprise, while Locklear's face lit up. 'I think so,' said Jimmy noncommittally.

Motioning the boys to follow as the Prince's party began to head inside, Arutha said, 'Well then, we'll have to drop in and see how it goes, won't we?'

Jimmy winked at Locklear. Then Arutha said, 'Besides, if you boys lose that bet, your skins won't be worth a tanner's trouble by the time the other squires get through with you.'

Jimmy said nothing while they moved toward the great hall and the reception for the nobles before the commoners were admitted to the feast in the courtyard. Then he whispered to Locklear, 'That man has an irritating habit of always knowing what's going on around here.'

The celebration was in full swing, nobles mingling with those commoners granted admission to the palace courtyard. Long tables stood heavily laden with food and drink, and for many in attendance this was the finest meal they would eat this year. While formality was forgotten, the commoners were still deferential to Arutha and his party, bowing slightly and using formal address. Jimmy and Locklear hovered nearby, in case they were needed.

Carline and Laurie walked arm in arm behind Arutha and Anita. Since their own wedding, the new Duke and Duchess of Salador had settled down somewhat, in contrast to their well-reported and stormy romance at the King's court. Anita turned toward her sister-in-law and said, 'I'm pleased you could stay this long. It's so much a man's palace here in Krondor. And now with two boys . . .'

'It's going to get worse,' finished Carline. 'Being raised by a father and two brothers, I know what you mean.'

Arutha glanced over his shoulder at Laurie and said, 'It means she was spoiled shamelessly.'

Laurie laughed, but thought better of comment as his wife's blue eyes narrowed. Anita said, 'Next time, a daughter.'

'Then she can be shamelessly spoiled,' said Laurie.

'When are you going to have children?' asked Anita.

Arutha turned from the table with a pitcher of ale, filling both his own and Laurie's mugs. A servant hastened to present wine cups to the ladies. Carline answered Anita by saying, 'We'll have them when we have them. Believe me, it isn't for lack of trying.'

Anita stifled a laugh behind her hand, while Arutha and Laurie exchanged glances. Carline looked from face to face and said, 'Don't tell me you two are blushing?' To Anita she said, 'Men.'

'Lyam's last missive said Queen Magda might be with child. I expect we'll know for certain when he sends his next bundle of dispatches.'

Carline said, 'Poor Lyam, always such a one for the ladies, having to marry for reasons of state. Still, she's a decent sort, if a little dull, and he seems happy enough.'

Arutha said, 'The Queen isn't dull. Compared to you a fleet of Quegan raiders is dull.' Laurie said nothing, but his blue eyes echoed Arutha's comment. 'I just hope they have a son.'

Anita smiled. 'Arutha's anxious for another to become Prince of Krondor.'

Carline looked at her brother knowingly. 'Still, you'll not be done with matters of state. With Caldric dead, Lyam will rely more upon you and Martin than before.' Lord Caldric of Rillanon had died shortly after the King's marriage to Princess Magda of Roldem, leaving the office of Duke of Rillanon, Royal Chancellor – First Adviser to the King – vacant.

Arutha shrugged as he sampled food from his plate. 'I think he'll find no end of applicants for Caldric's office.'

Laurie said, 'That's exactly the problem. Too many nobles are seeking advantage over their neighbours. We've had three sizeable border skir- mishes between barons in the East – not anything to have Lyam send out his own army, but enough to make everyone east of Malac's Cross nervous. That's why Bas-Tyra is still without a duke. It's too powerful a duchy for Lyam to hand over to just anyone. If you're not careful, you'll find yourself named Duke of Krondor or Bas-Tyra should Magda give birth to a boy.'

Carline said, 'Enough. This is a holiday. I'll have no more politics tonight.'

Anita took Arutha's arm. 'Come along. We've had a good meal, there's a festival underway, and the babies are blessedly asleep. Besides,' she added with a laugh, 'tomorrow we have to start worrying over how we pay for this festival and the Festival of Banapis next month. Tonight we enjoy what we have.'

Jimmy managed to insinuate himself next to the Prince and said, 'Would your Highness be interested in viewing a contest?' Locklear and he exchanged worried glances, for the time for the game to begin was past.

Anita threw her husband a questioning glance. Arutha said, 'I promised Jimmy we'd go and see the barrel-ball match he's conspired to have played today.'

Laurie said, 'That might be more entertaining than another round of jugglers and actors.'

'That's only because most of your life has been spent around jugglers and actors,' said Carline. 'When I was a girl, it was considered the thing to sit and watch the boys beat each other to death in a barrel-ball game every Sixthday, while pretending not to watch. I'll take the actors and jugglers.'

Anita said, 'Why don't you two go along with the boys? We're all informal today. We'll join you later in the great hall for the evening entertainment.'

Laurie and Arutha agreed and followed the boys through the throng. They left the central courtyard of the palace and passed along a series of halls connecting the central palace complex with outer buildings. Behind the palace stood a large marshalling yard, near the stables, where the palace guards drilled. A large crowd had gathered and was cheering lustily when Arutha, Laurie, Jimmy and Locklear arrived. They worked their way toward the front, jostling spectators. A few turned to complain to those shoving past but, seeing the Prince, said nothing.

A place was made for them behind those squires not playing. Arutha waved to Gardan, who stood on the other side of the field with a squad of off-duty soldiers. Laurie watched the play a moment and said, 'This is a lot more organized than I remember.'

Arutha said, 'It's deLacy's doing. He wrote up rules for the game, after complaining to me about the number of boys too beat up to work after a match.' He pointed. 'See that fellow with the sandglass? He times the contest. The game lasts an hour now. Only a dozen boys to a side at a time, and they must play between those chalk lines on the ground. Jimmy, what are the other rules?'

Jimmy was stripping off his belt and dagger in preparation. He said, 'No hands, like always. When one side scores, it falls back past the midpoint line and the other side gets to bring the ball up. No biting, grabbing an opponent, or weapons allowed.'

Laurie said, 'No weapons? Sounds too tame for me.'

Locklear had already rid himself of his overtunic and belt and tapped another squire on the shoulder. 'What's the score?'

The squire never took his eyes from play. A stableboy, driving the ball before him with his feet, was tripped by one of Jimmy's teammates, but the ball was intercepted by a baker's apprentice, who deftly kicked it into one of the two barrels situated at each end of the compound. The squire groaned. 'That puts them ahead four counts to two. And we've less than a quarter hour to play.'

Jimmy and Locklear both looked to Arutha, who nodded. They dashed onto the field, replacing two dirty, bloody squires.

Jimmy took the ball from one of the two judges, another of deLacy's innovations, and kicked the ball toward the mid-line. Locklear, who had stationed himself there, quickly kicked it back to Jimmy, to the surprise of the several apprentices who bore down upon him. Lightning-fast, Jimmy passed them before they could recover, ducking an elbow aimed at his head. He loosed a kick at the barrel's mouth. The ball struck the edge and bounced out, but Locklear broke free of the pack and kicked the rebound in. The squires and a large number of minor nobles were on their feet cheering. Now the apprentices led by only one count.

A minor scuffle broke out and the judges quickly intervened. With no serious damage having been done, play resumed. The apprentices brought the ball up; Locklear and Jimmy fell back. One of the larger squires threw a vicious block, knocking a kitchen boy into the one with the ball. Jimmy pounced like a cat, kicking the ball toward Locklear. The smaller squire deftly moved it upfield, passing it on to another squire who immediately kicked it back as several apprentices swarmed over him. A large stableboy rushed Locklear. He simply lowered his head and took Locklear, himself, and the ball across the field boundary rather than trying to tackle the ball. At once a fight broke out and, after the judges had separated the combatants, they helped Locklear to his feet. The boy was too shaken to continue, so another squire took his place. As both players had been beyond bounds, the judge ruled the ball free and tossed it into the centre of the field. Both sides attempted to recover the ball as elbows, knees and fists flew.

'Now this is how barrel-ball should be played,' commented Laurie.

Suddenly a stableboy broke free, no one between himself and the squires' barrel. Jimmy took off after him and seeing no hope of intercepting the ball, launched himself at the boy, repeating the technique used against Locklear. Again the judge ruled the ball free and another riot ensued at midfield.

Then a squire named Paul had the ball and began to move it toward the apprentices' goal with unexpected skill. Two large baker's apprentices intercepted him, but he managed to pass the ball seconds before being levelled. The ball bounced to Squire Friedric, who passed it to Jimmy. Jimmy expected another rush from the apprentices, but was surprised as they fell back. This was a new tactic, employed against the lightning passing Jimmy and Locklear had brought to the game.

The squires on the sidelines shouted encouragement. One yelled, 'There's only a few minutes left.'

Jimmy motioned Squire Friedric to his side, shouted quick instructions, and then was off. Jimmy swept to the left and then dropped the ball back to Friedric, who moved back toward midfield. Jimmy cut to his right, then took a well-aimed pass from Friedric toward the barrel. He dodged a sliding tackle and kicked the ball into the barrel.

The crowd shouted in appreciation, for this match was bringing something new to barrel-ball: tactics and skill. In what was always a rough game, an element of precision was being introduced.

Then another fight broke out. The judges rushed to break it up, but the apprentices were unbending in their reluctance to end the scuffle. Locklear, whose head had stopped ringing, said to Laurie and Arutha, 'They're trying to hold up the game until time runs out. They know we'll win if we get another crack at the ball.'

Finally order was restored. Locklear judged himself fit enough to return and replaced a boy injured in the scuffle. Jimmy waved his squires back, quickly whispering instructions to Locklear as the apprentices slowly brought the ball up. They attempted the passing demonstrated by Jimmy, Friedric, and Locklear, but with little skill.

They nearly kicked the ball out of bounds twice before regaining control of errant passes. Then Jimmy and Locklear struck. Locklear feigned a tackle toward the ball handler, forcing him to pass, then darted toward the barrel. Jimmy came sweeping in behind, the others acting as a screen, and picked up the badly passed ball, kicking it toward Locklear. The smaller boy took the ball and broke toward the barrel. One defender attempted to overtake him, but couldn't catch the swifter squire. Then the apprentice took something from his shirt and threw it at Locklear.

To the surprised onlookers, it seemed the boy simply fell face down and the ball went out of bounds. Jimmy rushed to the side of his comrade, then suddenly was up and after the boy who was attempting to bring the ball onto the field. With no pretence of playing a game, Jimmy struck the apprentice in the face, knocking him back. Again a fight erupted, but this time several apprentices and squires from the two sides joined the fray.

Arutha turned to Laurie and said, 'This could get ugly. Think I should do something?'

Laurie watched the fight pick up in tempo. 'If you want a squire left intact for duty tomorrow.'

Arutha signalled to Gardan, who waved some soldiers onto the field. The seasoned fighting men quickly restored order. Arutha walked across the field and knelt next to where Jimmy sat, cradling Locklear's head in his lap. 'The bastard hit him in the back of the head with a piece of horseshoe iron. He's out cold.'

Arutha regarded the fallen boy, then said to Gardan, 'Have him carried to his quarters and have the chirurgeon examine him.' He said to the timekeeper, 'This game is over.' Jimmy seemed on the verge of protesting, then seemed to think better of it.

The timekeeper called out, 'The score is tied at four counts apiece. No winners.'

Jimmy sighed. 'Nor losers, at least.'

A pair of guards picked up Locklear and carried him away. Arutha said to Laurie, 'Still a pretty rough game.'

The former singer nodded. 'DeLacy needs a few more rules before they start cracking heads.'

Jimmy walked back to where his tunic and belt lay while the crowd wandered off. Arutha and Laurie followed. 'We'll have another go, sometime,' remarked the youngster.

'It could be interesting,' said Arutha. 'Now that they know about that passing trick of yours, they'll be ready.'

'So we'll just have to come up with something else.'

'Well, then I guess it might be worthwhile to make a day of it. Say in a week or two.' Arutha placed his hand on Jimmy's shoulder. 'I think I'll have a look at these rules of deLacy's. Laurie's right. If you're going to be dashing pell-mell up and down the field, we can't have you tossing irons at each other.'

Jimmy seemed to lose interest in the game. Something in the crowd caught his eye. 'See that fellow over there? The one in the blue tunic and grey cap?'

The Prince glanced in the indicated direction. 'No.'

'He just ducked away when you looked. But I know him. May I go and investigate?'

Something in Jimmy's tone made Arutha certain this was not another ploy to escape duty. 'Go on. Just don't be away too long. Laurie and I will be returning to the great hall.'

Jimmy ran off to where he last saw the fellow. He halted and looked about, then noticed the familiar figure standing near a narrow stairway into a side entrance. The man leaned against the wall, hidden in shadows, eating from a platter. He only glanced up when Jimmy approached. 'There you are, then, Jimmy the Hand.'

'No longer. Squire James of Krondor, Alvarny the Quick.'

The old thief chuckled. 'And that also no longer. Though I was quick in my day.' Lowering his voice so anyone else was unlikely to overhear, he said, 'My master sends a message for your master.' Jimmy knew at once something major was afoot, for Alvarny the Quick was the Daymaster of the Mockers, the Guild of Thieves. He was no common errand runner but one of the most highly placed and trusted aides of the Upright Man. 'By word only. My master says that birds of prey, thought gone from the city, have returned from the north.'

A chill visited the pit of Jimmy's stomach. 'Those that hunt at night?'

The old thief nodded as he popped a lightly browned pastry into his mouth. He closed his eyes a moment and made a satisfied sound. Then his eyes were on Jimmy, narrowing as he spoke. 'Sorry I was to see you leave us, Jimmy the Hand. You had promise. You could have been a power in the Mockers if you'd kept your throat uncut. But that's water gone, as they say. To the heart of the message. Young Tyburn Reems was found floating in the bay. There are places near where smugglers used to ply their trade; one is a place that smells and is of little importance to the Mockers and, therefore, is neglected. It may be that is where such birds are hiding. Now then, there's an end to the matter.' Without further conversation, Alvarny the Quick, Daymaster of the Mockers and former master thief, sauntered off into the crowd, vanishing among the revellers.

Jimmy did not hesitate. He dashed back to where Arutha had been only a few minutes before and, not finding him, headed for the great hall. The number of people before the palace made it difficult to move quickly. Seeing hundreds of strange faces in the corridors suddenly filled Jimmy with alarm. In the months since Arutha and he had returned from Moraelin with Silverthorn to cure the stricken Anita, they had become lulled by the commonplace, everyday quality of palace life. Suddenly the boy saw an assassin's dagger in every hand, poison in every wine cup, and a bowman in every shadow. Struggling past celebrants, he hurried on.

Jimmy darted through the press of nobles and other less distinguished guests in the great hall. Near the dais a clot of people were deep in conversation. Laurie and Carline were speaking with the Keshian Ambassador, while Arutha mounted the steps toward his throne. A band of acrobats was hard at work in the centre of the hall, forcing Jimmy to skirt the clearing made for them, while dozens of citizens looked on in appreciation. As he moved through the press, Jimmy glanced up at the windows of the hall, the deep shadows within each cupola haunting him with memories. He felt anger at himself as much as anyone. He above all others should remember what a menace could lurk in such places.

Jimmy darted past Laurie and reached Arutha's side as the Prince sat on his throne. Anita was nowhere in sight. Jimmy glanced at her empty throne and inclined his head. Arutha said, 'She's gone to look in on the babies. Why?'

Jimmy leaned near Arutha. 'My former master sends a message. Nighthawks have returned to Krondor.'

Arutha's expression turned sombre. 'Is this speculation, or a certainty?'

'First, the Upright Man would not send whom he sent unless he counted the matter critical, needing quick resolution. He exposed one high in the Mockers to public scrutiny. Second, there is – was – a young gambler by name Tyburn Reems who was often seen about in the city. He had some special dispensations from the Mockers. He was permitted things few men not of our guild are permitted. Now I know why. He was a personal agent of my former master. Reems is now dead. My guess is the Upright Man was alerted to the possibility of the Nighthawks' return and Reems was sent to discover their whereabouts. They are once again hidden somewhere in the city. Where, the Upright Man does not know, but he suspects somewhere near the old smugglers' warren.'

Jimmy had been speaking to the Prince while glancing about the hall. Now he turned to look at Arutha and words failed him. Arutha's face was a hard mask of controlled anger, almost to the point of a grimace. Several nearby had turned to stare at him. In a harsh whisper he said to Jimmy, 'So it's to begin again?'

Jimmy said, 'So it would seem.'

Arutha stood. 'I'll not become a prisoner in my own palace, with guards at every window.'

Jimmy's eyes roamed the hall, past where the Duchess Carline stood charming the Keshian Ambassador. 'Well and good, but this one day your house is overrun with strangers. Common sense dictates you retire to your suite early, for if ever there was a golden chance to get close to you, it is now.' His eyes kept passing from face to face, seeking some sign that something was amiss. 'If the Nighthawks are again in Krondor, then they are in this hall or en route as night approaches. You may find them waiting between here and your own quarters.'

Suddenly Arutha's eyes widened. 'My quarters! Anita and the babies!'

The Prince was off, ignoring the startled faces about him, Jimmy at his heels. Carline and Laurie saw something was wrong and followed.

Within moments a dozen people trailed behind the Prince as he hurried down the corridor. Gardan had seen the hasty exit and had fallen in beside Jimmy. 'What is it?'

Jimmy said, 'Nighthawks.'

The Knight-Marshal of Krondor needed no further warning. He grabbed at the sleeve of the first guard he met in the hall, motioning for another to follow. To the first he said, 'Send for Captain Valdis and have him join me.'

The soldier said, 'Where will you be, sir?'

Gardan sent the man off with a shove. 'Tell him to find us.'

As they hurried along, Gardan gathered nearly a dozen soldiers to him. When Arutha reached the door to his quarters, he hesitated a moment, as if fearful to open the door.

Pushing open the door, he discovered Anita sitting next to the cribs wherein their sons slept. She looked up and at once an expression of alarm crossed her features. Coming to her husband, she said, 'What is it?'

Arutha closed the door behind him, motioning for Carline and the others to wait without. 'Nothing, yet.' He paused a moment. 'I want you to take the babies and visit your mother.'

Anita said, 'She would welcome that,' but her tone left no doubt she understood there was more here than she was being told. 'Her illness is past, though she still doesn't feel up to travel. It will be a treat for her.' Then she fixed Arutha with a questioning look. 'And we shall be more easily protected in her small estate than here.'

Arutha knew better than to attempt to hide anything from Anita. 'Yes. We again have Nighthawks to worry about.'

Anita came to her husband and rested her head against his chest. The last assassination attempt had nearly cost her life. 'I have no fear for myself, but the babies . . .'

'You leave tomorrow.'

'I'll make ready.'

Arutha kissed her and moved toward the door. 'I'll return shortly. Jimmy advises I keep in quarters until the palace is free of strangers. Good advice, but I must remain on public view a while longer. The Nighthawks think us ignorant of their return. We cannot let them think otherwise, yet.'

Finding humour amid the terror, Anita said, 'Jimmy still seeks to be First Adviser to the Prince?'

Arutha smiled at that. 'He's not spoken of being named Duke of Krondor for nearly a year. Sometimes I think he'd be better suited than many others likely to come to that office.'

Arutha opened the door and found Gardan, Jimmy, Laurie, and Carline waiting. Others had been moved away by a company of the Royal Household Guard. Next to Gardan, Captain Valdis waited. Arutha told him, 'I want a full company of lancers ready to ride in the morning, Captain. The Princess and the Princes will be travelling to the Princess Mother's estates. Guard them well.'

Captain Valdis saluted and turned to issue orders. To Gardan, Arutha said, 'Begin to slowly place men back at post throughout the palace and have every possible hiding place searched. Should any inquire, say Her Highness is feeling poorly and I am staying with her for a while. I'll return to the great hall shortly.' Gardan nodded and left. Then Arutha added to Jimmy, 'I have an errand for you.'

Jimmy said, 'I'll leave at once.'

Arutha said, 'What do you think you're going to do?'

'Go to the docks,' said the boy with a grim smile.

Arutha nodded, again both pleased and surprised at the boy's grasp of things. 'Yes. If you must, search all night. But as soon as you can, find Trevor Hull and bring him here.'

• CHAPTER TWO •

Discovery

JIMMY SEARCHED THE ROOM.

The Fiddler Crab Inn was a haunt of many who wished a safe harbour from questions and prying eyes. As the sun began to set the room was crowded with locals, so Jimmy was at once the source of curiosity, for his clothing marked him out of place. A few native to the city knew him by sight – after the Poor Quarter, the docks had been a second home to him – but no small number of those in the inn marked him as a rich boy out on the evening, perhaps one with some gold to be shaken loose.

One such man, a sailor by the look of him, drunken and belligerent, barred Jimmy's passage through the room. 'Here and now, such a fine young gentleman as yourself'll be having a spare coin or two to buy a drink in celebration of the little Princes, wouldn't you think?' He rested his hand upon his belt dagger.

Jimmy adroitly sidestepped the man and was half past him, saying, 'No, I wouldn't.' The man reached for Jimmy's shoulder and tried to halt him. Jimmy came around in a fluid movement, and the man found the point of a dirk levelled at his throat. 'I said I don't have any extra gold.'

The man backed away, and several onlookers laughed. But others began to circle the squire. Jimmy knew at once he had made an error. He'd had no time to scrounge up clothing to fit his present environment, but he could have made a show of turning over a half-empty purse to the man. Still, once begun, such a confrontation could not be aborted. A moment before, Jimmy's purse had been at risk, now it was his life.

Jimmy backed up, seeking to place his back to a wall. His expression was hard and revealed no hint of fear, and a few who surrounded him suddenly understood that here was someone who knew his way about the docks. Softly he said, 'I'm looking for Trevor Hull.'

At once the men stopped advancing upon the boy. One turned and indicated with his head a back door. Jimmy hurried toward it and pulled aside the hanging cloth cover.

A group of men sat gambling in a large, smoke-filled room. From the pile of betting markers on the table, it was for high stakes. The game was lin-lan, common to the southern Kingdom and northern Kesh. A colourful display of cards was unfolded and players bet and dealt in turn, determining odds and payoffs by which cards were turned. Among the gamblers were two men, one with a scar from forehead to chin, running through a milk-white right eye, and the other a bald, pock-faced man.

Aaron Cook, the bald man and first mate on the customs cutter *Royal Raven*, looked up as Jimmy pushed toward the table. He nudged the other man, who sat regarding his cards with disgust, throwing them down. When he saw the youth, the man with the white eye smiled then, as he took note of Jimmy's expression, the smile faded. Jimmy spoke loudly, over the noise in the room. 'Your old friend Arthur wants you.'

Trevor Hull, onetime pirate and smuggler, knew at once who Jimmy meant. Arthur was the name Arutha had used when Hull's smugglers and the Mockers had joined forces to get Arutha and Anita out of Krondor while Guy du Bas-Tyra's secret police had been combing the city for them. After the Riftwar, Arutha had pardoned Hull and his crew for past crimes and had enlisted them in the Royal Customs Service.

Hull and Cook stood as one and left the table. One of the other gamblers, a heavyset merchant of some means by his dress, spoke around a pipe. 'Where are you off to? The hand's not played out.'

Hull, his shock of grey hair fanning out around his head like a nimbus, shouted, 'It is for me. Hell, I only have a run in blue and a pair of four counts to play,' and he reached back and turned over all his cards.

Jimmy winced as men around the table began to curse and throw in their cards. In the common room, as they headed for the door, Jimmy observed, 'You're a mean man, Hull.'

The old smuggler turned customs officer laughed an evil laugh. 'That fat fool was ahead, and on my gold. I just wanted to take some wind out of his sails.' The nature of the game was such that as soon as he revealed his hand, play was disrupted. The only fair thing would be to leave the bets out and redeal the entire hand, a prospect not appreciated by those with good cards left to play.

Outside of the inn, they hurried along the streets, past celebrants as the festival began to pick up while afternoon shadows lengthened.

Arutha stood looking down at the maps on the table. The maps were from his archives, provided by the royal architect, and showed the streets of Krondor in detail. Another, showing the sewers, had been used before in the last raid against the Nighthawks. For the past ten minutes Trevor Hull had been carefully studying them all. Hull had headed the most prosperous gang of smugglers in Krondor before taking service with Arutha, and the sewers and back alleys had been his means of bringing contraband into the city.

Hull conferred with Cook, then the older man rubbed his chin. His finger pointed at a spot on the map where a dozen tunnels came together in a near-maze. 'If the Nighthawks were living down in the sewers, the Upright Man would have spotted them before they could have dug in. But it may be they're using the tunnels as a way in and out' – his finger moved to another spot on the map – 'here.' His finger lingered over a portion of the docks resembling a crescent along the bay. Halfway along the curve the docks ended and the warehouse district began, but also nestled against the water was a small section of the Poor Quarter, like a pie-shaped wedge driven between the more prosperous trading areas.

'Fish Town,' said Jimmy.

'Fish Town?' echoed Arutha.

'It's the poorest section of the Poor Quarter,' said Cook.

Hull nodded. 'It's called Fish Town, Divers' Town, Dockside, and other things as well. Used to be a fishing village a long time ago. As the city grew northward along the bay, it was surrounded by businesses, but there're still some fisher families living there. Mostly lobstermen and mussel rakers who work the bay, or clam diggers who work the beaches north of the city. But it's also located near the tanners, dyers, and other foul-smelling sections of Krondor, so no one who can afford better lives there.'

Jimmy said, 'Alvarny said the Upright Man thought they were hiding in a place that smells. So he thinks of Fish Town as well.' Jimmy shook his head as he considered the map. 'If the Nighthawks are hiding in Fish Town, finding them will be difficult. Even the Mockers don't control Fish Town as firmly as they do the rest of the Poor Quarter and the docks. There's a lot of places to get lost in there.'

Hull agreed. 'We used to run in and out near there, through a tunnel to a landing once used to carry cargo into the harbour from some merchant's basement.' Arutha studied the map and nodded: he knew where that landing lay. 'We used a number of different locations, moving things in and out, varying where we kept them from time to time.' He looked up at the Prince. 'Your first problem is the sewers. There are maybe a dozen conduits leading up from the docks to Fish Town. You'll have to block each one. One of them is so big you'll need to block it with a crew in a boat.'

Aaron Cook said, 'The trouble is we don't know where in Fish Town they're hiding.'

'If that's where they are,' said Arutha.

Cook said, 'I doubt if the Upright Man would even mention it had he not a good notion that they're down there somewhere.'

Hull nodded agreement. 'That's a fact. I can't think of any place else in the city they could be hiding. The Upright Man would've pinned down the location as soon as a Mocker caught a glimpse of the first Nighthawk. Even though the thieves use a lot of the sewers to skulk about in, there are parts they don't pass through much. And Fish Town is worse. The older fisher families are independent and tough, almost clannish. If someone took up residence in one of the old shacks near the docks, kept to himself . . . Even the Mockers only get silence from the Fish Town folk when they ask questions. Should the Nighthawks have infiltrated slowly, no one but the locals might have a hint. It's a regular warren there, little streets all twisted about.' He shook his head. 'This part of the map's useless. Half the buildings shown here are burned down. Shacks and hovels built anywhere there's room. It's a mess in there.' He looked at the Prince. 'Another name for Fish Town is the Maze.'

Jimmy said, 'Trevor's right. I've been in Fish Town as much as anyone in the Mockers, and that's not much. There's nothing worth stealing in there. But he's wrong about one thing. The biggest problem isn't blocking escape routes. It's locating the Nighthawks. There are a lot of honest folk living in that part of town and you just can't ride in and kill everyone. We've got to find their hideout.' He considered. 'From what I know of the Nighthawks, they'll want some place that's first of all defensible, then easy to flee. They'll probably be here.' His finger pointed to a spot on the map.

Trevor Hull said, 'It's a possibility. That building is nestled against those two walls, so they've only two fronts to cover. And there's a network of tunnels below the streets there, and those tunnels are all small and difficult to navigate unless you've been there before. Yes, it's a likely place.'

Jimmy looked at Arutha. 'I'd better go change.'

Arutha said, 'I don't like the need, but you're the best equipped to scout.'

Cook looked at Hull, who nodded slightly. 'I could come along.'

Jimmy shook his head. 'You know parts of the sewers better than I, Aaron, but I can slip in and out without making the water ripple. You haven't the knack. And there's no possible way you can get into Fish Town unnoticed, even on a noisy night like this. I'll be safer if I go alone.'

Arutha said, 'Shouldn't you wait?'

Jimmy shook his head. 'If I can locate their warren before they know they've been discovered, we may be able to clean them out before they know what hit them. People do funny things sometimes, even assassins. It being a festival day, their sentries will probably not expect someone nosing around. And, with the city in celebration, there will be lots of noises filtering down from the streets. Odd and out-of-place sounds will be less likely to alert anyone below the buildings. And if I have to poke around above ground, a strange poor boy in Fish Town isn't as likely to be noticed this night as much as other nights. But I need to go at once.'

'You know best,' said Arutha. 'But they'll react should they discover someone's seeking them out. One glimpse of you and they'll come straight after me.'

Jimmy noticed Arutha didn't seem troubled by that fact alone. It seemed to Jimmy the Prince wouldn't mind an open confrontation. No, Jimmy knew what bothered him was his concern for the safety of others. 'That goes without saying. But chances are excellent they're coming after you tonight anyway. The palace is crawling with strangers.' Jimmy looked out the window at the late afternoon sunset. 'It's almost seven hours after noon. If I were planning an attack on you, I'd wait about another two or three hours, just when the celebration is at its height. Performers and guests will be going in and out of the

46

gates. Everyone will be half-drunk, tired from a day-long celebration, and feeling very relaxed. But I wouldn't wait much after that or your guards might notice a late arriving guest entering the grounds. If you stay alert you should be safe enough while I snoop around. I'll report back as soon as I have a hint.'

Arutha indicated permission for Jimmy to withdraw. Quickly Trevor Hull and his first mate followed, leaving a troubled, seething Prince alone with his thoughts. Arutha sat back, balled fist held before his mouth as his eyes stared off into nothing.

He had faced the minions of Murmandamus near the Black Lake, Moraelin, but the final contest was yet to come. Arutha cursed himself for becoming complacent over the last year. When he had first returned with Silverthorn, the key to saving Anita from the effects of the Nighthawks' poison, he had been nearly ready to return at once to the north. But the affairs of court, his own marriage, the trip to Rillanon to attend his brother's wedding to Queen Magda, then Lord Caldric's funeral, the birth of his sons, all these had come and gone without his attending to the business north of the Kingdom. Beyond the great ranges lay the Northlands. There lay the seat of his enemy's power. There Murmandamus marshalled his forces. And from that seat far to the north he was reaching down again to touch the life of the Prince of Krondor, the Lord of the West, the man fated by prophecy to be his undoing, the Bane of Darkness. Should he live. And again Arutha found himself struggling within the confines of his own demesne, the battle carried to his own door. Striking his palm with his fist, Arutha voiced a low, harsh curse. To himself and whatever gods listened, he vowed that when this business in Krondor was finished, he, Arutha conDoin, would carry the struggle northward to Murmandamus.

The darkness hid a thousand treasures amid a million pieces of worthless garbage. The waters in the sewers flowed slowly, and often large clumps of debris would gather in a jam called a tof. The tofsmen who picked over such floating refuse earned their living gleaning valuables lost into the sewers. They also kept the refuse flowing by breaking up the jams of garbage that threatened to back up the sewers. Little of this concerned Jimmy, save that a tofsman was standing less than twenty feet away.

The young squire had dressed all in black, save for his old, comfortable boots. He had even purloined an executioner's black hood from the torture chamber. Beneath the black he wore more simple garb, needed to blend into the Poor Quarter. The tofsman looked directly at the boy several times, but for all his peering, Jimmy did not exist.

For the better part of half an hour, Jimmy had stood motionless in the deep shadows of an intersection, while the old tofsman picked over the smelly mess passing by. Jimmy hoped this wasn't the man's chosen location to work, otherwise he could be there for hours. Jimmy even more fervently hoped the tofsman was real and not a disguised Nighthawk lookout.

Finally the man wandered off, and Jimmy relaxed, though he did not move until the tofsman had had ample time to vanish down a side tunnel. Then, with stealth bordering on the unnatural, Jimmy crept along the tunnel toward the area below the heart of Fish Town.

Down a series of tunnels he travelled silently. Even as he stepped into water, he managed to disturb it only slightly. The gifts of nature – lightning-fast reflexes, astonishing coordination, and the ability to make decisions, to react nearly instantaneously – had been augmented by training from the Mockers and forged in the harshest furnace: the daily life of a working thief. Jimmy made each move as if his life depended upon remaining undetected, for it did.

Down the dark conduits of the sewers he journeyed, his senses extended into the darkness. He knew how to ignore the faint sounds coming down from the streets above and how the slight echoes of rippling water rebounding from the stonework should sound; the slightest variation would warn of anyone lurking out of view. The noisome air of the sewer masked any potentially warning odours, but the air was almost motionless, so he would have a betraying hint of movement close by should anyone suddenly come at him.

A sudden shift in the air, and Jimmy froze. Something had changed, and the boy immediately shrank down into the sheltering darkness of a low, overhanging brickwork. From a short distance ahead, he heard the faint grind of leather on metal and knew someone was descending a ladder from the street above. A slight disturbance in the water caused the boy to tense. Someone had stepped into the sewer and was walking in his direction, someone who moved almost as silently as he.

Jimmy hunkered down, as small as he could make himself in the dark, and watched. In the gloom, black against black, he could half-see, half-sense a figure moving toward him. Then, from behind, light showed and Jimmy could see the approaching man. He was slender, wearing a cloak, and armed. He turned and whispered harshly, 'Cover that damn lantern.'

But in that instant, Jimmy could see a face well known to him. The man in the sewer was Arutha – or at least resembled him enough to fool any but his closest intimates.

Jimmy held his breath, for the bogus Prince was passing only a few feet away. Whoever followed shut the lantern, and darkness enveloped the tunnel, hiding Jimmy from discovery again. Then he heard the second man pass. Listening for sounds indicating others, Jimmy waited until he felt certain no one else was coming. He quickly, but quietly, rose from his hiding spot and went to where the two men had emerged from the gloom. Three tunnels intersected, and he would have to spend time determining which had provided entrance to the sewers for the false Prince and his companion. Jimmy weighed his options briefly, then placed the need to follow the pair above the need to discover the entrance to the sewer employed.

Jimmy knew this part of the sewers as well as any in Krondor, but if he fell too far behind he would lose them. He slipped through the dark, listening at each intersection for the sounds that told him where his quarry moved.

Through the murky passages under the city the boy hurried, slowly overtaking the two men. Once he caught a glimpse of light, as if the shuttered lantern had been uncovered slightly so the travellers might gain their bearings. Jimmy followed after it.

Then Jimmy rounded a corner, and a sudden movement in the air gave warning. He dodged and felt something pass close to where his head had been, accompanied by a grunt of exertion. He pulled his dirk and turned toward the sound of breathing, holding his own breath. Fighting in the dark was an exercise in controlled terror. Each man could die from an overactive imagination as he sought a clue to the exact position of his opponent. Sounds, illusory movement seen from the corner of the eye, a feeling about where the foe stood, all could cause a miscue that would give away a location, bringing sudden death. Both men stood frozen for a long moment.

Jimmy sensed a scurrying and instantly recognized the presence of a rat, a large one by the sound, moving away from trouble. He aborted a lunge in that direction before it was begun and waited. His opponent also heard the rat, but lashed at it, striking the stone. The ring of steel on stone was all Jimmy needed and he thrust with his dirk, feeling the point strike deep. The man stiffened, then with a low sigh collapsed into the water. The combat had taken three blows, from the first at Jimmy in the dark to the one that ended it.

Jimmy pulled his dirk free and listened. There was no sign of the man's companion. The youngster swore silently. While he was free of another attack, it had also allowed the other man freedom to escape. Jimmy sensed a source of heat nearby and almost burned his hand on the metal lantern. Uncovering the shutter, he examined his foe. The man was a stranger, but Jimmy knew he was a Nighthawk. No other possible explanation could account for his presence in the sewers with an exact double of the Prince. Jimmy checked the body and found the ebon hawk worn next to the skin and the black poison ring. There was no longer any doubt. The Nighthawks were back. Jimmy steeled himself and quickly cut open the man's chest, removing the heart and casting it into the sewer. With the Nighthawks one never knew which were likely to rise again and serve their master, so it was best to take no chances.

Jimmy abandoned the lantern, left the body to float toward the sea with the other garbage, and began his return to the palace. He hurried, regretting the time lost in dealing with the corpse. Splashing noisily toward the nearest exit back to the surface, Jimmy was confident the false Prince was long gone. As he rounded a corner, a sudden alarm sounded in his head, for an echo had rung false. Dodging, he was a moment late. He avoided a sword blade slash but took a blow to the head from the hilt. He was knocked hard against the wall, his head striking brick. Pitching forward, he landed in the centre of the sewer channel, going under muck-covered water. Half-dazed, he managed to roll over, getting his face above the scum. Through a grey haze, he could hear someone splashing in the water a short distance away. In a strange detached way he knew someone was looking for him. But the lantern lay back where the first man had fallen, and in the dark the boy drifted away from the man who vainly sought to find him and end his life.

Hands shook at the boy, dragging him from an odd half-dream. He had thought it strange he should be floating in the darkness, for he had to meet with the Prince of Krondor. But he couldn't find his good boots and Master of Ceremonies deLacy would never allow him into the great hall in his old ones.

Opening his eyes, Jimmy discovered a leathery face hovering over his own. A toothless smile greeted his return to full consciousness. 'Well, well,' said the old man with a chuckle. 'You're back with us again, you are. I've seen all manner of things floating in the sewers over the years. Never thought I'd see the royal hangman tossed into the scumways, though.' He continued to chuckle, his face a grotesque dancing mask in the guttering candlelight.

Jimmy couldn't make sense of the old man's words, until he remembered the hood he had worn. The old man must have removed it. 'Who . . .?'

'Tolly I'm called, young Jimmy the Hand.' He chuckled. 'Must have come to some difficulty to find yourself in such a fix.'

'How long?'

'Ten, fifteen minutes. I heard the splashing about and went to see what's to-do. Found you floating. Thought you dead. So I pulled you away to see if you carried gold. That other one was fit to bust he couldn't find you.' Again the chuckle. 'He'd have found you certain if you'd been left to float. But I hauled you to this little tunnel I uses for a hidey and I'd lit no light till he was on his way. Found this,' he said, returning Jimmy's pouch.

'Keep it. You've saved my life, and more. Where's the nearest way to the street?'

The man helped Jimmy to his feet. 'You will find stairs to the basement of Teech's Tannery. It's abandoned. It's on the Avenue of Smells.' Jimmy nodded. The street was Collington's Road, but all in the Poor Quarter called it the Avenue of Smells because of the tanneries, slaughterhouses, and dyers located there.

Tolly said, 'You're gone from the guild, Jimmy, but word's come down you might be poking about here and there, so I'll tell you the password tonight is "finch". I don't know who those blokes fighting you were, but I've seen an odd crew down here the last three days. I guess things move apace.'

Jimmy realized this simple tofsman was trusting to the higher-ups in the Mockers to deal with the intruders in his domain. 'Yes, they will be dealt with in a matter of days.' Jimmy considered. 'Look, there's more than thirty gold in that pouch. Take word to Alvarny the Quick. Tell him matters are as suspected and my new master will act at once, I'm certain. Then take the gold and have some fun for a few days.'

The man fixed Jimmy with a squint, grinning his toothless grin. 'Stay clear is what you're saying? Well then, I might spend a day or two drinking up your gold. That enough?'

Jimmy said, 'Yes, two days will see this business over.' As he moved toward the tunnel that would lead to his exit to the streets, he added, 'One way or the other.' He looked about in the gloom and discovered he had been pulled back toward the place where he had first encountered the two Nighthawks. Pointing toward the intersection, he asked, 'Is there a metal ladder nearby?'

'Three that can be used.' He indicated their locations.

'Thanks again, Tolly. Now, quickly, carry my message to Alvarny.'

The old tofsman waded away into a large tunnel, and Jimmy began his inspection of the nearest ladder. It was rusty and dangerous, as was the second, but the third was newly repaired and firmly anchored in the stones. Jimmy quickly climbed to the top and examined the trapdoor above.

It was wood and therefore part of a building floor. Jimmy considered his position relative to Teech's Tannery. If his sense of direction wasn't off, he was under the building he had thought likely to be the Nighthawks' hideout. He listened at the trap for a long minute, hearing nothing.

Gently he pushed upward, peeking through the tiny crack made by the rising door. Directly before his nose was a pair of boots, crossed at the ankles. Jimmy froze. When the feet didn't move, he pushed the trap an inch higher. The feet in the boots belonged to a nasty-looking customer who was sound asleep, a half-empty bottle clutched tightly to his chest. From the cloying odour in the room, Jimmy knew the man had been drinking *paga* – a potent brew, heavily spiced and laced with a perfume-sweet mild narcotic, imported from Kesh. Jimmy chanced a quick glance about. Aside from the sleeping sentry the room was empty, but faintly heard voices came from the single door in the nearby wall.

Jimmy drew a silent breath and noiselessly emerged from the trap, avoiding touching the sleeping guard. He moved with a single step to the door and listened. The voices were faint. A tiny crack in the wooden door allowed Jimmy to peek through.

He could see only the back of one man and the face of another. From the manner in which they were speaking, it was clear there were others in the room as well, and from the sound of movement, some number of them, perhaps a dozen. Jimmy glanced about and nodded to himself. This was the headquarters of the Nighthawks.

53

And these men were Nighthawks, beyond doubt. Even if he hadn't seen the ebon hawk on the man he had killed, those in the next room were nothing like the common folk of Fish Town.

Jimmy wished he could better scout the building, for there were at least a half-dozen other rooms, but the restless sounds of the sleeping man alerted the former thief that time was quickly running out. The false Prince would be inside the Palace soon, and while Jimmy could run down the streets whereas the false Arutha had to slog through the sewers, it would be a close thing who would be at the palace first.

Jimmy quietly left the door and moved back to the trap. He gently lowered it overhead. As he reached a point halfway between the trap and the sewer, he heard voices from directly overhead. 'Matthew!'

Jimmy's heart leaped as the other voice said, 'What!'

'If you've drunk yourself asleep, I'll have your eyes for dinner.'

The other voice answered irritably, 'I only closed my eyes for a minute, just as you walked in, and don't threaten me or the crows will have your liver.'

Jimmy heard the trap being lifted, and without hesitation swung himself around to the side of the ladder. He hung in midair, only one hand and boot on the small rungs as he flattened himself against the wall, barely holding on to scant hand- and footholds in the rough stones. He trusted his black clothing in the gloom – and the fact the eyes of those above would take time to adjust to the darkness of the sewer – to hide him. A light was shone from above and Jimmy averted his face, the only part of him not black, and held his breath. For a long, terror-filled moment he hung in space, arm and leg burning with fatigue with the strain of holding himself motionless. Not daring to look upward, he could only imagine what the two Nighthawks above might be doing. Even at this moment they could be drawing weapons. A crossbow could be aiming at his skull and in an instant he could be dead, his life blotted out without warning. He heard feet scuffling about and laboured breathing above where he hung and then a voice said, 'See? Nothing. Now, leave it, or you'll be floating with the other garbage.'

Jimmy almost flinched when the trap was slammed close above him. He silently counted to ten, then quickly scampered down the ladder to the water and moved off.

With the bickering voices fading behind, Jimmy headed towards Teech's Tannery, and the way back to the palace.

The night was half over, but the celebration was still in full swing. Jimmy hurried through the palace, ignoring the startled people he passed. This apparition in black was a most uncommon sight. He was battered, an angry lump decorating his visage, and he reeked of the sewer. Twice Jimmy asked the guards about the Prince's whereabouts and was informed the Prince was en route to his private quarters.

Jimmy passed a startled pair of familiar faces as Gardan and Roald the mercenary stood speaking. The Knight-Marshal of Krondor looked tired from a long day yet unfinished and Laurie's boyhood friend looked half-drunk. Since returning from Moraelin, Roald had been a guest in the palace, though he still refused Gardan's constant offer of a place in Arutha's guard. Jimmy said, 'You'd better come along.' Both took the boy at his word and fell into step. Jimmy said, 'You won't believe what they're up to this time.' Neither man had to be told who 'they' were. Gardan had just informed Roald of the Upright Man's warning. And both men had faced the Nighthawks and Black Slayers of Murmandamus at Arutha's side before.

Rounding the corner, the three found Arutha about to open the door to his quarters. The Prince halted, waiting for the three to come close, an expression of open curiosity on his face.

Gardan said, 'Highness, Jimmy's discovered something.'

Arutha said, 'Come along. I have a few things I must attend to at once, so you'll have to be brief.'

The Prince pushed open the door and led them through the ante-chamber to his private council room. As he reached for the door, it opened.

Roald's dark eyes widened. Before them stood another Arutha. The Prince in the door looked at them, saying, 'What . . .?' Suddenly both

Aruthas were drawing weapons. Roald and Gardan hesitated; what their eyes told them was impossible. Jimmy watched as the two Princes engaged each other in combat, the 'second' Arutha, the one who had come from within, leaping back into the council chamber, gaining room to fight. Gardan shouted for guards and in a moment a full dozen were approaching the door.

Jimmy watched closely. The resemblance was uncanny. He knew Arutha as well as he knew anyone else in the Palace, but while the two men fought a furious duel, he couldn't tell them apart. The impostor even fought with the same skill with the blade as the Prince. Gardan said, 'Seize them both.'

Jimmy shouted, 'Wait! If you grab the wrong one first, the impostor may kill him.' Gardan instantly countermanded his own order.

The two combatants thrust and parried, moving about the room. Each man's face was set in a mask of grim determination. Then Jimmy raced across the room, no hesitation marking his lunge for one of the men. Striking out with his dirk, Jimmy knocked him backward. Guards flooded into the room, seizing the other combatant as Gardan ordered. The Knight-Marshal was uncertain what Jimmy was doing, but he was taking no chances. Both men would be held until the matter was sorted out.

Jimmy grappled on the floor with one of the Aruthas, who struck out with a backhand blow, stunning Jimmy and knocking him aside. That Arutha began to rise to his feet, then halted as Roald levelled his sword point at the man's throat. The man on the floor shouted, 'The boy's gone mad. Guards! Seize him!' Then, as he rose, he clutched at his side. His hand came away covered in blood. The man looked pale and began to wobble. He appeared on the verge of fainting. The other Arutha stood quietly, enduring the restraining hands of the guards.

Jimmy shook his head, clearing it from the effects of the second serious blow of the day. Seeing the condition of the wounded man, Jimmy yelled, ''Ware a ring!'

As the boy spoke, the wounded man placed his hand before his mouth, and as Roald and a guard seized him, he slumped down, unconscious. Roald said, 'His royal signet is false. It's a poison ring such as the others wore.'

The guards released the real Arutha who said, 'Did he use it?'

Gardan inspected the ring. 'No, he passed out from his wound.'

Roald said, 'The likeness is unbelievable. Jimmy, how'd you know?'

'I saw him in the sewers.'

'But how did you know he was the impostor?' asked Gardan.

'The boots. They're covered in muck.'

Gardan looked at Arutha's polished black boots and the impostor's mud-encrusted pair. Arutha said, 'It's a good thing I didn't take a walk through Anita's newly planted garden today. You'd have had me in my own dungeon.'

Jimmy studied the fallen impostor and the real Prince. Both men wore the same cut and colour of clothing. Jimmy said to Arutha, 'When we came through the door, were you with us or already in the room?'

'I entered with you. He must have come into the palace with the late celebrants and simply walked into my quarters.'

Jimmy agreed. 'He hoped to catch you here, kill you, dump your body in one of the secret passages or down the sewer, and take your place. I don't think he could have maintained the charade long, but if only for a few days he could have bollixed things up around here to a fare-thee-well.'

'You've done well one more time, Jimmy.' He asked Roald, 'Will he live?'

Roald examined him. 'I don't know. These lads have a bothersome habit of dying when they shouldn't, then not staying dead when they should.'

'Get Nathan and the others. Take him to the east tower. Gardan, you know what to do.'

Jimmy watched while Father Nathan, a priest of Sung the White and one of Arutha's advisers, examined the assassin. Each person who was admitted to the tower selected to house the prisoner was astonished at the likeness. Captain Valdis, a broad-shouldered man who had been Gardan's chief lieutenant and had succeeded him as head of Arutha's guard, shook his head. 'No wonder the lads did nothing but salute when he walked in the palace, Highness. He's your exact double.'

The wounded man lay tied to the bedposts. As before when a Nighthawk had been captured, he had been stripped of his poison ring and any other possible means of committing suicide. Nathan stood away from the prisoner's side. The stocky priest said, 'He's lost blood and his breathing's shallow. It would be touch and go under normal circumstances.'

The royal chirurgeon nodded agreement. 'I'd say he'd make it. Highness, if I hadn't seen their willingness to die before.' He looked out the window of the room as the morning light began to pour through. They had worked for hours repairing the damage done by Jimmy's dirk.

Arutha considered. The last attempt at interrogating a Nighthawk had produced only an animated corpse who had killed several guards and had almost murdered the High Priestess of Lims-Kragma and the Prince himself. He said to Nathan, 'If he regains consciousness, use what arts you can to discover what he knows. If he dies, burn the body at once.' To Gardan, Jimmy, and Roald he said, 'Come with me,' and to Valdis, 'Captain, double the guards at once, quietly.'

Leaving the heavily guarded room, he led his companions toward his own quarters. 'With Anita and the babies safely on their way to her mother's, I need only worry about rooting out these assassins before they find another way to reach me.'

Gardan said, 'But Her Highness hasn't left yet.'

Arutha spun. 'What? She bade me goodbye at first light an hour ago.'

'Perhaps, Sire, but it seems a thousand details are still left. Her baggage was only loaded a little while ago. The guards have been ready for two hours, but I don't think the carriages have left yet.'

'Then hurry and make sure they're safe until they've gone.'

Gardan ran off and Arutha, Jimmy, and Roald continued on their way. Arutha said, 'You know what we face. Of all here, only those of us who were at Moraelin truly know what sort of enemy stands behind this. You also know it is a war without quarter, until one side or the other ends in utter defeat.'

Jimmy nodded, a little surprised at Arutha's tone. Something in this latest attack had touched a nerve. Since Jimmy had known the Prince, Arutha had always been a cautious man, careful to consider all the information at his disposal in making the best judgments he was able. The only exception Jimmy had witnessed had been when Anita lay injured by Laughing Jack's errant crossbow bolt. Then Arutha had changed. Now, as when Anita was nearly killed, he again seemed a man on the edge of possession, a man full of rage at this invasion of his sanctum. The well-being of his person and his family was in jeopardy and he showed a barely controlled killing rage toward those responsible.

'Find Trevor Hull again,' he told Jimmy. 'I want his best men ready to move after sundown tonight. Have him come with Cook as soon as possible. I'll want plans made with Gardan and Valdis.

'Roald, your task is to keep Laurie busy today. He's sure to tumble something's amiss when I don't hold court this afternoon. Keep him preoccupied with something, perhaps with a visit to old haunts in the city, and keep him away from the east tower.' Jimmy looked surprised. 'Now that he and Carline are married, I'll risk only one member of her family. He's just foolish enough to want to come along.'

Roald and Jimmy exchanged glances. Both anticipated what the Prince planned for tonight. Arutha's expression became thoughtful. 'Go on, I've just remembered something I need to discuss with Nathan. Send word when Hull's returned.' Without further discussion, they headed off to their appointed tasks while Arutha returned to the room to speak with the priest of Sung.

• CHAPTER THREE •

Murder

*A*RMED MEN STOOD READY.

Krondor was still celebrating, for Arutha had proclaimed a second day of festival, with the weak explanation that as there were two sons, there should be two days of Presentation. The announcement had been greeted with enthusiasm by all in the city save the palace staff, but Master of Ceremonies deLacy had quickly got things under control. Now, with the celebrants still crowding inns and alehouses, as the festive mood of the day before seemed to increase, the passing of many men – seemingly off duty, upon one errand or another, not acknowledging one another – was scarcely noticed. But by midnight they had gathered in five locations: the common room of the Rainbow Parrot Inn, three widely scattered warehouses controlled by the Mockers, and aboard the *Royal Raven*.

At a prearranged signal, the incorrect ringing of the time by the city watch, the five companies would begin to make their way toward the stronghold of the brotherhood of assassins.

Arutha led the company assembling at the Rainbow Parrot. Trevor Hull and Aaron Cook commanded the seamen and soldiers entering the sewers by boats. Jimmy, Gardan, and Captain Valdis would lead the companies hiding in the old warehouses through the streets of the Poor Quarter.

Jimmy glanced around as the last soldiers slipped quietly through the narrowly opened doors of the warehouse. The Mockers' storage house for stolen goods was now thoroughly crowded. He returned his attention to the single window, through which he observed the street that led straight to the Nighthawks' stronghold. Roald consulted an hour glass he had turned when the last hour had been rung by the city watch. Soldiers listened by the door of the warehouse. Jimmy again glanced at the assembled company. Laurie, who had unexpectedly appeared with Roald an hour before, gave Jimmy a nervous smile. 'It's more comfortable than the caves below Moraelin.'

Jimmy returned a half-smile to the uninvited participant in the night's raid. 'Right.' He knew the singer turned noble was laughing off the worry they all felt. They were ill prepared in many ways and had no sense of how many servants of Murmandamus they faced. But the appearance of the false Prince had heralded a new round of assaults by the moredhel's agents and Arutha had been emphatic about the need for speed. It had been Arutha's decision to assemble his raiders quickly and attack the Nighthawks before another dawn came to Krondor. Jimmy had urged more time to scout the area, but the Prince had remained intractable. Jimmy had made the mistake of confiding to Arutha how close he had come to being discovered. Also, Nathan reported the impostor now dead, and Arutha had said they had no way of knowing if he had accomplices in the palace, or his compatriots other means of learning of his success or failure. They ran the risk of discovering an ambush or, worse yet, an empty nest. Jimmy understood the Prince's impatience, but still wished for one more scouting trip. They couldn't even be certain they'd blocked all avenues of escape.

They had sought to increase their chances of success by sending large amounts of ale and wine into the city, 'gifts' from the Prince to the citizens. They were aided by the Mockers, who diverted a disproportionate number of barrels and casks into the Poor Quarter, especially Fish Town. The honest population of Fish Town – however small a number that might be, thought Jimmy ruefully – would be happily in its collective cups by now. Then someone said, 'Watch bell's ringing.'

Roald glanced at the glass. There was still a quarter hour's sand in it. 'That's the signal.'

Jimmy was first through the door, leading the way. His company of seasoned soldiers would reach the Nighthawks' lair first. Jimmy was the only one who had had even a glimpse of the interior of the building, so he volunteered to flush them out. Gardan and Valdis's companies would be in close support, flooding the streets surrounding the target building with soldiers in the Prince's tabards as Jimmy's men assaulted the stronghold. The companies under Arutha and Trevor Hull had already entered the sewers through the basement trapdoor in the Rainbow Parrot and the smugglers' tunnel at the dock. They were already closing in below the Nighthawks and would be responsible for blocking any escape routes in the sewers the assassins would likely take.

Soldiers fanned out to either side, hugging the shadows as they moved quickly down the narrow street. The orders had called for stealth if possible, but with this many armed men moving at once, speed was more important. And the orders had been to attack at once should they be spotted. Jimmy scouted about after reaching the intersection closest to the Nighthawks' building and discovered no guards in sight. He waved toward two narrow side streets, indicating the need to block them, and soldiers hurried to comply. When they were in position, Jimmy moved toward the entrance of the building. The last twenty yards to the door were the trickiest, for there was little cover in sight. Jimmy knew the Nighthawks probably kept the area before the door free of concealing debris against the possibility of a night such as this. He also knew there was likely at least one lookout in the second floor corner room overlooking the two streets leading to the intersection where nestled the building. A distant sound of metal on stone echoed from the other approach to the building, and Jimmy knew Gardan's men were also approaching, just as Valdis's company would be coming up behind Jimmy's. He saw movement in the second storey window and froze a moment. He had no idea if he had been spotted, but knew if he had, someone would be out quickly to investigate unless he could allay suspicions. He staggered away from the wall a moment, then fell forward, arms outstretched to support himself, another drunk vomiting excess wine from a tormented stomach. Turning his head, he knew Roald was only a short distance behind in the gloom. Between loud retching noises, he softly said, 'Get ready.'

After a moment he resumed a staggering walk toward the corner building. He paused once more, then continued on. The entire way, he sang a simple ditty, as if to himself, hoping he passed for a late celebrant on his way home. Nearing the entrance of the building, he staggered away, as if to turn the corner to the next street, then jumped to the wall next to the door. Jimmy held his breath and listened. A muffled sound, as if someone spoke, could be discerned. There seemed no tone of alarm. Jimmy nodded, then staggered out, a short way down the connecting street to where Gardan's company waited. He leaned against the wall and feigned being sick again, then yelled something mindless and happy. He hoped that yell would momentarily distract the lookout.

A dozen men quickly came up the street, carrying a light ram, and positioned themselves, while four bowmen nocked arrows behind them. They had a direct line of fire into the windows on the second floor as well as the entrance to the building. Jimmy staggered back toward the building, then when he reached a point below the window, he could see an inquisitive head stick out to follow his progress. The sentry had watched his performance and had not noticed the approaching raiders. Jimmy hoped Roald knew what to do.

An arrow sped through the night, showing the mercenary had

seized the moment. If there was a second lookout above, they lost nothing by killing the first, but if not, they gained additional moments of surprise. The lookout seemed to lean further out, as if attempting to follow Jimmy's movement along the wall. He kept coming out the window, until he fell into the street a few feet behind the youngster. Jimmy ignored the body. One of Gardan's men would be cutting the man's heart out soon enough.

Jimmy reached the door, pulled his rapier, and signalled. The six men with the ram, a beam with a fire-hardened end, stepped forward. They quietly rested the end against the door, pulled back, took three swings, then on the fourth crashed the ram against the door. The door had been bolted, not barred, and exploded inward, sending splinters flying from around the lockplate and men scrambling for weapons. Before the men who held the ram could let it fall and draw weapons, a flight of arrows sped past them. Roald and his men were through the door as the ram struck the stones and bounced.

The sounds of fighting, screams, and oaths filled the room as other voices shouted questions from other parts of the building. Jimmy took in the layout of the room with a single glance and swore in frustration. He spun to confront the sergeant leading the second company. 'They've opened doors to buildings on the other side of the walls behind this one. There're more rooms there!' He pointed to two doors through which questioning shouts had issued. The sergeant led his detachment off at once, splitting his squad and sending men through both doors. Another sergeant led his group up the stairs, while Roald and Laurie's men overwhelmed the few assassins in the first room and began searching for trapdoors in the floor.

Jimmy ran to the door that he was certain led to the room above the sewer. He kicked open the door and found a dead Nighthawk and Arutha's men coming up through the trap. There was a second door out of the room and Jimmy thought he saw someone duck around a corner. Jimmy followed after, shouting for someone to follow him, and turned the corner. He dodged to one side, but no expected ambush remained. The last time they had fought the Nighthawks,

Arutha's raiders had found the assassins determined to die rather than be captured. This time they seemed more determined to flee.

Jimmy ran down the corridor, a half-dozen soldiers at his heels. He pushed open a side door and found three dead Nighthawks on the floor of a room behind the first they had entered. Already soldiers prepared torches. Arutha's orders had been specific. All the dead were to have their hearts cut from their bodies and burned. No Black Slayers would rise from the grave this night to kill for Murmandamus.

Jimmy shouted, 'Did anyone run by here?'

One soldier looked up. 'Didn't see anyone, squire, but we were busy up to a moment ago.'

Jimmy nodded once and ran down the hall. Rounding a corner, he discovered a hand-to-hand struggle under way in a connecting corridor. He dodged between guardsmen who were quickly over-whelming the assassins and ran toward another door. It was not entirely closed, as if someone had slammed it behind him but not stopped to see if it was shut. Jimmy shoved it wide and stepped into a broad alley. And across from him were three open and unguarded doors. Jimmy felt his heart sink. He turned to discover Arutha and Gardan behind him. Arutha cursed in frustration. What had once been a large burnt-out building had been replaced by several smaller ones, and where a solid wall had been, now doors invited passage. And not one of Arutha's soldiers had arrived in time to prevent anyone from fleeing by this route. 'Did anyone escape this way?' asked the Prince.

'I don't know,' answered Jimmy. 'One, I think, through one of these doors.'

A guard turned to Gardan and asked, 'Shall we pursue, Marshal?'

Arutha turned back into the house as shouts of inquiry came from nearby buildings, from citizens of Fish Town awakened by the fighting. 'Don't bother,' said the Prince flatly. 'As certain as the sunrise, there are doors to other streets in those homes. We've failed this night.'

Gardan shook his head. 'If anyone was already here, they might have bolted as soon as they heard us attack.'

Other guards came up the narrow alley, many with bloodied

clothing. One ran to the Prince. 'We think two escaped down a side street, Highness.'

Arutha pushed past the man and re-entered the building. Reaching the main room, he found Valdis overseeing the guards as they conducted the grisly work of ensuring no undead assassins rose again. Grimly the men cut deeply into the chest of each dead man and removed his heart. The hearts were burned at once.

A breathless sailor appeared and said, 'Your Highness, Captain Hull says you should come quick.'

Arutha, Jimmy, and Gardan left the room, as Roald and Laurie came into view, weapons still in hand. Arutha regarded his blood-spattered brother-in-law and said, 'What are you doing here?'

'I just came along to keep an eye on things,' he answered. Roald looked sheepishly at the Prince as Laurie added, 'He could never learn to lie with a straight face. As soon as he asked me to go gambling, I knew something was up.'

Arutha waved away further comment and followed the sailor to the room leading to the sewer, and down the ladder, the others coming after him. They moved down a tunnel to where Hull and his men waited in their boats. Hull motioned for Arutha to board, and he and Gardan entered one boat, Jimmy, Roald, and Laurie another.

They were rowed to a large convergence of six channels. A boat was tethered to a mooring ring in the stone, and from a trap in the ceiling above hung a rope ladder. 'We stopped three boats of them coming out, but this one got past. When we reached here, they had all escaped.'

'How many?' asked the Prince.

'Maybe half a dozen,' answered Hull.

Arutha swore again. 'We lost maybe two or three down a side street and now we know this lot got away. We may have as many as a dozen Nighthawks loose in the city.'

He paused a moment, then looked at Gardan, his eyes narrowing in controlled anger as he said, 'Krondor is now under martial law. Seal the city.'

* * *

For the second time in four years, Krondor endured martial law. When Anita had escaped from her captivity in her father's palace and Jocko Radburn, Guy du Bas-Tyra's captain of secret police, had sought her out, the city had been sealed. Now the Princess's husband searched out the city for possible assassins. The reasons might be different, but the effects on the populace were the same. And coming on the heels of celebration, martial law was a doubly bitter draught for the people to swallow.

Within hours of the order for martial law being given, the merchants began to troop to the palace to lodge their complaints. First came the ship brokers, whose commerce was the first disrupted as their vessels were held in port or denied entrance to the harbour. Trevor Hull led the squadron assigned to blockade duty, since the former smuggler knew every trick used to run a blockade. Twice ships attempted to leave and both times they were intercepted and boarded, their captains were arrested and their crews confined to ship. In both cases it was quickly determined that the motive had been profit and not escape from Arutha's retribution. Still, since it was not known who they were searching for, any man arrested was kept in the city jail, the palace dungeon, or the prison barracks.

Soon the ship brokers were followed by the freight haulers; then the millers, when farmers were kept out of the city; then others, each with a reasonable request to have the quarantine of the city lifted for just his special case. All were denied.

Kingdom law was based upon the concept of the Great Freedom, the common law. Each man freely accepted service to his master, except the occasional criminal condemned to slavery or bondsman serving his indenture. Nobles received the benefits of rank in exchange for protecting those under their rule, and the network of vassalage rose from common farmer paying rent to his squire or baron, who paid taxes to his earl. In turn, the earl served his duke, who answered to the crown. But when the rights of free men were abused, those free men were quick to voice their displeasure. There were too many enemies within and without the boundaries of the Kingdom for an abusive noble to keep his position overly long. Raiding pirates from the Sunset Islands, Quegan privateers, goblin bands, and, always, the Brotherhood of the Dark Path – the dark elves – demanded some internal stability in the Kingdom. Only once in its history had the populace borne oppression without open protest, under the rule of mad King Rodric, Lyam's predecessor, for the ultimate recourse to grievance was the crown. Under Rodric, lese majesty had been re-instated as a capital crime and men could not express their grievances publicly. Lyam had again struck that offence from the laws of the land; as long as treason was not espoused, men were free to speak their minds. And the free men of Krondor spoke their displeasure loudly.

Krondor became a city in turmoil, her stability a thing of the past. For the first few days of martial law, there had been grumbling, but as the seal on the city entered its second week, shortages became commonplace. Prices rose as demand exceeded supply. When the first alehouse near the docks ran out of ale, a full scale riot ensued. Arutha ordered curfew.

Armed squads of the Royal Household Guard patrolled the streets alongside the normal city watch. Agents of both the Chancellor and the Upright Man eavesdropped on conversations, listening for hints to where the assassins lay.

And free men protested.

Jimmy hurried down the hall toward the Prince's private chambers. He had been sent to carry messages to the commander of the city watch and was returning with the commander at his side. Arutha had become a man driven by his need to find the hidden assassins. He had put aside all other matters. The daily business of the Principality had slowed, then had finally come to a halt, while Arutha searched for the Nighthawks.

Jimmy knocked upon the door to the Prince's chamber; he and the commander of the watch were admitted. Jimmy went to stand next to Laurie and Duchess Carline while the commander came to attention before the Prince. Gardan, Captain Valdis, and Earl Volney were arrayed behind the Prince's chair. Arutha looked up at the commander. 'Commander Bayne? I sent you orders; I didn't request your presence.'

The commander, a greying veteran who had begun service thirty years before, said, 'Highness, I read your orders. I came back with the squire to confirm them.'

'They are correct as written, Commander. Now, is there anything else?'

Commander Bayne flushed, his anger apparent as he bit off each word. 'Yes, Highness. Have you lost your bloody mind?' Everyone in the room was stunned by the outburst. Before Gardan or Volney could censure the commander's remarks, he continued, 'This order as written means I'll be putting over a thousand more men in the lockup. In the first place—'

'Commander!' snapped Volney, recovering from his surprise.

Ignoring the stout Earl, the commander plunged forward with his complaint. 'In the first place, this business of arresting anyone "not commonly or well known to at least three citizens of good standing" means every sailor in Krondor for the first time, traveller, vagabond, minstrel, drunk, beggar, whore, gambler, and just plain stranger are to be whisked away without hearing before a magistrate, in violation of the common law. Second, I don't have the men to do the job properly. Third, I don't have enough cells for those who are to be picked up and questioned, not even enough for those who will stay on due to unsatisfactory answers. Hell, I can barely find room for the ones who are already behind bars. And last, the whole thing stinks to high heaven. Man, are you daft? You'll have open rebellion in the city within two weeks. Even that bastard Radburn never tried anything like this.'

'Commander, that will be enough!' roared Gardan.

'You forget yourself!' said Volney.

'It's His Highness who forgets himself, my lords. And unless lese majesty's been returned to the list of felonies of the Kingdom, I'll speak my mind.'

Arutha fixed the commander with a steady gaze. 'Is that all?'

'Not by half,' snapped the commander. 'Will you rescind this order?'

Showing no emotion, Arutha said, 'No.'

The commander reached for his badge of rank and pulled it from his tunic. 'Then find another to punish the city, Arutha conDoin. I'll not do it.'

'Fine.' Arutha took the badge. He handed it to Captain Valdis and said, 'Locate the senior watchman and promote him.'

The now former commander said, 'He'll not do it, Highness. The watch is with me to a man.' He leaned forward, knuckles on Arutha's conference table, until his eyes were level with the Prince's. 'You'd better send in your army. My lads will have none of it. When this is over, it'll be them who'll be in the streets after dark, in twos and threes, trying to bring sanity back to a city gone mad and hateful. You brought this on; you deal with it.'

Arutha spoke evenly. 'That will be all. You are dismissed.' He said to Valdis, 'Send detachments from the garrison and take command of the watch posts. Any watchman who wishes to stay employed is welcomed. Any who refuses this order is to be stripped of his tabard.'

Biting back hot words, the commander stiffly turned and left the room. Jimmy shook his head and shot a worried glance at Laurie. The former minstrel would understand as well as the former thief what sort of trouble was brewing in the streets.

For another week Krondor stagnated under martial law. Arutha turned a deaf ear to all requests to end the quarantine. By the end of the third week every man or woman who could not be properly identified was under arrest. Jimmy had communicated with agents of the Upright Man who assured Jimmy that the Mockers were conducting their own housecleaning. Six bodies had been found floating in the bay so far.

Now Arutha and his advisers were ready to conduct the business of interrogating the captives. A large section of warehouses in the north end of the city near the Merchants Gate had been converted to jails. Arutha, surrounded by a company of grim-faced guards, looked over the first five prisoners brought forward.

Jimmy stood off to one side and could hear a soldier mumble to another, 'At this rate we'll be here a year talking to all these lads.'

For a while Jimmy watched as Arutha, Gardan, Volney, and Captain Valdis questioned prisoners. Many were obviously simple fellows caught up in some business they didn't understand, or they were consummate actors. All looked filthy, ill fed, and half-frightened, half-defiant.

Jimmy became restless and left the scene. At the edge of the crowd he discovered that Laurie had taken a seat on a bench outside an ale house. Jimmy joined the Duke of Salador, who said, 'They've only some homemade left, and it's not cheap, but it's cool.' He looked on while Arutha continued the interrogations under the summer sun.

Jimmy wiped his forehead. 'This is a sham. It accomplishes nothing.'

'It lessens Arutha's temper.'

'I've never seen him like this. Not even when we were racing to Moraelin. He's . . .'

'He's angry, frightened, and feeling helpless.' Laurie shook his head. 'I've learned a lot from Carline about my brothers-in-law. One thing about Arutha, if you don't already know: being helpless is something he can't abide. He's walked into a blind alley and his temper won't allow him to admit he's facing a stone wall. Besides, if he lifts the seal on the city, the Nighthawks are free to come and go at will.'

'So what? They're in the city in any event, and no matter what Arutha thinks, there's no guarantee they're locked up. Maybe they've infiltrated the court staff the way they did the Mockers last year. Who knows?' Jimmy sighed. 'If Martin was here or maybe the King, we might have this business at an end.'

Laurie drank, and grimaced at the bitter taste. 'Maybe. You've named the only two men in the world he's likely to listen to. Carline and I've tried to talk to him, but he just listens patiently, then says no. Even Gardan and Volney can't budge him.'

Jimmy watched the Prince's interrogation for a little longer while three more groups of prisoners were brought out. 'Well, some good's come of this. Four men have been turned loose.'

'And if they're picked up by another patrol, they'll be tossed into another lockup and it might be days before anyone gets around to checking out their claims to having been turned loose by the Prince. And the other sixteen have been returned to the lockup. All we can hope for is Arutha's realizing soon that this will gain him nothing. The Festival of Banapis is less than two weeks off, and if the seal isn't lifted by then, there'll be a citywide riot.' Laurie's lips tightened in frustration. 'Maybe if there was some magic way to tell who is a Nighthawk or not . . .'

Jimmy sat up. 'What?'

'What what?'

'What you just said. Why not?'

Laurie turned slowly to face the squire. 'What are you thinking?'

'I'm thinking it's time to have a chat with Father Nathan. You coming?'

Laurie put aside his mug of bitter beer and rose. 'I've a horse tied up over there.'

'We've ridden double before. Come along, Your Grace.'

For the first time in days, Laurie chuckled.

Nathan listened with his head tilted to one side while Jimmy finished his idea. The priest of Sung the White rubbed his chin a moment, looking more a former wrestler than a cleric, while he thought. 'There are magic means of impelling someone to tell the truth, but they are time consuming and not always reliable. I doubt we'd find such means any more useful than those presently being employed.' His tone revealed he didn't think much of the means presently being employed.

'What of the other temples?' inquired Laurie.

'They have means differing little from our own, small things in the way spells are constructed. The difficulties do not lessen.'

Jimmy looked defeated. 'I had hoped for some way to pluck the assassins from the mass wholesale. I guess it isn't possible.'

Nathan stood up behind the table in Arutha's conference room, appropriated while the Prince was overseeing the questioning. 'Only when a man dies and is taken into Lims-Kragma's domain are all questions answered.'

Jimmy's expression clouded as a thought struck; then he brightened. 'That could be it.'

Laurie said, 'What could be it? You can't kill them all.'

'No,' said Jimmy, dismissing the absurdity of the remark. 'Look, can you get that priest of Lims-Kragma, Julian, to come here?'

Nathan remarked dryly, 'You mean High Priest Julian of the Temple of Lims-Kragma? You forget he rose to supremacy when his predecessor was rendered mad by the attack in this palace.' Nathan's face betrayed a flicker of emotion, for the priest of Sung himself had defeated the undead servant of Murmandamus, at no little cost. Nathan was still plagued by nightmares from that event.

'Oh,' said Jimmy.

'If I request, he may grant us an audience, but I doubt he'll come running here just because I ask. I may be the Prince's spiritual adviser, but in temple rank I am simply a priest of modest achievements.'

'Well then see if he will see us. I think if he'll cooperate, we might find an end to all this madness in Krondor. But I'll want to have the Temple of Lims-Kragma's cooperation before I blab the idea to the Prince. He might not listen otherwise.'

'I'll send a message. It would be unusual for the temples to become involved in city business, but we've had closer relationships with each other and the officers of the Principality since the appearance of Murmandamus. Perhaps Julian will be kindly disposed to cooperate. I assume there's a plan in this?'

'Yes,' said Laurie, 'just what have you got up that voluminous sleeve of yours?'

Jimmy cocked his head and grinned. 'You'll appreciate the theatre of it, Laurie. We'll whip up some mummery and scare the truth out of the Nighthawks.'

The Duke of Salador sat back and thought on what the boy had said; after a moment of consideration, his blond beard was slowly parted by a widening grin. Nathan exchanged glances with the two as understanding came and he, too, began to smile, then to chuckle. Seeming to think he forgot himself, the cleric of the Goddess of the One Path composed himself, but again broke into an ill-concealed fit of mirth.

Of the major temples in Krondor, the one least visited by the populace was that devoted to the Goddess of Death, Lims-Kragma – though it was commonly held that the goddess sooner or later gathered all to her. It was usual to give votive offerings and a prayer for the recently departed, but only a few worshipped with regularity. In centuries past, the followers of the Death Goddess had practised bloody rites, including human sacrifice. Over the years these practices had moderated and the faithful of Lims-Kragma had entered the mainstream of society. Still, past fears died slowly. And even now enough bloody work was done in the Death Goddess's name by fanatics to keep her temple tainted by a patina of horror for most common men. Now a band of such common men, with perhaps a few uncommon ones hidden among them, was being marched into that temple.

Arutha stood silently by the entrance to the inner sanctum of the Temple of Lims-Kragma. Armed guards surrounded the antechamber while temple guards in the black and silver garb of their order filled the inner temple. Seven priests and priestesses stood arrayed in formal attire, as if for a high ceremony, under the supervision of the High Priest, Julian. At first the High Priest had been disinclined to participate in this charade, but as his predecessor had been driven past the brink of insanity by confronting the agent of Murmandamus, he was sympathetic to any attempts to balk that evil. Reluctantly he had agreed at the last.

The prisoners were herded forward, toward the dark entrance. Most held back and had to be shoved by spear-wielding soldiers. The first band contained those judged most likely to be members of the brotherhood of assassins. Arutha had grudgingly agreed to this sham, but had insisted on having all suspected of being Nighthawks in the first batch to be 'tested', in case the deception was revealed and word leaked back to the other prisoners being held.

When the reluctant prisoners were arraigned before the altar of the Goddess of Death, Julian intoned, 'Let the trial commence.' At once the attending priests, priestesses, and monks began a chant, one that carried a dark and chilling tone.

Turning to the fifty or so men held by the silent temple guards, the High Priest said, 'Upon the altar stone of death, no man may speak falsehood. For before She Who Waits, before the Drawer of Nets, before the Lover of Life, all men must swear to what they have done. Know then, men of Krondor, that among your number are those who have rejected our mistress, those who have enlisted in the ranks of darkness and who serve evil powers. They are men who are lost to the grace of death, to the final rest granted by Lims-Kragma. These men are despisers of all, holding only to their evil master's will. Now they shall be separated from us. For each who lies upon the stone of the Goddess of Death will be tested, and each who speaks true will have nothing to fear. But those who have sworn dark compacts will be revealed and they shall face the wrath of She Who Waits.'

The statue behind the altar, a jet stone likeness of a beautiful, stern-looking woman, began to glow, to pulse with strange blue-green lights. Jimmy was impressed, as he looked on with Laurie. The effect added a strong sense of drama to the moment.

Julian motioned for the first prisoner to be brought forward and the man was half dragged to the altar. Three strong guards lifted him up onto the altar, used ages past for human sacrifice, and Julian pulled a black dagger from his sleeve. Holding it over the man's chest, Julian asked simply, 'Do you serve Murmandamus?'

The man barely croaked out a reply in the negative and Julian removed the dagger from over the man. 'This man is free of guilt,' intoned the priest. Jimmy and Laurie exchanged glances, for the man was one of Trevor Hull's sailors, ragged and rough looking in the extreme, but above suspicion and, judging from the performance just given, not a mean actor. He had been planted to lend credibility to the proceedings, as had the second man, who was now being dragged to the altar. He sobbed piteously, yelling to be left alone, begging for mercy.

Behind an upraised hand, Jimmy said, 'He's overdoing it.'

Laurie whispered, 'It doesn't matter; the room stinks with fear.'

Jimmy regarded the assembled prisoners, who stared with fascination at the proceedings while the second man was judged innocent of being an assassin. Now the guards grabbed the first man to be truly tested. He had the half-captivated look of a bird confronting a snake and was led quickly to the altar. When four other men were led without protest, Arutha crossed to stand next to Laurie and Jimmy. Shielding them from the gaze of the prisoners by turning his back on the proceedings, he whispered, 'This isn't going to work.'

Jimmy said, 'We may not have dragged a Nighthawk up there yet. Give it time. If everyone comes through the test, you still have them all under guard.'

Suddenly a man near the front of the prisoners made a dash for the door, knocking aside two temple guards. At once Arutha's guards at the door blocked his exit. The man hurled himself at them, forcing the guards back. In the scramble he reached for a dagger and attempted to strip it from a guard's belt. His hand was struck, and the dagger skittered freely across the floor, while another guard smashed him across the face with the haft of a spear. The man dropped to the stone floor.

Jimmy, like the others, was intent upon the attempt to restrain the man. Then, as if time slowed, he saw another prisoner calmly bend over and pick up the dagger. With cool purpose the man stood, turned, reversed the dagger, and held the blade between thumb and forefinger. He pulled back his arm, and, as Jimmy's mouth opened to shout a warning, he threw the dagger.

Jimmy sprang forward to knock Arutha aside, but he was a moment too late. The dagger struck. A priest cried, 'Blasphemy!' at the attack.

Then all looked toward the Prince. Arutha staggered, his eyes widening with astonishment as he stared down at the blade protruding from his chest. Laurie and Jimmy both caught his arms, holding him up. Arutha looked at Jimmy, his mouth moving silently as if trying to speak were the most difficult task imaginable. Then his eyes rolled up into his head and he slumped forward, still held up by Laurie and Jimmy.

Jimmy sat quietly while Roald paced the room. Carline sat opposite the boy, lost in her own thoughts. They waited outside Arutha's bedchamber while Father Nathan and the royal chirurgeon worked feverishly to save Arutha's life. Nathan had showed no regard for rank as he had ordered everyone out of Arutha's room, refusing even to let Carline glimpse her brother. At first Jimmy had judged the wound serious but not fatal. He had seen men survive worse, but now the time was dragging on and the young man began to fret. By now Arutha should have been resting quietly, but there had been no word from within his chambers. Jimmy feared this meant complications.

He closed his eyes and rubbed at them a moment, sighing aloud. Again he had acted, but too late to stave off disaster. Fighting back his own feelings of guilt, he was startled when a voice next to him said, 'Don't blame yourself.'

He looked to find Carline had moved to sit beside him. With a faint smile he said, 'Reading minds, Duchess?'

She shook her head, fighting back tears. 'No. I just remembered how hard you took it when Anita was injured.'

Jimmy could only nod. Laurie came in and crossed to the door of the bedchamber to speak quietly to the guard. The guard quickly entered and returned a moment later, whispering an answer. Laurie went over to his wife, kissed her lightly on the cheek, and said, 'I've dispatched riders to fetch Anita back and lifted the quarantine.' As senior noble in the city, Laurie had assumed a position of authority, working with Volney and Gardan to restore order to a city in turmoil. While the crisis was likely over, certain restraints were kept in force, to prevent any backlash from angry citizens. Curfew would stay in effect for a few more days, and large gatherings would be dispersed.

Laurie spoke softly. 'I've more duties to discharge. I'll be back shortly.' He rose and left the antechamber. Time dragged on.

Jimmy remained lost in thought. In the short time he had been with the Prince his world had changed radically. From street boy and thief to squire had entailed a complete shift in attitudes toward others, though some vestige of his former wariness had stood him in good stead when dealing with court intrigue. Still, the Prince and his family and friends had become the only people in Jimmy's life who meant something to the boy, and he feared for them. His disquiet had grown in proportion to the passing hours and now bordered on alarm. The ministrations of the chirurgeon and the priest were taking far too long. Jimmy knew something was very wrong.

Then the door opened and a guard was motioned inside. He appeared a moment later, hurrying down the hall. In short order, Laurie, Gardan, Valdis, and Volney were back before the door. Without taking her eyes from the closed portal, Carline reached out and clutched at Jimmy's hand. Jimmy glanced over and was startled to see her eyes brimming with tears. With dread certainty, the young man knew what was happening.

The door opened and a white-faced Nathan appeared. He looked around the room and began to speak, but halted, as if the words were too difficult to utter. At last he simply said, 'He's dead.'

Jimmy couldn't contain himself. He sprang from the bench and pushed past those before the door, not recognizing his own voice crying, 'No!' The guards were too startled to react as the young squire forced his way into Arutha's chamber. There he halted, for upon the bed was the unmistakable form of the Prince. Jimmy hurried to his side and studied the still features. He reached out to touch the Prince, but his hand halted scant inches from Arutha's face. Jimmy didn't need to touch him to know without doubt that the man on the bed, whose features were so familiar, was indeed dead. Jimmy lowered his head to the bed quilting, hiding his eyes as he began to weep.

CHAPTER FOUR

Embarkation

*T*OMAS AWOKE.

Something had called to him. He sat up and looked about in the dark, his more than human eyes showing him each detail of his room as if it were twilight. The apartment of the Queen and her consort was small, carved from the living bole of a mighty tree. Nothing appeared amiss. For an instant he felt fear that his mad dreams of yesterday were returning, then as wakefulness fully came to him, he dismissed that fear. In this place, above all others, he was master of his powers. Still, old terrors often sprang unexpectedly to the mind.

Tomas regarded his wife. Aglaranna slept soundly. Then he was on his feet, moving to where Calis lay. Almost two years old now, the boy slept in an alcove adjoining his parents' quarters. The little Prince of Elvandar slept soundly, his face a mask of repose.

Then the call came again. And Tomas knew who called him. Instead of being reassured by the source of that call, Tomas felt a strange sense of fate. He crossed to where his white and gold armour hung. He had worn this raiment only once since the end of the Riftwar, to destroy the Black Slayers who had crossed into Elvandar. But now he knew it was time to wear battle garb again.

Silently he took down the armour and carried it outside. The summer's night was heavy with fragrance as blossoms filled the air with gentle scents, mingled with the preparations of elven bakers for the next day's meals.

Under the green canopy of Elvandar, Tomas dressed. Over his undertunic and trousers he drew on the golden chain-mail coat and coif. The white tabard with the golden dragon followed. He buckled on his golden sword and picked up his white shield then donned his golden helm.

For a long moment he stood again mantled in the attire of Ashen-Shugar, last of the Valheru, the Dragon Lords. A mystic legacy that crossed time bound them together, and in odd ways Tomas was as much Valheru as human. His basic nature was that of a man raised by his father and mother in the kitchen of Castle Crydee, but his powers were clearly more than human. The armour no longer held that power; it had been but a conduit fashioned by the sorcerer Macros the Black, who had conspired to have Tomas inherit the ancient powers of the Valheru. Now they resided in Tomas, but he still felt somehow lessened when he forwent the gold and white armour.

He closed his eyes and, with arts long unused, willed himself to travel to where his caller awaited.

Golden light enveloped Tomas and suddenly, faster than the eye could apprehend, he flew through the trees of the elven forest. Past unsuspecting elven sentries he sped, until he reached a large clearing far to the northwest of the Queen's court. Then he again stood in corporeal form, seeking the author of the call to him. From out of the trees a black-robed man approached, one whose face was familiar to Tomas. When the short figure had reached him, the two embraced, for they had been foster brothers as children.

Tomas said, 'This is a strange reunion, Pug. I knew your call like a signature, but why this magic? Why not simply come to our home?'

'We need to speak in private. I have been away.'

'So Arutha reported last summer. He said you stayed upon the Tsurani world to discover some cause behind these dark attacks by Murmandamus.'

'I have learned things over the last year, Tomas.' He led Tomas to a fallen tree and they sat upon the trunk. 'I am certain now, beyond doubt, that what stands behind Murmandamus is what the Tsurani know as the Enemy, an ancient thing of awesome abilities. That terrible entity seeks entrance to our world and manipulates the moredhel and their allies – toward what particular ends I do not know. How a moredhel army gathering or assassins killing Arutha can aid the Enemy's entrance into our space-time is beyond my under-standing.' For a moment he fell into a reflective mood. 'So many things I still don't understand, despite my learning. I almost came to an end to my searching in the library of the Assembly, save for one thing.' Looking at his boyhood friend, he seemed possessed by a deep urgency. 'What I found in the library was barely a hint, but it led me to the far north of Kelewan, to a fabulous place beneath the polar ice.

'I have lived for the last year in Elvardein.'

Tomas blinked in confusion. 'Elvardein? That means . . . "elvenrefuge", as Elvandar means "elvenhome". Who . . .?'

'I have been studying with the eldar.'

'The eldar!' Tomas appeared even more confused. Memories of his life as Ashen-Shugar came pouring back. The eldar were those elves most trusted by their Dragon Lord masters, those who had access to many tomes of power, pillaged from the worlds the Dragon Lords raided. Compared to their masters, they were weak. Compared to other mortals upon Midkemia, they were a race of powerful magicians. They had vanished during the Chaos Wars and were thought to have perished beside their masters. 'And they live upon the Tsurani homeworld?'

'Kelewan is no more homeworld to the Tsurani than it is to the eldar. Both races found refuge there during the Chaos Wars.' Pug paused, thinking. 'Elvardein was established as a watch post by the eldar against the need of such a time as this.

'It is much like Elvandar, Tomas, but subtly different.' He remembered. 'When I first arrived, I was made welcome. I was taught by the eldar. But it was a different sort of teaching than any I had undergone before. One elf, called Acaila, seemed responsible for my education, though many taught me. Never once in the year I spent under the polar ice did I ask a question. I would dream.' He lowered his eyes. 'It was so alien. Only you among men might understand what I mean.'

Tomas placed his hand on Pug's shoulder. 'I do understand. Men were not meant for such magic.' He then smiled. 'Still, we've had to learn, haven't we?'

Pug smiled at that. 'True. Acaila and the others would begin a spell and I would sit and watch. I spent weeks not understanding they were conducting lessons for me. Then one day I . . . joined in. I learned to weave spells with them. That was when my education began.' Pug smiled. 'They were well prepared. They knew I was coming.'

Tomas's eyes widened. 'How?'

'Macros. It appears he told them a "likely student" might be coming their way.'

'That indicates some connection between the war and these odd occurrences of the last year.'

'Yes.' Pug fell silent. 'I've learned three things. The first is that there is no truth to our concept of there being many paths of magic. All is magic. Only the limits of the practitioner dictate what path is followed. Second, despite my learning, I am but just beginning to understand all that was taught to me. For while I never asked a question, the eldar also never gave an answer.' He shivered. 'They are so different from . . . anything else. I don't know if it's the isolation, the lack of normal congress with others of their kind, or what, but Elvardein is so alien it makes Elvandar feel as familiar as the woods outside Crydee.' Pug sighed. 'It was so frustrating at times. Each day I would arise and wander the woods, waiting until an opportunity to learn presented itself. I now know more of magic than any on this world, now that Macros is gone, but I know nothing more about what we face. Somehow I was forged as a tool, without fully understanding my purpose.'

'But you have suspicions?'

'Yes, though I will not share them, not even with you, until I am sure.' Pug stood. 'I have learned much, but I need to learn more. This is certain – it is the third thing I told you I had learned – both worlds face the gravest threat since the Chaos Wars.' Pug rose, looking Tomas in the eyes. 'We must be going.'

'Going? Where?'

'All of that will become apparent. We are poorly equipped to enter the struggle. We are ill informed and knowledge is slow in coming. So we must go seek knowledge. You must come with me. Now.'

'Where?'

'To where we may learn that which may gain us advantage: to the Oracle of Aal.'

Tomas studied Pug's face. In all the years they had known each other, Tomas had never seen the young magician so intense. Quietly Tomas said, 'To other worlds?'

'That is why I need you. Your arts are alien to mine. A rift to Kelewan I can manage, but to travel to worlds I know only through millennia-old tomes . . .? Between the two of us, we have a chance. Will you aid me?'

'Of course. I must speak to Aglaranna . . .'

'No.' Pug's tone was firm. 'There are reasons. Mostly, I suspect something even more dread than what I know. If what I suspect is true, then no one beyond the two of us may know what we undertake. To share the knowledge of this quest with another is to risk the ruination of everything. Those you seek to comfort will be destroyed. Better to let them doubt awhile.'

Tomas weighed Pug's words. One thing was certain to the boy from Crydee turned Valheru: one of the few beings in the universe worthy of complete, utter trust now spoke to him. 'I dislike this, but I will accept your caution. How shall we proceed?'

'To traverse the cosmos, perhaps even to swim the time-stream, we need a steed only you may command.'

Tomas looked away, peering into the darkness. 'It has been . . . ages. Like all the former servants of the Valheru, those you speak of have become stronger-willed over the centuries and are unlikely to serve willingly.' He thought, remembering images of long ago. 'Still, I will try.'

Moving to the centre of the clearing, Tomas closed his eyes and raised his arms high above his head. Pug watched silently. For long moments there was no movement by either man. Then the young man in white and gold turned to face Pug. 'One answers, from a great distance, but she comes with great speed. Soon.'

Time passed, and the stars overhead moved in their course. Then in the distance the sound of mighty wings beating upon the night air could be heard. Soon the sound was a loud rush of wind and a titanic shape blotted out the stars.

Landing in the clearing was a gigantic figure, its descent swift and light, despite its size. Wings spanning over a hundred feet on each side gently landed a body bulking larger than any other creature on Midkemia. Silver sparkles of moonlight danced over golden scales as a greater dragon settled to the earth. A head the size of a heavy wagon lowered, until it hung just above and before the two men. Giant eyes of ruby colour regarded them. Then the creature spoke. 'Who dares summon me?'

Tomas answered. 'I, who was once Ashen-Shugar.'

The creature's mood was apparent. Irritation mixed with curiosity. 'Thinkest thou to command me as my forebears were commanded by thine? Then know we of dragonkind have grown in power and cunning. Never willingly shall we serve again. Standest thou ready to dispute this?'

Tomas raised hands in a sign of supplication. 'We seek allies, not servants. I am Tomas, who, with Dolgan the dwarf, sat the deathwatch with Rhuagh at the last. He counted me as a friend, and his gift was that which has made me again Valheru.'

The dragon considered this. Then she answered. 'That song was well sung and loudly, Tomas, friend of Rhuagh. In our lore, no more marvellous thing has occurred, for when Rhuagh passed, he coursed the skies one last time, as if his youth had been restored, and he sang his death song with vigour. In it he spoke of thee and the dwarf Dolgan. All of the greater dragons listened to his song and gave thanks. For that kindness, I will listen to thy need.'

'We seek places barred from us by space and time. Upon your back I may breach such barriers.'

The dragon seemed leery of the notion of one of her kind again carrying a Valheru, despite Tomas's reassurance. 'For what cause dost thou seek?'

It was Pug who spoke. 'A grave danger is gathering to strike this world, and even unto dragonkind it poses a threat terrible beyond imagining.'

'There have been strange stirrings to the north,' said the dragon, 'and an ill-aspected wind blows across the land these nights.' She paused, pondering what had been said. 'Then I think it may be thou and I a bargain shall strike. For such purposes thou hast spoken shall I be willing to carry thee and thy friend. I am called Ryath.' The dragon lowered her head, and Tomas adroitly mounted, showing Pug where to step so as not to cause the giant creature any discomfort. When both were mounted, they sat in a shallow depression where neck joined shoulder, between the wings.

Tomas said, 'We are in your debt, Ryath.'

The dragon gave a mighty beat of her wings and took to the sky. As they rapidly climbed above Elvandar, Tomas's magic kept Pug and himself firmly seated on Ryath's back. The dragon spoke. 'Debts of friendship are not debts. I am of Rhuagh's get; he was to me what in thy world thou wouldst term a father, I to him a daughter. While we do not count such kinship vital as do humans, still such things have some importance.

'Come, Valheru, it is time for thee to take command.'

Drawing on powers not employed for millennia, Tomas willed a passage into that place beyond space and time where his brothers and sisters had once roamed at will, visiting destruction upon worlds unnumbered. For the first time in long ages, a Dragon Lord flew between worlds.

Tomas mentally directed Ryath's course. As need came, he discovered abilities not used in this life. Again he felt the persona of Ashen-Shugar within, but it was nothing like the all-consuming madness he had endured before he finally overcame the heritage of the Valheru to regain his humanity.

Tomas maintained an illusion of space about himself, Pug, and the dragon, again almost instinctively. All about them the glory of a thousand million stars illuminated the darkness. Both men knew they were not in what Pug had come to call 'true space', but were rather in that grey nothingness he had experienced when he and Macros had closed the rift between Kelewan and Midkemia. But that greyness had no substance, existing as it did between the very strands of the fabric of space and time. They could age here while appearing back at the point of departure an instant after having left. Time did not exist in this nonspace. But the human mind, no matter how gifted, had limits, and Tomas knew Pug was human, regardless of his powers, and that now was not the time to test his limits. Ryath appeared indifferent to the illusion of true space around her. Tomas and Pug sensed the dragon change directions.

The dragon's ability to navigate in this nothingness was a source of interest to Pug. He suspected Macros might have gained some insight into how to move between worlds at will from his time of study with Rhuagh years ago. Pug made a mental note to search through Macros's works back at Stardock for that information.

They emerged in normal space, thundering into existence with a loud report. Ryath beat her wings strongly, flying through angry skies, dark with rain clouds, above a rugged landscape of ancient mountains.

The air held a bitter metallic tang, a hint of something foul blown along by a stinging, frigid wind. Ryath sent a thought to Tomas. *This place is of an alien nature. I like it not.*

Aloud so that Pug might hear, Tomas answered, 'We shall not tarry here, Ryath. And here we need fear nothing.'

I have nothing to do with fear, Valheru. I simply care not for such odd places.

Pug pointed past Tomas, who turned to follow the magician's gesture. With mental commands, Tomas directed the dragon to follow Pug's instructions. They sped between jagged peaks, a nightmare landscape of twisted rock. In the distance mighty volcanoes spewed towers of black smoke that fanned upward, their undersides glowing orange from reflected light. The mountain slopes were aglow with flowing superheated rock. Then they came upon the city. Once-heroic walls lay rent, the gaps framed by shattered masonry. Proud towers occasionally still rose above the destruction, but mostly there was ruination. No signs of life could be seen. Over what had once been a plaza they banked, circling the heart of the city, where throngs once gathered. Now only the sound of Ryath's wings could be heard over the icy wind.

'What place is this?' asked Tomas.

'I do not know. I know this is the world of the Aal, or once was in the past. It is ancient. See the sun.'

Tomas observed an angry white spot behind blowing clouds. 'It is strange.'

'It is old. Once it shone like ours, brilliant and warm. Now it fades.'

Valheru lore, long dormant, returned to Tomas. 'It is near the end of its cycle. I have knowledge of these. Sometimes they simply dwindle to nothing. Other times . . . they explode in titanic fury. I wonder which this will be.'

'I don't know. Perhaps the oracle knows.' Pug directed Tomas toward a distant range of mountains.

Toward the mountains they sped, Ryath's powerful wings carrying them swiftly. The city had stood on the edge of tableland, once cultivated, they suspected. But nothing hinting of farms remained, save a single stretch of what seemed an aqueduct, standing isolated in the centre of the broad plain, a silent monument to a long dead people. Then Ryath began to climb as they approached the mountains. Once again they flew between mountain peaks, these old and worn by wind and rain.

'There,' said Pug. 'We have arrived.'

Following Tomas's mental instructions, Ryath circled above a peak. Upon the south-facing rocks a clear flat place was revealed, before a large cave. There was no room for the giant dragon to land, so Tomas used his powers to levitate himself and Pug from her back. Ryath sent a message that she would fly to hunt, returning at Tomas's call. Tomas wished her success, but expected the dragon to return hungry.

They floated through a damp, windblown sky, so darkened by the storm there was little difference between day and night. They alighted upon the ledge before the cave.

They watched Ryath speed away. Pug said, 'There is no danger here, but we may yet travel to places of great peril. Do you think Ryath truly without fear?'

Tomas turned to Pug with a smile. 'I think her so. In my dreams of ancient days I touched the minds of her ancestors, and this dragon is to them as they were to your Fantus.'

'Then it is good she joins us willingly. It would have been difficult to persuade her otherwise.'

Tomas agreed. 'I could have destroyed her, without a doubt. But bend her to my will? I think not. The days of the Valheru ruling without question are long since vanished.'

Pug studied the alien landscape below the ledge. 'This is a sad and hollow place. In the tomes harboured in Elvardein this world is described. It was once adorned with vast cities, homes to nations; now nothing is left.'

Tomas asked quietly, 'What became of those people?'

'The sun waned; weather changed. Earthquakes, famine, war. Whatever it was, it brought utter destruction.'

They turned to face the cave as a figure appeared in the entrance, shrouded from head to foot in an all-concealing robe; only one thin arm appeared from a sleeve. That arm ended in a gnarled old hand holding a staff. Slowly the man, or so he appeared to be, approached, and when he stood before them, a voice as thin as an ancient wind issued from within the dark hood. 'Who seeks out the Oracle of Aal?'

Pug spoke. 'I, Pug, called Milamber, magician of two worlds.'

'And I, Tomas, called Ashen-Shugar, who has lived twice.'

The figure motioned for them to enter the cave. Tomas and Pug passed into a low, unlit tunnel. With a wave of his hand, Pug caused light to appear about them. The tunnel opened into a monstrous cavern.

Tomas halted. 'We were but scant yards below the peak. This cavern cannot be contained within . . .'

Pug placed his hand upon Tomas's arm. 'We are somewhere else.'

The cavern was lit by faint light issuing from the walls and ceiling, so Pug ended his own spell. Several more figures in robes could be seen in distant corners of the cavern, but none approached.

The man who had greeted them upon the ledge walked past them, and they followed. Pug said, 'What should we call you?'

The man said, 'Whatever pleases you. Here we have no names, no past, no future. We are simply those who serve the oracle.' He led them to a large outcropping of rock, upon which rested a strange figure. It was a young woman, or, more appropriately, a girl, perhaps no more than thirteen or fourteen, perhaps a few years older; it was difficult to judge. She was nude, covered in dirt, scratches, and her own excrement. Her long brown hair was matted with filth. Her eyes widened as they approached, and she scampered backward across the rocks, shrieking in terror. It was obvious to both men she was entirely mad. The shrieking continued while she hugged herself, then it descended the scale, changing into a mad laugh. Suddenly the girl gave the men an appraising look and began to pull at her hair, in a pitiful imitation of combing, as if she was suddenly concerned about her appearance.

Without words, the man with the staff indicated the girl. Tomas said, 'This, then, is the oracle?'

The hooded figure nodded. 'This is the present oracle. She will serve until her death, then another will come, as she came when she who was oracle before died. So it has always been and so will it always be.'

'How do you survive on this dead world?'

'We trade. Our race has perished, but others, such as yourselves, seek us out. We abide.' He pointed to the cowering girl. 'She is our wealth. Ask what you will.'

'And the price?' inquired Pug.

The hooded man repeated himself. 'Ask what you will. The oracle answers as she chooses, when she chooses. She will name a price. She may ask for a sweet, a fruit, or your still-beating heart to eat. She may ask for a bauble with which to play.' He indicated a pile of odd devices, cast off in the corner. 'She may ask for a hundred sheep, or a hundredweight of grain or gold. You must decide if the knowledge you seek is worth the price asked. She sometimes answers without a price. And ofttimes she will not answer, no matter what is offered. Her nature is capricious.'

Pug stepped up to the cowering girl. She stared at him a long moment, then smiled, absently playing with her stringy hair. Pug said, 'We seek to learn the future.'

The girl's eyes narrowed and suddenly there was no hint of madness within. It was as if another person instantly inhabited her. In a calm voice she answered, 'To learn this, then, will you give me my price?'

'Name your price.'

'Save me.'

Tomas looked at the guide. From deep within the hood the dry voice said, 'We do not truly understand what she means. She is trapped within her own mind. It is that madness which grants her the gift of oracularity. Free her of that madness and she no longer will be the oracle. So she must have another meaning.'

Pug said, 'Save you from what?'

The girl laughed, then the calm voice returned. 'If you do not understand, you cannot save me.'

The figure in robes seemed to shrug. Pug considered, then said, 'I think I do understand.' He reached out, seizing the girl's head between his hands. She stiffened, as if about to scream, but Pug sent a comforting mental message. What he was about to attempt was something formerly thought to be solely the province of clerics, but his time with the eldar at Elvardein had taught him that the only real limits to magic were those of the practitioner.

Pug closed his eyes and entered madness.

Pug stood in a landscape of shifting walls, a maze of maddening colours and shapes. The horizon changed with each step and perspective was nonexistent. He looked down at his hands and watched them suddenly grow larger, until they were the size of melons, then just as rapidly shrink, until they were smaller than a child's. He looked up and could see the walls of the maze receding and approaching, seemingly at random, while their colour and pattern flashed through a dozen changes. Even the ground beneath his feet was a red and white chessboard one moment, a pattern of black and grey lines the next, then large blue and green spots on red. Angry, flashing lights sought to blind him.

Pug took hold of his own perceptions. He knew he was still within the cavern and this illusion was an extension of his own need for a physical analogue in dealing with the girl's madness. First he stabilized himself so the strange shifting of limbs halted. To act rashly at any point could destroy the girl's brittle mind, and he had no way to judge what that would do to him, given his present contact with that mind. He might somehow be trapped in her madness, an unpleasant prospect. Over the last year Pug had learned a great deal about controlling his arts, but he had also learned their limits and he knew what he did carried some risk.

Next he stabilized the immediate area around him, changing the shifting, vibrating walls and dazzling lights. Realizing that any direction was as valid as another, he set out. Walking was also illusory, he knew, but the illusion of movement was required for him to reach the seat of her consciousness. Like any problem, this one required a frame of reference, and it would be one the girl would provide. Pug could only react to whatever her demented mind dreamed up for him.

Abruptly he was plunged into darkness, so silent that only death could match that stillness. Then a single, odd sound came to him. A moment later, another came, from a different direction. Then a faint pulse in the air. With more rapidity, the darkness was punctuated with movement in the air and odd sounds. At last the blackness was full of pulsing noises and fetid odours. Strange breezes blew across his face and odd feathery things brushed against him, moving away too quickly for him to seize. He created light and discovered himself in a large cavern, much like the real one in which he and Tomas now stood. Nothing else stirred. Within the illusion he called out. No answer.

The landscape shuddered and shifted, and he stood upon a beautiful greensward, lined by graceful trees, too perfect to exist in reality. They formed boundaries that pointed toward an impossibly lovely palace of white marble adorned with gold and turquoise, amber and jade, opal and chalcedony, a place so startlingly wonderful that Pug could only stand in mute appreciation. The image was emotionally laden with the feeling that this was the most perfect place in the universe, a sanctuary where no trouble intruded, where one could wait out eternity in absolute contentment.

Again the landscape shifted, and he stood within the halls of a palace. From the white marble floors flecked with gold to pillars of ebony, it was the most lavish image of wealth he had ever perceived, surpassing even the palace of the Warlord in Kentosani. The ceiling was carved quartz, admitting sunlight with a rosy glow, and the walls were bedecked with rich tapestries, woven with gold and silver threads. Ebony doors with ivory trim and studdings of precious stones were common to every portal, and wherever Pug looked, he saw gold. In the centre of this splendour a white circle of light illuminated a dais, upon which stood two figures, a woman and a girl.

He stepped toward them. Suddenly warriors erupted from the floor like plants springing from the ground. Each was a powerful creature of terrible aspect. One looked like a boar made human, another like a giant mantis. A third seemed a lion's head upon a man, a fourth wore the face of an elephant. Each was armed and armoured in rich metals and jewels, and they bellowed fearsomely. Pug stood quietly.

The warriors attacked and Pug remained motionless. As each nightmare creature struck, its weapon passed through Pug, and the creatures vanished. When they were gone, Pug stepped toward the dais upon which the two figures stood.

The dais began to move away, as if upon tiny wheels or legs, picking up speed. Pug walked directly toward it, willing himself to overtake it. Soon the landscape about him was a blur in passing, and he judged the illusion of the palace must be miles in subjective size. Pug knew he could halt the fleeing dais with its two passengers, but to do so might be harmful to the girl. Any overt act of violence, even one as minor as commanding the pair of fugitives to halt, could permanently scar her.

Now the dais began a careening, banging passage through an obstacle course of rooms, and Pug was forced to dodge and move to avoid objects hurled into his path. He could also have destroyed anything that blocked his way, but the effect would have been as harmful as if he had ordered the pair to halt. No, he thought, when you enter another's reality, you observe her rules.

Then the dais halted and Pug overtook the pair. The woman stood silently, studying the approaching magician, while the girl sat at her feet. Unlike her real appearance, here the girl was beautifully clothed in a gown of soft, translucent silk. Her hair was gathered atop her head in a magnificent fashion, held by pins of silver and gold, each bearing a jewel. While it was impossible to judge how the girl looked in truth beneath the dirt, here she was a young woman of astonishing beauty.

Then the beautiful girl stood and grew, changing before his eyes to a horror of gigantic proportions. Large hairy arms sprouted from soft shoulders, while her head became that of an enraged eagle. Lightning cascaded from her ruby eyes as claws came crashing down upon Pug.

He stood motionless. The claws passed harmlessly through him, for he refused to take part in this reality. Suddenly the monster vanished and the girl was as he had seen her in the cave, nude, filthy, and mad.

Looking at the woman, Pug said, 'You are the oracle.'

'I am.' She was regal, proud, and alien. While she looked entirely human, Pug guessed that was part of the illusion. She would be something else in truth . . . or had been when she was alive. Pug now understood.

'If I free her, what of you?'

'I must find another, and soon, or I will cease my existence. That is as it has always been and how it must be.'

'So another must succumb to this?'

'That is as it has always been.'

'If I free her, what of her?'

'She will be as she was when brought here. She is young and will regain her sanity.'

'Will you resist me?'

'You know I cannot. You see through the illusions. You know these are only monsters and treasures of the mind. But before you rid her of me, understand something, magician.

'At the dawn of time, when the multitude of universes were forming, we were born, we of the Aal. When your Valheru companion and his kin raged across the heavens, we were old and wise beyond their understanding. I am the last female of my race, though that is a convenient label and not a description. Those in the cavern are males. We labour to maintain that which is our grandest heritage, the power of the oracle, for we are the husbanders of truth, the handmaidens of knowledge. It was found in ages past that I could continue to exist within the minds of others, but at the price of their own sanity. It was considered a necessary evil to corrupt a few members of lesser

94

races in exchange for maintaining the power of the Aal. We would that it were otherwise, but it is not, for I need living minds in which to exist. Take the girl, but know that I will soon have another to reside within. She is nothing, a simple child of unknown parentage. On her homeworld she would have become at best the drudge of some peasant, at worst a whore for men's amusement. Within her mind I've given her riches beyond the dreams of the most powerful kings. What will you give her in its place?'

'Her own fate. But I think another sort of salvation was spoken of, one for you both.'

'You are perceptive, magician. The star around which this world moves is close to dying. Its erratic cycle is the cause of this planet's ruination. Already we endure an age of vulcanism not seen for aeons. Within a hand's span of years this world will end in fiery death. We stand upon the third world to be called home by the Aal. But now our race has vanished into time, and we lack the means of finding a fourth world. To answer your needs, you must be willing to answer ours.'

'Relocating you to another world is no difficulty. There are less than a dozen of you. It is agreed. Perhaps we may even find a way to prevent another's mind being sacrificed.' He inclined his head toward the figure of the cowering girl.

'That would be preferable, but we have not as yet discovered means. Still, if you will find us a haven, I will answer your queries. A bargain has been set.'

'This, then, I propose. Upon my world I have means to ensure a place of safekeeping for you and yours. I am counted kin to our King by adoption, and he will be favourably disposed to my request. But know that my world stands in peril, and you will share that risk.'

'That is unacceptable.'

'Then we shall have no bargain, and all will perish. For I will fail in my undertaking, and this world will vanish in a cloud of flaming gases.'

The woman remained grave in appearance. After a long silence she said, 'I shall amend our bargain. I will provide you with the power of the oracle, in exchange for this safe haven, when you have completed your quest.'

'Quest?'

'I read the future, and as we near agreement, the lines of probability resolve themselves and the most likely future is revealed to my sight. Even as we speak, I see what you will undertake, and it is a way fraught with perils.' She stood silently for a moment, then softly said, 'Now I understand what you face. I agree to these terms, as you must.'

Pug shrugged. 'Agreed. When all has been favourably resolved, we shall carry you to a place of safety.'

'Return to the cavern.'

Pug opened his eyes. Tomas and the servants of the oracle stood as they had done when he had begun the mind contact. He asked Tomas, 'How long have I been standing here?'

'A few moments, no longer.'

Pug stepped away from the girl. She opened her eyes, and her voice was strong, untainted by madness, but carrying a hint of the alien woman's speech. 'Know that darkness unfolds and gathers, coming from where it has been confined, seeking to regain that which was lost, to the utter ruination of all you love, to the redemption of all you hold in terror. Go and find the one who knows all, who has from the first understood the truth. Only he can guide you to the final confrontation, only he.'

Tomas and Pug exchanged glances, and even as Pug spoke, he knew the answer to his question. 'Whom must I seek?'

The girl's eyes seemed to pierce his soul. Calmly she said, 'You must find Macros the Black.'

CHAPTER FIVE

Crydee

MARTIN CROUCHED.

He motioned for those behind to remain quiet as he listened for movement in the deep thicket. Sundown was approaching and animals should have been appearing at the edge of the pond. But something had driven away most of the game. Martin hunted the source of that disruption. The woods were silent except for the sound of birds overhead. Then something rustled in the brush.

A stag leaped forward, bounding over the edge of the clearing. Martin dodged to his right, avoiding the stag's antlers and flying hooves as the frightened animal sprang past. He could hear the scurrying of his companions as they avoided being trampled by the fleeing animal. Then Martin heard a deep grumbling sound issuing from where the stag had fled. Whatever had spurred the animal into flight was approaching through the undergrowth. Martin waited, his bow ready.

He watched as the bear limped into view. At a time it should be getting fat and glossy, this animal was weak and scrawny, as thin as if it had just emerged from a long winter's sleep. Martin studied it as it lowered its head to drink from the pool. Some injury had lamed the animal, sickening it and preventing it from getting the food it needed. Two nights before the bear had mauled a farmer who had attempted to defend his milk cow. The man had died and Martin had been tracking the bear since. It was a rogue and had to be killed.

The sound of horses carried through the woods, and the bear's muzzle came up as it sniffed the air. A questioning growl escaped its throat as it rose on hind legs, followed by an angry roar as it smelled horses and men. 'Damn!' said Martin as he stood, drawing his bow. He had hoped to get a cleaner shot, but the animal would turn and flee in a moment.

The arrow sped across the clearing, taking the bear below the neck in the shoulder. It was not a quick killing shot. The animal pawed at the shaft, its growls a bubbling, liquid sound. Martin came around the pond, his hunting knife out, his three companions behind. Garret, now Huntmaster of Crydee, let fly his own arrow as Martin raced toward the bear. The second shaft took the beast in the chest, another serious but not yet fatal wound. Martin sprang at the bear while it pawed at the arrows embedded in its thick fur. The Duke of Crydee's large hunter's knife struck deep and true, taking the weak and confused animal in the throat. The bear died as it hit the ground.

Baru and Charles followed, their bows at the ready. Charles, short and bandy-legged, wore the same green leather clothing as Garret's, the uniform of a forester in Martin's service. Baru, tall and muscular, wore a plaid of green and black tartan – signifying the Iron Hills Clan of the Hadati – slung over one shoulder, leather trousers, and buckskin boots. Martin knelt over the animal. He worked at the bear's shoulder with his knife, turning his head slightly at the sweetish, rotting stench that came up from the gangrenous wound, then he sat back, showing a bloody, pus-covered arrowhead. He said to Garret in disgust, 'When I was Huntmaster for my father, I often ignored a little poaching here and there during a lean year. But if you find the man who shot this bear, I want him hung. And if he has anything of value, give it to the farmer's widow. He murdered that farmer as much as if he had shot him instead of the bear.'

Garret took the arrowhead and examined it. 'This arrowhead is home-cast, Your Grace. Look at this odd line running down the side of the head. The man who cast these doesn't file the heads. He's as sloppy in his fletchery as his hunting. If we find a quiver of arrowheads with the same flaw, we have our man. I'll pass word to the trackers.' Then the long-faced Huntmaster said, 'If Your Grace had reached that bear before I'd hit it, we might have had two murders to charge the poacher with.' His tone was disapproving.

Martin smiled. 'I had no doubt of your aim, Garret. You're the only man I know who's a better shot than I. It's one of the reasons you're Huntmaster.'

Charles said, 'And because he's the only one of your trackers who can keep up with you when you decide to hunt.'

'You do set a fast pace, Lord Martin,' agreed Baru.

'Well,' said Garret, not entirely appeased by Martin's answer, 'we might have had one more good shot before the bear ran.'

'Might, might not. I'd rather jump it here in the clearing, with you three coming, than try to follow it into the brush, even with three arrows in it.' He motioned toward the thicket a few yards away. 'It could get a little tight in there.'

Garret looked at Charles and Baru. 'No argument as to that, Your Grace.' He added, 'Though it got a mite close out here.'

A calling voice sounded a short way off. Martin stood. 'Find out who is making all that noise. It almost cost us this kill.' Charles hurried off.

Baru shook his head as he regarded the dead bear. 'The man who wounded this bear is no hunter.'

Martin looked about the woods. 'I miss this, Baru. I might even forgive that poacher a little for giving me an excuse to get away from the castle.'

Garret said, 'It's a thin excuse, my lord. By rights you should have left this to me and my trackers.'

Martin smiled. 'So Fannon will insist.'

Baru said, 'I understand. For almost a year I stayed with the elves and now you. I miss the hills and meadows of the Yabon Highlands.'

Garret said nothing. Both he and Martin understood why the Hadati had not returned. His village had been destroyed by the moredhel chieftain Murad. And while Baru had avenged it by killing Murad, he no longer had a home. Someday he might find another Hadati village in which to settle, but for the time being he chose to wander far from home. After his wounds had healed at Elvandar, he had come to Crydee to guest for a while with Martin.

Charles returned, a soldier of Crydee behind. The soldier saluted and said, 'Swordmaster Fannon requests you return at once, Your Grace.' Martin exchanged a quick glance with Baru. 'What's afoot, I wonder?'

Baru shrugged.

The soldier said, 'The Swordmaster took the liberty of sending extra mounts, Your Grace. He knew you'd left on foot.'

Martin said, 'Lead on,' and they followed the soldier to where others waited with mounts. As they readied themselves for the return to Castle Crydee, the Duke felt a sudden disquiet.

Fannon stood waiting for them as Martin dismounted. 'What is it, Fannon?' said Martin as he slapped at the road dust on his green leather tunic.

'Has Your Grace forgotten Lord Miguel will arrive this afternoon?'

Martin looked at the lowering sun. 'Then he's late.'

'His ship was sighted beyond the point at Sailor's Grief an hour ago. He'll be passing Longpoint lighthouse into the harbour within the next hour.'

Martin smiled at his Swordmaster. 'You're right, of course. I had forgotten.' Almost running up the stairs, he said, 'Come and talk with me, Fannon, while I change.'

Martin hurried toward his quarters, once occupied by his father, Lord Borric. Pages had drawn a hot tub and Martin quickly stripped off his hunter's garb. He took the strongly scented soap and washing stone and said to the page, 'Have plenty of cold fresh water here. This scent is something my sister might like, but it cloys my nose.' The page left to fetch more water.

'Now, Fannon, what brings the illustrious Duke of Rodez from the other side of the Kingdom?'

Fannon sat upon a settee. 'He is simply travelling for the summer. It is not unheard of, Your Grace.'

Martin laughed. 'Fannon, we're alone. You can drop the pretence. He's bringing at least one daughter of marriageable age.'

Fannon sighed. 'Two. Miranda is twenty and Inez is fifteen. Both are said to be beauties.'

'Fifteen! Gods, man! She's a baby.'

Fannon smiled ruefully. 'Two duels have been fought already over that baby, according to my information. Remember, these are easterners.'

Martin stretched out to soak. 'They do tend to get into politics early back there, don't they?'

'Look, Martin, like it or not, you are Duke – and brother to the King. You've never married. If you didn't live in the most remote corner of the Kingdom, you'd have had sixty social visits since your return home, not six.'

Martin grimaced. 'If this turns out like the last, I'm going to return to the forests and the bears.' The last visit had been from the Earl of Tarloff, vassal to the Duke of Ran. His daughter had been charming enough, but she tended to the flighty and had giggled, a trait that set Martin's teeth on edge. He had left the girl with vague promises to visit Tarloff someday. 'Still,' he said, 'she was a pretty enough thing.'

'Pretty has little to do with it, as you well know. Things are still reeling in the East, even though it's approaching two years since King Rodric's death. Guy du Bas-Tyra's out there somewhere doing what only the gods know. Some of his faction still wait to see who will be named Duke of Bas-Tyra. With Caldric dead and the office of Duke of Rillanon also vacant, the East is a tower of sticks. Pull the wrong one and it will all come down on the King's head. Lyam is well advised by Tully to wait for sons and nephews. Then he can put more allies in office. It would do well for you not to lose sight of the facts of life for the King's family, Martin.'

'Yes, Swordmaster,' Martin said, with a regretful shake of his head. He knew Fannon was right. Once Lyam had elevated him to the position of Duke of Crydee, he had lost a great deal of his freedom, with even greater losses to come, or so it seemed.

Three pages entered with buckets of cold water. Martin stood and let them pour the water over him. Shivering, he wrapped himself in a soft towel, and when the pages were gone, he said, 'Fannon, what you say is obviously right, but . . . well, it's not even a year since Arutha and I returned from Moraelin. Before that . . . it was that long tour of the East. Can't I have a few months just to live quietly at home?'

'You did. Last winter.'

Martin laughed. 'Very well. But it would seem to me that there is a lot more interest in a rural duke than is required.'

Fannon shook his head. 'More interest than is required in the brother to the King?'

'None of my line could claim the crown, even if three, maybe soon four, others didn't stand in succession before me. Remember, I abdicated any claim for my posterity.'

'You are not a simple man, Martin. Don't play the woodsy with me. You may have said whatever you wished on the day of Lyam's coronation, but should some descendant of yours be in a position to inherit, your vows won't count a tinker's damn if some faction in the Congress of Lords wishes him King.'

Martin began to dress. 'I know, Fannon. That was meant only to keep people from opposing Lyam in my name. I may have spent most of my life in the forests, but when I dined with you, Tully, Kulgan, and Father, I kept my ears open. I learned a lot.'

A knock came and a guard appeared at the door. 'Ship flying the banner of Rodez clearing Longpoint light, Your Grace.'

Martin waved the guard out. He said to Fannon, 'I guess we'd better hurry to meet the Duke and his lovely daughters.' Finishing his dressing, he said, 'I will be inspected and courted by the Duke's daughters, Fannon, but for the gods' love and patience, I hope neither of them giggles.' Fannon nodded in sympathy as he followed Martin from the room.

Martin smiled at Duke Miguel's jest. It concerned an eastern lord Martin had met only once. The man's foibles might have been a source of humour to the eastern lords, but the joke was lost on Martin. Martin cast a glance at the Duke's daughters. Both girls were lovely: delicate features, pale complexions framed by nearly black hair, and both had large dark eyes. Miranda sat engaged in conversation with young Squire Wilfred, third son of the Baron of Carse and newly come to the court. Inez sat regarding Martin with frank appraisal. Martin felt his neck begin to colour and turned his attention back to her father. He could see why she had been the excuse for a duel between hotheaded youths. Martin didn't know a great deal about women, but he was an expert hunter and he knew a predator when he saw one. This girl might be only fifteen years of age, but she was a veteran of the eastern courts. She would find a powerful husband before too long, Martin didn't doubt. Miranda was simply another pretty lady of the court, but Inez hinted at hard edges Martin found unattractive. This girl was clearly dangerous and already experienced in twisting men to her will. Martin determined to keep that fact uppermost in mind.

Supper had been quiet, as was Martin's usual custom, but tomorrow there would be jugglers and singers, for a travelling band of minstrels was in the area. Martin had little affection for formal banquets after his eastern tour but some sort of show was in order. Then a page hurried into the room, skirting the tables to reach Housecarl Samuel's side. He spoke softly, and the Housecarl came to Martin's chair. Leaning down, he said, 'Pigeons just arrived from Ylith, Your Grace. Eight of them.' ·

Martin understood. For so many birds to have been used the message would be urgent. It was usual to employ only two or three against the possibility of a bird not finishing the dangerous flight over the Grey Tower Mountains. It took weeks to send them back by cart or ship, so they were used sparingly. Martin rose. 'If Your Grace will excuse me a moment?' he said to the Duke of Rodez. 'Ladies?' He bowed to the two sisters, then followed the page out of the hall.

In the antechamber of the keep, he found the Hawkmaster, in charge of the hawk mews and the pigeon coop, standing with the small parchments. He handed them to Martin and withdrew. Martin saw the tiny message slips were sealed, with the royal crest of Krondor drawn on the roll of paper about them, indicating only the Duke was to open them. Martin said, 'I'll read these in my council chamber.'

Alone in his council room, Martin saw that the slips had been numbered one and two. Four pairs. The message had been sent four times to ensure it arrived intact. Martin unfolded one of the slips marked one, then his eyes widened as he fumbled to open another. The message was duplicated. He then read a number two, and tears came unbidden to his eyes.

Long minutes passed as Martin opened every slip, hoping to find something different, something to tell him he had misunderstood. For a long time, he could only sit staring at the papers before him as a cold sickness visited the pit of his stomach. Finally a knock came at the door, and he said weakly, 'Yes?'

The door opened and Fannon entered. 'You've been gone near an hour—' He stopped when he saw Martin's drawn expression and red eyes. 'What is it?'

Martin could only wave his hand at the scraps. Fannon read them, then half staggered backward to sit in a chair. A shaking hand covered his face for a long minute. Both men were silent. At last he said, 'How could this be?'

'I don't know. The message only says an assassin.' Martin let his gaze wander around the room, every stone in the wall and piece of furniture associated with his father, Lord Borric. And of his family, the most like their father had been Arutha. Martin loved them all, but Arutha had been a mirror of Martin in many ways. They had shared a certain way of seeing things and had endured much together: the siege of the castle during the Riftwar while Lyam had been absent with their father, the long dangerous quest to Moraelin to find Silverthorn. No, in Arutha Martin had discovered his closest friend in many ways. Elven-taught, Martin knew the inevitability of death, but he was mortal and felt an empty place appear within himself. He regained his composure as he stood. 'I had best inform Duke Miguel. His visit is to be short. We leave for Krondor tomorrow.'

Martin looked up as Fannon reentered the room. 'It will take all night and morning to get ready, but the captain says your ship will be able to leave on the afternoon tide.'

Martin motioned for him to take a chair and waited a long moment before speaking. 'How can it be, Fannon?'

The Swordmaster said, 'I can't answer that, Martin.' Fannon was thoughtful a moment, then softly said, 'You know I share your grief. We all do. He, and Lyam, were like my own sons.'

'I know.'

'But there are other matters that cannot be put off.'

'Such as?'

'I'm old, Martin. I suddenly feel the weight of ages upon me. News of Arutha's death . . . makes me again feel my own mortality. I wish to retire.'

Martin rubbed his chin as he thought. Fannon was past seventy now, and while his mental capacity was undiminished, he lacked the physical stamina required of the Duke's second-in-command. 'I understand, Fannon. When I return from Rillanon—'

Fannon interrupted. 'No, that's too long, Martin. You will be gone several months. I need a named successor now, so I can begin to ensure he is capable when I leave office. If Gardan were still here, I'd have no doubt as to a smooth transition, but with Arutha stealing him away' – the old man's eyes filled with tears – 'making him Knight-Marshal of Krondor, well . . .'

Martin said, 'I understand. Who did you have in mind?' The question was asked absently, as Martin struggled to keep his mind calm.

'Several of the sergeants might serve, but we've no one of Gardan's capabilities. No, I had Charles in mind.'

Martin gave a weak smile. 'I thought you didn't trust him.'

Fannon sighed. 'That was a long time back, and we were fighting a war. He's shown his worth a hundred times since then, and I don't think there's a man in the castle more fearless. Besides, he was a Tsurani officer, about equal to a knight-lieutenant. He knows warcraft and tactics. He has often spent hours speaking with me about the differences between Tsurani warfare and our own. I know this: once he learns something, he doesn't forget. He's a clever man and worth a dozen lesser men. Besides, the soldiers respect him and will follow him.'

Martin said, 'I'll consider it and decide tonight. What else?'

Fannon was silent for a time, as if speaking came with difficulty. 'Martin, you and I have never been close. When your father called you to serve I felt, as did others, that there was something strange about you. You were always aloof, and you had those odd elvish ways. Now I know that part of the mystery was the truth of your relation-ship to Borric. I doubted you in some ways, Martin. I'm sorry to admit that . . . But what I'm trying to say is . . . you honour your father.'

Martin took a deep breath. 'Thank you, Fannon.'

'I say this to ensure you understand why I say this next. This visit from Duke Miguel was only an irritation before; now it is an issue of weight. You must speak to Father Tully when you reach Rillanon, and let him find you a wife.'

Martin threw back his head and laughed, a bitter, angry laugh. 'What jest, Fannon? My brother is dead and you want me to look for a wife?'

Fannon was unflinching before Martin's rising anger. 'You are no longer the Huntmaster of Crydee, Martin. Then no one cared should you ever wed and father sons. Now you are sole brother to the King. The East is still in turmoil. There is no duke in Bas-Tyra, Rillanon, or Krondor. Now there is no Prince in Krondor.' Fannon's voice became thick with fatigue and emotion. 'Lyam sits upon a perilous throne should Bas-Tyra venture back to the Kingdom from exile. With only Arutha's two babes in the succession now, Lyam needs alliances. That is what I mean. Tully will know which noble houses need to be secured to the King's cause by marriage. If it's Miguel's little hellcat Inez, or even Tarloff's giggler, marry her, Martin, for Lyam's sake and the sake of the Kingdom.'

Martin stifled his anger. Fannon had pressed a sore point with him, even if the old Swordmaster was correct. In all ways, Martin was a solitary man, sharing little with any man save for his brothers. And he had never done well with the company of women. Now he was being told he must wed a stranger for the sake of his brother's political health. But he knew there was wisdom in Fannon's words. Should the traitorous Guy du Bas-Tyra be plotting still, Lyam's crown was not secure. Arutha's death showed all too clearly how mortal rulers were. Finally Martin said, 'I'll think about that as well, Fannon.'

The old Swordmaster rose slowly. Reaching the door, he turned. 'I know you hide it well, Martin, but the pain is there. I'm sorry if it seems I add to it, but what I said needed to be said.' Martin could only nod.

Fannon left and Martin sat alone in his chamber, the sole moving thing the shadows cast by the guttering torches in the wall sconces.

Martin stood impatiently watching the scurrying activity in preparation for his and the Duke of Rodez's departure. The Duke had invited Martin to accompany them aboard his own ship, but Martin had managed a barely adequate refusal. Only the obvious stress of dealing with Arutha's death had allowed him to rebuff the Duke without serious insult.

Duke Miguel and his daughters appeared from the keep, dressed for travel. The girls were poorly hiding their irritation at having to resume travel so soon. It would be a full two weeks or more before they were again in Krondor. Then, as a member of the peerage, their father would be hurrying to Rillanon for Arutha's burial and state funeral.

Duke Miguel, a slight man of fine manners and dress, said, 'It is tragic we must quit your wonderful home under such grim circumstances, Your Grace. If I may, I would gladly extend the hospitality of my own home to you should Your Grace wish to rest awhile after your brother's funeral. Rodez is but a short journey from the capital.'

Martin's first impulse was to beg off but, keeping Fannon's words of the night before in mind, he said, 'Should time and circumstances permit, Your Grace, I'll be most happy to visit you. Thank you.' He cast a glance at the two daughters and determined then and there that should Tully advise an alliance between Crydee and Rodez, it would be the quiet Miranda he would court. Inez was simply too much trouble gathered together in one place.

The Duke and his daughters rode out in a carriage toward the harbour. Martin thought back to when his father had been Duke. No one in Crydee had need of a carriage, which served poorly on the dirt roads of the Duchy, often turned to thick mud by the coastal rains. But with the increasing number of visitors to the West, Martin had ordered one built. It seemed the eastern ladies fared poorly on horseback while in court costume. He thought of Carline's riding like a man during the Riftwar, in tight-fitting trousers and tunic, racing with Squire Roland, to the utter horror of her governess. Martin sighed. Neither of Miguel's girls would ever ride like that. Martin wondered if there was a woman anywhere who shared his need for rough living. Perhaps the best he could hope for would be a woman who would accept that need in him and not complain over his long absences while he hunted or visited his friends in Elvandar.

Martin's musing was interrupted by a soldier accompanying the Hawkmaster, who held out another small parchment. 'This just arrived, your Grace.'

Martin took the parchment. Upon it was the crest of Salador. Martin waited until the Masterhawker had left to open it. Most likely it was a personal message from Carline. He opened it and read. He read again, then thoughtfully put the parchment in his belt pouch. After a long moment of reflection, he spoke to a soldier at post before the keep. 'Fetch Swordmaster Fannon.'

Within minutes the Swordmaster was in the Duke's presence. Martin said, 'I've thought it over and I agree with you. I'll offer the position of Swordmaster to Charles.'

'Good,' said Fannon. 'I expect he will agree.'

'Then after I'm gone, Fannon, begin at once to instruct Charles in his office.'

Fannon said, 'Yes, Your Grace.' He started to turn away but turned back toward Martin. 'Your Grace?'

Martin halted as he had just begun to walk back to the keep. 'Yes?'

'Are you all right?'

Martin said, 'Fine, Fannon. I've just received a note from Laurie informing me that Carline and Anita are well. Continue as you were.' Without another word he returned to the keep, passing through the large doors.

Fannon hesitated before leaving. He was surprised at Martin's tone and manner. There was something odd in the way he looked as he left.

Baru quietly faced Charles. Both men sat upon the floor, their legs crossed. A small gong rested to the left of Charles and a censer burned between them, filling the air with sweet pungency. Four candles illuminated the room. The only furnishings were a mat upon the floor, which Charles preferred to a bed, a small wooden chest, and a pile of cushions. Both men wore simple robes. Each had a sword across his knees. Baru waited while Charles kept his eyes focused upon some unseen point between them. Then the Tsurani said, 'What is the Way?'

Baru answered. 'The Way consists of discharging loyal service to one's master, and of deep fidelity in associations with comrades. The Way, with consideration for one's place upon the Wheel, consists of placing duty above all.'

Charles gave a single curt nod. 'In the matter of duty, the code of the warrior is absolute. Duty above all. Unto death.'

'This is understood.'

'What, then, is the nature of duty?'

Baru spoke softly. 'There is duty to one's lord. There is duty to one's clan and family. There is duty to one's work, which provides an understanding of duty to one's self. In sum they become the duty that is never satisfactorily discharged, even through the toil of a lifetime, the duty to attempt a perfect existence, to attain a higher place on the Wheel.'

Charles nodded once. 'This is so.' He picked up a small felt hammer and rang a tiny gong. 'Listen.' Baru closed his eyes in meditation, listening to the sound as it faded, diminishing, becoming fainter. When the sound was fully gone, Charles said, 'Find where the sound ends and silence begins. Then exist in that moment, for there will you find your secret centre of being, the perfect place of peace within yourself. And recall the most ancient lesson of the Tsurani: duty is the weight of all things, as heavy as a burden can become, while death is nothing, lighter than air.'

The door opened and Martin slipped in. Both Baru and Charles began to rise, but Martin waved them back. He knelt between them, his eyes fixed on the censer upon the floor. 'Pardon the interruption.'

'No interruption, Your Grace,' answered Charles.

Baru said, 'For years I fought the Tsurani and found them honourable foemen. Now I learn more of them. Charles has allowed me to take instruction in the Code of the Warrior, in the fashion of his people.'

Martin did not appear surprised. 'Have you learned much?'

'That they are like us,' said Baru with a faint smile. 'I know little of such things, but I suspect we are as two saplings from the same root. They follow the Way and understand the Wheel as do the Hadati. They understand honour and duty as do the Hadati. We who live in Yabon had taken much from the Kingdom, the names of our gods, and most of our language, but there is much of the old ways we Hadati kept. The Tsurani belief in the Way is much like our own. This is strange, for until the coming of the Tsurani, no others we met shared our beliefs.'

Martin looked at Charles. The Tsurani shrugged slightly. 'Perhaps we only find the same truth on both worlds. Who can say?'

Martin said, 'That sounds the sort of thing to take up with Tully and Kulgan.' He was quiet a moment, then said, 'Charles, will you accept the position of Swordmaster?'

The Tsurani blinked, the only sign of surprise. 'You honour me, Your Grace. Yes.'

'Good, I am pleased. Fannon will begin your instruction after I'm gone.' Martin looked up at the door, then lowered his voice. 'I want you both to do me a service.'

Charles didn't hesitate in agreeing to serve. Baru studied Martin closely. They had forged a bond on the trip to Moraelin with Arutha. Baru had almost died there, but fate had spared him. Baru knew his fortune was intertwined in some way with those who had quested for Silverthorn. Something lay hidden behind the Duke's eyes, but Baru would not question him. He would learn what it was in time. Finally he said, 'As will I.'

Martin sat between the men. He began to speak.

Martin gathered his cloak about him. The afternoon breeze was chilly, blowing down from the north. He looked sternward as Crydee disappeared behind the headlands of Sailor's Grief. With a nod to the ship's captain, he descended the companionway from the quarterdeck. Entering the captain's cabin, he locked the door behind. The man who waited there was one of Fannon's soldiers, named Stefan, equal in height and general build to the Duke, and wearing a tunic and trousers of the same colour as Martin's. He had been sneaked aboard in the early hours before dawn, dressed as a common sailor. Martin took off his cloak and handed it to the man. 'Don't come up on deck except after night until you're well past Queg. Should anything force the ship ashore at Carse, Tulan, or the Free Cities, I don't want sailors speaking of my disappearance.'

'Yes, Your Grace.'

'When you get to Krondor, there'll be a carriage waiting for you, I expect. I don't know how long you can continue the masquerade. Most of the nobles who've met me will already be en route to Rillanon, and we're enough alike to casual observation that most of the servants won't know you.' Martin studied his bogus counterpart. 'If you keep your mouth closed, you might pass as me all the way to Rillanon.'

Stefan looked disquieted by the prospect of a long siege of playing nobility but said only, 'I will try, Your Grace.'

The ship rocked as the captain ordered a change of course. Martin said, 'That's the first warning.' Quickly he stripped off his boots, tunic, and trousers, until all he wore was his underbreeches.

The captain's cabin had a single, hinged window, which opened with a protest. Martin hung his legs over the edge. From above he heard the captain's angry voice. 'You're coming too close to the shore! Hard a starboard!'

A confused-sounding helmsman answered, 'Aye, captain, hard a starboard.'

Martin said, 'Good fortune be with you, Stefan.'

'And with you, Your Grace.'

Martin dropped from the captain's cabin. The captain had warned him of the danger of hitting the large tiller, so Martin easily avoided it. The captain had brought him as close to shore as was safe, then turned out for deeper waters. Martin saw the beach less than a mile off. He was an indifferent swimmer but a powerful man and he set out for the shore in a series of easy strokes. The rolling swells made it unlikely anyone in the rigging would notice the man who was falling far behind them.

A short time later, Martin staggered up onto the beach, breathing hard. He looked about, locating landmarks. The action of the currents had carried him farther south than he had wished. Taking a deep breath, he turned up the beach and began to run.

After less than ten minutes, three riders came over a low bluff, moving rapidly down to the sand. Upon seeing them, Martin halted. Garret was the first to dismount, while Charles led an extra horse. Baru kept an alert eye out for sign of anyone in the area. Garret handed Martin a bundle of clothing. The run up the beach had dried Martin off and he dressed quickly. Behind the saddle of the extra horse hung an oilskin-covered longbow.

As Martin dressed, he said, 'Did anyone see you leave?'

Charles answered, 'Garret was already gone from the castle with your horse before dawn, and I simply instructed the guards I was riding a short way with Baru as he returned to Yabon. No comment was made by anyone.'

'Good. As we learned the last time we faced Murmandamus's agents, secrecy is paramount.' Martin mounted and said, 'Thank you for your help. Charles, you and Garret had best return quickly, before anyone becomes suspicious.'

Charles said, 'Whatever fate brings, Your Grace, may it also bring honour.'

Garret only said, 'Good fortune, Your Grace.'

The four riders were off, two returning up the coast road to Crydee, two heading away from the sea, toward the forest, bound for the northeast.

The forests were quiet, but still punctuated by the normal bird calls and small animal noises that indicated things were as they should be. Martin and Baru had ridden hard for days, pushing their horses to the limit of their endurance. They had crossed the river Crydee hours earlier.

From behind a tree a figure emerged, dressed in a green tunic and brown leather breeches. With a wave he said, 'Well met, Martin Longbow, Baru Serpentslayer.'

Martin recognized the elf, though he didn't know him well. 'Greetings, Tarlen. We come seeking counsel with the Queen.'

'Then travel on, for you and Baru are always welcome in her court. I must stand watch here. Things have become somewhat strained since last you guested.'

Martin recognized the tone of the elf's words. Something had the elves distressed, but Tarlen wouldn't speak of it. Martin would need to see the Queen and Tomas to discover what it was. He wondered. The last time the elves had seemed this disturbed over something, Tomas had been at the height of his madness. Martin spurred his horse forward.

Later the two riders approached the heart of the elven forests, Elvandar, ancient home to the elves. The tree city was awash with light, for the sun was high overhead, crowning the massive trees with brilliance. Leaves of green and gold, red and white, silver and bronze sparkled across the canopy of Elvandar.

As they dismounted, an elf approached. 'We shall care for your mounts, Lord Martin. Her Majesty wishes you to come at once.'

Martin and Baru hurried up the stairs cut from the bole of a tree into the city of the elves. Across high arches on the backs of branches and upward they climbed. At last they reached the large platform that was the centre of Elvandar, the court of the Queen.

Aglaranna sat quietly upon her throne, her senior adviser, Tathar, at her side. Around the court the elder Spellweavers sat, the Queen's council. The throne beside her was empty. Her expression was unreadable to most, but Martin understood elven ways and saw the strain in her eyes. Still, she was beautiful and regal and her smile a beacon of warmth as she said, 'Welcome, Lord Martin. Welcome, Baru of the Hadati.'

Both men bowed; then the Queen said, 'Come, let us talk.' She rose and led them to a chamber, accompanied by Tathar. Inside she turned and bade them sit. Wine and food were brought but ignored as Martin said, 'Something is wrong.' It was not a question.

Aglaranna's expression of concern deepened. Martin had not seen her this troubled since the Riftwar. 'Tomas is gone.'

Martin blinked. 'Where?'

Tathar answered. 'We do not know. He vanished in the night, a few days after the Midsummer's Festival. Occasionally he would wander off to be with his own thoughts, but never for more than a day. When he did not appear after two days, trackers were dispatched. There were no tracks from Elvandar, though that is not surprising. He has other means of travelling. But in a glade to the north we found marks from his boots. There were signs of another man there, sandal prints in the dirt.'

Martin said, 'Tomas went to meet with someone, then didn't return.'

'There was a third set of tracks,' said the Elf Queen. 'A dragon's. Once again the Valheru flies upon the back of a dragon.'

Martin sat back, understanding. 'You fear a return of the madness?'

'No,' said Tathar instantly. 'Tomas is free of that and, if anything, is stronger than he suspects. No, we fear Tomas's need to depart in such a manner without word. We fear the presence of another.'

Martin's eyes widened. 'The sandals?'

'You know what power is needed to enter our forests undetected. Only one man before has had the ability: Macros the Black.'

Martin pondered. 'Perhaps he's not the only one. I understand Pug to have stayed upon the Tsurani world to study the problem of Murmandamus and what he called the Enemy. Perhaps he has returned.'

'Which sorcerous master it is proves of little import,' said Tathar.

It was Baru who spoke next. 'What is important is that two men of vast powers are about upon a mission of mystery, at a time when it seems troubles have returned from the north.'

Aglaranna said, 'Yes.' She said to Martin, 'Rumours have reached us of the death of one who was close to you.' In the elven way she avoided naming the dead.

'There are things I may not speak of, lady, even to one as highly regarded as you. I have a duty.'

'Then,' asked Tathar, 'may I ask where you are bound, and what brings you here?'

'It is time to go north again,' said Martin, 'to finish what was started last year.'

'It is well you came this way,' said Tathar. 'We have seen signs from the coast to the east of massive goblin migrations northward. Also the moredhel are bold with their scouting along the edge of our forests. They seem intent on discovering if any of our warriors pass beyond our normal boundaries. There have been sightings of bands of renegade humans riding northward, close to the boundary with Stone Mountain, as well. The gwali have fled south into the Green Heart, as if fearing something approaching. And for months we have been visited by some ill-aspected wind of evil, which carries some mystic quality, as if power were being drawn to the north. We are concerned over many things.'

Baru and Martin exchanged glances. 'Things move at swift pace,' said the Hadati.

Further conversation was halted when a shout went up from below and an elf appeared at the Queen's elbow. 'Majesty, come, a Returning.'

Aglaranna said, 'Come, Martin, Baru, witness something miraculous.'

Tathar followed his Queen, turning to say, 'If it is indeed a true Returning and not a ruse.'

The Queen and Tathar were joined by her other advisers as they hurried down to the forest floor. When they reached ground level, they were greeted by several warriors who surrounded a moredhel. The dark elf looked somehow odd to Martin, showing a calmness beyond what was normal for the dark elves.

The moredhel saw the Queen and bowed before her, lowering his head. Softly he said, 'Lady, I have returned.'

The Queen nodded to Tathar. He and others of the Spellweavers gathered about the moredhel. Martin could feel a strange, fey sensation as if the air had suddenly become charged, and as if music could almost be heard. He knew the Spellweavers were working magic.

Then Tathar said, 'He has returned!'

Aglaranna said, 'What is your name?'

'Morandis, Majesty.'

'No more. You are Lorren.'

Martin had learned the year before that there was no true difference between the branches of elvenkind, separated only by the power of the Dark Path, that which bound the moredhel to a life of murderous hatred toward all not of their kind. But there was a subtle difference in attitude, stance, and manner between the two.

The moredhel rose and the elves surrounding him helped him remove his tunic, the grey of the moredhel forest clans. Martin had lived with elves all his life and fought the moredhel many times and could recognize the difference. But now his senses were confounded. One moment the moredhel seemed odd, somehow different from what they had expected, then suddenly he was a moredhel no longer. He was given a brown tunic and, miraculously, Martin saw an elf there. He had the dark hair and eyes common to the moredhel, but then so did a few other elves, just as an occasional moredhel was blond and blue-eyed. He was an elf!

Tathar observed Martin's reaction to the change and said, 'Occasionally one of our lost brothers breaks away from the Dark Path. If his kin do not discover the change and kill him before he reaches us, we welcome his return to his home. It is a cause for rejoicing.' Martin and Baru watched as every elf in the area came to embrace Lorren in turn, welcoming him home. 'In the past, the moredhel have attempted to send spies, but we can always tell the true from the false. This one has truly returned to his people.'

Baru said, 'Does it happen often?'

'Of all who abide in Elvandar, I am eldest,' said Tathar. 'I have seen only seven such Returnings before this one.' He was silent for a time. 'Someday we hope we shall redeem all our brothers in this fashion, when the power of the Dark Path is at last broken.'

Aglaranna turned to Martin. 'Come, we shall be celebrating.'

'We may not, Majesty,' answered Martin. 'We must be away to meet with others.'

'May we know your plans?'

'It is simple,' answered the Duke of Crydee. 'We shall find Murmandamus.'

'And,' added Baru without expression, 'we shall kill him.'

• CHAPTER SIX •

Leavetaking

*J*IMMY SAT QUIETLY.

He absently studied the list in his hand, attempting to keep his mind on the matter before him. But he was unable to concentrate on the task. The duty roster of squires for that afternoon's cortege was done, or as done as it was likely to be. Jimmy felt an emptiness inside, and the need to decide which squire was posted where seemed trivial in the extreme.

For two weeks Jimmy had been fighting the feeling that he was caught up in some horrible dream, one from which he could not shake himself. Nothing in his existence so far had affected him as deeply as Arutha's murder, and he still couldn't face his emotions. He had slept long each night, as if sleep were an escape, and when awake he was nervous and anxious to be doing something as if being busy would keep him from dealing with his grief. He kept it hidden away, to be confronted later.

Jimmy sighed. One thing the young man knew, this funeral was taking a hellishly long time getting organized. Laurie and Volney had postponed the departure of the funeral procession twice now. The bier had been placed aboard its carriage within two days after Arutha's death, awaiting his body. Tradition held the Prince's cortege should have started for Rillanon and his ancestral vault within three days after his death, but Anita had taken days returning from her mother's estates, then a few more days in recovering enough to depart, then they needed to wait for other nobles who were arriving, and the palace was in disorder and so on and so on. Still, Jimmy knew he wouldn't begin to get over this tragedy until after Arutha was carried away. Knowing he lay in the temporary vault Nathan had prepared, somewhere not too far from where the squire now sat, was just too much for Jimmy. He rubbed his eyes, lowering his head, as once more the threat of tears was forced down. In his short life, Jimmy had met only one man who had touched him deeply. Arutha should have been one of the last men in the world to care about the fate of a boy thief, but he had. He had proved a friend, and more. He and Anita had been the closest thing to family Jimmy had ever known.

A knock upon the door brought his head up and he saw Locklear standing before the entrance. Jimmy waved him in and the younger boy sat down on the other side of the writing desk. Jimmy tossed the parchment at him. 'Here, Locky, you do this.'

Locklear quickly scanned the list, and took quill from holder. 'It's almost ready, except Paul is down with the flux and the chirurgeon wants him in bed for the day. He needs rest. This is a mess. I'd better recopy it.'

Jimmy nodded absently. Through the blanket of grey sorrow that wrapped his thoughts, an irritant was gently scratching. Something had been nagging at the corner of the young man's mind for three days now. Everyone in the palace was still in shock at Arutha's death, but there was an odd note here and there; every so often someone said or did something that was somehow discordant. Jimmy couldn't put his finger on what that difference was, or even if it was important. With a mental shrug he pushed aside his worry. Different people reacted differently to tragedy. Some, like Volney and Gardan, threw themselves into their work. Others, like Carline, went off to cope with their grief in a private way. Duke Laurie was a lot like Jimmy. He just put his grief aside to be faced at some other time. Suddenly Jimmy understood one reason for his feeling of oddness about the palace. Laurie had been just about running the palace from the time Arutha lay stricken until three days ago. Now he was almost continuously absent.

Looking at Locklear as the younger boy wrote on the duty roster, Jimmy said, 'Locky, have you seen Duke Laurie about lately?'

Keeping his eyes on his work, Locklear said, 'This morning, very early. I was in charge of delivering meals to the visiting nobles for breakfast, and I saw him riding out the gate.' His head came up, a strange expression on his face. 'It was the postern gate.'

'Why would he leave by the postern gate?' Jimmy wondered.

Locklear shrugged and returned to the roster. 'Because that's the direction he was heading?'

Jimmy thought. What reason did the Duke of Salador have riding toward the Poor Quarter on the morning of the Prince's funeral procession? Jimmy sighed. 'I'm becoming suspicious in my old age.'

Locklear laughed, the first happy sound in the palace in days. Then, as if he had sinned, he looked up guiltily.

Jimmy stood. 'Done?'

Locklear handed over the parchment. 'Finished.'

'Good,' said Jimmy. 'Come along, deLacy will not show his usual forbearance if we're late.'

They hurried to where the squires were assembling. The usual jostling play and laughing whispers were absent, for the occasion was solemn. DeLacy arrived a few minutes after Jimmy and Locklear were in place and without preamble said, 'The roster.' Jimmy gave it to him and he glanced over it. 'Good, though either your penmanship is improving or you've acquired an assistant.' There was a slight shuffle among the boys, but no open mirthfulness. DeLacy said, 'I'm changing one assignment, though. Harold and Bryce will stand as coach attendants to the Princesses Alicia and Anita. James and Locklear will remain to assist the Steward of the Royal Household here at the palace.'

Jimmy was stunned. He and Locklear would not be in the cortege to the gates. They would stand idly by in case there was some minor problem the steward judged required a squire's presence.

DeLacy absently read the other assignments aloud, then dismissed the boys. Locklear and Jimmy exchanged glances, and Jimmy overtook the departing Master of Ceremonies. 'Sir . . .' Jimmy began.

DeLacy turned on Jimmy. 'If it's about the assignments, there will be no debate.'

Jimmy's face flushed angrily. 'But I was the Prince's Squire!' he answered hotly.

In an unusually bold moment, Locklear blurted, 'And I was Squire to Her Highness.' DeLacy looked at the younger boy in astonishment. 'Well, sort of . . .' he amended.

'That is of no consequence,' said deLacy. 'I have my orders. You must follow yours. That will be all.' Jimmy began to protest again, but was cut off by the old Master. 'I said that would be all, squire.'

Jimmy turned and began walking away. Locklear fell in beside him. 'I don't know what's going on here,' said Jimmy, 'but I intend to find out. Come on.'

Jimmy and Locklear hurried along, glancing about. An order from any senior member of the court would prevent this unexpected visit, so they took pains to avoid the scrutiny of anyone likely to find work for them. The funeral cortege would depart the palace in less than two hours, so there were ample tasks remaining for two squires. Once begun, there would be a slow parade through the city, a stop at the temple square, where public prayers would be said, then the long journey to Rillanon and the tomb of Arutha's ancestors. Once the funeral party was outside the city, the squires would return to the palace. But Jimmy and Locklear were being denied even that small part in the procession.

Jimmy approached the Princess's door and said to the guard without, 'If Her Highness can spare a moment?'

The guard's eyebrows rose, but he was not in a position to question even as minor a member of the court as a squire, so he would simply pass the message inside. As the guard pushed open the door, Jimmy thought he heard something out of place, a sound that ended before he could apprehend its nature. Jimmy tried to puzzle out what he had just heard, but the guard's return diverted his attention. A moment later, he and Locklear were admitted.

Carline sat with Anita, near a window, awaiting the summons to attend the funeral. Their heads were close together and they were speaking softly. Princess Mother Alicia hovered at her daughter's shoulder. All three were dressed in black. Jimmy came and bowed, Locklear at his side. 'I'm sorry to intrude, Highness,' he said softly.

Anita smiled at him. 'You're never an intrusion, Jimmy. What is it?'

Suddenly feeling it was petty to be concerned over his exclusion from the funeral, Jimmy said, 'A small thing, actually. Someone ordered me to remain at the palace today, and I wondered . . . well, did you ask for me to be kept here?'

A glance passed from Carline to Anita, and the Princess of Krondor said, 'No, I didn't, Jimmy.' Her tone was thoughtful. 'But perhaps Earl Volney did. You are Senior Squire and should stay in your office, or at least I'm sure that's what the Earl decided.'

Jimmy studied her expression. A discordant note was sounding here. Princess Anita had returned from her mother's estate displaying the grief expected. But soon after, there had been a subtle change in her. Further conversation was interrupted by a baby's cry, quickly followed by another. Anita rose. 'It's never just one of them,' she said, with affection clearly showing. Carline smiled at that, then suddenly her expression turned sombre.

Jimmy said, 'We have intruded, Highness. I am sorry to have troubled you over so petty a matter.'

Locklear followed Jimmy outside. Moving out of the guard's earshot, Jimmy said, 'Did I miss something in there, Locky?'

Locklear turned and regarded the door for a moment. 'Something's . . . odd. It's like we're being kept out of the way.'

Jimmy thought a minute. He now understood what had arrested his attention outside the door, just before they had been admitted. The sound that intruded had been the Princesses' voices, or rather the quality of those voices: chatty, lightly bantering. Jimmy said, 'I'm beginning to think you're right. Come along. We don't have much time.'

'Time for what?'

'You'll see.' Jimmy hurried off down the corridor and the younger boy had to scramble to catch up.

Gardan and Volney were hurrying toward the courtyard, accompanied by four guards, when the boys intercepted them. The Earl hardly spared a glance as he said, 'Aren't you two supposed to be in the courtyard.'

'No, sir,' answered Jimmy. 'We've drawn steward's duty.'

Gardan seemed mildly surprised at that, but all Volney said was, 'Then I expect you should hurry along in case you're needed there. We must begin the procession.'

'Sir,' said Jimmy, 'did you order us to remain?'

Volney waved off the question. 'Duke Laurie has been attending to those details with Master deLacy.' He turned his attention away from the boys as he and Gardan walked off.

Jimmy and Locklear halted as the Earl and Marshal vanished around a corner, the boot heels of their escorts clacking noisily on the stones. 'I think I'm beginning to understand,' said Jimmy. He grabbed Locklear by the arm. 'Come on.'

With a half frustrated note in his voice, Locklear said, 'Where?'

'You'll see,' came the answer, as Jimmy almost ran.

Locklear hurried after, mimicking, 'You'll see. You'll see. See what, damn it!'

Two guards stood at post. One said, 'And where are you young gentlemen off to?'

'Port Authority,' said Jimmy testily, handing over a quickly penned order. 'The steward can't find some ship manifest, and he's in a fury to get a copy.' Jimmy had been about to investigate something and was rankled by the need to run this errand. It also seemed an odd time for the steward to become obsessed with the need for a manifest.

The guard who had examined the paper said, 'Just a minute.' He signalled to another soldier near the guard officer's room by the main entrance to the palace. The guard hurried over and the first sentry said, 'Can you spare a bit of time to run these lads down to the port office and back? They need to fetch something for the steward.'

The guard looked indifferent. There and back would take less than an hour. He nodded and the three were off.

Twenty minutes later, Jimmy stood in the Port Authority office dealing with a minor functionary as everyone else was off to watch the cortege leave the city. The man grumbled as he thumbed through a stack of paper work, looking for a copy of the last manifest of goods delivered to the royal docks. While he fumbled, Jimmy cast a glance at another paper hanging on the wall of the office for all to look at. It was this week's schedules of departures. Something caught his eye and he crossed over to look. Locklear followed him. 'What?'

Jimmy pointed. 'Interesting.'

Locklear looked at the notation and said, 'Why?'

'I'm not sure,' answered Jimmy, pitching his voice lower, 'but think a minute about some of the things going on at the palace. We get held back from the procession, then we ask the Princess about it. We're out of her quarters less than ten minutes when we're sent on this useless errand. You tell me, doesn't it seem like we're being kept out of the way? Something's . . . odd.'

'That's what I said earlier,' said Locklear impatiently.

The clerk found and handed over the requested paper, and the guard escorted the boys back to the palace. Running past the gate guards, Jimmy and Locklear waved absently, then headed toward the steward's office.

Once inside the palace, they appeared at the office as the steward, Baron Giles, was leaving. 'There you are,' he said in an accusatory tone. 'I thought I was going to have to send guards to ferret you out of wherever you were lazing away the day.' Jimmy and Locklear exchanged glances. The steward seemed to have forgotten about the manifest entirely. Jimmy handed it to him.

'What's this?' He examined the paper. 'Oh yes,' he remarked, tossing the paper upon his desk. 'I'll deal with that later. I must be off to see the procession depart the palace. You will stay here. Should any emergency arise, one of you will remain in this office while the other will come and find me. Once the bier has left the gate, I will return.'

'Do you anticipate any problems, sir,' asked Jimmy.

Walking past the boys, the steward said, 'Of course not, but it always pays to be prepared. I shall return in a short time.'

After he left, Locklear turned to face Jimmy. 'All right. What's going on? And don't you dare say "You'll see."'

'Things are not what they seem to be. Come on.'

Jimmy and Locklear dashed up the stairs. Reaching a window overlooking the court, they quietly observed the preparations below. The funeral procession was assembling, the rolling bier moving into place, escorted by a hand-picked company of Arutha's Household Guard. It was pulled by a matched set of six black horses, each bedecked with black plumes and hand-led by a groom dressed in black. The soldiers fell in on each side of the bier.

A group of eight men-at-arms came from within the palace, bearing the casket containing Arutha. They moved to a rolling scaffolding that allowed them to raise the casket high atop the bier. Slowly, almost reverently, they hoisted the Prince of Krondor up onto the black shrouded structure.

Jimmy and Locklear looked down into the casket and, for the first time, could clearly see the Prince. Tradition held the procession should move out with the casket open so the populace could behold their ruler a last time. It would be closed outside the city gates, never to be opened again, save once more in the privacy of the family vault below the King's palace in Rillanon, where Arutha's family would bid him a final farewell.

Jimmy felt his throat tightening. He swallowed hard, moving the stubborn lump. He saw Arutha had been laid out in his favourite garb, his brown velvet tunic, his russet leggings. A green jerkin had been added, though he had rarely worn such. His favourite rapier was clasped between his hands, and his head remained uncovered. He seemed asleep. As he was moved out of view, Jimmy noticed the fine satin lounging slippers on the Prince's feet.

Then a groom came forward, leading Arutha's horse, which would follow behind the bier, riderless. It was a magnificent grey stallion, which tossed its head high and struggled against the groom. Another ran out and between the two of them they managed to quiet the fractious mount.

Jimmy's eyes narrowed. Locklear turned in time to notice the odd expression. 'What?'

'Damn me, but something's odd. Come on, I want to see a thing or two.'

'Where?'

But Jimmy was off, saying merely, 'Hurry, we only have a few minutes!' as he ran down the stairs. Locklear chased after, groaning silently.

Jimmy hid in the shadow near the stable. 'Look,' he said as he pushed Locklear forward. Locklear made a show of strolling past the stable entrance as the last of the honour guard's mounts were being led out. Nearly the entire garrison would be walking behind the Prince's bier, but once outside the city, a full company of Royal Lancers would act as escort all the way to Salador.

'Hey, you boy! Watch what you're about!' Locklear had to jump aside as a groom ran from the stable between two horses, holding their bridles. He had almost run Locklear down. Locklear ambled back and ducked around the corner beside Jimmy.

'I don't know what you expected to find, but no, it's not there.'

'That's what I expected to find. Come on,' ordered Jimmy as he dashed back toward the central palace.

'Where?'

'You'll see.'

Locklear stared daggers into Jimmy's back as they ran across the marshalling yard.

Jimmy and Locklear dashed up the stairs, taking the steps two at a time. Reaching the window overlooking the courtyard, they gasped for breath. The run to and from the stable had taken ten minutes, and the cortege was about to leave the palace. Jimmy watched closely. Carriages rolled up to the steps of the palace and pages ran forward to hold open the doors. By tradition only the royal family, by blood and marriage, would ride. All others would walk behind Arutha's bier as a sign of respect. Princess Anita and Alicia walked down and entered the first carriage, while Carline and Laurie hurried to the second, the Duke nearly skipping he was walking so fast. He almost leaped into the carriage after Carline, rapidly pulling the curtains over the windows on his side.

Jimmy regarded Locklear, who stood with an open expression of curiosity on his face over Laurie's behaviour. Seeing no need to comment to the other youngster, Jimmy remained silent.

Gardan took his place before the procession, his shoulders hung with a heavy black mantle. He signalled, and a single drummer began a slow tattoo upon a muffled drum. Without spoken order, the procession set out on the fourth beat of the drum. The soldiers moved in silent lockstep, while the carriages rolled forward. Suddenly the grey stallion bucked and an extra groom again had to hold the animal in place. Jimmy shook his head. He had an old familiar feeling: all the pieces of some odd puzzle were about to fall into place. Then slowly a smile of understanding spread across his face.

Locklear observed his friend's change of expression. 'What?'

'Now I know what Laurie's been up to. I know what's going on.'

With a friendly slap to Locklear's shoulder, he said, 'Come on, we've got a lot to do and little time to do it.'

Jimmy led Locklear through the secret tunnel, the guttering torch sending flickering shadows dancing in every direction. Both squires were dressed for travel and carried weapons, packs, and bedrolls. 'You sure they'll not have someone at the exit?' asked Locklear for the fifth time.

Impatiently Jimmy said, 'I told you: this is the one exit I never showed anyone, not even the Prince or Laurie.' As if trying to explain away this transgression of omission, he added, 'Some old habits are harder to break than others.'

They had gone about their duties all afternoon; after the squires had all retired, they had stolen away to where they had hastily stashed their travel packs. Now it was close to midnight.

Reaching a stone door, Jimmy pulled a lever and they both heard a click. Jimmy put out the torch and put his shoulder to the door. After several hard shoves, the protesting door moved, age having made it reluctant. They crawled through a small door – disguised as stonework – in the base of the wall beyond the Prince's marshalling yard, on the street closest to the palace. Less than half a block up the road stood the postern gate, with its attendant sentries. Jimmy tried to push the door shut, but it refused to budge. He signalled to Locklear, and the younger boy shoved in concert. It held, then with a sudden release slammed shut with an audible crash. From up by the gate came an inquiring voice. 'Here now, who's out there? Stand and be identified.'

Without hesitation Jimmy was off, Locklear half a step behind. Neither boy looked back to see if chase was being offered, but kept their heads down as they dashed along the cobblestones.

Soon they were lost in the warren of streets between the Poor Quarter and the docks. Jimmy halted to gain his bearings, then pointed. 'That way. We've got to hurry. The *Raven* leaves on the midnight tide.'

Both boys hurried through the night. Soon they were passing shuttered buildings near the waterfront. From the docks came the sound of men shouting orders as a ship made ready to depart.

'It's pulling out,' yelled Locklear.

Jimmy didn't answer, only picking up his pace. Both squires reached the end of the dock as the last line was cast off, and with desperate leaps they reached the side of the ship as it moved away from the quay. Rough hands pulled them over and in a moment they stood upon the deck.

'Here now, what is this?' came an inquiring voice, and a moment later, Aaron Cook stood before them. 'Well, then, Jimmy the Hand, are you so anxious for a sea voyage you'd break your neck to come aboard?'

Jimmy grinned. 'Hello, Aaron. I need to speak to Hull.'

The pock-faced man scowled at the squires. 'That's Captain Hull to any aboard the *Royal Raven*, Prince's Squire or not. I'll see if the captain has a moment.'

Shortly the squires stood before the captain, who fixed them with a baleful expression as he studied them with his one good eye. 'Deserting your post, eh?'

'Trevor,' Jimmy began, but as Cook scowled, he amended, 'Captain. We need to travel to Sarth. And we saw from the ships' list in the Port Authority you're beginning your northward patrol tonight.'

'Well now, you may think you need to travel up the coast, Jimmy the Hand, but you've not rank enough to come aboard my ship with no more than a by-your-leave, and you didn't even have that. And despite the public notice – for the benefit of spies, you should know – my course is westerly, for I've Durbin slave runners reported lying at sea ambush for hapless Kingdom traders, and there's always Quegan galleys nosing about. No, you'll be ashore with the pilot once we've cleared the outer breakwater, unless you've a better reason than simply wanting free transportation.' The former smuggler's expression revealed that while he might feel affection for Jimmy, he'd brook no nonsense aboard his ship.

Jimmy said, 'If I might have a word with you in private.'

Hull exchanged glances with Cook, then shrugged. Jimmy spent a full five minutes whispering with the old captain. Then suddenly Hull laughed, a genuinely amused sound. 'I'll be scuppered!'

A moment later he approached Aaron Cook. 'Have these lads taken below. As soon as we clear harbour, I want full sail. Make course for Sarth.'

Cook hesitated a minute, then turned to a sailor and ordered him to take the boys below. When they were gone, and the harbour pilot over the side in his longboat, the first mate called all hands aloft and ordered all sails out and set a northern course. He cast a glance rearward where Captain Hull stood next to the helmsman, but the captain only smiled to himself.

Jimmy and Locklear stood at rail's edge, waiting. When the boat was ready, they boarded. Trevor Hull came to stand beside them. 'Sure you don't want to put back to Sarth?'

Jimmy shook his head. 'I'd rather not be seen arriving aboard a Royal Customs ship. Attracts too much notice. Besides, there's a village near here where we can buy horses. There's a good place not a day's ride beyond there where we all camped last time. We can watch any who pass. It'll be easier to spot them there.'

'As long as they haven't passed already.'

'They only left a day before we did, and we sailed every night while they had to sleep. We're in front of them.'

'Well then, young lads, I'll wish you the protection of Kilian, who in her kinder moments watches over sailors and other reckless sorts, and of Banath, who does the same for thieves, gamblers, and fools.' In more serious tones, he said, 'Take care, boys.' Then he signalled the boat lowered.

It was still gloomy, as the coast fog had not been pierced yet by the sun. The longboat was turned toward the beach and the rowers pulled hard. Swiftly they headed in, until the bow of the longboat scraped sand, and Jimmy and Locklear were ashore.

* * *

The innkeeper hadn't wished to sell his horses at first, but Jimmy's serious attitude, his posture of authority, and the way he wore his sword, coupled with ample gold, changed his mind. By the time the sun had cleared the forest to the east of the village of Longroad, the two young men were mounted, well provisioned, and on their way up the road between Sarth and Questor's View.

By midday they were in place, at a narrow point in the road. To the east an upthrust of land, covered with heavy foliage, prevented anyone from passing, while to the west, the land dropped away quickly to the beach. From their vantage point, Jimmy and Locklear could see any travellers coming up the road or the beach.

They built a small fire against the damp and settled in to wait.

Twice in the three days that followed, they had been menaced. The first time had been by a band of unemployed bravos, mercenary guards, on their way south from Questor's View. But that band had been discouraged by the determination of the two young men, and the probability they had nothing to steal besides the two horses. One man tried to take a horse, but Jimmy's speed with a rapier dissuaded him. They left rather than spill blood over such trivial booty.

The second encounter had been considerably riskier, as both youngsters had stood side by side with weapons drawn, protecting their horses from three disreputable-looking bandits. Had the road agents had more numbers, Jimmy was certain the youths would have been killed, but the men had fled at the sound of approaching riders, which turned into a small patrol from the garrison at Questor's View.

The soldiers had questioned Jimmy and Locklear and had accepted their tale. They were travelling as sons of a minor squire, who was due to meet with them soon at this location. The boys and their father would then continue on south to Krondor, to follow after the Prince's funeral procession. The sergeant in charge of the patrol had wished them safe passage.

Late in the afternoon, the fourth day after arriving, Jimmy spotted three riders coming down the beach. He watched for a long moment, then said, 'There they are!'

Jimmy and Locklear quickly mounted and rode down the gap in the cliff to the beach. They halted, their mounts pawing the sand, as they waited for the riders to approach.

The three riders came into view, slowed, then approached warily. They looked tired and dirty, most likely mercenaries from their weapons and armour. All wore beards, though the two dark-haired men's were short and newly growing. The first rider swore an oath at the sight of the two youngsters. The second shook his head in disbelief.

The third rider edged his horse past the first two and came to halt before the boys. 'How did you . . .?'

Locklear sat with his mouth open, in stunned silence. In everything Jimmy had told him, this was the one thing the Senior Squire had not mentioned. Jimmy grinned. 'It's a bit of a story. We've a little camp up on the headland if you want to rest, though it's by the road.'

The man scratched at his two-week-old beard. 'Might as well. There's little point in travelling much more today.'

Jimmy's grin broadened. 'I must say, you're the liveliest-looking corpse I've ever seen, and I've seen a few.'

Arutha returned the grin. Turning to Laurie and Roald, he said, 'Come on, let's rest the horses and find out how these young rogues figured us out.'

The fire seemed to burn cheerfully as the sun disappeared over the ocean. They lay around the campfire, except Roald, who stood with a view of the road. 'It was a lot of little things,' said Jimmy. 'The Princesses both seemed more worried than grief-stricken. When we were kept away from the cortege, I became suspicious.'

Locklear added, 'It was something I said.'

Jimmy shot Locklear a hard glance, indicating it was his story. 'Yes, it was. He mentioned we were being kept away. Now I know why.

I'd have tumbled to the bogus Duke in the carriage in a minute. Then I'd have known he was heading north to finish with Murmandamus.'

Laurie said, 'Which is why you were kept away.'

Roald added, 'Which was the whole idea.'

Jimmy looked stung. 'You could have trusted me.'

Arutha looked caught halfway between amusement and irritation. 'It wasn't an issue of trust, Jimmy. I didn't want this. I didn't want you along.' With a mock groan, he said, 'Now I've two of you.'

Locklear looked at Jimmy with an expression of concern, but Jimmy's tone put him at ease. 'Well, even princes have an occasional lapse of judgment. Just remember what sort of fix you'd have been in if I hadn't sussed out that trap up at Moraelin.'

Arutha nodded in surrender. 'So you knew something strange was going on, then figured out Laurie and Roald were going north, but what gave away I was still alive?'

Jimmy laughed. 'First, the grey stallion was used in the procession, and your sorrel was missing from the stable. You never liked the grey, I remember you saying.'

Arutha nodded. 'He's too fractious. What else?'

'It hit me while we watched the body go past. If you were going to be buried in your favourite togs, you'd have your favourite boots on.' He pointed to the pair the Prince wore. 'But there were only slippers on his feet. That's because the boots the assassin wore into the palace were covered in sewer muck and blood. Most likely whoever dressed the body went looking for another pair rather than clean the assassin's boots and couldn't find any, or they didn't fit, so they just put the slippers on. When I saw that I figured it out. You didn't have the assassin's body burned, only the heart. Nathan must have put a spell on it to keep it fresh.'

'I didn't know what I was going to do with it, but thought it might come in useful. Then we had that attempt in the temple. That assassin's dagger was no sham' – he absently rubbed a sore side – 'but it was not a serious wound.'

Laurie said, 'Ha! Another inch higher and two to the right and he'd have had a real enough funeral after all.'

'We kept things at a low boil the first night, Nathan, Gardan, Volney, Laurie, and I, while we figured out what to do,' Arutha said. 'I decided to play dead. Volney held up the funeral procession until the local nobles arrived, which gave me time to heal enough to ride. I wanted to slip out of the city without anyone being the wiser. If Murmandamus thinks me dead, he'll stop looking for me. With this' – he held out the talisman given to him by the Ishapian Abbot – 'he'll not find me with magic means. I'm hoping to make him act prematurely.'

Laurie said, 'How'd you boys get here? You couldn't have passed us along the road.'

'I got Trevor Hull to bring us here,' replied Jimmy.

Arutha said, 'You told him?'

'But only him. Not even Cook knows you're alive.'

Roald said, 'Still too damn many for a secret.'

Locklear said, 'But, I mean, everyone who knows can be trusted . . . sir.'

'That's not the issue,' said Laurie. 'Carline and Anita know, as did Gardan, Volney, and Nathan. But even deLacy and Valdis were kept ignorant. The King won't know until Carline tells him in private when they reach Rillanon. Only those know.'

'What of Martin?' asked Jimmy.

'Laurie sent a message to him. He'll meet us in Ylith,' answered Arutha.

'That's risky,' said Jimmy.

Laurie said, 'No one but a few of us could understand the message. All it said was "The Northerner. Come fastest." It was signed "Arthur." He'll understand no one is to know Arutha lives.'

Jimmy revealed his appreciation. 'Only those of us here know the Northerner is the inn in Ylith where Martin wrestled with that Longly character.'

'Who's Arthur?' asked Locklear.

135

'His Highness,' said Roald. 'It's the name he used when last he travelled.'

'And I used it when I came to Krondor with Martin and Amos.'

Jimmy got a thoughtful look. 'This is the second time we ride north, and it's the second time I wish Amos Trask was with us.'

Arutha said, 'Well, he is not. Let's turn in. We've a long ride ahead, and I must decide what to do with you two young rogues.'

Jimmy wrapped his bedroll about him, as did the others, while Roald maintained the first watch. Then for the first time in weeks, Jimmy dropped quickly off to sleep, free of grief.

• CHAPTER SEVEN •

Mysteries

RYATH THUNDERED INTO FAMILIAR SKIES.

Above the forests of the Kingdom she wheeled. From her came the thought, *I must hunt.* The dragon preferred mind-speech while flying, though she spoke aloud upon the ground.

Tomas looked back at Pug, who answered. 'It is far to Macros's island. Nearly a thousand miles.'

Tomas smiled. 'We can be there more quickly than you imagine.'

'How far can Ryath fly?'

'Around the globe of this world without landing, though I think she'd judge there was no good reason to do so. Also, you've not seen a tenth of her speed.'

'Good,' answered Pug. 'Then, when we've landed upon Sorcerer's Isle.'

Tomas requested more forbearance from the dragon, who grudgingly agreed. Climbing high in the blue skies of Midkemia, Ryath followed Pug's directions, over the peaks of mountains, toward the

Bitter Sea. With mighty beats of her wings she climbed to where she could soar. Soon the landscape below sped away, and Pug wondered what the limits of the dragon's speed might be. They were moving more rapidly than a running horse and seemed to be picking up speed. There was a component of magic in Ryath's flying ability, for while the dragon appeared to soar, she was in fact increasing speed without a single beat of her wings. Faster and faster they flew. They were comfortable, owing to Tomas's magic; he protected them from wind and cold, though Pug was nearly dizzy from exhilaration. The forests of the Far Coast gave way to the peaks of the Grey Towers and then they were speeding over the lands of the Free Cities of Natal. Next they were flying over the waters of the Bitter Sea, highlights of silver and green glittering on the deep blue, and ships plying the summer trade routes from Queg to the Free Cities looked but a child's toys.

As they sped high above the island kingdom of Queg, they could see the capital and outlying villages, again looking like playthings from this height. Far below them winged shapes flew in formation over the edge of land, and from the dragon came a mirthful chuckle. *Know them, dost thou, Ruler of the Eagles' Reaches?*

Tomas said, 'They are not what they once were.'

Pug said, 'What is it?'

Tomas pointed downward. 'Those are descendants of the giant eagles I hunted – Ashen-Shugar hunted – ages past. I flew them as lesser men fly falcons. Those ancient birds were intelligent after a fashion.'

The island men train these and ride them as others do horses. They are a fallen breed.

Tomas seemed irritated. 'Like so much else, they are but a shadow of what they once were.'

With humour, the dragon answered, *Still there are those of us who are more, Valheru.*

Pug said nothing. Well as he understood his friend, there was much about him no one could ever fathom. Tomas was unique in all the world and had burdens upon his soul no other being could comprehend.

In a vague way Pug could understand how these descendants of the once proud eagles Ashen-Shugar had hunted could pain Tomas, but he chose not to comment. Whatever disquiet Tomas experienced, it was his alone.

A short time later another island came into view, tiny compared to the nation of Queg, but still large enough to house a sizeable population. But Pug knew only a few had ever abided there, for it was Sorcerer's Isle, home of Macros the Black.

As they sped over the northwestern edge of the island, they dipped lower, clearing a range of hills, then flew above a small vale. Pug said, 'It can't be!'

Tomas said, 'What?'

'There was an odd . . . place here before. A home with outbuildings. It's where I met Macros. Kulgan, Gardan, Arutha, and Meecham were all there, too.'

They swooped over tall trees. Tomas said, 'These oaks and bristlecone pines did not grow in even the near-dozen years since you first met the sorcerer, Pug. They are ancient in aspect.'

Pug said, 'Another of Macros's mysteries. Pray, then, the castle's still there.'

Ryath cleared another line of hills, putting them in sight of the only visible structure on the island, a lone castle. They banked over the beach where Pug and his companions had first landed upon the island, years before, and the dragon rapidly descended, landing upon a trail above the beach. Bidding her companions goodbye, she launched herself into the air, preparing to hunt. Tomas, watching as Ryath vanished into the azure sky, said, 'I had forgotten what it was to ride a dragon.' He appeared thoughtful as he faced Pug. 'When you asked me to accompany you, I was again fearful of awakening dormant spirits within.' He tapped his chest. 'I thought here Ashen-Shugar waited, only needing an excuse to rise up and overwhelm me again.' Pug studied Tomas's face. His friend was masking his emotions well, but Pug could still see them there, powerful and deep. 'But I know now there is no difference between Ashen-Shugar and Tomas. I am both.' He looked down for a moment, reminding Pug of how the boy had once looked when making excuses for some transgression before his mother. 'I feel as if I've both gained and lost.'

Pug nodded. 'We'll never again be the boys we once were, Tomas. But we've become so much more than we dreamed. Still, few things of worth are ever simple. Or easy.'

Tomas stared out to sea. 'I was thinking of my parents. I've not visited them since the end of the war. I am not who they once knew.'

Pug understood. 'It will be hard for them, but they are good people and will accept the change in you. They will wish to see their grandchild.'

Tomas sighed, then he laughed, part in pleasure, part in bitterness. 'Calis is different from what they would have expected, but then so am I. No, I do not fear to see them again.' He turned and looked at Pug. Softly he said, 'No, I fear I may never see them again.'

Pug thought of his own wife, Katala, and all the others at Stardock. He could only reach out and grip Tomas's arm for a long, thoughtful moment. Despite their strengths and abilities, talents unrivalled on this world, they were mortal and, even more than Tomas, Pug knew the dreadful nature of what they faced. And Pug held deeper suspicions and darker fears in private. The silence of the eldar during his training, their presence on Kelewan, and the insights gained from studying with them all pointed at possibilities Pug fervently hoped would prove false. There was a conclusion here he would not speak of until he had no other choice. Pushing aside his disquiet, he said, 'Come, we must seek Gathis.'

They stood overlooking the beach, at a point where two trails divided from one. Pug knew that one led to the castle, the other toward the small vale where the strange house and outbuildings the sorcerer had called Villa Beata had stood, the place he had first met Macros. Pug now wished when he and the others had returned to claim the legacy of Macros, the heart of the Academy at Stardock's library, they had visited the complex. For those buildings to have vanished, to be replaced by trees of ancient aspect . . . it was, as he had said, one more of the many mysteries surrounding Macros the Black. They followed the path toward the castle.

The castle stood upon a table of land, separated from the rest of the island by a deep ravine that fell away to the ocean. The crashing of waves through the passage echoed beneath them as they slowly crossed the lowered drawbridge. The castle was fashioned from unfamiliar dark stone, and around the great arch above the portcullis odd-looking creatures of stone perched, regarding Pug and Tomas with stony gaze as they passed below. The outside of the castle looked much as it had the last time Pug had been here, but once inside the castle, it was evident that everything else had changed.

Upon the last visit, the grounds and castle had appeared well tended, but now the stones at the base of the building exhibited weeds growing from cracks, and the grounds were littered with bird droppings. They hurried to the large doors to the central keep, which hung open. As they pushed them wide, the screeching of hinges testified to their rusty condition. Pug led his friend through the long hall and up the tower steps, until he reached the door into Macros's study. The last time he had been here, it had taken both a spell and answering a question in Tsurani to open the door, but now a simple push sufficed. The room was empty.

Pug turned and they hurried down the steps until they reached the great hall of the castle. In frustration, Pug cried, 'Hello, the castle!' His voice echoed hollowly off the stones.

Tomas said, 'It appears everyone is gone.'

'I don't understand. When we last spoke, Gathis said he would abide here, awaiting Macros's return and keeping his house in order. I only knew him briefly, but I would warrant he would keep this castle as we saw it last . . .'

Tomas said, 'Until he was no longer able. It may be someone had reason to visit the island. Pirates or Quegan raiders?'

'Or agents of Murmandamus?' Pug visibly sagged. 'I had hoped we would discover some clue from Gathis to begin our search for Macros.' Pug looked about and spied a stone bench before the wall.

Sitting down, he said, 'We don't even know if Macros lives yet. How are we to find him?'

Tomas stood in front of his friend, towering over him. He placed one boot upon the bench and leaned forward, crossed arms resting upon his knee. 'It is also possible this castle is deserted because Macros has already returned and left again.'

Pug looked up. 'Perhaps. There is a spell . . . a spell of the Lesser Path.'

Tomas said, 'As I understood such things—'

Pug interrupted. 'I have learned many things at Elvardein. Let me try this.' He closed his eyes and incanted, his words soft and low as he directed his mind into a path still strange to it as often as not. Suddenly his eyes snapped open. 'There's some sort of ensorcellment upon this castle. The stones – they're not right.'

Tomas looked at Pug, a question unspoken in his eyes. Pug rose and touched the stones. 'I used a spell that should have gleaned information from the very walls. Whatever occurs near an object leaves faint traces, energies that impact it. With skill, they can be read as you or I would read a scribe's writings. It is difficult but possible. But these stones show nothing. It is as if no living being had ever passed through this hall.' Suddenly Pug turned toward the doors. 'Come!' he commanded.

Tomas fell in beside his friend as Pug walked out to the heart of the courtyard. There he halted, raising his hands above his head. Tomas could feel mighty energies forming about them as Pug gathered power. Then Pug closed his eyes and spoke, rapidly and in a tongue both odd and familiar to Tomas. Then Pug's eyes opened and he said, 'Let the truth be revealed!'

As if a ripple moved outward, with Pug at the centre, Tomas found his vision shifting. The very air shimmered and on one side there was the abandoned castle, but as the ripple passed, the court was revealed as well tended. The circle widened rapidly as the illusion was dispelled, and suddenly Tomas discovered they were in an orderly courtyard. Nearby a strange creature was carrying a bundle of firewood. He halted, surprise evident upon his nonhuman face, and dropped the bundle.

Tomas had begun to draw his sword, but Pug said, 'No,' placing a restraining hand upon his arm.

'But it's a mountain troll!'

'Gathis told us Macros employed many servants, judging each upon its own merits.'

The startled creature, broad-shouldered, long-fanged, and fearsome in appearance, turned and ran in a stooping, apelike fashion toward a door in the outer wall. Another creature, nothing either man had seen upon this world, exited the stable and halted. It was only three feet tall and had a muzzle like a bear, but its fur was red-gold. Seeing the two humans regarding it, it set aside the broom it carried and slowly backed into the stable door. Pug watched until it was out of sight. Cupping his hands about his mouth, Pug cried, 'Gathis!'

Almost instantly, the doors to the great hall opened and a well dressed goblin-like creature appeared. Taller than a goblin, he possessed the thick ridges above the eyes and large nose of the goblin tribe, but his features were somehow more noble, his movements more graceful. Attired in blue singlet and leggings, with a yellow doublet and black boots, he hurried down the steps and bowed before the two men. With a sibilance to his speech, he said, 'Welcome, Master Pug.' He studied Tomas. 'This, then, would be Master Tomas?'

Tomas and Pug exchanged glances. Then Pug said, 'We seek your master.'

Gathis seemed to look distressed. 'That may prove a bit of a problem, Master Pug. As best as I can ascertain, Macros no longer exists.'

Pug sipped at his wine. Gathis had brought them to a chamber where refreshments were provided. The steward of the castle refused to sit, standing opposite the two men as they listened to his story.

'So, as I said when last we spoke, Master Pug, between the Black One and myself there is an understanding. I can sense his . . . state of being? Somehow I know he is always out there, somewhere. About a month after you left, I awoke one night suddenly feeling the absence of that . . . contact. It was most disturbing.'

'Then Macros is dead,' said Tomas.

Gathis sighed, in a very human way. 'I am afraid so. If not, he is somewhere so alien and remote it amounts to little difference.'

Pug considered in silence, while Tomas said, 'Then who fashioned that illusion?'

'My master. I activated it as soon as you and your companions left the castle after your last visit. Without the presence of Macros the Black to ensure our safety, he felt the need to provide us with "protective colouration," in a manner of speaking. Twice now bold pirates have combed the island for booty. They find nothing.'

Pug's head suddenly came up. 'Then the villa still exists?'

'Yes, Master Pug. It was also hidden by the illusion.' Gathis appeared disturbed. 'I must confess that while I am no expert in such matters, I would have thought the illusion spell beyond your ability to banish.' Again he sighed. 'Now I worry at its absence once you've left.'

Pug waved away the remark. 'I will reestablish it before we leave.' Something nagged at Pug's mind, a strange image of speaking with Macros in the villa. 'When I asked Macros if he lived in the villa, he said, "No, though I once did, long ago."' He looked at Gathis. 'Did he have a study, such as the one in the tower, at the villa?'

Gathis said, 'Yes, ages ago, before I came to this place.'

Pug stood. 'We must go there, now.'

Gathis led them down the path into the vale. The red tile roofs were as Pug had remembered. Tomas said, 'This is a strange place, though it seems pleasing enough in aspect. With fair weather, it would be a comfortable home.'

'So my master thought, once,' said Gathis. 'But he was gone for a long time, so he told me. And when he returned, the villa was deserted, those who had lived with him gone without explanation. At first he searched for his companions, but soon despaired of ever knowing their fate. Then he feared for the safety of his books and other works as well as the lives of the servants he planned to bring here, so he built the castle. And took other measures,' he added with a chuckle.

'The legend of Macros the Black.'

'Terror of evil magic serves ofttimes better than stout castle walls, Master Pug. The difficulties were not trivial: shrouding this rather sunny island in gloomy clouds and keeping that infernal blue light flashing in the high tower each time a ship approached. It was something of a nuisance.'

They entered the courtyard of the villa, surrounded by only a low wall. Pug paused to regard the fountain, where three dolphins rose upon a pedestal, and said, 'I fashioned the pattern in my transport room after this.' Gathis led him toward the central building, and suddenly Pug understood. There were neither connecting walkways nor roofs covering them, but this villa matched his own upon Kelewan in building size and placement. The pattern was identical. Pug halted, looking shaken.

Tomas said, 'What is it?'

'It seems Macros had his hand in many things far more subtle than we had known. I built my home upon Kelewan in the image of this one without knowing I had done so. I had no reason to, save it seemed the way to build it. Now I don't think I had much choice. Come, I will show you where the study lay.' He led them without error to the room that matched the location of his own study. Instead of the sliding cloth-covered doors of Kelewan, they faced a single door of wood, but Gathis nodded.

Pug opened the door and stepped inside. The room was identical in size and shape. A dust-covered writing table and chair rested where Pug had placed his low writing table and cushions in the matching room. Pug laughed, shaking his head in appreciation and wonder. 'The sorcerer had many tricks.' He moved to a small fireplace. Pulling upon a stone, he revealed a hidden nook. 'I had such a place built into my own hearth, though I never understood why. I had no reason to use it.' Within that nook a rolled parchment lay.

Pug withdrew it and inspected it. A single ribbon without seal tied the scroll.

He unrolled it and read, his face becoming animated. 'Oh, you clever man!' he said. Looking at Tomas and Gathis, he explained. 'This is written in Tsurani. Even if the spell of illusion was broken, and someone stumbled across this room, and found the nook and the parchment, there was almost no chance of them being able to read this.' He looked back at the parchment and began to read aloud. '"Pug, by reading this, know I am most likely dead. But if not, I am somewhere beyond the normal boundaries of space and time. In either case I am unable to provide you with the aid you seek. You have discovered something of the nature of the Enemy and know it imperils both Kelewan and Midkemia. Seek me first in the Halls of the Dead. If I am not there, then you know I live. If I am alive, I will be captive in a place difficult to find. Then you will make the choice, either to seek to learn more of the Enemy on your own, a most dangerous course in the extreme but one that may succeed, or to search for me. Whatever you do, know I wish you the blessings of the gods. Macros."'

Pug put away the scroll. 'I had hoped for more.'

Gathis said, 'My master was a man of power, but even he had his limits. As stated in his last missive to you, he could not pierce the veil of time once he entered the rift with you. From that point on, time was as opaque to him as to other men. He could only speculate.'

Tomas said, 'Then we must away to the Halls of the Dead.'

Pug said, 'But where are they to be found?'

'Attend,' said Gathis. 'Beyond the Endless Sea lies the southern continent, called Novindus by men. From north to south a range of mountains runs, called in the language of those men the Ratn'gari, which means "Pavilion of the Gods". Upon the two tallest peaks, the Pillars of Heaven, stands the Celestial City, or so men say, the home of the gods. Below those peaks, in the foothills stands the Necropolis, the City of the Dead Gods. The highest-placed temple, one that rests against the base of the mountains, honours the four lost gods. There you will find a tunnel into the heart of the Celestial Mountains. This is the entrance to the Halls of the Dead.'

Pug considered. 'We shall sleep the night, then call Ryath and cross the Endless Sea.'

Tomas turned without comment, beginning the trek back to Macros's castle. There was no discussion. They had no choice. The sorcerer had been nothing if not thorough.

Ryath banked. For hours they had flown faster than Pug had thought possible. The Endless Sea had rolled below, a vast ocean of seemingly uncrossable size. But the dragon had not hesitated an instant in accepting their destination. Now, hours later, they were flying over a continent on the other side of the world. They had moved from east to west as well as crossing to the southern hemisphere, so they had gained some daylight. In late afternoon, they had sighted the southern continent, Novindus. First they had crossed a great sand wasteland, bounded by high cliffs running for hundreds of miles along the seacoast. Any who landed from a ship on that northern coast would have days of travel and a dangerous climb before drinking water could be found. Then the dragon had cut across grasslands. Far below, hundreds of strange wagons surrounded by herds of cattle, sheep, and horses had been moving from north to south. Some nomadic people, a nation of herdsmen, was following the tracks of its ancestors, oblivious to the dragon high overhead.

Then they saw the first city. A mighty river, reminding Pug of the Gagajin on Kelewan, cut across the grasslands. On the southern shore a city had arisen, and farther south farmland could be seen. Far to the southwest, in the haze of evening, a range of mountains rose: the Pavilion of the Gods.

Ryath began to descend, and they soon approached the centre of the range, a pair of peaks that rose high above those surrounding, disappearing into clouds, the Pillars of Heaven. At the base of the mountains, deep forests hid anything that might have existed. The dragon spent the last minutes of light seeking a clearing in which to land.

The dragon set down, then said, 'I go to hunt. When I finish, I shall sleep. I would rest for a time.'

Tomas smiled. 'You will not be needed for the balance of this journey. Where we venture, we may not return and you would have difficulty finding us.'

The dragon projected a sense of amusement at that last remark. 'Thou hast lost some sense of things, Valheru. Else thou wouldst remember there is no place within the span of space I may not reach, should I have but a reason.'

'This place exists beyond even your ability to reach, Ryath. We enter the Halls of the Dead.'

'Then thou shalt indeed be beyond my ability to find, Tomas. Still, if thou and thy friend survive this journey, and return to the realms of life, thou hast but to call and I shall answer. Hunt well, Valheru. For I shall.' The dragon rose upward, extending her wings, then with a leap and a bound she launched herself into the darkening sky.

Tomas remarked, 'She is tired. Dragons usually hunt wild game, but I think some farmer may find a brace of sheep or a cow missing tomorrow. Ryath will sleep days with a full belly.'

Pug looked about in the deepening gloom. 'In our haste, we neglected such provision for ourselves.'

Tomas sat upon a deadfall and said, 'Such things never occurred in those sagas of our youth.'

Pug looked at his friend questioningly and Tomas said, 'Remember the woods near Crydee when we were boys?' His expression turned mirthful. 'In all our youthful dramas we conquered our foes in time to get home for dinner.'

Pug joined his friend in sitting. With a small chuckle, he said, 'I remember. You always played the fallen hero of some great tragic battle, bidding his loyal followers good-bye.'

Tomas's voice revealed a thoughtful tone. 'Only this time we don't simply get up and return to Mother's kitchen for a hot meal after we're killed.'

A long moment passed. Pug said, 'Still, we might as well make ourselves as comfortable as we can. This is as likely a spot to wait for dawn as any other. I suspect the Necropolis is overgrown, else we would have seen it from the air. We'll be better able to locate it tomorrow.' He added, with a faint smile, 'Besides, Ryath isn't the only one who's tired.'

'Sleep if you feel the need.' Tomas's eyes studied something in the brush. 'I've learned to ignore the need at will.' His expression caused Pug to turn his head, following Tomas's gaze. Something moved in the dark.

Then a roar erupted from the forests behind them. One moment the clearing had been silent, then something or someone was leaping out of the woods upon Tomas's back.

The half-cry, half-roar was answered by a dozen more. Pug sprang to his feet as Tomas was rocked forward by the impact of the thing upon his back. But while this creature or man seemed near Tomas's equal in size, no mortal upon Midkemia was his equal in strength. Tomas simply stood erect, gripping the thing on his back by a handful of fur. With a yank, he tossed it overhead as he would a child, sending it crashing into another creature running toward him.

Pug clapped his hands together overhead and the glade rang with the sound of a thunderclap centring upon him. It was deafening, and those nearby faltered. Blinding light erupted from Pug's upraised hands, and those surrounding Tomas and Pug froze.

They looked to be tigers, but their bodies had been altered into man shapes. Their heads were orange with black stripes, as were their arms and legs. Each wore a cuirass of blue metal and breeches ending at mid-thigh, of some blue-black material. Each carried a short sword, and a belt knife.

In the glare they crouched, blinded by the light of Pug's magic. He quickly incanted another spell and the tiger-men toppled. Pug staggered a little, inhaling with a loud sound as he sat upon the deadfall. 'That was almost too much. The spell of sleep cast on so many . . .'

Tomas seemed to listen with only half his attention. He had his sword out and his shield at the ready. 'There are more in the woods.'

Pug shook off his fogginess and rose. In the surrounding forest the sound of soft movement murmured like the gentle stirring of branches in a light breeze, but no wind blew this night. Then, as one, another dozen figures materialized from the gloom, all similar to the fallen. In a thick, slurred speech, one said, 'Put away your weapons, man. You are surrounded.' The others seemed crouched, ready to spring like the giant cats they resembled.

Tomas looked at Pug, who nodded. Tomas permitted one of the tiger-men to disarm him. The leader of the tiger-men waved at them, saying, 'Bind them!'

Tomas allowed himself to be tied, as did Pug. The leader said, 'You have slain many of my warriors.'

Pug said, 'They only sleep.'

One of the tiger-warriors knelt and examined a sleeper. 'Tuan, it is true!'

The one called Tuan examined Pug's face closely. 'You are a spell-caster, it seems, yet you allow yourself to be taken easily. Why?'

Pug said, 'Curiosity. And we have no wish to harm you.'

The surrounding tiger-men began to laugh, or something like it. Then Tomas simply parted his wrists. The bonds snapped instantly. He extended his hand toward the warrior holding his golden sword and the weapon flew from the startled creature's grasp into his own. The laughter died.

In a startled rage, the one called Tuan snarled and swung a clawed hand at Pug's face, fingers hooked and long talons extending from between them. Pug instantly raised his hand and a small golden light erupted on his palm. The creature's claws rebounded from that light as if from steel.

The surrounding creatures began to close upon them once more, two grabbing Tomas from behind. He simply tossed them aside and grabbed the one called Tuan by the scruff of the neck. Tuan stood six feet tall and more, but Tomas lifted him easily. Like any cat grabbed by the scruff, he dangled helplessly. 'Halt, or this one dies!' Tomas ordered.

The creatures hesitated. Then one of the tiger-warriors bent his knee. He was followed by the rest. Tomas released Tuan and let him fall. The leader of the tiger-men landed lightly and spun. 'What manner of being are you?'

'I am Tomas, once called Ashen-Shugar, Ruler of the Eagles' Reaches. I am of the Valheru.'

At that the tiger-men began to make small mewing noises, half growls, half whimpers. 'Ancient One!' was repeated several times. They huddled together in abject terror.

Pug said, 'What is this and who are these creatures?'

Tomas said, 'They are fearful of me, for I am a legend come to life before them. These are Draken-Korin's creatures.' Seeing Pug's look of incomprehension, he added, 'One of the Valheru. He was Lord of Tigers and bred these to stand as guards in his palace.' He looked about. 'I guess it would be in one of the caves in this forest.' To Tuan he said, 'Do you war on men?'

Tuan, still crouching, snarled. 'We war on all who invade our forest, Ancient One. It is our land, as you should know. It was you who made us a free people.'

Tomas's eyes narrowed, then opened wide. 'I . . . I remember.' His face turned slightly pale. He said to Pug, 'I thought I had remembered all of those days . . .'

Tuan said, 'We had thought you but men. The Rana of Maharta makes war upon the Priest-King of Lanada. His war elephants command the plains, but the forests are still ours. This year he is allied with the Overlord of the City of the Serpent River, who lends him soldiers. The Rana sends those against us. So we kill any who come here, dwarves, goblins, or serpent men.'

Pug said, 'Pantathians!'

Tuan said, 'So men call them. The land of the serpents lies some-where to the south, but they come north at times to do mischief. We treat them harshly.' He said to Tomas, 'Have you come to enslave us again, Ancient One?'

Tomas recovered from his reverie. 'No, those days are vanished in the past. We seek the Halls of the Dead, in the City of the Dead Gods. Guide us.'

Tuan waved away his warriors. 'I shall guide you.' To the others he spoke in a growling, guttural language. In scant moments they vanished into the gloom between the boles of the forest. When all were gone, he said, 'Come, we have far to go.'

Tuan led them throughout the night, and as they travelled, Pug asked many questions. At first the tiger-man was reluctant to speak to the magician, but Tomas indicated he should cooperate and the leader of the tiger-men did so. The tiger nation lived in a small city to the east of where the dragon had landed. Dragons had long been hated by the tigers, as they raided the herds raised by the tiger-men. So a full patrol had been sent in case the dragon needed to be driven away.

Their city had no name, being only the City of the Tigers. No man had seen this place and lived, for the tiger-men killed any invaders. Tuan revealed a great distrust of men and when queried said only, 'We were here before men. They took our forests to the east. We resisted. There has always been war between us.'

Of the Pantathians Tuan knew little, except they warranted killing on sight. When Pug asked how the tiger-men came to be or how Tomas had freed them, he was answered only by silence. As Tomas seemed equally reticent, Pug did not press the question.

After climbing the forested hills below the Pillars of Heaven, they came to a deep pass. Tuan halted. To the east the grey of dawn was approaching. 'Here live the gods,' he said. They looked upward. The tips of the mountains were receiving the first rays of sun. White clouds mantled the peaks of the Pillars of Heaven, wrapping them in glowing mists, which reflected the light in white and silver sparkles.

'How high are the peaks?' asked Pug.

'No one knows. No mortal has reached them. We allow pilgrims to pass this way unmolested if they stay south of our boundaries. Those who climb do not return. The gods prefer their privacy. Come.'

He led them into the pass, which descended into a ravine. 'Beyond this pass, the ravine widens to a broad plateau at the base of the mountains. There lies the City of the Dead Gods. It is now overgrown with trees and vines. Within the city is the great temple to the lost gods. Beyond is the abode of the departed. I will go no farther, Ancient One. You and your spellcaster companion may survive, but for mortals it is a journey without return. To enter the Halls of the Dead is to quit the lands of life.'

'We have no further need of you. Depart in peace.'

Tuan said, 'Hunt well, Ancient One.' Then Tuan was off, with a running, bounding gait.

Without conversation, Tomas and Pug entered the ravine.

Pug and Tomas walked slowly through the plaza. Pug took mental note of every wonder. Oddly shaped buildings – hexagonal, pentagonal, rhomboidal, pyramidal – were arranged in an apparently haphazard fashion, but one that seemed almost to make sense, as if the beholder was not quite sophisticated enough to comprehend the pattern. Obelisks of improbable design, great upthrusting columns of jet and ivory inscribed with runic carvings unknown to Pug stood at the four corners of the plaza. A city it was, but a city unlike any other, for it was a city without markets, or stables, a city lacking taverns or even the rudest hut for a man to dwell within. For in every direction they could travel, only tombs rose up. And upon each a single name was inscribed over the entrance.

'Who built this place?' Pug wondered aloud.

'The gods,' Tomas replied. Pug studied his companion and saw there was no jest in his words.

'Can this truly be so?'

Tomas shrugged. 'Even to such as us some things remain a mystery. Some agency constructed those tombs.' He pointed at one of the major buildings near the square. 'That bears the name Isanda.' Tomas looked lost in memory. 'When my kin rose up against the gods, I remained apart.' Pug did not fail to notice Tomas's reference to *his* kin; in the past he had spoken of Ashen-Shugar as a being apart.

Tomas continued. 'The gods were new then, coming into their power, while the Valheru were ancient. It was the passing of an old order and the birth of a new one. But the gods were powerful, at least those who survived. Of the hundred who were formed by Ishap, only sixteen survived, the twelve lesser and four greater gods. The others lie here.' He pointed again to the building. 'Isanda was the Goddess of Dance.' He looked about slowly. 'It was the time of the Chaos Wars.'

Tomas moved past Pug, clearly reluctant to speak more. Upon another building was inscribed the name Onanka-Tith. Pug said, 'What do you make of that?'

Tomas spoke quietly while he walked. 'The Joyful Warrior and the Planner of Battles were both mortally wounded, but by combining their remaining essences they survived in part, as a new being, Tith-Onanka, the War God with Two Faces. Here lie those parts of each which did not survive.'

Softly Pug observed, 'Each time I think I have witnessed a wonder unsurpassed . . . It humbles me.' After a long stretch of quiet, as they passed dozens of buildings upon which were inscribed names alien to Pug, the magician said, 'How is it that immortals die, Tomas?'

Tomas did not look at his friend as he spoke. 'Nothing is forever, Pug.' Then he looked at Pug, who saw a strange light in his friend's eyes, as if Tomas were poised for battle. 'Nothing. Immortality, power, dominance, all are illusions. Don't you see? We are simply pawns in a game beyond our understanding.'

Pug let his eyes sweep over the ancient city, its strange assortment of buildings half overgrown with lianas. 'That is what humbles me most.'

'Now, we must seek one who might understand this game. Macros.' He pointed at a gigantic edifice, a building dwarfing those about it. Upon it were carved four names, Sarig, Drusala, Eortis, and Wodar-Hospur. Tomas said, 'The monument to the lost gods.' He pointed to each name in turn. 'The lost God of Magic, who, it is thought, hid his secrets when he vanished. Which may be why only the Lesser Path rose upon this world among men. Drusala, the Goddess of

Healing, whose fallen staff was picked up by Sung, who keeps it against the day of her sister's return. Eortis, old dolphin-tail, the true God of the Sea. Kilian now holds sway over his dominion. She is now mother of all nature. And Wodar-Hospur, the Lorekeeper who, alone among all beings below Ishap, knew Truth.'

'Tomas, how do you know so much?'

Looking at his friend, he answered, 'I remember. I did not rise to challenge the gods, Pug, but I was there. I saw. And I remember.' There was a note of terrible, bitter pain in his tone, which he could not mask from his lifelong friend.

They began to walk on, and Pug knew Tomas would speak no more on this subject, at least for the present. Tomas led Pug into the vast hall of the four lost gods. A fey light illuminated the temple, filling the gigantic room with an amber glow. Even to the high vaulted ceiling, no shadows existed. On each side of the hall a pair of gigantic stone thrones sat empty and waiting. Opposite the entrance a vast cavern led away into darkness. Pointing at that black maw, Tomas said, 'The Halls of the Dead.'

Without comment, Pug began walking, and soon both were engulfed in darkness.

One moment they had existed in a real, albeit alien, world, the next they had entered a realm of the spirit. As if a coldness beyond enduring had passed through them, they each felt an instant of supreme discomfort and another instant of near-rapture. Then they were truly within the Halls of the Dead.

Shapes and distances appeared to have little meaning, for one moment they seemed in a narrow tunnel, then upon an endless sunlit field of grasses. Next they passed through a garden, with babbling brooks and fruit-laden trees. After that, they walked below an ice flow, a white-blue frozen cataract spilling from a cliff surmounted by a giant hall from which issued joyous music. Then they seemed to walk atop clouds. But at last they were in a dark and vast cavern, ancient dead rock vaulting away into a darkness beyond any eyes' ability to penetrate. Pug ran his hand over the rock and discovered the surface to have a slippery feel, as of soapstone. Yet when he rubbed thumb and fingers together, there was no residue. Pug put away his curiosity. A broad river slowly flowed across their path, and in the distance they could see another shore through dense mist. Then from out of the fog came a wherry, with a single figure hidden by heavy robes at the stern, propelling the craft by means of a scull. As the boat gently nudged the shore, the figure raised the large oar out of the water and motioned for Tomas and Pug to board.

'The ferryman?' said Pug.

'It is a common legend. At least here it is true. Come.'

They boarded, and the figure held out a gnarled hand. Pug removed two copper coins from his purse and deposited them in the outstretched hand. Pug sat, and was astounded to discover the wherry had reversed itself and was now heading across the river. He had felt no sensation of motion. A sound from behind caused him to turn, and over his shoulder he saw vague shapes on the shore they had left, quickly hidden by mist.

Tomas said, 'Those who fear to cross or who cannot pay the boatman. They abide upon the far shore for eternity, or so it is supposed.' Pug could only nod. He looked down into the river and was further astonished to see that the water glowed faintly, lit from below by a yellow-green light. And within its depth stood figures, each looking up to the boat as it passed overhead. Feebly they waved at the boat or reached out, as if seeking to grab hold, but the boat was too quickly past. Tomas said, 'Those who attempted to cross without the ferryman's permission. Trapped for all time.'

Pug spoke softly, 'Which way were they seeking to cross?'

Tomas said, 'Only they know.'

The boat bumped against the far shore, and the ferryman silently pointed. They disembarked, and Pug glanced back to discover the wherry gone from sight. Tomas said, 'It is a journey that may be taken in one direction only. Come.'

Pug hesitated, but realized the point of no return had just been crossed and reluctance was useless. He gazed at the river for a last, lingering moment and quickly followed Tomas.

They paused in their trek. One moment Pug and Tomas had been walking upon an empty plain of greys and blacks; the next, a vast building rose before them, if in fact it was a building. In each direction it stretched, to vanish at the horizon, more a wall of immense proportion. Upward into the strange grey which served as a sky in this forlorn place it rose, until the eye could no longer follow its lines. It was a wall in this reality; one with a door.

Pug looked over his shoulder and saw nothing but empty plain behind. He and Tomas had spoken infrequently since leaving the river some unknown time before. There had been nothing to comment on and somehow breaking the silence seemed inappropriate. Pug looked forward once more and discovered Tomas's eyes upon him.

Tomas pointed and Pug nodded and they mounted the simple stone steps to the large open portal before them. Crossing the threshold, they halted, for they were greeted by a sight that confounded their senses. In every direction, even behind them, a vast marble floor stretched away, upon which rows of catafalques were arrayed. Atop each rested a body. Pug approached the nearest and studied its features. The figure seemed asleep, for it was unmarked, but the chest was still. It was a girl no more than seven years of age.

Beyond lay men and women of every description from beggars in tatters to those wearing royal raiment. Bodies old and rotting, and those shattered or burned beyond recognition, lay beside bodies unmarked. Infants, dead at birth, lay beside withered ancient crones. Truly they were now within the Halls of the Dead.

Tomas said softly, 'It seems one direction is much the same as another.'

Pug shook his head. 'We are within the boundaries of eternity. I think we must discover a path, or we shall wander without let for ages. I do not know if time has any meaning here, but if it does we cannot afford to idle it away.' Pug closed his eyes and concentrated.

Above his head glowing mists gathered, forming into a pulsating globe that began to rotate rapidly. A faint white light could be seen within; then the conjuration vanished. Pug's eyes remained closed. Tomas watched quietly. He knew Pug was using some mystic sight to scout in moments what would have taken years on foot. Then Pug's eyes were open and he pointed. 'That way.'

Figures waited quietly without the portal to the next hall. It was an oddity of this place that from one angle more corpses could be seen stretching away in every direction, forming a chessboard of reclining figures, but from another angle a new wall was visible, one with another arched portal. Before it more than a thousand men and women, boys and girls, stood silently. While Pug and Tomas approached, one of the reclining figures sat up and dismounted the catafalque to walk past them and join with those waiting by the door. Pug looked back and saw another figure approaching from a different direction. He glanced at the just vacated catafalque and saw another body had appeared in place of the former occupant. Pug and Tomas moved past those who hovered by the door, discovering they took no notice of the newcomers' presence. Pug reached out and touched a child's shoulder, and the small boy absently brushed at Pug's hand, as if an insect had briefly alighted there. But the boy betrayed no other awareness of the magician. Tomas indicated with a jerk of his head they should continue. Through the door they found more people standing, in lines that led away beyond the limits of their perception. Again there was no reaction to their passing. Quickly the two men walked toward the head of the line.

For what seemed hours a light had been brightening before them. Thousands of figures formed silent lines facing that brilliance, each seemingly without impatience. They passed those who stood turned toward the light, expressions impossible to fathom upon their faces. Every so often Pug would notice those in one of the lines taking a step forward, but the lines moved at a snail's pace. As they approached the shining light, Pug glanced behind and noticed there were no shadows cast. Another oddity of this realm, he considered. Then at last they reached stairs.

Atop a dozen steps sat a throne, surrounded with golden brilliance. Something almost like music tickled at the edge of Pug's hearing, but it was not substantial enough to be apprehended. He lifted his eyes until he beheld the figure upon the throne. She was stunning in her beauty, yet frightening. Her features were impossibly perfect, but somehow daunting. She confronted the converging lines of humanity before her and studied each person at the head of the line for some time. Then she would point at one of the figures and motion. Most often the figures simply vanished, to whatever destiny the goddess had selected, but occasionally one would turn and begin the long trek back toward the plain of catafalques. After some time she turned to regard the two men, and Pug's gaze was captured by eyes like sooty coal, flat jet without any hint of warmth or light contained therein, the eyes of death. Yet for all her fearful demeanour, a face the colour of white chalk, she was a figure of incredible seduction, one whose lush form cried out to be embraced. Pug felt his being burn with the need to be gathered within the folds of her white arms, to be taken to her bosom. Pug used his powers to set aside those desires, and he stood his ground. Then the woman upon the throne laughed, and it was the coldest, deadest sound Pug had ever heard. 'Welcome to my domain, Pug and Tomas. Your means of arrival is unusual.' Pug's mind reeled and raced. Each word from the woman was an icy stab through his brain, a chilled pain, as if merely to comprehend the goddess's existence was something nearly beyond his ability. With certainty he knew that without his training and Tomas's heritage they would have been overwhelmed, swept away, most likely dead, by the force of her first uttered word. Still, he maintained his equilibrium and stood his ground.

Tomas spoke. 'Lady, you know our needs.'

The figure nodded. 'Indeed, better than yourselves, perhaps.'

'Then will you tell us what we need to know? We dislike being here as much as our presence displeases you.'

Again the bone-chilling laugh. 'You displease me not at all, Valheru. Of your kin I have often longed to take one to my service. But time and circumstances have never permitted. And Pug shall eventually come here, in time. Yet when that occurs, he shall be like these before me, standing in patient line for their turn to be judged. All wait upon my pleasure; some shall return for another turn of the Wheel; others shall be granted the ultimate punishment, oblivion, and fewer still will earn final rapture, oneness with the Ultimate.

'Still,' she said, as if thoughtful, 'it is not yet his time. No, we all must act as is foreordained. He whom you seek does not abide with me yet. Of all those within the mortal realms, he above all has been most astute in declining my hospitality. No, to find Macros the Black, you will need to look elsewhere.'

Tomas considered. 'May we know where he is?'

The lady upon the throne leaned forward. 'There are limits, Valheru, even to what I may attempt. Put your mind to the task and you shall know where the black sorcerer abides. There can be only one answer.' She turned her gaze again upon Pug. 'Silent, magician? You have said nothing.'

Softly Pug said, 'I wonder, lady. Still, if I may' – he waved a hand at those about him – 'is there no joy in this realm?'

For a moment the lady upon the throne regarded the silent lines of people arrayed before her. It was as if the question was new to her. Then she said, 'No, there is no joy in the realm of the dead.' She again studied the magician. 'But consider, there is also no sorrow. Now you must away, for the quick may abide here a short while only. And there are those within my realm who would distress you to apprehend. You must go.'

Tomas nodded and with a stiff bow, led Pug away. Past long lines they hurried, as the brilliance of the goddess dimmed behind. It seemed hours they walked. Suddenly Pug halted, transfixed by recognition. A young man with wavy brown hair stood quietly in line, his eyes fixed forward. In near-silent voice, Pug said, 'Roland.'

Tomas paused, studying the face of their companion from Crydee, dead for almost three years. He took no notice of his two former friends. Pug said, 'Roland, it's Pug!' Again there was no reaction. Pug shouted the squire from Tulan's name, and there was a nearly imperceptible flicker about the eyes, as if Roland heard a distant voice calling. Pug looked pained as his boyhood rival for Carline's affections took a step forward in the long line of those to be judged. Pug's mind ached for something to say to him. Then at last he shouted, 'Carline is well, Roland. She is happy.'

For a moment there was no reaction, then, faintly, the corners of Roland's mouth turned up for the briefest instant. But Pug thought he looked somehow more at peace as he stared blankly forward. Then Pug suddenly discovered Tomas's hand upon his arm, and the powerful warrior propelled his friend away from Roland. Pug struggled an instant, but to no avail, then walked in step with Tomas. A moment later, Tomas released his grip. Softly he said, 'They're all here, Pug. Roland. Lord Borric and his lady Catherine. The men who died in the Green Heart, and those taken by the wraith in Mac Mordain Cadal. King Rodric. All who died in the Riftwar. They're all here. That's what Lims-Kragma meant by saying there were those here who would cause us distress if we met.'

Pug only nodded. Again he felt a deep sense of loss for those whom fate had taken away from him. Turning his mind again to the cause of their strange travel, he said, 'Where are we bound now?'

'By not answering, the Lady of Death answered. There is only one place beyond her reach. It is an oddity outside the known universe. We must find the City Forever, that place which stands beyond the edge of time.'

Pug halted. Looking about, he noticed they had again passed into the vast plain of bodies, all arrayed in neat rows. 'Then the question is, how do we find it?'

Tomas reached out and placed his hand upon Pug's face, covering his eyes. A bone-wrenching chill passed through the magician, and he suddenly found his chest exploding in hot fire as he sucked in a lungful of air. His teeth chattered and he shook, a fierce, uncontrollable trembling as his body coiled and uncoiled in knots of pain. He moved and discovered he was lying on a cold marble floor. Tomas's hand was gone from his eyes and he opened them. He lay upon the floor in the Temple of the Four Lost Gods, just before the entrance to the dark cavern. Tomas rose on wobbly legs a short distance away, also pulling in ragged gasps of air. Pug saw that his friend's face was pale, his lips bluish. The magician regarded his own hands and saw the nails were blue to the quick. Standing, he felt warmth creep slowly back into his limbs, which ached and shook. He spoke, and his voice was a dry croak. 'Was it real?'

Tomas looked about, his alien features showing little. 'Of all mortal men on this world, Pug, you should know best how futile that question is. We saw what we saw. Whether it was a place or a vision in our mind, it doesn't matter. We must act upon what we experienced, so to that end, yes, it was real.'

'Now?'

Tomas said, 'I must summon Ryath, if she is not too deep in sleep. We must travel between the stars once again.'

Pug could only nod. His mind was numb, and dimly he wondered what possible marvels could await beyond that which was already behind.

CHAPTER EIGHT

Yabon

*T*HE INN WAS QUIET.

It was fully two hours before sundown and the hectic quality of evening revelry was not yet unleashed. For this, Arutha was thankful. He sat as deep in shadows as he could, Roald, Laurie, and the two squires occupying the other chairs. His newly cropped hair, shorter than he had worn in years and his thickening beard lent him a sinister appearance, giving credence to their impersonation of mercenaries. Jimmy and Locklear had purchased more common travel clothing in Questor's View, burning their squire's tunics. In all, the five of them looked to be nothing more than a simple crew of unemployed fighting men. Even Locklear was convincing, for he was no younger than some of those who passed through, aspiring young bravos seeking their first tour of duty.

They had been waiting three days for Martin, and Arutha was growing apprehensive. Given the timing of the message, he had expected Martin to reach Ylith first. Also, each day in the city increased the chance of someone's remembering them from their last encounter here. A tavern brawl ending in a killing, while not unique, was still something to cause a few to remember a face.

A shadow crossed the table and they looked up. Martin and Baru stood before them. Arutha rose slowly and Martin calmly extended his hand. They quietly shook, and Martin said, 'Good seeing you well.'

Arutha smiled crookedly. 'Good for me also.'

Martin's answering smile was his brother's twin. 'You look different.' Arutha only nodded. Then he and the others greeted Baru, and Martin said, 'How did he get here?' He pointed at Jimmy.

Laurie said, 'How can you stop him?'

Martin looked at Locklear and raised an eyebrow. 'This one's face I recognize, though I don't recall the name.'

'That's Locky.'

'Jimmy's protégé,' Roald added with a chuckle.

Martin and Baru exchanged glances. The tall Duke said, 'Two of them?'

Arutha said, 'It's a long tale. We should tarry here as little as possible.'

'Agreed,' answered Martin. 'But we'll need new horses. Ours are weary, and I expect we still have a long road before us.'

Arutha's eyes narrowed and he said, 'Yes. Very long.'

The clearing was little more than a widening in the road. To Arutha's party the roadhouse was a welcoming beacon, every window on both floors showing a merry yellow light that knifed through the oppressive gloom of night. They had ridden without incident since leaving Ylith, passing beyond Zūn and Yabon, and were now at the last outpost of Kingdom civilization, where the forest road turned northeast for Tyr-Sog. To travel directly north was to enter Hadati country, and the northern ranges beyond marked the boundary of the Kingdom. While there had been no trouble, all were relieved to be reaching this inn.

A sharp-eared stable boy heard them ride up and came down from his loft to open the barn – few travelled the forest roads after sundown and he had been about to turn in. They quickly cared for their animals, Jimmy and Martin occasionally watching the woods for signs of trouble.

When they were done, they gathered their bundles and headed for the roadhouse. As they crossed the clearing between barn and main building, Laurie said, 'It will be nice to have a warm meal.'

'Maybe our last for a while,' commented Jimmy to Locklear.

As they reached the front of the building, they could make out the sign over the door, a man sleeping atop a wagon while his mule had broken its traces and was making its getaway. Laurie said, 'Now for some hot food. The Sleeping Wagoneer is among the finest little country inns you'll ever visit, though at times you may find it occupied by a rather strange assortment.'

Pushing open the door, they entered a bright and cheery common room. A large open hearth contained a roaring fire, and three long tables stood before it. Across the room, opposite the door, ran a long bar, behind which rested large hogsheads of ale. And making his way toward them, a smile upon his face, came the innkeeper, a man of middle years and portly appearance. 'Ah, guests. Welcome.' When he reached them, his smile broadened. 'Laurie! Roald! As I live! It's been years! Glad I am to see you.'

The minstrel said, 'Greetings, Geoffrey. These are companions of mine.'

Geoffrey took Laurie by the elbow and guided him to a table near the bar. 'Your companions are as welcome as yourself.' He seated them at the table and said, 'Pleased as I am to see you, I wish you had been here two days ago. I could have done with a good singer.'

Laurie smiled at that. 'Trouble?'

A look of perpetual trial crossed the innkeeper's face. 'Always. We had a party of dwarves through here and they sang their drinking songs all hours. They insisted on keeping time to the songs by beating on the tables with whatever was at hand, winecups, flagons, hand axes, all in complete disregard for whatever was upon them. I've broken crockery and scarred tables all over. I only managed to return the common room to a semblance of order this afternoon, and I had to repair half of one table.' He fixed Roald and Laurie with a mock-stern expression. 'So don't start trouble, like the last time. One ruckus a week is plenty.' He glanced around the room. 'It is quiet now, but I expect a caravan through at any time. Ambros the silver merchant passes through this time of year.'

Roald said, 'Geoffrey, we perish from thirst.'

The man became instantly apologetic. 'Truly, I am sorry. Fresh in from the road and I stand jabbering like a magpie. What is your pleasure?'

'Ale,' said Martin, and the others echoed the request.

The man hurried away, and returned moments later with a tray of pewter jacks, all brimming with cool ale. After the first draught of the biting liquid, Laurie said, 'What brings dwarves this far from home?'

The innkeeper joined them at the table, wiping his hands on his apron. 'Have you not heard the news?'

Laurie said, 'We're just in from the south. What news?'

'The dwarves moot at Stone Mountain, meeting in the long hall of Chief Harthorn at village Delmoria.'

'To what ends?' asked Arutha.

'Well, the dwarves through here were up all the way from Dorgin, and from their talk it's the first time in ages the eastern dwarves have ventured up to visit their brethren in the West. Old King Halfdan of Dorgin is sending his son Hogne, and his rowdy companions, to witness the restoration of the line of Tholin in the West. With the return of Tholin's hammer during the Riftwar, the western dwarves have been pestering Dolgan of Caldara to take the crown lost with Tholin. Dwarves from the Grey Towers, Stone Mountain, Dorgin, and places I've never heard of are gathering to see Dolgan made King of the western dwarves. As Dolgan has agreed to moot, Hogne says it's a foregone conclusion he'll take the crown, but you know how dwarves can be. Some things they decide quickly, other things they take years to consider. Comes of being long lived, I guess.'

Arutha and Martin exchanged faint smiles. Both remembered Dolgan with affection. Arutha had first met him years ago when riding east with his father to carry news to King Rodric of the coming Tsurani invasion. Dolgan had acted as their guide through the ancient mine, the Mac Mordain Cadal. Martin had met him later, during the war. The dwarven chief was a being of high principle and bravery, possessing a dry wit and keen mind. They both knew he would be a fine King.

As they drank, they slowly discarded their travellers' accoutrements, putting off helms, setting aside weapons, and letting the quiet atmosphere of the inn relax them. Geoffrey kept the ale coming and, after a while, a fine meal of meats, cheeses, and hot vegetables and breads. Talk ran to the mundane, as Geoffrey repeated stories told by travellers. While they ate, Laurie said, 'Things are quiet this night, Geoffrey.'

Geoffrey said, 'Yes, besides yourselves I have only one other guest.' He indicated a man sitting in the corner farthest from them, and all turned in surprise for a moment. Arutha motioned for the others to resume their meal. All wondered how they had failed to notice him there all this time. The stranger seemed indifferent to the newcomers. He was a plain-looking fellow, of middle years, with nothing remarkable about him in either manner or dress. He wore a heavy brown cloak that hid any chain or leather armour he might be wearing. A shield rested against the table, its blazon masked by a plain leather cover. Arutha became curious, for only a disinherited man or one on some holy quest would choose to disguise his blazon – among honest men, Arutha added silently. He asked Geoffrey, 'Who is he?'

'Don't know. Name's Crowe. Been here for two days, coming just after the dwarves left. Quiet sort. Keeps to himself. But he pays his bill and makes no trouble.' Geoffrey began clearing the table.

When the innkeeper was gone to the kitchen, Jimmy leaned across the table as if to reach for something in a pack on the other side and said quietly, 'He's good. He makes no show, but he is straining to hear our conversation. Guard your words. I'll keep an eye on our friend over there.'

When Geoffrey returned, he said, 'Where are you bound, Laurie?'

Arutha answered, 'Tyr-Sog.'

Jimmy thought he noticed a flicker of interest in the sole occupant of the other table, but he couldn't be sure. The man seemed intent upon his meal.

Geoffrey clapped Laurie upon the shoulder. 'Not going back to see your family, are you?'

Laurie shook his head. 'No, not really. Too many years. Too many differences.' All save Baru and Locklear knew Laurie had been disowned by his father. As a boy, Laurie had proved an indifferent farmer, being more interested in daydreams and song. With so many mouths to feed, his father had tossed him out on his own at age thirteen.

The innkeeper said, 'Your father came through here two, no, almost three years back. Just before the end of the war. He and some other farmers were caravanning grain down to LaMut for the army.' He studied Laurie's face. 'He spoke of you.'

A strange expression crossed the former minstrel's face, one unreadable to those around the table. 'I had mentioned it had been years since you came by and he said, "Well then, ain't we the lucky ones? That worthless layabout hasn't pestered me in years either."'

Laurie erupted in laughter. Roald joined in. 'That's my father. I hope the old sod is still well.'

'I expect,' said Geoffrey. 'He and your brothers seem to be doing fine. If I can, I'll send word you were through. Last any of us heard of you, you were off somewhere with the army, and that was five or six years back. From where have you come?'

Laurie glanced at Arutha, both sharing the same thought. Salador was a distant eastern court, and word had not yet made its way to the frontier that a son of Tyr-Sog was now Duke there, married to the King's sister. Both were relieved.

Arutha tried to sound offhanded in his answer. 'Around, here and there. Most recently Yabon.'

Geoffrey sat at the table. Drumming his fingers on the wood, he said, 'You might do well to wait for Ambros to pass here. He'll be bound for Tyr-Sog. I am sure he could use a few more guards, and these roads are better travelled in large companies.'

Laurie said, 'Troubles?'

Geoffrey said, 'In the forest? Always, but more so of late. For weeks now there have been stories of goblins and brigands troubling travellers. It's nothing new, but there seems to be more of that going on than is usual, and something odd is the goblins and bandits almost always are reported as travelling northward.' He lapsed into silence for a moment. 'Then there's something the dwarves said when they first arrived. It was right strange.'

Laurie feigned amused uninterest. 'Dwarves tend to the strange.'

'But this was unusually so, Laurie. The dwarves claim they crossed the path of some Dark Brothers and, being dwarves, proceeded to have a bash at them. They claim they were chasing these Dark Brothers when they killed one, or at least should have. This one creature wouldn't have the decency to die, the dwarves avowed. Maybe these youngsters sought to pull a simple innkeeper's leg, but they said they hit this one Brother with an axe; damn near split his head in two, but the thing just sort of pushes the halves together and runs off after his companions. Shocked the dwarves so fierce they stopped in their tracks and forgot to chase after. That's the other thing. The dwarves said they've never met a band of Dark Brothers so intent on running away, like they had to get somewhere and couldn't take the time to fight. They're a mean lot as a rule and they don't like dwarves a little more than they don't like everybody else.' Geoffrey smiled and winked. 'I know the older dwarves are sombre sorts and not given to stretching the truth, but these youngsters were having me on a little, I think.'

Arutha and the others showed little expression, but all knew the story to be true – and that it meant the Black Slayers were again abroad in the Kingdom.

Arutha said, 'It probably would be best to wait for the silver merchant's caravan, but we've got to be off at first light.'

Laurie said, 'With only one other guest, I assume there's no trouble with rooms.'

'None.' Geoffrey leaned forward and whispered, 'I mean no disrespect toward a paying guest, but he sleeps in the commons. I've offered him a room at discount, since I've ample space, but he says no. What some will do to save a little silver.' Geoffrey rose. 'How many rooms?'

Arutha said, 'Two should provide comfort.'

The innkeeper seemed disappointed, but given travellers were often short of funds, he was not surprised. 'I'll have extra pallets brought into the rooms.'

As Arutha and his companions gathered up their belongings, Jimmy glimpsed the other man. He seemed intent on the contents of his wine cup and little else. Geoffrey brought over some candles and lit them with a taper from the fire. Then he led them up the dark stairs to their rooms.

Something woke Jimmy. The former thief's senses were more attuned to changes in the night than were his companions'. He and Locklear were bunking in with Roald and Laurie. Arutha, Martin, and Baru slept across the narrow hall, in a room over the common room, and as the soft sound that had awakened him came from outside, Jimmy was certain it hadn't roused the former Huntmaster of Crydee or the hillman. The young squire of the Prince's court strained his hearing to its limit. Again came a sound in the night, a faint rustling. He quietly got up from his pallet on the floor, next to Locklear's. Passing the sleeping forms of Roald and Laurie, he peered out the window between their beds.

In the darkness he caught a glimpse of movement, as if something or someone had just moved behind the barn. Jimmy wondered if he should wake the others but thought it would be foolish to raise alarm over nothing. He gathered up his own sword and quietly left the room.

His bare feet made no sound as he moved toward the stairs. At the landing atop the stairs another window opened on the front of the inn. Jimmy peeked through and in the gloom saw figures moving near the trees across the road. He counted it unlikely that anyone skulking out in the night was up to honest undertakings.

Jimmy hurried down the stairs and found the door unbolted. He puzzled at that, for he was near certain it had been bolted when they retired. Then Jimmy remembered the inn's other guest. He spun about and saw the man was gone.

Jimmy moved to a window, pulling aside a peep slide in the shutters, and saw nothing. Silently he let himself out the door, and dodged along the front of the building, trusting the gloom of the night to mask him. He hurried to the place he had last seen movement.

Jimmy's ability to walk quietly was hampered by having to negotiate the forest at night. While he had gained a little comfort in these environs from his journey with Arutha to Moraelin, he was still a city boy. He was forced to move slowly. Then he heard voices. Cautiously he approached the source of the conversation and saw a faint light.

He could begin to understand scraps of what was said, then he suddenly could see a half-dozen figures in a tiny clearing. The man in the brown cloak with the covered shield was speaking with a black armoured figure. Jimmy sucked in a chest full of air, to calm himself down. It was a Black Slayer. Four other moredhel stood quietly off to one side, three in the grey cloaks of the forest clans and one in the trousers and vest of the mountain clans. The man in brown was speaking. '. . . nothing, I say. Bravos from the look of them, with a minstrel, but . . .'

The Black Slayer interrupted him. His voice was deep and seemed to come from some distance, echoing with an odd breathiness. The voice was disquietingly familiar to Jimmy. 'You are not paid to think, human. You are paid to serve.' He punctuated that remark with a jabbing finger to the chest. 'See that I remain pleased with your work and we shall continue this relationship. Displease me and suffer the consequences.' The brown-cloaked fellow looked the sort not easily frightened, a tough fighting man, but he only nodded. Jimmy understood, for the Black Slayers were worthy of fear. Murmandamus's minions, even when dead, served him.

'You say there's a singer and a boy?' Jimmy swallowed hard.

The man tossed back his cloak, revealing brown chain mail, and said, 'Well, now that I think, you could more likely say there are two boys, but they're almost man-sized.'

This brought the Black Slayer out of his reverie. 'Two?'

The man nodded. 'Might be brothers from the look of them. About a size, though their hair colour's different. But they seem alike in some ways, like brothers do.'

'Moraelin. There was a boy there, but not two . . . Tell me, is there a Hadati among them?'

The man in brown shrugged. 'Yes, but hillmen're all over. This is Yabon.'

'This one would be from the northwest, near Lake of the Sky.' For a long moment there was only the sound of heavy breathing from behind the black helm as if the moredhel was lost in thought, or conversing with someone else. The Black Slayer hit his fist against his hand. 'It could be them. Was there one who looked cunning, a slender warrior with dark hair almost to his shoulders, quick in his movements, clean shaven?'

The man shook his head. 'There's a clean-shaven fellow, but he's big, and a slender one, but he's got short hair and a beard. Who do you think it is?'

'That is not for you to know,' said the Slayer. Jimmy eased his legs by slowly shifting his weight. He knew the Black Slayer was trying to connect this band to the one that raided Moraelin for Silverthorn the year before. Then the moredhel said, 'We shall wait. News reached us two days ago the Lord of the West is dead, but I am not foolish enough to count a man dead until I hold his heart in my hand. It may be nothing. Had an elf been with them, I would burn that inn to the ground tonight, but I cannot be sure. Still, remain alert. It could be his companions returning to do mischief, to avenge him.'

'Seven men, and two of them really boys. What harm?'

The moredhel ignored the question. 'Return to the inn and watch, Morgan Crowe. You are paid well and quickly for obedience, not questions. Should those in the inn leave, follow at a discreet distance. Should they remain upon the road to Tyr-Sog until midday, return to the inn and wait. Should they turn northward before then, I shall wish to know. Return here tomorrow night and tell me which. But tarry not, for Segersen brings his band north and you must meet him. Without the next payment, he takes his men home. I need his engineers. Is the gold safe?'

'Always with me.'

'Good. Now go.' For an instant the Black Slayer seemed to shudder, then wobble, then his movements returned. In a completely different voice, he said, 'Do as our master instructs, human,' then turned and walked away. In a moment the clearing was empty.

Jimmy's mouth hung open. Now he understood. He had heard that first voice before, in the palace where the undead moredhel had tried to kill Arutha, and again in the basement of the House of Willows when they had destroyed the Nighthawks in Krondor. The man called Morgan Crowe had been speaking not to the Black Slayer, but rather through him. And Jimmy had no doubt to whom. Murmandamus!

Jimmy's astonishment had caused him to hesitate, and suddenly he knew he could not return to the inn before Crowe. Already the man had quit the clearing, taking the lantern with him. In the dark, Jimmy had to move slowly.

By the time he reached the clearing near the road, Jimmy caught a glimpse of the red glow from the hearth in the common room as Crowe closed the door to the inn. He could hear the bolt driven home.

Hurrying silently along the edge of the clearing, Jimmy waited until he was opposite the window to his room. He hurried across and was quickly up the wall, the rough surface providing ample hand-and-foot-holds. From inside his tunic he retrieved twine and a hook and quickly fished open the simple bar locking the window. He pulled it open and stepped through.

Two sword points poked him in the chest and he halted. Laurie and Roald both lowered their weapons when they saw who it was. Locklear had his sword out and guarded the door. 'What's this? Looking for a new way to die: having your friends run you through?' asked Roald.

'What's that you have there?' Laurie pointed at the hook and twine. 'I thought you'd left all that behind.'

'Quietly,' said the boy, putting up his thieving tools. In hushed tones he said, 'You've not been a minstrel for almost a year, yet you still lug that lute with you everywhere. Now listen, we've got troubles. That fellow in the common room works for Murmandamus.'

Laurie and Roald exchanged glances. Laurie said, 'You'd better tell Arutha.'

Arutha said, 'Well, we know that they've heard the news of my death. And we know Murmandamus isn't certain, despite the show in Krondor.' All had come to Arutha's room, where they spoke quietly in the dark.

'Still,' Baru said, 'it seems he is acting upon the presumption you are dead until proven otherwise, despite any doubts he may harbour.'

Laurie said, 'He can't sit on a Brotherhood alliance indefinitely. He has to move soon or have everything fall apart around him.'

'If we continue for another day toward Tyr-Sog, then they'll leave us alone,' said Jimmy.

'Yes,' whispered Roald, 'but there's still Segersen.'

'Who is he?' Martin asked.

'Mercenary general,' answered Roald. 'But an odd sort. He doesn't have a large company, never a hundred men, often fewer than fifty. Mostly he employs experts: miners, engineers, tacticians. He's got the best crews in the business. His speciality is bringing down walls or keeping them up, depending on who's doing the paying. I've seen him work. He helped Baron Croswaith in his border skirmish with Baron Lobromill, when I was in Croswaith's employ.'

'I've heard of him, too,' said Arutha. 'He works from the Free

Cities or Queg, so he doesn't have to deal with Kingdom laws on mercenary service.

'What I want to know, though, is what Murmandamus needs a corps of high-priced engineers for. If he's working this far west, he must needs come through Tyr-Sog or Yabon. Farther east, the Border Barons. But he's still on the other side of the mountains and won't need them for months if he's going to siege.'

'Maybe he wants to make sure no one else hires this Segersen?' ventured Locklear.

'Maybe,' said Laurie. 'But most likely he needs something Segersen can provide.'

'Then we must make sure he doesn't get it,' said Arutha.

Roald said, 'We go half a day to Tyr-Sog, then turn back?'

Arutha only nodded.

Arutha signalled.

Roald, Laurie, and Jimmy moved slowly forward, while Baru and Martin moved off, to circle around. Locklear stayed behind to tend the horses. They had spent half the day moving along the road to Tyr-Sog; then at a little past noon, Martin had cut off the road and dropped back. He had returned with the news the man called Crowe had turned back. Now they stalked him through the night as the renegade met again with his moredhel employers.

Arutha moved up silently to look over Jimmy's shoulder. Again the Prince observed one of Murmandamus's Black Slayers. The iron-clad moredhel spoke. 'Did you follow that band?'

'They trundled up the road to Tyr-Sog, right proper. Hell, I told you they was nothing. Wasted a whole day tagging after.'

'You will do as our master orders.'

Jimmy whispered, 'That's not the same voice. That's the second voice.'

Arutha nodded. The boy had explained the two voices, and they had seen Murmandamus take control of his servants before. 'Good,' the Prince whispered back.

The moredhel said, 'Now wait for Segersen. You know—'

The Black Slayer seemed to leap forward, to suddenly be caught by Crowe, who held him a moment, then dropped him. The startled renegade could only stare in wide-eyed wonder at the cloth-yard shaft protruding from below the edge of the creature's helm. Martin's arrow had punched through the Black Slayer's neck coif of chain mail, killing him instantly.

Before the other four moredhel could pull weapons, Martin had a second down, and Baru was leaping from the woods, his long sword blurring as he struck a moredhel down. Roald was across the clearing and killed another. Martin shot the last moredhel while Jimmy and Arutha charged the renegade, Crowe. He made little attempt to defend himself, being shocked by the sudden attack and recognizing quickly he was outnumbered. He seemed confused, especially as he saw Martin and Baru begin to pull off the Black Slayer's armour.

Fear was replaced by shock as he saw Martin cut open the Slayer's chest and remove its heart. His eyes widened as he recognized who had taken the moredhel band. 'You, then—' His eyes searched each face as they gathered around him, then he studied Arutha's face. 'You! You're supposed to be dead!'

Jimmy quickly stripped him of hidden weapons and searched about his neck. 'No ebon hawk. He's not one of them.'

A feral light seemed to kindle in Crowe's eyes. 'Me, one of them? No, by no means, Your Worships. I'm only carrying messages, sir. Making a little gold for myself, is all, Your Kindness. You know how it can be.'

Arutha waved Jimmy off. 'Fetch Locky. I don't want him out there alone if there are other Dark Brothers about.' He said to the prisoner, 'What has Segersen to do with Murmandamus?'

'Segersen? Who's he?'

Roald stepped forward and, with a heavy dagger hilt in his gloved fist, struck Crowe across the face, bloodying his nose, and shattering his cheek.

'Don't break his jaw, for mercy's sake,' said Laurie, 'or he won't be able to tell us anything.'

Roald gave the man a kick as he lay writhing on the ground. 'Listen, laddie, I don't have time to be tender with you. Now, you'd best answer up, or we'll be taking you back to the inn in little pieces.' He stroked the edge of his dagger for emphasis.

'What has Segersen to do with Murmandamus?' Arutha repeated.

'I don't know,' said the man through bloody lips, and he yelled again when Roald kicked him. 'Honestly I don't. I was only told to meet him and give him a message.'

'What message?' asked Laurie.

'The message is simple. It was only "By the Inclindel Gap."'

Baru said, 'Inclindel Gap is a narrow way through the mountains, directly north from here. If Murmandamus has seized it, he can keep it open long enough for Segersen's crew to get through.'

'But we still don't know why Murmandamus needs a company of engineers,' observed Laurie.

Roald quipped, 'For whatever you use them for, I would think.'

Arutha said, 'What is there to siege? Tyr-Sog? It's too easy to reinforce from Yabon City, and he has to find a way past the Thunderhell nomads on the other side of the mountains. Ironpass and Northwarden are too far east of here, and he wouldn't need engineers to take on the dwarves or elves. That leaves Highcastle.'

Martin had finished his bloody work and said, 'Perhaps, but it's the largest of the Border Baron fortresses.'

Arutha said, 'I'd not bother with siege. It's designed to withstand raids. You can swarm it, and there is nothing we've seen of Murmandamus that indicates he's reluctant to spend lives. Besides, that would put him in the middle of the High Wold, with no place to go. No, this makes no sense.'

'Look,' said the man on the ground, 'I'm just a go-between, a fellow's paid to do a job. Now, you can't hold me responsible for what the Brotherhood's up to, can you, Your Kindness?'

Jimmy returned with Locklear in tow.

Martin said to Arutha, 'I don't think he knows anything else.'

A dark expression crossed Arutha's face. 'He knows who we are.'

Martin nodded. 'He does.'

Suddenly Crowe's face drained of colour. 'Look, you can rely on me. I'll keep my gob shut, Your Highness. You don't have to give me anything. Just let me go and I'll light out of these parts. Honestly.'

Locklear glanced about his grim-looking companions, comprehension escaping him.

Arutha noticed and nodded slightly to Jimmy. The older youth roughly grabbed Locklear by the upper arm and propelled him away. 'What—' said the younger squire.

A short distance away, Jimmy halted. 'We wait.'

'For what?' said the boy, confusion apparent on his face.

'For them to do what they have to do.'

'To do what?' insisted Locklear.

'To kill the renegade.'

Locklear looked sick. Jimmy's tone became short. 'Look, Locky, this is war and people are killed. And that Crowe is among the least of those who are going to die.' Locklear couldn't believe the harsh expression he was seeing on Jimmy's face. For over a year he had seen the rogue, the scoundrel, the charmer, but now he was seeing someone he had never expected to encounter, the cold, ruthless veteran of life, a young man who had killed and who would kill again. 'That man must die,' said Jimmy flatly. 'He knows who Arutha is, and do you think for a minute the Prince's life's worth spit if Crowe gets loose?'

Locklear appeared shaken, his face pale. He slowly closed his eyes. 'Couldn't we . . .'

'What?' demanded Jimmy savagely. 'Wait for a patrol of militia to pass so we can hand him over for trial in Tyr-Sog? Pop in to give testimony? Tie him up for a few months? Look, if it helps, just keep in mind Crowe is an outlaw and a traitor, and Arutha is dispensing High Justice. But any way you look at it, there's no choice.'

Locklear's mind seemed to spin, then a strangled cry came from the clearing and the boy winced. His confusion seemed to vanish, and he only nodded. Jimmy placed his hand upon his friend's shoulder and squeezed lightly. Suddenly, he knew Locklear would never seem quite so young again.

They had returned to the inn and waited, to the delight of the somewhat perplexed Geoffrey. After three days a stranger appeared who approached Roald, who had taken to occupying the spot formerly used by Crowe. The stranger had spoken briefly and then left in a rage, as Roald had told him the contract between Murmandamus and Segersen was cancelled. Martin had mentioned to Geoffrey that a famous and wanted general of mercenaries might be camped in the area, and he was sure there would be a reward to any who let the local militia know where to find him. They had left the next day, heading northward.

As they had ridden out of sight of the inn, Jimmy had remarked, 'Geoffrey's in for a pleasant surprise.'

Arutha had asked, 'Why?'

'Well, Crowe never paid for his last two days' bill, so Geoffrey took his shield as security against the debt.'

Roald laughed along with Jimmy. 'You mean one of these days he's going to look under that covering.'

When everyone looked confused except Roald, Jimmy said, 'It's gold.'

'That's why Crowe had so much trouble lugging it along but never left it behind,' added Roald.

'And why you buried everything save what Baru's using, but brought that back with you,' said Martin.

'It's the payment for Segersen. No one would bother a disinherited fighter without two coppers to rub together, now would they?' said Jimmy as everyone laughed. 'Seems proper Geoffrey should get it. Heaven knows, where we're going, we can't use it.'

The laughter died away.

Arutha motioned a halt.

They had been moving steadily northward from the inn for a week, twice staying in Hadati villages where Baru was known. He had been greeted with respect and honoured, for somehow his killing of Murad had become known throughout the Hadati highlands. If the hillmen had been curious about Baru's companions, they showed no sign. And Arutha and the others were certain no word of their passage would be spread.

Now they found themselves before a narrow trail leading up into the mountains, the Inclindel Gap. Baru, who rode next to Arutha, told him, 'Here we again enter enemy territory. If Segersen doesn't appear, perhaps the moredhel will withdraw their watch upon the place, but it may be we ride into their arms.'

Arutha only nodded.

Baru had tied his hair back behind his head and had wrapped his traditional swords in his plaid and hidden them in his bedroll. Now he wore Morgan Crowe's sword at his side and the renegade's chain mail over his tunic. It was as if the Hadati had ceased to exist and another common mercenary had taken his place. That was their story. They would be simply another band of renegades flocking to Murmandamus's banner, and it was hoped that story would withstand scrutiny. For days while travelling, they had discussed the problem of reaching Murmandamus. All had agreed that, even should he suspect Arutha to be still alive, the last thing Murmandamus would expect would be for the Prince of Krondor to come enlist in his army.

Without further conversation they moved out, Martin and Baru taking the lead, Arutha and Jimmy behind, Laurie and Locklear, then Roald. The experienced mercenary kept a constant watch to the rear as they rode higher into the Inclindel Gap.

For two days they rode upward, until the trail turned to the northeast. It seemed to follow the rise of the mountains somewhat, though it still ran along the south face of the mountains. In some strange sense they had yet to leave the Kingdom, for the peaks about them were where royal cartographers had chosen to indicate the boundaries between the Kingdom and the Northlands. Jimmy had no illusions about such things. They were in hostile territory. Anyone they met was likely to attack them on sight.

Martin was waiting at a bend in the road. He had resumed his habit from the trip to Moraelin of scouting on foot. The terrain was too rocky for the horses to move swiftly, so he could easily keep ahead of the party. He signalled, and the others dismounted. Jimmy and Locklear took the horses and began leading them a short way back down the trail, turning them in case it was necessary to flee. Though, Jimmy thought, that would prove a problem, for the trail was so narrow the only outlet was back where they had started.

The others reached the Duke, and he held his hand up for silence. In the distance, they could hear what had caused him to halt the party: a deep growl, punctuated by barking, and counterpointed by other, less familiar growling.

They drew weapons and crept forward. At a point less than ten yards beyond the turn they saw a meeting point of two trails, one continuing northeast, the other heading off to the west. A man lay upon the ground, whether dead or unconscious they could not judge. Over his still body stood a giant of a dog, resembling a bull mastiff but twice the size, standing almost waist-high to a man. Around his neck a leather collar studded with pointed iron spikes gave the impression of a steel mane, while he bared teeth and growled and barked. Before him crouched three trolls.

Martin let fly with a cloth-yard arrow, taking the rearmost troll in the head. The shaft punched through the thick skull and the creature was dead without knowing it. The others turned, which proved a fatal mistake to the troll nearest the dog, for he leaped at it, setting terrible fangs in the creature's throat. The third tried to flee when it saw the five men charging, but Baru was quickest to leap over the confusion of bodies on the ground and the troll died swiftly.

In a moment the only sound was that of the dog worrying the dead troll. As the men approached, the dog released the dead troll and backed away, standing guard once more over the prone man.

Baru regarded the animal, emitted a low whistle, and half whispered, 'It is not possible.'

Arutha said, 'What?'

'That dog.'

Martin said, 'Possible or not, if that man isn't dead already, he may die because this monster won't let us near him.'

Baru spoke a strange-sounding word and the dog's ears perked up. He turned his head slightly and ceased growling. Slowly the dog moved forward, and then Baru was kneeling, scratching the animal behind the ears.

Martin and Arutha hurried to examine the man, while Roald and Laurie helped the boys bring the horses along. When everyone was gathered, Martin said, 'He's dead.'

The dog looked at the dead man, and whined a bit, but allowed Baru to continue petting him.

'Who is this?' asked Laurie aloud. 'What brings a man and a dog to such a desolate spot?'

'And look at those trolls,' added Roald.

Arutha nodded. 'They are armed and armoured.'

'Mountain trolls,' said Baru. 'More intelligent, cunning, and fierce than their lowland cousins. Those are little more than beasts; these are terrible foemen. Murmandamus has recruited allies.'

'But this man?' said Arutha, pointing at the corpse on the ground.

Baru shrugged. 'Who he is I cannot say. But what he is I may venture a guess.' He regarded the dog before him, who sat quietly, eyes closed in contentment as Baru scratched behind the ears. 'This dog is like those in our villages, but greater, larger. Our dogs are descended from his breed, a breed not seen in Yabon in a century. This animal is called a Beasthound.

'Ages ago, my people lived in small, scattered villages throughout these mountains, and the hills below. We had no cities, gathering in moot twice a year. To protect our herds from predators, we bred these, the Beasthounds. His master was the Beasthunter. The dogs were bred to a size to give even a cave bear pause.' He indicated the folds of skin around the eyes. 'The dog will set teeth in an opponent's neck, these folds channelling blood away from his eyes. And he will not release that hold until the opponent's dead, or his master commands. This spiked collar prevents a larger predator from biting it about the neck.'

Locklear looked astonished. 'Larger! That thing's near the size of a pony!'

Baru smiled at the exaggeration. 'They used them to hunt wyverns.'

Locky asked, 'What's a wyvern?'

Jimmy answered. 'A small, stupid dragon – only about twelve feet high.' Locky looked to the others to see if Jimmy was joking. Baru shook his head, indicating he wasn't.

Martin said, 'That man there was his master?'

'Most likely,' agreed Baru. 'See the black leather armour and coif. In his pack you should find an iron mask, with leather bands for the head, so he can wear it over the coif. My father had such in his lodge, a reminder of the past handed down from our ancestors.' He glanced about and sighted something over by the fallen trolls. 'There, fetch that.'

Locklear ran over and came back with a giant crossbow. He handed it over to Martin, who whistled aloud. 'That's the damnedest thing.'

'It's half again the size of the heaviest crossbow I've ever seen,' remarked Roald.

Baru nodded in agreement. 'It is called a Bessy Mauler. Why it is named after Bessy is not known, but it is indeed a mauler. My people used to employ a Beasthunter at every village, to protect the herds from lions, cave bears, griffins, and other predators. When the Kingdom came to Yabon, and your nobles built cities and castles, and your patrols rode out and pacified the countryside, the need for a Beasthunter lessened, then died out. The Beasthounds were also allowed to diminish in size, bred as pets and to hunt smaller game.'

Martin put down the crossbow. He examined a quarrel the man had in a hip quiver. It was steel-tipped and twice the size of a normal bolt. 'This looks like it would punch a hole through a castle wall.'

Baru smiled slightly. 'Not quite, but it will put a dent the size of your fist in a wyvern's scales. It might not kill the wyvern, but it would make him think twice about raiding a herd.'

Arutha said, 'But you say there are no more Beasthunters.'

Baru patted the dog on the head and stood. 'Or so it was supposed. Yet there lies one.' He was silent for a long moment. 'When the Kingdom came to Yabon, we were a loose association of clans, and we were divided on our treatment of your people. Some of us welcomed your ancestors, some did not. For the most part, we Hadati kept to our old ways, living in the highlands and herding our sheep and cattle. But those in the towns quickly were absorbed as your countrymen came in increasing numbers, until there was little difference between Yabon city men and those of the Kingdom. Laurie and Roald are born of such stock. So Yabon became Kingdom.

'But some resented the Kingdom, and resistance became open war. Your soldiers came in numbers, and the rebellion was quickly crushed. But there is a story, not well believed, that some chose neither to bow before the King nor fight. Rather they chose to flee, going north to new homes beyond the control of the Kingdom.'

Martin regarded the dog. 'Then it may be the story is true.'

'So it seems,' said Baru. 'I think I have distant kin out here somewhere.'

Arutha studied the dog for a moment. 'And we find allies. These trolls were Murmandamus's servants, certainly, and this man was their foeman.'

'And the enemy of our enemy is our ally,' said Roald.

Baru shook his head. 'Remember, these people fled the Kingdom. They may have little love yet for you, Prince. We may be exchanging one trouble for another.' The last was added with a wry smile.

Arutha said, 'We have no choice. Until we know what lies beyond these mountains, we must seek out whatever aid chance brings us.' He permitted a brief pause while the body of the fallen Beasthunter was covered with rocks, forming a rude cairn. The dog stood stoically while this was being done. When it was finished, the dog refused to move, laying his head upon his master's grave.

'Do we leave him?' asked Roald.

'No,' answered Baru. Again he spoke in the odd tongue, and reluctantly the dog came to his side. 'The language used to command our dogs must be still the same, for he obeys.'

'How, then, do we proceed?' asked Arutha.

'With caution, but I think it best to let him lead us,' answered the hillman, indicating the dog. He spoke a single word, and the dog's ears perked and he began trotting up the trail, waiting at the limit of their vision for them to follow.

Quickly they mounted and Arutha said, 'What did you say?'

Baru said, 'I said "home". He will lead us to his people.'

CHAPTER NINE

Captives

*T*HE WIND HOWLED.

The riders pulled cloaks tightly about themselves. They had been following the Beasthound for more than a week. Two days after finding the dog they had passed over the crest of the Great Northern Mountains. Now they moved along a narrow trail just below a high ridge, running toward the northeast.

The dog had come to accept Baru as his master, for he obeyed every command the Hadati gave, while he ignored any spoken by the others. Baru called the dog Blutark, which he said meant, in the old Hadati tongue, an old friend rediscovered or come back from a long journey. Arutha hoped it was a favourable omen, and that those who bred the dog would feel similarly toward Arutha's company.

Twice the dog had proven useful, signalling dangers along the trail. He could smell what even Baru and Martin's hunters' eyes missed. Both times they had surprised goblins camped along the trail. It was clear that Murmandamus controlled this route into the Northlands.

Both encounters had taken place at junctions with trails clearly heading downward.

The trail had run southeasterly from Inclindel, then turned east, hugging the north side of the mountain ridges. In the distance they could see the vast reaches of the Northlands, and they wondered. To most men of the Kingdom, 'the Northlands' was a convenient label for that unknown place the other side of the mountains, the nature of which could only be speculated upon. But now they could see the Northlands below them, and the reality of the place dwarfed any speculation, for it was an immense reality. To the northwest a vast plain stretched away into the distant mists, the Thunderhell. Few men of the Kingdom had ever trod upon that grassy domain, and then only with the consent of the nomads who called the Thunderhell home. At the eastern edge of the Thunderhell a range of hills rose, and beyond were lands never seen by men of the Kingdom. Each turn in the road, each jog in the trail, and a new vista opened before them.

That the dog refused to descend caused them concern, for Martin avowed they would have more cover in the hills below than upon this open trail. Weaving along the north ridges of the mountains, they only now and then descended below the timberline. Upon three occasions they had noticed indications that this trail was not entirely natural, as if someone had once, long ago, undertaken to connect sections of it.

Not for the first time, Roald remarked, 'That hunter wandered quite a distance from home, that's for certain.' They were easily a hundred miles to the east of where they had found the body.

Baru said, 'Yes, and that is a strange thing, for the Beasthunters were given the defence of an area. Perhaps he had been pursued for some time by those trolls.' But he knew, as did the others, that such a pursuit would be a matter of miles, not tens of miles. No, there was another reason that hunter had been so far from his home.

To pass the time, Arutha, Martin, and the boys had undertaken to learn Baru's Hadati dialect, against the day of meeting Blutark's owner's kin. Laurie and Roald spoke fluent Yabonese and a smattering of the

Hadati patois already, so it came quickly to them. Jimmy had the most difficulty, but he was able to make simple sentences.

Then Blutark came bounding back down the trail, his stubby tail wagging furiously. In atypical behaviour he barked loudly, and spun in place. Baru said, 'It is strange . . .'

The dog normally went on point when sensing danger, until he was attacked or ordered to attack by Baru. Baru and Martin rode past the others, the Hadati ordering the dog forward. Blutark dashed ahead, around a bend between high walls of stone, as the trail cut downward again.

They rounded the turn and pulled up, for in a clearing Blutark faced another Beasthound. The two dogs sniffed at each other and wagged tails. But behind the second dog stood a man in black leather armour, an odd iron mask over his face. He sighted at them down a Bessy Mauler, mounted upon a single long wooden pole. He spoke, the words made unintelligible by the blowing wind.

Baru raised his hands and shouted something, most of the words lost upon the others, but his friendly intentions clear. Suddenly, from above, nets descended, ensnaring all seven riders. A dozen brown-leather-clad soldiers leaped down upon them, and quickly wrestled Arutha's party from their mounts. In short order all seven were trussed up like game birds. The man in black armour broke down his pole, folding it, and slung it with the crossbow across his back. He approached and gave his own dog and Blutark both friendly pats.

The sound of horses accompanied another detachment of men in brown, this time riders. One of the men in brown spoke to them, in heavily accented King's Tongue. He said, 'You will come with us. Do not speak aloud, or we will gag you. Do not try to escape, or we will kill you.'

Baru nodded curtly to his companions, but Roald began to say something. Instantly hands jammed a gag into his mouth and tied a cloth over his face, silencing him. Arutha looked about, but only nodded to the others. The captives were roughly placed back in their saddles, their feet tied to their stirrups. Without further words the riders turned back down the trail, leading Arutha and the others along.

For a day and a night they rode. Short halts were ordered to rest the horses. While the horses were being tended, Arutha and his companions would have their bindings loosened to lessen the cramping they were all experiencing. A few hours after they had set out, Roald's gag was removed, much to his relief, but it was clear their captors wouldn't permit them to speak.

After dawn they could see they had negotiated nearly half the distance between the trail along the crest of the mountains and the foothills below. They passed a small herd of cattle, with three watchful and armed herdsmen who waved, and approached a walled hill community.

The outer wall was sturdy, heavy logs lashed together and sealed with dried mud. The horsemen were forced to make a circular approach by deep trenches about the wall, coming up the hill on a switchback trail. On both sides of the trail the trenches revealed fire-hardened wooden spikes, ready to impale any horseman who faltered. Roald looked about and whispered, 'They must have some charming neighbours.'

One of the guards immediately rode in next to him, the gag ready, but the leader waved him back as they approached the gate. The gate swung open, and they discovered a second wall behind the first. There was no barbican, but the entire area between the walls was effectively a killing ground. As they passed through the second gate, Arutha admired the simple craftsmanship. A modern army could take this village quickly, but it would cost lives. Bandits and goblins would be repulsed easily.

Inside the walls, Arutha observed his surroundings. It was a village of no more than a dozen huts, all of wattle-and-daub construction. In the compound, children played, but with serious eyes. They wore gambeson armour or, in the case of a few of the older children, leather. All carried daggers. Even the old men were armed, and one hobbled past using a spear instead of a walking staff. The leader of the company said, 'Now you may speak, for the rules of the trail do not apply here.' He continued to speak King's Tongue. His men cut the straps binding the captives' feet to the stirrups and helped them dismount. He then motioned for them to enter a hut.

Inside, Arutha and the others faced the commander of the patrol. Blutark, who had continued to run at Baru's side, lay at the Hadati's feet, his large tongue lolling out as he panted.

'That dog is a rare breed, of particular importance to our people,' said the commander of the patrol. 'How do you come to have him?'

Arutha nodded to Baru. 'We found his master killed by trolls,' said the Hadati. 'We killed the trolls and the dog chose to come with us.'

The man considered. 'Had you harmed his master, that dog would have killed you or died in the attempt. So I must believe you. But that breed is trained to obey only a few. How do you command?'

The hillman spoke a word and the dog sat up, ears perked. He spoke another and the dog lay down, at rest. 'My village had dogs of similar breed, though not so large as this.'

The commander's eyes narrowed. 'Who are you?'

'I am Baru, called the Serpentslayer, of Ordwinson's family of the Iron Hills Clan. I am Hadati.' He spoke in the Hadati patois as he loosened his long bedroll and removed his tartan and swords.

The commander nodded. He answered in a language similar enough to Baru's that the others could understand. The differences between the two languages seemed mainly to be pronunciation and otherwise trivial. 'It has been many years since one of our Hadati kin has come over the mountains, Baru Serpentslayer, nearly a generation. This explains much. But men of the Kingdom usually come here to cause mischief and of late we've had more than our share of such men. I think you other than renegades, but this is a matter for the Protector's wisdom.' He rose. 'We shall rest here tonight, then tomorrow we shall depart. Food will be brought. There is a bucket for night soil in the corner. Do not leave this hut. Should you attempt it, you will be bound, should you resist, killed.'

As he reached the door, Arutha asked, 'Where are you taking us?'
The man looked back. 'Armengar.'

At first light they rode out, heading downward out of the highlands into a heavy forest, Blutark loping along easily beside Baru's horse. Their captors again instructed them not to speak, but their weapons had been returned. To Arutha it seemed their captors assumed they would act as comrades on the road should trouble start. As the only likely encounters would be with Murmandamus's servants, Arutha thought it a safe assumption. It was clear the forest had been logged in places, and the path seemed one used regularly. Coming out of a stand of woods, they passed a meadow where a small herd of cattle grazed, with three men standing watch. One was the Beasthunter, who had left the village the night before. The others were herdsmen, but each was armed with a spear, sword, and shield.

Twice more that day, they passed herds, one of cattle, one of sheep. All were tended by warriors, several of whom were women. They came at sundown to another village and were given a place to stay, again with instructions not to leave the building.

The morning of the next day, the fourth of their captivity, they entered a shallow canyon, following a river out of the mountains. They paralleled its course until past noon, then came to a long rise. The road circled around a large hill rather than follow the river, which cut its way through the rock, so their view of all below them was blocked for nearly an hour. When they cleared the hill, Arutha and his friends all exchanged glances in silent wonder.

The leader of the party, who they had learned was called Dwyne, turned and said, 'Armengar.'

The city could not be seen in detail, but what could be seen was staggering. The outer wall was a full fifty or sixty feet high. Bartizans atop the wall were placed every fifty feet or so, allowing overlapping fields of fire for archers placed in them. As they closed upon the wall, more details emerged. The barbican was immense, fully a hundred feet across. The gates seemed more like movable sections of the wall than gates. The river they had followed out of the mountains became a moat that flowed along the wall, not giving more than a foot of ground between its bank and the base of the wall.

As they approached the city, the gates opened with surprising swiftness given their ponderous appearance, and a company of riders appeared from within. They rode at good pace toward Arutha's escorts. As the two companies passed, the riders of each raised right hands in salute. Arutha saw they were attired in identical fashion. Men and women both wore leather coifs over their heads. Their armour was leather or chain, with no plate in view. Each wore a sword and carried a shield, and spears and bows appeared in equal proportion. There were no tabards or devices upon shields. Soon they were past, and Arutha's attention returned to the city. They were crossing a bridge, which appeared to be permanent, over the moat.

As they entered the city gate, Arutha caught a glimpse of a banner flying from an outer corner of the barbican. He could discern only its colours, gold and black, not its markings, but something about that banner caused him to feel an instant's disquiet. Then the outer gates were closing. They seemed to swing shut of their own accord, and Martin said, 'There must be some mechanism that moves them from within the walls.' Arutha only watched silently. 'You could have a full hundred, hundred fifty horsemen sally forth without opening the inner gates,' said Martin as he regarded the size of the killing ground in the barbican. Arutha nodded. It was the largest he had ever seen. The walls seemed an impossible thirty feet thick. Then the inner gates swung open and they entered Armengar.

The city was separated from the walls by a bailey a hundred yards wide. Then began a tightly packed array of buildings, shot through with narrow streets. There was nothing like the broad boulevards of Krondor in sight, and no signs upon any building betraying its purpose. They followed their escort and noticed that few people loitered about the doorways. If there were businesses here, they were not apparent to Arutha's companions. Everywhere they looked, the people walked in armour and wore weapons. Only once did they see an exception to the armour, a woman obviously in the late stages of pregnancy, yet her belt sash held a dagger. Even children who looked above the age of seven or eight were under arms.

The streets twisted and turned, intercepting others at random intervals. 'This city seems without plan,' said Locklear.

Arutha shook his head. 'It is a city with great plan, a clear purpose. Straight streets benefit merchants and are easy to build, if the terrain is flat or easily worked. You see twisting streets only where it is too difficult to cut straight ones, such as in Rillanon, which is situated upon rocky hills, or near the palace in Krondor. This city is built upon a plateau, which means these meandering streets are intentional. Martin, what do you think?'

'I think that should the walls be breached, you could place an ambush every fifty feet from here to the other end of the city.' He pointed upward. 'Notice every building is of equal height. I warrant the roofs are flat and accessible from within. A perfect place for archers. Look at the lower floor.'

Jimmy and Locklear looked and saw what the Duke of Crydee meant. Each building had only a single door on the ground floor, heavy wood with iron bands, and there were no windows. Martin said, 'This is a city designed for defence.'

Dwyne turned and said, 'You are perceptive.' He then returned his attention to their passage through the city. Citizens watched for a moment while the strangers rode by, then went back to their business.

They emerged from the press of buildings into a market. Everywhere they looked, booths were placed and people moved about them, buying and selling. Arutha said, 'Look,' as he pointed toward a citadel. It seemed to grow from the very face of a gigantic cliff, against which the city was nestled. It rose up a full thirty stories high. Another wall, thirty feet in height, circled the citadel, and around the wall another moat. Jimmy looked and said, 'They must expect some bad company.'

'Their neighbours tend to be an irksome lot,' commented Roald.

At that a few of the guards who understood the Kingdom language laughed openly, nodding agreement. Arutha said, 'If the booths come down, we ride across another bailey, giving those on the walls an open field of fire. Taking this city would cost a fortune in lives.'

Dwyne said, 'As it was meant to.'

They entered the citadel and were ordered to dismount, and their horses were led away. They followed Dwyne down to a dungeon, though it seemed clean and fairly spacious. They were shown to a large common cell, illuminated by a brass lantern. Dwyne motioned they should enter. He said, 'You shall wait here. If you hear an alarm, come to the common court above and you will be told what to do. Otherwise, wait here until the Protector sends for you. I will have food sent down.' With that he left.

Jimmy looked about and said, 'They don't lock the door or take our weapons?'

Baru sat down. 'Why bother?'

Laurie heaved himself across an old blanket placed upon straw. 'We certainly can't go anywhere. We can't pretend to be native to this city, and we couldn't hide. And I'm not about to fight my way out of here.'

Jimmy sat down next to Laurie. 'You're right. So what do we do now?'

Arutha removed his sword. 'We wait.'

For hours they waited. Food was brought and they ate. When the meal was finished, Dwyne returned. 'The Protector approaches. I would know your names and your purpose.'

All eyes turned to Arutha, who said, 'I think we gain nothing by hiding the truth, and may gain something if we are forthright.' He said to Dwyne, 'I am Arutha, Prince of Krondor.'

Dwyne said, 'That is a title?'

'Yes,' Arutha said.

'We remember little of the Kingdom, we of Armengar, nor do we have such titles. It is important?'

Roald nearly burst. 'Damn it, man, he's brother to the King, as is

Duke Martin here. He's the second most powerful lord in the Kingdom.'

Dwyne seemed unimpressed. He was given the others' names, then he asked, 'Your purpose?'

Arutha said, 'I think we shall wait to speak of this with your Protector.' Dwyne seemed not in the least offended by the answer and left.

Another hour went by, and then the door flew open. Dwyne entered, a blond man a step behind. Arutha looked up expectantly, for perhaps this was the Protector. This was the first man they had seen not attired in brown armour. He was dressed in a long coat of chain over a red, knee-length gambeson. A chain coif had been thrown back, leaving his head uncovered. He wore his hair cut short and was clean-shaven. His face was one that would have been counted open and friendly by most, but there was a hardness around the eyes as he regarded the captives. He said nothing, simply looking from face to face. He studied Martin, as if noting something familiar in him. Then he looked at Arutha. For a long minute he stared at the Prince, his eyes betraying no reaction. With a single nod to Dwyne he turned and left.

Martin said, 'There's something about that one.'

Arutha said, 'What?'

'I don't know how, but I could swear I've seen him before. And he wore a blazon upon his breast, though I couldn't make it out through the chain.'

A short time later the door opened again. Whoever stood before it remained outside, only his silhouette visible. Then a familiar, ear-shattering bellow of a laugh erupted and the man stepped forward. 'I'll be the son of a saint! It is true,' he said, a broad grin splitting his grey-shot beard.

Arutha, Martin, and Jimmy all sat staring up in disbelief. Arutha rose slowly, not able to trust his senses. Before him stood the last man he had expected to see entering this cell. Jimmy jumped up and said, 'Amos!'

Amos Trask, onetime pirate, and companion to Arutha and Martin during the Riftwar, stepped into the cell. The burly sea captain engulfed Arutha in a bear hug, then did the same for Martin and Jimmy. He was quickly introduced to the others. Arutha said, 'How did you get here?'

'That's a tale, son, one with great sagas, but not for now. The Protector is expecting the pleasure of your company, and he's not given to be kept waiting gracefully. We can exchange histories after. For the moment you and Martin must come with me. The others are to wait here.'

Martin and Arutha followed Amos down the hall and up the stairs to the courtyard. He quickly crossed into the citadel's main building and began to hurry. 'I can't tell you much, except we must hurry,' he said as he reached an odd platform in some sort of tower. He motioned them to stand beside him. He pulled on a rope and suddenly the platform was rising.

'What's this?' inquired Martin.

'A hoisting platform, a lift. We need to carry heavy missiles to the catapults on the roof. It's powered by some horses on a winch below. It also keeps a fat former sea captain from having to dash up twenty-seven courses of stairs. My wind's not what it once was, lads.' His tone turned serious. 'Now, listen. I know you've a hundred questions, but they must go begging for the moment. I'll explain everything after you speak to One-eye.'

'The Protector?' asked Arutha.

'That's him. Now, I don't know how to tell you, but you're in for a shock. I want you to keep your temper in check until you and I can sit and talk. Martin, keep a close line on the lad.' He put his hand upon Arutha's shoulder and leaned close. 'Shipmate, remember, here you are not a prince. You're a stranger, and with these people that usually means crowbait. Strangers are rare and seldom welcomed in Armengar.'

The lift halted and they got off. Amos hurried down a long corridor. Along the left wall was a series of vaulted windows, providing an unobstructed view of the city and the plain beyond. Martin and Arutha could only afford a quick glance at the vista but it was impressive. They hurried as Amos turned and motioned for them to keep up. The blond man was waiting for them before a door. 'Why didn't you say anything?' he asked Amos in a harsh whisper.

Jerking his thumb toward the door, Amos said, 'He wanted a full report from you. You know how he can be. Nothing personal until business is finished. He doesn't show it, but he's taking it hard.'

The blond man nodded, his face a grim mask. 'I can scarcely believe it. Gwynnath dead. It's a heavy blow to us all.' He had removed the chain mail coat. Upon his gambeson, over his heart, was a small red and gold device, but he turned away and passed through the door before Arutha could comprehend the particulars of that crest. Amos said, 'The Protector's patrol was ambushed and some people died. He's in a rare foul mood, for he blames himself, so tread lightly. Come, he'll have my ears if we wait any longer.'

Amos pushed open the door and motioned for the brothers to enter. They were in a conference chamber of some sort, a large round table dominating the room. Against the far wall a massive fireplace sent forth warmth and light. Many maps covered the walls, save the left wall, which had more of the large windows, and overhead a circular candle holder provided more light.

Before the fireplace stood the blond man speaking with another, who wore all black, from tunic to trousers to the chain he still hadn't removed. His clothing was covered in dust and his face was dominated by a large black patch over his left eye. His hair was grey and black in equal proportion, but his carriage showed nothing of age. For an instant Arutha was struck by a certain resemblance. He glanced at Martin, who returned the look. He saw it as well. More in bearing and manner than in physical appearance, this man resembled their father.

Then the man stepped forward, and Arutha could see clearly the blazon upon his tabard. A golden eagle spread his wings upon a sable field. Arutha knew the cause of the discomfort he had felt at glimpsing the flag atop the gate. Only one man in the world wore that crest. He was once counted the finest general in the Kingdom, then branded traitor by the King as being responsible for the death of Anita's father. Here was their own father's most hated enemy. The man called Protector by the men of Armengar waved toward a pair of seats. His voice was deep and commanding, though his words were spoken softly. 'Won't you be seated . . . cousins?' asked Guy du Bas-Tyra.

Arutha's hand tightened upon the hilt of his sword an instant, but he said nothing as he and Martin sat. His mind reeled as a hundred questions crashed together. Finally he said, 'How –?'

Guy interrupted him as he took a chair. 'It is a long story; I'll leave it to Amos to tell you. I have other concerns for the moment.' A strange, pained look was briefly revealed. He turned away for an instant, then back to the brothers. He studied Martin. 'You look a little like Borric did when young, do you know that?'

Martin nodded.

Guy said to Arutha, 'You favour him somewhat, but you also look like . . . your mother. The shape of the eyes . . . if not the colour.' He said the last softly. Then his tone shifted as a soldier brought in mugs and ale. 'We have no wine in Armengar, the making of it is a lost art here, as the climate is ill suited for grape arbours. But they do make stout ale, and I'm thirsty. Join me if you wish.' He poured himself a mug and let Arutha and Martin serve themselves. Guy drained his mug, and for a moment his mask fell again and he said, 'Gods, I'm tired.' Then he looked at the brothers. 'Well then, when Armand reported who Dwyne had fetched in, I could scarcely believe my ears. Now my eyes bear witness.'

Arutha's gaze flicked to where the tall blond man hovered by the fire. 'Armand?' He studied the blazon, a shield bend dexter, with a crouching red dragon chief on field gold, and an upraised lion's claw in gold upon a field red.

Martin said, 'Armand de Sevigny!' The man inclined his head toward the Duke.

'Baron of Gyldenholt? Marshal of the Knights of St Gunther?' wondered Arutha.

Martin swore. 'I'm an idiot. I knew I had seen him. He was at the palace in Rillanon in the days before you joined us, Arutha. But he was not there the day of the coronation, the day you arrived.'

The blond man smiled slightly. 'At your service, Highness.'

'Not, as I recall. You were not among those who swore fealty to Lyam.'

The blond man shook his head. 'True.' His expression seemed almost one of regret.

Guy said, 'Again, part of the story of how we came here. For the moment, I need concern myself with why you are here, and if that reason poses any threat to this city. Why did you come north?'

Arutha sat silently, his arms crossed before him, studying du Bas-Tyra through narrowed eyes. He was off balance from finding Guy du Bas-Tyra in control of this city. He hesitated in answering the question. The importance of finding Murmandamus might in some way run counter to what Guy saw as his best interests. And, Arutha was suspicious of anything involving Guy. Guy had most openly plotted to seize the throne for himself, almost precipitating a civil war. Anita's father had died by his order. Du Bas-Tyra was everything Arutha had been taught to dislike and mistrust by his father. He was a true eastern lord, shrewd, cunning, and well practised in the subtleties of intrigue and treachery. Of de Sevigny Arutha knew little, save he had been numbered among the most capable rulers in the East, but he was Guy's vassal and always had been. And while the Prince liked and trusted Amos, Trask had been a pirate and was not above lawbreaking. No, there was ample reason for caution.

Martin watched Arutha, waiting for an answer. The Prince's manner was truculent to all outward appearances, but that was only what the others in the room saw. Martin knew that his brother was wrestling with the unanticipated shock of the moment and the desire that nothing interfere with his mission to find and kill Murmandamus. Martin glanced around the room and could see that

Amos and Armand both seemed concerned at the lack of a quick response from Arutha.

When no answer was forthcoming, Guy slammed his hand down on the table. 'Play not with my patience, Arutha.' He pointed his finger. 'You are not a prince in this city. In Armengar only one voice commands, and that voice is mine!' He sat back, his face flushed behind the black eye patch. Softening his voice, he said, 'I . . . mean no rudeness. I have my mind on other things.' He lapsed into thoughtful silence while he stared at them for a long time. At last he said, 'I have no idea what you are doing here, Arutha, but something of the oddest nature is dictating your choices, or you didn't learn a damn thing from your father. The Prince of Krondor and two of the most powerful dukes in the Kingdom, Salador and Crydee, riding into the Northlands with a mercenary, a Hadati hillman, and two boys? Either you're totally without wit or you're clever far beyond my understanding.'

Arutha remained silent, but Martin said, 'There have been changes since you were last in the Kingdom, Guy.'

Guy again lapsed into silence. 'I think there is a story here I need to know. I cannot promise you aid, but I think our purposes may prove compatible.' He said to Amos, 'Find them better quarters and feed them,' and to Arutha, 'I'll give you until the morning. But when we speak next, do not again tempt my patience. I must know what brought you here. It is vital. You may seek me out before tomorrow if you decide to speak.' His voice again became heavy with some emotion. 'I should be here most of the night.'

With a wave he indicated that Amos was to lead them away. Arutha and Martin followed the seaman out of the hall, and Amos halted once the door was closed. He looked at Arutha and Martin for a long moment. 'For a couple of bright lads, you both did right well in showing how to be stupid.'

Amos wiped his mouth with the back of his hand. He belched and then stuffed another slice of bread and cheese into his mouth. 'Then what?'

'Then,' answered Martin, 'when we got back, Anita had Arutha's pledge within an hour and Carline and Laurie were betrothed not long after.'

'Ha! Remember that first night out of Krondor aboard the *Sea Swift*? You told me your brother was a hooked fish – never stood a chance.'

Arutha smiled at the remark. They were all sitting around a large basket of food and a hogshead of ale, in a spacious room in a suite given over to their use. There were no servants – food had been brought by soldiers – and they served themselves. Baru scratched absently at Blutark's ear while the dog chewed on a joint of beef. No one had seemed concerned about the Beasthound's staying with the Hadati. Then Arutha said, 'Amos, we've been chatting for a half hour. Will you tell us what's going on? How in the world did you get here?'

Amos looked about. 'What's going on is you're prisoners, of sorts, and so you'll stay until One-eye changes things. Now, I've seen my share of cells, and this is the nicest I've ever seen.' With a sweep of his hand he indicated the large and spacious room. 'No, if you've a mind to be in prison, this here's a good one.' His eyes narrowed. 'But don't lose sight it is a prison, laddie. Look, Arutha. I spent enough years with you and Martin here to know something about you. I don't remember you being such a suspicious lot, so I expect some things over the last two years have caused you to trim sails that way. But here you've got to live, breathe, and eat trust, or you're dead. Do you understand me?'

'No,' answered the Prince. 'Just what do you mean?'

Amos thought a long moment, then said, 'This is a city of people surrounded by nothing but enemies. Trust of your neighbour is a way of life if you want to keep breathing.' He paused and considered. 'Look, I'll tell you how we came here and then maybe you'll understand.'

Amos settled back, poured himself another mug of ale and began his story. 'Well, the last I saw you two was as I was sailing out of the harbour aboard your brother's ship.' Martin and Arutha both smiled in remembrance. 'Now, if you'll recall, you had everyone in the city out looking for Guy. You didn't find him, because he was hiding somewhere no one thought to look.'

Martin's eyes opened in wonder, one of the few unguarded reactions any of those in the room had ever seen in him. 'On the King's ship!'

'When he heard King Rodric had named Lyam the Heir, Guy cut from Krondor and ran for Rillanon. He had hopes of seeing something of his plans salvaged when the Congress of Lords met to ratify the succession. By the time Lyam got to Rillanon, enough of the eastern lords had gathered for Guy to judge the lay of the land. It was clear Lyam would be King – this was before anyone knew about you, Martin – so Guy resigned himself to being tried for treason. Then, the morning of the convocation and coronation, word came about Martin's being legitimized, so Guy waited to see what would happen later that afternoon.'

'Waiting to seize the moment,' commented Arutha.

'Don't be so quick to judge,' snapped Amos; then he continued in softer tones. 'He was worried over a civil war and if it came, he was ready to fight. But while he waited to see what would happen, he knew Caldric's men were out snooping about. He had been dodging them – barely, a couple of times. Guy still had friends in the capital, and some of them smuggled him and Armand aboard the *Royal Swallow* – gad, what a pretty craft she was – just about the time the Ishapian priests reached the palace to start up the coronation. Anyway, when I . . . borrowed the ship, we discovered we had passengers.

'Now, I was ready to toss Guy and Armand over the side, or turn about and deliver them trussed up to you, but Guy can be a convincing enough rogue in his way, so I agreed to take him to Bas-Tyra, in exchange for a healthy price.'

'So he could plot against Lyam?' asked Arutha incredulously.

'Damn it, boy,' bellowed Amos, 'I let you out of my sight for a pissing two years and you go and get downright thick-headed on me.' Looking at Martin, he said, 'Must be the company you've been keeping.'

Martin said to his brother, 'Let him finish.'

'No, it wasn't to plot treason. It was so he could put his affairs in order. He figured Lyam'd ordered his head, so he was going to tidy up some things, then I was going to bring him back to Rillanon, so he could *give himself up*.'

Arutha looked stunned.

'About the only thing he really wanted was to get pardon for Armand and his other followers. Anyway, we reached Bas-Tyra and stayed a few days. Then came word of the banishment. Guy and I had become a little more friendly by then, so we talked and made another deal. He wanted to leave the Kingdom, to seek a place. He's a fine general, and there are many who would have given him service, especially Kesh, but he wanted to go someplace so remote he would never have to face Kingdom soldiers in the field. We figured to head east, then turn south, and make for the Keshian Confederacy. We might have made a name for ourselves down there. He was going to be a general and I thought I'd take a bash at being an admiral. We had a spot of trouble with Armand, for Guy wanted to send him back home to Gyldenholt, but Armand's a funny one. He'd sworn fealty to Guy, years before, and as he had not sworn to Lyam he'd not quit his liege lord's service. Damnedest argument I've ever heard. Anyway, he's still with us. So we set sail for the Confederacy.

'But three days out of Bas-Tyra, a fleet of Ceresian pirates took out after us. I'd be willing to take on two, even three of the bastards, but five? The *Swallow* was a fast lady, but the pirates stayed right on her heels. For four days it was all clear skies, unlimited visibility, and fair winds. For Kingdom Sea pirates, they were a canny lot. They spread out across each following quarter, so I couldn't lose them at night. Each night I'd sail around, this way and that, then come morning, there'd be five sails on the horizon. They were like lampreys. I couldn't shake them. Then we hit weather. A line squall came roaring out of the west, driving us east for a day and a half, then a full gale blew up carrying us north along uncharted coast. The only good thing about that storm is we shook loose of the Ceresians at last. By the time I found safe harbour, we were in waters I'd never heard of, let alone seen.

'We lay up and took stock. The ship was in need of some repair, not serious enough to sink her, but enough to make sailing damned inconvenient. I took her up a big river, must have been somewhere east of the Kingdom proper.

'Well, the second night we were at anchor, a damn army of goblins swarmed the ship, killing the sentries and capturing the rest of us. Bastards fired the *Swallow* and burned her down to the waterline. Then they marched us to a camp in the woods where some Dark Brothers were waiting. They took charge of us and we were all marched north.

'The lads I'd recruited were a crusty lot, but most of them died on the march. Damn goblins didn't care spit. We got almost nothing to eat, and if a man took sick and couldn't walk, they killed him on the spot. I got a touch of the belly flux and Guy and Armand carried me for two days, and believe me that wasn't pleasant for any of us.

'We moved northwest, heading up into the mountains, then over them. Lucky for us it was late summer, or we'd all have frozen to death. Still, it was touch and go. Then we met with some other Dark Brothers with more prisoners. Most of the prisoners spoke an odd tongue, a lot like Yabonese, but a few others spoke the King's Tongue, or languages from the eastern kingdoms.

'Twice more we joined with other bands of Brothers with human prisoners, all marching west. I lost track of the time, but we must have travelled for over two months by then. By the time we were ready to cross the plain – which I now know to be the plain of Isbandia, it was starting to snow. I know where we were headed now, though then I didn't. Murmandamus was gathering slaves at Sar-Sargoth to pull his siege machines.

'Then one night our guards were hit by a company of horsemen from here. Of the two hundred or so slaves, only twenty survived, for the goblins and Dark Brothers took to killing us as soon as the horsemen struck the camp. Guy strangled one with his chains as it tried to run me through with a sword. I picked up the sword and killed another just after it clawed the Protector's eye out. Armand was wounded but not quite enough to kill him. He's a tough bastard. But we three and two others were the only survivors from the *Swallow*.

'From there we were brought here.'

Arutha said, 'An incredible tale.' He sat back against the wall. 'Still, these are incredible times.'

Martin said, 'How is it an outlander came to rule here?'

Amos took another drink. 'These are a strange folk, Martin. As honest and fine as you'll find anywhere, in some ways, but they're as alien as those Tsurani in other ways. They have no hereditary rank here, instead placing great store in ability. Within a few months it was clear Guy was a first-rate general, so they gave him a company to command. Armand and I served under him. Within a few more months it was clear he was by far the best commander they had. They've got nothing like the Congress of Lords here, Arutha. When something needs to be decided, they call everyone into a meeting in the great square, where the market's held. They call the meeting the volksraad, and they all vote. Otherwise, all decisions are left to those elected by the volksraad. They summoned Guy and told him he was now Protector of Armengar. It's like being named the King's Marshal, but also something like being responsible for the safety of the city as well, a chief sheriff, constable, reeve, and bailiff all rolled up in one.'

Arutha said, 'What did the previous Protector think of this?'

'She must have thought it was a good idea; she proposed it.'

'She?' said Jimmy.

Amos said, 'That's another thing around here takes a bit of getting used to. Women. They're just like men. I mean when it comes to giving and taking orders, voting in the volksraad . . . other things. You'll see.' Amos's expression got distant. 'Her name was Gwynnath. She was as fine a woman as I've met. I'm not ashamed to admit I was a little in love with her myself, though' – his tone turned a little lighter – 'I'll never settle down. But if I ever did, that's the sort for me.' He looked down into his ale mug. 'But she and Guy . . . I know some things about him, learned slowly over the last two years, Arutha. I can't betray a trust. If he tells you himself, fine. But let's say they were something like man and wife there at the end, deeply in love. She was the one to step aside and turn over her city to him. She would have died for him. And he for her. She rode beside him and fought like a lioness.' His voice softened. 'She died yesterday.'

Arutha and Martin exchanged looks with the others. Baru and Roald remained silent. Laurie thought of Carline and shivered. Even the boys could sense something of the loss Amos felt. Arutha remembered what Amos had said to Armand just before they had met Guy. 'And Guy blames himself.'

'Yes. One-eye's much like any good captain: if it happened under his command, it's his responsibility.' Amos sat back, his face a thoughtful mask. 'The goblins and the Armengarians used to keep things pretty simple for a long time. Run out, break a few heads, then retreat. The Armengarians were a lot like the Tsurani, fierce warriors, but no real organization. But when Murmandamus showed up, the Brothers got downright organized, even to the company level. Now they can coordinate two, three thousand warriors under a single commander. The Brotherhood was punishing the Armengarians regularly when we showed up. Guy proved a blessing to the Armengarians, knowing modern warcraft. He's trained them, and now they're damn good cavalry and fair mounted infantry, though getting an Armengarian off his horse can be a chore. Still, Guy makes progress. They're back to holding their own with the Brothers. But yesterday . . .' Nobody spoke for a long while.

Martin said, 'We have some serious matters to discuss, Amos. You know we wouldn't be here unless something of the gravest consequence was happening in the Kingdom.'

'Well, I'll let you alone for a while. You were good companions, and I know you to be honourable men.' He got to his feet. 'But one thing more. The Protector is the most powerful man in the city, but even his power is limited to matters of safety for Armengar. If he said he'd an old debt with you, no one would interfere while you fought a duel, man to man. If you won, you'd be cut loose to make your own way and no one in the city'd raise a hand against you. But all he has to do is to call you spies and you'd be dead before you turned around. Arutha, Martin, I know there's bad blood between you and Guy, because of your father, and because of Erland. And I now know some of what lay behind that. I'll leave that for Guy to sort out with you in time. But you must know something of how the weather turns up here. You are free to come and go as long as you don't break a law, or as long as Guy doesn't order you tossed out, or hung, or whatever. But *he* takes the responsibility. He guarantees your good behaviour, all of you. If you betray the city, his life is forfeit along with your own. As I said, these folk can be fairly strange in their way, and their ways can be harsh. So understand what I say when I tell you this: betray Guy's trust, even if you think it's for the good of the Kingdom, and these people will kill you. And I'm not sure I'd even try to stop them.'

'You know we'd not break trust, Amos,' answered Martin.

'I know, but I wanted you to understand how strongly I feel. I'm fond of both you lads, and would dislike seeing your throats cut almost as much as you would.' Saying nothing more, Amos left.

Arutha settled back, considering all that Amos had told him, and suddenly realized he was bone-tired. He looked to Martin and his brother nodded. No further discussion was required. Arutha knew he would tell the complete story to Guy in the morning.

Arutha and his companions waited as the lift rose, then halted at the floor of the Protector's council room. It had been late morning, almost noon, before the call to Guy's council had arrived. They walked a short way down the hall, then stopped. The guard who had come for them waited while they stared out the window in wonder at the vista below. Armengar spread out beyond the moat about the citadel and across the open market, to the huge city wall. But beyond the wall they could see a vast plain stretching northeast into the distant mist. On either side of the city the mountains rose high into the heavens.

From the west white billowing clouds blew through a deep blue sky, as amber-highlighted green grasses stretched away to the limit of their view. It was an incredible view. Jimmy glanced over and saw a strange expression on Locklear's face. 'What?'

'I was just thinking about all that land,' he said, pointing toward the plain.

'What about it?' asked Arutha.

'You could grow a lot on such land.'

Martin let his gaze wander the horizon. 'Enough wheat to feed the Western Realm,' he commented.

Jimmy said, 'You, a farmer?'

Locklear grinned. 'What do you think a baron does in a small place like Land's End? Mostly he settles squabbles between farmers, or sets fair taxes on crops. You have to know about such things.'

The guard said, 'Come, the Protector waits.'

As Arutha and his companions entered, Guy looked up. With him were Amos, Dwyne, Armand de Sevigny, and a woman. Arutha looked at his brother and saw that Martin had halted in his tracks. The Duke of Crydee was staring at the woman in unabashed appreciation. Arutha touched Martin's arm and he moved to follow his brother. Arutha glanced at the woman again, and could appreciate his brother's distraction. At first blush, she seemed a plain-looking woman, but as soon as she moved, her bearing added another dimension to her appearance. She was striking. She wore leather armour, brown tunic and trousers, like most of the others in the city. But the bulky covering couldn't disguise the fact she was trimly built, and her carriage was erect, even regal. Her hair was deep brown, with a startling streak of grey at the left temple, and was tied back with a rolled green scarf, and her eyes were blue. And from the red-rimmed state of those eyes, it was clear she had been crying.

Guy indicated that Arutha and his companions should sit. Arutha introduced everyone, and Guy in turn said, 'You know Amos and Armand. This is Briana' – he indicated the woman – 'one of my commanders.' Arutha nodded, but saw the woman had recovered from whatever had caused her to cry and was returning Martin's appraising look.

Quickly, with economy, Arutha told Guy his story, starting with the return from the long trip with Lyam to the East, then of the first attack by the Nighthawks, through the revelations at the Abbey at Sarth and the quest for Silverthorn, to the false death of the Prince of Krondor. He ended by saying, 'To end it, we've come to kill Murmandamus.'

At that, Guy shook his head in disbelief. 'Cousin, it's a bold plan, but . . .' He turned to Armand. 'How many infiltrators have we tried to get into his camp?'

'Six?'

'Seven,' said Briana.

'But they weren't Kingdom men, were they?' asked Jimmy, taking out an ebon hawk on a chain. 'And they didn't carry the Nighthawks' talisman, did they.'

Guy looked at Jimmy in near-exasperation. 'Armand?'

The former Baron of Gyldenholt opened a drawer in a cabinet and took out a pouch. He untied the pouch and poured a half dozen of the talismans on the table. 'We've tried it, Squire. And yes, some were Kingdom men, for there are always a few among those saved by the Armengarians when they raided the Brothers' slave coffles. No, there's something missing. They know who the true brigands are and who are spies.'

Arutha said, 'Magic, most likely.'

Guy said, 'That's a problem we've faced before. We number no spellcasters, whether magicians or priests, in this city. It seems constant warfare, with everyone expected to fight, does not permit the sort of placidity such study requires – or it kills off all the teachers. But whatever the reason, on those few occasions when Murmandamus or his snake has taken a hand, we've paid a dear price.' He added thoughtfully, 'Though for some reason he seems reluctant to use his powers against us, thank the gods.'

Guy sat back. 'You and I share an interest, cousin. To give you some sense of it, let me tell you about this place. You know that the ancestors of the Armengarians came over the mountains when the Kingdom annexed Yabon. They discovered a rich land, but one already inhabited, and those who were here first tended to look upon the incursion of the Armengarians with disfavour. Briana, who built this city?'

The woman spoke, her voice a soft contralto. 'The legend is that the gods ordered a race of giants to build this city, then left it abandoned. We took it as we found it.'

'No one knows who lived here,' said Guy. 'There is another city, far to the north, Sar-Sargoth. It is a city twin to this one, and Murmandamus's capital.'

Arutha said, 'So if we are to seek him out, there is where we'll find him.'

'Seek him out and he'll see your heads on pikes,' snorted Amos.

Guy indicated agreement. 'We have other needs, Arutha. Last year he marshalled an army in excess of twenty thousand. As much might as the Armies of the East at full muster during peaceful times. We braced ourselves for a full-scale onslaught, but nothing materialized. Now, I expect your friend here' – he pointed to Baru – 'killing off Murmandamus's favourite general might have aborted the campaign. But this year he's back and he's even stronger. We estimate he may have more than twenty-five thousand goblins and Dark Brothers under his banner, with more arriving every day. I expect upward of thirty thousand when he marches.'

Arutha looked at Guy. 'Why hasn't he marched yet?'

Guy spread his hands, inviting comment from anyone. 'He's waiting for your death, remember?' instructed Jimmy. 'It's a religious thing.'

Arutha said, 'He has word by now. That's what he told that renegade Morgan Crowe.'

Guy's one good eye narrowed. 'What's this?'

Arutha told of the renegade at the inn on the road to Tyr-Sog, and of the plan to hire Segersen's engineers.

'That's what he was waiting for,' said Guy, slapping the table. 'He has his magic, but for some reason won't use it against us.

Without Segersen's engineers he can't bring down our walls.' When Arutha looked uncertain of Guy's meaning, Guy said, 'If he could bring down Armengar's walls he wouldn't be trying to hire Segersen. No one knows who built those walls, Arutha, but whoever it was had some skills beyond any other I've knowledge of. I've seen fortification of all manner, but none like Armengar. Segersen's engineers might not be able to breach the walls, but they are the only ones I know of with half a chance to do it.'

'So, with Segersen not coming, you're in good position to defend.'

'Yes, but there are other matters coming to bear as well.' Guy stood. 'We've more to discuss, and can continue later; I've a meeting with a city council now. For the present, you are free to come and go within Armengar at will.' He took Arutha aside and said, 'I need to speak with you in private. Tonight, after the evening meal.'

The meeting broke up, with Briana, Armand, and Guy leaving. Dwyne and Amos lingered behind. Amos approached Arutha and Martin while the Duke watched the woman leave. 'Who is she, Amos?' asked Martin.

'One of the city's better commanders, Martin. Gwynnath's daughter.'

'Now I understand the look of grief,' said the Duke.

'She just learned of her mother's death this morning.' Amos pointed toward the city. 'Her patrol was to the west, along the line of steadings and kraals, and she just returned hours ago.' Martin's expression was quizzical. 'The farm communities are steadings and the cattle-and sheepherder communities are kraals. No, she's dealing with Gwynnath's loss. It's Guy who has me worried.'

Arutha said, 'He hides his grief well.'

Arutha felt conflicting emotions. The dislike for Bas-Tyra he had learned at his father's knee fought his sympathy at the man's grief. He had almost lost Anita, and he could feel that terror and pain echoing as he considered Guy's lot. Yet Guy had ordered Anita's father imprisoned, which had killed him. And Guy was a traitor. Arutha pushed aside those feelings, for they troubled him. He walked with Amos and Martin while Martin continued asking questions about Briana.

CHAPTER TEN

Accommodation

JIMMY POKED LOCKLEAR IN THE RIBS.

They were strolling through the market, attempting to see what little of Armengar was worth seeing. Boys their own age were rare, and those few who they did see were armed and armoured. What interested Jimmy was the differences between this market and those in Krondor.

'We've been here an hour or more, and I'll swear I've not seen a beggar or thief in the lot,' said Jimmy.

'Makes sense,' said Locklear. 'From what Amos said, trust is essential to the existence of this city. No thieves, 'cause they all have to hang together, and where would you hide anyway? I don't know much about cities and such, but it seems to me this place is more a garrison than a city, despite its size.'

'You have that right enough.'

'And there are no beggars because they probably take care of everyone, like in the army.'

'Mess and infirmaries?'

'Yes,' agreed Locklear.

They wandered past booths and Jimmy judged the worth of the items displayed. 'Notice any real luxuries?' Locklear indicated he had not. The booths were devoted to foodstuffs, simple cloth and leather goods, and weapons. All prices were low, and there seemed little if any haggling.

After a short time of walking, Jimmy sat on a door stoop at the edge of the market. 'This is boring.'

'I see something that's not boring.'

Jimmy said, 'What?'

'Girls.' Locklear pointed. Two girls had emerged from the press of shoppers and were examining goods at a booth near the edge of the market. They appeared about the same age as the boys. Both were similarly attired, leather boots, trousers, tunics, leather over-vests, belt knives, and swords. Each wore a rolled scarf to hold her shoulder-length dark hair out of her eyes. The taller girl noticed Jimmy and Locklear watching them and said something to her companion. The second girl regarded the boys while the two whispered, heads together. The first girl put back the items she had been holding, and she and her friend walked over to Jimmy and Locklear.

'Well?' said the taller, her blue eyes regarding them frankly.

Jimmy got to his feet and was surprised to find the girl almost as tall as he was. 'Well what?' he responded in halting Armengarian.

'You were staring at us.'

Jimmy glanced down at Locklear, who stood. 'Is there something wrong with that?' asked the younger boy, who spoke the language better than Jimmy.

The two girls exchanged glances and laughed, little more than giggles. 'It is rude.'

'We're strangers,' ventured Locklear.

The two girls laughed openly at that. 'That is clear. We heard of you. Everyone in Armengar has heard of you.'

Locklear blushed. It only took a moment's thought to realize that he and Jimmy were markedly different in appearance from everyone in sight. The second girl studied Locklear with dark eyes and said, 'Do you stare at girls where you come from?'

With a sudden grin, Locklear said, 'Every chance I get.'

All four laughed. The taller girl said, 'I am Krinsta; this is Bronwynn. We serve in the Tenth Company. We have liberty until tomorrow night.'

Jimmy didn't know the significance of the reference to company, but he said, 'I'm Squire James – Jimmy. This is Squire Locklear.'

'Locky.'

Bronwynn said, 'You have the same name?'

Locklear said, ' "Squire" is a title. We are in service to the Prince.'

The girls exchanged questioning looks. Krinsta said, 'You speak of outlandish things we do not understand.'

In a fluid motion, Jimmy slipped his arm inside hers and said, 'Well then, why don't you show us the city and we'll explain our outlandish ways.'

Awkwardly Locklear followed his friend's example, but it wasn't clear who grabbed whose arm first, he or Bronwynn.

With girlish laughter, Bronwynn and Krinsta took the boys in tow and they made their way through the streets of the city.

Martin ate quietly, studying Briana while he listened to the dinner conversation. Arutha's company, except for Jimmy and Locklear, sat around a large table with Guy, Amos, and Briana. Another of Guy's commanders, Gareth, also dined with them. The boys' absence was no cause for alarm, Amos had assured them, for there was no trouble in the city they could find without the Protector hearing about it at once. And there was no way they could leave the city, even for one as gifted as Jimmy. Arutha was not as sure of that as Amos, but forwent comment.

Arutha knew he and Guy would quickly have to come to an understanding, and he had some sense of what it would be, but he deferred speculation until he heard what Guy had to say in private. Arutha studied the Protector. Guy had fallen into a black mood, which in a strange way reminded Arutha of his father when in a similar frame of mind. Guy had eaten little, but had been steadily drinking for an hour.

Arutha turned his attention to his brother, who had been behaving in a most unusual fashion since morning. Martin could be quiet for long periods of time, a trait they both shared, but since meeting Briana he had become almost mute. She had arrived with Amos in Arutha's suite for the noon meal, and since then Martin hadn't uttered a dozen words to anyone. But over this meal, as over that earlier one, his eyes had spoken volumes, and if Arutha could judge such things, Briana answered. At least, she seemed to spend more time observing Martin than anyone else at the table.

Guy had said little during the course of the evening. If Briana's mother had been anything like her, Arutha understood Guy's loss, for in the short hours he had observed her, he had come to count her a rare woman. He also could understand Martin's being attracted to her. There was nothing pretty about her, but as different as she was from his beloved Anita, there was a powerful appeal in her, a rough, determined quality of competence that was magnetic. She seemed without artifice, and in Arutha's judgment there was something in her manner that suggested her nature was a match for his brother's. Arutha's attention had been focused for a long time upon grave considerations, but he still had a moment for amusement; he judged Martin was quickly sinking in deep waters.

The meal was somewhat strange to Arutha and Martin, for there were no servants in Guy's hall, or in any part of Armengar. Soldiers brought food to the Protector's quarters as a courtesy, but he served himself, as did his guests. Amos had remarked that most nights he and Armand would lug the serving ware back down to the scullery and give a hand washing it. Everyone in the city helped.

When the meal was finished, Amos said, 'I, Gareth and Armand are due to make rounds of the walls. We're spared the scullery this night so we might act the proper hosts. Would you care to join us?' It was a general invitation to all at the table. Roald, Laurie, and Baru asked to join them, the Hadati especially wishing to see more of his distant kin.

Martin rose and, in what appeared a heroic effort for him, said to Briana, 'Perhaps the commander would show me the city?' He seemed equally pleased and distressed when she agreed.

Arutha motioned for him to go with the woman, indicating he would stay behind to speak with Guy. Martin hurried out of the hall as Briana led the way.

In the long hall that led to the lift, Martin paused to look at the city lights below. A thousand glittering points shone in the sable darkness. 'As often as I pass this way,' said Briana, 'I never tire of the sight.' Martin nodded agreement. 'Is your home like Armengar?'

Martin didn't look at her. 'Crydee?' he thought aloud. 'No. My castle is tiny compared to this citadel, and the town of Crydee is but a tenth the size of this city. We have no giant wall about it, nor are all its people constantly under arms. It is a peaceful place, or so it seems now. Before, I used to shun it as much as I could, staying in the forests, to hunt and be alone with my thoughts. Or I would go to the tallest tower of my castle and watch the sun set over the ocean. That is the best time of day. In the summer the breeze from off the water cools the heat of day while the sun plays colours across the water. In the winter the towers are draped in white and it seems a storied place. You can see mighty clouds rolling in from the ocean. And even more magnificent are the lightning storms, with flashes and booming thunder, as if the sky were alive.' He looked down and saw her studying him. Suddenly he felt foolish, and smiled slightly, his only sign of embarrassment. 'I ramble.'

'Amos has told me of oceans.' She tilted her head a little, as if considering. 'It seems a strange thing, all that water.'

Martin laughed a little, feeling his nervousness diminish. 'It is a strange thing, strange and powerful. I've never liked ships, but I've had to sail them, and after a while you appreciate how beautiful the sea can be. It is like . . .' He halted, words not coming. 'Laurie should tell you, or Amos. Both have a flair for words I lack.'

She placed her hand upon his arm. 'I would rather hear them from you.' She turned toward the window, her face sculptured by orange torchlight, her hair a black crown in the half-light. She was silent for a long moment and then looked at Martin. 'Are you a good hunter?'

Suddenly Martin was grinning, feeling like a fool. 'Yes, very good.' Both knew there was no false boasting, just as there would be no false modesty. 'I am elven-taught and know only one man who may be a fairer archer than I.'

'I enjoy the hunt but rarely have time, now that I command. Perhaps we may steal away some time and look for game. It is more dangerous here than in your Kingdom, perhaps, for while we hunt, others may be hunting us.'

Coolly Martin said, 'I have dealt with the moredhel before.'

She regarded him frankly. 'You are a strong man, Martin.' Placing her hand upon his arm, she said, 'And I think a good man, as well. I am Briana, daughter of Gwynnath and Gurtman, of the line of Alwynne.' These were formal words, yet there was something else in them, as if somehow she was revealing herself to him, reaching out to him.

'I am Martin, son of Margaret . . .' For the first time in years he thought of his mother, a pretty serving girl in Duke Brucal's court. '. . . and Borric, of the line of Dannis, first of the conDoins. I am called Martin Longbow.'

She looked long at his face, as if studying each feature. Her expression changed as she smiled. Martin felt heat burst in his chest at the sight of it. Then she laughed. 'That name suits you, Martin Longbow. You are as tall and powerful as your weapon. Have you a wife?'

Martin spoke softly. 'No. I . . . I had never met anyone . . . I've never had a way with words . . . or women. I've not known many.'

She placed her fingertips on his lips. 'I understand.'

Suddenly Martin found her in his arms, her head on his chest, how he didn't know. Gently he held her, as if the slightest motion would cause her to flee. 'I do not know how things are done in your Kingdom, Martin, but Amos says you avoid speaking openly of things we take for granted in Armengar. I do not know if this is such a thing. But I do not wish to be alone this night.' She looked again at his face, and he saw both desire and fear there and understood her needs. Softly, almost inaudibly, she said, 'Are you as gentle as you are strong, Martin Longbow?'

Martin studied her face and knew no words were needed. He held her for a long time in silence, until she slowly moved away, took his hand, and led him off toward her quarters.

For a long time Arutha sat watching Guy. The Protector of Armengar was lost in his own thoughts, drinking absently from his ale cup, the fire's crackle the only sound in the room. Then at last Guy said, 'The thing I miss most is the wine, I think. There are times when it suits a mood, don't you agree?'

Arutha nodded, sampling his own ale. 'Amos told us of your loss.'

Guy waved absently, and Arutha could see he was a little drunk, his movements not as sure, not quite as controlled. But his voice betrayed no slurring of speech. He sighed deeply. 'More your loss than mine, Arutha. You never met her.'

Arutha didn't know what to say. He suddenly felt irritated by this, as if he was being forced to watch something private, somehow being forced to share a bond of grief with a man he should hate. 'You said we needed to speak, Guy.'

Guy nodded, pushing aside his cup. He still stared off into the distance. 'I have need of you.' He turned to face Arutha. 'I have need of the Kingdom, at least, and that means Lyam.' Arutha motioned for Guy to continue. 'It makes little difference to me personally if I possess your good opinion or not. But it is clear I need your acceptance as the leader of these people.' He lapsed into thoughtfulness. Then he said, 'I thought your brother would marry Anita. It was the logical thing to do to bolster his claim. But then, he was King before he knew it. Rodric did us all a favour by having one lucid moment before he died.' He looked hard at Arutha. 'Anita is a fine young woman. I had no desire to wed her, only a need at the time. I would have let her find her own . . . satisfactions. It is better this way.' He sat back. 'I'm drunk. My mind wanders.' He closed his eye, and for a moment Arutha thought he might be drifting off to sleep.

Then Guy said, 'Amos told you how we came to Armengar, so I'll not repeat that tale. But there are other matters I think he did not touch upon.' Again he was silent. Another long period without words was followed by 'Did your father ever tell you how there came to be so much bitterness between us?'

Arutha kept his voice calm. 'He said you were at the heart of every conspiracy in court against the Western Realm, and you used your position with both Rodric and his father to undermine Father's position.'

To Arutha's astonishment, Guy said, 'That's mostly true. A different interpretation of my actions might give a softer label to what I did, but my actions under the reigns of Rodric and his father before him were never in the interest of your father or the West.

'No, I speak of . . . other things.'

'He never spoke of you except to brand you as an enemy.' Arutha considered, then went on, 'Dulanic said you and Father were friends once.'

Guy again looked at the fire. His manner was distant, as if remembering. Softly he said, 'Yes, very good friends.' Again he fell into silence, then just as Arutha was about to speak, he said, 'It started when we were both young men at court, during the reign of Rodric the Third. We were among the very first squires sent to the royal court – Caldric's innovation was to produce rulers who know more than their fathers.' Guy considered. 'Let me tell you how it was. And when I'm done, maybe you'll understand why you and your brother were never sent to court.

'I was three years younger than your father, who was barely eighteen, but we were of a size and temper. At first we were thrown together, for he was a distant cousin, and I was expected to teach manners to this son of a rustic duke. In time we became friends. Over the years we gambled, wenched, and fought together.

'Oh, we had differences, even then. Borric was a frontier noble's son, more concerned with old concepts of honour and duty than in understanding the true causes of events around him. I, well . . .' He drew his hand down over his face, as if stirring himself awake. His tone became more brisk. 'I was raised in the eastern courts, and I was marked to command from an early age. My family is as old and honoured as any in the Kingdom, even yours. Had Delong and his brothers been slightly less gifted generals and my forebears slightly better ones, the Bas-Tyras would have been kings instead of the conDoins. So I had been taught from boyhood how the game of politics is played in the realms. No, we were very different in some ways, your father and I, but in my life there has never been a man I've loved more than Borric.' He looked hard at Arutha. 'He was the brother I never had.'

Arutha was intrigued. He had no doubt Guy was colouring things to suit his purpose, suspecting even the drunkenness was a pose, but he was curious to hear of his father's youth. 'What, then, caused the estrangement between you?'

'We competed, as young men do, in the hunt, gambling, and for the affection of the ladies. Our political differences led to hot words from time to time, but we always found a way to gloss over arguments and reconcile ourselves. Once we even came to blows over some thoughtless remarks I made. I had said your great-grandfather had been nothing more than the disgruntled third son of a king, seeking to gain by strength of arms that which could not be found within the existing Kingdom. Borric saw him a great man who planted the banner of the Kingdom in Bosania.

'I held that the West was a sap upon the resources of the Kingdom. The distances are too great for proper administration. You rule in Krondor. You know you govern an independent realm, with only broad policy coming from Rillanon. The Western Realm is almost a separate nation. Anyway, we argued about that, then fought.

Afterward we relented in our anger. But that was the first sign of how deep were the differences we felt over the policies of the realms. Still, even those differences did nothing to lessen the bond between us.'

'You make it sound a reasonable disagreement between honourable men over politics. But I knew Father. He hated you and his hate ran deep; there must be more.'

Guy again studied the firelight for a time. Softly he said, 'Your father and I were rivals in many things, but most bitterly for your mother.'

Arutha sat forward. 'What?'

'When your uncle Malcom died of the fever, your father was called home. As older brother, Borric would inherit, which is why he had been sent to court for an education, but with Malcom dead your grandfather was alone. So your grandfather had the King name your father Warden of the West and send him back to Crydee. Your grandfather was aging – your grandmother had already died, and with Malcom's death he seemed to fade quickly. It was less than two years later that he died and Borric became Duke of Crydee. By then Brucal had returned to Yabon, and I was Senior Squire of the King's court. I looked forward to Borric's return – for he was to present himself to the King to swear fealty as all new dukes are required to do during the first year of their office.'

Arutha calculated and realized that had to be the time his father had visited Brucal at Yabon, on his way to the capital. It was during that visit that Borric's fancy was caught by a pretty serving maid, and from that union came Martin, a fact not known to Borric until five years later.

Guy continued speaking. 'The year before Borric's return to Rillanon, your mother came to court, to be a lady-in-waiting to Queen Janica, the King's second wife – Prince Rodric's mother. That's when Catherine and I met. Until Gwynnath, she was the only woman I've ever loved.'

Guy lapsed into silence, and suddenly Arutha felt an odd sense of shame, as if he had somehow forced Guy to reexamine two painful losses. 'Catherine was rare, Arutha. I know you understand that; she was your mother, but when I first saw her she was as fresh as a spring morning, with a blush in her cheeks and a hint of playfulness in her shy smile. Her hair was golden, with a shine to it. I fell in love with her the first moment I saw her. And so did your father. From that moment on, our competition for her attention became fierce.

'For two months we both courted her, and by the end of the second, your father and I were not speaking, so bitter was our rivalry for Catherine. Your father kept putting off his return to Crydee, choosing to stay and woo Catherine. We vied desperately for her favour.

'I was to have gone riding with Catherine one morning, but when I reached her quarters, she was readying to travel. She was first cousin to Queen Janica and, as such, a prize in the game of court intrigue. The lessons I had taught your father the years before had paid handsomely, for while I had been riding and walking in the garden with Catherine, he had been speaking to the King. Rodric directed your mother to wed your father, as was his right as her guardian. It was a politically expedient marriage, for even then the King had doubts as to his son's ability and his brother's health. Damn it, but Rodric was an unhappy man. His three sons from his first marriage had died before reaching manhood, and he never got over their deaths or the death of his beloved Queen Beatrice. And his younger brother, Erland, was a late child and sickly with the lung flux. He was but ten years older than Prince Rodric. The court knew that the King wished to name your father Heir, but Janica had given him a son, a shy boy whom Rodric despised. I think he forced your mother to marry your father to strengthen the tie to the throne, so he might name him Heir, and heaven knows he spent the next twelve years trying to either make the Prince a better man or break him in the trying. But the King never did name an Heir before he died, and we were left with Rodric the Fourth, a sadder, more broken man than his father.'

Arutha looked on, his cheeks flushed. 'What do you mean, the King forced my mother to marry my father?'

Guy's one good eye blazed. 'It was a political marriage, Arutha.'

Arutha's anger rose up. 'But my mother loved my father!'

'By the time you were born, I'm sure she had learned to love him. Your father was a good enough man and she a loving woman. But in those days, she loved me.' His voice became thick with old emotions. 'She loved me. I had known her a year before Borric's return. We had already vowed to wed when my tenure as a squire was through, but it was a secret thing, a pledge between children made in a garden one night. I had written to my father, asking him to intercede with the Queen, to gain me Catherine's hand. I never thought to speak to the King. I, the clever son of an eastern lord, had been bested by the country noble's boy in a court intrigue. Damn, I had thought I was so wily. But I was then only nineteen. It was so long ago.

'I fell into a rage. In those days my temper was a match for your father's. I dashed from your mother's room and sought Borric out. We fought; in the King's palace, we duelled and almost killed each other. You must have seen the long wound upon your father's side, from under the left arm across his ribs. I gave him that scar. I bear a similar wound from him. I almost died. When I recovered, your father was a week gone to Crydee, taking Catherine with him. I would have followed, but the King forbade it on pain of death. He was correct, for they were married. I took to wearing black as a public mark of my shame. Then I was sent to fight Kesh at Deep Taunton.' He laughed a bitter laugh. 'Much of my reputation as a general came from that encounter. I owe my success in part to your father. I punished the Keshians for his having robbed me of Catherine. I did things no general in his right mind should do, leading attack after attack. I think now I hoped to die then.' His voice softened, and he chuckled. 'I was almost disappointed when they asked for quarter and terms of surrender.'

Guy sighed. 'So much of what happened in my life stems from that. I ceased holding ill will toward Borric, eventually, but he . . . turned a bitter side up when she died. He rejected the idea of sending his sons to the King's court. I think he worried I might take revenge upon you and Lyam.'

'He loved Mother; he was never a happy man after her death,'

Arutha said, feeling somehow both uncomfortable and angry. He did not need to justify his father's behaviour to his most bitter enemy.

Guy nodded. 'I know, but when we are young we cannot entertain the idea another's feelings can be as deep as our own. Our love is so much loftier, our pain so much more intense. But as I grew older, I realized Borric loved Catherine as much as I did. And I think she did love him.' Guy's good eye fixed on a point in space. His tone became softer, reflective. 'She was a wonderful, generous woman with room in her life for many loves. Yet, I think deep in his heart your father harboured doubts.' Guy regarded Arutha with an expression of mixed wonder and pity. 'Can you imagine that? How sad it must have been? Perhaps, in a strange way, I was the luckier, for I *knew* she loved me. I had *no* doubt.' Arutha noticed a faint sheen of moisture in Guy's good eye. The Protector brushed away the gathering tear in an unselfconscious gesture. He settled back, closing his eye, his hand to his forehead, and quietly added, 'There seems little justice in life at times.'

Arutha pondered. 'Why are you telling me this?'

Guy sat up, shedding his mood. 'Because I need you. And there can be no doubts on your part. To you I am a traitor who sought to take control of the Kingdom for his own aggrandizement. In part, you are correct.' Arutha was again surprised at Guy's candour.

'But how can you justify what you did to Erland?'

'I am responsible for his death. I cannot disavow that. It was my captain who ordered his continued confinement after I had ordered his release. Radburn had his uses, but tended to be overzealous. I can understand his panic, for I would have punished him for letting Anita and you escape. I needed her to gain a foothold in the succession, and you would have been a useful bargaining piece with your father.' Seeing surprise on Arutha's face, he said, 'Oh yes, my agents knew you were in Krondor – or they reported to me when I returned – but Radburn made the error of thinking you'd lead him to Anita. It never occurred to him you might have nothing to do with her escape. The fool should have clapped you in jail and kept the search on for her.'

Arutha felt a return of his distrust and a lessening of sympathy. Despite Guy's forthright speech, his callous references to using people rankled. Guy continued, 'But I never wished Erland dead. I already had the Vice-royalty from Rodric, giving me full command over the West. I didn't need Erland, only a link to the throne: Anita. Rodric the Fourth was mad. I was one of the first to know – as was Caldric – for in kings people overlook and forgive behaviour they would not tolerate in others. Rodric could not be allowed to rule much longer. The first eight years of the war were difficult enough in the court, but in the last year of his reign, Rodric was almost totally without reason. Kesh always has an eye turned northward, seeking signs of weakness. I did not wish the burdens of kingship, but even with your father as heir after Erland, I simply felt I was better able to rule than anyone in a position to inherit.'

'But why all this intrigue? You had backing in the congress. Caldric, Father, and Erland barely overruled your attempt to become Prince Rodric's regent before he reached majority. You could have found another way.'

'The congress can ratify a King,' answered Guy, pointing a finger at Arutha. 'It cannot remove him. I needed a way to take the throne without civil war. The war with the Tsurani dragged on, and Rodric would not give your father the Armies of the East. He wouldn't even give them to me, and I was the only man he trusted. Nine years of a losing war and a mad King, and the nation was bleeding to death. No, it had to end, but no matter how much backing I had, there were those like Brucal and your father who would have marched against me.

'That's why I wanted Anita for my wife and you as a bargaining piece. I was ready to offer Borric a choice.'

'What choice?'

'My preference was to let Borric rule in the West, to divide the Kingdom and let each realm follow its own destiny; but I knew none of the western lords would have permitted that. So my offer to Borric was to allow him to name the Heir after me, even if it were Lyam or you. I would have named whoever he chose Prince of Krondor, and I would have ensured I had no sons to contest for the crown. But your father would have had to accept me as King of Rillanon and swear fealty.'

Suddenly Arutha understood this man. He had put aside all questions of personal honour after he had lost Arutha's mother to Borric, but he had kept one honour above all others: his honour for the Kingdom. He had been willing to do anything, even commit regicide – to go down in history as a usurper and traitor – in exchange for removing a mad king. It left a bad taste in Arutha's mouth.

'With Rodric's death and Lyam being named Heir, all that became meaningless. Your brother is not known to me, but I expect he shares some of your father's nature. In any event, the Kingdom must be in better hands than when Rodric sat the throne.'

Arutha sighed. 'You have given me much to think about, Guy. I don't approve of your reasoning or your methods, but I understand some of it.'

'Your approval is immaterial. I repent nothing of what I have done, and will admit my decision to claim the throne myself, ignoring your father's place in succession, was done in part from spite. If I couldn't have your mother, Borric couldn't have the crown. Beyond selfish considerations, I also held the firm conviction I would have made a better king than your father. What I do best is rule. But it doesn't mean I feel good about what I've had to do.

'No, what I want is your understanding. You don't have to like me, but you must accept me for who and what I am. I need your acceptance to secure the future of Armengar.'

Arutha became silent, feeling discomforted. A memory of a conversation two years previous flooded back into his mind. After a long silence, he said, 'I am not in a position to judge. I'm remembering a conversation with Lyam in our father's burial vault. I was ready to see Martin dead rather than risk civil war. My own brother . . .' he added softly.

'Such judgments are a necessary consequence of ruling.' He sat back, regarding Arutha. At last he said, 'How did your decision about Martin make you feel?'

Arutha seemed reluctant to share that with Guy. Then after a long silence had passed, he looked directly at the Protector. 'Dirty. It made me feel dirty.'

Guy extended his hand. 'You do understand.' Slowly Arutha took the proffered hand and shook. 'Now, to the heart of the matter.

'When we first came here, Amos, Armand, and I were sick, injured, and near-starved. These people healed us, strangers from an alien land, without questions. When we were fit, we volunteered to fight, then discovered it was expected that all who are able serve without question. So we took our place in the garrison of the city and began to learn of Armengar.

'The Protector before Gwynnath had been an able commander, as was Gwynnath, but both knew little of modern warfare. Nevertheless, they kept the Brotherhood and the goblins under control, keeping a bloody balance of sorts.

'Then Murmandamus came and things changed. When I arrived, the Brotherhood was victorious three out of four encounters. The Armengarians were losing, being routinely defeated for the first time in their history. I taught them modern warfare, and again we hold our own. Now nothing comes within twenty miles of the city without being seen by one of our scouts or patrols. But even with that, it is too late.'

'Why too late?'

'Even if Murmandamus weren't coming to crush us, this nation couldn't last another two generations. This city is dying. As best I can judge, two decades ago, there were perhaps fifteen thousand souls living within the city and in the surrounding countryside. Ten years ago, it was eleven or twelve thousand. Now it's more like seven or perhaps even less. Constant warfare, women of childbearing age being killed in battle, children dying when a steading or kraal is overrun: it all adds up to a declining population, a decline that seems to be accelerating. And there's more. It's as if years of constant warfare have sapped the strength from these people. For all their willingness to fight, they seem somehow indifferent to the needs of daily living.

'The culture is twisted, Arutha. All they have is struggle and, in the end, death. Their poetry is limited to sagas of heroes, and their music is simple battle chants. Have you noticed there are no signs in the city? Everyone knows where everyone else lives and works. Why signs? Arutha, no one born in Armengar can read or write. They don't have the time to learn. This is a nation slipping inexorably into barbarism. Even should there have been no Murmandamus, in another two decades there would be no nation. They would be as the nomads of the Thunderhell. No, it's the constant fighting.'

'I can see how that could give one a sense of futility. What can I do to help?'

'We need relief. I will gladly turn the governance of this city over to Brucal—'

'Vandros. Brucal retired.'

'Vandros, then. Bring Armengar into the Duchy of Yabon. These people fled the Kingdom, ages ago. Now they would not hesitate to embrace it, should I but order it, so much have they changed. But give me two thousand heavy foot from the garrison at Yabon and Tyr-Sog, and I'll hold this city against Murmandamus for another year. Add a thousand more and two thousand horse, and I'll rid the Plain of Isbandia of every goblin and Dark Brother. Give me the Armies of the West, and I'll drive Murmandamus back to Sar-Sargoth and burn the city down with him inside. Then we can have commerce and children can be children, not little warriors. Poets will compose and artists paint. We will have music and dancing. Then maybe this city will grow again.'

'And will you wish to remain as Protector, or as Earl of Armengar?' asked Arutha, not fully rid of his distrust.

'Damn it,' said Guy, slamming his hand down on the table. 'If Lyam has the brains of a bag of nails, yes.' Guy sagged back into his chair. 'I'm tired, Arutha. I'm drunk and tired.' His good eye brimmed. 'I've lost the only thing I've cherished in ages, and all

I've left is the need of these people. I'll not fail them, but once they're safe . . .'

Arutha was stunned. Before him Guy bared his soul, and what he saw was a man without much reason left to live. It was sobering. 'I think I can persuade Lyam to agree, if you understand what his attitude toward you will be.'

'I don't care what he thinks of me, Arutha. He can have my head, for all of it.' His voice again betrayed his fatigue. 'I don't think I care at all anymore.'

'I'll send messages.'

Guy laughed, a bitter, frustrated laugh. 'That, you see, is the problem, dear cousin. You don't think I've been sitting here for the last full year hoping a Prince of Krondor might blunder into Armengar? I've sent a dozen messages to Yabon, and toward Highcastle, outlining in detail what the situation here is and what I've proposed to you. The difficulty is that while Murmandamus lets anyone come north, no one – nothing – goes south. That Beasthunter you found was one of the last to try for the south. I don't know what happened to the messenger he escorted, but I can imagine . . .' He let the thought drift off.

'You see, Arutha, we're cut off from the Kingdom. Utterly, totally, and unless you've an idea we've not thought of, without a prayer.'

Martin awoke sputtering, spitting out a mouthful of water. Briana's laughter filled the room as she tossed a towel at him and replaced the now empty water pitcher. 'You're as difficult to wake as a bear in winter.'

Blinking as he dried himself off, Martin said, 'I must be.' He fixed her with a black look, then found his anger slip away as he regarded her smiling face. After a moment he smiled in return. 'Out in the woods I'm a light sleeper. Indoors I relax.'

She knelt upon the bed and kissed him. She was dressed in tunic and trousers. 'I must ride out to one of our steadings. Care to come? It is only for the day.'

Martin grinned. 'Certainly.'

She kissed him again. 'Thank you.'

'For what?' he asked, clearly confused.

'For staying here with me.'

Martin stared at her. 'You're thanking me?'

'Of course, I asked you.'

'You are of a strange people, Bree. Most men I know would happily slit my throat to have had my place here last night.'

She turned her head slightly, a puzzled look on her face. 'Truly? How odd. I could say the same about most of the women here and you, Martin. Though no one would fight over something like bed rights. You are free to choose your partners, and they are free to answer yes or no. That is why I thanked you, for saying yes.'

Martin grabbed her and kissed her, half-roughly. 'In my land we do things differently.' He let her go, suddenly concerned he had been too rough. She seemed a little uncertain but not frightened. 'I'm sorry. It's just that . . . it was *not* a favour, Bree.'

She leaned close and rested her head upon his shoulder. 'You speak of something beyond the comforts of the bedchamber.'

'Yes.'

She was silent for a long time. 'Martin, here in Armengar, we know the wisdom of not planning too far into the future.' There was a catch in her speech and her eyes gleamed. 'My mother was to have wed the Protector. My father has been dead eleven years. It would have been a joyous union.' Martin could see the wetness spreading down her cheeks. 'Once I was betrothed. He rode to answer a goblin raid on a kraal. He never returned.' She studied his face. 'We do not lightly make promises. A night shared is not a vow.'

'I am not a frivolous man.'

She studied his face. 'I know,' she said softly. 'And I am not a frivolous woman. I choose partners carefully. There is something here building quickly between us, Martin. I know that. It will . . . come to us as time and circumstances permit, and to worry what the outcome of these things will be is wasted effort.' She bit her lower lip as she struggled for her next words. 'I am a commander, privy to knowledge most in the city are ignorant of. For the moment I can only ask you not to expect more than I can freely give.' Seeing his mood darken, she smiled and kissed him. 'Come, let us ride.'

Martin quickly dressed, uncertain of what had been accomplished, but certain it had been important. He felt both relieved and troubled: relieved he had stated his feelings, then troubled he had not done so clearly and her answer had been clouded. Still, he had been reared by elves, and as Briana had said, things would come to pass in their own good time.

Arutha finished recounting the previous night's conversation to Laurie, Baru, and Roald. The boys had been gone for a day. Martin had not returned to their quarters, and Arutha thought he knew where he had spent the night.

Laurie thought long on what Arutha had said. 'So the population is falling.'

'Or so Guy says.'

'He's right,' said a voice from the door.

They looked and discovered Jimmy and Locklear standing there, each with his arm about the waist of a pretty girl. Locklear appeared unable to keep his face in repose. No matter how hard he tried, his mouth seemed determined to set itself in a grin.

Jimmy introduced Krinsta and Bronwynn, then said, 'The girls showed us the city. Arutha, there are entire sections standing empty, home after home with no one living there.' Jimmy looked about and, discovering a plate of fruit, attacked a pear. 'I guess upward of twenty thousand people lived here once. Now I guess less than half of that.'

'I've already agreed in principle to help Armengar, but the problem is getting messages back to Yabon. It seems Murmandamus may be lax in letting people in, but he's rigorous in seeing no one gets out.'

'Makes sense,' said Roald. 'Most of those coming north are heading for his camp anyway. So what if a few blunder into this city and help. He's massing his army and can probably drive past here if he chooses.'

Baru said, 'I think I can get through, if I go alone.' Arutha looked interested and Baru said, 'I am a hillman, and while these people are kin they are also city people. Only those in the few high steadings and kraals might have my skill. Moving at night, hiding during the day, I should be able to cross over into the Yabon Hills. Once there, no moredhel or goblin would be able to keep pace with me.'

'Getting into the Yabon Hills would be the problem,' said Laurie. 'Remember how those trolls had chased that Beasthunter for what, days? I don't know.'

'I'll think on it, Baru,' said Arutha. 'It may be that desperate gamble is all we have, but perhaps there's another way. We might mount a raiding party to get someone up to the crest, then turn and fight our way back, giving whoever goes south as much of a head start as possible. It may not be possible, but I'll discuss it with Guy. If we can't discover another choice, I'll permit you to try. Though I don't think alone is necessarily the best. We managed all right in a small company getting in and out of Moraelin.' He rose. 'If any of you can conceive a better plan, I'll welcome it. I am going to join Guy in inspecting the battlements. If we're stuck here when the assault comes, we might as well lend all the aid we may.' He left the room.

Guy's hair blew wildly as they looked out over the plain beyond the city. 'I've inspected every inch of this wall, and I still don't believe the quality of engineering.'

Arutha could only agree. The stones used had been cut to a precision undreamed of by the Masterbuilders and stonemasons of the Kingdom. Running his hand over a joint, he could barely feel where one stone ended and another began. 'It is a wall that might have defied Segersen's engineers had they come.'

'We had some good engineers in our armies, Arutha. I can't see how this wall could be brought down short of a miracle.' He took out his sword and struck hard enough to make the blade ring, then pointed to the merlon where he had struck. Arutha inspected the place and saw only a slight lighter-colour scratch. 'It seems a blue granite, like ironstone, but even harder. It's a stone common enough to these mountains, but harder to work than anything I've seen. How it was worked is unknown. And the footings below the plinth are twenty feet into the earth, thirty feet from front to back. I can't even guess how the blocks were moved from the quarries in the mountains. If you could tunnel under it, the best that might happen is the entire wall section might sink down and crush you. And you can't even do that, because the wall sits atop bedrock.'

Arutha leaned back against the wall, looking at the city and the citadel beyond. 'This is easily the most defensible city I have ever heard of. You should be able to handle up to twenty-to-one odds.'

'Ten-to-one's the conventional figure for overrunning a castle, but I'm inclined to agree. Except for one thing: Murmandamus's damn magic. He may not be able to bring these walls down, but I'll warrant he's got a means to get past them. Somehow. Else he wouldn't be coming.'

'You're certain? Why not bottle you up with a small harrying force and move his army south?'

'He can't leave us at his back. He had his way with us for a year before I took command, and could have bled us to death by now if I hadn't changed the rules of the game. Over the last two years I've taught our soldiers everything I know. With Armand and Amos helping them learn, they now have the advantages of modern warcraft. No, Murmandamus knows he has an army of seven thousand Armengarians ready to jump on his rear if he turns his back. He can't leave us behind his lines. We'd hamstring him.'

'So he must rid himself of you first, then turn to the Kingdom.'

'Yes. And he must do it soon, or he loses another season. It turns to winter quickly up here. We see snow weeks before the Kingdom. The passes become blocked in days, sometimes in only hours. Once he has moved south, he must be victorious, for he cannot move his army north again until spring. He is on a timetable. He must come within the next two weeks.'

'So we must get word out soon.'

Guy nodded. 'Come, let me show you some more.'

Arutha followed the man, feeling a strange sense of divided loyalties. He knew he must help the Armengarians, but he still was not comfortable with Guy. Arutha had come to understand why Guy had done what he did, and in a strange way he even grudgingly admired him, but he didn't like him. And he knew why he didn't like him: Guy had made him see a similarity of nature common to them, a willingness to do what must be done regardless of cost. So far, Arutha had never gone to the lengths Guy had, but he now understood he might have acted in much the same way had he been in Guy's place. It was a discovery about himself he didn't particularly like.

They moved through the city, and Arutha asked about those details observed when they had first entered Armengar. 'Yes,' said Guy. 'There are no clear lines of fire, so that every turn can hide an ambush. I've a city map in the citadel, and the city is as it is by design rather than chance. Once you see the pattern, it's easy to know which directions to choose to reach any given point in the city, but without knowing what the pattern is, it's easy to get turned about, to be led back toward the outer wall.' He pointed at a building. 'Every house lacks windows on the street, and every roof is an archery platform. This city was built to cost any attackers dearly.'

Soon they were inside the citadel, and saw the boys coming across the courtyard. 'Where are the girls?' Arutha asked.

Locklear looked disappointed. 'They had to go do some things before they reported back for duty.'

Guy studied the two squires. 'Well then, come with us if you've nothing better to do.'

They followed Guy into the first floor and down to the lift. Guy rang the bell, giving the code to raise them to the highest roof. Reaching it, they looked down upon the city and plain beyond. 'Armengar.' His hand swept across the horizon. 'There,' he pointed, 'is the Plain of Isbandia, cut across by the Vale of Isbandia, the limit of our holdings to the north and northwest. The plain beyond that is Murmandamus's. To the east, the Edder Forest, almost as vast as the Blackwood or the Green Heart. We don't know much about it, save we can safely lumber at the edges. Anyone who goes more than a few miles deep tends not to be seen again.' He pointed to the north. 'Beyond the vale is Sar-Sargoth. If you're especially bold, you can climb the hills at the north edge of the vale and look across the plain to see the lights of this city's twin.'

Jimmy studied the war engines upon the roof. 'I don't know a lot about this, but can those catapults shoot beyond the outer wall?'

'No,' was all Guy said. 'Come along.'

They all moved back to the lift and Guy pulled the cord. Arutha noticed there was some code to indicate up or down, and, he supposed, the number of floors.

They descended to the ground floor, then lower yet. They reached a subbasement, several levels below the ground, and Guy led them from the platform. They passed a giant winch arrangement with a team of four horses hitched to a large wheel, which Arutha supposed was the power source for the lift. It certainly looked impressive, with large tongue and grooved wheels, and strange multiple rope and pulley arrangements. But Guy ignored the horse team and drivers, walking past them. He pointed at a large door, barred from the inside. 'That's the bolt hole out of here. We keep it sealed, for by some fluke or other, when the door's open a constant breeze blows through here, something to be avoided.' Opposite the large door stood another, which he opened, leading them into a natural tunnel. He took a strange-looking lantern from beside the door, one that glowed with a lower level of light than expected. Guy said, 'This thing uses some sort of alchemy to give off light. I don't understand it fully, but it works. We risk no flames here. You'll see why.'

Jimmy had been examining the walls and pulled off a white, flaky wax substance. He rubbed it between his thumb and forefinger and sniffed. 'I understand,' he said, making a face. 'Naphtha.'

'Yes.' Guy looked at Arutha. 'He's a sharp one.'

'So he's quick to remind me. How did you know?'

'Remember at the bridge south of Sarth, last year? The one I fired to keep Murad and the Black Slayers from crossing? That's what I used, distillation of naphtha.'

'Come,' said Guy taking them through another door.

The reek of tar assailed their noses as they entered the chamber. Strange-looking, large buckets were hung from chains. A dozen shirtless men laboured to manoeuvre the buckets down into a huge pool of black liquid. The odd lanterns burned about the cavern, but mostly the place was shrouded in darkness. 'We've tunnels honeycombing this entire mountain, and this stuff is found in all of them. There's some natural source of naphtha below and it constantly bubbles to the surface. We must keep taking it off, or it seeps upward into the basements of the city, through cracks in the bedrock. If work was halted, the stuff would be pooling in the cellars of the city within a few days. But as the Armengarians have been doing this for years, it's under control.'

'I can see why you don't want to risk a fire,' said Locklear, in open wonder.

'Fires we can handle. We've had dozens, as recently as last year, briefly. What we've discovered, or rather what the Armengarians have discovered, is some uses for this stuff we don't have in the Kingdom.' He motioned them into another chamber, where odd looking coils of tubing ran between vats. 'Here we do the distillation, and some of the other mixing. I understand a tenth of it, but the alchemists can explain. They make all manner of things from this naphtha, even some odd salves that keep wounds from festering, but one thing they've found is the secret of making Quegan fire.'

'Quegan fire!' Arutha exclaimed.

'They don't call it that, but it's the same stuff. The walls are limestone, and it's limestone dust that turns naphtha into Quegan fire oil. Fling it from a catapult and it burns and even water won't put it out. That's why we have to be so careful, for it doesn't just burn.' He looked at Locklear. 'The fumes are heavy, hugging the ground, but if you let the fumes build up, vent them with a lot of air, then hit a spark, the fumes explode.' He pointed toward a far cavern, loaded up with wooden barrels. 'That storage cave wasn't there ten years ago. When a barrel is emptied, it is filled again, or put under water until used. Some dolt left three empties standing about and somehow a spark hit one and . . . Just the amount of that stuff which soaks into the wood, then evaporates, can give off a tremendous explosion. That's why we keep the doors closed. The breeze off the mountains through the bolt hole can vent this entire complex in a day or two. And if all this went up at once . . .' He let their imaginations provide the picture. 'I've had the Armengarians making this for two years now, to give Murmandamus a warm welcome when he comes.'

'How many barrels?' asked Arutha.

'Over twenty five thousand.'

Arutha was staggered. When he had met Amos, the pirate had had two hundred barrels in the hold of his ship, a fact not known to the Tsurani raiders who had set fire to his ship. When it had gone up, it had blown a column of flames hundreds of feet into the air, engulfing the ship in an instant, incinerating it within minutes. The light of the flames had been seen for miles up and down the coast. If half the town hadn't already been burned by Tsurani raiders the fire would have devastated Crydee. 'That's enough . . .'

'To fire the entire city,' finished Guy.

'Why so much?' asked Jimmy.

'Something you must understand, all of you. The Armengarians have never thought of leaving here. In their judgment, there's no other place to find refuge. They came north to flee the Kingdom, so they thought they couldn't return south. On every side they saw enemies. Should the worst occur, they'll fire this city rather than let Murmandamus capture it. I've developed a plan beyond that, but in either case, a lot of fire could prove useful.' He returned toward the tunnel leading to the lift, the others following behind.

Martin sat resting against a tree. He kissed Briana's hair as she sank deeper into his arms. She stared off into some unseen place. Before them a small brook wound its way through a stand of woods, shrouding them in soft, cool shadows. Her patrol had broken for a noontime meal, which was being provided by the local farmers. She and Martin had stolen away to spend the time alone. The woodland setting put Martin more at ease than he had been in months, but still he was troubled. They had made love under the trees and now were simply finding pleasure in each other's company, but Martin still felt a lack inside. In her ear he said, 'Bree, I wish this could go on forever.'

She sighed and wiggled a little. 'I also, Martin. You are such a man as . . . another I knew. I think I could not wish for more.'

'When this is finished—'

She cut him off. 'When this is finished. Then we can talk of things. Come, we must get back.' She dressed quickly, Martin openly admiring her. She had none of the frail beauty of the women he had known at home. There was leather toughness to her makeup, tempered by a deep feminine quality. She was not a pretty woman by any standards, but she was striking and, with those arresting qualities of self-confidence and self-reliance Martin saw in her, she was stunning, even beautiful. In all ways, he had become captivated by her.

He finished dressing and before she could move away reached out and took her by the arm, turning her and bringing her to him. With a deep passion he kissed her, then said, 'I need not speak, but you know my need and my desire. I have waited for you too long.'

She looked up into his dark eyes. She reached up and touched his face. 'And I you.' She kissed him gently. 'We must return.'

He let her lead him back to the village. A pair of guardsmen were walking toward them when they left the woods. They halted and one said, 'Commander, we were about to come fetch you.'

She regarded the second man, not one of her company. 'What is it?'

'The Protector commands all the patrols to ride out and order the steadings and kraals abandoned. Everyone is to move at once to the city. Murmandamus's army is on the march. They will stand outside the walls within the week.'

Briana said, 'Orders to ride. We shall split the patrol. Grenlyn, you'll take half and head down to the lowland kraal and the river steadings. I'll take the ones higher up along the ridge. The moment you finish, ride back as soon as possible. The Protector will need all the scouts he can muster. Now go.' She looked back at Martin. 'Come, we have much to do.'

CHAPTER ELEVEN

Discovery

*G*AMINA SAT UP, SCREAMING.

Within moments Katala was in the child's room, holding her. Gamina sobbed for a short while, then quieted, as a sleepy William came into her room, followed by a grumpy-looking firedrake. Fantus padded past William and placed his head on the bed by Katala. 'Was it a bad dream, baby?' asked Katala.

Gamina nodded. Softly she said, 'Yes, Mama.' She was finally learning to speak, not always relying upon the mental speech that had marked her as a special talent since birth.

With her family dead, Gamina had been reared by Rogen the blind seer, before he brought her to Stardock. Rogen had aided Pug in discovering that the Enemy was behind all the troubles besetting the Kingdom, though he had suffered injury in uncovering this secret. He and Gamina had stayed with Pug's family while he recovered, and over the last year had come to be as members. Rogen had been as a grandfather to William, while to Gamina, Katala was a mother and

William a brother. The old man had died peacefully in his sleep three months before, but at the last he had been happy his ward had found others besides himself whom she could love and trust. Katala hugged and caressed the child while she calmed down.

Meecham, the tall franklin, hurried into the room looking for the source of any danger. He had returned from Kelewan with Hochopepa and Elgahar of the Assembly shortly after Pug had departed in search of the Watchers. Their other companion, Brother Dominic, had returned to the Ishapian abbey at Sarth. Meecham had taken it upon himself to act as protector of Pug's family while the magician was upon Kelewan. For all his fierce appearance and stoic demeanour, he was one of Gamina's favourites. She called him Uncle Meecham. He stood behind Katala, smiling one of his very rare smiles at the tiny girl.

Hochopepa and Kulgan entered the room, the two magicians of different worlds, alike in so many ways. Both came and fussed over the girl while Katala said, 'Still up working?'

Hochopepa said, 'Certainly, it's still early.' He looked up. 'Isn't it?'

Meecham said, 'No, unless you mean early in the morning. It's an hour past midnight.'

Kulgan said, 'Well, we were involved in some interesting discourse, and—'

'You lost track of time,' Katala said. Her tone was slightly disapproving, slightly amused. Pug was title holder to the property of Stardock and since he had left she had assumed control of the community. Her calm nature, intelligence, and ability to deal with people tactfully had made her the natural leader of the diverse community of magic users and their families, though occasionally Hochopepa was overheard calling her 'that tyrannical woman.' No one minded, for they knew he spoke with respect and affection.

Kulgan said, 'We were discussing some reports sent by Shimone at the Assembly.' By agreement, the rift between the worlds was opened for brief periods on a regular schedule so messages could be exchanged between the Academy at Stardock and the Assembly of Magicians on Kelewan.

Katala looked up expectantly, but Hochopepa said, 'Still no word of Pug.'

Katala sighed and, suddenly irritated, said, 'Hocho, Kulgan, you may do as you like in your research, but poor Elgahar seems almost ready to drop. He does almost all the training of the new Greater Path magicians, and he never complains. You should bend some of your efforts to helping him.'

Kulgan took out his pipe and said, 'We stand properly corrected.' He and Hochopepa exchanged glances. Both knew Katala's brusque manner was born from frustration over a husband absent a year.

Hochopepa said, 'Indeed.' He also unlimbered a pipe, a habit acquired in his year of working beside Kulgan. As Meecham had once observed, the two magicians were two peas in a pod.

Katala said, 'And if you intend to light those foul-smelling things, take them and yourselves out of here. This is Gamina's bedchamber, and I'll not have her room reeking of smoke.'

Kulgan was on the verge of lighting his and halted. 'Very well. How is the child?'

Gamina had ceased her crying and spoke softly. 'I'm all right.' Since she had learned to speak, her voice had never been raised above a soft, childish whisper, save for her scream of a few moments before. 'I . . . had a bad dream.'

'What sort of dream?' asked Katala.

Gamina's eyes began to brim with tears. 'I heard Papa calling me.'

Kulgan and Hochopepa both looked down at the girl intently. 'What did he say, child?' asked Kulgan softly so as not to frighten the girl.

Katala went ashen, but showed no other signs of fear. She was born of a line of warriors and she could face anything, anything save this not knowing how her husband fared. Gently she said, 'What did he say, Gamina?'

'He was—' As she did when under stress, she changed to mind-speech. *He was in a strange place, far away. He was with somebody? somebodies? else. He said, he said—*

'What, child?' said Hochopepa.

He said we must wait for a message, then something – changed. He was – gone? in an empty? place. I became frightened. I felt so alone.

Katala held the girl closely. She controlled her voice, but she felt fear as she said, 'You're not alone, Gamina.' But inwardly Katala echoed the girl's thoughts. Even when Pug had been taken from her by the Assembly to become a Great One, she had not felt this alone.

Pug closed his eyes in fatigue. He let his head fall forward until it rested upon Tomas's shoulder. Tomas looked back. 'Did you get through?'

With a heavy sigh, Pug said, 'Yes, but – it was more difficult than I had thought, and I frightened the child.'

'Still, you got through. Can you do it again?'

'I think so. The girl's mind is unique and should be easier to reach next time. I know more about how this process works. Before I only had the theory. Now I've done it.'

'Good. We may need that skill.'

They were speeding through the greyness they had come to call 'rift-space', that place between the very strands of time and the physical universe. Tomas had instructed Ryath to go there the moment Pug had signalled the end of his contact with those at Stardock. Now the dragon sent a mind message. *Where dost thou wish, Valheru?*

Tomas spoke aloud. 'To the City Forever.'

Ryath seemed to shudder as she took control of that nothingness around her and bent it to her needs in travel. The featureless grey about them pulsed, and somehow they changed directions within this boundless dimension, this no place. Then the fabric of grey about them rippled once more and they were somewhere else.

An odd spot appeared before them in the grey, the first hint of any reality within rift-space. It grew as rapidly as if Ryath were speeding through some physical plane, then they were above it. It was a city, a place of terrible and alien beauty. It possessed towers of twisted symmetry, minarets impossibly slender, oddly designed buildings that sprawled below the vaulting arches between the towers. Fountains of complex fashion spewed forth drops of liquid silver that turned to crystals, filling the air with tinkling music as they shattered upon the tiles of the fountain, becoming liquid again and running into drains.

The dragon banked and sped downward, flying above the centre of a magnificent boulevard, nearly a hundred yards wide. The entire street was tiled, and the tiles glowed with soft hues, each subtly different from the next, so that over a distance it appeared a gradually changing rainbow. And as the dragon's shadow passed over, the tiles blinked and glowed, then shifted colour, and music filled the air, a theme of majestic beauty, bringing a stab of longing for green fields beside sparkling brooks while soft pastel sunsets coloured magnificent mountains. The images were nearly overwhelming and Pug shook his head to clear it, putting aside a soft sadness that such a wonderful place could never be found. They flew under heroic arches, a thousand feet above their heads, and tiny flower petals of sparkling white and gold, glowing rose and vermilion, pastels green and blue fell about them, a softly caressing rain scented of wild flowers, as they made for the heart of the city.

'Who built this wonder?' asked Pug.

'No one knows,' said Tomas, 'Some unknown race. Perhaps the dead gods.' Pug studied the city as they flew over it. 'Or perhaps no one built it.'

'How could that be?' asked Pug.

'In an infinite universe, all things are not only possible but, no matter how improbable, certain to exist somewhere at some time. It may be this city sprang into existence at the very moment of creation. The Valheru first found it ages ago, exactly as you see it. It is one of the greatest mysteries of the many universes the Valheru have travelled. No one lived here, or we Valheru never found them. Some have come here to abide awhile, but none stay long. This place is never changing, for it stands where there is no true time. It is said the City Forever may be the only truly immortal thing in the universes.' With a sad and rueful note he said, 'A few of the Valheru attempted to destroy it, out of pique. It also may be the only thing impervious to their rage.'

Then a flicker of motion arrested Pug's attention, and suddenly a swarm of creatures leaped from atop a distant building, took wing, and banked in their direction. He pointed toward them and Tomas said, 'It seems we are expected.'

The creatures came speeding at them, larger red versions of the elemental beings that Pug had destroyed on the shores of the Great Star Lake the year before. They were man-shaped, and their large crimson bat wings beat the wind as they sped toward the two dragon riders. Calmly Pug said, 'Should we land?'

'This is but the first test. It will amount to little.'

Ryath screamed a battle clarion and the demon host recoiled, then dived at them. On the first pass, Tomas's golden blade arced outward and two creatures fell in screaming agony to the stones below as his sword severed batlike wings. Pug cast blue energies which danced from creature to creature, causing them to contort in pain as they fell, unable to fly. As each struck the ground, it vanished in green flame and silver sparks. Ryath unleashed a blast of fire, and all those within the blast were withered to ash. In moments the creatures were gone.

Now the dragon turned and flew toward a sinister building of black stone, squatting like some brooding malignancy in the midst of beauty. Tomas said, 'Someone makes it painfully obvious where we must hie to. It will clearly be a trap.'

Pug said, 'Will we need to protect Ryath?'

The dragon snorted, but Tomas said, 'Only against the most powerful magic and should that come to pass, we shall be dead and she may flee back to the real universe. Do you hear?'

I hear and understand, answered the dragon.

They swooped down over a brick courtyard and the dragon circled. Tomas used his power to lift himself and Pug from Ryath's back and lower them to the stones. 'Return to the fountains and rest. The water is sweet and the surroundings soothing. Should anything go amiss, depart as you will. If we need you, here or upon Midkemia, you'll hear my call.'

I will answer, Tomas.

The dragon departed and Tomas turned to Pug. 'Come, we should find an interesting reception ahead.'

Pug looked at his boyhood friend. 'Even as a child, your view of the interesting was somewhat broader than mine. Still, there is no choice. Will we find Macros within?'

'Probably not, for this is where we have been brought. I doubt the Enemy would make it easy for us.'

They entered the only door to the vast black building, and the moment they were both beyond the portal, a vast stone door descended, blocking their retreat. Tomas looked back with amusement. 'So much for an easy retreat.'

Pug measured the stone. 'I can deal with this if needs be, but it will take time.'

Tomas nodded. 'I thought as much. Let us go on.'

They moved down a long corridor, and Pug created a light, which glowed brightly in a circle about them. The walls were without features, smooth and unmarked, leading only in one direction. The floor seemed fashioned of the same material.

The end of the corridor produced a single door without markings or means to open. Pug studied it and invoked a spell. With a grinding note of protest the door rose upward, permitting them to pass. They entered a vast hall, with doors in a circle. As they entered, those doors flew open and a horde of creatures came tumbling out, snarling and screeching. Apes with the heads of eagles, giant cats with turtle shells, serpents with arms and legs, men with extra arms – an army of horrors came pouring forth. Tomas drew his sword, raised his shield, and shouted, 'Make ready, Pug.'

Pug incanted and a ring of crimson flames exploded upward about them, engulfing the first rank of creatures, who exploded in searing hot silver flashes. Many of the creatures held back, but those that could leap or fly cleared the top of the flames, to meet destruction from Tomas's golden sword. As he struck them, they vanished in a shower of glowing silver sparkles, accompanied by a stench of rotting decay. The press of creatures continued, with more and more coming from the doors. As they pressed forward, those before them were pushed into Pug's mystic flames and exploded in brilliance for an instant before vanishing. Pug said, 'There seems no end of them.'

Tomas nodded as he cut down a giant rat with eagle's wings. 'Can you close the portals?'

Pug worked magic, and a loud wail of grinding metal and stone filled the chamber as the doors to the hall were forced closed. Creatures seeking to push through were crushed between door and wall, dying with loud piteous cries, shrieks, and hootings. Tomas dispatched all the monsters that had cleared the flames, and for a moment he and Pug stood alone within the circle of fire.

Tomas panted slightly. 'This is irritating.'

Pug said, 'I can finish this.' The burning circle began to expand outward, and each creature it touched died. Soon it pressed to the very walls of the hall, and as the last creature died in an explosion and shriek, the flames winked out of existence. Pug looked about. 'Each door holds dozens of those beasts behind. Which way do you think?'

Tomas said, 'I think down.'

Pug reached out and Tomas slung his shield over his back. He took Pug's hand while still gripping his sword. Another incantation was mouthed, and Tomas saw his friend becoming transparent. He looked down and saw he could view the floor through his own body. Pug spoke and sounded distant. 'Do not release my hand until I say, or it will be difficult to get you back.'

Then Tomas saw the floor rise, or rather they were sinking. Darkness engulfed them as they passed down into the rock. After a long time it was light again as they entered another chamber. Something sped through the air, and Tomas felt pain erupt in his side. He looked down and saw a warrior standing below, a thing of powerful shoulders with a boar's head, wearing gaudy blue plate armour on back and chest. The creature bellowed, spittle dripping from long tusks, as he swung a wicked looking double-bladed axe at Tomas, who barely managed to turn it with his own blade. Pug shouted, 'Let go!'

Tomas released Pug's hand and instantly was solid again. He fell to the floor, landing lightly before the man-boar as the creature brought his axe crashing down. Tomas parried again, and retreated, seeking to free his shield. Pug landed upon his feet and began incanting a spell. The boar thing moved rapidly for something so large, and Tomas could only just defend. Then the Valheru countered a blow with a parry and a thrust and the thing was wounded. It backed away, bellowing in anger.

Pug sent forth a slowly expanding rope of pulsing smoke, which moved like a snake. It travelled only a few feet in the first several seconds, but began picking up speed. Then, like a striking cobra, the smoke lashed out and hit the boar thing in the legs. Instantly the smoke became solid, encasing the creature in boots as heavy as rock. The thing bellowed in rage as it tried to move. With no ability to retreat, the man-boar was quickly dispatched by Tomas. Tomas cleaned off his blade. 'Thank you for the help. It was annoying me.'

Pug smiled, seeing that his boyhood friend still hadn't changed in some ways. He knew Tomas would have dispatched the creature eventually, but there was no point in wasting time.

Tomas winced as he examined his side. 'That axe had some unexpected mystic power to strike while we were insubstantial.'

'Rare, but not unheard of,' agreed Pug. Tomas closed his eyes and Pug saw the wound begin to heal. First blood ceased flowing and then the skin gathered itself together. A puckered red scar showed. That began to fade, until unbroken skin was shown. Soon even the golden chain and white tabard were mended. Pug was impressed.

He glanced about, feeling discomforted. 'This seems too easy. For all the fury and noise, these traps are pitiful.'

Tomas patted his side. 'Not all that pitiful, but in general, I agree.

I think we are supposed to become overbold and fall prey to incaution.'

'Then let us be wary.'

'Now, where next?'

Pug looked about. The chamber was carved from stone, without any apparent purpose except to provide a meeting place for several tunnels. Where they led was unknown. Pug sat upon a large rock. 'I will send out my sight.' He closed his eyes and another of the strange whitish spheres appeared above his head, spinning rapidly. Then suddenly it was off down one of the tunnels. In a few moments it was back, then down another. After almost an hour Pug recalled the device, and with a wave of his hand it vanished. He opened his eyes. 'The tunnels all lead back upon themselves and empty out here.'

'This is an isolated place?'

Pug got to his feet. 'A labyrinth. A trap for us, no more. Again we must go down.'

They gripped hands and once more Pug allowed them to pass through the solid rock. For what seemed a very long time they moved downward in darkness. Then they were floating just below the roof of a vast cavern. Below and some distance away, a huge lake was surrounded on all sides by a ring of fire, which lit the cavern in a red-orange glow. Beyond the fire, a boat rocked at the edge of the shore, a clear invitation. In the centre of the lake they could see an island, upon the shores of which a host of human-shaped beings waited, all in battle dress. They surrounded a single tower, with but one door on the ground floor and a single window at the top.

Pug lowered them to the ground and made them solid again. Tomas looked at the burning circle and said, 'I expect we're supposed to battle through the fire, take the boat, and evade whatever lurks below the water, then defeat all those warriors just to reach the tower.'

'That looks like what we're supposed to do,' said Pug, sounding tired. He walked to the edge of the fire, and said, 'But I think not.' Pug waved his hand in a circular motion, then repeated the gesture a second time. The air began to stir in the cavern, following the circle described by Pug's hand, moving along the curve of the vast stone dome above their heads. At first it was a simple gust, a breeze with some life, then quickly a zephyr. Again Pug motioned. Rapidly the wind picked up tempo, and the flames began to dance, illuminating the cavern in mad lights and flickering shadows. Another gesture from Pug and the wind blew faster and harsher until the fire was being blown backward. Tomas watched, able to stand against the pressure of the air without difficulty. The blaze began to sputter and lapse, as if it could not keep burning before the press of wind. Pug made a larger, broader circular motion with his arm, almost spinning himself about with the furious gesture. The water foamed as whitecaps appeared upon the lake. Wind-whipped water blew high into the air as spindrift leaped in capering dance and the water ran up the shores of the island. Swelling waves rolled, and soon the boat was overturned and sank below the surface, the fire hissing into nothing as the surf swept over the banks. Pug shouted a word, and a clear white light illuminated the cavern in place of the red fire glow. Now Pug spun his arm about like a child playing a game, imitating a gale-driven windmill. Within minutes the warriors upon the island were staggering back under the force of the wind, unable to keep their footing. One's boot touched the water and something green and leathery rose up and seized the warrior's leg. The screaming fighter was dragged below the water. Again and again this scene was repeated as more and more of the warriors were forced into the water, to be taken by the denizens of the lake. Then, as the windstorm reached a crescendo of fury, shrieking in their ears, Pug and Tomas saw the last figure upon the island stagger backward into the water, to be seized by whatever lay below the frothy surface of the lake. With a clap of his hands, Pug halted the wind and said, 'Come.'

Tomas used his ability to fly them over the water's surface to the door of the tower. They pushed it open and entered.

Pug and Tomas spent a full five minutes discussing what they were likely to discover at the top of the tower. The stairway leading upward was narrow enough so that it could be climbed only single file as it wound along the inside wall of the tower. At last Pug said, 'Well, we are as ready as we are ever likely to be. There's nothing to do but go up.' He followed his friend as the white-and-gold clad warrior mounted the steps. Near the top, Pug glanced down and discovered it a fair fall to the stones below as Tomas reached the trapdoor at the top.

Tomas pushed open the door and vanished upward through the opening. Pug followed. There was a single room atop the tower, a simple setting of a bed, a chair, and a window. Sitting on the chair was a man, wearing a brown robe cinched at the waist by a whipcord belt. He sat reading a book, which he closed as Pug joined Tomas. Slowly he smiled.

Pug said, 'Macros.'

Tomas said, 'We've come to take you back.'

The sorcerer stood, weakly, as if injured or tired. He faltered as he stepped toward the pair. He staggered. Pug moved forward to catch him, but Tomas was faster. He got his arm about Macros's waist.

Then the sorcerer bellowed an alien sound, as if a roar were being heard through a distant windstorm. His arm contracted, gripping Tomas in a rib shattering hug as the trapdoor slammed shut. For a moment Tomas threw back his head and screamed in agony, then Macros threw him with stunning force against the wall. Pug froze an instant and began to mouth an incantation, but the sorcerer was too quick in moving toward him. The brown-clad figure reached out, picked up Pug with ease, and threw him against the opposite wall. Pug hit with a bone-jarring impact, his head striking stone, and fell hard to the floor. He slumped down, obviously dazed.

Tomas was up, his sword drawn when Macros spun. Then in an instant the sorcerer was gone and a creature of nightmarish aspect stood poised for attack. In outline only was it seen, seven feet high and easily twice Tomas's weight, with large feathered wings extending outward. As it moved, a vague hint of horns upon the head and large upswept ears could be seen. A featureless charcoal mask regarded the Valheru with ruby glowing eyes. Fully cloaked in smoky darkness, it had only a red-orange glow showing through the eyes and mouth, as if revealing some inner fire. Otherwise it was a thing of ebon shadow, each detail of face and form only a suggestion. Tomas struck outward with his sword, and the blade passed through the creature without apparent harm. Tomas retreated as the creature advanced.

'Puny thing,' came a whispering voice, a distant echo caught upon mocking breezes. 'Did you think that which opposes you did not prepare fully for your destruction?'

Tomas crouched, sword at the ready. Narrowed eyes under the golden helm regarded the thing as he said, 'What manner of creature are you?'

The whispering voice said, 'I, warrior? I am a child of the void, brother to the wraith and spectre. I am a Master of the dread.' With startling quickness, it reached out and seized Tomas's shield, crushing it with a single twist and ripping it away from him. Tomas swung in answer, but it reached up and gripped his sword arm at the wrist. Tomas howled in pain. 'I am summoned here to end your existence,' said the shadowy thing. Then with ease it yanked and tore Tomas's arm from his shoulder. With a shower of blood, Tomas fell to the stones, screaming in agony.

The thing said, 'I am disappointed. I was warned you were to be feared. But you are as nothing.'

Tomas's face was white and drenched in perspiration, his eyes wide with pain and terror. 'Who . . .' he gasped. 'Who warned you?'

'Those who know your nature, man-thing.' The dread stood holding Tomas's arm and sword. 'They even understood how you would come here, rather than seek the sorcerer's true prison.'

'Where is he?' gasped Tomas, seeming on the verge of fainting.

With a whisper of evil the thing said, 'You have failed.'

Evidently near collapse, Tomas forced himself alert, almost snarling when he spoke. 'Then you don't know. For all your posturing you are nothing but a servant. You know nothing but what the Enemy tells you.' With contempt, he spat, 'Slave.'

With a muted howl of glee, the dread spoke. 'I stand high. I know where the sorcerous one is hidden. He abides where you should have expected: at that place most unlikely to be a prison, therefore the most likely place. He lives in the Garden.'

Suddenly Tomas jumped to his feet, grinning. The thing faltered, for the arm it was holding faded into insubstantiality as it reappeared upon Tomas's body, while the shield untwisted itself with metallic complaint and sped across the room to rest again upon his left arm. The thing moved toward Tomas, but the warrior in white slashed out with his sword with blinding quickness and this time the blade bit with fury, exploding on contact with a spray of golden sparks and a loud hiss. Bitter smoke came from the contact, and the creature shrieked its muted cry of pain. 'It seems I am not the only one given to arrogant presumption,' said Tomas as he drove the thing back with a fury of blows. 'Nor are your masters the only ones capable of casting illusions. Foolish thing, don't you know that it was I along with my brethren who cast you and yours from this universe? Do you think that I, Tomas called Ashen-Shugar, fear such as you? I, who once vanquished the Dreadlords?'

The thing cowered in terror and anger, its cries distant echoes. Then, with a musical tinkling, glowing clear crystalline gems erupted in the air about the creature. Each elongated rapidly, forming a latticework of transparent bars around the creature. Tomas grinned as Pug finished the mystic cage about the night black being. The dread lashed out and sounded a muted howl of agony as it touched the transparent bars. Pug got up from where he had feigned unconsciousness and came to stand next to the creature, which attempted to reach between the glass-like bars, but recoiled instantly it touched one. It shrieked and howled, its alien voice an odd raucous whispering. 'What is this thing?' asked Pug.

'A Dreadmaster, one of the Unliving. A thing whose nature is alien even to the essence of our being. It comes from a strange universe at the farthest reaches of time and space, one that only a few beings can breach and survive. It eats the very substance of life, as do all its kind when they enter this universe. It will wither grass should it step upon it. It is a creature of animated destruction, second in power only to the Dreadlords, who are beings even the Valheru are cautious of. That this thing was even brought to the City Forever shows that the Enemy and Murmandamus have callous regard for the potential destruction they might unleash.' He paused, a look of concern on his face. 'It also makes me wonder what more is involved with this Enemy than we have understood so far.' He looked at Pug. 'How are you?'

Pug stretched and said, 'I think I broke a rib.'

Tomas nodded. 'It was lucky that was all you broke. Sorry, but I expected to keep it busy.'

Pug shrugged and winced. 'What do we do with it?' He indicated the softly howling creature.

'We could drive it back to its own universe, but that would be time consuming. How long will that cage stand?'

Pug said, 'Normally, centuries. Here, perhaps forever.'

'Good,' said Tomas, starting for the door.

A terrified cry erupted from the thing of blackness. 'No, master!' it shouted. 'Don't leave me here! I will wither for ages before I die! It will be constant pain! Even now I hunger! Release me and I will serve you, master!'

Pug said, 'Can we trust it?'

Tomas said, 'Of course not.'

Pug said, 'I hate to visit torment on anything.'

'You always did have a tender side to your nature,' said Tomas, hurrying down the stairs. Pug came after as shrieks and curses followed them. 'Those beings are the most destructive in the universes,' said Tomas, 'anti-life. Once set free, the common dread are difficult enough to deal with; the Dreadmasters are impossible to control.'

They reached the door and went outside. Tomas said, 'Do you feel up to getting us back to the surface?'

Pug stretched slowly, testing his tender side. 'I'll manage.'

He incanted his spell and, holding Tomas's hand, rose into the air, insubstantial again as they passed the rock ceiling of the cavern. With their departure the only sound in the vast cave was the faint inhuman screams that came from the top of the tower upon the island.

'What is the Garden?' asked Pug.

Tomas said, 'It is a place which is of the city, but apart from it.' He closed his eyes, and shortly after, Ryath descended from the sky. They mounted and Tomas said, 'Ryath, the Garden.'

The dragon beat into the sky and soon they were again speeding over the odd landscape of the City Forever. More alien buildings rolled by beneath them, hinting at functions but not revealing them. In the distance, if distance could be judged in this impossible place, Pug saw seven pillars rising from the city. At first they appeared black, but as they drew closer, Pug could see tiny flecks of light contained within.

Noticing his interest, Tomas said, 'The Star Towers, Pug.' He sent a mental command to Ryath, and the dragon banked, coming very close to one of the pillars, which were arranged in a circle around a mighty, open plaza, easily miles across.

As they passed, Pug was astonished to discover that the pillars were composed of tiny stars, comets, and planets, miniature galaxies swirling within the confines of the pillar, locked in a void as black as true space. Tomas laughed at Pug's astonishment. 'No, I don't know what they are. No one does. It may be art. It may be a tool of understanding.' He paused and added, 'It may be the true universe is contained within those pillars.'

As they flew away, Pug looked back at the Star Towers. 'Another mystery of the City Forever?'

Tomas said, 'Yes, and not even the most spectacular. Look there.' He pointed to the horizon, where a red glow could be seen. As they raced toward it, it resolved into a wall of flames, topped by a heat shimmer that distorted everything seen beyond. As they passed over the flames, waves of scorching heat rose to meet them.

'What was that?'

Tomas said, 'A wall of flames. It runs roughly a mile along a straight line. It has no apparent purpose, no reason, no use. It's simply there.'

They continued their flight until they approached land free of buildings of any sort. The dragon descended toward a green area. As they dropped in altitude, Pug could see a dark circular shape outlined against the grey of rift-space, floating at the edge of the city. 'It is the oddest feature of this very odd place,' said Tomas. 'Had I your discerning nature, I might have thought of the Garden when we first came here. It is a floating place of plants. Assuming Macros's powers could have been neutralized, this is the last place from which he could escape. There are many unexpected treasures hidden throughout the City Forever. Besides gold and other obvious items of wealth, there are alien machines of vast power, arcane items of might, perhaps means to return to true space. But even should means of return to Midkemia exist in the city, Macros can't get there.'

Pug looked down. They were a thousand feet above the city and descending rapidly. Beyond the boundaries of the City Forever, the grey of rift-space could be seen. As they approached the border of the Garden, Pug could see misty falls of water descending from several points along the edge. The garden was surrounded by what Pug could think of only as a moat. But instead of water flowing along the edges of the Garden, there was literally nothing – the void of rift-space.

They passed above the edge of the Garden, and Pug could see that somehow a large circle of land floated beside the city. Atop this circle of earth a garden of lush vegetation sat, fully covering every inch of the surface. It brimmed with meandering streams, which spilled over the edge. Fruit trees of every description could be seen. Pug said, 'This is indeed a most improbable place.'

Tomas indicated a stone artifact. 'A bridge should stand there.' At once Pug could see that a span had indeed once arched above the moat. It had been shattered, leaving a stone foundation on the ground. Across the moat, the twin of that foundation squatted. 'If this place once existed upon some real world, then whoever or whatever brought it here neglected to include the river that ran around the Garden. With the bridges destroyed, there's no way to leave the Garden.'

They began a search, skimming over the trees. Not only the

varieties known to Pug from Midkemia, but also many he knew from Kelewan were planted there, along with a host of bowers from other worlds, never seen before. They flew past one stand of large tubular plants that began a haunting fluting, almost a musical sound, in the wind from the dragon's wings. They sped above a wine coloured stand of flowers that exploded in white, as seed pods were thrown skyward to drift upon the breeze of their passing. And as Tomas had predicted, other bridges along the perimeter of the Garden were also shattered.

Small animals could be seen scurrying below the brush, hiding from the potential predator that flew above. Then another shape appeared in the heavens, heading toward them.

Faster than an arrow's flight, something hurtled through the sky at them. In the instant before it closed, Ryath bellowed a bone wrenching battle cry. It was answered.

A giant black dragon attacked, claws extended, head craning forward with sheets of fire exploding from its maw. Tomas erected a barrier that prevented Pug and himself from being harmed by the flame.

Ryath answered the attack and the two creatures joined in battle. They grappled with claw and fang as they hovered above the garden. Tomas slashed out with his blade, but could not reach the other dragon. 'This is an ancient beast,' shouted Tomas. 'His kind no longer exist upon Midkemia. No greater black has lived there in ages.'

'Where did it come from?' shouted Pug, but Tomas seemed unable to hear the question. Pug felt the buffeting of the black's wings, but Tomas's spellcraft was sufficient to keep them both safely seated. They would have difficulty only should Ryath not win the contest, for while Pug thought he had some idea of how the beast flew between worlds, he didn't wish to have to put those theories into practice. If Ryath fell, they might be stranded here.

But the golden dragon was equal in might to the black and Tomas punished the black every time it came close enough to be struck. Pug incanted and launched an attack of his own. As crackling energies struck the enemy dragon, the beast screamed in rage and pain, throwing back its head. Ryath seized the opening and bit upon the black's neck, bringing claws up to rip at the less protected belly. The golden dragon's fangs could only dent the heavy scales of the neck, not break them, but the claws were doing considerable damage to the black's underside. The battle carried the two mighty dragons away from the heart of the Garden, until they hovered near the moat.

Now the black sought to escape, but Ryath's jaws held tight. Pug and Tomas felt the gold falter and begin to be dragged down. Then suddenly they were moving upward again. The black had collapsed, ceasing its hovering. The sudden added weight had pulled Ryath down, but she had released in time to prevent them all from being dragged downward.

Pug watched as the black fell past the edge of the Garden, to vanish into the moat between it and the city. As he watched, the black dragon continued to fall, below the city, until at last it was simply a spot of black against the grey, then at last gone from sight. Pug heard Tomas say, 'You fought well, Ryath. I have never ridden one so accomplished, even the mighty Shuruga.'

Pug felt the beaming pride the dragon projected as she said, *Thou art fairly spoken, Tomas. I thank thee for thy words. But that one was an ancient male, one less mighty than I, so it was less a contest than it appeared. Had thou and Pug not crouched upon my back, I would have been less cautious. Still, thine aid and Pug's counted much.*

They circled above the island in the sky and began their search again. It was a large place, and the foliage was dense, but at last Pug pointed and shouted, 'Tomas!'

Tomas followed his friend's direction and there, in the centre of a clearing, a figure jumped up and down, waving his arms above his head. They waved back as Tomas instructed the dragon to descend. The figure staggered back, covering his eyes from the wind the huge wings caused. He was holding a staff and wore the familiar brown homespun. It was Macros. He continued to wave at them as they came to land.

His face registered resignation as the dragon touched ground.

There was an odd, strangely quiet moment, and they could hear him sigh. Then he said, 'I wish you hadn't done that.'

The universe collapsed and came crashing down upon them.

It felt as if the ground had fallen out from under them. Pug staggered a moment, then righted himself and saw Tomas doing the same. Macros leaned upon his staff, looking about, then sat down upon a rock. The falling sensation slowed, then ceased, but the sky above changed, as the grey of rift-space was replaced by a dazzling display of stars in an inky void. Macros said, 'You should do something about the air above this island, Pug. In a moment we'll not have it.'

Pug didn't hesitate, but incanted quickly and closed his eyes. Above them the others could see a faint glowing canopy come into existence. Pug opened his eyes again.

Macros said, 'Well, you couldn't have known.' Then his eyes narrowed and his voice rose in anger. 'But you should have been clever enough to have anticipated this trap!'

Pug and Tomas suddenly both felt such guilt as they had when boys, being reprimanded by Tomas's father for some failing in the kitchen. Pug shrugged off the feeling and said, 'We thought it all right, seeing you waving to us.'

Macros closed his eyes and leaned his head against the staff a moment, then heaved a deep sigh. 'One of the problems with being my age is you look at everyone who is younger as children, and when *everyone* else around you is younger, it means you live in a universe of children. So you tend to scold more than is proper.' He shook his head. 'I am sorry to be so short with you. I was trying to warn you off. If you'd thought to use one of the abilities you learned from the eldar, we could have spoken despite the noise of the dragon. Then Tomas could have lifted me up to the dragon, and we wouldn't be in this mess.'

Pug and Tomas exchanged guilty glances again. Then Macros said, 'Still, there's nothing to be done, and no gain from recriminations. At least you got here on time.'

Tomas's eyes narrowed. 'On time? You knew we were coming?'

Pug said, 'Your message to Kulgan and me said you could no longer read the future.'

Macros smiled. 'I lied.'

Pug and Tomas were both mute in astonishment. Macros stood up and began to pace. 'The truth is when I penned my last missive to you, I could see the future, but now I really can't anymore. I lost the ability to know what was to happen when my powers were stripped away.'

'Your powers are gone?' said Pug, understanding at once what a staggering loss that would be to Macros. Above all others, Macros was the master of magic arts, and Pug could only imagine what it would feel like to be suddenly stripped of that which gave definition to your being, your existence and nature. A magician without magic was a bird without wings. Pug locked eyes with Macros for a moment, and they both knew there was a bond of understanding.

In a lighter tone, Macros said, 'Those that put me here couldn't destroy me – I'm still a tough old walnut – but they could neutralize me. Now I am powerless.' He pointed to his head. 'But I've my knowledge and you've the power. I can guide you like no other in the universe, Pug.' He took a deep breath. 'I can gauge the situation based on superior information to that which you presently possess. I know more of what faces us than anyone in the universe, save the gods. I can help.'

'How did you come to this place?' asked Pug.

Macros motioned for them to sit and they did. To Ryath the mage said, 'Daughter of Rhuagh, there is game, though scant, upon this island of plants. If you are clever, you shall not starve.'

The dragon said, 'I shall hunt.'

''Ware the limit of the protective shell I've erected about the Garden,' warned Pug.

'I shall,' answered the dragon as she took wing.

Macros looked at the pair and said, 'When you and I closed the rift, Pug, you directed shattering energies for my use. As a by-product of that business, I was suddenly a beacon in the black to that which strove to pierce the barrier between worlds.'

'The Enemy,' said Pug.

Macros nodded. 'I was seized and a battle ensued. Fortunately, as powerful as what I face is, I am . . . was not without powers of my own.'

Pug said, 'I remember watching you, in the vision upon the Tower of Testing, turning aside the warped rift that threatened to allow the Enemy to regain that universe.'

Macros shrugged. 'You live long enough, you learn a few things. And I may be unkillable.' The last was said with a note of regret. 'In any event, we battled for some time. How long I cannot judge, for, as you've no doubt noticed, time has little meaning between worlds.

'But at last I was forced to take a stand here in the Garden, and my powers were limited. I could not quite reach the city, for there I have means to augment some of my powers with clever devices. So, we battled to a standstill, until my powers were stripped from me and the trap was set. Then the Enemy destroyed the bridges and left. So I was forced to wait until you arrived.'

'Then why didn't you say something in your last message?' asked Pug. 'We could have come sooner.'

'I couldn't have you two coming after me before it was time. Tomas, you needed to come to terms with yourself, and, Pug, you needed the training only the eldar could give. And I've used the time to some purpose. I've healed some wounds and' – he pointed to his staff – 'I've even taken up wood carving. Though I don't recommend using rocks as tools. No, everything had to move at its proper pace. Now you are fit weapons for the coming battle.' He looked about. 'If we can manage to escape this trap.'

Pug regarded the glowing shell above their heads. Through it they could see the stars, but there was something odd in the way they appeared, as if they flickered in odd rhythms. 'What sort of trap have we encountered?'

'The most clever sort,' said Macros. 'A time trap. The moment you set foot upon the Garden, it was activated. Those who set it are sending us backward in time, at the rate of one day's movement backward for each true day's passing. Right about now, you two are sitting upon the dragon looking for me, I should think. In about five minutes, you'll be battling the black dragon. So on and so forth.'

Tomas said, 'What must we do?'

Macros seemed amused. 'Do? At present, we are isolated and rendered helpless, for those who oppose us know we did not defeat them in the past, for nature puts limits on such paradox, so our only hope is to break free somehow and return to our proper time . . . before it is too late.'

'How do we do that?' asked Pug.

Sitting again upon the rock, Macros rubbed his beard. 'That's the problem. I don't know, Pug. I just don't know.'

• CHAPTER TWELVE •

Messengers

*A*RUTHA WATCHED THE HORIZON.

Companies of horsemen galloped toward the gate, while behind them the sky was thick with dust. Murmandamus's army was marching on Armengar. The last of those coming from the kraals and steadings were reaching the gates, with herds of cattle and sheep, wagons loaded with crops, all lumbering into the city. With the decline in population over the years there was ample housing for everyone, even space for livestock.

For three days Guy, Amos, Armand de Sevigny, and the other commanders had been leading skirmish parties to slow the advancing columns while those called to Armengar reached the city. Arutha and the others had ridden out with them from time to time, lending aid when possible.

At Arutha's side, Baru and Roald watched as the last company of horsemen to quit the field before Murmandamus's host came thundering out of the dust. Baru said, 'The Protector.'

'One-eye's cutting it close this time,' said Roald. Behind the dashing horsemen, goblins on foot and moredhel cavalry followed closely. The dark elves quickly left their goblin allies behind as they chased Guy's company. But just as they overtook the last rider, archers from another company wheeled and began shooting over Guy's men, raining arrows down upon the moredhel. They broke and retreated and both Armengarian companies were again dashing for the gate.

Arutha spoke quietly. 'Martin was with them.'

Jimmy and Locklear came hurrying along, Amos a short distance behind. The former sea captain said, 'De Sevigny says that if anyone is going to make the run to Yabon, they have to leave tonight. After that, all the patrols in the hills will fall back to the redoubts upon the cliff tops. By midday tomorrow there will be only Dark Brothers and goblins in the hills out there.'

Arutha had at last agreed with Baru's plan to carry word south. 'All right, but I want some last words with Guy before we send anyone.'

'If I know One-eye,' said Amos, 'and I do, he'll be standing by your side within minutes of the gate's closing.'

True to Amos's prediction, as soon as the last stragglers were safely through the gates, Guy was up on the wall studying the approaching army.

He signalled and the bridge across the moat was retracted, slowly disappearing into the foundation of the wall. Looking down, Roald said, 'I was wondering how that would be taken care of.'

Guy motioned toward the now unbroken moat. 'A drawbridge can be lowered from the outside. This one has a winch below the gate-house which can be operated only from there.' He said to Arutha, 'We have miscalculated. I thought we'd face only twenty-five thousand or perhaps thirty.'

'How many do you judge?' asked Arutha.

Martin and Briana came up the stairs as Guy said, 'Closer to fifty.'

Arutha looked at his brother as Martin said, 'Yes, I've never seen so many goblins and moredhel, Arutha. They're coming down the slopes and out of the woods like a flood. And that's not all. Mountain trolls, entire companies. And giants.'

Locklear's eyes widened. 'Giants!' He threw Jimmy a black look as the older boy elbowed him quiet.

'How many?' asked Amos.

Guy said, 'It appears several hundred. They stand a good four or five feet above the others. In any event, if they are scattered about in equal numbers, several thousand have come to Murmandamus's banner. Even now the bulk of his army is still in camp north of the Vale of Isbandia, at least a week away. This coming toward us is only the first element. By tonight ten thousand will camp opposite our walls. Within ten days there will be five times as many.'

Arutha looked out over the wall in silence for a while, then said, 'So what you're saying is you cannot hold until reinforcements arrive from Yabon.'

'If this were any normal army, I'd say we could,' answered Guy. 'But past experience tells us Murmandamus will bring some tricks to bear. By my best guess he's allowed only four weeks for sacking the city, otherwise he won't have enough time to cross the mountains. He's got to flood a dozen lesser passes with soldiers, reform his army on the other side and move straight south to Tyr-Sog. He can't move west to Inclindel, for it would take too long to reach the city and dispose of the garrisons before reinforcements arrive from Yabon City and Loriél. He needs to establish himself in the Kingdom quickly, to ready for a spring campaign. If he tarries here even more than a week beyond that schedule, he risks the possibility of being caught in the mountains with early snows. Time is his biggest enemy now.'

Martin said, 'The dwarves!'

Arutha and Guy looked at the Duke of Crydee. Martin said, 'Dolgan and Harthorn moot at Stone Mountain with all their kin. There must be two, three thousand dwarves there.'

Guy said, 'Two thousand dwarven warriors could tip the balance until Vandros's heavy foot can cross the mountains from Yabon. Even if we can only hold up Murmandamus for an additional two weeks,

I think his campaign will have to be aborted. Otherwise it's likely he'll have an army stuck in the Yabon Hills in winter.'

Baru looked from Arutha to Guy. 'We'll leave an hour after nightfall.'

Martin said, 'I'm going with Baru and will travel to Stone Mountain. Dolgan knows me.' With a wry grin he added, 'I've no doubt he'd be loath to miss this fight. Then I'll go to Yabon.'

'Can you reach Stone Mountain in two weeks?' asked Guy.

'It will be difficult but possible,' answered the Hadati. 'A small band, moving quickly . . . yes, it is possible.' No one needed to add 'barely.' All knew it meant better than thirty miles a day.

Roald said, 'I'd like to try as well. Just in case.' He didn't say what, but everyone knew it was against the possibility that either Martin or Baru would not survive.

Arutha had agreed to Martin going with Baru, for the Duke of Crydee was only slightly less gifted travelling through the hills than the Hadati, but the Prince didn't know about Roald. He was about to say no, when Laurie said, 'I'd better go as well. Vandros and his commanders know me, and should the messages be lost, we'll need to do some convincing. Remember, everyone thinks you're dead.'

Arutha's expression darkened. Laurie said, 'We all made it to Moraelin and back, Arutha. We know what it's like to travel in the mountains.'

At last the Prince said, 'I'm not sure it's a good idea, but I don't have a better one.' He looked out at the approaching army. 'I don't know how much I believe in prophecy, but if I am the Bane of Darkness, then I must stay and confront Murmandamus.'

Jimmy and Locklear exchanged glances, but Arutha preempted any volunteering. 'You two will stay. This may not be the healthiest of places in a few days, but it's a damn sight safer than scampering across the mountain ridges through Murmandamus's army at night.'

Guy said to Martin, 'I'll make sure you have some cover for a while. We'll have enough activity until dawn in the ridges behind the city to cover your escape. Our redoubts above the city still control a good portion of the hills behind Armengar. Murmandamus's cutthroats won't be behind us in strength for several days. Let us hope they'll assume everyone is heading toward the city and won't be too careful in looking for those heading in the other direction.'

Martin said, 'We'll leave on foot. Once we're free of patrols, we'll appropriate some horses.' He smiled at Arutha. 'We'll make it.'

Arutha looked at his brother and nodded. Martin took Briana by the arm and left. Arutha knew how much the woman had come to mean to Martin and realized his brother would want to spend his last hours in Armengar with her. Without thinking, Arutha reached out and placed a hand upon Jimmy's shoulder. Jimmy looked up at the Prince then followed his gaze to the plain before the city, where under clouds of rolling dust an army approached.

Martin held Briana closely. They had retired to her quarters for the afternoon. She had left word with her second-in-command she was to be disturbed only in case of grave need. Their lovemaking had been frenzied at first, then gentle. At the last they simply held each other, waiting as the moments slipped by.

Martin at last spoke. 'I must go soon. The others will be gathering at the tunnel door into the hills.'

'Martin,' she whispered.

'What?'

'I just wanted to say your name.' She studied his face. 'Martin.'

He kissed her and tasted the salt of tears upon her lips. She clung to him and said, 'Tell me about tomorrow.'

'Tomorrow?' Martin felt a sudden, unexpected confusion. He had laboured to honour her request in not speaking of the future. His elven-tempered nature offered patience, but his feelings for her demanded commitment. He had put aside the conflict that resulted from this contradiction and had lived for the present. He softly said, 'You said we must not think about tomorrow.'

She shook her head. 'I know, but now I want to.' She closed her eyes and spoke softly. 'I told you once I was a commander, privy to knowledge most of the city are ignorant of. What I know is that we most likely will not hold this city and must needs flee into the hills.' She was silent for a moment, then said, 'Understand, Martin, we know nothing save Armengar. The possibility of living somewhere else never occurred to any here until the Protector came among us. Now I have faint hope. Tell me about tomorrow and the day after and the day after that. Tell me of all the tomorrows. Tell me how it will be.'

He nestled down into the covers, gently cradling her head upon his chest, feeling a hot flush of love and urgency rise up within himself. 'I will get through the mountains, Bree. There is no one who can stop me. I will bring Dolgan and his kin. That old dwarf would take it personally if he weren't invited to this battle. We'll hold Murmandamus at bay and ruin his campaign for a second year. His army will desert and we'll hunt him down like the rabid animal he is and destroy him. Vandros will send his army from Yabon to bolster yours and you'll be safe. You'll have time for your children to be children.'

'And what of us?'

Ignoring the tears that coursed down his cheeks, he said, 'You'll leave Armengar and come to Crydee. You will live there with me and we will be happy.'

She cried, 'I want to believe.'

He gently pushed her away and lifted her chin. Kissing her he said, 'Believe, Bree.' His voice was hoarse with emotion. Never in his life had he thought he could feel such bittersweet happiness, for to discover that his love was returned was a joy shrouded by the shadow of coming madness and destruction.

She studied his face, then closed her eyes. 'I want to remember you this way. Go, Martin. Don't say anything.'

Quickly he rose and dressed. He silently wiped away the tears, turning his feelings inward in the elven fashion as he prepared to face the perils of the trail. With a long last look at her, he quit her chambers. When she heard the door close, she turned her face into the covers and continued to cry softly.

* * *

The patrol moved up toward a canyon. It had ridden out as if making a final sweep of the area before retreating behind the upper redoubts that protected the cliffs above the city. Martin and his three companions crouched down in the shelter of a large rock formation, waiting. They had left the city by the secret passage from the keep that cut through the mountain behind Armengar. Reaching a position along the patrol's route, they hid in a narrow draw a short distance from the canyon. Blutark lay silently, Baru's hand upon his head. The Hadati had discovered the source of Armengarian indifference to his possession of the dog. It was the first time a Beasthound had survived its master in the memory of those of Armengar, and as the dog seemed to accept Baru as his master, no one objected.

Martin whispered, 'Wait.'

Long moments dragged by, then the soft footfalls coming out of the darkness could be heard. A squad of goblins hurried by, moving with no light and little noise, as they shadowed the route of the patrol. Martin waited until they vanished down the ravine, then signalled.

At once Baru and Blutark were up, running across the draw. The Hadati jumped to the upper edge of the shallow wash and reached down as Blutark leaped. With a helping hand from the hillman the huge Beasthound cleared the rim of the small depression. Laurie and Roald sprang for the edge, followed a moment later by Martin. Then Baru was leading them along a naked ridge. For terrible long moments they ran in a crouch, exposed to the view of anyone who might look their way, until they could jump down into a small crevice.

Baru looked one way and the other as his companions landed beside him. With a curt nod he led them away, toward the west and Stone Mountain.

For three days they moved, making cold camp at first light, hiding in a cave or in a blind draw, until nightfall, when they would be off again. Knowing the way helped, for they avoided many of the false trails and other paths which would lead them away from the true route. All about them was proof Murmandamus's army was sweeping the hills, ensuring they were clear of Armengarians. Five times in three days they had lain in hiding as mounted or foot patrols passed by. Each time the fact of their hiding motionless, rather than fleeing for Armengar, saved them. Arutha had been right. The patrols were looking for stragglers heading for the city, not for messengers on the way out. Martin was sure that was not always going to be the case.

The next day Martin's fears were borne out, for a narrow pass, impossible to get around, was guarded by a company of moredhel. A half-dozen hill-clan moredhel sat about a campfire, while two more were posted as guards near their horses. Baru had only narrowly avoided being spotted, the warning from Blutark the only reason he had blundered into view. The Hadati lay back against a boulder, holding up eight fingers. He motioned that two stood atop rocks, and pantomimed looking. He then held up six fingers and squatted, panto-miming eating. Martin nodded. He motioned passing around the position. Baru shook his head.

Martin unlimbered his bow. He took out two arrows, putting one between his teeth as he nocked the other. He held up two fingers and pointed to himself, then pointed to the others and nodded. Baru held up six fingers and motioned he understood.

Martin calmly stepped out into view and let fly with his first arrow. One of the dark elves flew backward from the top of his stone perch, while the other started to jump down. He had an arrow in his chest before he landed.

Baru and the others were already past Martin, weapons drawn. Baru's blade whistled through the air as he slashed out, killing another moredhel before he could close. Blutark had another down on the ground. Roald and Laurie engaged two others, while Martin dropped his bow and pulled his sword.

The fight was furious, as the moredhel quickly recovered from the surprise. But as Martin engaged another, the sound of hoofbeats could be heard. One moredhel had been left without an opponent and he had chosen to leap to his saddle. He spurred his horse and rode past the attackers before he could be prevented. In short order, Martin and his companions had dispatched the other moredhel and the campsite was silent. 'Damn!' Martin swore.

Baru said, 'It could not be helped.'

'If I'd stayed with my bow, I could have brought him down. I was impatient,' he said, as if that was the worst possible error. 'Well, there's nothing for it now, as Amos would say. We've their horses, so let's use them. I don't know if there are more camps beyond, but we'll need speed now, not stealth. That moredhel will be back here shortly with friends.'

'His sort of friends,' Laurie added as he mounted.

Roald and Baru were also quickly up and Martin cut the cinches on the remaining three horses. 'They can have the horses, but they'll have to ride them bareback.'

The others said nothing, but this petty act of vandalism indicated most clearly how angry Martin was with himself over the moredhel's escape. The Duke of Crydee signed, and Baru ordered Blutark out ahead. The dog ran down the trail, and the riders followed quickly after.

The giant turned his head as Martin's arrow struck between the shoulders. The ten-foot-tall creature staggered back as another arrow took him in the neck. His two companions lumbered toward Martin while he fired a third arrow into the stricken giant as he collapsed.

Baru had ordered Blutark to stand, for the huge humanoids wielded swords the size of a human great-sword, easily sufficient to cleave the large dog in two with a single blow. For all their shambling movement, the hairy creatures could lash out with enough speed to make them very dangerous. Baru ducked to a squat as the sword passed over his head, then lashed out with his sword as he leaped past his towering opponent. In a single stroke he hamstrung the creature, causing it to fall. Between them Roald and Laurie had the third giant on the defensive, and they kept him backing up until Martin could kill him with the bow.

When all three lay dead, Laurie and Roald fetched the horses.

Blutark sniffed at the corpses, growling low in his throat. The giants looked roughly manlike, but averaged ten to twelve feet tall. They bulked heavier than a human in proportion and were all uniform with their black hair and beards. The Hadati said, 'The giants are usually aloof from men. What power do you think Murmandamus holds over them?'

Martin shook his head. 'I don't know. I've heard of them, and there are some in the mountains near the Free Cities. But the Natalese Rangers also say they avoid contact with others and do not usually cause trouble. Perhaps they are simply no more immune to the blandishments of wealth and power than other creatures.'

'Legend says they were once men such as you or I, but that something changed them,' commented Baru.

As they mounted, Roald said, 'That I find difficult to believe.'

Martin signalled that the march should resume, and they rode forward, the second encounter with Murmandamus's guards successfully passed.

Blutark's low growl indicated something up the trail. They were reaching that point above the Inclindel Gap where they would be leaving the ridge and heading down into Yabon. They had covered ground as fast as possible for three days. They were bone-weary, drifting off to sleep in the saddle, but they kept on. The horses were losing weight, for the grain carried by the moredhel had run out two days before, and there was no forage to speak of. They would have to let the animals graze when they reached some grasses, but Martin knew that, with the demands placed upon the animals, they would have to have more than grass if they were to finish out the journey. Still, he was thankful for the horses, for the three days of riding had turned their chances from desperate to fair. Two more days of riding and, even should the horses die, they would be certain to reach Stone Mountain in time.

Baru motioned for the others to hold position. He inched forward along the narrow trail, disappearing around a turn. Martin remained motionless, his bow at the ready, while Laurie and Roald held the mounts.

Baru reappeared and motioned them back down the trail. 'Trolls,' he whispered.

'How many?' asked Laurie.

'A full dozen.'

Martin swore. 'Can we get around them?'

'If we leave the horses, and move along the ridges, there may be a way, but I don't know.'

'Try surprise?' asked Roald, knowing what the answer would be.

'Too many,' said Martin. 'Three to one on a narrow trail? Mountain trolls? Even without weapons, they can bite your arm off. No, we'd better try to move around them. Get what you need from the horses and let them loose back up the trail.' Martin silently cursed the change in luck. Leaving the horses now severely reduced their chances of reaching the dwarves in time.

They stripped what gear they needed and Laurie and Roald led the mounts away, while Baru and Martin kept a keen watch for any signs that the trolls might venture up the trail. Suddenly Laurie and Roald were coming back at a run. 'Dark Brothers,' said Roald.

'How close?' asked Martin.

'Too close to stand here and talk about it,' said Roald as he began climbing the ridges alongside the trail. They scampered up the rocks, the dog able to keep pace, and moved toward the downslope side of the crest, keeping the ridges between themselves and the trail, hoping to bypass the trolls.

They reached a point along the trail where it had suddenly doubled back. Baru looked along its length. He signalled and they moved farther down the slope and jumped back down to the trail. Suddenly they heard distant shouting. 'The moredhel have reached the trolls and most likely have our mounts.' He signalled and they started to run down the trail.

They ran until their lungs ached, but behind they could hear the sound of riders. Martin dodged around a tall stand of rocks on one side, and shouted, 'Here!' When the others had stopped, he said, 'Can you get up there and push those rocks down here?'

Baru leaped and clambered up the side of the trail until he crouched behind the precarious outcropping. He motioned for Laurie and Roald to join him.

Riders came into view and the first spurred his mount when he saw Martin and the dog; the other riders appeared an instant later. The Duke of Crydee quietly drew a bead upon the charging lead rider. Martin let fly as the horseman reached the narrowest part of the trail, and a broad-head shaft struck the charging horse in the chest. The animal went down as if poleaxed and the moredhel rider flew forward over the animal's neck, to hit the ground with back-breaking impact. The second horse struck the fallen one and threw another rider. Martin saw that rider dead with another arrow. Behind, confusion reigned as the horses were thrown into a roadblock of dead animals and riders. Two other horses appeared injured, but Martin couldn't be sure. Then Baru shouted. At once Blutark sprang down the trail.

Martin ran after the dog as the sound of rocks coming loose filled the air. With an almost explosive release, the rockslide came down in a torrent. Martin could hear his companions swearing and yelling as a rain of small rocks bounced down the trail beside him.

Martin halted to observe the fall of rock. Dust filled the air, clouding his vision. Then, as the dust began to settle, he could hear Laurie calling his name. He dashed back and began to climb the slide. At the top, hands grabbed him, and through watering eyes he saw Laurie. 'Roald,' he said, pointing.

The mercenary had lost his footing, sliding down the hillside to land on the wrong side of the rocks blocking the road. He sat with his back to the fall, facing up the trail to where the moredhel and trolls regrouped. 'We'll cover for you,' shouted Martin.

Roald turned and with a grim smile shouted, 'Can't. My legs are broken.' He pointed to where his legs stretched out before him, and Martin and Laurie could see the blood beginning to pool. Bone was visible through one trouser leg. He sat with his sword in his lap, daggers held ready to throw. 'Get along. I'll hold them up a few minutes. Get away.'

Baru came up beside Laurie and Martin. 'We must get away,' said the Hadati.

Laurie said, 'We won't leave you!'

Roald shouted, but his eyes were fixed up the trail where vague shapes moved through the dust. 'I always wanted to die a hero. Don't spoil it for me, Laurie. Make up a song. Make up a good one. Now get out of here!'

Baru and Martin pulled Laurie down the rocks, and after a moment, he came willingly. When they reached the place where Blutark waited, Laurie was the first to begin the run down the trail. His face was a grim mask, but his eyes were now dry. Behind they could hear the shouts of the trolls and moredhel, accompanied by cries of pain, and they knew Roald was giving a good account of himself. Then the sounds of struggle ceased.

· CHAPTER THIRTEEN ·

First Blood

*T*RUMPETS SOUNDED.

Armengarian bowmen looked out upon the host that stood ready to assault the city. For six days they had waited for the attack, and now it was under way. Again a goblin trumpeter sounded the call, answered up and down the line by other horns. Drums beat and the order for attack was given. The line of attackers rolled forward, a living wave ready to beat against the walls of Armengar. At first they moved slowly, then as those in the van began to run, the host surged forward. Guy raised his hand and signalled for the catapults to loose their deadly missiles upon those beyond the walls. Stones flew overhead in a high arc, to crash down upon the attackers. Goblins sprang over the bodies of fallen comrades. This was their third assault upon the city since dawn. The first attack had broken before they had reached the wall. The second had carried the attackers to the moat, but there they had broken and run.

They came forward until they were at the limit of the archers' range. Guy ordered the bowmen to fire. A rain of arrows descended upon the goblins and moredhel. Hundreds fell, some dead, others wounded, but all were trampled under the boots of those who came behind.

And still they came forward. Orders were given, and scaling ladders were brought up, to be placed upon heavy platforms thrown across the moat. The ladders were raised only to be pushed back by long poles. In futile effort, the goblins were again and again seeking to climb the ladders, while death rained down from above. Guy signalled and buckets and cauldrons of scalding-hot oil were poured down upon the attackers. The rain of stones, arrows, oil, and flame became too intense for the attackers to survive. Within minutes, trumpets sounded from behind the lines and Murmandamus's forces were in full retreat. Guy ordered a cease-fire.

He looked down at the litter of bodies below the castle, hundreds of dead and wounded. Turning to Amos and Arutha, he said, 'Their commander is without imagination. He wastes lives.'

Amos pointed to where a company of moredhel sat atop a hillock, observing the assault. 'What he does is count our bowmen.'

Guy swore. 'I must be slipping. I didn't see them.'

Arutha said, 'You've gone without sleep for two days. You're tired.'

Guy said, 'And I'm not as young as I used to be.'

Amos laughed. 'You never were.'

Armand de Sevigny came up and reported, 'There's no activity along any sector and the redoubts along the back of the cliff report nothing of note behind us.'

Guy studied the setting sun. 'We'll be done with them for this day. Order the companies down in turn and get them fed. I'll want watches of one in five this night. We're all tired.'

Guy walked along the wall to the stairs leading downward, the others following. Jimmy and Locklear came hurrying up the stairs, wearing leather armour provided by the Armengarians. Arutha said, 'Pulling first watch?'

'Yes,' said Jimmy. 'We traded with a couple of fellows we met.'

Locklear said, 'The girls are on first watch, too.'

Arutha roughly tousled the grinning Locklear's hair and sent him after Jimmy. Reaching the bottom of the stairs, he said, 'We've got a full-blown war raging around us, and he thinks of girls.'

Amos nodded. 'We were that young once, though I'd be hard pressed to remember that far back. Though, it does remind me of this time I was sailing down the lower Keshian delta, near the Dragonlands . . .'

Arutha smiled as they headed for the common kitchen. Some things had not changed and Amos's storytelling was one of them, and at this time that was a welcome fact.

The second day the moredhel and goblin host attacked in the morning and were beaten back without difficulty. Each time only a single thrust was made, then a retreat. By late afternoon it was clear the besiegers were settling down. Near sunset, Arutha and Guy watched from the wall, and Amos came running toward them. 'The lookouts on the top of the citadel see movement across the plains behind these lads. Looks like the bulk of Murmandamus's army's on the march. They should be here by midday tomorrow.'

Guy looked at his two companions. 'It'll take them a full day to get into position. So we gain two more days. But the day after tomorrow, even as dawn comes, he'll hit us with everything he's got.'

The third day passed slowly, while the defenders watched thousands of moredhel soldiers and their allies take position in the camps about the city. After sunset moving lines of torches showed that new companies were still arriving. Throughout the night the sound of marching soldiers filled the dark, and Guy, Amos, Arutha, and Armand repeatedly came to look out upon the sea of campfires across the plain of Armengar.

But the fourth day came and the besieging army only settled in, seemingly willing to bide their time. For the entire day the full army of defenders held to their places upon the walls, waiting for the assault.

Near sundown, Arutha said to Amos, 'You don't think they're going to try that Tsurani trick of attacking at night to divert our attention from sappers?'

Amos shook his head. 'They're not that clever. They wanted Segersen's boys because they don't have engineers. If they've got sappers tunnelling under these walls, I'd like to meet those lads: they'd have to be rock-eating gophers. No, they're up to something, but nothing fancy. I just think his grand bastardhood has no sense he's got trouble here. That arrogant swine-lover plans on overrunning us in one attack. That's what I think.'

Guy listened, but his good eye was fixed upon the mass of enemies who camped upon the plain. At last he said, 'We gain another day for your brother to get to Stone Mountain, Arutha.' Martin and the others had been gone ten days now.

'There is that,' agreed Amos. They watched in silence as the sun set behind the mountains. They remained watching until darkness had completely taken hold, then slowly they left the wall to eat and, if possible, to rest.

At dawn a thunderous cheer erupted from the besieging host, a mixture of shouts, shrieks, the rattle of drums, and the blowing of horns. But instead of the anticipated attack, the van of the army opened and a large platform rolled forward. It was moved by the strength of a dozen giants, the tall hairy creatures pushing it effortlessly. Upon the platform rested a gold encrusted throne, upon which sat a single moredhel dressed in a short white robe. Behind him crouched a figure whose features were hidden by a bulky robe and deep hood. The platform came toward the wall at a leisurely pace.

Guy leaned forward, his arm resting upon the blue stones of the wall, while Arutha stood at his side, arms crossed. Amos shaded his eyes with his hands against the rising sun. The seaman spat over the wall. 'I think we finally meet the grand high royal bastard himself.'

Guy only nodded. A company subcommander came up and said, 'Protector, the enemy takes position opposite all sectors of the wall.'

'Any attempt to reach the mountain redoubts?' Guy indicated the section of cliff behind the citadel.

'Armand reports only weak thrusts toward the outposts in the rocks. They seem unwilling to climb and fight.'

Guy nodded and returned his attention to the field. The platform halted and the figure on the throne stood. By some act of magic his voice filled the air, heard by everyone on the wall as if he were standing only a few feet away. 'O my children,' he said, 'hear my words.' Arutha looked at Amos and Guy in wonder, for this Murmandamus spoke music. The very sounds of his words were etched with the warmth of a lute's melody. 'We share the destiny of tomorrow. Stand in opposition to fate's will and you risk utter destruction. Come, come. Let old differences be put aside.'

He signalled and a company of human riders came trotting up to stand behind him. 'Here, can you see? With me already are those of your kindred who understand our destiny. I welcome all who will willingly serve. With me you shall find a place of greatness. Come, come, let us put aside the past. You are but my misguided children.'

Amos snorted. 'My old pa was a scoundrel, but that's an insult.'

'Come, I welcome any who will join.' His words were sweet, seductive and those on the walls exchanged glances, and unspoken questions.

Guy and Arutha looked about, and du Bas-Tyra said, 'There's art and power in his voice. Look, my own soldiers are thinking maybe they won't have to fight.'

Amos said, 'Ready catapults.'

Arutha stepped beside him. 'Wait!'

'For what?' asked Guy. 'So he can sap the resolve of my army?'

'Stall for time. Time is our ally, and his enemy.'

Murmandamus shouted, 'But those who oppose, those who will not stand aside and who block our march toward destiny, those shall be crushed utterly.'

Now, the tone of his voice carried a warning, a note of menace, and those upon the walls were visited by a feeling of utter futility. 'I give you a choice!' He stretched his arms away from his body, and his short white robe fell away, revealing a body of incredible power, with the purple dragon birthmark clearly seen. He wore only a white loincloth. 'You may have peace and serve in the cause of destiny.' Servants ran forward and quickly fitted his armour to his body: iron plates and greaves, chain and leather; a black helm, with the upswept wings of a dragon on either side. Then the human riders moved away, and behind, a full company of Black Slayers could be seen. They rode forward and assumed positions about Murmandamus. Murmandamus took up a sword and pointed it toward the wall. 'But if you resist, you will be obliterated. Choose!'

Arutha whispered in Guy's ear. At last the Protector shouted back, 'I may not order any to quit the city. We must meet in volksraad. We will decide tonight.'

Murmandamus paused, as if the answer was unexpected. He began to speak but was interrupted by the serpent priest. With a curt gesture he silenced the priest. Turning back toward the wall, Arutha imagined he could see a smile below the eye guards of Murmandamus's black helm. 'I will wait. At first light tomorrow, open the gates of the city and come forth. You will be embraced as returning brethren, o my children.' He signalled and the giants pulled back the platform. In a few moments he had vanished into the huge host.

Guy shook his head. 'The volksraad will not do anything. I will knock down any fool who thinks there is a single shred of truth in that monster's words.'

Amos said, 'Still we gain another day.'

Arutha leaned back against the wall. 'And Martin and the others are one day closer to Stone Mountain.'

Guy remained silent, watching as the morning sun rose, and as the besieging army stood down, returning to camp, but still isolating the city. For hours the Protector and his commanders just watched.

* * *

Torches burned brightly all along the wall. Soldiers kept vigil on all fronts, under the command of Armand de Sevigny. The bulk of the populace assembled in the great market.

Jimmy and Locklear moved through the crowd. They found Krinsta and Bronwynn and moved alongside the girls. Jimmy began to speak, but Krinsta motioned for silence as Guy, Arutha, and Amos stepped onto the platform. With them stood an old man, dressed in a brown robe that appeared as ancient as its wearer. He held an ornate staff, incised with scrollwork and runic symbols along its entire length, in the crook of his arm.

'Who's he?' asked Locklear.

'The Lawkeeper,' whispered Bronwynn. 'Hush.'

The old man raised his free hand and the crowd became silent. 'The volksraad meets. Hear, then, the law. What is spoken is true. What is counselled is heeded. What is decided is the will of the folk.'

Guy raised his hands above his head. He spoke. 'Into my care you have given this city. I am your Protector. I now counsel this: our foe awaits without and seeks to gain with fine-sounding words what he will not gain by strength of arms. Who will speak to his cause?'

A voice from the crowd said, 'Long have the moredhel been the enemies of our blood. What service can we take in their cause?'

Another answered, 'Still, may we not hear again this Murmandamus? He speaks fairly.' All eyes turned toward the Lawkeeper.

The Lawkeeper closed his eyes and was silent for a time. Then he spoke. 'The Law says that the moredhel are beyond the conventions of men. They have no bond with the folk. But in the Fifteenth Year the Protector Bekinsmaan did meet with one called Turanalor, chieftain of the Clan Badger moredhel in the Vale of Isbandia, and a truce during Banapis was established. It lasted for three midsummers. When Turanalor vanished in the Edder Forest, during the Nineteenth Year, his brother, Ulmslascor, became chieftain of Clan Badger. He violated the truce, killing the entire population of Dibria's Kraal.' He seemed to evaluate the traditions as he knew them. 'It is not unprecedented to listen to the words of the moredhel, but caution is urged, for they are treacherous.'

Guy motioned toward Arutha. 'This man you have seen. He is Arutha, a prince of the Kingdom that once you counted enemy. He is now our friend. He is a distant kinsman of mine. He has had dealings with Murmandamus before. He is not of Armengar. Will he be given voice in the volksraad?'

The Lawkeeper raised his hand in question. A chorus of affirmation sounded, and the Lawkeeper indicated the Prince could speak. Arutha stepped forward. 'I have battled against this fiend's minions before.' In simple words he spoke of the Nighthawks, the wounding of Anita, and the journey to Moraelin. He spoke of the moredhel chieftain, Murad, who was slain by Baru. He spoke of the terrors and evils seen, all fashioned by Murmandamus.

When he was done, Amos raised his hands and spoke. 'I came to you sick and wounded. You cared for me, a stranger. Now I am one of you. I speak of this man Arutha. I lived with him, fought beside him, and learned to count him friend for four years. He is without guile. He has a generous heart and his words can be counted as bond. What he has said can only be the truth.'

Guy shouted, 'What can our answer be?'

Swords were lifted and torches brandished as a chorus of shouts echoed across the great market. '*No!*'

Guy waited while the host of Armengar cried out their defiance to Murmandamus. He stood with hands fisted, black gauntlets held high above his head while the sound of Armengar's thousands washed over him. His single eye seemed alight and his face was alive, as if the courage of the city's populace was sweeping away his fatigue and sorrows. To Jimmy, he looked a man renewed.

The Lawkeeper waited until the din died, then said, 'The volksraad has decreed the law. This is the law: no man will quit the city to serve this Murmandamus. Let no man violate the law.'

Guy said, 'Return to your places. Tomorrow the battle begins in earnest.'

The crowd began to disperse and Jimmy said, 'I didn't doubt this would happen for a minute.'

Locklear said, 'Still, that Dark Brother with the beauty mark has a way with words.'

Bronwynn said, 'True, but we have fought the moredhel since the beginning of Armengar. There can be no peace between us.' She looked at Locklear, a serious expression on her pretty face. 'When are you to report?'

He said, 'Jimmy and I have duty at first light.'

She and Krinsta exchanged glances and nods. Bronwynn took Locklear by the hand. 'Come with me.'

'Where?'

'I have a house we may stay in tonight.' Firmly she led him away from his friend, through the evaporating press of the volksraad.

Jimmy glanced at Krinsta. 'He's never—'

She said, 'Neither has Bronwynn. She has decided if she is to die tomorrow, she will at least know one man.'

Jimmy thought a moment. 'Well, at least she's picked a gentle lad. They'll be good to each other.'

Jimmy began to move and was halted by Krinsta's restraining hand. He looked back to find her studying his face in the torchlight. 'I also have not known the pleasures of the bedchamber,' she said.

Jimmy suddenly felt the blood rise in his face. For all the time spent together, Jimmy had never been able to get Krinsta off alone. The four had spent hours together, with some mock passion in dark doorways, but the girls had always managed to keep the two squires under control. And always there had been a sense that it was all somehow play. Now, suddenly, Jimmy knew there was no more play. There was a serious note of approaching doom and a desire to live more intensely, even if only for one night. At last he said, 'I have, but only twice.'

She took his hand. 'I also have a house we may use.' Silently she led Jimmy away. As he followed he was aware of a new feeling inside. He felt a sense of the inevitability of death, for it had been etched in bold relief against this desire to affirm life. And with it came fear. Jimmy squeezed Krinsta's hand tightly as he walked with her.

Couriers raced along the wall, carrying messages. The Armengarian tactic was simple. They waited. As dawn broke, they had seen Murmandamus ride forth, his white horse prancing as it moved back and forth before his assembled host. It was clear he waited for an answer. The only answer he received was silence.

Arutha had convinced Guy to do nothing. Each hour gained before the attack was another hour relief might be coming. If Murmandamus expected the gates to open, or a defiant challenge, he was disappointed, for only the sight of silent lines of Armengarian defenders atop the wall greeted him. At last he rode forward, until he stood at midpoint between his army and the walls. Again by arcane arts his voice could be clearly heard.

'O my reluctant children, why do you hesitate? Have you not taken counsel? Do you not see the folly in opposing? What, then, is your answer?'

Silence was his only reply. Guy had given orders that no one was to speak above a whisper, so that any who were tempted to shout taunts would be halted. There would be no excuse for Murmandamus to order an attack one moment before necessary. Again the horse pranced in a circle. 'I must know!' shrieked Murmandamus. 'If an answer is not forthcoming by the time I return to the lines of my host, then shall death and fire be visited upon you.'

Guy slammed his gloved fist against the walls. 'Damn me if I'll wait five more minutes. Catapults!'

By signal he ordered them fired. A hail of stones the size of melons arced overhead and came crashing down about Murmandamus. The white stallion was struck and collapsed in a bloody shower. Murmandamus rolled free and was struck repeatedly by stones. A wild cheer went up from the walls.

Then it died as Murmandamus regained his feet. Unmarked,

he strode toward the walls, until he was within bow range. 'Spurn my largess and my bounty. Refuse my dominion. Then know destruction!'

Archers fired, but the arrows bounced away from the moredhel as if he were enveloped in some sort of protective shell. He pointed his sword and a strange, dull explosive sound came from it as blasts of scarlet fire shot forth. The first blast erupted along the edge of the walls, and three archers screamed in agony as their very bodies exploded in flames. Others ducked below the wall as blast after blast struck. With the entire force of defenders crouching, no further damage was sustained. With a bellow of rage, Murmandamus turned to face his army and shrieked, 'Destroy them!'

Guy glanced over a crenel and saw the moredhel striding away while his army poured across the plain past him. Like a calm island in a sea of chaos he walked back toward the waiting platform and throne.

Then Guy ordered the war engines loosed, and a rain of destruction began. The assaulting forces faltered, but regained momentum as they approached the walls. The moat had been cluttered with debris and platforms from earlier assaults, and again more platforms were thrown across the water. More scaling ladders were lifted and again attackers swarmed upward.

Giants ran forward, pushing odd-looking boxes, some twenty feet on a side and ten feet high. These rolled on wheeled platforms, with long poles extending to the front and rear, bumping over the rough terrain and fallen bodies. When they were near the wall, some mechanism was triggered, for the poles moved under the boxes, lifting them upward to a level with the top of the wall. Suddenly the fronts of the boxes fell forward, forming a platform, and goblins came swarming out to stand upon the walls of Armengar, while rope ladders were lowered from the boxes so more invaders might climb up. At dozens of points along the wall, this tactic was repeated until hundreds of moredhel, goblins, and trolls fought in bloody hand-to-hand combat with the defenders of the city.

Arutha dodged a blow by a goblin and ran the green-skinned creature through, causing it to fall screaming to the stones of the bailey below. Armengarian children ran forward with drawn daggers and ensured the creature was dead. Everyone who could serve in the battle did so.

The Prince of Krondor ran past Amos, who struggled with a moredhel, each holding the other's wrist. Arutha hit the moredhel in the head with his hilt and continued to move along the wall. The dark elf staggered and Amos grabbed it by the throat and crotch. He lifted and tossed the creature over the wall, knocking down several more attempting to climb a ladder. He and another defender then pushed the ladder away from the wall.

Jimmy and Locklear dashed along the wall, dealing blows where needed to win past attackers who sought to slow them. Reaching the point where Guy had his command, Jimmy said, 'Sir, Armand says there is a second wave of those boxes coming forward.'

Guy turned to look at his defence. The walls were being swept clear of attackers and almost all the ladders had been overturned. 'Poles and burning oil!' he shouted and the command was passed along the wall.

When the second wave of boxes rose to the wall, long poles, pole arms, and spears were used to hold the falling front sections up, though several attempts to do so failed. But those that held were followed by leather bags of oil, which were tossed by strong-armed Armengarians upon the sides of the boxes. They were fired by burning arrows and quickly the boxes were ablaze. Screaming attackers jumped to their death below rather than burn inside the boxes.

Those few companies of moredhel who gained the walls were quickly disposed of, and within an hour of the first assault the retreat sounded from the field.

Arutha looked about and turned to Guy. The Protector was breathing heavily, more from tension than from the fighting. His command position had been heavily defended so he could issue orders along the walls. He looked back at the Prince. 'We were lucky.'

Rubbing his face with his hands, he said, 'Had that fool sent both waves at once, he could have cleared a section before we knew what to do. We'd be retreating through the streets.'

Arutha said, 'Perhaps, but you've a good army here, and they fought well.'

Guy sounded angry. 'Yes, they fought well, and they die damn well, too. The problem is keeping them alive.'

Turning to Jimmy and Locklear and several other couriers, he said, 'Call officers to the forward command post. Ten minutes.' He said to Arutha, 'I'd like you to join us.'

Arutha washed his bloody arms in fresh water provided by an old man pulling a cart full of buckets, and said, 'Of course.'

They left the walls and descended the stairs to a home that had been converted to Guy's forward command post. Within minutes every company commander and Amos and Armand were in his presence.

As soon as everyone was there, Guy said, 'Two things. First, I don't know how many such assaults we can safely repel, or if they have the capacity for another like the last. Had they been a little more intelligent in their use of those damn boxes, we'd be fighting them in the streets now. We might repulse a dozen more such attacks, or the next could finish us. I want the city evacuation begun at once. The first two stages are to be finished by midnight. Horses and provisions to the canyons, and the children made ready. And I want the final two stages ready at my command anytime after. Second, should anything occur, the order of command after me will be Amos Trask, Armand de Sevigny, and Prince Arutha.'

Arutha half expected the Armengarian commanders to protest, but without a word they left to begin the work ordered. Guy interrupted Arutha before he could speak. 'You're a better field commander than any of the city men, Arutha. And if we must quit the city, you may find yourself in charge of one portion or another of the populace. I want it known you are to be obeyed. This way, even if one of the local commanders be with you, your orders will be followed.'

'Why?'

Moving toward the door, Guy said, 'So that perhaps a few more of my people can get to Yabon alive. Come along; just in case, you should know what we're planning here.'

The second major assault began while Guy was showing Arutha the deployment of units in the citadel, against the fall of the city proper. They rushed back to the walls, while old men and women were rolling barrels through the streets. As they reached the outer bailey, Arutha saw dozens of barrels being placed at each corner.

They reached the top of the wall, finding heavy fighting along every foot. Blazing boxes teetered in the breeze a short distance from the walls, but no company of moredhel, goblin, or troll had safely passed the parapets.

Gaining his command post, Guy found Amos supervising the deployment of reserve companies. Without waiting for Guy's request, Amos began relating the situation. 'We've had two dozen more of those box contraptions rolled out. This time we shot them full of fire arrows and heaved the oil after, so they went up farther away from the walls. Our lads are peppering them heavily and we should take their measure this time. His unholy bastardness is fit to be tied.' He pointed to the distant hill where Murmandamus sat. It was difficult to see, but there was a vague hint the moredhel leader was less than pleased with the assault. Arutha wished for Martin's hunter's eye, for he couldn't quite see what Murmandamus was doing.

Then Amos shouted, 'Down! All down!' Arutha crouched below the merlons on the wall as Amos's warning was echoed by others, and again scarlet fire exploded over their heads. Another blast followed, then a third. The distant sound of trumpets could be heard and Arutha chanced a glimpse over the wall. The surrounding army was in retreat, heading back for the safety of their own lines. Guy got up and said, 'Look.'

All below them, incinerated corpses lay, smoking from the blast of Murmandamus's mystic flames. Amos surveyed the damage and said, 'He doesn't take too kindly to defeat, does he?'

Arutha studied the walls. 'He's killed his own soldiers and done little harm to ours. What manner of enemy is this?'

Amos placed his hand upon Arutha's shoulder. 'The worst sort. Insane.'

Smoke covered the field and the defenders almost collapsed from fatigue and lack of clean air. Large constructions of wood and brush, fashioned in such a manner as to allow quick ignition, had been brought forward on wagons and placed before the walls. They had been set afire and had sent up a foul black smoke. A different manner of scaling had been attempted, long ladders set atop platforms. Companies of goblins ran forward carrying these. To the defenders it seemed a wall of black smoke had obscured the air, then suddenly a ladder would loom out of the smoke before them. While they vainly tried to push aside the fixed ladders, attackers swarmed up them. The attackers wore cloths over their mouths and noses, treated with some mixture of oils and herbs, which filtered out the smoke. Several positions along the wall were overrun, but Arutha helped direct reinforcements, which soon pushed the attackers back. Guy had ordered naphtha poured down upon the fires, causing them to explode beyond the ability of the attackers to control. Soon an inferno blazed at the base of the wall, and those upon the platform ladders were left to die in burning agony. When the fire had at last died down, not a ladder was left intact.

The late afternoon sun sank behind the citadel and Guy motioned Arutha to his side. 'I think they're done for the day.'

Arutha said, 'I don't know. Look how they stand.'

Guy saw that the attacking host had not retired to camps as they had before. Now they reformed in attack positions, their commanders moving before them, directing replacements into the line. 'They can't mean to attack at night, can they?'

Amos and Armand had approached. 'Why not?' said Amos. 'The way they're throwing their men at us, it matters little who can see who.

The silly swine-lover doesn't give spit for who lives and who dies. It'll be pure butchery, but they may wear us down.'

Armand surveyed the wall. The wounded and dead were being carried down to infirmaries set up within the city. 'We've lost a total of three hundred twenty soldiers today. We may find the number higher when all the reports are re-checked. That leaves us with a standing force of six thousand two hundred and about twenty five.'

Guy swore. 'If Martin and the others reach Stone Mountain in the fastest possible time and get back here as fast, it will not be soon enough. And it seems our friends out there have something planned for tonight.'

Arutha leaned against the stones of the wall. 'They don't seem to be readying for another assault.'

Guy looked back toward the citadel. The sun was now behind the mountains, but the sky was still bright. Banners and torches could both be seen on the plain before the city. 'They seem to be . . . waiting.'

Guy said, 'Have the companies stand down, but feed them at the forward positions.' He and de Sevigny left without ordering a sharp watch. There was no need.

Arutha remained on the wall with Amos. He felt some strange sense of anticipation, as if the time for him to play his part, whatever that would prove to be, was rapidly approaching. If the ancient prophecy told him by the Ishapians at Sarth was true, he was the Bane of Darkness and it would fall to him to defeat Murmandamus. He rested his chin on his arms, upon the cold stones of the wall. Amos took out a pipe and began filling it with tabac, humming a sea chanty. As they waited, the army beyond was cloaked in darkness.

'Locky, no,' said Bronwynn, pushing the boy away.

Looking confused, the squire said, 'But we're off duty.'

The tired girl said, 'I've been running messages all day, the same as you. I'm hot and sticky, covered with dirt and smoke, and you want to lie with me.'

Locklear's voice betrayed a note of hurt. 'But . . . last night.'

'Was last night,' said the girl gently. 'That was something I wanted, and I thank you for it. But now I'm tired and dirty, and not in the mood.'

Stiffly the boy said, 'Thank you! Was . . . that a favour?' His wounded pride showed and his voice was thick with youthful emotion. 'I love you, Bronwynn. When this is over you must come with me to Krondor. I'm going to be a rich man someday. We can be married.'

Half-impatiently, half-tenderly, the girl said, 'Locky, you speak of things I don't understand. The pleasures of the bedchamber are . . . not promises. Now I must rest before we are called back to duty. Go. Maybe some other time.'

Feeling stung, the boy backed away, his cheeks burning. 'What do you mean, some other time?' Colour rose in his face as he almost shouted. 'You think this is some game, don't you. You think I'm just a boy.' He spoke defiantly.

Bronwynn looked at him with sadness in her eyes. 'Yes, Locky. You're a boy. Now go.'

His temper rising, Locky shouted, 'I'm no damn boy, Bronwynn. You'll see. You're not the only girl in Armengar. I don't need you.' Awkwardly he stepped through the door, slamming it behind him. Tears of humiliation and anger ran down his cheeks. His stomach churned with cold fury and his heart raced. Never in his life had he felt so much confusion and pain. Then he heard Bronwynn shout his name. He hesitated a moment, thinking the girl might want to apologize, or afraid she might simply want him for some errand. Then she screamed.

Locklear pushed open the door and saw the girl clutching her ribs while she awkwardly held a dagger in her hand. Blood poured down her arm and along her side and thigh. Before her crouched a mountain troll, his sword upraised. Locklear's hand flew to his rapier as he shouted, 'Bronwynn!' The troll faltered as the boy leaped toward him, but even as Locklear raised his own weapon, the troll's blade came down.

In blind rage Locklear slashed out, cutting the troll across the back of the neck. The creature staggered and attempted to turn, but the boy ran it through, the point of the rapier finding a place under the arm where no armour protected the creature. The troll shuddered and its sword fell from limp fingers as it collapsed to the floor.

Locklear stabbed it one more time, then was past it to Bronwynn's side. The girl lay in a pool of blood and instantly Locklear knew she was dead. Tears ran down the boy's face as he cradled her in his arms, hugging her close. 'I'm sorry, Bronwynn. I'm sorry I was mad,' he whispered in the dead girl's ear. 'Don't be dead. I'll be your friend. I didn't mean to shout. Damn!' He rocked back and forth as Bronwynn's blood ran down his arms. 'Damn, damn, damn.'

Locklear wept aloud, his pain a hot iron in his stomach and groin, his heart pounding and his muscles knotted. His skin flushed, as if hatred and rage sought to leach through the pores of his skin, and his eyes seemed to burn inside his head, suddenly too hot and dry for tears.

Then the sound of alarm brought him from his private grief. He rose and gently placed the girl upon the bed they had shared the night before. Then he took his rapier and opened the door. He took a deep breath, and something froze inside him, as if mountain ice replaced the burning agony of the moment before.

Before him a woman held a child as a goblin advanced, his sword upraised. Locklear stepped calmly forward and ran the goblin through the side of the neck, twisting his sword savagely, so the creature's head fell from his shoulders. Locklear looked about and saw a brief shimmer in the night air, and suddenly a moredhel warrior appeared before him. Without hesitation Locklear attacked. The moredhel took a wound in the side, but managed to avoid being killed by the boy. Still the wound had been serious and Locklear was a swordsman of above-average skill. And now he had come to command a cold, controlled rage, a disregard for his own safety that made him the most fearful of opponents, one willing to take risks because he didn't

293

care if he lived. With astonishing fury the boy drove the moredhel back to the wall of the building and ran him through.

Locklear spun about, looking for another opponent, and saw another form appear in the street a half block down. The boy ran toward the goblin.

Everywhere in the city, the invaders suddenly appeared. Once the alarm had been sounded, the defenders had dealt with them, but a few goblins and moredhel had joined in force and were now fighting from pockets within the city. As the invasion of magically transported warriors reached its peak, the army outside the walls attacked. Suddenly there was the risk of enough soldiers being pulled from the walls to deal with the teleported soldiers to allow those without to find a point of defence they could breach.

Guy ordered one reinforcement company to the point of heaviest attack upon the wall, and another off the wall to aid those in the city. Hot oil and arrows quickly turned back those at the wall, but the constant appearances within the city continued. Arutha fought off numbing fatigue and watched his father's most bitter rival, wondering how the man found the reserve of strength to carry on. He was a much older man, yet Arutha found himself envying Guy his energy. And the speed with which he made decisions showed a complete understanding of where every unit at his disposal was at any time. Arutha still couldn't bring himself to like this man, but he respected him and, more than he cared to admit, even admired him.

Guy watched the distant hill, the place where Murmandamus oversaw his army. There was a faint flicker of light; after a moment, another; then a third. Arutha followed Guy's gaze and, after witnessing the lights for a time, said, 'That's where they're coming from?'

'I'd bet on it. That witch-king or his snake priest is behind this.'

Arutha said, 'He's too far for even Martin's bow, and I'll wager none of your archers can reach him. Nor can your catapults.'

'The bastard's just out of range.'

Amos came along the wall to say, 'Things seem to be under control, but they keep popping up everywhere. I've a report of three in the citadel, and one appeared in the moat and sank like a stone, now . . . What are you looking at?'

Arutha indicated the hill and Amos watched for a while. 'Our catapults can't reach it. Damn.' Then the old seaman's face split in a grin. 'I've an idea.'

Guy waved toward the bailey, where an astonished looking troll had suddenly appeared, to be overwhelmed by three soldiers. But while he died, another came into existence and dashed away down a street. 'Anything. Sooner or later, they're going to gather into a large enough company to cause serious trouble.'

Amos hurried away, toward a catapult platform. He issued instructions and soon a cauldron was heating. He oversaw the preparations and returned. Leaning upon the wall, he said, 'Anytime now.'

'What?' said Guy.

'The wind will change. Always does this time of night.'

Arutha shook his head. He was tired and suddenly was visited with a funny image. 'Are we going to sail closer, Captain?'

Abruptly a troll was upon the rampart, blinking in confusion. Guy struck it with the back of his fist, knocking it to the cobbles far below. It landed with a thump of finality. 'It seems they have a moment or two of disorientation, which is a damn good thing,' said the Protector. 'Otherwise that one might have had your leg for lunch, Amos.'

Amos stuck a finger in his mouth, then raised it. With a satisfied 'Ah' he shouted, 'Catapult! Fire!'

The mighty war engine uncoiled, throwing its missile with such force as to make it leap upon the wall. Into the dark the missile silently sped.

For a long moment no effect was visible, then shrieks filled the night from the distance. Amos let out a satisfied howl of glee. Arutha watched for a moment and saw no more flashes of light. 'Amos, what did you do?' asked Guy.

'Well, One-eye, it's a trick I learned from your old friends the Keshians. I was in Durbin when a tribe of desertmen had an uprising and decided to take the city. The governor-general, that old fox Hazara-Khan, found the walls being swept with bow fire, so he ordered up hot sand and threw it at them.'

'Hot sand?' said Arutha.

'Yes, you just heat it until it glows red and toss it at them. The wind carries it a fair piece, and if it hasn't cooled too much when it hits – it burns like unholy blazes. Gets in your armour, under your tunic, in your boots, your hair, everywhere. If Murmandamus was looking this way, we might have blinded the impotent son of a poxy rat. Anyway, it'll take his mind off spells for an hour or two.'

Arutha laughed. 'I think only for a time, however.'

Amos took a pipe from his tunic and a taper which he lit from a torch. 'Yes, there's that.' His tone turned serious. 'There is that.'

The three looked out again into the dark, seeking some sign of what would be next.

CHAPTER FOURTEEN

Destruction

*T*HE WIND BLEW DUST ACROSS THE WALL.

Arutha squinted as he watched riders move along the lines of the assembled host, heading for Murmandamus's banner. The attacks had continued unabated for three days before ceasing. Some sort of war council was being held in Murmandamus's camp, or so it seemed to Arutha.

For an hour the conference had been taking place. Arutha considered the situation. The last assaults had been intense, as much as any before. But they had lacked the disquieting element of the sudden appearance by those warriors transported by magic inside the walls. The lack of magic assaults had Arutha puzzled. He speculated there was some compelling reason for Murmandamus not to use his arts again, or some limit on what he was able to do for any length of time. Still, Arutha suspected something was about to break for Murmandamus to be calling all his chieftains together.

Amos wandered along the wall, inspecting the soldiers on duty.

It was late in the day, and already men were relaxing, for it was apparent there would be little chance of attack before morning. The enemy's camp was not standing ready, and it would take hours for them to muster. Amos reached Arutha's side and said, 'So, then, if this was your command, what would you be doing?'

'Had I the men, I'd roll out the bridge, sally forth, and hit them before they could marshal their forces. Murmandamus pitches his command post far too close to the front, and without apparent thought a company of goblins has been moved down the line, leaving an almost clear path to his pavilion. Lead with mounted archers and with luck you could have several of his captains dead before they could organize resistance. By the time they were roused, I'd be back inside the city.'

Amos grinned. 'Well, what a bright lad you are, Highness. If you want, you can come play with us.'

Arutha regarded Amos questioningly, and the seaman inclined his head. Arutha looked past him to the bailey and saw horsemen riding into position before the inner gate of the barbican. 'Come along. I've an extra horse for you.'

Arutha followed Amos down the stairs to the waiting mounts. 'And what if Murmandamus has another magic trick to toss at us?'

'Then we will all die and Guy will be sad for having lost the best company he's had in the last twenty years: me.' Amos mounted. 'You worry too much, lad. Have I told you that?'

Arutha smiled his crooked half-smile as he mounted. Guy, waiting by the gates, said, 'Be doubly careful. If you can hurt them, fine, but no heroic suicide assaults just on the chance to get at Murmandamus. We need you back.'

Amos laughed. 'One-eye, I'm the last candidate for hero you're ever likely to meet.' He signalled and the inner gate was opened. The rumble of the bridge being run out could be heard as the inner gate closed. Suddenly the outer gate swung open and Amos was leading the company out. Quickly outriders took their position on the flanks as the main element of Amos's force advanced upon the besieging army. At first it was as if the enemy didn't understand that a sally was being undertaken, for no alarm was given. They were almost upon the first elements of Murmandamus's army when a trumpet sounded. By the time the goblins and trolls were scrambling for weapons, Amos and his raiders were racing by them.

Arutha rode straight for the hill where Murmandamus's commanders were in conference, three Armengarian archers at his side. He didn't know what drove him, but suddenly he was filled with a need to meet this dark lord. A squad of riders, those closest to the raiders, galloped to intercept the Armengarians with Arutha. Arutha found himself facing a human renegade, who grinned as he slashed at Arutha. Arutha killed him quickly and efficiently. Then the fight was fully joined.

Arutha looked toward the command pavilion and saw Murmandamus standing in plain view, his snake companion at his side. The moredhel leader seemed indifferent to the carnage being visited upon his forces. Several Armengarians attempted to close upon the pavilion, but they were intercepted by renegade and moredhel horsemen. One archer pulled up his mount and coolly sent bow shafts at the pavilion. Having learned the lesson of Murmandamus's invulnerability, he chose other targets. He was quickly joined by another bowman and suddenly two of Murmandamus's chieftains were down, one clearly dead from an arrow in the eye. Another company of foot soldiers ran toward the spot where Arutha laid about with his sword, cutting down goblins, trolls, and moredhel, attempting to protect the archers while they attacked the chieftains. For some endless time the ringing of steel and the pounding of blood in his ears were all Arutha heard. Then Amos shouted, 'Begin the withdrawal!' The cry was taken up by other horsemen, until every raider had heard the call.

Arutha cast a glance past where Amos sat his horse and saw another company of riders was headed toward them. Arutha slashed out with his sword, unseating another renegade, and headed toward Trask. The newly arriving renegades struck Amos's raiders, halting their movement. Then the raiders wheeled as a body and attacked

Murmandamus's cavalry. Slowly the raiders began to fight their way out of the camp, killing everyone who stood between them and escape. A break appeared in the mass around them, a clear path back to the gates. Arutha spurred his mount forward and joined with the others in headlong flight back to the city. He glanced over his shoulder. A company of black-clad riders sped past Murmandamus's pavilion, following in hot pursuit. To Amos he shouted, 'Black Slayers!'

Amos signalled and several riders peeled off to turn and engage the Black Slayers. They charged and met with a ringing clash of steel, and several riders from both sides were unhorsed. Then the melee dissolved as the Armengarians disengaged, while another company of moredhel advanced upon the conflict. Most of the Armengarians who fell regained their saddles, but not all. A full dozen soldiers lay upon the sandy soil of the plain.

The gates were open when Amos's company reached the wall, and they spun in place once inside the barbican. Behind, the rear guard was hurrying, engaged in a running fight with the Black Slayers and other moredhel. A dozen Armengarians sought to escape from more than thirty pursuers.

Amos sat next to Arutha as the Black Slayers cut down a pair of riders. 'Ten,' said Amos, counting the remaining riders. As they rode for the gate, Amos said, 'Nine, eight,' then, 'seven.' Upon the dusty plain a wave of black-armoured riders overwhelmed a half-dozen fleeing soldiers and Amos said, 'Six, five, four.' Then, with a note of anger in his voice, he shouted, 'Close the gate!'

As the gate began to swing shut, Arutha continued his count. 'Three, two . . .' The last two riders from the raiding party were cut down.

Then from above came the sound of catapults launching. A moment later the screams of dying moredhel and horses filled the air. As the inner gates opened, Amos spurred his horse forward and said, 'At least the bastards paid. I saw at least four chieftains down, two clearly dead.' Amos glanced back, as if he could see through the massive gates. 'But why didn't the bastard use magic? That's what I don't fathom. He could have had us, you know?'

Arutha could only nod. He also wondered. He gave his horse to a boy detailed to care for the mounts and hurried up the stairs to Guy's command location. 'Damn me!' greeted him as he joined the Protector.

Several prostrate figures in black armour were rising, in jerky awkward motion, moving back toward their own lines. Quickly their movement smoothed out and they were soon running as fast as if they had been uninjured.

'When you told me of those . . .' began Guy.

'. . . you couldn't believe,' finished Arutha. 'I know. You have to see it to understand.'

'How do you kill them?'

'Fire, magic, or by cutting their hearts out. Otherwise even the pieces find a way to rejoin and they just get stronger by the minute. They are impossible to stop by other means.'

Guy looked out at the retreating Black Slayers. 'I never had your father's fascination for things magic, Arutha, but now I'd give half my duchy – my former duchy – for a single talented magician.'

Arutha considered. 'Something here has me concerned. I know little of these things, but it seems that, for all his powers, Murmandamus does little to truly trouble us. I remember Pug – a magician I know – telling me of some things he has done . . . well, they far outstripped what we've seen so far. I think Pug could pull the gates from the city walls if he'd a mind to do so.'

'I don't understand such things,' admitted Guy.

Amos was standing behind them, having approached at the last. 'Maybe the king of pigs doesn't want his army relying too heavily upon him.' Guy and Arutha both regarded Amos with open curiosity. 'It might be a matter of morale.'

Guy shook his head. 'Somehow I think it more complicated.'

Arutha watched the confusion in the enemy camp. 'Whatever it is, we'll most likely know soon.'

Amos leaned on the wall. 'It's been two weeks since your brother and the others left. If all has gone as planned, Martin's at Stone Mountain today.'

Arutha nodded, 'If all has gone as planned.'

Martin crouched down in the depression, his back tight against wet granite. The scraping sound of boots on the rocks above told him his pursuers were looking for signs of him. He held his bow before him, regarding the broken string. He had another in his pack, but no time to restring. If discovered, he would drop the weapon and pull his sword.

He breathed slowly, attempting to stay calm. He wondered if fate had been kind to Baru and Laurie. Two days before, they had reached what appeared to be the Yabon Hills proper. They had seen no sign of pursuit until today, when, a little after sunrise, they had been overtaken by a patrol of Murmandamus's riders. They had avoided being run down by climbing up into the rocks alongside the trail, but the moredhel had dismounted and followed. By poor chance, Martin and the others were on opposite sides of the trail and Laurie and Baru were forced southward, while Martin ran to the west. He hoped they had enough sense to continue south toward Yabon, and not to attempt to rejoin him. The chase had lasted throughout the day. Martin glanced upward, noting the sun moving behind the mountains. He judged only two more hours of light left. If he could avoid capture until dark, he would be safe.

The sound of boots grew faint and Martin moved. He left the shelter of the rock overhead and scampered along at a half-crouch, half-run, following a rill upward. He judged he was close to Stone Mountain, though he had never come there from the northeast before. But some of the landmarks looked vaguely familiar, and had he not had other concerns to occupy his attentions at this time, he was sure he could easily find the dwarves.

Martin rounded a curve and suddenly a moredhel warrior loomed up before him. Without hesitation Martin lashed out with his bow, striking the dark elf in the head with the heavy yew weapon. The surprised moredhel staggered, and before he could recover, Martin had his sword in hand and the moredhel lay dead.

Martin spun about, seeking signs of the moredhel's companions. In the distance he thought he saw movement but couldn't be sure. He quickly hurried upward then discovered another bend. Peering around the bend, Martin found a half-dozen horses tied. He had somehow managed to double behind the pursuers and stumble across their mounts. Martin ran forward and gained the saddle of one of the horses. He used his sword to cut the reins of the others and slapped them across the flanks with the flat of his blade to drive them off.

He spun his horse and spurred it forward. He could race down the wash and reach the trail. Then he could outrun the moredhel to Stone Mountain.

A dark shape launched itself from atop a rock as Martin rode past, dragging him from the saddle. Martin rolled and came up in a fighter's crouch, his sword out as a moredhel did the same. The two combatants faced each other as the moredhel cried out in his harsh elven dialect to his companions. Martin attacked, but the moredhel was a skilled swordsman and kept Martin at sword's length. Martin knew if he turned to flee, he'd get a blade in the ribs for his troubles, but if he stayed, he'd soon be facing five moredhel. Martin kicked rocks and pebbles at the moredhel, but the warrior was an experienced fighter who moved sideways, avoiding dust in the eyes.

Then the sound of boots pounding over the rocks could be heard from both directions. The moredhel shouted again and was answered from Martin's left, to the south. From the right the sound of armour and boots grew louder. The moredhel's eyes flickered in that direction, and Martin launched his attack. The dark elf barely avoided the blow, getting a slight cut in the arm for his troubles. Martin pushed his slight advantage, and while the moredhel was off balance, he struck out with a risky thrust that left him open for a riposte if he missed. He didn't. The moredhel stiffened and collapsed as Martin pulled his blade free.

Martin didn't hesitate. He leaped for the rocks, seeking high ground before he was overrun from both sides. Moredhel warriors came rushing into view from the southern end of the wash, and one had his sword back, to slash at Martin.

Martin kicked out unexpectedly and the warrior ducked, causing him to mistime his blow. Then, equally unexpectedly, a hand reached down and gripped Martin's tunic.

A powerful pair of arms lifted the Duke of Crydee and dragged him over the lip of the wash. Martin looked up to discover a grinning face, with a thick red beard regarding him. 'Sorry for the rough handling, but things are about to get nasty down there.'

The dwarf pointed past Martin, who turned to see a dozen dwarves dashing down the ravine from the north. The moredhel saw the superior number of dwarven warriors and turned to flee, but the dwarves were upon them before they moved ten yards. The fight was quickly over.

Another dwarf joined the one at Martin's side. The first handed Martin a waterskin. Martin stood and took a drink. He looked down at the pair of dwarves, their being barely five feet, and said, 'Thanks to you.'

'No bother. The Dark Brothers have been poking about here of late, so we keep this area heavily patrolled. As we have guests' – he indicated some dwarves who were climbing up to join them – 'we have no shortage of lads willing to go out and have a bash at them. Usually the cowards run, knowing they're too close to our home, but this time they were a mite slow. Now, if you don't mind me asking, who might you be and what are you doing at Stone Mountain?'

Martin said, 'This is Stone Mountain?'

The dwarf pointed behind Martin and the Duke turned about. Behind him, above the edge of the wash he had crouched in, a stand of trees reared up. Following the woods, he saw they blanketed the sides of a great peak that rose high into the clouds. He had been so intent on the pursuit of the last day, so intent on hiding, that he had seen only the rocks and the gullies. Now he recognized the peak. He was standing with a half day's walk of Stone Mountain.

Martin regarded the assembling dwarves. He removed his right glove and displayed his signet. 'I am Martin, Duke of Crydee. I need to speak with Dolgan.'

The dwarves looked sceptical, as if it was improbable for a lord of the Kingdom to come in this fashion to their halls, but they simply looked to their leader. 'I'm Paxton. My father is Harthorn, Warleader of the Stone Mountain clans, and Chieftain of village Delmoria. Come along, Lord Martin, we'll take you to see the King.'

Martin laughed. 'So he did take the crown.'

Paxton grinned. 'In a manner of speaking. He said he'd take the job of King, after we nagged at him a couple of years, but he won't wear a crown. So it sits in a chest in the long hall. Come along, Your Grace. We can be there by nightfall.'

The dwarves set off, and Martin fell in beside them. He felt safe for the first time in weeks, but now his mind returned to thoughts of his brother and the others at Armengar. How long could they hold? he wondered.

The camp reverberated with a cacophony of drums, trumpets and shouts. From every quarter came the response to the order to marshal. Guy watched the display as the false dawn gave way to the light of morning. He said to Arutha, 'Before the globe of the sun is at noon, they'll hit us with everything they have. Murmandamus may have felt the need to hold back some forces against the invasion of Yabon, but he can't afford even another day's delay. Today they will come in strength.'

Arutha nodded as he watched every company on the field before the city marshal for battle. He had never felt so bone tired. The killing of Murmandamus's captains had thrown the enemy camp into turmoil for two days before order had been restored. Arutha had no idea what bargains had been struck or what promises made, but finally they had come again, three days later.

For a week after, the assaults had continued, and each time more attackers had gained the walls. The last assault of the day before had required the entire force of reserves being thrown into a potential breach to keep the integrity of the wall intact. Another few minutes, and the attackers would have had a position upon the walls to hold, so that more warriors could have scaled ladders in safety, unleashing a potential fatal flood of invaders into the city. Arutha thought, it has been twenty-seven days since Martin had left. Even if help was coming, it would be too late.

Jimmy and Locklear waited close by, ready for messenger duty. Jimmy regarded his young friend. Since Bronwynn's death Locklear had become possessed. He sought out the fighting at every turn, often ignoring instructions to stay behind for courier duty. Three times Jimmy had seen the boy involve himself in combat where he should have avoided it. His skills with the sword and his speed had counted for much, and he had survived, but Jimmy wasn't sure how long Locklear could keep surviving, or even if he really wished to. He had tried to speak to Locklear about the girl, but the younger squire had refused. Jimmy had seen too much death and destruction by the time he had reached sixteen. He had grown callous in many ways. Even when he thought Anita or Arutha dead, he had not withdrawn the way Locklear had. Jimmy wished he understood more of such things, and worried for his friend.

Guy gauged the strength of the army before him and at last, in a quiet voice, said, 'We can't hold them at the wall.'

Arutha said, 'I thought as much.' In the four weeks since Martin's departure, the city had held, the soldiers of Armengar performing beyond even Arutha's most optimistic assessment. They had given all they had, but attrition was at last sapping the army's reserve. Another thousand soldiers had been killed or rendered unable to fight in the last week. Now the defenders were spread out too thinly to deal with the full force of the attackers, and it was clear from the careful way Murmandamus was staging that he indeed planned to throw the full strength of his army at them today in one final, all-out assault. Guy nodded to Amos. The seaman said to Jimmy, 'Carry word to the company commanders: begin the third stage of evacuation now.'

Jimmy nudged Locklear, who seemed almost in a trance, and led his friend off. They ran along the wall, seeking out the company commanders. Arutha watched as a few chosen soldiers left the wall once word was passed. They hurried down the steps to the bailey and began to sprint toward the citadel.

Arutha said, 'What mix did you decide upon?'

Guy said, 'One able-bodied fighter, two armed old men or women, three older children, also armed, and five little ones.' Arutha knew that within minutes dozens of such groups would begin slipping out into the mountains through the long tunnel from the cavern beneath the city. They were to work southward, seeking refuge in Yabon. It was hoped that this way at least some of the children of Armengar might survive. The single soldier would be in command of the party and each would carry orders to protect the children. And the soldiers also had orders to kill them rather than let them be captured by the moredhel.

Slowly the sun rose, moving at a steady pace, unconcerned with the conflict below. When it reached the noon position, still no signal was forthcoming. Guy wondered aloud, 'Why do they wait?'

Nearly a full two hours later, a faint thudding sound carried over the quiet army on the plain, to be barely heard by the defenders. It continued for almost a full half hour, then trumpets sounded along the line of attackers. Then from behind the lines odd figures loomed up against the bright blue sky. They appeared giant black spiders, or something akin. They began moving through the host, slowly, stately. Finally, they cleared the line of attackers, and approached the city. As they came closer, Arutha studied them. Questioning shouts came from along the wall, and Guy said, 'Gods, what are they?'

'Some manner of engine,' replied Arutha. 'Moving siege towers.' They appeared to be gigantic boxes, three or four times the size of the ones raised against the wall the previous week. They rolled on huge wheels, without any apparent motive source, for no giant, slave, or beast of burden pulled or pushed them. They moved under their own power, by some magic means. Their immense wheels thudded loudly when rolling over irregularities in the terrain.

'Catapults!' shouted Guy, and his hand dropped.

Stones hurled overhead, and crashed against the boxes. One was struck in a support, which shattered, causing the thing to teeter, and fall, striking the earth with a resounding crash. At least a hundred dead goblins, moredhel, and humans were thrown clear of the crash.

Arutha said, 'Each one of those things must hold two, three hundred soldiers.'

Guy counted quickly. 'There are nineteen more coming. If one in three gains the walls, that's fifteen hundred attackers on the wall at once. Oil and fire arrows!' he shouted.

The defenders sought to ignite the approaching boxes as they lumbered toward the wall, but something had been applied to the wood, and while the oil burned upon a few of the things, it only scorched and blackened the wood. Screams from within told of some damage done to the attackers by the flames, but the boxes were not halted.

'All reserves to the wall! Archers to the roofs beyond the bailey! Horse companies to their stations!'

Guy's orders were quickly carried out as the defenders awaited the approaching boxes. The magic siege towers filled the morning air with a loud grinding sound as the heavy wheels turned ponderously. The host of Murmandamus's army walked slowly behind the moving towers, keeping a discreet distance, for all defensive fire was directed at the rolling boxes.

Then the first of the boxes reached the wall. The side of the box facing the wall fell forward, as had happened with the smaller ones, and dozens of goblins and moredhel came leaping forward to engage the defenders. Soon there was frenzied combat along every foot of the wall. The attackers came flooding across the plain, behind their magic siege towers. The rear of the box opened as well, with long rope ladders being tossed out, and attackers in the field behind ran forward to clamber up the suddenly accessible entrances to the city. Long leather aprons were lowered from the centre of the boxes, only a foot in front of the ladders, confounding the bow fire directed at those climbing into the boxes. The catapult commanders continued to fire, and many of Murmandamus's soldiers died beneath the rocks, but with the archers ordered to the first row of houses and the other defenders engaged with the attackers from the towers there was no bow fire to harass the host below as they raised scaling ladders against the walls.

Arutha engaged a moredhel who had leaped over the body of a fallen Armengarian soldier, and slashed out, causing the dark elf to stumble backward. The moredhel fell off the parapet to the stones below.

The Prince spun about and saw Guy kill another. The Protector looked about and shouted, 'We can't hold them here! Pass the word to fall back to the citadel!'

Word was passed and suddenly defenders were scrambling away from those gaining the wall from outside. A select company of soldiers held each stairway while their companions fled toward the city. They were all volunteers and all were prepared to die.

Arutha ran across the bailey and saw the last of the defenders on the wall overwhelmed. As he reached the midway point across the large open area, attackers leaped from the stairs and headed for the gate. Suddenly a rain of arrows came from the roofs of the buildings opposite the gate and to the last the attackers died. Then Guy was at Arutha's side, with Amos running past.

'We can hold them off the gatehouse until they establish their own bowmen on the wall. Then our men will have to pull back.' Arutha looked up and saw that planks were being extended across the streets from the roofs of the buildings facing the bailey. When the archers quit the first line of buildings, they would pull the planks after them. The goblin host would have to use rams to break in doors, climb the stairs, and then engage the bowmen in a duel. By then the bowmen would have retreated to another line of houses. They would constantly fire down into the streets, forcing the invaders to pay for every foot gained. Over the last month, hundreds of quivers of arrows had been left under oilcloth upon those rooftops, along with replacement strings and additional bows. By Arutha's best judgment, it would cost Murmandamus no fewer than an additional two thousand casualties to travel from the first bailey to the second.

Running toward the bailey came a squad of men with large wooden mallets. They waited before heavy barrels placed at the corners, listening for the command. For a moment it appeared they would be overwhelmed, for a sea of goblins and their allies came swarming off the walls. Then a company of horsemen swept out of a side street, rolling back the invaders.

Arrows came flying past Guy and Arutha, and the Protector said, 'Their archers are in place. Sound retreat!'

A trumpet blast sounded from the squad of bowmen who were positioned halfway up the street, and the men with mallets struck the barrels, knocking small stoppers from bungs. Quickly the smell of oil mixed with the rusty odour of blood hanging in the air as the oil began slowly to leak out. The mallet-wielding soldiers at once began to race up the streets, where barrels waited at every corner.

Guy tugged at Arutha's sleeve. 'To the citadel. We begin the next phase.'

Arutha followed after Guy as the bloody house to house fighting began.

For two hours the terrible struggle continued, while Guy and Arutha watched from the first command post atop the wall of the citadel. In the city the shouts of fighting men could be heard, and the curses and screams continued unabated. At every turn in the city a company of archers waited, so that each block gained by the invaders was over the bodies of their comrades. Murmandamus would take the outer city, but he would pay a terrible price for it. Arutha revised his estimate of Murmandamus's casualties upward to three or four thousand soldiers to reach the inner bailey and the moat about the citadel. And he would still have to deal with the inner fortifications of Armengar.

Arutha watched in fascination. It was beginning to become difficult to see clearly, as the sun had fallen behind the mountains and the city was in shadow. Night was only an hour or so away; still, he could make out most of what occurred. The unarmoured, nimble archers were moving from rooftop to rooftop, by means of long planks which they pulled after themselves. A few goblins attempted to climb the outside of buildings but were shot down by bow fire from other buildings. Guy studied the continuing battle with a keen eye. Arutha said, 'This city was built for this sort of battle.'

Guy nodded. 'Had I to design one to bleed an opposing army, I couldn't have done better.' He looked hard at Arutha. 'Armengar will fall, unless aid arrives within the next few hours. We have until tomorrow morning at the longest. But we'll cut the bastard; we'll hurt him badly. When he marches against Tyr-Sog, he'll have lost a third of his army.'

Arutha said, 'A third? I would have said a tenth.'

With a grin devoid of humour, Guy said, 'Watch and you'll see.' The Protector of Armengar shouted to a signal man, 'How much longer?'

The man waved a white and blue cloth toward the top of the citadel. Arutha looked up and saw an answering wave with a pair of yellow cloths. The soldier said, 'No more than ten minutes, Protector.'

Guy thought, then said, 'Launch another catapult strike at the outer bailey.' Orders were given and a shower of heavy stones was launched at the far end of the city. Softly, almost to himself, he said, 'Let them think we've overextended our range, and maybe they'll hurry to get inside.'

Time passed slowly, and Arutha watched as the archers retreated from roof to roof. As day faded to twilight, a company of ambushers was dashing along the street, heading for the drawbridge and outer gate of the citadel's barbican. As the first company made for the lowered bridge, another, then a third company came into view. Guy watched as the gate commander ordered it retracted. The last soldier had just set foot upon it as it began to move across the moat. From the rooftops of the city more Armengarian archers fired down upon the invaders.

Arutha said, 'They are brave, to stay behind.'

Guy said, 'Brave, yes, but they're not planning to die.' Even as he spoke the archers on the rooftops were reaching the last line of houses. They lowered ropes to the street level and quickly slid down. They ran toward the citadel, tossing aside weapons as they ran. From behind, attackers swarmed after them. As the attackers were halfway across the open area used as a market, bowmen upon the wall of the citadel launched a flight of arrows. The Armengarians who were fleeing ran to the edge of the moat and dove in.

Arutha said, 'They'll be shot down if they try to climb the wall.' Then he saw they didn't surface.

Guy smiled. 'There are underwater tunnels into the gatehouse and other rooms contained in the wall. Our boys and girls will come up, then the entrances will be sealed.' A particular bold group of goblins came running after and leaped into the water. 'Even if those scum find the tunnels, they'll not be able to open the trapdoors. They'd better be part fish.'

Amos came from within the citadel. 'We've everything ready.'

'Good,' answered Guy, regarding the top of the citadel where Armand observed the fighting in the city.

A yellow banner was waved. 'Ready catapults!' shouted Guy. For a long time nothing happened; at last Guy said, 'What is de Sevigny waiting for?'

Amos laughed. 'He's watching Murmandamus leading his army through the gates, if we're lucky, or at least waiting for another thousand or so to come inside.'

Arutha was studying the nearest catapult, a giant mangonel, now loaded with a strange-looking assortment of barrels lashed loosely together. The barrels were similar to the small brandy casks used in inns and alehouses, holding no more than a gallon. Each bundle was composed of twenty or thirty such casks.

Amos said, 'The signal!'

Arutha watched as a red banner was waved and Guy shouted, 'Catapults! Fire!' Along the wall a dozen of the giant catapults heaved their cargo of barrels which arched high over the roofs of the city. As they travelled, the casks spread out, so that they struck the outer bailey in a shower of wood. The crew reloaded with a speed Arutha found astonishing for in less than a minute another launch was ordered and another flight of casks was sent. While a third flight of casks was prepared, Arutha noticed smoke coming from one quarter of the city.

Amos saw it, too, and said, 'The little darlings are doing some of our work for us. They must have started a tidy fire to punish us for not staying around to die. It must be something of a shock to be standing next to it when it starts raining naphtha.'

Arutha understood. As he watched, the smoke increased rapidly and began spreading along a line indicating that the entire outer bailey area was catching. 'Those barrels at every corner?'

Amos nodded. 'Fifty gallons in each. The first block we broke the barrels, so it's all over the ground from the buildings to the wall. A lot of those murderers have been traipsing about in it and will likely find their feet and legs are covered. We have barrels in every building and one on every roof. At the time the horses were taken out of the city, during the second phase of evacuation, we also halted controlling the flow of oil upward. Every basement in the city is now ready to explode. The city's going to provide a warm reception for Murmandamus.'

Guy signalled and the third flight of casks was sent. But the centre pair of catapults heaved stones wrapped in burning oil-soaked rags, which coursed across the sky in a fiery arc. Suddenly an entire area near the barbican in the outer wall exploded with bright light. A tower of flames rose upward, climbing higher and higher. Arutha watched. A moment later he heard a dull thump, followed quickly by a hot breeze. The flames kept rising and for the longest time seemed likely never to stop. Then they began to subside, but a tower of black smoke continued to rise, flattening out in an umbrella over the city, reflecting the orange glow of the inferno below. 'The barbican is gone,' said Amos. 'We stored a few hundred barrels under the gate complex, with vents to let the flame in. They go with a bang. If we were half the distance closer to the wall, our ears would be ringing.'

Shouts and curses sounded from the city, as the flames began to spread. The catapults continued to launch their explosive cargo into the flames. 'Shorten the range,' Guy ordered.

Amos said, 'We'll drive them toward the citadel, so our bowmen can have some target practice with those that don't get roasted.'

Arutha observed the intensifying light. Another explosion came, followed quickly by another series, each echoed by a dull thud a moment later. Hot winds blew toward the citadel as spiralling towers of flames began to dance in the outer city. Again more explosions came, and from the dazzling display, it was evident a great store of the barrels had been left in strategic locations. Pounding at the ears, the dull rumbles of explosion after explosion indicated that flaming death marched rapidly from the outer bailey toward the citadel. Soon Arutha could tell the difference between a bunch of barrels igniting and a cellar explosion simply by the sound. It was, as Guy had said, a warm reception for Murmandamus.

'Signal,' said a soldier, and Guy looked up. Two red banners were being waved, now clearly seen in the blaze from the city despite the sun's having set.

'Armand's signalling that the entire outer city is in flames,' said Amos to Arutha. 'Impassable. Even those Black Slayers will be crisped if they're caught inside.' He grinned evilly as he stroked his chin. 'I just hope the grand high bilge-sucker himself was in a hurry to enter at the head of his army.'

From the city came shouts of terror and anger and the sound of running feet. The flames were marching in a steady course toward the inner bailey, their progress marked by dull explosions every few minutes as barrels at each corner ignited. The heat could now be felt, even upon the wall of the citadel. Arutha said, 'This fire storm will suck the air right out of their lungs.'

Amos nodded. 'We hope so.'

Guy looked down a minute, revealing the depth of his fatigue. 'Armand designed this final plan. He's a bloody genius, maybe the best field commander I've ever had. He was to wait until it appeared as many had entered as possible. We're going to have to attempt an escape through the mountains, so we must hurt them as much as we can.'

But Arutha saw, behind his matter-of-fact words, the defeated look of a commander whose position is about to be lost. Arutha said, 'You've conducted a masterful defence.'

Guy only nodded, and both Arutha and Amos knew he was silently saying, *It wasn't enough.*

Now the first of the fleeing invaders came running toward the citadel, halting when they realized they were exposed to the view of those upon the wall. They crouched in the lee of the last building, as if waiting for some miracle to deliver them. The number of Murmandamus's soldiers fleeing the flames increased as the fire continued its advance through the city. The catapults continued to feed the casks of naphtha to the fire, shortening their range every second launch so as to bring the flames closer and closer to the inner bailey. Now those upon the wall of the citadel could see flames exploding upon the rooftops only a half-dozen houses away from the market, then five houses, then four. Shouting moredhel, goblins, and humans, with a scattering of trolls and giants, began to fight among themselves, for as the press of those fleeing the impossible heat continued, more were being pushed into the open. Guy said to Amos, 'Order the archers to open fire.'

Amos shouted the command, and Armengarian archers began to fire. Arutha watched in stunned amazement. 'This isn't warfare,' he said softly. 'It's slaughter.' The invaders were so crowded together at the edge of the market that any arrow that reached them struck someone. They were falling over the dead as they were continuously pushed from behind. More casks of oil were thrown and the flames continued their inexorable march toward the citadel.

Arutha held up his hand, for the light of the conflagration was now near-blinding to look at and the heat was becoming uncomfortable. He realized how devastating it must be for those creatures at the edge of the market who were standing a hundred yards closer.

Then more barrels exploded, and with shrieks and cries there was a general break for the citadel. Many of those who raced across the bailey were shot down, but some number of them dove in the moat. Those wearing chain mail sank as they vainly tried to remove the armour underwater, and even some in leather sank. But many cleared the surface, paddling about like dogs.

Arutha judged a full two thousand lay dead in clear view. Another four or five thousand must have perished in the city. The Armengarian bowmen were beginning to tire so much they could hardly hit the targets clearly outlined against the flames.

Guy said, 'Open the pipes.'

An odd wheezing noise was heard as oil was discharged across the water in the moat. Cries of terror filled the air as those in the water came to understand what was occurring. As flames spread out across the bailey from the now completely burned out city, flaming bales were pushed over the walls, to fall to the moat. The surface of the water exploded in blue-white flames, which danced across the churning surface. Quickly the shrieks diminished, until at last it was over.

Arutha and the others were forced to pull back from the wall as waves of heat rose from the moat. When the flames burned out, he glanced down and saw black husks floating in the moat. He felt ill and saw his feelings were reflected in Guy's expression. Amos only looked on grimly. While the city burned out of control, Guy said, 'I feel the need of a drink. Come along. We only have a few more hours.'

Without words, Amos and Arutha followed the Protector of a dying city toward the inner building of the citadel.

Guy drained his flagon, then pointed to the map on the table. Arutha looked on beside a soot-stained Briana, who, along with the other commanders, was awaiting Guy's final orders. Jimmy and Locklear had come from their last duty station and were standing at Arutha's side. Even inside the council chamber they could feel the heat from the continuing fire as the catapults poured more naphtha into the blaze. Whatever part of Murmandamus's army that had escaped the trap was being forced to wait outside the outer wall by an inferno.

'Here,' said the Protector, indicating one of several green spots on the map, 'are where the horses are hidden.' He said to Arutha, 'They were moved out of the city during the second phase of evacuation.' He addressed the entire company. 'We don't know if the goblins have stumbled across any or all of them. But we hope several have remained safe. I think they assumed we had pulled back behind our redoubts up there at last, and felt no need to stay vigilant behind us. The secret tunnel out of the city is still secure; only one patrol of Dark Brothers has come remotely near it, and they were observed to have walked away without investigating that area. The general order is as follows:

'Each company will quit the city in turn, from First to Twelfth, with whatever auxiliaries were assigned to that company. They are to quit the tunnel only after it is clear the area around is secured. I want First Company to act as a perimeter unit, until the Second begins to replace it. When the Twelfth begins to leave the tunnel, the Eleventh will move out as well. Only those soldiers designated to remain here as the rear guard will be permitted to stay. I'll have no last-minute heroics jeopardizing this evacuation. I don't want any misunderstandings. Is everyone clear upon what they are to do?'

No one made any comment, so Guy said, 'Good. Now, make sure it is understood by everyone that once outside the city it is every man for himself. I want as many to reach Yabon as possible.' With cold anger in his voice, he said, 'Someday we shall rebuild Armengar.' He paused, as if the words were difficult. 'Begin the final phase of evacuation.'

The commanders left the room and Arutha said, 'When do you leave?'

Guy said, 'Last, of course.' Arutha looked at Amos, who nodded. 'Do you mind if I stay with you?'

Guy looked surprised. 'I was going to suggest you go out with the Second Company. First may find surprises, and the later ones may run into reinforcements called into the mountains. The last to leave stand the biggest chance of being overtaken.'

Arutha said, 'I don't know if I believe I'm some sort of champion destined to destroy Murmandamus, but if I am, I think perhaps I should stay.'

Guy pondered for a moment. 'Why not? You can't do more than you've done. Help is on the way or it isn't. Either way, it will come too late to save the city.'

Arutha glanced at Jimmy and Locklear. Jimmy seemed upon the verge of some quip, but Locklear simply said, 'We'll stay.'

Arutha was about to say something, then saw a strange expression on the face of the squire from Land's End. There was no longer the boyish uncertainty that had always lurked behind Locklear's ready smile. Now the eyes were older, somehow less forgiving, and, without any doubt, sadder. Arutha nodded.

They waited for some time, drinking a little ale to wash away the stench of the fire and to cool them from the heat. Occasionally a messenger would report back that another company had left the citadel. The hours dragged on, as night deepened, punctuated only by an occasional dull explosion as another basement was at last ignited. Arutha wondered how any could have lasted so long, but each time he thought the entire city burned out another explosion would announce the destruction still in progress.

When the Seventh Company had been reported safely away, a soldier entered the room. He was dressed in leather, but it was clear he was an auxiliary, one of the herders or farmers. His red hair was tied back, falling past his shoulders, and his face was covered by a full red beard. 'Protector! Come, see this!'

Guy and the others hurried out after the warrior to a window in the long hall, overlooking the burning city. The insane inferno had subsided, but fires still burned out of control throughout the city. It was supposed that it would be another hour before Murmandamus could send more soldiers in to make their way along the gutted streets. But now it seemed they had misjudged. Between the still burning buildings near the market, figures could be seen moving toward the citadel.

Guy quit the balcony, hurrying toward the wall. When he reached it, he could see a company of soldiers in black silhouette against the flames. They moved at slow pace, as if they were being careful to stay within a clearly defined area. While they watched, another courier reported that the Eighth Company was beginning to move out of the citadel. The approaching figures came to the edge of the outer bailey, and Guy swore. Large companies of goblins stood within protective fields, invisible except for an occasional glint of reflected light upon the surface. Murmandamus came riding into view.

Jimmy said, 'What is he?'

Without any apparent difficulty, the moredhel leader rode unprotected, ignoring the still-intense heat, and the beast upon which he rode was terrifying to behold. Shaped like a horse, it was covered in red glowing scales, as if some serpent skin of steel had been heated to near-melting. The creature's mane and tail were dancing flames and its eyes were glowing coals. Its breath seemed explosive steam. 'Daemonsteed,' said Amos. 'It's a legend. It's a mount that only a demon may ride.'

The creature reared and Murmandamus pulled out his sword. He waved it, and before the first companies of his army a black something came into existence. It was an inky darkness that obliterated light. It formed a pool on the stones of the bailey, flowing like quicksilver, then it ceased movement, forming a rectangle. After a moment it was apparent to those on the citadel wall that it had become a ten-foot-wide platform of jet blackness. Then it slowly rose, foot by foot, forming an ebon ramp above the moat. A piece of blackness broke away from the base of the ramp and flowed a short distance from the rising bridge. It stabilized into another block and began to grow. Another bridge began to form from it. After another wait, a third, then a fourth span began to form.

Guy said, 'Damn! He fashions some sort of bridges to the wall.' He shouted, 'Pass word to hurry the evacuation.'

When the ebon bridges were near the midpoint of the moat, the first companies of goblins mounted them and began to move slowly toward the leading edge. Foot by foot the black bridges advanced toward the defenders. Guy ordered the archers to fire.

The arrows sped across the gap but were deflected away, as if hitting a wall. Whatever protected the attackers from the heat also protected them from bow fire. Lookouts atop the citadel reported that the fires in the outer city were dying and more invaders were entering Armengar.

Guy shouted, 'Off the wall! Rear guard to the first balcony. All other units to evacuate at once! No one is to wait!'

The now orderly evacuation would soon turn into a headlong flight. The invaders were going to breach the last defence an hour or more before Guy had thought possible. Arutha knew it possible there would be room-to-room fighting within the citadel, and he made a mental promise to himself that if it came to that he'd wait to face Murmandamus.

They dashed across the countryard and hurried up the inner stairway to the first of the three balconies, to the sound of windows and doors being shuttered and barred. As they left the long front hallway, Arutha noticed a stack of barrels placed before the lift opening. More barrels were placed at each doorway, and everything that could burn had been left in doorways, all blocked open. Arutha knew that the last act of Guy du Bas-Tyra would be to fire the citadel in the hope that more of Murmandamus's army would be taken. For the sake of the Kingdom, Arutha hoped there was some limit on Murmandamus's ability to shield his soldiers from fire.

Soldiers came running down the hall, smashing odd-looking panels in the wall, covered by simple boards painted to match the white stones. Behind, black holes could be seen. The faint odour of naphtha could be detected as the breeze from the open bolt-hole pushed the pungent fumes up the vents. As they walked out upon the balcony,

Amos noticed Arutha looking back. 'They run from the basement to the roof. More air to feed the flames.'

Arutha nodded and watched as Murmandamus's first wave breasted the wall to the citadel. As soon as they stepped upon the wall, the field about them vanished and they spread out, ducking for cover as the archers upon the balcony opened fire. The catapults were useless, for the range was too short, but a dozen ballistae, looking like giant crossbows, hurled huge spearlike missiles at the foemen. Guy ordered the ballista crews to quit the balcony.

Guy watched as his bowmen held the invaders at bay. Arutha knew he counted every minute, for as each passed, another dozen of his people were leaving the city.

Behind the advancing goblins, more could be heard scaling the walls. Murmandamus's soldiers overran the gatehouse, extended the bridge, and opened the gate and an army came flooding in. The fires in the city were dying, so more companies of invaders were rapidly approaching the citadel. At the last, Guy shouted, 'It's over! Everyone to the tunnel!'

Each bowman took one last shot, then all turned and fled inside. At his word, Guy waited until everyone was inside before he came in, bolting the last door behind. Shutters covered every window on the balcony. The sound of pounding came from below as the invaders struggled with the bolted doors to the courtyard.

'The lift is rigged,' shouted Amos. 'We'll have to take the stairs.'

They rounded a corner into another corridor, slammed and barred a door, then ran down a narrow flight of stairs. At the bottom they reached the huge cavern. Every one of the special lanterns had been lit, illuminating the cavern with ghostly light. Arutha's eyes smarted from the sting of fumes, stirred up by the breeze from the bolt-hole tunnel, where the last of the reserve company was entering. Guy and the others ran toward the door and had to halt, for the tunnel could accommodate only two abreast. From above came the sound of shouting and pounding on the door at the top of the stairs.

Again Guy insisted on being the last to enter, and he closed the door behind, placing a huge iron bar across it. 'This should take them a few minutes to get past.' As he turned to flee up the tunnel, he said to Arutha, 'Pray none of those bastards brings a torch into that cavern before we clear the tunnel.'

They hurried along, closing several intervening doors, each being locked by the Protector. At last they reached the end of the tunnel, and Arutha entered a large cavern. A short way off, the yawning mouth of the cave revealed night. As Guy bolted this door a dozen bowmen of the rear guard remained ready against the possibility of the Protector's having been overtaken. Another three or four dozen soldiers were moving off, attempting to wait a minute or so before leaving, so that each group of men might not stumble upon the heels of those before. From the odd noises in the night, it was clear that a few of those fleeing had encountered units of the enemy. Arutha knew it was likely that most of those leaving the city would be spread throughout the hills by sundown tomorrow.

Guy waved the bowmen out of the cave, and soon the last of those not with the rear guard were off, and only they, Locklear, Jimmy, Arutha, and Amos stood with Guy. Guy then ordered the rear guard away, and soon only the five were in the cave. Another figure came out of the gloom, and Arutha could see it was the red-headed warrior who had brought news of Murmandamus's approach through the flames. 'Get away!' ordered Guy.

The soldier shrugged, seeming unconcerned with the order. 'You said every man for himself, Protector, I might as well stay.'

Guy nodded. 'Your name?'

'Shigga.'

Amos said, 'I've heard of you, Shigga the Spear. Won the Midsummer's games last year.' The man shrugged.

Guy said, 'Did you see de Sevigny?'

Shigga pointed toward the cave entrance with his chin. 'He and some others left just before you came out, as you ordered. They should be well past the highest redoubt, about a hundred yards down from here.'

The sound of wood tearing came faintly through the tunnel.

Guy said, 'They have reached the last door.' He grabbed a chain that ran from under the footing below the door, saying, 'Help me with this.' They all picked up the chain and helped him pull it taut, until he could attach it to a ballista pointing away from the door. The ballista had been fastened to the rock floor of the cavern. There was no bolt set in the war engine, but as soon as the chain was attached, Arutha saw its purpose.

'You fire the ballista and collapse the tunnel behind?'

Amos said, 'The chain runs under the supports of the tunnel, all the way back to the cavern, connecting them. It should all come down with several hundred of the scum covered rats inside. But there's more.'

Guy nodded. 'Start running from the cave, and when you reach the mouth, I'm going to pull this.'

A rhythmic pounding sounded on the last door; some sort of ram was being brought to bear. Arutha and the others hurried outside the cave mouth and halted to watch. Guy triggered the ballista and it seemed to hesitate, then with a jerk it snapped the chain forward only a few inches. It was enough. Abruptly the door erupted outward as Guy sprinted for the cavern mouth, a rolling cloud of dust behind. A few bloodied and pulped goblin bodies fell out as rocks came rushing out of the tunnel.

They all ran with Guy away from the cavern. He pointed up, where a path led above the cave. 'I want to go up there awhile. If you want to head out now, go, but I'm going to see this.'

Amos said, 'I wouldn't miss it,' and followed after. Arutha looked at them, then followed.

While they were climbing above the cave mouth, a rumbling beneath their feet could be felt as a series of dull explosions sounded. Amos said, 'The lifts were set to fall when the tunnel was collapsed. They should have ignited the barrels on each floor of the citadel, all the way down to the cavern.' Another series of explosions could be heard. 'Seems the damn contraption worked.'

Suddenly the ground heaved. A sound like the heavens opening rang in their ears as they were slammed to the earth, and a concussion of enormous power stunned them all for a moment. From beyond the edge of the prominence they were climbing, an astonishing, roiling ball of orange and yellow flames rushed heavenward. It rose at rapid rate, expanding as it went, and in the terrible beauty of its glow they could see trailing debris being lifted upward. Dull thuds rang through the ground beneath them as the last reservoirs of naphtha began to ignite, ripping the keep apart. Stones, charred fragments of wood, and bodies were being sucked skyward as if some giant wind blew straight up.

Arutha lay upon the ground, staggered by the display. A shrieking wind passed him, then there came an immense blast of heat. For a moment the air burned their noses and stung their faces, as if they stood within feet of the mouth of a giant furnace. Amos had to yell over the noise. 'The storage below the citadel blew. We were venting it all day and night, so it would become explosive.'

His words were faint, as ears rang, then were drowned out by another titanic explosion as the ground bucked and heaved under them, followed instantly by a series of lesser detonations, the concussion of the reports hammering at them like physical blows. They were still two hundred yards from the cliff overlooking the city, but the heat was nearly unbearable where they lay.

Guy shook his head to clear it and said, 'It's . . . so much more than we had thought.'

Locklear said, 'If we had reached the edge of the cliff we'd have been cooked.'

Jimmy cast a glance backward. 'It's a good thing we got out of the cave, as well.'

They all craned their heads around to look back to where he pointed. The ground continued to heave and more explosions sounded as rocks and debris rolled down the slopes past them. Below, the hillside had changed. The entire contents of the tunnel had been blown clear by the first massive explosion, covering the hillside opposite the cavern with a litter of body parts and rubble. Then the ground heaved and pitched as another massive explosion sounded. Again a fireball rose high overhead, though not as massive as the last.

There was a surging, rolling motion of the ground and a third tremendous explosion came, then some minor trembling. They all lay still, lest they be tossed down again by the shaking earth. After a time the ground only echoed with dull thuds, and they stood. Still two hundred yards or more from the edge of the cliff, they gathered and watched as the utter destruction of Armengar was accomplished. In only a few terrible moments the home of a people, the centre of their culture, had been swept away. It was an obliteration unmatched in the annals of Midkemian warfare. Guy watched the angry, glowing sky. He attempted to walk closer to the edge of the cliff, but the heat, an almost visible curtain of superheated air rising before the cliff face, forced him back. For a moment he stood, as if resolving to brave the inferno and glimpse the remains of his city, then he relented.

'Nothing could have survived that explosion,' said Arutha. 'Every goblin and Dark Brother between the citadel and the city wall must have been killed.'

Amos said, 'Maybe his bastardness got caught with his pants down. I'd love to think he had a limit on how much his magic could handle.'

Arutha said, 'His soldiers may have died, but I think he will somehow escape. I don't think that beast he rode minded the fire.'

Jimmy said, 'Look!' and pointed skyward.

The cloud of smoke that hung above them was glowing red from the reflected light of the fire below as a giant column of flames still rose toward the heavens. Against that angry backdrop a single figure could be seen riding in the air upon the back of a glowing red steed. It seemed to be descending, as if running downhill in a circle, and it was clearly making its way back to the heart of Murmandamus's camp.

'Son of a mangy bitch!' swore Amos. 'Can't anything kill that dungeater?'

Guy looked about. 'I don't know, but now we have other worries.' He began to climb down, and they discovered that the entire cavern had collapsed beneath them. Where the cave mouth had been, only a mass of rubble extending out into the gully could be seen. They picked their way through the debris, passing beyond several collapsed stone redoubts that had protected the city from attack from above, and at last reached the wash leading down into a canyon where horses were hidden.

Guy said, 'The first four or five canyons will have been picked clean by those first to flee. If we're to find mounts, we must look farther out.'

Arutha nodded. 'Still, we have a choice: west toward Yabon, or east toward Highcastle.'

'Toward Yabon,' answered Guy. 'If help's coming, we have a chance of meeting it along the road.' He scanned the area, looking for some sign of which was the most likely direction to travel. 'Whatever units Murmandamus had up here will likely be disorganized now. We may yet get free of them.'

Amos chuckled. 'Even his larger companies will be reluctant to stand in the way of a rout army. It isn't exactly healthy.'

Guy said, 'Still, if they find themselves cornered, they'll fight like the rats they are. And at first light there'll be thousands of reinforcements up here. We have only a few hours at best to get away.'

The sound of movement from the canyon caused all to draw weapons and move back into what little shelter was provided by the fallen rocks. Guy signalled for everyone to be ready.

They waited silently, and from around the corner a figure emerged. Guy sprang forward, halting his blow in midair.

'Briana!'

The commander of the Third Company looked slightly dazed, blood flowing from a cut upon her temple. Seeing Guy she relaxed. 'Protector,' she said with relief. 'We were forced to turn back. There was a patrol of trolls at the lower end of the canyon who were attempting to flee back to their own lines. We seemed to be fighting to get past each other. Then the explosion . . . we were showered with rocks. I don't know what happened to the trolls. I think they fled . . .' She pointed to her bleeding forehead. 'Some of us were hurt.'

'Who is with you?' he asked.

Arutha stepped forward as Briana shook her head to clear it, then motioned, and into the glow from the conflagration in the city came two more guards, one obviously wounded, and a dozen or more children. With wide, startled eyes they regarded Arutha, Guy, and the others.

Briana said, 'They had been trapped in a draw by some Dark Brothers. Some of my soldiers killed the Brothers, but we were separated. We've been finding stragglers for the last hour.'

Guy counted. 'Sixteen.' He turned to Arutha. 'What do we do now?'

Arutha said, 'Every man for himself or not, we can't leave them.'

Amos turned, alerted by some approaching sound. 'Whatever we do, we'd best do it somewhere else. Come along.'

Guy pointed over the rim of the draw and he and the others began helping the children climb. Soon they were all above the canyon rim and moving off toward the west.

Arutha was the last to reach the rim, and as the others vanished out of sight he dropped to his knees behind an outcropping of rock. Into view came a company of goblins, moving cautiously as if expecting attack at every turn while they attempted to return safely from their lines. From their bloodied appearance, it was clear they had already encountered some elements of the Armengarian rout. Arutha waited until he was sure the children were safely along, then took a rock and heaved it as far past the goblins as possible. The stone sped unobserved through the dark and clattered behind them. The goblins spun around and hurried along, as if fearing attack from behind. Arutha ducked along the ridge, running in a crouch, then jumped down to the next trail. Soon he overtook the last of their party, the man called Shigga, acting as rear guard.

Shigga motioned with his head. Arutha whispered, 'Goblins.'

The spearman nodded and they moved down the trail, following the band of tiny fugitives.

CHAPTER FIFTEEN

Flight

ARUTHA MOTIONED FOR A HALT.

Everyone, including the children, moved against the rocks, hiding from possible observation. The entire party crouched down in a gully, one they had been following for the night. Dawn was approaching, and after the fiery destruction of Armengar, the hills behind the city had become a no-man's land.

The fall of the city had been a victory for Murmandamus, but a vastly more costly one than he had expected. The hills behind Armengar had been thrown into chaos. The units already in place there had been overrun by the rout army fleeing the city. A large number of goblins and trolls had quit the hills and fled back toward Murmandamus's camp.

In the first few hours after the fall of the city, Arutha's party had seen few goblins or Dark Brothers, but it was obvious that Murmandamus had ordered a large number of his units back into the hills. At first Murmandamus's forces had no clear advantage once in the rocks. There was no coordination among commanders and not enough soldiers had come into the hills to put the fleeing Armengarians at a clear numerical disadvantage. Bands of goblins and moredhel ventured into the gullies and washes behind the city in the darkness, seeking to overtake the fugitives, but many never returned. Now, the balance was shifting; soon the area would be entirely in the enemy's control.

Arutha glanced back at the huddling children. Several of the little ones were close to exhaustion from a sleepless night and constant terror. The problem of finding a safe passage south was confounded by the inability of the youngest children to move quickly. And at each turn they ran the chance of encountering the enemy. Twice they had blundered into elements from the city, and Guy had ordered them along on their own, refusing to let this group become larger. Twice more they had discovered corpses, from both sides.

The sound of boots grew louder, and from the number and the lack of any attempt to hide their approach, Arutha judged this likely to be the enemy. He signalled and everyone faded back along the gully, until Arutha, Guy, Amos, Briana, and Shigga crouched down in the shadows before the huddling children. Jimmy and Locklear stayed in the midst of the children, keeping them quiet.

The patrol, led by a moredhel, consisted of trolls and goblins. The trolls were sniffing the air, but the heavy reek of smoke confounded their senses. They marched past the gully and down a large defile. When they were past, Arutha motioned and the company moved cautiously forward, travelling toward the west, away from the patrol's line of march.

Suddenly a child yelled in fright, and Arutha and the others whirled around. Jimmy was leaping past the children, Locklear at his side, weapons drawn as the trolls attacked. Whether they had discovered the fugitives or had simply decided to double back along the defile, Arutha did not know, but he knew they must dispose of this patrol quickly or they would alert others.

Arutha lunged over Locklear's shoulder and killed a troll forcing the boy back. Amos and Guy passed them and soon the entire company was engaged. Shigga thrust with his spear, killing another troll, while the moredhel faced Guy. The dark elf recognized the Protector of Armengar, for he shouted, 'One-eye!' He attacked with savage fury, pushing Guy backward, but Locklear duplicated Arutha's trick, striking past Guy, killing the moredhel.

Abruptly it was over, with five trolls, an equal number of goblins, and the moredhel dead. Arutha was breathing heavily when he said, 'It's a good thing this is a narrow gully. If they'd got around us, we'd never have survived.'

Guy regarded the greying sky and said, 'We have to find some place to hide. The children are ready to drop, and there's no place close where we can move over the mountains.'

Shigga said, 'My kraal is not far, so I've travelled here, Protector. There's a trail a mile more to the west, not often used. It leads to a shallow cave. Perhaps we can mask it. It's a difficult climb . . .'

'But we've no choice,' said Amos.

Guy said, 'Show us.'

Shigga set out at a trot, only slowing to glance around turns in the trail. When he at last climbed up on the rocks next to the defile, they began lifting the children. The last child had been handed up and Briana had climbed up after, when a shout came from the west. A half-dozen Armengarian soldiers were fighting a rearward action as a larger number of goblins pursued them toward Arutha and his companions.

Guy shouted to Briana, 'Get the children out of here!' Shigga crouched with his spear at the ready, while Briana hurried the children along toward the cave.

Arutha and the others joined with the Armengarians and blocked the defile, refusing to yield to the goblins. The goblins fought with a frantic quality, and suddenly Arutha shouted, 'They're fleeing from someone behind them!'

The pressure increased as goblins began to leap at the Armengarians. Guy ordered a slow withdrawal, and step by step they let the goblins push them back along the defile. Shigga crouched above the defile, guarding the slight trail to the cave from any goblin or troll who might attempt to climb toward the children, while Briana continued to usher the children upward. But the goblins chose to ignore them, seeking frantically to get past Guy's detachment.

Then a shout from the other side, beyond Arutha's vision, sounded, and several of the rearmost goblins began battling some other foe. The goblins ceased moving, as they were trapped between two groups of attackers.

A yell from behind caused Arutha to spin about. Jimmy and Locklear had been watching the rear, and another company of goblins was appearing at the far end of the defile. Without hesitation, Arutha shouted, 'Climb! Get out!'

He and the boys leaped for the rocks, then stabbed downward at the goblins to allow Amos and Guy a chance to climb upward. Now Arutha could see what had caused the first band of goblins to flee back toward him. A company of dwarves was battling furiously against the goblins. Behind the dwarves, two elves could also be seen, who drew bows and fired over the heads of their shorter companions. Arutha recognized one of the elves and shouted, 'Galain!'

The elf looked up and waved. He shouldered his bow and leaped up on the ridge, skirting the fighting in the gully below. With a long running leap he cleared another wash and landed on the side of the defile where Arutha stood. 'Martin has gone on to Yabon! Are you all right?'

Arutha nodded as he drew a deep breath. 'Yes, but the city's gone.'

The elf said, 'We know. Even miles away the explosion was seen. We've been encountering refugees all night. Most of the dwarves under Dolgan have formed a rough corridor along the high trail.' He pointed back down the main trail they had used in coming to Armengar. 'Most of those fleeing will get through.'

Guy said, 'There are children in that cave up there.' He waved to where Shigga crouched on the other side of the defile.

Galain called out, 'Arian! There are children up there.' He pointed toward the cave. The second detachment of goblins joined the fray and further conversation was halted. Several goblins attempted to climb up after those in the rocks, but Amos kicked one in the face and Jimmy ran another through, and the others thought better of it.

A momentary pause in the fight allowed Arian, the other elf, to yell, 'We'll get them out.' The elf continued to shoot at the goblins while two dwarves scrambled up the small trail, to aid Shigga, Briana, and the two remaining Armengarian soldiers in getting the children safely down.

Galain said, 'Calin sent a company of us to Stone Mountain, to honour Dolgan's accepting the crown. When Martin arrived and told of what was going on up here, Dolgan set off at once. Arian and I decided to come along while the rest returned to Elvandar with word of Murmandamus's march. Calin can't leave our forests unprotected with Tomas gone, but I suspect he'll send a company of archers to help the dwarves get the survivors over the mountain. The dwarves' corridor is well held, from the Inclindel Gap to about a mile west of here. Dolgan's warriors are all through the hills, so it'll be lively up here for a while.'

The dwarves fought a holding action from behind a shield wall while those above handed the children down to two dwarves at the rear, who quickly led them to safety. Jimmy tugged at Guy's sleeve and pointed to where a company of trolls was climbing up from below. Guy glanced about, seeing better than a dozen goblins still between himself and the dwarves, then pointed toward the east. He waved to Briana and Shigga, indicating they should flee with the children. Quickly Guy and the others scrambled behind the goblins, and leaped down. They ran back to the last intersection they had used, and moved down the shallow gully. Ducking into the same covering they had availed themselves of moments before, Guy said, 'Those trolls coming up from below will make it impossible to reach the dwarves. Perhaps we can drop lower and move along until we've circled around them.'

Galain said, 'It's pretty chaotic up here. I was with the most forward elements of Dolgan's army and they've come as far as they can. Now they'll begin withdrawing. If we don't overtake them quickly, we'll be left behind.'

Further conversation was interrupted by shouts from above as more of Murmandamus's forces ran along the ridges toward the invading dwarves. Guy signalled and they moved off at a crouched walk, deeper into the wash, heading down. After they had gone a few hundred more yards, Guy said, 'Where are we?'

They all exchanged looks and realized they had taken a different way from the one they had come, and now they were somewhere to the west of the cavern that had emptied out behind the city. Jimmy glanced up and began to rise, then ducked down again. He pointed. 'There's a glow in the sky still, over there, so that must be where the city is.'

Guy swore softly. 'We're not as far east as I thought. I don't know where this gully empties out.'

Arutha looked at the lightening sky. 'We'd better keep moving.' They hurried off, not certain where they were heading, but knowing that to be caught would be to die.

'Riders,' whispered Galain, who had been scouting ahead.

Arutha and Guy both pointed, and the elf said, 'Renegades. A half dozen. The louts are taking their ease about a campfire. You'd think it was a picnic.'

'Any signs of others?' asked Guy.

'Nothing. I saw some movement farther to the west, but I think we've moved behind Murmandamus's lines. If those lazing about the fire are any indication, things are pretty calm hereabouts.'

Guy gestured with his thumb across his throat. Arutha nodded. Amos pulled a belt knife and motioned for the boys to circle the camp. In a crouch they all moved along, until Jimmy signalled and he and Locklear climbed up above the trail. The two squires moved quickly and silently, while Arutha, Amos, Galain, and Guy waited. They heard a startled shout and dashed forward.

The two squires had jumped a guard at the far end of the small camp, and the five other men had their backs turned. Three died without knowing someone was coming behind them, and the other two quickly followed. Guy glanced about. 'Take their cloaks. If we're questioned, we'll likely be found out, but if we keep to the ridges, perhaps their sentries will think us only another band out looking for stragglers.'

The boys put cloaks of blue over their Armengarian brown leather. Arutha kept his own cloak of blue, while Amos donned one of green. Guy retained his black one. To a man the Armengarians wore brown, so the colours might disguise the fugitives for a while. Arutha tossed a grey cloak to Galain and said, 'Here, try to look like a Dark Brother.'

Dryly the elf said, 'Arutha, you do not know what a test of friendship that remark is. I must have Martin explain such things to you.'

Arutha said, 'Gladly, if it's back home over wine in the company of our families.'

The bodies were rolled down into a gully. Jimmy leaped atop the ridge above the camp and climbed up another ridge above that, standing so that he might get some sense of where they were. 'Damn!' he swore as he jumped back down.

Arutha said, 'What?'

'A patrol, about a half-mile back along the trail. It's not in any hurry, but it's coming this way. Thirty or more riders.'

Guy said, 'We leave now,' and they mounted the renegades' horses.

As they moved out, Arutha said, 'Galain, I've not had a moment to ask of the others who travelled with Martin.' He left the question unasked.

Galain said, 'Martin was the only one to reach Stone Mountain.' He shrugged. 'We know Laurie's boyhood friend is dead,' he said of Roald, not using the dead man's name in elven fashion. 'Of Laurie and Baru Serpentslayer, we know nothing.' Arutha could only nod. He felt regret at the death of Roald. The mercenary had proved a loyal companion. But he was more disturbed at Laurie's unknown fate; he thought of Carline. He hoped for her sake Laurie was well. He put aside that worry for more immediate concerns and motioned for Galain to lead the way.

They moved eastward, taking the higher trail whenever possible.

Galain rode in the van, and they did resemble a company of renegades led by a moredhel.

At a point where two trails met, they could again see the city. It squatted against the mountain, smoking rubble. The crater where the keep had stood still spewed forth black smoke. The rocks of the cliff face seemed to glow red in the early morning gloom. 'Is there nothing left of the keep?' Guy asked in quiet wonder.

Amos looked down, his face a stony mask. 'It was there,' he answered, pointing to a spot at the base of the cliff. Now only the raging inferno could be seen as the pool of naphtha burned unabated in the deep pit blown out of the rocks. Nothing which resembled the keep, the inner wall, moat, or the first dozen blocks of the city could be seen. Those buildings nearest the citadel still discernible were little more than piles of rubble. Only the outer wall remained intact, except where the barbican had been exploded. Everything was gutted, charred black, or glowing red. Amos said, 'It's all gone. Armengar is gone.' No building remained intact, and the entire mountainside was shrouded by a blue black haze of smoke. Even outside the walls, the litter of bodies was appalling.

It was clear that Murmandamus had taken a terrible beating in sacking the city, but still his host dominated the plain outside the walls. Banners flew and companies moved, as the moredhel warlord ordered his army to march. Amos spat. 'Look, he still has a larger army in reserve than he threw at us.'

Arutha said with fatigue in his voice, 'You cost him close to fifteen thousand dead—'

Guy interrupted. 'And he can still march more than thirty-five thousand against Tyr-Sog . . .' Elements were moving, and the scouts and outriders were already galloping toward their assigned places along the line of march. Guy studied it for a moment, then said, 'Damn me! He's not moving south! He's moving his army eastward!'

Arutha looked at Amos, then at Guy. 'But that makes no sense. He can hold the dwarves to the west, pushing them back until he's in Yabon.'

Jimmy said, 'To the east . . .'

'. . . lies Highcastle,' finished Arutha.

Guy nodded. 'He's going to march his army down Cutter's Gap, right into Highcastle's garrison.'

Arutha said, 'But why? He can overrun Highcastle in days, but he'll be left standing in the middle of the High Wold, unprotected on either flank. He's got no obvious goal.'

Guy said, 'If he strikes dead south, he can be in the Dimwood inside a month.'

'Sethanon,' said Arutha.

Guy said, 'I don't understand it. He can take Sethanon. Its garrison is little more than an honour company. But once there, what? He can winter, living on forage from the Dimwood and whatever city stores he captures, but come spring, Lyam can hit him from the east and your forces from the west. He'll be between the hammer and the anvil, with a five-hundred-mile retreat back into the mountains. It would mean his destruction.'

Amos spat. 'Let's not underestimate the nose-picker. He's up to something.'

Galain looked about. 'We'd best be going along. If he's moving east for certain, we'll never be able to double back and reach Inclindel. That patrol we saw will be a company of outriders. They'll stay up here along the entire line of march, following behind us.'

Guy nodded. 'Then we must reach Cutter's Gap before his advanced elements.'

Arutha spurred his horse and they began the ride eastward.

For the balance of the day they managed to keep ahead of any of Murmandamus's soldiers. Occasionally they would see flankers riding off from the main army, far below on the plain, and there were signs of movement behind them. But the trail began moving downward, and near sundown Arutha said, 'We're going to be riding smack into their outer pickets if we keep moving toward the plain.'

Guy said, 'If we continue riding past dark, we might slip into the woods at the bottom of the hills. If we hug the foot of the mountains and ride all night, we'll enter the forest proper. I doubt even Murmandamus will be sending large numbers of soldiers into the Edder Forest. He can circle it easily enough. The Edder is no place I'd like to be, but we'll have cover. If we ride all night, we might stay enough ahead of them to be safe . . . at least from them.'

Jimmy and Locklear exchanged questioning looks, then Jimmy said, 'Amos, what's he mean?'

Amos glanced at Guy, who nodded. 'The Edder's a bad place, boy. We can – could forest for about three miles or so into the woods along its edge. A little farther in a man could hunt. But farther than that, well – we don't know what's in there. Even the goblins and Dark Brothers skirt the place. Whoever goes deep into the forest just doesn't come back. We don't know what's in there. The Edder's pretty damn big, so just about anything could hide in there.'

Arutha said, 'We leap from the cauldron to the fire, then.'

'Perhaps,' answered Guy. 'Still, we know what we face if we ride the plain.'

Jimmy said, 'Maybe we could slip by, keeping our disguises.'

It was Galain who answered. 'There is no chance, Jimmy. One look and any moredhel knows an eledhel instantly. It is something we do not speak of, but simply believe me. There is an instinctive recognition.'

Amos spurred his mount forward. 'Then there's nothing else for it. Into the forest, lads.'

They rode as quietly as they could through woodlands dark and foreboding. Distant calls echoed from Murmandamus's army, camped for the night on the plains to the north. By moving throughout the night, Arutha judged they would be well ahead of Murmandamus's army by sunup. By midday they would be out of the forest, back upon the plain, able to pick up speed. Then if they could reach Cutter's Gap and Brian, Lord Highcastle, there was a chance of slowing Murmandamus all the way down the High Wold and through the Dimwood.

Jimmy spurred his horse forward and overtook Galain. 'I've got this funny itch.'

Softly the elf said, 'I feel it, too. I also sense something familiar about these woods. I can't put a name to it.' Then with elvish humour he added, 'But then, I'm only a youngster, barely forty years of age.'

Returning the dryness, Jimmy said, 'An infant.'

Guy, who rode next to Arutha, said, 'We might just get to Highcastle.' He was quiet for a while, then at last said, 'Arutha, returning to the Kingdom poses some problems for me.'

Arutha nodded in understanding, though the gesture was lost in the dark. 'I'll speak with Lyam. I assume once at Highcastle I'll have your parole. Until we sort this mess out, you'll be under my protection.'

Guy said, 'I'm not worried over my fate. Look, I've what's left of a small nation streaming down into Yabon. I just . . . just want to ensure they're well cared for.' His voice revealed a deep sense of despair. 'I vowed to rebuild Armengar. We both know that will never be.'

Arutha said, 'We'll work out something to bring your people into the Kingdom, Guy.' He studied the form that rode slowly beside him in the darkness. 'But what of yourself?'

'I have no concern for myself. But . . . look, consider interceding with Lyam on Armand's behalf . . . if he got out. He's a fine general and able leader. If I had taken the crown, he would have been the next Duke of Bas-Tyra. With no son of my own, I couldn't imagine a better choice. You'll need his sort, Arutha, if we're to weather all that's coming. His only fault is an overblown sense of personal loyalty and honour.'

Arutha promised to consider the request and they lapsed into silence. They continued riding until well after midnight, when Arutha and Guy agreed upon a halt. Guy approached Galain while they rested the horses and said, 'We're now farther into these woods than any Armengarian has travelled and returned.'

Galain said, 'I'll keep alert.' He studied Guy's face. 'I have heard of you, Guy du Bas-Tyra. At last recounting, you were something of an object of distrust,' he said with elven understatement. 'It seems the situation has changed.' He nodded toward Arutha.

Guy smiled a grim smile. 'For the moment. Fate and circumstance occasionally forge unexpected alliances.'

The elf grinned. 'That is true. You have an elf-like appreciation. I would like to hear the tale someday.'

Guy nodded. Amos approached and said, 'I thought I heard something that way.' Guy looked where he indicated. Then both discovered Galain gone.

Arutha came over. 'I heard it also, as did Galain. He'll return soon.'

Guy hunkered down, resting while alert. 'Let's hope he's able.'

Jimmy and Locklear tended the horses in silence. Jimmy studied his friend. In the gloom he could only see a little of the boy's expression, but he knew that Locklear still hadn't recovered from Bronwynn's death. Then Jimmy was visited by a strange sense of guilt. He hadn't thought of Krinsta since the retreat from the wall. Jimmy tried to shrug aside the irritation. Hadn't they been lovers from desire and entered freely into the relationship? Had any promises been made? Yes and no, but Jimmy felt nettled at his own lack of concern. He didn't wish any harm to Krinsta but he didn't see much sense in worrying about her. She was as able to take care of herself as any woman Jimmy had met, a soldier by training since childhood. No, what troubled Jimmy was the absence of concern. He vaguely sensed something was lacking. He became irritated. He'd had enough concern with others in his life, with Anita's injury and Arutha's mock death. Becoming involved with other people was a bloody inconvenience. Finally he felt his irritation grow to anger.

He moved up to Locklear and grabbed his friend roughly, swinging him about. 'Stop it!' he hissed.

Locklear's eyes widened in surprise. 'Stop what?'

'This bloody damn – silence. Bronwynn's dead and it wasn't your fault.'

Locklear's expression remained unchanged, but slowly moisture gathered in his eyes, then tears began to run down his face. Pulling his shoulder out from under Jimmy's hand with a shrug, he quietly said, 'The horses.' He moved away, his face still streaked with tears.

Jimmy sighed. He didn't know what had possessed him to act that way, but suddenly he felt stupid and thoughtless. And he wondered how Krinsta was faring, if she was still alive. He turned to the horses and struggled to push away strong emotions.

Galain returned at a silent run. 'A light of some sort, far into the woods. I ventured close, but heard movement. They were stealthy, almost passing unnoticed, but I did hear signs of their coming this way.'

Guy moved toward his horse, as did the others. Galain mounted, and when the others were ready, he pointed. He whispered, 'We must move to the edge of the forest, as far from the light as we can without being seen by Murmandamus's scouts.'

He spurred his horse and began to ride forward. He had moved about a dozen paces when a figure dropped out of the trees from above, knocking him from the saddle.

More attackers leaped down from the trees and all the riders were dragged from their horses. Arutha hit the ground and rolled, coming to his feet with his sword in hand. He regarded his opponent, looking into an elf-like face set in a mask of hatred. Then he saw the bowmen behind, drawing a bead upon him, and with a strange sense of finality, he thought, is this how it will end at the last? The prophecy was wrong.

Then the one sitting atop Galain pulled him up by the tunic, his other hand drawn back with a knife ready to kill him. He faltered, exclaiming, 'Eledhel!' followed by a sentence in a language unknown to Arutha.

Suddenly the attackers ran forward, but no attempt was made to kill Arutha's party. Hands restrained them while Galain's attacker helped him to his feet. They spoke rapidly in the other language, and Galain motioned to Arutha, then the rest. The others, dressed in grey hooded cloaks, nodded and pointed toward the east.

Galain said, 'We must go with them.'

In soft tones Arutha said, 'Do they think us renegades, and you one of them?'

The normal elven mask was dropped and Galain revealed confusion in the gloom. 'I don't know what wonder we have stumbled into,

Arutha, but these aren't moredhel. They're elves.' He glanced about the clearing. 'And I've never seen any of them before in my life.'

They were brought before an old elf, who sat upon a wooden seat, elevated by a platform. The clearing was seventy or so feet wide, and on all sides elves squatted or stood. The surrounding area was their home, a village of huts and small buildings of wood, but totally lacking the beauty and grace found in Elvandar. Arutha glanced about. The elves stood arrayed in unexpected garb. Grey cloaks, much like those worn by the moredhel, were common, and the warriors wore an assortment of leather armour and furs. Odd decorative jewellery of copper and brass, set with unpolished stones, or necklaces of animal teeth hung about many of the warrior's necks. The weapons were rude but efficient-looking, lacking the fine craftsmanship common to those elven weapons Arutha had seen before. That these were elves was certain, but they possessed a barbaric aspect that caused Arutha no small discomfort. The Prince listened as the leader of those who had captured them spoke to the elf upon the seat.

'*Aron Earanorn*,' whispered Galain to Arutha. 'That means King Redtree. They call that one their king.'

The King motioned for the prisoners to be brought forward and spoke to Galain. Arutha said, 'What did he say?'

The King said, 'What I said was that had your friend not been recognized, you'd all most likely be dead now.'

Arutha said, 'You speak the King's Tongue.'

The old elf nodded. 'As well as Armengarian. We speak the tongues of men, though we have nothing to do with men. We have learned it over the years from those we have captured.'

Guy seemed angered. 'It has been you who have been killing my people!'

'And who are you?' asked the King.

'I am Guy du Bas-Tyra, Protector of Armengar.'

The King nodded. 'One-eye, we have heard of you. We kill any who invade our forest, whether men, goblins, trolls, or even our dark kin. We have only enemies without the Tauredder. But this' – he pointed at Galain – 'is something new to us.' He studied the elf. 'I would know you and your line.'

'I am Galain, son of one who was brother to one who ruled,' he said, not using the names of the dead in elven fashion. 'My father was descended from he who drove the moredhel from our homes. I am cousin to Prince Calin and nephew to Queen Aglaranna.'

The old elf's eyes narrowed as he studied Galain. 'You speak of princes, yet my son was slain by the trolls seventy winters ago. You speak of queens, yet my son's mother died in the battle for Neldarlod, when our dark brothers last sought to destroy us. You speak of things I do not understand.'

Galain said, 'As do you, King Earanorn. I do not know where lies this Neldarlod you spoke of, nor have I heard of our people living north of the great mountains. I speak of those of our kin who live in our home, in Elvandar.'

Several elves said, 'Barmalindar!'

Arutha said, 'What is that word?'

Galain said, 'It means "golden home – place – land"; it's a place of wonder. They think of it as a fable.'

The King said, 'Elvandar! Barmalindar! You speak of legends. Our ancient home was destroyed in the Days of the Mad Gods' Rage.'

Galain was silent for a long while, as if deeply considering something. Finally he turned to Arutha and Guy. 'I am going to ask that you be taken from here. I must speak of things, things which I lack the wisdom to know if it is proper to share with you. I must speak of those who have gone to the Blessed Isle, and speak of the shame of our race. I hope you understand.' To the King he said, 'I would speak of these things, but they are for the eledhel only to hear. Will you take my friends to a place of safety while I speak?'

The King nodded and waved for a pair of guards, who escorted the five humans to another clearing. There was no place to sit, except upon the ground, so they hunkered down upon the damp soil. They could not hear Galain speak, but they caught the faint sound of his voice on the night wind. For hours the elves held council and Arutha drifted off into a doze.

Suddenly Galain was there, motioning for them to rise. 'I have spoken of things I'd thought I had forgotten, old lore taught to me by the Spellweavers. I think they believe now, though they are deeply shaken.'

Arutha looked at the two guards who waited some distance away, respecting Galain's privacy. 'Who are these elves?'

Galain said, 'I understand that when you and Martin passed through Elvandar on your way to Moraelin, Tathar told you of the shame of our race, the genocidal war conducted by the moredhel against the glamredhel. I think these are the surviving descendants of the glamredhel. They seem proper elves and are certainly not moredhel, but they have no Spellweavers or keepers of lore. They have become more primitive, little more than savages. They have lost many arts of our people. I don't know. Perhaps those who survived the last battle, when the first Murmandamus led the moredhel, came here and found refuge. The King spoke of their having lived for a long time in Neldarlod, which means "Place of the Beech Trees", so they are but recently come to Edder Forest.'

'They've been here long enough to make it impossible for the Armengarians to hunt or lumber deeply,' said Guy. 'At least three generations.'

'I'm speaking of elven things, an elven sense of years,' answered Galain. 'They've been here over two hundred years.' He regarded the two guards. 'And I don't think they're entirely free of the glamredhel heritage. They're much more warlike and aggressive than we of Elvandar, almost as much as the moredhel. I don't know. This King seems unsure of what should be done. He's taking counsel now with his elders, and I expect we'll hear what they wish in a day or two.'

Arutha looked alarmed. 'In a day or two, Murmandamus will again be between us and Cutter's Gap. We must be away this day.'

Galain said, 'I'll return to council. Perhaps I can explain a few things to them about the way the world works outside this forest.'

He left them and they sat, again resigned to having nothing to do but wait.

Nearly half the day had passed when Galain returned. 'The King will let us go. He'll even provide escort to the valley that leads to Cutter's Gap, along a clear trail, so we will reach it before Murmandamus's army. They'll have to go around the forest, while we'll go straight through.'

Arutha said, 'I was worried we might have trouble.'

'We did. You were going to be killed, and they were still deciding what to do with me.'

'What changed their minds?' said Amos.

'Murmandamus. I just mentioned that name and you would have thought someone had stuck a branch in a hornets' nest. They have lost much lore, but that is one name they remember. There is no doubt we have found the descendants of the glamredhel here. I judge about three or four hundred in the immediate area from the number of those in council. There are more living in distant communities, enough that it doesn't pay for anyone to bother them in any event.'

'Will they help with the fight?' asked Guy.

Galain shook his head. 'I don't know. Earanorn is a sly one. If he should bring his people to Elvandar they'd be welcomed but not entirely trusted. There's too much of the savage about them. It would be years before anyone was comfortable. He also knows that in the council of the true Elf Queen, he would be only a minor member, as he is not even a Spellweaver. He would be included, as a gesture to his people and also because he is among the oldest of the elves living in the Edder Forest. But, here he is a king, a poor king, but still a king. No, this will not be an easy or simple problem. But, that is the sort of question we elves are willing to spend years in pondering. I've given Earanorn clear instructions on the way to Elvandar, so that should his people wish to return to our mother forest, they may. They will come or not as pleases them, while for now we must make for Highcastle.'

Arutha rose and said, 'Good; at least we have one less problem.'

Jimmy followed Arutha toward the horses and said to Locklear, 'As if the ones we have left are such piddly little things.'

Amos laughed and clapped the boys on the shoulders.

The horses were at their limit, for Arutha and his companions had been riding them hard for almost a week. The tired animals were footsore and slow, and Arutha knew they had only just managed to stay ahead of the invaders. The day before, they had spotted smoke behind them, as Murmandamus's advanced scouts had made camp at day's end. This lack of caution at being spotted showed their contempt for the garrison between them and the Kingdom.

Cutter's Gap was at the south end of a wide valley, running through the Teeth of the World, rock-strewn and densely grown with brush for most of its length. Then it cleared, with no vestige of cover. Only scorched ground could be seen. Jimmy and Locklear glanced about, and Guy observed, 'We have reached the limit of Highcastle's patrols. He probably has a burn here every year, to keep the area uncovered so no one can approach undetected.'

As the sixth day since their leaving the Edder Forests was drawing to a close, the valley began to narrow and they entered the gap. Arutha slowed his horse as he looked about, softly observing, 'Remember Roald saying that thirty mercenaries held back two hundred goblins here?'

Jimmy nodded, thinking of the fun-loving mercenary. They rode into the gap in silence.

'Halt and identify yourselves!' came the cry from the rocks above.

Arutha and the others reined in and waited while the speaker revealed himself. A man stepped out from behind a rock above on the rim of the gap, a man wearing a white tabard with a red stone tor depicted upon it, still clear in the twilight of evening. A company of riders appeared from down the narrow canyon while bowmen rose up on all sides above.

Arutha slowly raised his hands. 'I am Arutha, Prince of Krondor.'

There were several laughs and the officer in charge said, 'And I'm your brother, the King. Nice and bold, renegade, but the Prince of Krondor lies dead in his family's vault in Rillanon. If you'd not been running weapons to the goblins you'd have heard.'

Arutha shouted back, 'Get me to Brian Highcastle.'

The leader of the horsemen rode up next to the Prince and said, 'Put your hands behind you, there's a good lad.'

Arutha removed his right gauntlet, and held out his signet. The man studied it, then shouted, 'Captain! Have you seen the Royal Seal of Krondor?'

'An eagle flying over a mountain peak.'

'Well, whether he's the Prince or not, he's wearing the ring.' Then the man looked at the others. 'And he's got an elf with him, too.'

'An elf? You mean a Dark Brother.'

The soldier looked confused. 'You'd better come down here, sir.' He said to Arutha, 'We'll get this straight in a minute . . . Your Highness,' he added in a soft voice, just in case.

The captain took several minutes to reach the floor of the gap, then came to stand next to Arutha. He studied the Prince's face. 'It's a good likeness, I'll warrant, but the Prince never wore no beard.'

Then Guy said, 'As thick-headed as you are, it's no wonder Armand sent you to Highcastle, Walter of Gyldenholt.'

The man regarded Guy for a long moment, then said, 'Bloody hell! It's the Duke of Bas-Tyra!'

'And this *is* the Prince of Krondor.'

The man called Walter kept looking back and forth; he said, 'But you're dead, or at least that's what the royal proclamation said.' He turned to Guy. 'And it's your head to return to the Kingdom, Your Grace.'

Arutha said, 'Get us to Brian and we'll straighten this out. His Grace is under my protection, as are these others. Now, can we stop this foolishness and ride on. There's an army of Dark Brothers and goblins a day or so behind us, and we think Brian would appreciate hearing about it.'

Walter of Gyldenholt motioned for the man who led the company to turn around. 'Take them to Lord Highcastle. And when it's all sorted out, come back and tell me just what the bloody hell is going on.'

Arutha put down the razor. He ran his hand over his again clean face and said, 'So we left the elves and rode straight here.'

Brian, Lord Highcastle, commander of the detachment at Cutter's Gap, said, 'An incredible tale, Highness. Were I not seeing you here with my own eyes, with du Bas-Tyra sitting there, I'd not have believed a word. The Kingdom thinks you dead. We had a day of memorial in your honour at the King's request.' He sat observing the weary travellers as they cleaned up and ate, in the barracks room he had given over to Arutha and his companions. The old commander was stiff in posture, as if he were constantly at attention. He looked more a parade ground soldier than a frontier commander.

Amos, who was busy gulping a flagon of wine, laughed. 'If you're going to have one of those, it's best to do it before you're dead so you can enjoy it. Shame you missed it, Arutha.'

Guy said, 'Have you many of my men with you?'

Highcastle said, 'Most of your officers were sent to Ironpass and Northwarden, but we've two of your better ones here: Baldwin de la Troville, and Anthony du Masigny. And a few remain at Bas-Tyra. Guiles Martine-Reems rules in your city now, as Baron du Corvis.'

Guy said, 'He'd like to be Duke, no doubt.'

Arutha said, 'Brian, I'd like to evacuate back to Sethanon. That's Murmandamus's obvious target and the city could benefit from your soldiers here. This position is untenable.'

Highcastle said nothing for a long moment, then said, 'No, Highness.'

Amos said, 'Say no to the Prince? Ha!'

The Baron cast a sidelong glance toward Amos, then said to Arutha, 'You know my charter and charge. I am vassal to your brother, no one else. I am given the security of this pass. I will not abandon it.'

'My gods, man!' said Guy. 'Will you not take our word? An army of more than thirty thousand is marching and you've what, one, two thousand soldiers spread over hills from halfway to Northwarden to halfway to Tyr-Sog. He'll overrun you in a half day!'

'So you say, Guy. I have no firsthand knowledge that what you say is true.'

Arutha was stunned, while Amos said, 'Now you're calling the Prince a liar!'

Brian ignored Amos. 'I have no doubt you've seen some heavy concentration of Dark Brothers up north, but thirty thousand seems unlikely. We've been dealing with them for years and our best intelligence is that there couldn't be any force of them larger than two thousand in the field under one commander. We can easily handle that many from this position.'

Guy spoke in controlled fury. 'Have you been daydreaming while Arutha's been speaking, Brian? Didn't he tell you we lost a city with a sixty-foot-high wall, approachable from only one side, defended by seven thousand battle-tested soldiers under my command!'

'And who has long been recognized as the finest military mind in the Kingdom?' asked Arutha.

Highcastle said, 'I know of your reputation, Guy, and against Kesh you've performed well. But we Border Lords face unusual situations as a matter of course. I'm sure we can deal with these Dark Brothers.' The Baron pushed himself away from the table and moved toward the door. 'Now, if you'll excuse me, I have my duties to see to. You may continue to rest here as long as you wish, but remember, here I am the supreme commander until the King decides otherwise. Now I judge you all need rest. Please feel free to dine with my officers and myself, in two hours. I'll send a guard to wake you.'

Arutha sat down at the table. After Highcastle had left, Amos said, 'The man's an idiot.'

Guy leaned forward, chin in hand. 'No, Brian's just doing his duty as he sees fit. Unfortunately, he's no general. His patent came from Rodric, as something of a joke. He's a southerner, a court noble with no prior battle training. And he's had little trouble with the goblins up here.'

'He came to Crydee once when I was a boy,' said Arutha. 'I thought him a dashing fellow. The Border Lords.' The last was said with bitter humour.

'He'll do as he wishes,' said Guy. 'And he's had mostly trouble-makers like Walter of Gyldenholt sent to his service. Armand sent him here five years ago for stealing from the company treasury. He had been a senior Knight-Lieutenant before that.

'But,' added Guy, 'because of politics, some good men are here as well. Baldwin de la Troville and Anthony du Masigny are both first-rate officers. They had the misfortune to be loyal to me. I'm sure it was Caldric who suggested to Lyam they be sent to the border.'

Amos said, 'Still, what good? Do you propose we incite a mutiny?'

Guy said, 'No, but at least when the butchering begins, the garrison will die under some competent officers along with the fools.'

Arutha leaned back in a chair, feeling fatigue course through his body. He knew they must do something soon, but what? His mind spun with confusion, and he knew it was dulled by lack of sleep and by tension. No one in the room spoke. After a moment Locklear rose and made his way to one of the bunks and lay down. Without words to the others, he was quickly asleep.

Amos said, 'That's the best idea I've heard in weeks.' He made his way to another bunk and, with a deep groan of satisfaction, settled into the soft embrace of the down comforter. 'I will see you at supper.' The others followed his example.

Soon all were asleep except Arutha, who tossed and turned, his mind visited by visions of hosts of goblins and moredhel overrunning his nation, killing and burning. His eyes refused to stay closed, and at last he sat up, a cold sweat upon his body. He glanced about and saw the others were all slumbering. He lay back and waited for sleep to come, but he was still awake when the call for supper came.

CHAPTER SIXTEEN

Creation

MACROS OPENED HIS EYES.

The sorcerer had entered a trance within minutes of discovering they were in the time trap, and had been motionless since. After watching him for several hours, Pug and Tomas had grown bored and turned their attentions to other matters. They had tried to discover all they could about the Garden, but as it was a mixture of alien plant and animal life, much of what they saw was difficult to understand. After what seemed days of exploration, the sorcerer hadn't stirred and they had resigned themselves to waiting.

'I think I've thought of a solution,' Macros said, stretching. 'How long have I been in trance?'

Tomas, who sat nearby on a large rock, said, 'I estimate about a week.'

Pug moved from where he had been observing, at Ryath's side, and said, 'Or it could be more. It's hard to tell.'

Macros blinked and stood up. 'Moving through time backwards

does make it somewhat academic, I'll admit. But I had no idea I'd been contemplating so long.'

Pug said, 'You haven't given us much idea of what is going on here. I tried several things to discover what is occurring about us, and have only gained a little notion of how this time trap works.'

'What have you learned about the trap?'

Pug's brow furrowed. 'It appears the spell was designed to reverse time in a field about us. As long as we're in that field, we are subject to its effect and cannot change it. We're carried along with the Garden, moving at a leisurely pace backward through the timestream.' Frustration showed clearly in his tone. 'Macros, we've plenty of fruit and nuts, but Ryath is hungry. She has managed to get by on some of the small game around here, and even has managed to eat some nuts, but she can't go on this way much longer. Within a short time she'll have hunted out the game, and then she'll begin to starve.'

Macros looked over to where the golden dragon lay in a doze, to conserve energy. 'Well, we must get out of here, then, by all means.'

'How?' said Tomas.

'It will be difficult, but I expect you two will be up to it.' He managed to smile, returning to something of the confidence he had exuded when both had known him before. 'Any trap has some weakness. Even something as simple as a rock dropped from above has a design flaw: it can miss. I think I've found the flaw in this trap.'

Pug said, 'It would prove refreshing. I've thought of a dozen things to do, if I were outside the field of this trap. Ryath has tried to take me outside and we've failed. And I can't think of a thing to do from the inside to fight our flight back through time.'

'The trick, dear Pug, is not to fight the flight backward through time but to accelerate it. We must travel faster and faster, moving at rates undreamed of.'

Tomas said, 'To what ends? We move back further from the conflict. What do we gain?'

'Think, Milamber of the Assembly,' Macros said, using Pug's Tsurani name. 'If we go back far enough . . .'

Pug said nothing for a while, then understanding began to dawn. 'We go back to the beginning of time.'

'And before . . . when time had no meaning.'

Pug said, 'Is this possible?'

Macros shrugged. 'I don't know, but as I can't think of anything else to try, I'm willing. I'll need your help. I have the knowledge but not the power.'

Pug said, 'Tell me what to do.'

Macros motioned for him to sit, and sat opposite him. Tomas stood behind his friend, observing with interest. Macros reached out and placed his hands upon Pug's head. 'Let my knowledge come into you.'

Pug felt his mind fill with images . . .

. . . and the universe as he knows it shudders. Only once before has he known this sense of panoramic awareness, that time he stood upon the Tower of Testing when he entered the ranks of the Great Ones. A more mature, more knowledgeable observer watches this time and understands so much more of what he sees: the symmetry, the order, the stunning magnificence that spin about him, all tied together in some plan beyond his ability to perceive. He stands in awe.

He casts his awareness about and again is astonished at the wonders of the universe about him. Now he again swims between the stars, again perceiving the mystic lines of force that bind together all things in the universe. He detects a tugging on those lines, and sees something striving to enter this universe from another. It is foul, a cancerous thing that threatens the order of all that is. It is a darkness, a blotting out. It is the Enemy. But it is weak and cautious. He ponders its nature as it falls away from his understanding. He is moving backward in time.

He observes the Garden. He can see himself sitting before the sorcerer, his boyhood friend behind. He knows what he must do. The flow of time about the Garden is stately, moving at rhythms matching the normal rhythm of space and time about him, but reciprocal in flow; for each passing second, a second in the Garden flows backward.

He reaches out, his mind finding the key to the timeflow, as real to the touch of his spirit being as a stone to his hand. He caresses it and feels the beat of the universe, the secret of the illusory dimension. He sees and he knows. He understands and manipulates that flow, and now for each second of passing time in the universe, two seconds pass in the Garden. He feels a calm joy, for he has just accomplished something that only recently he would have judged beyond the ability of any mortal magician. He puts aside his pride and concentrates on the task at hand. Again he manipulates, and for each true second, four now flow about Tomas, Macros, and himself. Again, and again, and again he duplicates his feat, and now for each hour that the universe ages, they flee backward more than a day. Again, and it is two days, then four, then more than a week. Thrice more, and they move at better than a month for each true hour. Again, again, and again, and soon they pass a year for each hour. He pauses and sends forth his awareness.

His mind soars across the cosmos like an eagle upon the wing, speeding between stars like the mighty bird of prey gliding past the peaks of the Grey Towers. He spies the hot and green-tinted star that is so familiar to him and for a brief instant understands. He is upon Kelewan, discovering the lost lore of the eldar. A year and more back in time have they moved. As fast as the time to think, he returns his consciousness to his personal here and now.

Again he manipulates the time flow, and now it is two years per hour, then four, eight, sixteen. Again he pauses and regards the universe.

The stars revolve in orderly fashion, hurtling through a cosmos so vast that their blinding speed appears little more than a crawl. But they move in odd pattern, their motions inverted, their travels reversed. He considers and again works upon the time frame. He is now master of this practice, possessing abilities to dwarf the wildest ambitions of even the most arrogant member of the Assembly. He is now certain of his own nature, so much more than he had thought, and he manipulates the time flow with ease. A wild thought passes through him: this is to be like a god! Then years of training surge up with the warning: beware pride! Remember, you are but a mortal, and the first duty is to serve the Empire. His teachers at the Assembly did their job well. He ignores the intoxication of his power, rediscovering his wal, the perfect centre of his being, and again manipulates the time flow. A year passes in reverse for each second in the true universe. Again and again he works his skills upon the time trap of the enemy, accelerating it beyond the expectations of those who fashioned it. Now a decade passes each second and he knows he lives before the time of his birth. In the time it takes to draw breath, he has passed back before the time when Duke Borric's grandfather invaded Crydee. He works another pass of time, and now the Kingdom is only half its future size, with the holdings of Baron von Darkmoor marking its western boundary. Twice more he accelerates the time factor, and the nations of his lifetime are little more than villages, peopled by simpler folks than those who will give rise to nations. Again and again he works his magic.

Then the universe rocks. The very fabric of reality is rent. Energies impossible to fathom explode about him, violent beyond his ability to apprehend, and he –

Pug opened his eyes. He felt a strange dislocation about him and for a moment his vision blurred. Tomas came to stand beside him and said, 'Are you all right?'

Pug blinked and said, 'Something out there . . . changed.'

Tomas looked skyward. 'There's something happening.'

Macros regarded the heavens. Odd patterns of energies whirled madly across the firmament while stars wobbled in the course. 'If we watch, we'll see things calm down in time. We're seeing this from back to front, remember.'

'Seeing what?' asked Pug.

Tomas answered, 'The Chaos Wars.' There was a haunted look in his eyes, as if something in what occurred touched him deeply in a place he had not expected. But his face remained a mask while he watched the mad skies above.

Macros nodded. Standing up, he pointed heavenward. 'See, even now we are passing into an epoch before the Chaos Wars, the Days of the Mad Gods' Rage, the Time of Star Death, and whatever other colourful names myth and lore have conjured up for that period.'

Pug closed his eyes and felt his mind cold and numb, his head throbbing with a dull ache.

Macros said, 'It appears we are moving at the rate of three, four hundred years a second in reverse time.' Pug nodded. 'So for every three seconds, about a millennium passes.' He calculated. 'That's a good start.'

'Start?' questioned Pug. 'How fast need we move?'

'By my best calculation, *billions* of years. At a thousand years per second, we'll get back to the beginning in our lifetime. But just barely. We need better.'

Pug nodded, clearly fatigued, but he closed his eyes. Tomas looked skyward. The stars could now be seen to move, though, given their vast distances, it was still a slow movement. But even seeing this much motion was disquieting. Then their movement seemed to accelerate, and soon it was noticeably faster. Then Pug was again with them.

'I've created a second spell within the structure of the trap. Each minute the rate will double without my intervention. We're now moving at a rate in excess of two thousand years per second. In a minute it will be four. Then eight, sixteen, and so forth.'

Macros's expression was one of approval. 'Good. That gives us a few hours.'

Tomas said, 'I think it's time for some questions, then.'

Macros smiled, his dark eyes piercing, as he said, 'What you mean is you think it's time for some answers.'

Tomas said, 'Yes, that is exactly what I mean. Years ago you coerced me into betraying the Tsurani peace treaty and on that night you told me you were the author of my current existence. You said you gave me all. Everywhere I look, I see signs of your handiwork. I would know more, Macros.'

Macros sat again. 'Well then, as we have some time to spend, why not? We are reaching a point in this unfolding drama where knowledge will no longer hurt you. What would you know?' He looked from Tomas to Pug.

Pug glanced at his friend, then looked hard at the sorcerer. 'Who are you?'

'I?' Macros seemed amused by the question. 'I'm . . . who am I?' The question seemed almost rhetorical. 'I've had so many names I can't recall every one.' He sighed in remembrance. 'But the one given at my birth translates into the King's Tongue simply as Hawk.' With a smile he said, 'My mother's people were a little primitive.' He pondered. 'I'm not sure where to begin. Perhaps with the place and time where I was born.

'On a distant world, a vast empire once ruled, at its height a match for Great Kesh and even Tsuranuanni. This empire was undistinguished in most ways – no artists, philosophers, or leaders of genius, save one or two who popped up at odd moments over the centuries. But it endured. And the one noteworthy thing it did was inflict peace upon its dominion.

'My father was a merchant, undistinguished in all ways, save he was thrifty, and held loan papers on many of the most powerful men in his community. This I tell you so you'll understand: my father was not someone about whom great sagas are composed. He was a most unremarkable, common man.

'Then, in the land of my father's birth, another common man appeared, but one with the ability of spellbinding oratory and an irritating habit of making people think. He raised questions that made those in power nervous, for while he was a peaceful man, he gathered followers, and some of them tended toward the radical and violent. So those who ruled levelled a false charge against him. He was brought to closed trial, where no man could raise a voice on his behalf. In the most extreme and harsh verdict, it was accounted he spoke treason – which was patently false – and he was ordered executed.

'His execution was to be public, in the fashion of that time, so many of the populace were there, including my father. That poor merchant of few gifts was there with some of his highly placed countrymen, and to please his rulers – who owed him money – he participated in mocking and ridiculing the condemned man upon his way to his death.

'For whatever reason, fate's whim or the gods' dry sense of humour, the condemned man paused in his walk to the place of execution and faced my father. Of all those about who were tormenting and berating him, he cast his eyes upon this one simple merchant. It may have been this man was a magician, or it could simply have been a dying man's curse. But out of all there upon the boulevard, he cursed my father. It was a strange curse, which my father dismissed as the ravings of a man gone mad with terror.

'But after the man had died and the years passed, my father noticed he wasn't getting any older. His neighbours and business associates were showing the ravages of the years, but my father looked much as he always did, a merchant of about forty years.

'When the differences became pronounced, my father fled his homeland, lest he be branded a companion of dark powers. He travelled for years. At first he put his time to good purpose, becoming a fair scholar. Then he learned the curse for what it really was. A serious accident occurred, leaving him bedridden for most of a year. He discovered death was denied him. Should he be wounded unto death, he would heal eventually.

'He began to long for the release of death, an end to the endless days. He returned to his homeland, to seek knowledge of this man who had cursed him.

'He discovered that myth now shrouded the truth and that the man now stood at the centre of religious debate. He was seen by some as a charlatan, by others as a messenger of the gods, by a few as a god himself, and by still others as a demon herald of damnation. That debate conspired to generate some strife within the empire. Religious wars are never pretty. But one story kept surfacing: that three magic artifacts associated with the dead man had the power to

357

cure, to bring peace, and finally, remove curses. As I understand it, they were a wand, a cloak, and a cup. My father began at once seeking those artifacts.

'Centuries passed, and at last my father came to a tiny nation at the frontier of this empire, where it was supposed the last of the three artifacts could be found – the other two being counted lost beyond recovery. The empire was at last dissolving, as all such things do, and this land was a wild place. Upon reaching that nation, my father was beset by brigands, who wounded him severely, leaving him for dead. But of course my father simply lay in mute agony, waiting to heal.

'A woman found him. Her husband had died in a fishing mishap, leaving her without resources. My father was of an ancient race, steeped in culture and history, but my mother's people, called the People of the Lizard, were barely more than savages. A widow was to be shunned, for any who gave to her assumed responsibility for her. So this woman of nearly nonexistent means nursed my father to health, then lay with him, for she was without a man of her own and my father was, by then, an obviously well learned man, and possibly an important one. The long and short of it was I was conceived.

'My father made his intent known to my mother, who professed no knowledge of the artifact my father sought, though it was a common enough legend even in that far land. I suspect she simply wished to keep her second husband close to home.

'So, for a time, my father stayed with my mother. In the canon of my father's people, it is said that the child will inherit the sins of the father, but whatever the cause, it is from this legacy I sprang. My father remained long enough to teach me his language and his history, and the rudiments of reading and writing. A rumour made its way to our land, a hint of the lost artifact, and my father resumed his quest, heading westward across a vast ocean. I never saw him again. For all I know, he quests still. So my mother packed me up and returned to the village of her birth.

'My mother was left with a son and no reasonable explanation from where he sprang, as far as her people were concerned, so she concocted some nonsense about mating with a demon. Because of my father's teachings, I was far more educated than the wisest elder among them, so my knowledge gave some credibility to these stories.

'In short, Mother gained significant influence in the community. She became a seer, though her abilities were more in the area of theatrics than divination. But I, well, I began seeing visions as a child.

'I left my mother when I was fourteen, wandering to where an ancient order of priests abided, in a land that seemed distant from my home at the time – a mere hop, step, and jump compared to the travelling I've done since. They trained me, vesting in me a dying lore. When I took my place within that brotherhood, I was transported in spirit.

'I was . . . taken somewhere, and some agency, perhaps the gods themselves, spoke to me. I was judged one among multitudes, a special vessel for rare powers. But there would be a price in taking that power for my own. I was given a choice. I might remain a simple mumbler of prayers, without much importance in the order of things, but I would have a safe and comfortable life, or I might truly learn magic arts. But it was clear there would be pain and danger along that path. I hesitated, but much as I wished for the peaceful existence of the monastic life, the lure of knowledge was too strong to resist. I chose the power, and the price was twofold. I was doomed, like my father, to live without hope of death, and was also given the gift – or curse – of foreknowledge. As I needed to know things, in order to act my part, that knowledge came to me. And from that day forward, I have lived my life in concert with that foreknowledge. I am destined to serve forces that work to bring sanity into the universes, and they are opposed by equally powerful agencies of destruction.'

Macros sat back. 'In short, I am a man who inherited a curse and gained some gifts.'

Pug said, 'I think I understand what you're saying. We have considered you the master behind some dark game, but the truth is you are the biggest pawn in the contest.'

Macros nodded. 'I alone have not had free will, or at least lacked the courage to challenge my foreknowledge. I have known from the day I left that priesthood that I would live for centuries and that many times I would be required to manipulate the lives of others, toward what ends I am only now beginning to understand.'

'What do you mean?' said Tomas.

Macros looked about. 'If things proceed as I suspect, we shall bear witness to that which no other mortal being in the universe, or even the gods themselves, have seen. If we survive, we will spend some time returning home. I think we can learn all we need during that time. For now, I am tired, as is Pug. I think I will sleep. Wake me.'

'When?' asked Tomas.

Macros smiled enigmatically. 'You'll know when.'

'Macros!'

Macros's eyes opened and he looked to where Tomas pointed. He stretched and rose, saying, 'Yes, it's time.'

Pug also awoke and his eyes widened. Above them the stars raced backward in flight as time ran counter to its normal course at furious speed. The skies were ablaze with fiery beauty, as rampaging energies were released in colours of splendid intensity. And light was more concentrated, as if everything seemed to be drawing together. At the centre of this loomed an utter void. It appeared they were rushing down a long, glittering, brightly streaked tunnel toward the darkest hole imaginable.

'This should prove interesting,' observed the sorcerer. 'I know you'll think this odd, but I find it strangely exhilarating not knowing what's coming next. I mean, I know what's likely to happen, but I haven't seen it.'

Pug said, 'That's fine, but what is this?'

'The beginning, Pug.' Even as he spoke, it appeared the matter about them was rushing faster and faster toward that total blackness. Now the colours were blending together to a pure white light almost painful to observe.

'Look behind!' said Tomas.

They did so, and where real space had been, now the utter grey of rift-space was seen. Macros applauded in obvious delight. 'Wonderful! It is as I thought. We shall elude this trap, my friends. We are approaching that place where time has no meaning. Watch!'

In a final rush of stunning majesty, all about them collapsed downward, as if being sucked into the maw of that black nothing. Macros said, 'Pug, halt our flight before we are pulled into all that.' Pug closed his eyes and did as he was bid. Faster and faster the last stuff of the universe was devoured by the giant thing before them, until the last vestige, the last mote of matter, vanished into the hole. Then Pug clutched at his temples and cried out in pain.

Macros and Tomas moved toward him as his legs buckled, and helped him to sit. After a moment he said, 'I'm all right.' His face was ashen and his brow was covered in sweat. 'It's just when the time trap ended, the spell of acceleration ended; it was painful.'

Macros said, 'Sorry. I should have anticipated that.' Almost to himself he added, 'But little of what we know will have any validity here and now.'

Macros pointed upward, where a vast and utter darkness could be seen. It seemed to curve, along a limitless line that moved off beyond the ability of the eye to apprehend. And the Garden and the City Forever hovered at the edge of that boundary.

Macros said, 'Fascinating. Now we know the City does exist outside of the normal order of the universe.' Macros regarded the massive thing above, counting silently to himself. 'I think it's about time, given how long ago Pug's spells were cancelled.'

'What is this?' asked Tomas, pointing to the impossible black orb against the grey.

'The sum of the universes, Tomas,' answered the sorcerer. 'The primal stuff everything else stems from. It *is* everything – except this little jot of land we stand on and the City itself. There is so much there that size and distance have no meaning. We are millions of times more distant from the surface of that matter than Midkemia is from its sun, but look how large it looms before us, blotting out more than half the sky. It's staggering to contemplate. Even light cannot escape it, for light has not been created. We are back before time, before the beginning. We are witnesses to the start of all things. Ryath, attend this!' The dragon woke from her torpor and stretched. She approached to stand behind the three men. Macros said, 'Keep watching.'

All turned to regard the utter darkness. For several minutes nothing occurred. As if no air moved in the Garden, there was a profound silence. The observers were acutely aware of their own being, feeling each sensation down to the rhythm of the blood coursing through their bodies. But no sound save their own breathing could they apprehend. Then came the note.

Each was transported, though they moved not a step. A filling joy, a profound sense of perfect rightness, washed over them, beauty too terrible to comprehend. It was as if music, a single flawless note, sounded and was felt rather than heard. Colours more vivid than any pigment were seen, yet only the dark void hung before their eyes. They felt crushed under the weight of indescribable wonder and terror. They were rendered so insignificant in an instant that each of them despaired and felt alone, yet in that crystalline instant each experienced exaltation, touched by something so wonderful it brought tears of joy flowing without stint.

It was impossible to comprehend. There was only a flickering, as if a million lines of force sprang across the surface of the void, but they were gone so quickly the watchers could not apprehend their passage. One instant all was black and formless, then a latticework of countless glowing lines spread across the magnificent void, and light filled the skies, staggering in its purity and strength. All were forced to avert their eyes from that blinding display for a moment. A blaze of stunning energies poured forth, as seen before, but now flowing outward. A strange emotion swept through Pug and his companions, one of completeness, as if what they had experienced was now at an end. All continued to weep in joy at the perfect beauty of the display.

'Macros, what was that?' asked Tomas softly, in awe.

'The Hand of God,' he whispered, his eyes wide with wonder. 'The Prime Urge. The First Cause. The Ultimate. I don't know what to call it. I know only this: one moment, there was nothing, the next, all existed. It is the First Mystery, and even now that I've seen it, I do not pretend to understand it.' The sorcerer laughed, a loud joyous sound, and did a little dance.

Pug and Tomas exchanged questioning looks, and Macros saw he was the object of their scrutiny. With an expression of genuine mirth, he said, 'It just occurred to me that there's more than one reason we're here.' When their expressions betrayed incomprehension, he said, 'I cannot imagine even a god to be without vanity, and were I the Ultimate, I'd want an audience for a show like that.'

Both Pug and Tomas began to laugh. Macros continued his little caper while he hummed a merry tune. 'Gods, I love a question I can't answer. It keeps things interesting, even after so many years.' Macros paused in his dance and his face clouded in concentration. After a moment, he said, 'Some of my powers return.'

Pug ceased his laughter. 'Some?'

'Enough so that I may more effectively manipulate your power when needed.' He gave a sly nod. 'And even add something to the total.'

Pug looked upward and regarded the splendour of a newly born universe spreading across the sky. 'Compared to that, all our troubles seem pitiful.'

'Well, they may be,' answered the sorcerer, regaining his usual manner. 'But there are a few people upon your homeworld who may feel different watching Murmandamus's army pouring down into the Kingdom. It may be a small planet, but it is the only one they have.'

Without knowing how, Pug felt them moving forward through time.

'We are free of the time trap,' confirmed Macros.

Pug sat in silent wonder. He had felt something spring into being when he had witnessed the Beginning. Now he gave voice to certainty. Looking at Macros, he said, 'I am like you.'

Macros nodded, an expression of warm affection upon his face. 'Yes, Pug, you are like me. I don't know what fate awaits you, but you are not like others. You are of neither the Lesser nor the Greater Path. You are a sorcerer, one who knows there are no paths, only magic. And magic may be limited only by the limits of one's gifts.'

Tomas said, 'Can you see your future?'

Pug said, 'No, I am spared that.'

Macros said, 'See, it's not an entirely unlucky thing, being a power. Compared to others, a minor power, but still one to be reckoned with. Now we must escape.' He scanned the madness above as the stuff of creation shot outward, filling the heavens with a staggering beauty. Green and blue swirls of gases, red orbs of fiery splendour, white and yellow streaks of light, sped by, obliterating the grey of rift-space, pushing back the boundaries of nothingness. Then Macros suddenly pointed. 'There!'

Following his hand, they saw what appeared to be a tiny ribbon stretching away from them, some vast distance off in the heavens. 'That is where we must go, and quickly. Hurry, mount Ryath and she will take us. Hurry, hurry.' They mounted upon the dragon's back, and while she was weakened by the meagre food, she was equal to the task. She took to the skies and they were suddenly speeding through the grey of rift-space. Then they again entered normal space and hung over the narrow strip of matter.

Macros ordered the dragon to hover and Tomas to lower them to the pathway. They stood upon a yellow-white roadway, marked by shimmering silver rectangles every fifty feet or so. Pug looked at the twenty-foot-wide strip and said, 'Macros, we may stand here, but there's the problem of Ryath.'

The sorcerer looked up and spoke rapidly. 'Ryath, there is little time. The Hidden Lore. You may either reveal it and trust Pug and Tomas, or perish to hide your race's secret. I argue for trust. You must decide, but quickly.'

The dragon's great ruby eyes narrowed as she regarded the sorcerer while she hovered. 'Was, then, my father so giving to thee, that the forbidden knowledge was shared with a human?'

'I know all, for I was one he counted friend.'

The dragon's eyes focused on Tomas and Pug. 'From thee and thy companion, Valheru, an oath: never to reveal that which you are about to witness.'

Tomas said, 'On my life.'

Pug nodded. 'I swear.'

A golden shimmering encompassed the dragon, faint at first, but growing more pronounced. Soon it was painful to look at. The light grew more intense, until it obscured all details of Ryath's form. Then the outlines began to move, to melt and flow, and contract down as she descended to the roadway. Rapidly the outlines grew smaller and smaller, until they were man-sized. The glow faded. Where the dragon had been there was a stunning woman with red-gold hair and blue eyes. Her figure was perfection as she stood before them unclothed.

Pug said, 'A shapeshifter!'

Ryath came toward them, and her voice was musical. 'It is not known to men, that we may come and go in their society at will. And only the greater dragons have the art. That is why thy people count our kind diminished, for we know it is better to look like this when confronting men.'

Tomas said, 'While I can appreciate such beauty, she'll cause quite a stir when we return home unless we find her some clothing.'

Ryath raised a lovely white arm and suddenly was attired in a yellow and gold travelling gown. 'I may accoutre myself as I wish, Valheru. My arts are far mightier than thou suspectest.'

'This is true,' agreed Macros. 'When I lived with Rhuagh he taught me magics unknown to any other mortal race. Never underestimate the scope of Ryath's skills. She has more than fang, flame, and talon to meet opposition.'

Pug regarded the lovely woman and found it difficult to believe that moments before she had bulked larger than the rooftops of buildings. He looked hard at Macros. 'Gathis once said you were always complaining about so much to learn and so little time to learn it. I think I'm beginning to understand.'

Macros smiled. 'Then you are truly beginning your education, Pug.' Macros glanced about them, an almost triumphant expression upon his face, a fiery spark in his eyes.

Pug said, 'What is it?'

'We were trapped, and we had no hope of victory. We still face the possibility of failure, Pug, but now at least we may take a hand – and we have a small chance of victory. Come, we have a long journey ahead.'

The sorcerer led them down the pathway, passing the shimmering rectangles. Between the rectangles were the rapidly receding stars of the new creation. Slowly the grey of rift-space was creeping about them. 'Macros,' said Pug, 'what is this place?'

'The strangest place of all, even compared to the City Forever. It is called the Universe Hall, the Star Walk, the Gateway Path, or, most often, the Hall of Worlds. To the majority who pass through it, it is simply the Hall. We have plenty of time to discuss many things as we walk. We shall return to Midkemia. But there are a few things I need to tell you first.'

'Such as?' asked Tomas.

'Such as the true nature of the Enemy,' said Pug.

'Yes, there is that,' agreed Macros. 'I've spared you some things until the last, for if we couldn't get free of that trap, why burden you? But now we must ready ourselves for the final confrontation, so you must have the rest of the truth.'

Both sorcerers looked at Tomas, who said, 'I don't understand your meaning.'

'Much of your past life is still hidden from you, Tomas. It is time for those veils to be lifted.'

He halted their walking and reached out his hand, speaking a strange word as he covered Tomas's eyes. Tomas stiffened as he felt memories returning.

* * *

A world spun through the void, orbiting a warm, nurturing star. Upon it life flourished in abundance and variety. Two beings straddled the world, each with an assigned task. Rathar took the multitudes of the fibres of life and power, and with care she wove each into the complex latticework of Order, forming a mighty single braided cord. Opposite Rathar stood another, Mythar, who gripped upon the cord, and with terrible wanton frenzy he tore apart the strands, letting them fly about in Chaos, until Rathar seized the strands and again wove them together. Each followed the dictates of his or her nature and to all others was indifferent. They were the Two Blind Gods of the Beginning. Such was the nature of the universe when it was in its infancy. In the endless process of the two deities' work, tiny strands of the fibres had eluded Rathar, falling to the soil of the world below. From these had come the most wondrous of creation's magic: life.

Ashen-Shugar was pulled from his mother's womb by the ungentle hands of the moredhel midwife. Hali-Marmora drew her sword and slashed the umbilical that tied her son to her. Her face was drawn with the pain of birth as she snarled, 'That is the last you'll have from me without a struggle.' The moredhel ran with the newborn Valheru and handed it over to an elf who waited without the mountain hall.

The elf knew his duty. No Valheru lived without struggle. It was the way of things. The elf carried the silent baby, who had not uttered a sound since birth. The infant had been born aware, a tiny thing, but not one without power.

The elf reached the place he had selected and left the baby exposed atop the rocks, facing the setting sun, unclothed and uncovered.

The infant Ashen-Shugar regarded his surroundings, names and concepts growing with each passing minute. A scavenger came sniffing toward the infant, and with a mental scream of rage the tiny Valheru sent it scurrying.

Toward evening a creature flew high above, soaring on broad wings. It regarded the thing upon the rocks and wondered if it was food. Circling lower, it was suddenly called upon by the infant.

Ashen-Shugar saw the giant eagle as it circled and knew it, that it was his creature to command. In primitive images he ordered the giant bird to land, then to hunt. Within minutes the bird returned with a flopping river fish, twice the baby's size, which it shredded with beak and talon, giving the scraps to the baby. As it was for all his kind, Ashen-Shugar's first meal was raw, bloody flesh.

For the first night the great eagle covered the infant with her wings, as she would her own young. Within days a dozen birds cared for the baby.

The Valheru grew, quickly, far faster than the children of other races. Within a summer's span the child could run down a deer, killing it with a stunning blast of the mind, and eating its flesh after tearing it from the carcass with bare hands.

Other minds occasionally touched the infant's, who would pull back. Instinctively he knew his own kind were the beings to be feared most, until he had sufficient power to carve his own place in their society.

His first conflict came as he ended his first year with the giant eagles. Another youth, Lowris-Takara, the so-called King of the Bats, arrived in the dead of night, using his servants to locate the youthful Ashen-Shugar. They struggled, each seeking to absorb the power of the other, but Ashen-Shugar finally prevailed. With the powers of Lowris-Takara added to his own, Ashen-Shugar began seeking out fit opponents. He hunted other youths, as Lowris-Takara had hunted him, and seven others fell before him. He grew in strength and power, taking the title Ruler of the Eagles' Reaches, and flew upon the back of a giant bird in the hunt. He tamed the first of the mighty dragons he would ride, and after destroying his mother in battle, he took her hall as his own. For years he grew in stature, and soon he was acknowledged one of the mightiest of his race.

He hunted and took sport with his moredhel women, and occasionally mated with one of his own kind when the heat came upon her and powerful lusts overrode the battle urge he felt toward his own kind. Of those unions only two offspring survived. His first child was Alma-Lodaka, whom he fathered in his early days, and the second was Draken-Korin, who resulted from his mating with Alma-Lodaka. Matters of relationship meant nothing to the Valheru, save as points of reference.

He raided across the heavens with his brethren when the need for plunder rose up within them like a thing of mindless want. He took his eldar servants with him, riding behind him on the backs of his dragons, to catalogue and care for his plunder. He knew the universe, and it trembled at the thunder of the Dragon Host when they roared into the skies. Other star-spanning races challenged the Valheru, but none survived. The Contemplators of Per, with their powers to manipulate the stuff of life, were cast down and their secrets lost with them. The Tyrant of the Cormoran Empire sent forth the might of a thousand worlds. Ships the size of cities sped through the void to unleash mighty engines of war upon the invaders. The Dragon Lords obliterated them without hesitation, and the Tyrant died screaming in the lowest basement of his palace while his world was destroyed above him. The Masters of Majinor and their dark magic were swept away by the Dragon Host. The Grand Alliance, the Marshals of Dawn, the Siar Brotherhood, all attempted to resist. All were destroyed. Of all who stood before the Valheru, only the Lorekeepers of the Aal, the supposed first race, managed to avoid destruction, but even the Aal could not oppose the Dragon Host. In the multitudes of universes, the Valheru were supreme.

For ages Ashen-Shugar lived as his people had always lived, fearing none, and worshipping only Rathar, She who was called Order, and Mythar, He who was called Chaos, the Two Blind Gods of the Beginning.

Then came the call, and Ashen-Shugar went to meet with his brethren. It was an odd call, one unlike any before, for there was no bloodlust rising in his breast to take them beyond the stars to raid other worlds. Instead it was a call to meeting, where the Valheru would gather, to speak to one another. It was a strange concept.

Upon the plain, south of the mountains and the great forest, they stood in a circle, the hundreds who were the race. In the centre stood Draken-Korin, who called himself Lord of Tigers. Two of his creatures waited one at each hand, powerful arms crossed, their tiger faces set in fierce snarls. They were as nothing to the Valheru, only posing as a reminder that Draken-Korin was, by commonly held opinion, the strangest of their kind. He had ideas of new things.

'The order of the universe is changing,' he said, pointing to the heavens. 'Rathar and Mythar have fled, or have been deposed, but for whatever cause, Order and Chaos have no more meaning. Mythar let loose the strands of power and from them the new gods arise. Without Rathar to knit the strands of power together, these beings will seize that power and establish an order. It is an order we must oppose. These gods are knowing, are aware, and are challenging us.'

'When one appears, kill it,' answered Ashen-Shugar, unconcerned by Draken-Korin's words.

'They are our match in power. For the moment they struggle among themselves, seeking each dominion over the others as they strive to gain mastery of that power left by the Two Blind Gods of the Beginning. But that struggle will end and then shall our existence be threatened. They *will* turn their might upon us.'

Ashen-Shugar said, 'What cause for concern? We fight as we have before. That is the answer.'

'No, there needs be more. We must fight in harmony, not each alone, lest they overwhelm us.'

Of late, an odd voice had come to Ashen-Shugar, a voice with a name. The name was lost upon him now, but the voice spoke. *You must be apart.*

The Ruler of the Eagles' Reaches said, 'Do what you will. I will have none of it.' He ordered his mighty golden dragon Shuruga into the sky and flew home.

Time passed, and Ashen-Shugar would occasionally return to the site of his brethren working. A strange thing, like the cities on other worlds, was fashioned by magic arts and the work of slaves. In it the Valheru resided, even as it was being fashioned. As never before in their history, they became for a time a cooperative society of beings, their combative nature stemmed by a compact, a truce. It was alien to Ashen-Shugar.

Shortly before the city was completed, Ashen-Shugar sat upon his dragon's back, regarding the work. It was a windy day, bitter cold as winter approached.

A roar from above caused Shuruga to trumpet a reply. *Do we fight?* asked the gold dragon.

'No. We wait.'

Ashen-Shugar ignored the disappointment he sensed in Shuruga. Another dragon, black as coal, landed and cautiously approached Ashen-Shugar.

'Has the Ruler of the Eagles' Reaches finally come to join us?' asked Draken-Korin, his black and orange striped armour glinting in the harsh light as he dismounted.

'No. I simply watch,' answered Ashen-Shugar, dismounting also.

'You alone have not agreed.'

'Joining to plunder across the cosmos is one thing, Draken-Korin. This . . . this plan of yours is madness.'

'What is this madness? I know not of what you speak. We are. We do. What more is there?'

'This is not our way.'

'It is not our way to let others stand against our will. These new beings, they contest with us.'

Ashen-Shugar looked skyward, regarding those signs that indicated Draken-Korin was correct about the struggle for power between the newly aborning gods. 'Yes, that is so.' He remembered those other star-faring races they had faced, the mortal beings who had fallen before the Dragon Host. 'But they are not like others. They also are formed from the very stuff of this world, as are we.'

'What does that matter? How many of our kin have you killed? How much blood has passed your lips? Whoever stands against you must be killed, or kill you. That is all.'

'What of those left behind, the moredhel and the elves?' He used the terms that had come to differentiate between the slaves of the household and the slaves of the fields and woods.

'What of them? They are nothing.'

'They are ours.' Ashen-Shugar felt a strange presence within himself and knew the other, the one whose name often eluded him, was causing him to be filled with alien cares.

'You have grown strange under your mountains, Ashen-Shugar. They are our servants. It is not as if they possessed true power. They exist for our pleasure, nothing more. What concerns you?'

'I do not know. There is something' – he paused, as if hearing a call to some other place – 'something wrong in the ordering of these events. I think we risk not only ourselves, but the very fabric of the universe.'

Draken-Korin shrugged and began returning to his dragon. 'What matter? If we fail, then we are dead. What matter if the universe ceases with us?' Draken-Korin returned to his dragon. Mounting, he said, 'You ponder issues that are meaningless.'

Draken-Korin flew off and Ashen-Shugar was left to face these odd, new feelings within himself.

Time passed, and the Ruler of the Eagles' Reaches watched the final work upon Draken-Korin's city. When it was done, Ashen-Shugar came and found his people once more in council. He walked along a broad avenue, one lined with tall pillars, each adorned with a tiger's head carving. He was mildly amused by Draken-Korin's vanity.

Walking down a long ramp, he reached the chamber within the earth. He found the vast hall filled with the Valheru. Alma-Lodaka, she who called herself Emerald Lady of Serpents, said, 'Have you come to join us, Father-Husband?' She was flanked by two of her servants, created in open imitation of Draken-Korin's. They were snakes given arms and legs, grown as large as the moredhel. Amber eyes flickered with nictitating membranes as they fixed upon Ashen-Shugar.

'I have come to witness folly.'

Draken-Korin drew his black blade, but another, Alrin-Stolda,

Monarch of the Black Lake, cried, 'Spill Valheru blood and the compact is void!'

The Lord of Tigers resheathed his sword. 'It is well you come late, or we should have seen an end to your mockery.'

Ashen-Shugar said, 'I have no fear of you. I only wish to see what you have fashioned. This is my world, and that which is mine is not to be threatened.'

The others regarded him with cold eyes and Alrin-Stolda said, 'Do what you will, but know our purpose cannot be balked. As mighty as you are, Ruler of the Eagles' Reaches, you cannot oppose us all. Watch as we do what we must.'

In concert, under Draken-Korin's direction, a great magic was forged. For an instant Ashen-Shugar felt a gut-wrenching pain, which passed almost instantly, leaving only a faint memory. A giant stone appeared upon the floor of the hall, a flat-topped, circular green thing with facets, glowing like an emerald lit with inner fire. Draken-Korin came to stand over it, and placed his hand upon it. It pulsed with energy as he said, 'Behold the final tool. The Lifestone.'

Without comment, Ashen-Shugar withdrew from the hall, marching back toward the waiting Shuruga. A voice from behind caused him to turn and he saw Alma-Lodaka hurrying after.

'Father-Husband. Will you not join us?'

He felt a strange urgency toward her, almost as when the heat came upon her, but different. He did not understand the odd feeling. *It is affection*, came the voice of the other. He ignored that voice and said, 'Daughter-Wife, our Brother-Son has begun that which spells final destruction. He is mad.'

She looked at him strangely. 'I don't know what you mean. I do not know that word. We do what we must. I had wished to have you at my side, for you stand as mighty as any of us, but do what you will. Oppose us at your risk.' With no further words, she left him and returned to the hall where the next great magic would be undertaken.

Ashen-Shugar mounted his dragon and returned to the Eagles' Reaches.

As Ashen-Shugar entered the hall of his mountain domicile, the skies above reverberated with the sound of distant thunder. And he knew the Dragon Host flew between worlds.

For weeks the skies were angry and without substance, as the stuff of creation flowed from horizon to horizon. Madness was without limit in the universe, as the Valheru rose up to challenge the new gods. Time was without meaning, and the very fabric of reality rippled and flowed, and in the centre of his hall, Ashen-Shugar brooded.

Then he summoned Shuruga and flew to that odd place on the plain, that city of Draken-Korin's making. And he waited.

Mad vortices of energy crashed across the heavens. Ashen-Shugar could see the very fabric of time and space rent and folding in upon itself. He knew it was almost time. He sat quietly upon the back of Shuruga and waited.

A clarion sounded, that alarm he had erected in concert with the world, which told him the moment he had awaited was upon him. Urging Shuruga upward, Ashen-Shugar searched for what he knew must appear before the mad display in the skies. The dragon stiffened under him and he saw his prey. The figure of Draken-Korin grew discernible as he slowed his black dragon. An odd something appeared in Draken-Korin's eyes, something alien. The other voice said, *It is horror.*

Shuruga sped forward. The great dragon roared his challenge, answered by Draken-Korin's black. Then the two clashed in the sky.

Quickly it was over, for Draken-Korin had surrendered too much of his essence to create the madness which filled the skies.

Ashen-Shugar landed lightly near the twisted body of his foeman and came to stand over him. The fallen Valheru looked up at his attacker and whispered, 'Why?'

Pointing upward, Ashen-Shugar said, 'This obscenity should never have been allowed. You bring an end to all we knew.'

Draken-Korin looked heavenward, where his brethren battled the gods. 'They were so strong. We could never have dreamed.' His face revealed his terror and hate as Ashen-Shugar raised his golden blade to end it. 'But I had the right!' he screamed.

Ashen-Shugar severed Draken-Korin's head from his shoulders, and suddenly both body and head vanished in a hiss of smoke. Leaving not a trace, the fallen Valheru's essence returned skyward, to mix with that mindless thing of anger which battled the gods. With bitterness Ashen-Shugar said, 'There is no right. There is only power.' Alone of his kind, he could understand the mocking irony in his words. He retired to his cavern to await the final outcome of the Chaos Wars.

Time was without meaning as time itself was a weapon in battle, but in some sense it passed while the new gods warred with what had been the Dragon Host. Then the gods moved in concert, those who had survived the internecine warfare whereby each had established his place in the hierarchy of things, and they focused their unified attention upon the Valheru. They moved as a force of power beyond the maddest dream of Draken-Korin, and as a body they cast the Valheru from the universe. They cast them into another dimension of space and time and moved to deny the Valheru a way back. In near-mindless rage the Valheru sought to return home, to reach that thing left against this day, that thing denied to them by one of their own. Ashen-Shugar had prevented their victory, and now they were being blocked from their homeworld. In their anger and anguish they turned their might upon the lesser races of the new universe. From world to world they rampaged, destroying anything and everything in their path. From world after world they tore the essence of life, the secrets of magics, and the powers of suns. Before them lay warm, verdant worlds circling living suns; behind them lay frigid, lifeless orbs spinning about burned out stars. In their frantic attempt to return to the world of their nurturance, they delivered utter ruination to all they touched. Lesser races banded together, attempting to oppose this raging thing. At first they were swept away, then they slowed it, then at last they found a way to escape. One lesser race, called human, turned its full attention to escape, and ways were found to flee. Mankind and other races discovered a haven. Gates were opened to other worlds, and the races fled, scattering themselves through time and space.

Great holes in the fabric of the universe were opened. Dwarves and men, goblins and trolls, all came through the cracks in reality, the rifts between one universe and another. New races, new creatures, came to Midkemia, and upon this world they sought a place.

Then the gods moved to close off the world of Midkemia to the Dragon Lords for eternity. They turned to the rifts they had allowed to form, and they sealed them. Suddenly the last route between the stars was closed off. A barrier was erected. The Dragon Host tried in vain to penetrate this curtain, but to no avail. They were denied return to Midkemia's universe and they raged in frustration, vowing to find means of entrance.

Then it was over. The Chaos Wars, the Days of the Mad Gods' Rage, the Time of Star Death: by whatever name it would come to be called, the clash between that which was and that which followed was finished. When it was over, and the skies had again been cleansed of insanity, Ashen-Shugar left his cavern. Returning to the plain before the city of Draken-Korin, he observed the aftermath of the mightiest struggle recorded. He landed Shuruga, then allowed the dragon to hunt. For a long time he silently waited for something, he couldn't be sure what.

Hours passed, then at last the other voice spoke. *What is this place?*

'The Desolation of the Chaos Wars. Draken-Korin's monument, the lifeless tundra that was once great grasslands. Few living things abide here. Most creatures flee to the south and more hospitable climes.'

Who are you?

Ashen-Shugar felt amusement. Laughing, he said, 'I am what you are becoming. We are as one. So you have said many times.' His laughter ceased. He was the first of his race to laugh. There was a sadness underlying the humour, for to understand humour marked Ashen-Shugar as something beyond any Valheru, and he knew he was witness to the beginning of a new era.

I had forgotten.

Ashen-Shugar, last of the Valheru, called Shuruga back from

376

his hunt. Mounting his steed, he glanced at the spot where Draken-Korin had been defeated, marked only by ash. Shuruga took to the skies, high above the aftermath of destruction.

It is worthy of sorrow.

'I think not,' said the Valheru. 'There is a lesson, though I cannot bring myself to know it. Yet I sense you do.' Ashen-Shugar closed his eyes a moment as his head throbbed. The other voice had again vanished from his mind. Ignoring the wonder of this odd personality who had come to influence him over the years, he turned his attention to his last task. Over mountains the Valheru rode, seeking those things enslaved by his kind. Within the forests of the southern continent, Ashen-Shugar raced over the stronghold of the tiger-men. In a voice loud enough to be heard, he cried, 'Let it be known that from this day you are a free people.'

The leader of the tiger-men called back, 'What of our master?'

'He is gone. Your destiny is in your own hands. By my word I, Ashen-Shugar, say this is so.'

Then to the south, to where the serpent race created by Alma-Lodaka resided, he went. And there his words were greeted with hisses of terror and anger. 'How may we survive without our mistress, she who is our goddess-mother?'

'That is for you to decide. You are a free people.'

The serpents were not pleased and set about to discover means how their mistress could again be recalled. As a race they made a vow, that until the end of time they would work to bring back her who was their mother and their goddess, Alma-Lodaka. From that day forward, the priesthood became the ultimate power within the society of the Pantathian serpent people.

Around the world he flew, and everywhere he passed, the words were spoken: 'Your destiny is your own. All are a free people.' At last he reached the strange place fashioned by Draken-Korin and the others. There gathered were the elves. Landing upon the plain, the Valheru said, 'Let the word go forth. From this moment you are free.'

The elves looked among themselves, and one said, 'What does this mean?'

'You are free to do as you wish. No one will care for you or direct your lives.'

The spokesman bowed and said, 'But, master, those who are wisest among us have gone with your brethren, and with them goes the lore, the knowledge, and the power. We are weak without the eldar. How, then, will we survive?'

'Your destiny is now your own to forge as best you may. Should you be weak you will perish. Should you be strong, you will survive. And mark you well, there are new forces let loose upon the land. Creatures of alien nature are come here, and with them shall you strive or make peace, as you will, for they also seek their destiny. But there will be a new order, and in it must you find a place. It may be you shall need raise yourself above others and exercise dominion, or it may be they will destroy you. Or perhaps peace is possible between you. That is for you to decide. I am done with you all, save this one last command. This place is forbidden, upon pain of my wrath. Let none enter it again.' With a wave of his hand he fashioned mighty magic and the small city of the Valheru slowly sank under the ground. 'Let the dusts of time bury it and let none remember it. This is my will.'

The elves bowed and said, 'As it is willed, master, so you will be obeyed.' The eldest of the elves turned to his brethren and said, 'None may enter this place: let none approach. It is vanished from mortal eye; it is not remembered.'

Ashen-Shugar said, 'Now you are a free people.'

The elves, those who had lived most removed from their masters, said, 'We shall go, then, to a place where we may live at peace.' They moved to the west, seeking a place where they could live in harmony.

Others said, 'We shall be wary of these new beings, for we are those who have the right to inherit the mantles of power.'

Ashen-Shugar turned and said, 'Pitiful creatures, have you not observed how power means nothing? Find another path.' But the moredhel were already leaving, his words unheard, as they began to dream the dreams of power. They had set foot upon the Dark Path even as they began to follow their brothers to the west. In time their brothers would drive them off, but for now they were as one.

Others moved silently away, ready to destroy any who opposed them, not content to seek out their master's power, certain of their own ability to take by force of arms whatever they wished. Those elves had been twisted by the forces let loose during the Chaos Wars and were already drawing away from their brethren. They would be called the glamredhel, the mad elves, and as they set out for the north, they turned suspicious eyes upon those moving westward. They would hie themselves away, using science and sorcery plundered from alien worlds to build giant cities in imitation of their masters, to protect themselves from their kindred, while plotting to make war upon them.

Disgusted by their behaviour, Ashen-Shugar returned to his hall, to reside until that time when he was to leave this life, preparing the way for the other. The universe was changed, and within his hall Ashen-Shugar felt himself alien to the newly-forged order. As if reality itself rejected his nature, he fell into torpor, a coma-like sleep, where his being grew and diffused and began to suffuse his armour, the power being passed into artifacts, to await another who would come to wear his mantle.

At the last he stirred and said, 'Have I erred?'

Now you know doubt.

'This strange quietness within, what is it?'

It is death approaching.

Closing his eyes, the last Valheru said, 'I thought as much. So few of my kind lived beyond battle. It was a rare thing. I am the last. Still, I would like to fly Shuruga once more.'

He is gone. Dead ages past.

Ashen-Shugar struggled with vague memories. Weakly he said, 'But I flew him this morning.'

It was a dream. As is this.

'Am I then also mad?' The thought of what was seen in Draken-Korin's eyes haunted Ashen-Shugar.

You are but a memory, said the other. *This is but a dream.*

'Then I will do what is planned. I accept the inevitable. Another will come to take my place.'

So it has happened already, for I am the one who came, and I have taken up your sword and put upon your mantle; your cause is now mine. I stand against those who would plunder this world, said the other.

The one called Tomas.

Tomas opened his eyes and then closed them again. He shook his head, as if clearing it. To Pug he had been silent for only a moment, but the magician suspected that many things had passed through Tomas's mind. At last Tomas said, 'I have the memories now. Now I understand what is occurring.'

Macros nodded. He said to Pug, 'In all my dealings with the Ashen-Shugar-Tomas paradox, that most difficult of all was how much knowledge to permit Tomas. Now he is ready to deal with the greatest challenge of his existence, and now he must know the truth. And you as well, though I suspect you have already deduced what he has learned.'

Softly Pug replied, 'At first I was misled by the enemy's use of ancient Tsurani when it spoke in Rogen's vision. But now I realize that was simply because that was the language of humans it knew at the time of the Escape across the golden bridge. Once I discarded the idea that the Enemy was somehow linked to the Tsurani, when I considered the presence of the eldar upon Kelewan, then I understood. I know what we face, and why the truth was hidden from Tomas. It is the worst possible nightmare come to life.'

Macros looked to Tomas. Tomas looked long at Pug, and there was pain in his eyes. Quietly, he said, 'When I first remembered the time of Ashen-Shugar I thought I . . . I thought my heritage had been left against the Tsurani invasion. But that was only a small part of it.'

'Yes,' said Macros. 'There is more. You now know how a dragon thought extinct for generations – an ancient black – could guard me.'

Tomas's expression was openly one of doubt and worry. With an almost resigned note, he added, 'And I now know the purpose of Murmandamus's masters.' He waved his hand around them. 'The trap was less to prevent Macros from reaching Midkemia than it was to bring us here, keeping us away from the Kingdom.'

'Why?' asked Pug.

Macros said, 'For in our own time Murmandamus commands an army and strikes into your homeland. Even as you searched for me in the City Forever, I wager he was overrunning the garrison at Highcastle. And I know his purpose in invading the Kingdom. He needs to reach Sethanon.'

'Why Sethanon?' asked Pug.

'Because by chance that city is built over the ruins of the ancient city of Draken-Korin,' answered Tomas. 'And within that city lies the Lifestone.'

The sorcerer said, 'We'd best continue walking while we discuss these problems, Pug, for we've got to return to Midkemia and our own era. Tomas and I can tell you of the city of Draken-Korin and the Lifestone. That part you are ignorant of, though you know the rest; the Enemy, that thing you learned of upon Kelewan, is not a single being. It is the combined might and mind of the Valheru. The Dragon Lords are returning to Midkemia, and they want their world back.' With a humourless grin he said, 'And we've got to keep them from taking it.'

CHAPTER SEVENTEEN

Withdrawal

*A*RUTHA STUDIED THE CANYON.

He had ridden out before first light with Guy and Baron Highcastle to observe the advancing elements of Murmandamus's forces. From the spot where he and his companions had been intercepted by Highcastle's men, they could see campfires in the distance.

Arutha pointed. 'Do you see, Brian? There must be a thousand fires, which means, five, six thousand soldiers. And that is only the first elements. By this time tomorrow there will be twice that number. Within three days Murmandamus will be throwing thirty thousand or more at you.'

Highcastle, ignoring Arutha's tone, leaned forward over his horse's neck, as if straining to see more clearly. 'I only see fires, Highness. You know it is a common trick to build extra fires, so the enemy can't gauge your strength or disposition.'

Guy swore under his breath and turned his horse around. 'I'll not wait to explain the obvious to idiots.'

'And I'll not sit and be insulted by a traitor!' Highcastle shot back.

Arutha rode between them, saying, 'Guy, you swore no oath of fealty to me, but you're alive this minute because I've accepted your parole. Don't let this become an issue of honour. I don't need duels now. I need you!'

Guy's one good eye narrowed and he seemed ready for more hot words, but at last he said, '*I apologize . . . my lord*. The rigours of a long journey. I'm sure you understand.' At the last, he spurred his horse back toward the garrison.

Brian Highcastle said, 'The man was an insufferably arrogant swine when he was Duke, and it seems two years wandering about the Northlands hasn't changed him in the least.'

Arutha spun his horse around and faced Lord Highcastle. His words showed he was at the limit of his patience. 'He's also the finest general I've ever known, Brian. He just watched his command overrun; his city *utterly* destroyed. He has thousands of his people scattered throughout the mountains and *he doesn't know how many survived*. I'm sure you can appreciate his shortness of temper.' The sarcasm of the last remark revealed his own frustration.

Lord Highcastle was silent. He turned and regarded the camp of the enemy as the dawn came.

Arutha tended his horse, the one taken from the brigands in the mountains. A bay mare, she was resting and regaining lost weight; Arutha had used one loaned him by Baron Highcastle that morning. In another day the mare would be fit to ride south. Arutha had expected the Baron at least to offer him an exchange of animals, but Brian, Lord Highcastle, seemed to be taking delight in pointing out at every opportunity that as a vassal to Lyam he had no obligation to Arutha, save being barely civil. Arutha was not sure if Brian would even offer to send an escort. The man was an insufferable egotist, not terribly perceptive, and stubborn – qualities not unexpected in a man shunted off to the frontier to hold against small bands of badly organized goblins, but hardly those of the commander one would wish to oppose a battle-hardened, well-led invading army.

The stable door opened and Locklear and Jimmy walked in. They halted when they saw Arutha, then Jimmy approached. 'We were coming to check the horses.'

Arutha said, 'I cast no blame on your stewardship, Jimmy. I simply like to see to such things for myself when I can afford the time. And it gives me a chance to think.'

Locklear sat down on a hay bale between Arutha's mount and the wall. He reached out and patted the mare's nose. 'Highness, why is this happening?'

'You mean why the war?'

'No, I think I can understand someone wanting to conquer, or at least I've heard enough about such wars in the histories. No, I mean the place. Why here? Amos was showing us some Kingdom maps upstairs and . . . it doesn't make any sense.'

Arutha paused in combing his mount. 'You've just touched upon the single biggest cause for concern I have. Guy and I have discussed it. We just don't know. But one thing to be sure of is, if your enemy is doing something unexpected, it's for a reason. And you had best be quick in understanding what that is, Squire, for if you don't, it's likely to be the means of your defeat.' His eyes narrowed. 'No, there is a reason Murmandamus is heading this way. Given the timetable for what he is able to do before winter, he must be making for Sethanon. But why? There is no apparent motive for him to go there, and once there, he can only hold until spring. Once spring comes, Lyam and I will crush him.'

Jimmy pulled an apple from his tunic and cut it in two, giving half to the horse. 'Unless he figures to have this business over and done with before spring.'

Arutha looked at Jimmy. 'What do you mean?'

Jimmy shrugged and wiped his mouth. 'I don't know exactly, except what you said. You have to guess what the enemy is up to. Given the indefensibility of the city, he might be counting on everyone pulling out. Like you said, come spring you can crush him. So, I guess he knows that, too. Now, if I was making straight for some place I could get smashed the next spring, it'd be because I didn't plan on being there in the spring. Or maybe there was something there that gave me an edge – either made me so powerful that I didn't have to worry about being caught between two armies, or kept the armies from coming at all. Something like that.'

Arutha rested his chin upon his arm on the back of the horse as he thought. 'But what?'

Locklear said, 'Something magic?'

Jimmy laughed. 'We've had no shortage of that since this whole mess began.'

Arutha ran his finger along the chain holding the talisman given him by the Ishapian monks at Sarth. 'Something magic,' he muttered. 'But what?'

Quietly Jimmy said, 'It'll be something big, I'd guess.'

Arutha fought rising irritation. In his belly he knew Jimmy was right. And he felt frustration close to rage in not understanding the secret behind Murmandamus's insane invasion.

Abruptly trumpets sounded, and were answered almost immediately by the pounding of boot heels upon the cobbles as soldiers rushed to their posts. Arutha was out of the stables in an instant, the boys just behind.

Galain pointed. 'There.'

Guy and Arutha looked down from the highest tower of the keep, overlooking the barbican of the fortification. Beyond, in the deep canyon called Cutter's Gap, the first elements of Murmandamus's army could be seen. 'Where's Highcastle?' asked Arutha.

'Down on the wall with his men,' answered Amos. 'He rode in a short time ago, all bloodied and battered. Seems the Dark Brothers were up in the hills above his advance position and swarmed down over him. He had to cut his way out. Looks like he lost most of the detachment out there.'

Guy swore. 'The idiot. That was where he could have bottled up

Murmandamus's army for a few days. Here, on the walls, it'll be a bloody damned farce.'

The elf said, 'It was foolish to underestimate the ability of the mountain moredhel once they get into the rocks. These are not simple goblins he's facing.'

Arutha said, 'I'm going to see if I can talk to him.' The Prince hurried down through the keep and within a few minutes was standing beside Lord Highcastle. The Baron was bloodied from a scalp wound, received when his helm had been knocked off his head. He had not put another on, and his hair was matted with dried blood. The man was pale and shaky, but he still supervised his command without hesitation. Arutha said, 'Brian, can you see what I was talking about?'

'We'll bottle them up here,' he answered, pointing to where the narrow canyon came together before the wall. 'There's no room to stage, so his men will be stopped before the wall. We'll cut them down like wheat before a scythe.'

'Brian, he's bringing an army of thirty thousand against you. What have you here? Two? He doesn't care about losses! He'll pile his soldiers against your walls, then walk over their corpses to reach you. They'll come and come and come again and wear you down. You can't hold out for more than a day or two at the longest.'

The Baron's eyes locked upon Arutha's. 'My charter is to defend this position. I may not quit it save by leave of the King. I am charged to hold at all costs. Now, you are not part of my command; please leave the wall.'

Arutha remained motionless for a moment, his face flushed. He left the wall and hurried back to the tower. When he had rejoined those upon the tower, he said to Jimmy, 'Go saddle the horses and get all we need for a long ride. Steal what you must from the kitchen. We may have to make a quick exit.'

Jimmy nodded and took Locklear by the sleeve, leading the other boy away. Arutha, Guy, Galain, and Amos watched as the leading edge of the invading army moved closer, coming down the canyon like a slow-moving flood.

It began as Arutha had predicted, a wave of soldiers attacking down the narrow draw. The fortress had been built as a staging point for the garrison, with little thought that it would need to withstand a massive attack from an organized army. Now just such an army advanced upon it.

Arutha joined his companions atop the tower, watching as Highcastle's bowmen began slaughtering Murmandamus's advance elements. Then the front ranks of the attackers opened, and goblins with heavy shields hurried forward at a crouch, forming a shield wall. Moredhel bowmen ran and took refuge behind them, then rose and began answering the archers upon the wall. The first flight of arrows took a dozen of Highcastle's bowmen off the wall, and the attackers streamed forward. Again and again the two sides exchanged missile fire and the defenders stood firm. But the attackers continued to advance toward the wall.

Step by bloody step they came, moving past the bodies of those who had fallen. Each wave came and fell, but moved closer to the walls than the last. An archer would die and another would run forward to take his place. Then, as the sun breasted the high wall of the canyon, the attackers had halved the distance to the wall. By the time the sun had made the narrow transit from wall to wall overhead, the distance was narrowed to less than fifty yards. The next wave was unleashed.

Scaling ladders were carried forward, and the defenders exacted a heavy toll on those who carried them, but as each goblin or troll fell, another took his place carrying the ladder. At last they rested against the wall. Pole arms were employed to topple them, but others were put in place, and goblins scrambled up to be greeted by steel and flame. Then the battle of Highcastle was truly joined.

Arutha watched as the ragged defenders held again. The final wave had breasted the wall to the south of the barbican, but the reinforcement company had filled the breach and driven them back. With sunset, the trumpets sounded withdraw, and Murmandamus's host pulled back up the canyon.

Guy swore. 'I've never seen such carnage and waste in the name of duty.'

Arutha was forced to agree. Amos said, 'Bloody hell! These border lads might be the dregs and outcasts of your armies, Arutha, but they're a tough and salty crew. I've never seen men give better account of themselves.'

Arutha agreed. 'You don't serve on the border for long and not get toughened. Few big battles, but constant fighting. Still, they're doomed if Brian keeps this up.'

Galain said, 'We should leave before dawn if we are to get away, Arutha.'

The Prince nodded. 'I'm going to speak one last time with Brian. If he still refuses to listen to reason, I'll ask permission to quit the garrison.'

'And if he doesn't?' asked Amos.

Arutha said, 'Jimmy's already got us provisions and a way out. We'll leave on foot if we must.'

The Prince left the tower and hurried back to where he had last seen Highcastle. Looking about, he saw no sign of the Baron. Inquiring of a guard, he was told, 'Last I saw of the Baron was an hour ago. He might be down in the courtyard with the dead and wounded, Highness.'

The soldier's words were prophetic, for Arutha found Brian, Lord Highcastle, with the dead and wounded. The chirurgeon was kneeling over him, and when the Prince approached, he looked up, shaking his head. 'He's dead.'

Arutha spoke to an officer standing by the body. 'Who's second?'

The man said, 'Walter of Gyldenholt, but I think he fell during the overrunning of the forward position.'

'Then who?'

'Baldwin de la Troville and I, Highness, are both ranked behind Walter. We arrived upon the same day, so who is senior I do not know.'

'Who are you?'

'Anthony du Masigny, formerly Baron of Calry, Highness.'

Arutha recognized the man from Lyam's coronation after hearing the name. He had been one of Guy's supporters. He still affected a trim appearance, but two years on the frontier had rid him of much of the manner of the court dandy he had displayed at Rillanon.

'If you've no objections, send for de la Troville and Guy du Bas-Tyra. Have them meet with us in the Baron's chambers.'

'I've no objections,' said du Masigny. He surveyed the carnage along the walls and in the courtyard. 'In fact I would welcome a little sanity and order about now.'

Baldwin de la Troville was a slender, hawkish man, in contrast to du Masigny's neatly trimmed, softer appearance. As soon as both officers were present, Arutha said, 'If either of you has any notion of that nonsense about being vassals only to the King and defending this fortress to the death, say so now.'

Both exchanged glances, and du Masigny laughed. 'Highness, we were sent here by order of your brother for' – he cast a glance at Guy – 'certain former political indiscretions. We are in no hurry to throw our lives away in futile gesture.'

De la Troville said, 'Highcastle was an idiot. A brave, almost heroic man, but still an idiot.'

'You'll accept my orders?'

'Gladly,' they both said.

'Then from now forward, du Bas-Tyra is my second in command. You'll accept him as your superior.'

Du Masigny grinned. 'That is hardly new to either of us, Highness.'

Guy nodded and returned the smile. 'They're good soldiers, Arutha. They'll do what needs to be done.'

Arutha ripped a map off the wall and laid it upon the table. 'I want half the garrison in saddle within an hour, but all orders are to be by whisper, no trumpets, no drums, no shouts. As soon as possible, I want squads of a dozen men each slipped out the postern gates at one-minute intervals. They're to ride for Sethanon. I think even as we speak Murmandamus is slipping his soldiers through the rocks on either side of the pass to cut off retreat. I don't think we have more than a few hours, certainly not past dawn.'

Guy's finger touched the map. 'If we send a small patrol to this point, then this point, just for show, it would slow down any infiltrators and cover some of the noise.'

Arutha nodded. 'De la Troville, lead that patrol, but don't engage any enemy forces. Run like a rabbit if needs be, and be sure to be back by two hours before dawn. By sunrise this garrison is to be evacuated, not a living man left behind.

'Now, the first squads leaving will consist of six able bodies and six wounded. Tie the wounded to their horses if you must. After today's slaughter, there should be enough mounts for each squad to take two or three extra, and I want each to carry as much grain as possible. Not all the horses will make Sethanon, but between the grain and rotating the mounts, most should.'

'Many of the wounded won't survive, Highness,' said du Masigny.

'The ride to Sethanon will be a killer, but I want everyone safely away. I don't care how badly hurt they are, we're not leaving one man behind for the butchers. Du Masigny, I want every dead soldier to be put back on the wall, propped up in the crenels. When dawn comes, I want Murmandamus to think he faces a full garrison.' He turned to Guy. 'That might slow him down a little. Now prepare messages for Northwarden, telling him of what is occurring here. If memory serves, Michael, Lord Northwarden, is far brighter than the late Baron Highcastle. Perhaps he'll agree to send some soldiers to harass Murmandamus's flanks along his line of march. I want messages to Sethanon—'

'We have no birds for Sethanon, Highness,' said de la Troville. 'We are expecting some to be coming by caravan within the month.' He looked embarrassed for his former commander. 'An oversight.'

'How many birds do you have left in the coops?'

'A dozen. Three for Northwarden. Two each for Tyr-Sog and Loriél, and five for Romney.'

Arutha said, 'Then at least we can spread the word. Tell Duke Talwyn of Romney to send word to Lyam in Rillanon. I want the Armies of the East to march on Sethanon. Martin will already be in the field with Vandros's army. As soon as he encounters the survivors from Armengar and learns Murmandamus's route, he'll turn his forces around and send the army from Yabon to Hawk's Hollow, where they can cut through the mountains and march this way. We'll send word to Tyr-Sog to get gallopers out to tell him exactly where we are. The garrison from Krondor will march as soon as Gardan receives word from Martin. He'll pick up troops along the way at Darkmoor.' He seemed vaguely hopeful. 'We may yet survive at Sethanon.'

'Where's Jimmy?'

Locklear said, 'He said he had something to do and would be right back.'

Arutha looked about. 'What nonsense is he about now?' It was nearly first light and the last detachment of soldiers was ready to ride out of the garrison. Arutha's party, the last fifty soldiers, and two dozen extra horses were poised at the gate, and Jimmy was off somewhere.

Then the boy dashed into sight, waving for them to be off. He jumped into the saddle, and Arutha signalled for the postern gates to be opened. They were pushed wide and Arutha led the column out. As Jimmy overtook him, Arutha said, 'What kept you?'

'A surprise for Murmandamus.'

'What?'

'I put a candle on top of a small barrel of oil I found. It's on a bunch of straw and rags and things. Should go up in a half hour or so. Won't do much but make a lot of smoke, but it will burn for a few hours.'

Amos laughed in appreciation. 'And after Armengar, they won't be so quick to rush toward a fire.'

Guy said, 'That's a bright one, Arutha.'

Jimmy looked pleased at the praise. Arutha said dryly, 'Sometimes too bright.'

Jimmy's expression turned dark, while Locklear grinned.

They gained a day. From the time they left the first morning until sundown, they saw no sign of pursuers. Arutha decided Murmandamus must have ordered a thorough search of the empty fortress and would then have to reorder his army for the trek across the High Wold. No, they had stolen the march on the invaders, and they were likely to stay ahead of all but his fastest cavalry.

They could push the horses, rotating the remounts they led, and make between thirty-five and forty miles a day. Some horses were sure to go lame but with luck they would be across the vast, hilly High Wold in a week. Once in the Dimwood, they would have to slow, but the chances of being overtaken would also be less, for those behind would have to be cautious of ambush from among the thick trees.

On the second day they began passing the bodies of those wounded who could not withstand the punishment of the hard ride. Their comrades had followed orders and cut the dead loose from their saddles, not wasting time to bury them, not even stripping them of weapons and armour.

On the third day they saw the first signs of pursuit, vague shapes on the horizon near sundown. Arutha ordered an extra hour's ride, and there were no signs of those behind at dawn.

On the fourth day they saw the first village. The soldiers riding past before them had alerted everyone of the danger, and it was now deserted. Smoke came from one chimney and Arutha sent a soldier to investigate. A well-banked fire still smouldered, but no one was left. A little seed grain was found and brought along, but all other foodstuffs were gone. There was little to comfort the enemy, so Arutha ordered the village left alone. Had the villagers not picked the place clean, he would have ordered it burned. He expected Murmandamus's soldiers would see to that, but he still felt better for leaving the place as he had found it.

Near the end of the fifth day, they saw a company of riders approaching from behind, and Arutha ordered his company to halt and make ready. The riders came close enough to be clearly marked as a dozen moredhel scouts, but they veered off and moved back toward their main army rather than accept the offer to fight the larger force.

On the sixth day they overtook a caravan, heading south, already warned of the approaching danger by the first units of the garrison to ride past. The caravan drivers were moving at a slow, steady pace, but it was certain they'd be overtaken by Murmandamus's advanced units within another day, two at the most. Arutha rode to where the merchant who owned the wagons sat and, riding alongside, shouted, 'Cut your horses loose and ride them. Otherwise you cannot escape the Dark Brothers who follow!'

'But my grain!' complained the merchant. 'I'll lose everything!'

Arutha signalled a halt. When the wagons were stopped, he shouted to his command. 'Each man take a sack of this merchant's grain. We'll need it for the Dimwood. Burn the rest!'

The protesting merchant ordered his bravos to defend his cargo, but the mercenaries took a single look at the fifty soldiers from Highcastle and moved away, allowing them to take the grain.

'Cut the horses loose!' ordered Guy.

The soldiers cut the horses from their traces, and led them away. Within minutes the sacks of grain had been removed from the first wagon and passed among the soldiers, including an extra sack for each of the merchant's horses. The rest of the wagons and grain were fired.

Arutha said to the merchant, 'There are thirty thousand goblins, Dark Brothers, and trolls on the march this way, master merchant. If you think I've done you an injustice, consider what you would face trundling these wagons along the trails of the Dimwood in the midst of such company. Now take the grain for your mounts and ride for the south. We shall stand at Sethanon, but if you value your skin, I'd ride past the city and make for Malac's Cross. Now, if you want to be paid for this grain, stay in Sethanon, and if we all manage somehow to survive the invasion, I'll recompense you. That's your risk to decide. I've no more time to waste on you.'

Arutha ordered his column forward and, minutes later, was not surprised to find the merchant and his mercenaries riding after them, staying as close to the column as their tired mounts would allow. After a short while, Arutha yelled to Amos, 'When we halt, get them some fresh horses from the remounts. I don't want to leave them behind.'

Amos grinned. 'They're just about scared enough to behave. Let's let them fall just a little farther behind, then when they catch up with us tonight they'll be bright and cooperative lads.'

Arutha shook his head. Even in the face of this backbreaking ride, Amos appreciated the humour of the moment.

On the seventh day they entered the Dimwood.

The sounds of fighting caused Arutha to order a halt. He motioned for Galain and a soldier to ride toward the source of the sound. They returned minutes later, the elf saying, 'It's over.'

They rode to the east to find soldiers from Highcastle in a clearing. A dozen moredhel bodies lay about. The sergeant in charge saluted when he saw Arutha approaching. 'We were resting our mounts when they hit us, Highness. Luckily, another squad was just west of here and came running.'

Arutha looked at Guy and Galain. 'How the hell did they get ahead of us?'

Galain said, 'They didn't. These have been here all summer, waiting.' He looked about. 'Over there, I think.' He led Arutha to a deadfall, which hid the entrance to a low hut, cleverly concealed by brush. Within the hut were stores: grain, weapons, dried meats, saddles, and other supplies.

Arutha inspected everything quickly, then said, 'This campaign has been long in planning. We can now be certain that Sethanon has always been Murmandamus's objective.'

'But we still don't know why,' observed Guy.

'Well, we'll have to proceed without regard to why. Take anything here that we can use, then destroy the rest.'

He said to the sergeant, 'Have you sighted other companies?'

'Yes, Highness. De la Troville had a camp a mile's ride to the northeast last night. We encountered one of his pickets and were ordered to continue on, so as not to concentrate too many men in one place.'

Guy said, 'Dark Brothers?'

The sergeant nodded. 'The woods are swarming with them, Your Grace. If we ride past, they give us little trouble. If we stop, we've snipers to deal with. Luckily they don't usually come in bands as large as this one. Still, it might do well for us to stay on the move.'

Arutha said, 'Take five men from my column and begin to head east. I want word passed that everyone is to keep a watchful eye for these stores of Murmandamus. I expect you'll find them guarded, so look for places where the Dark Brothers begin to object to your trespassing. Anything that can help him is to be destroyed. Now you'd better ride.'

Arutha then ordered another dozen men to ride a halfday to the west, then turn south, so that word of the caches of arms could be spread. He said to Guy, 'Let's get on the march. I can almost feel his vanguard stepping on our heels.'

Du Bas-Tyra nodded and said, 'Still, we might be able to slow him a bit along the way.'

Arutha looked about. 'I've been waiting for a place for an ambush. Or a bridge to burn behind us. Or a narrowing in the trail where we can fell a tree. But there hasn't been a single likely place.'

Amos agreed. 'This is the most bloody damn accommodating forest I've seen. You can march a parade through here and not one man in twenty would miss a step for having to dodge a tree.'

Guy said, 'Well, we take what we can get. Let's be off.'

The Dimwood was a series of interconnecting woodlands rather than a single forest such as the Edder or the Green Heart. After the first three days' travel, they passed a series of meadows, then entered some truly dark and foreboding woods. Several times they waited while Galain mismarked moredhel trail signs. The elf thought some of the moredhel scouts might wander a bit before discovering they were being misled. Three more times they came across caches of Murmandamus's stores. Dead moredhel and soldiers showed their locations. The swords had been tossed into fires to rob them of temper, while the arrows and spears were burned. The saddles and bridles had been cut up and the grain was scattered about the ground or burned. Blankets, clothing, and even foodstuffs had gone to feed the fires.

Late in the second week in the forest, they smelled smoke and had to flee a forest fire. Some overzealous ravaging of one of Murmandamus's caches had resulted in the fire breaking loose in the woods, now dry from the hot summer. As they rode away from the advancing blaze, Amos shouted, 'That's what we should do. Wait until his magnificent bastardness gets into the woods and burn it down around him. Ha!'

Arutha had lost six horses by the time they left the Dimwood, entering cultivated lands, but not one man, including the merchant and his mercenaries. They crossed twenty miles of farmland, then made camp. After sunset a faint glow on the southern horizon appeared.

Amos pointed it out to the boys. 'Sethanon.'

They reached the city and were halted at the gate by soldiers of the local garrison. 'We're looking for whoever's in command!' shouted the sergeant in charge, his chevrons clearly shown in gold upon the finely tailored green and white tabard of the Barony of Sethanon.

Arutha signalled, and the sergeant said, 'We've had soldiers from Highcastle drifting in for the last half day. They're being given compound in the marshalling yard. The Baron wants to see whoever's in charge of this lot.'

'Tell him I'm on my way as soon as these men are quartered.'

'And who should I tell him that is?'

'Arutha of Krondor.'

The man's mouth opened. 'But . . .'

'I know, I'm dead. Still, tell Baron Humphry I'll be up to his keep within the hour. And tell him I've Guy du Bas-Tyra with me. Then send a runner to the marshalling yard and find out if Baldwin de la Troville and Anthony du Masigny are safely here. If so, have them join me.'

The sergeant was motionless for a moment, then saluted. 'Yes, Highness!'

Arutha signalled for his column to enter the city, and for the first time in months saw the normal sights of the Kingdom, a city busy with the business of citizens who thought they were safely kept from harm by a benevolent monarch. The streets thronged with people busy with the concerns of the market, commerce, and celebration. In every direction Arutha could see only the commonplace, the expected, the mundane. How soon that would change.

Arutha ordered the gates closed. For the last week those who had chosen to take their chances and flee southward had been allowed to leave. Now the city was to be sealed. More messages had been sent, by pigeon and riders, to the garrisons at Malac's Cross, Silden, and Darkmoor, against the possibility of the other messages not reaching those commanders. Everything that could be done had been done, and all they could do was wait.

The scouts who had been positioned to the north had reported that Murmandamus's army was now completely in control of the Dimwood. Every farm between the woodlands and the city had been evacuated and all the inhabitants brought inside the walls. The Prince had instructed everyone to follow a strict schedule. All food was brought to Sethanon, but when time ran out, Arutha had ordered every farm put to the torch. The fall crops not yet harvested were fired, and unpicked gardens were dug up or poisoned and all herds too distant to be brought to the city were ordered scattered to the south and east. Nothing was left behind to aid the advancing host. Reports from the soldiers who had reached Sethanon indicated that at least thirty of Murmandamus's caches of stores had been discovered and looted or destroyed. Arutha harboured no illusions. At best he had stung the invaders, but no real damage had been accomplished save inconvenience.

Arutha sat in council with Amos, Guy, the officers from Highcastle, and Baron Humphry. Humphry sat in his armour – uncomfortably, for it was a gaudy contraption of fluted scrollwork, designed for show and not for combat – his golden plumed helm held before him. He had readily acknowledged Arutha's preemption of his command, for given its location, the garrison of Sethanon lacked any real battlefield commanders. Arutha had installed Guy, Amos, de la Troville, and du Masigny in key positions. They sat reviewing the disposition of troops and stores. Arutha concluded reading the list and spoke. 'We could withstand an army of Murmandamus's size up to two months, under normal circumstances. With what we saw at Armengar and Highcastle, I'm sure the circumstances will not be normal. Murmandamus must be within the city by two weeks, three at longest; otherwise he faces the possibility of an early freeze. The rainy fall weather is beginning, which will slow his assaults, and once winter comes, he'll find a starving army under his command. No, he must quickly enter Sethanon, and prevent us from using up or destroying our stores.

'If the very best of situations comes to pass, Martin will be now leaving the foothills of the Calastius Mountains below Hawk's Hollow with the army from Yabon, upward of six thousand soldiers. But he'll be at least two weeks away. We might see soldiers from Northwarden or from Silden about the same time, but at best we must hold for no less than two weeks and perhaps as long as four. Any longer, and help will be too slow in coming.'

He rose. 'Gentlemen, all we may do now is wait for the enemy to come. I suggest we rest and pray.'

Arutha walked out of the conference room. Guy and Amos came after. All paused, as if considering what they had been through so far, then drifted off their separate ways, to wait for the attackers.

CHAPTER EIGHTEEN

Homeward

*T*HEY WALKED THE HALL.

It seemed a straight thoroughfare, a yellowish white roadway with more glowing silver doors at about fifty-foot intervals. Macros made a sweeping motion with his arm. 'You walk in the midst of a mystery to match the City Forever, the Hall of Worlds. Here you may walk from world to world, if you but know the way.' He indicated a silver rectangle. 'A portal, giving passage to and from a world. Only a select few among the multitudes may discern them. Some learn the knack through study, others stumble upon them by chance. By altering your perceptions, you may see them wherever they lie. Here' – he waved at a door as they passed – 'is a burned-out world circling a forgotten sun.' Then he pointed to the door on the other side of the Hall. 'But there is a world teeming with life, a hodgepodge of cultures and societies, but with only one intelligent race.' He halted a moment. 'At least, that is what they will be in our own time.' He continued walking. 'At present, I expect these doors empty into swirls of hot gases only slightly more dense than nothing.

'In the future, a complete society exists who travel the Hall, conducting commerce between worlds, yet there are worlds whose entire populations have no knowledge of this place.'

Tomas said, 'I knew nothing of this place.'

'The Valheru had other means to travel,' Macros answered, inclining his head in Ryath's direction. 'Without the need, they never paused to apprehend the existence of the Hall, for surely they had the ability. Luck? I don't know, but much destruction was avoided by their remaining ignorant.'

'How far does the Hall extend?' said Pug.

'Endlessly. No one knows. The Hall appears straight, but it curves, and should I walk a short distance, I would vanish from your sight. Distances and time have little meaning between the worlds.'

He began leading them down the hall.

Following Macros's instructions, Pug had managed to bring them forward in time, to what Macros judged was near their own era. After having accelerated the Dragon Lord time trap, Pug had no difficulty following Macros's direction. The mechanics of the spells used were but logical extensions of what Pug had used to speed up the trap. Pug could only guess if the proper amount of time had passed, but Macros had reassured him that when they started to approach Midkemia, he would know how much adjustment Pug would have to make.

They had been walking and Pug had studied each door in passing. After a while he discovered there was a faint difference between each door, a slight spectral oddity in the shimmering silver light, which provided the clue to which world the door led to. 'Macros, what would occur if one were to step off between doors?' asked Pug.

The sorcerer said, 'I suspect you'd be quickly dead if you did so unprepared. You would float in rift-space without the benefit of Ryath's ability to navigate.'

He halted before a door. 'This is a necessary shortcut, across a planet, which will more than halve our travel time to Midkemia. The distance between here and the next gate is less than a hundred yards, but be advised: this world's atmosphere is deadly. Hold your breath for here magic has no meaning and you may not protect yourself with arts.' He breathed heavily for a moment, then with a great intake of breath, dashed through the door.

Tomas came next, then Pug, then Ryath. Pug squinted and almost exhaled as burning fumes assaulted his eyes and sudden, unexpected weight seemed to pull him down. They were sprinting across a barren plain of purple and red rocks, while overhead the air hung heavy with grey haze in orange skies. The earth trembled, and giant clouds of black smoke and gases were spewed heavenward by the bleeding mountains, glowing with reflecting orange light from volcanoes. The stuff of the world flowed down the sides of those peaks and the air hung heavy with oppressive heat. Macros pointed and they ran into a rock face, which returned them to the Hall.

Macros had been silent for hours, lost in thought. He pulled up short, coming out of his reverie, as he halted before a portal. 'We must cut across this world. It should be pleasant.'

He led them through a gate into a lovely green glade. Through trees they could hear the pounding of waves on the rocks and smell the tang of sea salt. Macros led them along a bluff overlooking a magnificent view of an ocean.

Pug studied the trees about them, finding them similar to those upon Midkemia. 'This is much like Crydee.'

'Warmer,' said Macros, inhaling the fragrance of the ocean. 'It's a lovely world, though no one lives upon it.' With a sad look in his eyes, he said, 'Perhaps someday I'll retire here.' He shook off the reflective mood. 'Pug, we are close to our own era, but still slightly out of phase.' He glanced about. 'I think it a year or so before your birth. We need a short burst of temporal acceleration.'

Pug closed his eyes and began a long spell, which had no

discernible effect, save that shadows began moving rapidly across the ground as the sun hurried its course across the sky. They were quickly plunged into darkness as night descended, then dawn followed. The pace of time's passage increased, as day and night flickered, then blurred into an odd grey light.

Pug paused and said, 'We must wait.' They all settled in, for the first time apprehending the loveliness of the world about them. The mundane beauty provided a benchmark against which to measure all the strange and marvellous places they had visited. Tomas seemed deeply troubled. 'All that I have witnessed makes me wonder at the scope of what we are confronting.' He was silent for a time. 'The universes are . . . such imponderable, immense things.' He studied Macros. 'What fate befalls this universe, if one little planet succumbs to the Valheru? Did my brethren not rule there before?'

Macros regarded Tomas with an expression of deep concern. 'True, but you've grown either fearful or more cynical. Neither will serve us.' He looked hard at Tomas, seeing the deep doubt in the eyes of the human turned Valheru. At last he nodded and said, 'The nature of the universe changed after the Chaos Wars; the coming of the gods heralded a new system of things – a complex, ordered system – where before only the prime rules of Order and Chaos had existed. The Valheru have no place in the present scheme of things. It would have been easier to bring Ashen-Shugar forward in time than to undertake what was required. I needed his power, but I also needed a mind behind that power that would serve our cause. Without the time link between him and Tomas, Ashen-Shugar would have been one with his brethren. Even with that link, Ashen-Shugar would have been beyond anyone's control.'

Tomas remembered. 'No one can imagine the depth of the madness I battled during the war with the Tsurani. It was a close thing.' His voice remained calm, but there was a note of pain in it as he spoke. 'I became a murderer. I slaughtered the helpless. Martin was driven to the brink of killing me, so savage had I become.' Then he added,

'And I had come to but a tenth part of my power then. On the day I regained my . . . sanity, Martin could have sent his cloth-yard shaft through my heart.' He pointed at a rock a few feet away and made a gripping motion with his hand. The rock crumbled to dust as if Tomas had squeezed it. 'Had my powers then been as they are now I could have killed Martin before he could have released the arrow – by an act of will.'

Macros nodded. 'You can see what the risks were, Pug. Even one Valheru alone would be almost as great a danger as the Dragon Host; he would be a power unrestrained in the cosmos.' His tone held no reassurance. 'There is no single being, save the gods, who could oppose him.' Macros smiled slightly. 'Except myself, of course, but even at my full powers, I could only survive a battle with them, not vanquish them. Without my powers . . .' He let the rest go unsaid.

'Then,' said Pug, 'why haven't the gods acted?'

Macros laughed, a bitter sound, and waved at all four of them. 'They are. What do you think *we're* doing here? *That* is the game. And we are the pieces.'

Pug closed his eyes and suddenly the odd grey light was replaced by normal daylight. 'I think we're back.'

Macros reached out and gripped Pug's hand, closing his eyes as he felt the flow of time through the younger sorcerer's perceptions. After a moment Macros said, 'Pug, we are close enough to Midkemia that you may be able to send messages back home. I suggest you try.' Pug had told Macros of the child and his previously unsuccessful attempts at reaching her.

Pug shut his eyes and attempted to contact Gamina.

Katala looked up from her needlework. Gamina sat with eyes fixed, as if seeing something in the distance. Then her head tilted, as if listening. William had been reading an old, musty tome Kulgan had given him, and he put it down and looked hard at his foster sister.

Then softly the boy said, 'Mama . . .'

Calmly Katala put down her sewing and said, 'What, William?'

The boy looked at his mother with eyes wide and said in a whisper, 'It's . . . Papa.'

Katala came to kneel beside her son and put her arm around his shoulders. 'What about your father?'

'He's talking to Gamina.'

Katala looked hard at the girl, who sat as if enraptured, all around her forgotten. Slowly Katala rose and crossed to the door to the family's dining room and softly she pulled it open. Then she was through it at a run.

Kulgan and Elgahar sat over a chessboard, while Hochopepa observed, offering unsolicited advice to both players. The room was thick with smoke, for both the stout magicians were sucking on large, after-dinner pipes, enjoying their effects fully, oblivious to the reactions of the others. Meecham sat nearby putting an edge on his hunting knife with a whetstone.

Katala pushed open the door and said, 'All of you, come!'

Her tone and the urgency of her manner caused all questions to be put aside as they followed her back down the corridor to where William sat studying Gamina.

Katala knelt before the girl and slowly passed her hand before the glassy eyes. Gamina didn't respond. She was in some sort of trance. Kulgan whispered, 'What is this?'

Katala whispered back, 'William says she's talking to Pug.'

Elgahar, the usually reserved Greater Path magician, moved past Kulgan. 'Perhaps I may learn something.' He crossed to kneel before William. 'Would you do something with me?'

William shrugged noncommittally. The magician said, 'I know you can sometimes hear Gamina, just as she can hear you when you speak to animals. Could you let me hear what she's saying?'

William said, 'How?'

'I've been studying how Gamina does what she does, and I think I might be able to do the same. There's no risk,' he said, looking at Katala.

Katala nodded while William said, 'Sure. I don't mind.'

Elgahar closed his eyes and put his hand upon William's shoulder, and then after a minute he said, 'I can only hear . . . something.' He opened his eyes. 'She's speaking to someone. I think it is Milamber,' he said, using Pug's Tsurani name.

Hochopepa said, 'I wish Dominic hadn't returned to his abbey. He might be able to listen in.'

Kulgan held up his hand for silence. The girl let out a long sigh and closed her eyes. Katala reached for her, afraid she might faint, but instead the girl opened her eyes wide, then gave a broad smile and leaped up.

Gamina nearly danced around the room, so excited were her movements as she shouted in mind-speech, *It was Papa! He talked to me! He's coming back!*

Katala put her hand upon the girl's shoulder and said, 'Gently, daughter. Now, stop jumping about and tell us what you said, and speak, Gamina, speak.'

For the first time ever, the girl spoke above a whisper, in excited shrieks punctuated with laughter. 'I spoke to Papa! He called me from someplace!'

'Where?' asked Kulgan.

The child paused in her excited dance and tilted her head, as if thinking. 'It was . . . just someplace. It had a beach and was pretty. I don't know. He didn't say where it was. It was just someplace.' She jiggled up and down again and started to push on Kulgan's leg. 'We have to go!'

'Where?'

'Papa wants us to meet him. At a place.'

'What place, little one?' asked Katala.

Gamina jumped a little. 'Sethanon.'

Meecham said, 'That's a city near the Dimwood, in the centre of the Kingdom.'

Kulgan shot him a black look. 'We know that.'

Unabashed, the franklin indicated the two Tsurani magicians, and said, 'They didn't . . . Master Kulgan.' Kulgan's bushy eyebrows met over the bridge of his nose as he cleared his throat, a sign his old friend was right. It was the only sign Meecham would get.

Katala attempted to calm the girl. 'Now, slowly, who is to meet Pug at Sethanon?'

'Everyone. He wants us all to go there. Now.'

'Why?' asked William, feeling neglected.

Suddenly the girl's mood shifted and she calmed. Her eyes widened and she said, 'The bad thing, Uncle Kulgan! The bad thing from Rogen's vision! It's there!' She clutched Kulgan's leg.

Kulgan looked at the others in the room, and finally Hochopepa said, 'The Enemy?'

Kulgan nodded and hugged the child to him. 'When, child?'

'Now, Kulgan. He said we must go now.'

Katala spoke to Meecham. 'Pass word through the community. All the magicians must ready to travel. We must leave for Landreth. We'll get horses there and ride north.'

Kulgan said, 'No daughter of magic would depend on such mundane transportation.' His mood was light in an attempt to relieve the tension. 'Pug should have married another magician.'

Katala's eyes narrowed, for she was in no mood to banter. 'What do you propose?'

'I can use my line-of-sight travel to move myself and Hocho to locations in jumps, up to three miles or more. It will take time, but far less than by horse. In the end we can establish a portal, near Sethanon, and you and the others can walk through from here.' He turned to Elgahar. 'That will give all of you time to prepare.'

Meecham said, 'I'll come, too, in case you pop into an outlaw camp or some other trouble.'

Gamina said, 'Papa said to bring others.'

'Who?' asked Hochopepa, placing his hand on the child's delicate shoulder.

'Other magicians, Uncle Hocho.'

Elgahar said, 'The Assembly. He would ask for such a thing only if the Enemy was indeed upon us.'

'And the army.'

Kulgan looked down at the little face. 'The army? Which army?'

'Just the army!' The girl seemed at the end of her young patience, standing with small fists upon her hips.

Kulgan said, 'We'll send a message to the garrison at Landreth, and another to Shamata.' He looked at Katala. 'Given your rank as Princess of the royal house by marriage, it might be time to go dig out that royal signet you routinely misplace. We'll need it to emboss those messages.'

Katala nodded. She hugged Gamina, who was quieting down, and said, 'Stay here with your brother,' then hurried out of the room.

Kulgan looked to his Tsurani colleagues. Hochopepa said, 'Now, at last. The Darkness comes.'

Kulgan nodded. 'To Sethanon.'

Pug opened his eyes. Again he felt fatigue, but nothing as severe as the first time he had spoken to the girl. Tomas, Macros, and Ryath observed the younger sorcerer and waited. 'I think I got through enough that she'll be able to give instructions to the others.'

Macros nodded, pleased. 'The Assembly will prove little match for the Dragon Lords should they manage to break into this space-time, but they may aid in keeping Murmandamus at bay, so we can gain the Lifestone before him.'

'If they reach Sethanon in time,' commented Pug. 'I don't know how we stand with time.'

'That,' agreed Macros, 'is a problem. I know we are in our own era, and logic says we must be there sometime after you last left, to avoid one of the knottier paradoxes possible. But how much time has passed since you left? A month? A week? An hour? Well, we'll know when we reach there.'

Tomas added, 'If we're in time.'

'Ryath,' said Macros, 'we need to travel some distance to the next gate. There are no mortal eyes upon this world to apprehend the transformation. Will you carry us?'

Without comment, the woman glowed brightly and returned to her dragon form. The three mounted and she took to the sky. 'Fly to the northeast,' shouted Macros as the dragon banked and headed in the indicated direction.

For a while they were silent as they flew, no one feeling the need to speak. They sped away from the bluffs and beach, over rolling plateaus covered with chaparral-like growth. Above, a warm sun beat down.

Pug weighed everything Macros had said in the last hour. He quickly incanted, so they could speak without shouting. 'Macros, you said even one Valheru would be a force unleashed in the universe. I don't think I understand what you meant.'

Macros said, 'There is more at stake here than one world.' He looked down as they sped over a river emerging from a canyon of staggering proportions, running to the southwest to join the sea. He said, 'This wonderful planet stands at risk equal to Midkemia. As does Kelewan, and all other worlds, sooner or later.

'Should the Valheru's servants win this war, their masters will return, and chaos will again be loose in the cosmos. Every world will stand open for the Dragon Host to plunder, for not only will they be unmatched in their wanton destruction, they will be unmatched in might. The very act of returning to this space-time will provide them with a source of mystical power heretofore unthought of, a source of power that would make just one Dragon Lord an object of fear for even the gods.'

'How is such a thing possible?' said Pug.

Tomas spoke. 'The Lifestone. It was left against the final battle with the gods. If it is used . . .' He left the thought unfinished.

They were now flying high above mountains, entering a land of lakes, to the north of rolling plains, as the sun sank in the west. Pug found it difficult to contemplate concepts of utter destruction while flying above this splendid world. Macros pointed and said, 'Ryath! That large island, with the twin bays facing us.'

The dragon descended and landed where Macros instructed. They leaped off her back and waited while she transformed herself back to human form. Then Macros was off, leading them toward a large upthrusting of rock near a stand of pinelike trees. They were before another door, upon the face of the large boulder. Macros stepped through. Tomas followed, then Pug. As Pug returned to the Hall, a dread shrieked its haunting whisper of rage and struck out at Macros, knocking him to the floor.

Tomas jumped forward, drawing his blade as the life stealer attempted to finish Macros. He ducked as another of the dread attempted to grapple him from behind. Pug was knocked to one side by Ryath as she came through the door. A third dread lunged at the human form dragon and seized her arm above the elbow. Ryath screamed in pain.

Then Tomas's blade lashed out and the dread who sought to close upon Macros was rent and cried in whispering rage, spinning to face his adversary. He howled and ripped out with his talons. Golden sparks rippled along the front of Tomas's shield as he blocked the strike.

Ryath's blue eyes glowed, turning angry red, and suddenly the dread that was holding her arm shrieked. Foul grey smoke rose from the unliving's hand, but he seemed unable to release his hold. The dragon woman's eyes continued to glow and she stood motionless, with only a slight trembling in her body. The dread seemed to be shrinking, its whispering cries reduced to a reedy fluting.

Pug finished an incantation and the third dread was seized by some sort of fit. He arched backward and his black wings quivered as he fell to the stones of the Hall. Then he rose upward, Pug's slight hand motion the only sign he was using his arts upon the creature. Pug gestured and the creature was moved to a place between worlds, vanishing into the grey void.

Tomas struck out again and again and the dread he faced fell back. Each time the golden sword bit into the black nothingness, hissing energies were released. Now the thing appeared weakened and it sought to escape. Tomas thrust with his blade, impaling the dread as it tried to flee, holding it motionless.

While Pug watched, Ryath and Tomas disposed of the two remaining dread, somehow draining them of their life essences, as the dread suck out the life of others.

Pug moved to where Macros lay stunned. He helped the sorcerer to his feet and asked, 'Are you injured?'

Macros cleared his head with a shake and said, 'Not to any degree. Those creatures can be difficult for a mortal, but I've dealt with them before. That they were stationed before this door shows that the Valheru fear what aid we may bring to Midkemia. If Murmandamus reaches Sethanon and finds the Lifestone . . . well, the dread are but a faint shadow of the destruction that will be unleashed.'

Tomas said, 'How far to Midkemia?'

'That door.' Macros pointed to the one opposite the one they entered. 'Through it and we are home.'

They entered a vast hall, cold and empty. It was fashioned from massive stones, fitted together by master crafters. A single throne reared above the hall upon a dais, and along both walls deep recesses were set, as if ready to receive statuary.

The four walked forward, and Pug said, 'It is chilly here. Where upon Midkemia are we?'

Macros seemed mildly amused. 'We are in the fortress city Sar-Sargoth.'

Tomas spun about to face the sorcerer. 'Are you mad? This is the ancient capital of the original Murmandamus. I know that much of the moredhel lore!'

Macros said, 'Calm yourself. They are all down invading the Kingdom. Should any moredhel or goblins be hanging about, they'll certainly be deserters. No, we can dispose of any obstacles here. It is at Sethanon we must be ready to deal with the ultimate challenge.'

He led them outside, and Pug faltered. Arrayed in every direction were stakes of a uniform ten feet in height. Atop each was a human head. Perhaps as many as a thousand stretched away in every direction. Pug whispered, 'Heaven's pity, but how can such evil exist?'

'This, then, completes your understanding,' answered Macros. Looking at his three companions, he said, 'There was a time Ashen-Shugar would have thought this nothing more than an object lesson.'

Tomas glanced about, and nodded absent agreement.

'Tomas, as Ashen-Shugar, can remember a time when no moral issues existed in the universe. There was no thoughts of right or wrong, only of might. And in that universe all other races were of similar mind, save the Aal, and their view of things was odd even by the standards of those days. Murmandamus is a tool, and he resembles his masters.

'And beings far less evil than Murmandamus have done far worse than this one wanton act. But they do so with some knowledge of their deeds relative to a higher moral principle. The Valheru don't understand good and evil; they are totally amoral, but they are so destructive we must count them a near-ultimate evil. And Murmandamus is their servant, so he is also evil. And he is but the palest shadow to their darkness.' Macros sighed. 'It may be only my vanity, but the thought I fight such evil . . . it lightens my burdens.'

Pug took a deep breath as he gained further insight into the tormented soul who sought to preserve all Pug held dear. At last he said, 'Where to? Sethanon?'

Macros said, 'Yes. We must go and discover what has come to pass, and with luck we shall be able to help. No matter what, Murmandamus must not be allowed to reach the Lifestone. Ryath?'

The dragon shimmered and soon was again her true form. They mounted and she took to the skies. Moving high above the Plain of Isbandia, she circled. She banked and flew to the southwest, and Macros bid her pause as they inspected the destruction of Armengar. Black smoke still issued from the pit where the keep had once stood. 'What is that place?' asked Pug.

'Once called Sar-Isbandia, it was last called Armengar. It was built by the glamredhel, as was Sar-Sargoth, long before they fell into barbarism. Both were made in imitation of the city of Draken-Korin, using sciences plundered from other worlds. They were vain constructions, won by the moredhel in battle at great cost: first Sar-Sargoth, which became Murmandamus's capital, then Sar-Isbandia. But Murmandamus was killed in the Battle of Sar-Isbandia, when the glamredhel were reputedly obliterated. Both cities were abandoned by the moredhel after his death. Only recently have the moredhel returned to Sar-Sargoth. Men lived in Armengar.'

'There is nothing left,' commented Tomas.

'The present incarnation of Murmandamus paid a price to take it, it seems,' agreed Macros. 'The people who lived here were tougher and more clever than I had thought. Perhaps they have hurt him enough that Sethanon still stands, for he must have passed beyond the mountains by now. Ryath! South, to Sethanon.'

CHAPTER NINETEEN

Sethanon

S UDDENLY THE CITY WAS UNDER SIEGE.
   Nothing had happened for a week after Arutha had secured the city, then the eighth day after the gates had been closed, guards reported Murmandamus's army on the march. By midday the city was surrounded by elements of his advance cavalry, and by nightfall picket fires burned along every quarter of the horizon.

Amos, Guy, and Arutha observed the invaders from their command post upon the southern barbican, the main entrance to the city. After a while Guy said, 'It'll be nothing fancy. He'll hit us from all sides at once. These piddling little walls will not hold. He'll be inside the city after the first or second wave unless we can think of something to slow him down.'

'The defensive barriers we built will help, but only a little. We must depend upon the men,' said Arutha.

'Well, those we brought south with us are a solid crew,' observed Amos. 'Maybe these parade soldiers here will pick up a thing or two.'

'That's why I spread the men from Highcastle out among the city garrison. Just maybe they'll prove the difference.' Arutha didn't sound hopeful.

Guy shook his head, then rested it on his arms, against the wall. 'Twelve hundred seasoned men, including the walking wounded returned to duty. Three thousand garrison, some local militia, and city watch – most of whom have never seen anything more extreme than a tavern brawl. If seven thousand Armengarians couldn't hold from behind sixty-foot-high walls, what can this lot do here?'

Arutha said, 'Whatever they must.' He said no more as he returned his attention to the fires across the plain.

The next day passed into night, and still Murmandamus staged his army. Jimmy sat with Locklear upon a bale of hay near a catapult position. They, and the squires of Lord Humphry's court, had been carrying buckets of sand and water to every siege engine along the city walls all day, against the need to douse fires. They were all bone-tired.

Locklear watched the sea of torches and campfires outside the walls. 'It somehow looks bigger than at Armengar. It's like we never hurt them at all.'

Jimmy nodded. 'We hurt them. It's just they're closer, that's all. I overheard du Bas-Tyra saying they'll come in a rush.' He was silent for a while, then said, 'Locky, you've not said anything about Bronwynn.'

Locklear looked at the fires on the plains. 'What's to say? She's dead and I've cried. It's behind. There's no use in dwelling on it. In a few days I might be dead, too.'

Jimmy sighed, as he leaned back against the inner wall, glimpsing the host around the city through the crenellation in the stones. Something joyous had died in his friend, something young and inno-cent, and Jimmy mourned its loss. And he wondered if he had ever had that young and innocent thing in himself.

* * *

With dawn, the defenders were ready, poised to answer the attackers when they came. But as he did at Armengar, Murmandamus approached the city. Lines of soldiers carrying the banners of the confederations and clans marched out, then opened their line to let their supreme commander come to the fore. He rode a huge black stallion, equal in beauty to the white steed he had ridden the last time. His helm was silver trimmed black and he held a black sword. Little in his appearance offered a reassuring image, yet his words were soft. They carried to everyone in the city, projected by Murmandamus's arts. 'O my children, though some of you have already opposed me, yet am I ever ready to forgive. Open your gates and I will offer solemn vow: any who wishes may quit and ride away, untroubled and unharried. Take whatever you desire, food, livestock, riches, and I'll offer no obstacle.' He waved behind him and a dozen moredhel warriors rode forward to sit behind. 'I will even offer hostages. These are among my most loyal chieftains. They will ride unarmed and unarmoured with you until you are safe within the walls of whatever other city you wish. Only this I ask. You must open your gates to me. Sethanon must be mine!'

Upon the walls the commanders observed this and Amos muttered, 'The royal pig-lover is certainly anxious to get within the city. Damn me if I don't almost believe him. I almost think we could all ride away if we would only give him the bloody place.'

Arutha looked at Guy. 'I almost believe him too. I've never heard of any Dark Brother offering hostages.'

Guy ran his hand over his face, his expression one of worry and fatigue, a tiredness born of long suffering and not simply lack of sleep. 'There's something here he wants badly.'

Lord Humphry said, 'Highness, can we deal with the creature?'

Arutha said, 'It is your city, my lord Baron, but it is my brother's Kingdom. I'm sure he'd be quite short with us if we went about giving portions of it away. No, we'll not deal with him. As sweet as his words are, there's nothing about him that makes me believe he'd honour his vows. I think he'd willingly sacrifice those chieftains of his without a thought. He's never been bothered by his losses before. I've even come to think he welcomes the blood and slaughter. No, Guy's right. He simply wants inside the walls as quickly as possible. And I would give a year's taxes to know what it is he's after.'

Amos said, 'And I don't think those chieftains look happy with the offer either.' Several moredhel leaders were exchanging hurried words with one another behind Murmandamus's back. 'I think things are rapidly becoming less than harmonious among the Dark Brothers.'

'Let us hope,' said Guy flatly.

Murmandamus's horse spun and danced nervously as he shouted, 'What, then, is your answer?'

Arutha stepped up on a box, so he might better be seen above the wall. 'I say return to the north,' he shouted. 'You have invaded lands that hold no bounty for you. Even now armies are marching against you. Return to the north before the passes are choked with snow and you die a cold and lonely death, far from your home.'

Murmandamus's voice rose as he said, 'Who speaks for the city?'

There was a moment's silence, then Arutha shouted, 'I, Arutha conDoin, Prince of Krondor, Heir to the throne of Rillanon,' and then he added a title not officially his, 'Lord of the West.'

Murmandamus shrieked an inhuman cry of rage and something else, perhaps fear, and Jimmy nudged Amos. The former thief said, 'That's torn it. He's definitely not amused.'

Amos only grinned and patted the young man on the shoulder. From the ranks of Murmandamus's army there arose a murmuring as Amos said, 'It sounds as if his army doesn't like it either. Omens that turn out false can undermine a superstitious lot like these.'

Murmandamus cried, 'Liar! False Prince! It is known the Prince of Krondor was slain! Why do you prevaricate? What is your purpose?'

Arutha stood higher, his features clear to see. The chieftains rode about in milling circles, engaged in animated discussion. He removed his talisman, given by the Abbot at Sarth, and held it forth. 'By this talisman am I protected from your arts.' He handed it down to Jimmy. 'Now you know the truth.'

Murmandamus's constant companion, the Pantathian serpent priest, Cathos came forward at a shambling run. He tugged upon the stirrup of his master's saddle, pointing at Arutha and speaking at a furious rate in the hissing language of his people. With a shriek of rage, Murmandamus kicked him away, knocking him to the ground. Amos spat over the wall. 'I think that convinced them.'

The chieftains looked angry and moved as a group toward Murmandamus. He seemed to recognize the moment was slipping away from him. He spun his mount in a full circle, the warhorse's hooves striking the fallen serpent priest in the head, rendering him senseless. Murmandamus ignored his fallen ally and the approaching chieftains. 'Then, foul opposer,' he cried toward the wall, 'death comes to embrace you!' He spun to face his army, and pointed back at the city. 'Attack!'

The army was poised for the assault and moved forward. The chieftains could not countermand the order. All they could do was ride at once to take charge of their clans. Slowly the horsemen moved up behind the advancing elements of infantry, ready to rush the gates.

Murmandamus rode to his command position as the first rank of goblins walked over the unconscious body of the serpent priest. It was not clear if the Pantathian had died from the horse's kick or not, but by the time the last rank had passed over, only a bloody carcass lay in a robe.

Arutha raised his hand and held it poised, dropping it when the first rank came within catapult range. 'Here,' said Jimmy, handing back the talisman. 'It might come in handy.'

Missiles struck the advancing host and they faltered, then continued forward. Soon they were running toward the walls, while bowmen offered covering fire from behind shield walls. Then the first rank hit trenches hidden by canvas and dirt and fell upon the buried, fire-hardened stakes. Others threw shields upon their writhing comrades and ran over their impaled bodies. The second and third ranks were decimated, but others came forward, and scaling ladders were placed against the walls, and the battle for Sethanon was joined.

*   *   *

The first wave swarmed up the ladders and were met with fire and steel by the defenders. The men of Highcastle provided the leadership and example that kept the inexperienced defenders of the city from being swept away. Amos, de la Troville, du Masigny, and Guy were linchpins for the defence of the city, always appearing where needed.

For nearly an hour the battle teetered as if poised upon the point of a dagger, with the attackers only barely able to gain a foothold upon the battlements before they were thrown back. Still as one rush was repulsed, another would be mounted from a different quarter and soon it was apparent that all would hinge upon some chance of fate, for the two opposing forces were in equilibrium.

Then a giant ram, fashioned within the dark glades of the Dimwood, was rolled forward, toward the southern gate of the city. Without a moat, there were only the traps and trenches to slow its advance and those were quickly covered with wooden planking laid over the bodies of the dead. It was a tree bole, easily ten feet in diameter. It rolled on six giant wheels and was pulled by a dozen horsemen. A dozen giants pushed from behind using long poles. The thing gathered speed as it rumbled toward the gate. Soon the horses were cantering and the riders peeled off, turning away from the answering hail of arrows. The sluggish giants were replaced by faster goblins, whose primary task was to keep the thing on course and moving. It rolled toward the outer gates of the barbican, and nothing the defenders could do would stop it.

It struck the gates with a thunderous crash, the shattering of wood and protests of metal hinges torn from the walls heralding a breach in the city's defences. The gates were flung back into the barbican, twisting as they fell under the wheels of the ram. The front end of the ram lifted as it bounced off the tilting gates, momentum carrying it upward as it struck against the right wall of the barbican. Suddenly the invaders were provided with a clear entrance to the city. Up the tottering ram and leaning gates the goblins swarmed, gaining the top of the barbican. Suddenly the balance was tipped.

Atop the barbican the defenders were forced back. The invaders reached a point above the inner gate as more goblins and moredhel swarmed up the accidental ramps. Arutha called the reinforcement company forward. They hurried to where the first goblins were dropping into the courtyard before the massive bar that held the inner gates in place. The fighting before the gates was fierce, but soon goblin bowmen were driving the defenders away, despite the fire directed at them from other parts of the wall. The bar was being hoisted when shrieks and cries went up from outside. The fighting slowed, as those engaged sensed something odd was occurring. Then all eyes looked heavenward.

Descending from the sky was a dragon, its scales glinting in the sun. Upon its back three figures could be seen. The giant animal swooped downward with an astonishing roar, as if about to pounce upon the attackers before the gates and the goblins began to flee.

Ryath spread her wings and swooped into a low glide above the heads of the attackers, as Tomas waved his golden sword aloft. She trumpeted her battle cry and the goblins beneath her broke and ran.

Tomas looked about, seeking signs of this Murmandamus, but could see only a sea of horsemen and infantry in all directions. Then arrows began to speed past. Most were harmlessly bouncing off the dragon's scales, but the Prince Consort of Elvandar knew a well-placed shot could strike between the overlapping plates or in the eye and the dragon could be injured. He ordered Ryath to enter the city.

The dragon landed in the market, some distance from the gate, but Arutha was already running toward them, with Galain behind. Pug and Tomas both leaped lightly down, while Macros was more sedate in his dismount.

Arutha gripped Pug's hand. 'It is good to see you again, and making so timely an entrance.'

Pug said, 'We hurried, but we had some delays upon the way.'

Tomas had been greeted by Galain, and Arutha in turn clasped his hand, both of them obviously pleased to see each other alive. Then Arutha saw Macros. 'So you didn't die, then?'

Macros said, 'Apparently not. It is good to see you again, Prince Arutha. More pleasant than you can imagine.'

Arutha looked at the signs of battle about him and considered the relative quiet. From distant quarters the sounds of battle carried, signifying only that the assault upon the gate had ceased. 'I don't know how long they'll wait before they rush the barbican again.' He glanced down the street toward the gate. 'You gave them a start, and I think Murmandamus is having trouble with some of his chieftains, but not enough to benefit us, I'm afraid. And I don't think I can hold them here. When they come again, they'll swarm over that ram.'

'We can help,' said Pug.

'No,' said Macros.

All eyes turned toward the sorcerer. Arutha said, 'Pug's magic could counter Murmandamus's.'

'Has he used any spellcraft against you so far?'

Arutha thought. 'Why no, not since Armengar.'

'He won't. He must harbour it against the moment he has won into the city. And the bloodshed and terror benefit his cause. There is something here he wants, and we must keep him from getting it.'

Arutha looked at Pug. 'What is happening here?'

A messenger came running toward them. 'Highness! The enemy masses for another attack on the gate.'

Macros said, 'Who is your second?'

'Guy du Bas-Tyra.'

Pug looked startled at the news but said nothing. Macros said, 'Murmandamus will not use magic, except perhaps to destroy you if he can, Arutha, so you must turn command of the city over to du Bas-Tyra and come with us.'

'Where are we going?'

'Some place near here. If all else fails, it will be our cause to prevent the complete destruction of your nation. We must keep Murmandamus from his final goal.'

Arutha considered a moment. He said to Galain, 'Orders to du

Bas-Tyra. He is to take command. Amos Trask is to assume his role as second-in-command.'

'Where will Your Highness be?' asked the soldier next to the elf.

Macros took Arutha by the arm. 'He'll be someplace where no one can reach him. If we are victorious, we shall all meet again.' He didn't bother saying what would happen if they were defeated.

They hurried down the street, past shuttered doors as the citizens huddled safely within their homes. One bold boy looked out a second floor window just as Ryath lumbered past, and with wide eyes slammed the window. The sounds of battle came from the walls as they rounded a corner into an alley. Macros spun to face the Prince. 'What you see, what you hear, what you learn must always remain a trust. Besides yourself, only the King and your brother Martin may know the secrets you'll learn today – and your heirs,' he added with a dry note, 'if any. Swear.' It was not a request.

Arutha said, 'I swear.'

Macros said, 'Tomas, you must discover where the Lifestone lies, and, Pug, you must take us there.'

Tomas looked about. 'It was ages ago. Nothing resembles . . .' He closed his eyes. He appeared to the others to be in some trance state. Then he said, 'I feel it.'

Without opening his eyes, he said, 'Pug, can you take us . . . there!' He pointed down and to the centre of the city. He opened his eyes. 'It is below the entrance to the keep.'

Pug said, 'Come, join hands.'

Tomas looked toward the dragon, saying, 'You have done all you can. I thank you.'

Ryath said, 'With thee I shall come, one more time.' She regarded the sorcerer and then Tomas. 'With certainty do I know my fate. I must not seek to avoid it.'

Pug looked at his companions and said, 'What does she mean?' Arutha's expression mirrored Pug's.

Macros did not speak. Tomas said, 'You have not told us before.'

'There was no need, friend Tomas.'

Macros interrupted. 'We can speak of this once we've reached our destination. Ryath, once we have ceased moving, come to us.'

Tomas said, 'The chamber will be large enough.'

'I shall.'

Pug pushed his confusion aside and took Arutha's hand. The other was joined with Tomas's, and Macros completed the circle. They all became insubstantial and began to move.

They sank, and light was denied them for a time. Tomas directed Pug, using mind-speech, until after long minutes in the dark, Tomas spoke aloud. 'We are in an open area.'

With returning solidity, they all felt cold stone beneath their feet and Pug created light about himself. Arutha looked up. They were in a gigantic chamber, easily a hundred feet in every direction, with a ceiling twice that high. About them rose columns and next to them stood an upraised dais.

Then suddenly, with a booming displacement of air, the dragon bulked above them. Ryath said, 'It is near time.'

Arutha said, 'What is the dragon speaking of?' He had seen so many wonders over the last two years the sight of a talking dragon was making no impression on him.

Tomas said, 'Ryath, like all the greater dragons, knows the time of her death. It is soon.'

The dragon spoke. 'While we fared between worlds, it was possible I would die of causes removed from thee and thy friends. Now it is clear I must continue to play a part in this, for our destiny as a race is always tied with thine, Valheru.'

Tomas only nodded. Pug looked about the chamber, saying, 'Where is this Lifestone?'

Macros pointed to the dais. 'There.'

Pug said, 'There is nothing there.'

'To ordinary appearances,' said Tomas. He asked Macros, 'Where shall we wait?'

Macros was silent for a moment, then said, 'Each to his place. Pug, Arutha, and I must wait here. You and Ryath must go to another place.'

Tomas indicated understanding and used his arts to lift himself upon the dragon's back. Then, with a thunderous crash, they vanished.

Arutha said, 'Where did he go?'

'He is still here,' answered Macros. 'But he is slightly out of phase with us in time – as is the Lifestone. He guards it, the last bastion of defence for this planet, for should we fail, then he alone will stand between Midkemia and her utter destruction.'

Arutha looked at Macros, then Pug. He moved toward the dais and sat. 'I think you had better tell me some things.'

Guy signalled and a shower of missiles came down upon the heads of the goblins rushing the gate. A hundred died in an instant. But the flood was unleashed and du Bas-Tyra shouted to Amos, 'Ready to quit the walls! I want skirmish order back to the keep, no rout. Any man who tries to run is to be killed by the sergeant in charge.'

Amos said, 'Harsh,' but he didn't argue the order. The garrison was on the verge of breaking, the untested soldiers close to panic. Only by frightening them more than the enemy could was there a shred of hope of maintaining an orderly retreat back to the keep. Amos glanced back as the population of the city fled toward the keep. They had been kept out of the streets so that companies could move from section to section without impediment, but now they had been ordered to leave their homes. Amos hoped they would be safely out of the way before the retreat from the walls began.

Jimmy came running through the melee evolving to the west of where Galain, Amos, and Guy stood, and shouted, 'De la Troville wants reinforcements. He's hard pressed upon the right flank.'

Guy said, 'He'll have none. If I pull anyone from their own sections, it will open a floodgate.' He pointed to where the goblins had cleared the breach through the outer gate of the barbican once more and were now climbing up the inner gate. The covering fire from moredhel archers was murderous. Jimmy began to leave and Guy grabbed him. 'Another messenger is passing the word to quit the walls on signal. You'll not be able to reach him in time. Stay here.'

Jimmy signalled understanding, his sword at the ready, then suddenly a goblin appeared before him. He slashed out, and the blue skinned creature fell, only to be replaced by another.

Tomas looked down. His friends had vanished, though he knew they were still in the same place, but slightly out of phase with him in time. Part of Ashen-Shugar's attempt to hide the gem had been to put the ancient city of Draken-Korin into a different frame of time. He looked across the vast hall where the Valheru had held their last council, then regarded the giant glowing green gem. He altered his perceptions and saw the lines of power spreading outward, touching, he knew, every living thing on the planet. He considered the importance of what he was to do, and calmed himself. He felt the dragon's mood and acknowledged it. It was a willingness to accept whatever fate brought, but without a resignation to defeat. Death might come, but with it might also come victory. Tomas was somehow reassured by this thought.

Arutha nodded. 'You have told me it is important. Now tell me why.'

'It was left against the day of the Valheru's returning. They understood that the gods were fashioned of the stuff of the world, a part of Midkemia. Draken-Korin was a genius among his race. He knew that the power of the gods depended upon the relationship they had with all other living things. The Lifestone is the most powerful artifact upon this world. If it is taken and used, it will drain all power from all creatures down to the tiniest being, giving that power to the user. It can be used to bring the Valheru into this space and time. It does so by providing a surge of energy so vast it cannot be equalled, and at the same time it drains away the source of power for the gods. Unfortunately, it will also destroy all life upon this planet. In one instant, everything that walks, flies, swims, or crawls across Midkemia will die, insects, fish, the plants that grow, even living things too small to see.'

Arutha was astonished. 'Then what will the Valheru have with a dead planet?'

'Once back in this universe, they can war upon other worlds, bringing slaves, livestock, and plants, life in all forms, to reseed. They have no concern for the other beings here, just their own needs. It is truly a Valheru view of things, that all may be destroyed to protect their interests.'

'Then Murmandamus and the invading moredhel will die as well,' said Arutha, horrified at the scope of the plan.

Macros considered. 'That is the one thing about this that puzzles me, for to utilize the Lifestone, the Valheru must have entrusted much lore to Murmandamus. It seems impossible that he doesn't know he will die when he opens the portal. The Pantathian serpent priests I can understand. They have worked since the time of the Chaos Wars to bring back their lost mistress, the Emerald Lady of Serpents, whom they regard as a goddess. They have become a death cult and believe that with her return, they will achieve some sort of demigod-head for themselves. They embrace death. But this attitude is unlikely for a moredhel. So I don't understand Murmandamus's motives, unless guarantees have been made. I don't know what they could be, as I don't know what this use of the dread can herald, for they will not perish with the others. And if the Valheru no longer wish them upon this world as they reseed the planet, it will be difficult for the Valheru to rid themselves of the dread. The Dreadlords are powerful beings, and this makes me wonder at the possibility of a compact.' Macros sighed. 'There is still so much we don't know. And any one thing could prove our undoing.'

Arutha said, 'In all this there's one other thing I don't understand. This Murmandamus is an archmage of some sort. If he needs to come here, why not shape-change, sneak into Sethanon looking like any human and come here unnoticed? Why this marching of armies and wholesale destruction?'

Macros said, 'It is the nature of the Lifestone. To reach its proper frame of reference in time and to open the gate to admit the Valheru require an enormous mystic power. Murmandamus feeds off death.' Arutha nodded, remembering a comment Murmandamus had made when he had first confronted Arutha through the dead body of one of his Nighthawks, back in Krondor. 'He sucks energy from each death near him. Thousands have died in his service and opposing him. Had he no need to harbour those energies to open the gateway, he could have blown down the walls of this city like a thing of sticks. Even such a small matter as keeping his barrier up against personal injury costs him valuable energies. No, he needs this war to bring back the Valheru. He would gladly see his entire army to the last soldier die just so long as he can reach this chamber. Now we must seek to block his masters' entrance back into this universe.' He stood up. 'Arutha, you must remain vigilant against mundane attack.' He came to Pug and said, 'We must aid him, his foe will prove mighty: most surely, Murmandamus will come to this room.'

Pug took Macros's hand and watched as the sorcerer reached out and gripped the Ishapian talisman. Arutha nodded, and Macros took it from the Prince. Macros closed his eyes and Pug felt powers within himself being manipulated by another, a feat again new and startling to him. Whatever skills he had, were still as nothing to those lost to Macros. Then Arutha and Pug watched as the talisman began to glow. Softly, Macros said, 'There is power here.' He opened his eyes and said, 'Hold out your sword.'

Arutha did so, hilt first. Macros released Pug's hand and carefully placed the talisman below the hilt, so the tiny hammer lay next to the forte of the blade. He then gently closed his hand around the blade and hammer. 'Pug, I have the skill, but I need your strength.' Pug took Macros's hand and the sorcerer again used the younger mage's magic to augment his own diminished powers. Macros's hand began to glow with a warm, yellow-orange light, and all heard a sizzling sound while smoke came off the sorcerer's hand. Arutha could feel the blade warm to the touch.

After a few moments the glow vanished and Macros's hand opened. Arutha looked at the blade. The talisman had been somehow embedded into the steel, now appearing only as a hammer-shaped etching in the forte. The Prince looked up at Macros and Pug.

'That blade now holds the power of the talisman. It will guard you from all attacks from mystic sources. It will also wound and kill creatures of dark summoning, piercing even Murmandamus's protective spells. But its power is limited to the strength of will within the man who holds it. Falter in your resolve and you will fall. Remain steadfast and you shall prevail. Always remember that.

'Come, Pug, we must ready ourselves.'

Arutha watched as the two sorcerers, one ancient and robed in brown and one young and wearing the black robes of a Tsurani Great One, stood facing each other, next to the dais. They joined hands and closed their eyes. A disquieting silence fell over the chamber. After a minute, Arutha pulled his attention from the two magic users and began inspecting his surroundings. The chamber seemed empty of any artifact or decoration. One small door, waist-high in the wall, seemed the only means of entrance. He pulled it open, and glanced in, seeing a hoard of gold and gems lying in the next chamber. He laughed to himself. Ancient treasure, riches of the Valheru, and he'd trade it all to have Lyam's army on the horizon. After a moment of poking about the treasure, he settled in to wait. He absently tossed and caught a ruby the size of a plum, wishing he knew how his comrades above were faring in the battle for Sethanon.

'Now!' shouted Guy, and the company directly under his command began to fall back from the barbican, while behind them trumpeters sounded the call to withdraw. In every quarter of the city the call was answered and, in as coordinated a retreat as possible, the walls were surrendered to the attackers. Rapidly the defenders fell back, gaining the cover of the first block of houses beyond the bailey, for the moredhel archers upon the wall began taking a heavy toll.

Companies of Sethanon archers waited to offer answering fire over the heads of the retreating skirmishers, but it was only through exceptional bravery that a total rout was avoided.

Guy pulled Jimmy and Amos along, watching over his shoulder while his squad fell back to new positions. Galain and three other archers offered covering fire. As the front rank of attackers reached the first major intersection, a company of riders erupted from the side street. Sethanon cavalry, under the command of Lord Humphry, rode among the goblins and trolls, trampling them underfoot. In a few minutes the attackers were being slaughtered and began withdrawing the way they had come.

Guy waved to Humphry, who rode over. 'Shall we harry them, Guy?'

'No, they'll regroup shortly. Order your men to ride the perimeter, covering where necessary, but everyone is to fall back to the keep as quickly as possible. Don't do anything too heroic.'

The Baron acknowledged his orders, and Guy said, 'Humphry, tell your men they did well. Very well.' The stout little Baron seemed to perk up and saluted smartly, riding off to take command of his cavalry.

Amos said, 'That little squirrel's got teeth.'

'He's a braver man than he looks,' answered Guy. He quickly surveyed his position and signalled his men back. In a moment they were all running toward the keep.

When they reached the inner bailey of the city, they ran toward the keep. The outer fence was a decorative thing of iron bars, which would be torn down in moments, but the inner, ancient fortress wall still looked difficult to attack. Guy hoped so. They gained the first parapet overlooking the battle and Guy sent Galain to see if his other commanders had reached the keep. When the elf had gone, he said, 'Now, if I could only know where Arutha has vanished to?'

Jimmy wondered as well. And he also wondered where Locklear was.

Locklear hugged the wall, waiting until the troll turned his back to him at the sound of the scream. The girl was no more than sixteen and the other two children considerably younger. The troll reached for the girl, and Locklear leaped out and ran him through from behind. Without saying anything, he reached out and grabbed the girl's wrist. He tugged and she followed, leading the other two children.

They hurried toward the keep, but the squire halted when a squad of horsemen was driven backward across their path. Locklear saw that Baron Humphry was the last man to quit the fray. The Baron's horse stumbled and goblin hands reached up and pulled Humphry from his saddle. The stout little ruler of Sethanon lashed out with his sword, cutting down two of his assailants before finally being overwhelmed by the goblins he faced. Locklear pulled the frightened girl and her companions into an abandoned inn. Once inside, he searched until he spied the trapdoor to the cellar. He opened it and said, 'Quickly, and be silent!'

The children obeyed and he followed after. He felt about in the dark and found a lamp, with steel and flint next to it. In a short moment he had a light burning. He glanced around while sounds of fighting filtered down from the street above. He pointed toward a large pair of barrels and the children hurried over to crouch between them. He pushed on another barrel and rolled it slowly before the others, creating a small place to hide. He took his sword and the lamp and climbed over to sit with the others.

'What were you doing running down the street?' he asked in a harsh whisper. 'The order for noncombatants to leave came a half hour ago.'

The girl looked frightened but spoke calmly. 'My mother hid us in the cellar.'

Locklear looked incredulous. 'Why?'

The girl regarded him with mixed expression and said, 'Soldiers.'

Locklear swore. A mother's concern over her daughter's virtue could cost all three of her children their lives. He said, 'Well, I hope she prefers you dead to dishonoured.'

The girl stiffened. 'She's dead. The trolls killed her. She fought them while we ran.'

Locklear shook his head, wiping his dripping forehead with the back of his hand. 'Sorry.' He studied her for a moment, then recognized she was indeed pretty. 'I really am sorry.' He was silent, then added, 'I've lost someone, too.'

A thump on the floor above, and the girl stiffened more, fear making her eyes enormous as she bit the back of her hand to keep from screaming. The two smaller children clung to each other and Locklear whispered, 'Don't make a sound.' He put his arm about the girl and blew out the lamp and the cellar was plunged into darkness.

Guy ordered the inner gate to the keep closed, and watched as those too slow to reach it safely were cut down by the advancing horde. Archers fired from the battlements, and anything that could be hurled at the attackers was thrown – boiling water and oil, stones, heavy furniture – as the last, desperate attempt to resist the onslaught began.

Then a shout went up from the rear of the invading army and Murmandamus came riding forward, trampling his own soldiers as often as not. Amos waited beside Guy and Jimmy, ready for the first scaling ladders to be brought forward. He looked at the frantically hurrying moredhel leader and said, 'The dung-eater still seems in a hurry, doesn't he? He's a bit rough on the lads who happen to be in his way.'

Guy shouted, 'Archers, there's your target!' and a storm of arrows descended about the broad-shouldered moredhel. With a scream the horse was down and the rider fell and rolled. He leaped to his feet, unharmed, and pointed toward the keep doors. A dozen goblins and moredhel raced forward, to die under bow fire. Most bowmen concentrated upon the moredhel leader, but none could harm him. The arrows would harmlessly strike some invisible barrier and bounce off.

Then a ram was carried forward, and while dozens of invaders died, it at last reached the doors and was brought to bear. Moredhel archers kept the defenders down, while the rhythmic pounding began.

Guy sat with his back to the stones, as flight after flight of moredhel arrows sped overhead. 'Squire,' he said to Jimmy, 'hurry downstairs and see if de la Troville has his company together. Order him to be ready at the inner door. I think we have less than ten minutes before they're inside.' Jimmy hurried off, and Guy said to Amos, 'Well, you pirate . . . it looks like we gave them a good run.'

Hunkering down beside Guy, Amos nodded. 'The best. All things considered, we did all right. A little more luck here or there, and we'd have had his guts on a stick.' Amos sighed. 'Still, there's no use dwelling on the past, I always say. Come along, let's go bleed some of those miserable land rats.' He leaped to his feet and grabbed the throat of a goblin who had just cleared the wall. The creature had not seen any defenders, and suddenly there was Amos, seizing him by the throat. With a jerk he crushed the creature's windpipe, and cast him back down the ladder, dislodging three more who were right behind him. Amos pushed the ladder away as Guy slashed with his sword at another who climbed through a crenel beside Amos.

Amos stiffened and gasped and, looking down, discovered an arrow in his side. 'Damn me!' he said, apparently astonished by the fact. Then a goblin breasted the wall, and struck out with his sword, the impact nearly spinning Amos around. The former sea captain's knees buckled, and he fell hard to the stones. Guy cut the goblin's head from his shoulders with a savage blow.

He knelt next to Amos and said, 'I've told you to keep your damn head down.'

Amos smiled up at him. 'Next time I'll listen,' he said weakly, then his eyes closed.

Guy whirled as another goblin came over the wall, and with an upward thrust he gutted the creature. The Protector of Armengar, former Duke of Bas-Tyra, slashed right and left, bringing death to any goblin, troll, or moredhel who came close to him. But the outer wall of the keep was breached, and more invaders swarmed over, and Guy saw himself being slowly surrounded. Others on the wall heard the call for retreat and hurried down the stairs to stand within the great hall, but Guy stood over his fallen friend with sword ready, not moving.

Murmandamus walked over the bodies of his own soldiers, ignoring the cries of the dying and wounded around him. He entered the barbican of the keep, passing the shattered outer doors. With a curt motion of his hand he ordered his soldiers forward with the ram to begin the assault upon the inner door. He moved to one side while they began beating on the door, their comrades seeking to rid the walls of Sethanon archers. For an instant all within the killing ground of the barbican were intent upon the splintering door, and Murmandamus stepped back into the shadows, silently laughing at the folly of other creatures. With each death he had gained power and now he was ready.

A moredhel chieftain ran into the killing ground seeking his master. He brought word of the battle in the city. Fighting over spoils had broken out between two rival clans, and while they had been distracted, a pocket of defenders had escaped certain annihilation. The master's presence was required to keep order. He grabbed one of his underlings and asked Murmandamus's whereabouts. The goblin pointed, and the chieftain shoved the creature away, for the dark corner he indicated was empty. The goblin ran forward to work upon the ram, for another soldier had fallen to arrows from above, while the moredhel chieftain continued to look for his master. He asked about, and all said that Murmandamus had vanished. Cursing all omens, prophecies, and heralds of destruction, the chieftain hurried back toward the section of the city where his own clan battled. New orders were about to be given.

Pug heard Macros's words in his mind. *They are trying to break through.*

Pug and Macros's minds were linked, with a rapport beyond anything Pug had experienced in his life. He knew the sorcerer, he understood him, he was one with Macros. He remembered things from the sorcerer's long history, foreign lands with alien people, histories of worlds far distant, all was his. And so was the knowledge.

With his mystic eye, he could 'see' the place they would attempt to enter. It existed between their physical world and the place where Tomas waited, a seam between one time frame and another. And something like sound was building, something that he could not hear but could feel. A pressure was rising, as those who sought to enter this world began their final assault.

Arutha tensed. One moment he had been watching Pug and Macros standing like statues, then suddenly another moved in the vast hall. From out of the shadows came the giant moredhel, his face a thing of beauty and horror as he removed his black dragon helm from his sweating brow. Bare of armour, his chest revealed the dragon birthmark of his heritage, and in his hand he held a black sword. He fixed his eyes upon Macros and Pug and moved toward them.

Arutha stepped out from behind a pillar, standing between Murmandamus and the two motionless mages. He held his sword at the ready. 'Now, baby killer, you have your chance,' he said.

Murmandamus faltered, his eyes growing wide. 'How—' Then he grinned. 'I thank the fates, Lord of the West. You are now mine.' He pointed his finger and a silver bolt of energy shot forward, but it was warped to strike the blade of Arutha's sword, where it danced like incandescent fire, pulsing with white-hot fury. Arutha flicked his wrist and the point of the blade touched the stone floor. The fire winked out.

The moredhel's eyes again widened, and with a shriek of rage he leaped toward Arutha. 'I will not be denied!'

Arutha narrowly avoided a blow of stunning savagery, which caused blue sparks to leap when the black blade struck the stones. But as he moved back, his own sword flicked out and he cut the moredhel upon the arm. Murmandamus shrieked as if some grave injury had been done, and staggered back a moment. He righted himself as Arutha followed the blow with another, and was able to parry the Prince's second thrust. With a look of madness, Murmandamus clutched the wound, then regarded the crimson wetness upon his palm. The moredhel said, 'It is not possible!'

With catlike quickness Arutha lashed out, and another cut appeared upon the moredhel, this one across his bare chest. Arutha smiled a smile without humour, one as savage as the moredhel's had been. 'It is possible, scion of madness,' he said with studied purpose. 'I am the Lord of the West. I am the Bane of Darkness. I am your destruction, slave of the Valheru.'

Murmandamus roared in rage, the sound of a vanished age of insanity returning into the world, and launched his attack. Arutha stood his ground and they began to duel in earnest.

Pug.

I know.

They moved in concert, weaving a pattern of power, erecting a lattice of energies against the intruder. It was not so mighty a work as that used to close off the great rift at the time of the golden bridge, but then this rift hadn't been opened yet. But there was pressure and they were being tested.

The pounding on the door continued as the wood began to splinter. Then came the sound of distant thunder, growing louder. The pounding on the door halted for a moment, then resumed. Twice more the booming sounded, as if coming closer, as the sounds of fighting seemed to be increasing. Then from outside came unexpected cries, and the pounding of the ram on the door ceased. Then an explosion rocked the hall. Jimmy leaped forward. He pulled aside the slide that covered the peephole, then yelled back at de la Troville, 'Open this door!'

The commander of the company signed his men forward as the sounds of fighting reached his ears, and it took the strength of most of the men to move the half-detached door. Then they heaved and it opened and de la Troville and Jimmy raced through. Before them men in brightly coloured armour ran through the streets, battling moredhel and goblins on every hand. Jimmy shouted, 'Tsurani! By damn, it's an army of Tsurani!'

'Can it really be?' said de la Troville.

'I've heard enough stories from Duke Laurie to know what they're supposed to look like. Little fellows, but tough, all in bright coloured armour.'

A squad of goblins turned before the keep retreating from a larger company of Tsurani, and de la Troville led his own men out, taking them in the rear. Jimmy hurried past, and heard another loud explosion. Down a broad avenue he could see a black-robed magician standing before a smoking pile of barrels and an overturned wagon that had been used as a breastwork. The magician began conjuring. Within a moment there flowed from his hands a heavy rolling ball of energy which struck some target beyond Jimmy's line of sight, exploding in the distance.

Then a company of horsemen came galloping into view, and Jimmy recognized the banner of Landreth. Riding alongside came Kulgan, Meecham, and two black-robed magicians. They reined in and Kulgan left his mount, nimbly for one so stout. He approached Jimmy, who said, 'Kulgan! I've never been so glad to see anyone in my life, I think.'

'Have we arrived in time?' asked Hochopepa. Jimmy had never met the black-robed man, but, given his arrival with Kulgan, Jimmy assumed he had some authority. 'I don't know. Arutha vanished some hours ago with Pug, Macros, Tomas, and a dragon, if you can believe Galain's report to du Bas-Tyra. Guy and Amos Trask are around here somewhere.' He pointed toward some fighting in the distance and said, 'Du Masigny and the others are over there somewhere, I think.' He looked around, his eyes wide with terror and exhaustion. His voice began to sound thick with emotions held too long in check, rising with a near-frantic note. 'I don't know who's left alive.'

Kulgan put his hand on Jimmy's shoulder, realizing the boy was close to collapse. 'It's all right,' he said. Looking at Hochopepa and Elgahar, he said, 'You'd better look inside. I don't think this battle is truly over yet.'

Jimmy said, 'Where are all the Dark Brothers? There were thousands around here only a . . . few minutes ago?'

Kulgan led the boy away, while the two black-robed magicians ordered a squad of Tsurani soldiers to accompany them into the keep, where the sounds of fighting could still be heard. To Jimmy, the green-robed magician said, 'Ten magicians of the Assembly came to join us, and the Emperor sent part of his army, so much did they fear the appearance of the Enemy upon this world. We created a gate between the portal on Stardock and a place less than a mile from the city, but out of sight of Murmandamus's army. We marched three thousand Tsurani here along with the fifteen hundred horse from Landreth and Shamata, and more are coming.'

Jimmy sat. 'Three thousand? Fifteen hundred? They ran from that?'

Kulgan sat next to him. 'And the Black Robes, whose magic they cannot oppose. And the news that Martin is upon the plain with the army from Yabon, four thousand strong, less than an hour away to the northwest. And I'm sure their scouts saw the dust from the southwest, where the soldiers from Darkmoor are marching beside those from Malac's Cross, followed by Gardan's regiments from Krondor. And all can see the banners of Northwarden to the northeast, and in the east the King comes with his army, one or two days away at most. They are surrounded, Jimmy, and they know it.' Kulgan's voice turned thoughtful. 'And something had already disturbed them, for even as we approached we saw bands of Dark Brothers quitting the city, fleeing for the Dimwood. At least three or four thousand seemed to have already abandoned the attack. And many of those between the gate and here were not organized, and some even seemed to be falling out among themselves, with one band fighting another. Something has happened to blunt the attack at the moment of victory.'

Then into view came a detachment of Keshian dog soldiers, running rapidly toward the sound of battle. Jimmy looked at the magician and began to laugh as tears started to run down his cheeks. 'I guess that means Hazara-Khan's come to play, too?'

Kulgan smiled. 'He *happened* to be camped near Shamata. He claims it was coincidence he was having dinner with the governor of Shamata when Katala's message to come to Stardock with the garrison arrived. And of course the facts that he convinced the governor to let him bring along some observers and that his people were ready to march within an hour are also coincidence.'

'How many observers?'

'Five hundred, all armed to the teeth.'

'Arutha's going to die an unhappy man if he can't get Abdur to admit there is an Imperial Intelligence Corps.'

Kulgan said, 'But what I can't fathom is how does he know what's going on at Stardock?'

Jimmy laughed a genuinely amused laugh. He sniffed as his nose began to run and smiled. 'You must be joking. Half your magicians are Keshian.' He sighed and sat back. 'But there must be more to it, mustn't there?' He closed his eyes, and tears of fatigue again ran down his face.

Kulgan said, 'We still haven't found Murmandamus.' Kulgan looked to where more Tsurani soldiers ran down the street. 'Until we do, it's not over.'

Arutha ducked a savage slashing backhand blow and thrust in return, but the moredhel jumped backward. Arutha's breath came with difficulty, for this was the most cunning and dangerous opponent he had ever faced. He was incredibly strong and only slightly slower than Arutha. Murmandamus bled from a half-dozen minor wounds, cuts which would have weakened a normal opponent, but which seemed to bother him only a little. Arutha gained no advantage, for the battle and this duel were bringing him to the edge of exhaustion. It took all the Prince's skills and speed to stay alive. He had a limit on his ability to fight, for he had to keep himself between Murmandamus and the two sorcerers, who laboured over some mystic duty. The moredhel had no such concern.

The duel had fallen into a rhythm, each swordsman taking the measure of the other. Now they moved almost in lockstep, each thrust answered with a parry, each riposte with a disengage. Sweat poured off each and made hands slippery, and the only sounds heard were the grunts of exertion. The fight was coming to the stage where the first to make a mistake would be the one to die.

Then a shimmering filled the air to the left, and for an instant Arutha glanced away, only catching himself at the last. But Murmandamus didn't remove his eyes from his opponent and seized the moment, levelling a blow that skidded along the Prince's ribs. Arutha gasped in pain.

The moredhel drew back to slash at Arutha's head, and as his hand came forward, it was brought crashing against an invisible barrier. The moredhel's eyes widened as Arutha staggered upright and thrust, skewering Murmandamus through the stomach. The moredhel howled in a dull ululation, staggered, then fell backward, pulling Arutha's sword from weakened fingers.

Arutha slumped to the floor as two black-garbed men ran forward to grip him. They hovered over the Prince. Arutha's vision clouded and cleared, focused and unfocused, until the room was stable again. He saw Murmandamus smile, as the moredhel spoke in a menacing whisper. 'I am a thing of death, Lord of the West. I am ever the servant of Darkness.' He laughed weakly and blood flowed down his chin, to drip upon the dragon birthmark. 'I am not what I seem. In my death you accomplish your destruction.' He closed his eyes and fell back, his death rattle filling the room. The two men in black looked on as from Murmandamus's body a strange keening sound came. The figure on the stones puffed up, seeming to swell as if suddenly inflated. Like an overripe pod, from forehead to crotch, Murmandamus's body ripped, revealing an inner body of green scales. Thick black liquid and red blood, with clots of meat and gouts of white pus, were spewn about the room as the green-scaled body seemed to burst from within the husk that was Murmandamus, flopping on the floor like a freshly landed fish. In this terrible convulsion a leaping flame of bright red appeared, evil and filling the hall with a stench of ages of decay. Then the flame vanished and the universe opened around them.

Macros and Pug staggered where they stood, each somehow aware of a change in the fighting nearby. All their attentions were focused upon the place between the universes where the aborning rift was beginning. Each time a thrust came from the other universe, they answered with a patch of energy. The battle had reached its peak a moment before, and now the thrusts were weakening. But still there was danger, for Pug and Macros were also exhausted. It would require the utmost concentration to keep the rift between universes from opening. Then pain exploded in their minds as a silver note, a shrieking whistle, sounded a signal. From another quarter a different, unexpected attack came, and Pug could not answer. A thing of captured lives, taken in terrible death and held against this moment came flowing toward the rift, dancing like a mad and stinking red flame. It struck the barriers Pug had erected and shattered them. It tore open the rift and somehow moved between Pug's perceptions and the place where the battle raged, obscuring his sense of what occurred there. Pug felt slightly dazed. Then a warning cry from Macros refocused his attention on the rift, which now stood open. Pug worked frantically, and from some deep hidden reservoir of strength he drew forth the energy to grip the shredding fabric that held the universes apart. The rift closed violently. Again came the thrust, and again Pug barely held, but he held. Then from Macros came the warning, *Something got through*.

Something has come through, came the warning from Ryath.

Tomas leaped down from the dragon's back and waited behind the Lifestone. A darkness grew within the hall, vast and powerful, a thing of nightmare taking form. Then it stood forth. It was ebon, without feature and definition, a being of hopelessness, and it was aware. Its outline hinted at a man shape, but it bulked nearly as large as Ryath. Its shadow wings spread, casting gloom about the hall like a palpable black light, and about its head, like a crown, burned a circle of flames, angry red-orange and seeming to cast no illumination.

Tomas yelled to Ryath, 'It is a Dreadlord! Beware! It is a stealer of souls, an eater of minds!'

But the dragon bellowed in rage and attacked the monstrous thing of nightmare, bringing its magic to play as well as talons and flame. Tomas started forward, but a presence, another being entered this phase of time.

Tomas moved back into the shadow while a figure he had never seen before, but one as well known to him as Pug, emerged into the light of the gem. The newcomer dodged away from the towering battle that rocked the hall. With quick steps the figure moved toward the Lifestone.

Tomas appeared out of shadow, standing over the stone so that he was now visible. The figure halted, and a snarl of rage escaped.

Splendid in his orange-and-black armour, the Lord of Tigers, Draken-Korin, confronted a vision beyond his understanding. The Valheru shouted, 'No! It is impossible! You cannot still live!'

Tomas spoke and his voice was Ashen-Shugar's. 'So, you've come to see it finished.'

With the snarl of a tiger, lost in the shrieks and bellows of the larger battle in the hall, the returned Dragon Lord drew his black sword and leaped forward, and for the first time in his existence Tomas faced an enemy with the power to truly destroy him.

The battle was coming to an end as the host of Murmandamus streamed out of the city, fleeing toward the Dimwood. The word of Murmandamus's disappearance had spread as if blown through Sethanon by a sudden wind. Then, without warning, the Black Slayers, no matter where they were, collapsed as if their lives had been sucked out of their armour. This, along with the arrival of the Tsurani and the magicians and reports of more armies on the horizon, had caused the attack to falter and then fail. Chieftain after chieftain ordered his clans away, quitting the battle. With leadership evaporating, the goblins and trolls were slaughtered, until the still-larger invading army was in complete rout.

Jimmy hurried through the halls of the keep, looking among the dead and wounded for anyone he knew. He dashed up the stairs to the wall overlooking the killing ground and found a clot of Tsurani blocking the way. He slipped through them and saw a chirurgeon from Landreth standing over two bloody men who slumped against the wall. Amos had an arrow still sticking from his side, but was grinning. Guy was covered in gore and had a terrible-looking cut along his scalp. The cut had severed the cord holding the patch over his eye, and the angry, empty red socket could be seen. Amos laughed and almost choked. 'Hey, boy. Good to see you.' He looked about the wall. 'Look at all these little peacocks.' He waved one hand weakly at the brightly clad Tsurani soldiers, who looked on with unreadable expressions. 'Damn me, but they're the prettiest things I've ever seen.'

Then from below came a grinding, followed by a soul-chilling thunderous roar, as if some terrible host of madness was suddenly escaping from hell. Jimmy looked around in startled wonder, and even the Tsurani exhibited surprise. A trembling filled the keep as the walls began to shake. 'What's that!' shouted Jimmy.

'I don't know, and I don't plan on staying here to find out,' said Guy. Gesturing to be helped to his feet, he took the outstretched hand of a Tsurani warrior and got up. He motioned to what appeared a Tsurani officer, who ordered men to pick up Amos. Guy said to Jimmy, 'Order whoever's alive to evacuate the keep.' Then the rolling motion below increased and he staggered, while the howling sound grew in volume. 'No, tell whoever's alive to evacuate the city.'

Jimmy ran along the battlement, heading for the stairs.

• CHAPTER TWENTY •

Aftermath

*A*GAIN THE ROOM TREMBLED AND SHOOK.

Arutha listened, clutching his bleeding side. It sounded a distant battle, with titanic forces unleashed. He went to where Pug and Macros stood, with the two black-robed magicians next to them. He sighed as he nodded to them. 'I am Prince Arutha,' he said.

Hochopepa and Elgahar introduced themselves and Elgahar said, 'These two are undertaking to hold some power at bay. We must aid them.' The two Black Robes placed their hands upon Macros's and Pug's shoulders and closed their eyes. Arutha found he was alone again. He looked toward the grotesque husk of Murmandamus slumped in the corner. Crossing to where it lay, Arutha reached down and pulled his sword from the serpent man. Arutha studied the slime-covered form of the serpent priest and laughed bitterly. The reincarnated leader of the moredhel nations was a Pantathian! It had all been a ruse – from the centuries-old prophecy, to the marshalling of the moredhel and their allies, to the assault upon Armengar and Sethanon. The Pantathians

442

had simply been using the moredhel, at the command of the Dragon Lords, hoarding the magic of spent lives to reach the Lifestone and use it. In all of it, the moredhel had been used more cruelly than anyone else. It was an irony of heroic proportion. Arutha was astonished by the realization, though he was too tired to do more than weakly scan the room, as if looking for someone with whom to share the revelation. Suddenly a rent appeared in the wall with the small door, and gold, gems, and other treasures were spilled upon the floor. In his fatigue, Arutha hardly wondered how this had come to be, for he had heard no sound of masonry collapsing.

Arutha let his sword point drop and turned to walk back to the magicians. Seeing no exit from the vault, he sat upon the dais and watched the four motionless spellcasters as they stood with hands joined. He examined his wound and saw the blood flow had lessened. It was painful, but not serious. He leaned back, getting as comfortable as possible, for he could do nothing but wait.

Brickwork and masonry were smashed to dust as Ryath's tail drove through the wall. With shrieks of pain and rage, the dragon worked her magic upon the Dreadlord, while fang and talon inflicted injury. But the Dreadlord struggled mightily and the dragon paid a heavy toll in return.

Tomas lashed out, keeping his body between the Lifestone and Draken-Korin. The screaming, snarling Valheru had come at Tomas like the tiger on his tabard. Tomas had not possessed the savage fury of his opponent since the days of madness had been upon him during the Riftwar. But he was a practised warrior and he kept his wits about him.

Draken-Korin shouted, 'You cannot deny us again, Ashen-Shugar. We are the lords of this world. We must return.'

Tomas parried, turning the blade away, then slashed out and was rewarded with a shower of sparks as his blade hit Draken-Korin's armour, rending his tabard. 'You are a decayed artifact of a former age. You are a thing that hasn't the wits to know you're dead. You'd destroy all to win a lifeless planet.'

Draken-Korin swung a looping blow toward the head, but Tomas ducked and thrust, and his sword point took the Valheru in the stomach. Draken-Korin staggered back, and Tomas was upon him like a cat upon a rat. Blow after blow rained down upon the Lord of Tigers and Tomas held the upper hand.

'We shall not be turned away,' screamed Draken-Korin and he redoubled his fury, halting Tomas, then driving him back. In an instant there was a shimmering, and where Draken-Korin had been, Alma-Lodaka now stood, but her attack was no less fierce. 'You underestimate us, Father-Husband. We are all the Valheru, you are but one.' Then the face and body changed, as one and another Valheru opposed Tomas. Quickly they shifted, until a blur of faces appeared before Tomas. Then Draken-Korin was back. 'You see, I am a multitude, a legion. We are power.'

'You are death and evil, but you are also the father of lies,' answered Tomas with contempt. He struck out, and Draken-Korin barely parried. 'Had you the power of the race, I would have been taken in a mere instant. You may shift your form, but I know you are only a single agent, a small part of the whole, slipped here to use the Lifestone to open the portal, so the Dragon Host might enter.'

Draken-Korin's only answer was a renewed attack. Tomas took the black blade upon his golden one, knocking it aside. At the other side of the hall, the struggle between the dragon and the Dreadlord was nearing a finish, for the sounds of battle were faint and occasional. Then from behind came silence and a terrible presence.

Tomas felt the Dreadlord approach and knew Ryath had fallen to it. As Ashen-Shugar he had faced the Dreadlord before, and if unencumbered he would not have feared it, but to face it would free Draken-Korin to act, and to ignore it would give it the chance to incapacitate him.

Tomas knocked aside Draken-Korin's next strike and leaped forward, unexpectedly, chancing a blow. The black blade snapped forward, but only glanced against the chain mail under the white tabard. Tomas's teeth clenched in pain as the ebon blade severed the golden links, cutting his side, but he gripped Draken-Korin's arm.

With a wrenching twist, he reversed their positions, pushing the Lord of Tigers directly into the Dreadlord's path.

The Dreadlord attempted to halt, but the dragon had exacted a toll before succumbing. The Dreadlord was injured and dazed and his blow struck Draken-Korin from behind, stunning him. Draken-Korin screamed in agony, for he had not erected any protection against the life-draining touch of the Dreadlord.

Tomas thrust and tore a gaping wound in the stomach of the black-and-orange clad Valheru, weakening him more. Draken-Korin stumbled and was again forced to brush against the near-mindless Dreadlord, who shoved him aside. That inadvertent strike propelled Draken-Korin toward the Lifestone.

'No!' shouted Tomas, leaping forward. The Dreadlord lashed out, gripping Tomas for an instant. Pain flooded Tomas's being, and he struck out with his sword, causing a hissing shower of sparks where he hit the night-dark creature. It echoed a windy cry and let go. Quickly Tomas lashed out at the heart of the unliving creature, a near-mortal wound which caused it to stagger back. Tomas spun toward where Draken-Korin attempted to reach his goal.

Draken-Korin stumbled and fell forward across the Lifestone, as if to embrace it. He laughed, even as he felt his energies begin to dissipate, for he still had time to work his arts and open the gate, allowing the rest of his collective consciousness to return to the world of their creation. He would be whole again.

Then with a mighty bound, Tomas leaped above him, sword held with both hands, point downward, and with all his remaining energies he drove the blade down in one terrible blow. There was an ear-shattering shriek as Draken-Korin arched backward, like a bow being drawn. The golden sword passed through him and into the Lifestone.

Then the wind came. From somewhere a compelling current of air appeared, blowing from all directions into the Lifestone. The mortally stricken Dreadlord trembled at the breeze's touch, then quivered. It suddenly became a thing of smoke and insubstance and was carried along on the wind as it was sucked into the stone. The form of the Lord of Tigers shivered, then shook violently, as a golden glow spread from Tomas's magic blade to engulf Draken-Korin. The golden nimbus began to pulse and Draken-Korin became insubstantial and like the Dreadlord vanished into the stone.

Pug staggered as if from a blow, and the rift was torn open, but not from the other side. It was as if a giant hand had reached out and moved his magic blocks aside, then reached into the rift, pulling something through. Pug felt Macros's mind and recognized that somehow Hochopepa and Elgahar were there as well. Then the rift exploded toward them and they were cast back into normal awareness.

The room shifted about Tomas. Suddenly Macros, Pug, two black-robed men, and Arutha were there.

He looked back and saw Ryath, huddled in the corner, a mass of terrible, smoking wounds. The dragon appeared dead, or if still alive, then only for a short while longer. She had met her destiny as she had foretold, and Tomas vowed she would be remembered. Beyond her recumbent form, the Valheru treasure vault had been torn open in the struggle between dragon and Dreadlord, emptying its contents of gold and gems, books and artifacts, across the floor.

Arutha leaped to his feet and asked, 'What has happened?'

'I think it is almost over,' Tomas said as he jumped down.

Macros staggered, and Pug and the others moved, as the sound of shrieking winds became a terrible force buffeting the ears. Suddenly all covered their ears as a terrible concussion sounded, and the very roof of the chamber exploded upward, destroying the very soil above the ancient vault, and the cellars and lower floors of the keep as well, blowing toward the heavens through the now open crater. A geyser of masonry and stone, the fragments of two buildings, were carried high into the sky, to be strewn outward into the city. High in the air above them an opening, a grey sparkling nothing, appeared against the blue. And from within it, a blaze of many colours could be seen.

Pug, Hochopepa, and Elgahar had all seen such a display once before, each in turn when upon the Tower of Testing in the City of Magicians. It was the vision of the Enemy seen at the time of the golden bridge, when the nations had fled to Kelewan during the Chaos Wars. 'It is coming through!' shouted Hochopepa.

Macros shouted above the terrible howling sound from the gem, 'The Lifestone! It's been activated.'

Pug looked about in confusion. 'But we're still alive!'

Tomas pointed to where his golden sword was still stuck upright into the Lifestone. 'I killed Draken-Korin before he could finish utilizing the Lifestone. It is only partly active.'

'What will happen?' shouted Pug over the ear-shattering noise.

'I don't know.' Macros joined the others in covering his ears. At the top of his lungs he shouted, 'We need a force barrier!'

At once Pug knew what was needed and attempted to fashion the magic that would keep them from being destroyed. 'Hocho, Elgahar, aid me!'

He began his incantation and the others joined in, to fashion a protective barrier around them. The sound increased to the pitch where Arutha found his hands over his ears did no good; he gritted his teeth in pain, fighting against the urge to scream, wondering if the magicians could finish their incantations. The light from the Lifestone grew in intensity, to a blinding pure white with silver flares about the edge. It seemed ready to unleash some terrible destruction. The Prince was nearly numb from fatigue and the horror of what had occurred in the last few hours. He dully wondered what it would be like for the planet to die. Then he could stand the pain no longer and began to scream . . .

. . . as Pug finished the incantation, and the room exploded.

A ragged trembling commenced in the ground, a rolling surging like an earthquake, and Guy turned to regard the city. The soldiers of Shamata, Landreth, and the Tsurani were fleeing alongside those from Sethanon and Highcastle. Mixed in were goblins, trolls, and a few steadfast Dark Brothers, but all combat was forgotten as every creature in the city fled a feeling of impending doom, a terror palpable down to the fibre of their being. Black emotions, dark horror and despair had suddenly washed over every living creature, robbing them of any urge to fight. To the last, each wished only to put as much distance as possible between himself and the source of that desperate fear.

Then a low rolling pulse began, a stunning noise of grating, painful quality. All within earshot of the sound fell to their knees. Men vomited as their stomachs constricted from a horrible sense of directionlessness, as if suddenly the force that held them to the ground vanished. Eyes watered and ears ached as they seemed to rise upward. All felt as if they were floating for an instant, then they were wrenched to the ground, slammed as if struck by a giant hand. Then came the explosion.

Any who were struggling to stand were again thrown down as a light of impossible brilliance shot straight upward. As if the sun had exploded, it hurled shards of stone, earth, and wood skyward, a monstrous upheaval of energies. High above Sethanon, a red sparkle grew, a blinding light that dulled quickly to a point of grey nothingness. There came an unexpected silence, while vortices of energy danced within the greyness. As if the fabric of heaven were being turned back upon itself, the edges of the rent in the sky peeled backward, revealing another universe in the skies. The cascading colours that were the might, the energy, the very life of the Dragon Lords, could be seen pulsing and surging forward, as if seeking to pass the last barrier between themselves and their final goal. Then came a sound.

A silver trumpet note of incredible volume sounded, piercing every being within miles of the city, as if a wind of needles passed through their bodies. The agony of final hopelessness overwhelmed them all. A thing of despair again sounded through the minds of every creature within sight of Sethanon, as each was suddenly aware their life was somehow tied to what they witnessed. Panic rose up in each observer, even to the most battle-tested soldier, and to a man all wept and cried out, for they were seeing the last moments of their existence. Then all noise ceased.

In the eerie silence, something formed in the blaze of colours in the skies. The grey nothingness had spread outward, until the whole of the heavens seemed blanked out by it, and in the heart of that insane display the Enemy appeared. At first it seemed dull blotches of colour, pulsing and shifting as it pushed itself through the gap between worlds. But as it began to pass through, it began to dissolve into smaller blots of bright colours, shifting energy forms that solidified into distinct shapes. Soon all on the ground could see individual beings, man-shaped creatures, each mounted upon the back of a dragon, in the heart of the rift. With an explosion surpassing all before, the Dragon Host sprang through the rift in the sky, thundering into the world of their birth. Hundreds of beings, each mystically linked with the others, swept out of the rift, crying ancient battle cries. They were images of terrible beauty, magnificent beings of astonishing power, in armour of bright colour and splendid form, riding upon the backs of ancient dragons. Incredible beasts, many gone ages from Midkemia, beat gigantic wings across the heavens. Great black, green, and blue dragons, extinct upon their homeworld, soared beside the gold and bronze creatures whose descendants were still alive. Reds, whose like were common, glided next to silver dragons, unseen in Midkemia in ages. The Valheru's faces were masks of gleeful joy as they seized the moment of victory and savoured it. Each seemed a vessel of unsurpassed power, ruler of all he surveyed. They *were* power. As they appeared, a pain of nearly unendurable intensity was felt within the body of each creature upon the planet, as if their strand of life was somehow being pulled.

Then at the moment of deepest terror, when all hope seemed abandoned, a force rose upward. From deep within the crater below the keep a surge of energy fountained above the city, twisting in confusion and leaping across the roof-tops. It danced a furious jig in mad abandon as green fire sped outward, pouring like liquid flame into ever-widening circles. Then with a dull thumping sound, loud but not painful to the ears, a gigantic cloud of dust was hurled skyward, and all noise ceased.

Something answered the chaos in the skies. It was unseen but felt, a thing of titanic dimensions, a rejection of all the black and evil despair experienced only moments before. As if all the love and wonders of creation had given voice to a song, it rose to challenge the Dragon Host. A green light, brilliant to match that red light of a moment before, sprang upward from the crater in the ground, to strike at the rift. Those in the van of the Dragon Host were engulfed in green light, and as each was touched, it became a thing of insubstantiality, a wraith of a past epoch, a shadow of an earlier era. The Dragon Lords became clouds of coloured smoke, beings of mist and memory. They trembled and danced, as if held in thrall by opposing and equal forces, then they were suddenly sucked downward, as if being pulled into the ground by an irresistible wind. The riderless dragons screamed and wheeled, flying furiously away from the wind, now free of their masters' commands. Toward all points of the compass they dispersed. The earth shook beneath those who watched in stunned wonder, and the sound of that wind was both fearsome and beautiful to hear, as if the gods themselves had composed a death song. Then the tear in the sky vanished in a single instant, with no display, no hint it had existed. The wind ceased.

And the silence was stunning.

Jimmy looked around. He found himself crying, then laughing, then crying. Suddenly he felt as if all the horrors he had known, all the pain he had experienced had been banished. Suddenly he felt right, to the deepest centre of his being. He felt connected with every living thing upon the planet. He felt his being filled with life, and with love. And he knew that, at last, they had won. Somehow at the moment of their triumph, the Valheru had been overcome, had been defeated. The young squire stood upon wobbly legs, laughing in joy as tears fell unashamedly down his face. He found himself with his arm around a Tsurani soldier who also grinned and cried at once.

Guy was helped again to his feet and regarded the scene about him. Goblins, trolls, and Dark Brothers, and an occasional giant, were staggering northward, but no one was yet giving chase. The soldiers of the Kingdom and the Tsurani simply watched the spectacle of the city, for now a dome of impossible green light glowed over Sethanon, a green so bright it was visible in the sunlight of a clear autumn day, and so beautiful it filled all who watched with a wonder of overpowering intensity. A song of awesome joy sounded within the hearts of all who saw the dome, felt rather than heard. At every hand, men wept openly as they regarded something of sublime perfection, filling them with a joy beyond description. The green dome seemed to flicker, but that might have been the result of the dust passing in clouds around it. Guy watched, unable to take his eye from it. Even the goblins and trolls who staggered past were changed, as if drained of any desire to fight.

Guy sighed and felt the joy within begin to lessen, and was visited with the certainty that never again in his life would he know such a perfect moment of joy, such a wondrous rapture. Armand de Sevigny came hurrying toward his old ally, Martin and a dwarf a short way behind. 'Guy!' he said, taking the place of one of the Tsurani, holding his former commander and friend upright as he hugged him fiercely. Both men rocked back and forth with arms around each other, laughing and weeping.

Quietly du Bas-Tyra said, 'Somehow we've won.'

Armand nodded, then said, 'Arutha?'

Guy shook his head sadly. 'Nothing could have survived inside that. Nothing.'

Martin and Dolgan arrived at the head of a band of dwarven warriors. The King of the Dwarves of the West came to stand next to Guy and Armand. He spoke quietly. ''Tis a thing of terrible and infinite beauty.' Now the dome of light seemed to take on the appearance of a giant gem, as if composed of hexagonal facets. Each facet shone brightly but dimmed at a different rate, giving the dome the appearance of sparkling. The feelings of perfection were dimming, as was the surging joy, but still a calm wonder could be felt by all who looked upon it.

Martin tore his eyes from the sight and said, 'Arutha?'

Guy said, 'He vanished in there with three men who came by dragon-back. The elf knows their names.'

As the vision before them pulsed, Guy forced his attention back to mundane concerns. 'Gods, what a mess. Martin, you'd better have some men chase those Dark Brothers home, before they can re-form and come back.'

Dolgan quietly removed a pipe from his belt pouch. 'My lads are already seeing to that, but they won't mind company. Though somehow I don't think the moredhel and their servants will need much urging. Truth is, I doubt any here today have much itch for fighting left.'

Then, outlined against the glowing green sphere, through the dust, came the silhouettes of six men, half-walking, half-limping. Martin and the others were silent as the six came nearer, each rendered almost featureless by a thick mantle of dust. Then when they were halfway between the city gates and the onlookers, Martin shouted, 'Arutha!'

At once men were hurrying forward, to give aid to Arutha and his companions. Each had a pair of soldiers offering to help them walk, but Arutha only halted and embraced his brother. Martin put his arm about his brother's shoulder, crying in open relief at seeing him alive again. After a long moment they separated and turned to regard the glowing dome over the city.

A sudden renewal of the sensation of harmony with all life and love washed over them, a wondrous feeling of sublime perfection. Then it vanished.

The green lights of the dome winked out of existence, and the dust began to settle.

Macros spoke in a hoarse croak. 'It's finally over.'

Lyam moved through the camp, inspecting the ragged remains of those who fought at Highcastle and Sethanon. Arutha walked at his side, still sore and battered from the struggle. The King said, 'This tale is astonishing. I can believe it only because proof lies before my eyes.'

Arutha said, 'I lived it and can scarcely believe what I saw.'

Lyam glanced about. 'Still, from everything you've said, we're lucky to be seeing anything at all. I guess we have much to be thankful for.' He sighed. 'You know, when we were boys, I'd have sworn being King would be a grand thing.' He looked thoughtfully at Arutha. 'Just as I would have sworn that I was as smart as you and Martin.' With a rueful smile he said, 'The proof that I'm not was that I didn't follow Martin's example and renounce the crown.

'Nothing but messes. I've got Hazara-Khan prowling about, engaging in chitchat with half the nobles in the Kingdom, and no doubt picking up state secrets like they were seashells on the beach. Now the rift is reopened, I need to communicate with the Emperor and see if I can arrange for a prisoner exchange. Except we don't have any, having made them all free men, so Kasumi and Hokanu tell me we'll probably have to buy the captives back, which means raising taxes. And I've got a hundred or more dragons, some not seen on this world in many ages, flying in every direction, who may land wherever they will – when they get hungry. Then there's the problem of an entire city being ruined—'

Arutha said, 'Consider the alternative.'

'But if that isn't enough, you handed me du Bas-Tyra to deal with and, from what you said, he's a hero in the bargain. Half the lords of the Kingdom want me to find a tree and hang him, and the other half are ready to hang me if he tells them to do so.' He regarded his brother with a sceptical eye. 'I think I should have taken a hint when Martin renounced, and dropped the crown on you. Give me a decent pension and I still might.' Arutha's expression turned dark and cloudy at even a hint he would have more responsibility. Lyam looked about as Martin shouted greeting. 'Anyway,' he said to Arutha, 'I think I know what I'll do about the last.' Lyam waved to Martin, who hurried over. 'Did you find her?'

The Duke of Crydee grinned. 'Yes, she was with a group of auxiliaries from Tyr-Sog that marched a halfday behind me all the way here, the ones who came along with Kasumi's LaMutians and Dolgan's dwarves.'

Lyam had been touring the site of the battle for a day and a half with Arutha, since he had arrived. His army had been the last to reach the battlefield, for winds from Rillanon to Salador had been unfavourable. With a jerk of his thumb over his shoulder, he indicated where the nobles of the Kingdom had gathered, near his pavilion. 'Well,' he said, 'they're all dying to know what we do now.'

'Have you decided?' asked Arutha of Martin. The Prince had stayed in council all night with Lyam, Pug, Tomas, Macros, and Laurie – while Martin had combed the camp looking for Briana – discussing the disposition of many matters, now that the threat from Murmandamus was averted.

Martin looked positively jubilant. 'Yes, we're to be married as soon as possible. If there's a priest of any order left among the city refugees, then tomorrow.'

Lyam said, 'I think you'll have to stem your passion long enough for some sort of state wedding.' Martin's expression began to cloud over. Lyam burst into laughter. 'Hell, now you look just like he does!' and pointed at Arutha. The King was suddenly overcome with a deep affection for his brothers and threw his arms about their necks. Hugging them fiercely, he spoke in a voice thick with emotion. 'I'm so proud of you both. I know Father would be.' For a long moment the three of them stood with their arms about each other. Brightening his tone, Lyam said, 'Come, let us restore some order to our Kingdom. Then we can celebrate. Damn me, but if we don't have a reason, no one ever has.' He gave both a playful shove and, with all three laughing, herded them toward his pavilion.

Pug watched as Lyam entered with his brothers. Macros leaned upon his staff beside Kulgan, with the other magicians from Stardock and the Assembly clustered behind. Katala hung on to her husband, as if unwilling to let him go, while William and Gamina clung to his robe. He tousled the girl's hair, pleased to discover he had inherited a daughter in the time he'd been gone.

Off to one side, Kasumi spoke quietly with his younger brother. For the first time in three years they were together. Hokanu and the soldiers most loyal to the Emperor had been those sent to aid the Black Robes of the Assembly when they had come. Both brothers of the Shinzawai had been interviewed by Lyam earlier that day, for, as he had said, the return of the rift between worlds had created some difficulties.

Laurie and Baru joined Martin, who kept his arm around Briana's waist. The redheaded warrior called Shigga leaned upon his spear behind them, quietly observing the proceedings, despite his inability to understand what was being said. They had arrived with Briana, as had other survivors of Armengar, marching with the army under Vandros of Yabon. Most of the Armengarian soldiers were out with the dwarves, chasing the host of Murmandamus back north. Next to them Dolgan and Galain watched, the dwarf seeming to have aged not one day. The only indication of his rise to the throne of the western dwarves was the Hammer of Tholin, which hung at his belt. Otherwise he looked exactly as Pug remembered him from the time they had braved the mines under the Grey Tower Mountains. He spied Pug from across the tent and gave him a smile and wave.

Lyam held up his hand. 'Many things have been told to us since our arrival, wondrous tales of bravery and heroism, narratives of duty and sacrifice. With the upheaval here, some issues become resolved. We have spoken with many of you, taking good counsel, and now we have some proclamations to make. In the first, though the people of the city of Armengar are foreign to our nation, they are brethren to our people of Yabon. We welcome them back as brothers returned and offer them a place alongside their kin. They may count themselves as citizens of the Kingdom. If any wish to return to the north, to settle again in that land, we shall aid them in whatever way we may, but we hope they will stay.

'And we also offer deep thanks to King Dolgan and his followers for their timely aid. I also wish to thank Galain the elf for his willingness to help our brother. And let it be known that our lords the Prince of Krondor and the Dukes of Crydee and Salador have served their Kingdom beyond any measure and the crown is in their debt. No king could ever demand of his subjects what they so freely gave.' Then, in a precedent-making display, Lyam led a cheer for Arutha, Laurie, and Martin. The pavilion rang with the cheers of the assembled nobles. 'Now let Earl Kasumi of LaMut and his brother, Hokanu of the Shinzawai, approach.'

When the two Tsurani had come before him, Lyam said, 'Kasumi, first of all relay to your brother, and through him to the Emperor and his soldiers, our undying gratitude for their generous and valiant efforts in saving this nation from grave peril.' Kasumi began to translate for his brother.

Pug felt a hand upon his shoulder and turned to find Macros inclining his head. Pug kissed Katala and whispered, 'I'll be back shortly.'

Katala nodded and held on to her children, knowing that for once her husband was not just saying that. She watched while Macros took Tomas and Pug away a short distance.

Lyam said, 'Now that the way has been opened, we shall permit those of the garrison of LaMut who wish to return to their homeland to do so, freeing them of vassalage to us.'

Kasumi bowed his head. 'My liege, I am pleased to inform you that most of the men have elected to remain, saying that while your generosity overwhelms them, they are now men of the Kingdom, with wives, families, and ties. I shall also remain.'

'We are pleased, Kasumi. We are very pleased.'

The two withdrew and Lyam said, 'Now let Armand de Sevigny, Baldwin de la Troville, and Anthony du Masigny come forward.'

The three men came and bowed. Lyam said, 'Kneel,' and the three men bent knees before their King.

'Anthony du Masigny, you are herewith granted again your titles and lands in the Barony of Calry, taken from you when you were sent to the north, and add to them the title and lands once held by Baldwin de la Troville. We are pleased with your service. Baldwin de la Troville, we have need of you. As we have given your office of Squire of Marlsbourough to du Masigny, we have another for you. Will you accept the post of commander of our outpost at Highcastle?'

De la Troville said, 'Yes, sire, though if it pleases the crown I'd like to winter in the south, now and again.'

From the crowd a laugh answered, as Lyam said, 'Granted, for we shall also grant you the titles formerly held by Armand de Sevigny. Rise, Baldwin, Baron of Highcastle and Gyldenholt.' He looked at Armand de Sevigny and said, 'We have plans for you, my friend. Let the former Duke of Bas-Tyra be brought forth.' Guards in the colours of the King came with Guy du Bas-Tyra, half escorting him, half carrying him from within the King's pavilion, where he had been convalescing with Amos Trask. When Guy halted next to the kneeling Armand, the King said, 'Guy du Bas-Tyra, you have been branded traitor and banished, not to return to our nation upon pain of death. We understand you had little choice in the matter of your return.' He cast a glance at Arutha who smiled ruefully. 'We hereby rescind the order of banishment. Now, there is a matter of title. We are giving the office of Duke of Bas-Tyra to the man our brother Arutha has judged most fit for it. Armand de Sevigny, we hereby grant unto you the office of Lord of the Duchy of Bas-Tyra, with all rights and obligations pertaining thereunto. Rise, Duke Armand de Sevigny.'

Lyam turned his gaze upon Guy. 'Even without your hereditary office, we think we shall still keep you busy. Kneel.' Guy was helped to kneel by Armand. 'Guy du Bas-Tyra for your deep concern for the welfare of the Kingdom despite her having cast you out and your bravery in the defence of both Armengar and this Kingdom, we offer to you the office of First Advisor to the King. Will you accept?'

Guy's good eye widened, and then he laughed. 'This is a grand jest, Lyam. Your father's having a fit somewhere. Yes, I'll take it.'

The King shook his head and smiled, remembering his father. 'No, we think he understands. Rise, Guy, Duke of Rillanon.'

Next Lyam said, 'Baru of the Hadati.' Baru left Laurie, Martin, and Briana, and knelt before his King. 'Your bravery is without peer, both in destroying the moredhel Murad and in accompanying our brother Martin and Duke Laurie over the mountains to bring us warning of Murmandamus's invasion. We have thought long and hard and are at a loss as to what reward to offer. What may we do to show you our pleasure at your service?'

Baru said, 'Majesty, I desire no reward. I have many new kinsmen come into Yabon and would make my home with them, if I may.'

Lyam said, 'Then go with our blessings, and should you need anything within our power to grant, to ease the relocation of your kinsmen, you have but to ask.'

Baru rose and returned to stand by his friends, who all smiled. Baru had found a new home and a purpose in life.

Other rewards were given and the business of the court continued. Arutha remained apart, wishing that Anita could be with him, but knowing he was only days away from her. He saw Macros off in the distance, speaking with Pug and Tomas. The three figures stood in shadow, as the day was coming to a close, evening rapidly approaching. Arutha sighed in fatigue and wondered what they were concerned with now.

Macros said, 'Then you understand.'

Pug said, 'Yes, but it is still a hard thing.' He didn't need to speak any more. He had full measure of the knowledge gained when he and the sorcerer had been joined. Now he was Macros's equal in power, and almost his equal in knowledge. But he would miss the presence of the sorcerer, now he knew his fate.

'All things come to an end, Pug. Now it is the end of my time upon this world. With the ending of the Valheru presence, my powers have returned fully. I will move on to something new. Gathis will join me, and the others at my island are cared for, so I have no more duties here. I must move onward, just as you must stay here. There will be kings to counsel, little boys to teach, old men to argue with, wars to avoid, wars to be fought.' He sighed, as if again he wished for a final release. Then his tone lightened. 'Still, it is never boring. It is never that. Be sure the King knows what we have done here.' He regarded Tomas. The human turned Valheru looked somehow different since the final battle, and Macros spoke softly. 'Tomas, you have the eldar returning home at last, their self-imposed exile in Elvardein at an end. You'll need to aid your Queen in ruling a new

Elvandar. Many of the glamredhel will be seeking you out, now that they know Elvandar exists, and you'll also find an increase in Returnings, I think. Now that the influence of the Valheru is confined, the lure of the Dark Path should weaken. At least, we can hope so. Seek inward, as well, Tomas, for I think you'll find much of your power is now gone with those who were Ashen-Shugar's brethren. You still stand with the most powerful of mortals, but I wouldn't seek to master dragons, if I were you. I think they might give you a shock.'

Tomas said, 'I felt myself change . . . at the last.' He had seemed subdued since his battle with Draken-Korin. 'Am I again mortal?'

Macros nodded. 'You always were. The power of the Valheru changed you, and that change will not be reversed, but you were never immortal. You were simply close to it. But do not worry, you've retained a great deal of the Valheru heritage. You'll live out a long life beside your Queen, at least as long as any of elvenkind are allotted by fate.' At these words Tomas seemed reassured.

'Keep vigilant, both of you, for the Pantathians spent centuries planning and executing this deceit. It was a plot of stunning detail. But the powers granted to the one who posed as Murmandamus were no mean set of conjurer's illusions. He was a force. To have created such a one and to have captured and manipulated the hearts of even a race as dark as the moredhel required much. Perhaps without the Valheru influence across the barriers of space and time, the serpent people may become much as others, just another intelligent race among many.' He looked off into the distance. 'Then again, perhaps not. Be wary of them.'

Pug spoke slowly. 'Macros . . . at the end I was certain we had lost.'

Macros smiled an enigmatic smile. 'So was I. Perhaps the Valheru's manipulation of the Lifestone was prevented from reaching fruition by Tomas's sword stroke. I don't know. The rift was opened, and the Dragon Host allowed to enter, but . . .' The old sorcerer's eyes seemed alight with some deep emotion. 'Some wonder or another, beyond my understanding, intervened at the last.' He looked downward. 'It was as if the very stuff of life, the souls of all that lived upon this world, rejected the Valheru. The power of the Lifestone aided us, not them. That was from where I drew strength at the last. It was that which captured the Dragon Host and the Dreadlord and closed the rift. It was that which protected us all, keeping us alive.' He smiled. 'You should seek, with care, to learn as much as you can about the Lifestone. It is a wonder beyond what any of us suspected.'

Macros was silent for a time, then looked at Pug. 'You are as much a son to me, in a strange sort of way, as any I may have called that over the ages. At least you are my heir, and husbander of all the magic lore I have accumulated since coming to Midkemia. That last case of books and scrolls I held at my island will come soon to Stardock. I suggest you hide that fact from Kulgan and Hochopepa, until you've reviewed what's there. Some of it is beyond any on this world but you, and whoever may follow you in our unusual calling. Train those around you well, Pug. Make them powerful, but make them loving, generous men and women as well.' He paused as he looked at the two boys grown to men, those lads from Crydee whom twelve years ago he had begun to mould to save a world and more. At last he said, 'I have used both of you, ungently at times. But in the end it proved necessary. Whatever pain you may have endured is, I like to think, offset by the gains. You have achieved things beyond your boyhood dreams. You are now the caretakers of Midkemia. You have whatever blessing I may give.' With an unusual catch in his voice, his eyes moist and glowing, he softly said, 'Good-bye and thank you.' He stepped away from them, then slowly turned. Neither Pug nor Tomas could bring himself to say good-bye. Macros began walking toward the west, into the sunset. Not only did he move away from them, but with the first step he seemed somehow to become less solid. With each additional step he became more insubstantial, transparent, and soon he was like mist, then less than the mist. Then he was gone.

They watched him go, saying nothing for a while. Then Tomas wondered, 'Will he ever know peace, do you think?'

Pug said, 'I don't know. Perhaps someday he'll find his Blessed Isle.'

They were again silent for a time. Then they returned to the King's Pavilion.

There was a celebration in full swing. Martin and Briana had announced their plans to wed, to the obvious approval of everyone. Now, while others revelled in life and survival and the simple joy of living, Arutha, Lyam, Tomas, and Pug picked their way through the rubble that was Sethanon. The populace was housed in the less damaged western section, but they were only a distant presence. Still they moved cautiously, lest anyone observe them.

Tomas led them through a large crack in the ground, to what appeared a cave opening below the rubble of the keep. 'Here,' said Tomas, 'a fissure has opened, leading down to the lower chamber, the centre of the ancient city. Step carefully.'

Slowly they descended, seeing by a dim light of Pug's magic arts, and soon they entered the chamber. Pug waved his hand and a brighter light sprang forth. Tomas motioned the King forward. Figures in robes stepped out of the shadows, and Arutha drew his sword.

A woman's voice came from the dark. 'Put up your sword, Prince of the Kingdom.'

Tomas nodded and Arutha resheathed his mystic blade. From out of the dark came an enormous figure, bejewelled and brilliant as light danced across a myriad of facets. It was a dragon, but none like any seen, for in place of scales once golden a thousand gemstones gleamed. With each movement, a rainbow of dazzling beauty washed over the monstrous form.

'Who are you?' asked the King calmly.

'I am the Oracle of Aal,' came the soft voice from the Dragon's mouth.

'We struck a bargain,' said Pug. 'We needed to find her a proper body.'

Tomas said, 'Ryath was rendered mindless, her soul gone at the hands of the Dreadlord. Her body still lived, though damaged severely and hovering close to death. Macros healed her, replacing the destroyed scales with new ones fashioned from the gems of the treasure hidden here, using some unique property of the Lifestone. With his restored arts he brought the Oracle and her servants here. Now the Oracle lives within the emptied mind.'

'It is a more than satisfactory body,' said the Oracle. 'It will live for many centuries. And it possesses many powers.'

'And,' added Pug, 'she will remain forever vigilant over the Lifestone. For if any were to tamper with it, she would perish along with everyone else upon the planet. Until we find a way to seek out and deal with the Pantathians, the risk still exists that the Valheru could be recalled.'

Lyam regarded the Lifestone. The pale green gem glowed softly, seeming to pulse with a warm inner light. And from its centre a golden sword protruded. 'We do not know if this destroyed the Dragon Lords or merely holds them in thrall,' said Pug. 'Even the magics I learned from Macros may not penetrate all its mysteries. We are fearful of removing Tomas's sword, for to do so might cause no harm at all or it might unleash what is trapped within.'

Lyam shuddered. Of all he had heard, the power of the Lifestone had made him feel the most helpless. He approached it and slowly put forth his hand. The stone proved warm to the touch and contact filled him with a mild, relaxing pleasure. There was a sense of rightness in the stone. The King faced the mighty form of the bejewelled dragon. 'I have no objection to your stewardship, lady.' He thought, then spoke to Arutha. 'Start some rumour that the city's now cursed. Brave little Humphry's dead, and there's no heir to his title. I'll move what's left of the populace and pay them indemnity. The city's more than half destroyed already. Let's empty it out, and the Oracle will remain undisturbed. Let us leave, lest we are missed at revel and someone comes seeking after us.' To the dragon he said, 'Lady, I wish you well in your office. Should you have any need, send a message, by means magic or mundane, and I shall seek to meet it. Only we four, and my brother Martin, shall know the truth of you, and from this time forward, only our heirs.'

'You are gracious, Majesty,' answered the Oracle.

Tomas led them out of the cavern, and upward, to the surface.

Arutha entered his tent, and was startled to find Jimmy sleeping in his bed. He shook him gently. 'What is this? I thought you were given quarters?'

Jimmy looked at the Prince with an ill-concealed grumpiness at being awakened. 'It's Locky. The whole damn city's coming down about our ears and he finds another girl. It's getting to be a habit. Last night I slept on the ground. I just thought to catch a nap. I'll find another place.'

Arutha laughed and pushed the youngster back into the cot as he began to rise. 'Stay here. I'll bunk in the King's Pavilion. Lyam was busy handing out rewards this evening, while you slumbered and Locky . . . well, did whatever he was doing. In all the confusion I overlooked you two. What should I do to reward you scoundrels.'

Jimmy grinned. 'Make Locky Senior Squire so I can go back to the quiet life of a thief.' He yawned. 'Right now, I can't think of a damn thing I want except a week of sleep.'

Arutha smiled. 'All right. Get some sleep. I'll come up with something for you young rogues.' He left Jimmy and made his way back toward Lyam's tent.

As he approached the entrance, a shout of announcement and a trumpet flourish accompanied the arrival of a dusty carriage bearing the royal crest. Anita and Carline quickly stepped out. Arutha showed astonishment as his wife and sister rushed forward to hug and kiss him. 'What's this?'

'We followed Lyam,' said a tearful Anita. 'We couldn't wait in Rillanon to find out if you and Laurie were alive. As soon as messages reached us you were well, we broke camp and hurried here.'

Arutha hugged her as Carline listened to singing a moment and said, 'Either that's a nightingale in love, or my husband is forgetting he's now a duke.' She kissed Arutha once more on the cheek and said, 'You're going to be an uncle again.'

Arutha laughed and hugged his sister. 'Much love and happiness, Carline. Yes, that's Laurie. He and Baru arrived today with Vandros.'

She smiled. 'Well, I think I'll go give him some grey hairs.'

Arutha said, 'What does she mean "again"?'

Anita looked up into her husband's face. 'The Queen is with child – the announcement was made while you were gone – and Father Tully sends word to Lyam that it seems all signs indicate a prince. Tully claims he's too old for the road now. But his prayers have been with you.'

Arutha grinned. 'So I can be done with being Heir soon.'

'Not too soon, the baby won't be here for another four months.'

A cheer from within told them Carline had passed along the news of her own pregnancy to her husband, and another cheer said that Tully's message had been given as well.

Anita hugged her husband and whispered, 'Your sons are well and getting big. They miss their father, as I have done. Can we slip away soon?'

Arutha laughed. 'As soon as we make an appearance. But I've had to give my quarters to Jimmy. It seems Locky's developed an amorous nature and Jimmy had nowhere else to sleep. So we'll have to use one of the guest tents in this pavilion.' He walked inside with his wife, and the assembled nobles rose in greeting to the Prince and Princess of Krondor.

The Keshian Ambassador, Lord Hazara-Khan, bowed, and Arutha extended his hand. 'Thank you, Abdur.' He introduced Anita to Hokanu and again repeated thanks. Dolgan was speaking with Galain, and Arutha congratulated the dwarf on his assumption of the crown of the western dwarves. Dolgan threw him a wink and a smile, then they all fell silent as Laurie began to play.

They listened closely while Laurie sang; it was a sad song, yet brave, a ballad he had composed in honour of his friend Roald. It spoke of Laurie's sorrow at his passing, but it ended on a major chord, a note of triumph, then a silly little coda that made all who knew Roald laugh, for it somehow captured his raffish nature.

Then Gardan and Volney came up and the Earl of Landreth said, 'If we may have a brief word with you, Highness.'

Anita indicated she didn't mind, and Arutha let the two men who had ruled in his absence lead him into the room next to the King's chamber. A bulky figure lay upon the bed, breathing heavily, and Arutha raised his fingers to his lips, indicating quiet.

Gardan craned his neck and whispered, 'Amos Trask?'

Arutha said softly, 'It's a very long story, and I'll let him tell it. He'd never forgive me if I didn't. Now, what is it?'

In a low voice, Volney said, 'Highness, I want to return to Landreth. With your supposed death, the city's been a rats' warren to administer. I've done my best for the last three years, but this is enough. I want to go home.'

Arutha said, 'I can't spare you, Volney.' The stout Earl's voice started to rise, and Arutha hushed him. 'Look, there's going to be a new Prince of Krondor soon, so we'll need a Principate Regent.'

Volney said, 'That's impossible. That's an eighteen year commitment. I refuse.'

Arutha looked at Gardan, who grinned and held up his hands. 'Don't look at me. Lyam promised me I could return to Crydee with Martin and his lady. With Charles the new Swordmaster, I can leave the soldiering to my son. I plan on spending my days fishing off the breakwater at Longpoint. You're going to need a new Knight-Marshal soon.'

Arutha swore. 'That means if I don't find someone soon, Lyam's going to name me Duke of Krondor and Knight-Marshal both. I am going to try to get him to give me some quiet Earldom, like Tuckshill, and never leave home again.' He thought hard and silently, then said, 'I want ten more years, from both of you.'

'Absolutely not!' said Volney. The stout noble's voice rose in indignation. 'I'm willing to stay one year, to aid any transition in administration, but no more.'

Arutha's eyes narrowed. 'Six, six more years from each of you. If you agree, you can retire to Landreth, Volney, and you to Crydee, Gardan. If not, I'll find some way to drag you off to nothing but trouble.'

Gardan laughed. 'I have Lyam's permission already, Arutha.' Seeing the Prince's anger growing, he said, 'But if Volney stays, I'll also stay on a year – all right, two, but no more, until you get things under control.'

An almost evil light entered Arutha's eyes. To Gardan he said, 'We're going to need a new ambassador to the Tsurani court, now that the rift is again opened,' and to Volney, 'and we'll need another ambassador to Great Kesh.'

Both men exchanged glances and Volney said, in a harsh whisper, 'All right, blackmailer, three years. What are we going to do for three years?'

Arutha smiled his crooked smile. 'I want you to take Jimmy and Locky's training in hand, personally, Volney. You teach them everything about administration you can. Pile the work on until they're ready to drop, then give them more. I want those overactive minds turned to good use. Make them the best administrators you can.

'Gardan, when they're not in the office, learning how to govern, turn them into soldiers. That young bandit asked for a reward a year ago, and now he's got to show me if he really is a match for that request. And his young partner in crime has too much talent to let him go back to Land's End. Locky's the youngest son, so he'd simply go to waste there. With you two gone, we're going to need a new Duke and Knight-Marshal and, with me gone as well, he's going to be acting as Principate Regent; he'll need an able Chancellor to help him shoulder the burdens of office. So I don't want either of them to have five loose minutes in the next four years.'

'Four years!' shouted Volney, 'I said three!'

Then from the bed came a chuckle and a sigh as Amos said, 'Arutha, you have an odd idea of reward. Whatever gave you such a nasty turn of mind?'

Arutha grinned openly as he said, 'Get some rest, Admiral.'

Amos fell back heavily on the bunk. 'Ah, Arutha, you still take all the fun out of life.'

Chères lectrices,

Je ne sais pas si vous êtes comme moi, mais un des moments que je préfère est celui où j'ouvre un nouveau livre, pour entrer doucement dans le monde inconnu qui va m'abriter pendant des jours, des semaines, voire des mois. Vous l'avez compris, je suis une incorrigible lectrice, amoureuse d'histoires, dévoreuse de contes en tout genre, et lorsque je plonge dans un roman, c'est tête la première et avec l'envie, s'il me passionne, d'en ressortir le plus tard possible. Pour cela mes goûts me portent volontiers vers les romans-fleuves, mais j'aime aussi beaucoup les histoires à suivre. Quoi de plus excitant en effet que l'arrivée soudaine du nouveau tome d'une saga que vous avez interrompue la mort dans l'âme, et dont l'histoire depuis ne vous a pas quittée ?

Voilà bien le genre de rendez-vous que votre collection vous propose régulièrement. Ainsi, ce mois-ci, vous allez découvrir une trilogie d'un style nouveau : « Amies et rivales », une série écrite par trois auteurs de grand talent : Emilie Richards, Celeste Hamilton et Erica Spindler. Prenant la plume à tour de rôle, elles se sont relayées pour vous raconter l'histoire de trois jeunes femmes, liées dans leur jeunesse par une amitié qu'elles croyaient indestructible et séparées à la suite d'un terrible drame. Mais je vous laisse en découvrir le premier volet, il s'intitule *Les années dérobées* (Amours d'Aujourd'hui n° 840) et vous laissera, j'en suis persuadée, vibrante d'émotion et d'impatience jusqu'à la parution du deuxième volume : *Les chemins de l'espoir* (n° 844) en octobre 2003.

Bonne lecture à toutes !

La responsable de collection

L'amour en partage

LYNNETTE KENT

L'amour en partage

HARLEQUIN

AMOURS D'AUJOURD'HUI

Cet ouvrage a été publié en langue anglaise
sous le titre :
LUKE'S DAUGHTERS

Traduction française de
JULIETTE BOUCHERY

HARLEQUIN®

est une marque déposée du Groupe Harlequin
et Amours d'Aujourd'hui®
est une marque déposée d'Harlequin S.A.

Illustration de couverture :
© MASTERFILE

Toute représentation ou reproduction, par quelque procédé que ce soit, constituerait une contrefaçon sanctionnée par les articles 425 et suivants du Code pénal.
© 2000, Cheryl Bacon. © 2003, Traduction française : Harlequin S.A.
83-85, boulevard Vincent-Auriol, 75013 PARIS — Tél. : 01 42 16 63 63
Service Lectrices — Tél. : 01 45 82 47 47
ISBN 2-280-07842-2 — ISSN 1264-0409

1.

Ce fut d'abord la voix qui fit réagir Sarah. Une voix masculine au timbre grave et chaleureux, mêlée au grondement des vagues. Elle ne distinguait pas ce que disait l'homme, mais quand cette voix résonna en elle, elle ouvrit les yeux, repoussa son chapeau de paille en arrière… et ne put retenir un cri d'admiration.

Quel spectacle, en effet ! Un bel inconnu en smoking sur une plage quasi déserte… C'était inattendu et merveilleux. Il avait remonté le bas de son pantalon à bande de satin et déboutonné les manches de sa chemise qui vibrait au vent du large. Tout en retenant ses longs cheveux noirs d'une main, il riait avec ses compagnes : deux petites princesses en robes de brocard rose et vert, manches gonflées, cols montants et longues jupes amples. Leurs têtes blondes brillaient au soleil. Quand elles levèrent le visage vers lui, Sarah remarqua qu'on avait tressé des fleurs dans leurs cheveux : des petits boutons de roses.

Automatiquement, elle tendit la main vers son appareil photo, et se mit au travail. Dans le cadre, entre ciel et mer, elle saisit la douceur avec laquelle l'homme prenait la main des petites filles pour les aider à descendre le talus surplombant le sable, puis leur façon de relever soigneusement leur robe pour traverser le bras d'eau peu profond qui s'étirait au cœur de la dune. Sur fond de coucher de soleil, le contraste entre leurs tenues splendides et ce décor sauvage était étonnamment poétique.

Quand les trois promeneurs s'approchèrent d'elle, elle laissa l'appareil retomber sur ses genoux, craignant de paraître indiscrète.

D'où venaient-ils ? Ces hautes herbes séparaient la plage publique du Sandspur Country Club. Des lumières brillaient derrière les fenêtres ; l'établissement semblait bondé.

Là était l'explication ! Ils se trouvaient à une réception. Prenant sans doute en pitié les deux petites filles qui s'ennuyaient, l'homme les avait emmenées au bord de l'océan.

Sur la pelouse, Sarah distinguait les petites taches noires et blanches de leurs sandales et de leurs socquettes abandonnées.

Quand l'objectif de son appareil photo les trouva de nouveau, les petites se penchaient sur le seau d'un pêcheur, et regardaient sa prise avec admiration.

Quant à l'homme qui les accompagnait, il se tenait très droit, et contemplait le large, les cheveux rejetés en arrière, son profil ciselé découpé sur le ciel.

Sarah prit la photo, tout en se félicitant d'avoir emporté son *zoom*. Quelle expression sombre pour un jour de fête !

Au bout de quelques instants, l'inconnu se retourna pour dire quelque chose aux fillettes. Aussitôt, elles rebroussèrent chemin et se dirigèrent vers le club, sautant et dansant comme d'adorables fées. L'homme les suivit, la tête baissée, les mains dans les poches, traînant ses pieds nus dans le sable. Il s'en allait ! Vite, Sarah fourra son appareil photo dans son étui, trouva deux cartes professionnelles et un stylo, et sauta sur ses pieds. Le temps de traverser le petit bras d'eau tiède, les gamines atteignaient les rochers, et l'homme arrivait à sa hauteur.

— Excusez-moi ! lança-t-elle.

Il tourna la tête vers elle. Il était plus grand qu'elle ne l'avait cru.

— Je m'appelle Sarah Randolph, dit-elle en lui tendant sa carte. Je suis photographe.

— Ah ? dit-il, l'air distant.

Brusquement, elle se fit l'effet d'une intruse. Elle dut prendre sur elle pour poursuivre :

— Vous formiez un tableau exceptionnel, tous les trois, sur la plage, dans cette tenue.

— Ce n'était pas délibéré.

Un soupçon d'accent du Sud colorait sa voix, comme un fil de caramel moelleux dans du très bon chocolat.

— Moi, ça m'a sauté aux yeux. Et j'ai pris des photos.

Son regard gris se fit plus froid.

— Et vous voudriez que je vous les paie ? Désolé, dit-il en allongeant le pas pour rejoindre les enfants. Je ne suis pas intéressé.

Elle dut courir pour le rattraper.

— Je ne cherche pas à me faire payer !

— Qu'est-ce que vous cherchez, alors ? Je dois ramener les petites.

— Ce sont vos filles ?

— Ouais. Mes filles, dit-il, la bouche crispée.

Surprise par son attitude, elle s'efforça de sourire.

— Vous comprenez, j'aurai peut-être l'occasion de me servir de ces photos, professionnellement. Et, pour ça, il me faut une autorisation de votre part.

— Je ne crois pas...

— Non, écoutez, je vous demande juste de signer un papier disant que vous acceptez que ces photos soient publiées, le cas échéant. Ça n'arrivera peut-être jamais... elles ne donneront peut-être rien, une fois développées. Mais, si je les utilise, je serai ravie de vous en offrir un jeu, en échange de votre autorisation… S'il vous plaît !

Pendant un moment, il contempla ses filles qui inspectaient un rocher noir à la forme bizarre. Enfin, il soupira.

— Il faudrait d'abord que je voie les photos.

— Très bien. Pas de problème, dit Sarah en lui tendant sa carte et un stylo. Notez votre adresse ici et je vous les apporterai d'ici quelques jours.

Le visage sévère, il prit la carte, la lut, griffonna quelque chose au dos.

— Heureux de vous avoir rencontrée, mademoiselle, dit-il poliment.

Avant qu'elle ne pût répondre — ou même lire ce qu'il avait inscrit —, il s'éloigna d'elle à grands pas, et entraîna ses filles avec lui dans l'enceinte du club.

Erin et Jennifer trouvèrent leur mère au cœur de la foule. La jeune femme se retourna instantanément vers elles. Kristin était une maman fantastique : ses filles passaient toujours en premier. C'était l'une des choses qu'il aimait chez elle.

Elle faisait une mariée adorable dans sa robe ivoire au corsage de dentelle et à la jupe en cloche. Sous le voile opulent, sa chevelure blonde brillait comme un soleil. Erin lui expliquait quelque chose. Elle se mit à rire, glissa une mèche folle derrière l'oreille de Jennifer, et leva les yeux vers son nouveau mari. Le regard qu'ils échangèrent sortait tout droit d'un roman d'amour. Comme le baiser échangé à la fin de la cérémonie, qui aurait mérité d'être accompagné par un feu d'artifice…

Il prit une grande inspiration, et tourna les talons. Ça suffisait. Il avait joué son rôle, préservé les apparences. S'il s'en allait maintenant, il ne manquerait à personne.

— Luke ! Je t'avais demandé d'attacher tes cheveux.

Il se retourna vers sa mère.

— J'ai dû perdre l'élastique, dit-il d'une voix neutre. Nous sommes allés faire un petit tour, les filles et moi. Il y a du vent.

Elena Brennan haussa les sourcils d'un air surpris.

— Tu les a emmenées sur la plage ? Habillées comme elles sont ?

— Nous avons fait attention. Nous avons laissé les chaussures…

— Il n'y a que toi pour te montrer aussi irresponsable ! lança-t-elle, tandis que son accent cultivé du Sud devenait plus marqué sous l'effet de la contrariété. Le photographe n'a pas encore terminé ! Une fois dans ta vie, une seule, j'aimerais que tu réfléchisses avant de…

Puis elle haussa les épaules en signe de renoncement, et se dirigea vers les filles, sans doute pour évaluer les dégâts. Même exaspérée, elle conservait son apparence élégante et raffinée.

— Encore une mauvaise idée, mon garçon !

Luke tourna la tête vers son père qu'il n'avait pas vu approcher.

— Je n'ai rien fait de particulier, marmonna-t-il. Les filles n'en pouvaient plus de jouer les poupées de porcelaine. Je les ai emmenées s'amuser un peu.

— Tu dois comprendre l'importance de ce mariage pour ta mère.

Luke pensait encore à la plage, à cette sensation de liberté… et au regard si chaleureux d'une inconnue.

— Je sais, oui, répondit-il avec amertume.

Une nuit — huit ans plus tôt —, Luke avait disparu, et il était revenu, quelques jours plus tard, marié à une jeune femme qui portait son enfant. Un procédé inacceptable dans

11

la bonne société de Chuckton où Elena Calhoun Brennan avait grandi.

— Nous n'avons rien fait de mal, répéta Luke. Ni à l'instant… ni à l'époque.

Son père lui posa la main sur l'épaule pour l'entraîner dans la pièce.

— Ce qui est fait est fait. Arrange-moi ces fichus cheveux, enfile ta veste et viens prendre une coupe de champagne, comme tout le monde.

Les trente ans qu'il avait passés dans l'armée transformaient chacune de ses paroles en sommation. Ils avaient la même silhouette haute et mince, mais le colonel Brennan dominait toujours son entourage.

Là-bas, Kristin embrassait son nouveau mari sur un dernier pas de valse…

— Non merci, répondit Luke.

Les yeux gris du Colonel se firent très froids.

— Ecoute-moi bien. J'attends de toi que tu coopères.

Luke recula pour échapper à la main qui serrait toujours son épaule.

— Qu'est-ce que je peux faire de plus ? Je leur laisse les filles ! Et il me semble avoir parfaitement joué le rôle que vous avez écrit pour moi, aujourd'hui.

Baissant la voix pour s'assurer que ses paroles ne seraient entendues de personne d'autre que son père, il ajouta :

— Mais si vous pensez que je fais tout ça de gaieté de cœur, vous vous trompez. Pas question que je boive à leur mariage ni que je leur donne ma bénédiction !

— Luke…

Des doigts de fer serraient son coude.

Au même instant, des acclamations retentirent à l'autre bout de la salle. Perchée sur une chaise, Kristin riait, et relevait sa robe pour révéler une jambe mince, élégamment cambrée dans un escarpin à talon haut. Resplendissant dans son uniforme d'apparat, son mari lui retira sa jarretelle de dentelle bleue et blanche. Puis, sous les applaudissements, il se redressa en brandissant son trophée.

— Tous les célibataires devant ! clama-t-il avec un large sourire. Cette belle dame est à moi, et je ne partagerai pas. Mais, si vous attrapez sa jarretelle, vous trouverez la vôtre !

Quand, soudain, son regard rencontra celui de Luke, il exprima une profonde hostilité. Autour de lui, la foule riait trop fort.

Luke détourna les yeux et s'adressa à son père.

— Il y a des limites, marmonna-t-il en tournant les talons. Votre fils préféré vient d'aller trop loin.

Puis il s'enfuit, poursuivi par ses démons.

— Tu as bientôt fini, mamie ?

— Je n'aurai jamais fini si tu ne te tiens pas tranquille.

Mamie Brennan était plutôt sévère. Chez elle, on ne mettait pas les pieds sur les chaises ni les coudes sur la table. En tout cas, pas à sept ans. Les bébés de quatre ans pouvaient encore se permettre de faire quelques caprices, comme Jenny en ce moment…

— Je veux garder cette robe ! Je veux aller voir Mickey comme ça !

— C'est impossible, Jenny. On va monter dans un avion : tu ne peux pas porter une robe comme ça dans un avion.

La petite se mit à pleurer.

— Je veux maman !

Erin, quant à elle, était ravie de se débarrasser de son déguisement ridicule. Elle fit vivement passer la robe par-dessus sa tête, et la jeta sur le sol.

— Oh, génial ! J'ai horreur des robes !

Les bras étendus, elle tourna comme une toupie au milieu de la pièce. Mamie secoua la tête d'un air réprobateur, puis ramassa la robe verte et rose, et l'accrocha sur un cintre.

— Enfile ton short, Erin. Vous allez bientôt partir.

— A Disney World ?

— Oui.

La fillette se précipita vers le fauteuil où l'on avait préparé ses vêtements, et enfila son short préféré. Comme les fleurs que l'on avait fixées dans ses cheveux se prenaient dans son T-shirt, elle les arracha aussi.

— Où sont mes chaussures ?

— Ici, dit mamie Brennan en lui montrant une paire de sandales blanches à fleurs roses.

— C'est pas les miennes, celles-là ! Je veux les baskets rouges que papa m'a achetées.

— Celles-ci iront mieux avec ta tenue, ma chérie, répliqua mamie en lui apportant les sandales.

Erin croisa les bras sur sa poitrine.

— Je veux mes baskets.

Elle n'allait pas pleurer comme Jenny, mais elle n'irait nulle part avec ces horribles sandales.

Soudain, la porte de la chambre s'ouvrit, et maman apparut. Les deux fillettes se précipitèrent vers elle, mais, bien entendu, ce fut Erin qui arriva la première.

— Dis-lui que je ne suis pas obligée de mettre ça, maman ! Je veux mes baskets rouges.

— Je veux mettre ma robe pour Mickey ! clama Jenny en se jetant dans leurs jambes.

Maman se mit à genoux, et prit ses deux filles dans ses bras.

— Erin, mon cœur, tes baskets sont dans la valise, sous la fenêtre.

14

Erin se précipita, trouva les baskets et entreprit de les enfiler.

— Avec des chaussettes ! lui conseilla sa mère.

— Oui, m'man, dit la petite, à contrecœur.

En un temps record, elle enfila des socquettes, puis noua ses lacets. Papa lui avait appris, pendant les vacances de Pâques.

Maintenant que maman était là, c'était facile de se préparer. Jenny enfila sa robe jaune sans faire d'histoires, et se laissa coiffer. Quelques minutes plus tard, elles étaient prêtes.

Le nouveau mari de maman les attendait dans le couloir.

— Alors, c'est parti pour Disney World ?

Pour toute réponse, Jenny fourra son pouce dans sa bouche et cacha son visage dans le cou de sa mère.

Se tournant vers Erin, il demanda :

— Qu'est-ce que tu en dis ? C'est le grand jour ?

Erin lui rendit son regard. Une fois, il lui avait proposé de l'appeler Matt, mais maman trouvait que papa Matt, ce serait mieux, maintenant qu'il faisait partie de la famille. Pour faire plaisir à maman, Erin essayait de s'en souvenir, mais Matt ne lui faisait pas du tout l'effet d'un papa. Il était grand, carré — plus carré que papa, qui était son frère —, et il avait plutôt le caractère de mamie Brennan.

Avec papa, on pouvait jouer, rire, raconter des histoires drôles. Papa Matt, lui, il parlait surtout de ce qu'on n'avait pas le droit de faire.

Tout à coup, Erin n'eut plus très envie d'aller à Disney World.

— Maman, où il est, papa ?

— Mais… sous ton nez, ma chérie !

— Non, je veux dire mon papa. Il faut que je lui dise quelque chose.

Erin vit le regard que maman jetait à papa Matt. Celui-ci vint s'accroupir près d'elle.

— Il a dû aller… travailler, Erin.

Papa Matt avait des yeux très bleus qui restaient toujours sérieux, même quand il souriait.

— Il espère que tu vas beaucoup t'amuser en Floride. Il va penser à toi tout le temps, il me l'a dit, et vous vous verrez dès ton retour. D'accord ?

Quand on a presque sept ans, on sait généralement quand ça ne vaut pas la peine de protester. Comprenant qu'elle ne reverrait pas son père avant le départ, elle hocha la tête avec un soupir.

— Bon, on y va ?

Papa Matt se remit debout, et lui prit la main. Maman et Jenny marchaient de l'autre côté. Quand ils émergèrent de la porte d'entrée, tous les gens qui étaient venus au mariage se mirent à crier en leur jetant des graines pour les oiseaux qu'ils puisaient dans les petits sachets qu'Erin avait noués avec sa grand-mère. Puis on galopa vers la grosse voiture garée le long du trottoir.

Une fois à l'intérieur, Erin aida sa petite sœur à s'installer dans son siège auto, et boucla sa propre ceinture de sécurité, comme papa le lui avait appris.

A l'avant, maman et papa Matt riaient en agitant la main. La voiture partit, laissant les invités sur place.

— Prochain arrêt : l'aéroport ! s'écria papa Matt.

Jenny bâilla et ferma les yeux. Erin regarda par la vitre sans répondre, en se demandant pourquoi elle ne se sentait pas plus excitée à l'idée de ce grand voyage.

Sarah observa les clichés qu'elle venait de développer. Pour la deuxième fois, elle était éblouie par la beauté de Luke

Brennan et l'élégance de son attitude. Quant aux fillettes, elles étaient aussi adorables que dans son souvenir, aussi photogéniques qu'elle l'avait espéré ! La vitalité qui se dégageait d'elles illuminait chaque photo.

— Joli !

Sarah sursauta, lâcha un juron et se pencha pour ramasser la pince qui venait de lui échapper.

— Tu m'as fait peur ! Tu ne pourrais pas frapper, Chuck ? Tu aurais pu tout gâcher.

Son associé leva les yeux au ciel.

— La porte était déjà ouverte : j'ai pensé qu'il n'y avait pas de danger. Ça fait des heures que tu es là-dedans !

Elle connaissait Chuck depuis toujours. Ils avaient hérité ensemble du magasin de photo où elle développait ses clichés.

Il passa devant elle, croisa les bras sur son ventre rebondi, et contempla les photos qui étaient en train de sécher.

— Voilà qui tranche sur ton style habituel. C'est pour un calendrier des postes ?

Ce petit ton supérieur, méprisant… Chuck ne manquait jamais une occasion de dénigrer son travail.

— Non, répondit-elle. Ce sont des photos que j'ai prises hier, un peu par hasard. Quelle heure est-il ?

— 19 heures passées. J'ai fermé le magasin. Tu comptes rester encore longtemps ?

Elle avait développé les photos en grand format ; certaines méritaient des agrandissements encore plus importants.

— Je crois que je vais travailler encore un peu. Mais tu peux fermer : j'ai ma clé.

— Je sais, oui, dit-il avec un petit sourire déplaisant. Ça ne te dérange pas de rester seule à cette heure-ci ? Le quartier est désert, le dimanche soir.

— Pas de problème, répondit-elle avec assurance.

Il haussa les sourcils d'un air sceptique, puis tourna les talons et quitta la chambre noire.

Quelques minutes plus tard, la jeune femme entendit la porte de derrière se refermer, puis le rugissement de la Cadillac de Chuck. Elle était enfin seule !

Tout en s'attaquant à ses agrandissements, elle se demanda ce qu'elle ferait de ces photos. *Events*, l'hebdomadaire d'actualité pour lequel elle travaillait, ne publiait pas de « jolies » photos. A la rédaction, on recherchait plutôt le réalisme le plus brut, et c'était exactement ce qu'elle leur fournissait depuis six ans, en courant d'Afrique en Europe de l'Est, d'Irlande du Nord en Afghanistan.

Ils travaillaient en tandem, James Daley et elle, même après qu'elle eut mis un terme à leurs brèves fiançailles. Avec le temps, la colère et l'humiliation qu'elle avait éprouvées à cause des infidélités de James s'étaient effacées. Ils se respectaient beaucoup, et avaient pleinement conscience que leur collaboration était précieuse. Ensemble, ils s'étaient fait une réputation solide ; on pouvait compter sur eux pour assurer un reportage pointu sur chaque événement.

Et puis, un soir… Elle marchait à moins d'un mètre derrière James quand il était tombé. Et elle s'était retrouvée seule. Elle s'efforçait d'éloigner d'elle le souvenir de ses yeux morts, de l'odeur du sang, de la poudre, de l'unique cri tremblant qu'il avait jeté… Elle s'était accrochée : elle voulait à toute force terminer le reportage — pour lui, pour eux deux. Et elle avait tenu le coup… jusqu'à ce matin terrible où elle s'était retrouvée devant un charnier, près de Kaboul. Devant ce cratère rempli de corps de femmes et de jeunes filles, elle s'était mise à trembler avec une violence inouïe. C'était incontrôlable. Elle se sentait aspirée par cette tombe ; elle entendait la voix des morts, et notamment de James, se lamenter, l'appeler.

Prenant une grande inspiration tremblante, elle revint au présent. Elle n'était pas au Moyen-Orient, dans un champ violé par la guerre, mais à Myrtle Beach, en Caroline du Sud. Ici, le soleil se couchait paisiblement derrière les dunes, jetant une lueur dorée sur des fillettes qui dansaient sur la plage dans des robes de conte de fées.

Les yeux fermés, Sarah se concentra sur cette scène lumineuse, évoquant avec minutie chaque détail charmant. Peu à peu, ses tremblements s'apaisèrent. Voilà ! C'était passé. Six mois de thérapie lui avaient rendu sa capacité à gérer le quotidien. A son retour aux Etats-Unis, elle ne pouvait même pas dormir, malgré son épuisement ; les rêves lui semblaient encore pires que les souvenirs. Maintenant, tout cela était derrière elle. Elle se sentait reposée. Bientôt, elle pourrait envisager de reprendre son travail. Si elle revoyait périodiquement certaines images, c'était normal, et elle refaisait surface de plus en plus rapidement. Elle avait travaillé dur pour décrocher ce poste de photographe reporter, et elle n'y renoncerait pas. Elle accepterait tout ce qu'on lui proposerait.

Le fait qu'elle eût pris ces photos, hier, prouvait bien qu'elle progressait. C'était la première fois, depuis… depuis ce jour-là. Elle pouvait remercier Luke Brennan et ses adorables petites filles.

Elle rangea la chambre noire en jetant de fréquents regards à ses photos. Un homme difficile à oublier avec son rire chaleureux et ses yeux assombris par un chagrin profond. Que lui était-il arrivé ? Quelle était la cause de sa souffrance ? Elle ne le saurait sans doute jamais. Et, de toute façon, même si elle découvrait son secret, elle serait bien la dernière à pouvoir l'aider. La vie quotidienne représentait déjà pour elle un véritable défi !

Voilà, tout était en ordre. Après s'être assurée que les portraits étaient secs, elle les glissa dans une chemise, puis dans sa serviette. Demain, elle irait demander à Luke l'autorisation de les publier, et elle en enverrait un jeu à son agent. S'il trouvait un acheteur, parfait. Sinon, elle pourrait au moins se féliciter d'avoir repris son travail. Six mois, ça faisait vraiment de très longues vacances.

Dans la kitchenette, la jeune femme lava sa tasse et celle de Chuck, puis elle remplit la machine à café pour qu'il n'eût plus qu'à la brancher, le lendemain matin. Enfin, elle sortit par la porte de derrière, sa serviette et son sac sous le bras.

La nuit de juin l'accueillit comme une eau tiède. On entendait, au loin, des cris et des rires qui venaient de la fête foraine. Là-bas, près du port, des lumières multicolores brillaient dans la nuit, des projecteurs fouillaient le ciel. Myrtle Beach n'était plus le gros bourg endormi où elle passait ses vacances d'été quand elle était enfant...

Tout en sifflotant, elle se dirigea vers sa jeep. Avec l'explosion du tourisme, la petite ville était devenue aussi étouffante qu'une autre. Pourtant, ces petites filles sur la plage grandissaient librement, sans connaître le danger...

Sarah entendit des pas derrière elle, une course désordonnée. Elle voulut se retourner, mais... elle n'eut même pas le temps de crier. Un corps d'homme la percuta de plein fouet, la jetant à genoux. Elle chercha à se débattre, mais il était déjà trop tard : le souffle rauque de l'homme sifflait à son oreille, et il pesait sur elle de tout son poids. Elle se cabra. Ses paumes glissaient sur le gravier. Il lui saisit les poignets, la poussa brutalement. Son visage heurta le sol, et sa joue la brûla.

Elle eut beau se tordre de toutes ses forces, il était assis sur son dos, ses genoux pesaient sur ses épaules. Puis il referma les mains autour de son cou. Affolée, Sarah voulut le poignarder avec ses clés de voiture qu'elle tenait toujours à la main. Il lui arracha le trousseau, resserra encore sa prise sur sa gorge.

Cette fois, elle se sentait faiblir. Elle hoqueta, se débattit encore, s'efforça de soulever le poids qui l'écrasait... puis un brouillard noir se referma sur elle, et elle cessa de lutter.

2.

Las de sa propre compagnie, Luke arriva au commissariat en avance, le dimanche soir. Il ne prenait son service qu'à 23 heures.

— Brennan, tu es le seul flic que je connaisse avec des cheveux pareils ! lança cordialement son sergent en lui appliquant une claque sur l'épaule. Tu fais honte à ton uniforme.

— Ces cheveux *sont* mon uniforme, vieux.

Luke alla se servir un café dont il n'avait aucune envie, et s'assit sur le bureau le plus proche, en visiteur.

— On a quelque chose, ce soir ?

Nick Rushe, son partenaire au boulot comme au handball, se carra confortablement sur sa chaise.

— La routine habituelle : des bagarres d'ivrognes, un gamin perdu à la fête foraine... Oh, et puis une agression.

— Où ça ?

— A quatre rues d'ici. Une femme s'apprête à monter dans sa voiture, un type la jette par terre, prend son sac, la tabasse. Jordan est en train de prendre sa déposition.

Luke se retourna à demi vers le bureau de Hank Jordan. Recroquevillée sur une chaise, les yeux baissés, le visage presque entièrement caché par la serviette qu'elle pressait contre sa joue, la victime répondait à ses questions. Cette cascade de boucles châtain doré lui disait quelque chose.

La jeune femme leva la tête pour répondre à une question, et Luke reconnut ses yeux vert et or aux longs cils soyeux. C'était Sarah quelque chose, la femme de la plage. Celle qui prenait des photos !

Il s'avança.

— Vous allez bien ?

Elle leva vers lui son visage tuméfié. Ses lèvres s'entrouvrirent, mais aucun son ne sortit de sa bouche. Croyant qu'elle avait peur de lui, il posa doucement sa main sur la sienne. Elle eut une grimace de douleur. Atterré, il s'accroupit devant elle et la regarda au fond des yeux.

— Sarah, tout va bien. Je ne vais pas vous faire de mal. Je peux voir ce qu'il vous a fait ?

Elle le fixa si longtemps qu'il se demanda si elle avait compris. Puis ses épaules se détendirent un peu, et elle retira la serviette avec précaution. Entre les bleus, les chairs enflées et les éraflures, le côté gauche de son visage était méconnaissable. Son T-shirt blanc était déchiré, taché de terre et de sang, et ses genoux étaient presque aussi abîmés que son visage.

— Vous avez vu un médecin ?

— Elle est venue jusqu'ici à pied, tu te rends compte ? lança Hank. On aurait dit qu'elle arrivait de la morgue, c'est dire si elle va mieux !

Jordan était un bon flic, mais il manquait singulièrement de tact. Sans relever, Luke lui demanda :

— Tu as tout ce qu'il te faut ?

— Ouais, mais ça ne fait pas grand-chose. Pas de mobile : elle ne connaît quasiment personne en ville, et elle ne peut pas faire de description du type qui l'a agressée.

— On trouvera un moyen de le coincer, dit Luke en se redressant. Sarah, je vais vous emmener à l'hôpital. Vous devez voir un médecin.

Le regard de la jeune femme refléta alors une véritable panique, et elle secoua la tête.

— Je ne crois pas… chuchota-t-elle.

— Vous êtes en sécurité avec moi, lui dit-il en sortant son identification. J'aurais dû vous le dire : je suis flic. Mon partenaire peut venir avec nous, si vous préférez.

Il fit un signe de tête vers Nick, qui répondit d'un salut réglementaire.

Sarah hocha la tête.

— D'accord, souffla-t-elle. Ne dérangez pas votre collègue…

Doucement, il prit son coude pour l'aider à se lever. Elle se tourna alors vers Hank d'un air hésitant.

— Merci, chuchota-t-elle de sa voix étrange.

Jordan agita la main en rougissant.

— Pas de problème. Prenez bien soin de vous. On vous contactera si… quand… on aura appris quelque chose.

Ils mirent longtemps à traverser la grande salle du commissariat. Sarah marchait à petits pas. Luke ouvrait les portes, écartait les obstacles. En la voyant se tasser, inerte, sur la banquette de sa voiture, il mesura l'effort qu'elle avait dû fournir. Sans lui demander l'autorisation, il boucla sa ceinture de sécurité à sa place, en évitant soigneusement de la toucher. Elle lui offrit alors un regard et un pâle sourire.

— Merci. Pour le coup de main…

Il lui rendit son sourire. Maintenant qu'elle lui faisait confiance, il se sentait tout à fait à l'aise avec elle. C'était même étonnant, comme une sorte de… connivence. Puis la lumière du réverbère lui révéla ce qu'il n'avait pas encore remarqué : de vilaines marques sombres tout autour de sa gorge. Des marques de doigts.

— On y sera dans quelques minutes, dit-il.

Allumant son gyrophare, il prit le chemin de l'hôpital.

L'attente fut longue. Enfin, après avoir examiné la jeune femme, le médecin des urgences vint le trouver.

— Pas de fractures, pas de lésions sérieuses. Seulement des blessures superficielles. Elle va surtout avoir mal pendant une dizaine de jours.

— Il a essayé de l'étrangler, n'est-ce pas ?

— Oui, répondit le médecin en secouant la tête d'un air consterné. Sa gorge est enflée ; elle mettra plusieurs jours à retrouver sa voix. Empêchez-la de trop parler.

— Vous pouvez me dire autre chose sur l'agression ?

— A part le fait que le type qui l'a frappée est un salaud ?

— A part ça, oui.

Le médecin fronça les sourcils, et considéra Luke un instant.

— Elle a de la chance qu'il ne l'ait pas tuée, dit-il enfin.

Luke la retrouva dans une petite pièce tout au fond du service des urgences, assise sur une table d'examen, les mains croisées sur les genoux. Des pansements couvraient ses blessures les plus sévères.

— Bonsoir, chuchota-t-elle en le voyant.

Ses grands yeux étaient vagues, mais ils n'exprimaient plus ni douleur ni panique. Planté devant elle, Luke l'examina avec satisfaction.

— Ils disent que vous devez éviter de parler. Venez, nous pouvons partir.

Il l'aida à descendre de la table, et la soutint quand ses genoux fléchirent. Un peu affolée, elle s'accrocha à lui.

— Ils... m'ont donné un cachet. Je ne tiens plus debout...

— Nous prenons soin des drogués comme vous, dit-il en souriant. Je vais vous ramener chez vous.

Discrètement, il glissa un bras autour de sa taille. Elle chercha à se dégager, sans résultat notoire.

— Merci, c'est gentil, mais je peux prendre un taxi. Je vous assure...

— Pourquoi, puisque je vous propose de vous ramener ?

Elle voulut discuter, mais il l'entraîna doucement vers la sortie en expliquant :

— Vous n'avez tout de même pas envie d'attendre deux heures ? Nous ne sommes pas à New York, vous savez : il y a très peu de taxis, la nuit.

Cessant de résister, elle s'appuya contre lui. Ils franchirent les portes automatiques, émergeant dans la nuit fraîche.

— Alors, dites-moi : où allons-nous ?

— Oh... mes clés ! gémit-elle en fermant les yeux.

— Il les a prises, c'est ça ? Vous ne pouvez pas rentrer chez vous ? Vous avez des amis, en ville, chez qui vous pourriez dormir ?

A chaque question, elle hochait ou secouait la tête.

Quand ils atteignirent la voiture, Luke l'aida à s'installer, puis boucla encore une fois sa ceinture.

— Pas de cartes de crédit pour une chambre d'hôtel ?

— Non.

Il referma la portière côté passager, et contourna la voiture en réfléchissant. Le temps qu'il se glissât derrière le volant, sa décision était prise.

— Bon. Je vais vous emmener chez moi. Pour le reste, on verra demain matin.

Elle se redressa dans un sursaut, s'empêtra dans sa ceinture de sécurité.

— Oh, monsieur Brennan, non, c'est trop gênant...

Ce chuchotement rauque et douloureux faisait mal à entendre. Tout en manœuvrant pour sortir du parking, Luke expliqua à la jeune femme :

— Vous aurez la maison pour vous toute seule. Moi, je retourne au commissariat. Croyez-moi, c'est la solution la plus simple.

Il s'abstint d'évoquer les autres avantages : l'homme qui avait pris ses clés pouvait très bien être chez elle. Par contre, il n'aurait pas l'idée de venir la chercher chez un flic.

Heureusement, elle capitula sans qu'il eût besoin d'insister davantage.

— Bon, d'accord, murmura-t-elle. Merci.

Quelques instants plus tard, il s'aperçut qu'elle dormait.

Elle ne se réveilla pas quand il se gara devant chez lui et descendit pour aller déverrouiller la porte de la cuisine. Ni quand il la souleva et la porta avec précaution.

Sur le seuil, il hésita. Où devait-il la poser ? La chambre de Jen et Erin semblait avoir été dévastée par un cyclone. Prenant garde de ne pas heurter son fardeau, il franchit le seuil de sa propre chambre. Elle devait se reposer dans les meilleures conditions possibles. Elle aurait sans doute très mal, demain matin.

Délicatement, il l'allongea sur le côté du lit où il ne dormait pas. Puis, après un instant de réflexion, il disposa près d'elle un grand T-shirt et un mot l'invitant à ouvrir les tiroirs pour trouver ce dont elle pourrait avoir besoin.

Après ça, il recula vers la porte et resta quelques secondes immobiles, à regarder Sarah... — comment s'appelait-elle, déjà ? — à regarder Sarah dormir.

Dans la pénombre, elle avait un sourire détendu. Un sourire adorable que même les marques de coups ne pouvaient éteindre. Après une nuit d'horreur, elle s'était endormie comme une enfant. Bien sûr, la réaction interviendrait tôt ou tard. Certaines victimes craquaient tout de suite, d'autres attendaient d'être seules. Luke devinait que, comme lui, Sarah préférerait être seule pour affronter ses démons.

Cette idée lui rappela l'image de Kristin, en lune de miel avec Matt... Jen et Erin étaient en route pour Disney World avec leur mère et leur nouveau papa.

Le destin de sa femme et de ses enfants était désormais lié à celui d'un autre homme. A celui de son frère.

Luke eut soudain l'impression que les murs se resserraient autour de lui. Il n'y avait plus de lumière, plus d'oxygène. Il lutta pour reprendre son souffle, et sortit en se heurtant aux meubles. Respirer, retourner au boulot, retrouver une réalité supportable... Une réalité parfois dure, parfois dangereuse, mais qui lui épargnait au moins ce face-à-face avec le néant qui allait constituer le reste de sa vie.

Quand Luke rentra chez lui, à 7 heures du matin, un verre était posé sur l'égouttoir, et il entendait couler la douche. « Bravo ! pensa-t-il avec une certaine admiration. Elle reprend déjà le dessus. » Le voyant rouge du répondeur attira son regard. Il enfonça le bouton, et entendit une voix douce, reconnaissable entre toutes :

— Luke, bonsoir. C'est Kristin.

Le cœur serré comme dans un étau, il attendit la suite.

— Les filles voulaient t'appeler pour tout te raconter.

Il entendit une explosion de piaillements et de rires, puis la voix un peu grave d'Erin, aussi originale que sa propriétaire :

— Papa, salut, c'est moi ! On est allés au Monde de la Mer, hier, et c'était trop *cool*. Tu passes dans un tunnel sous l'eau et tu vois les poissons nager au-dessus de ta tête. Même les requins. La baleine nous a éclaboussés avec un milliard de litres d'eau : on était trempés. Maman et papa Matt ont juste rigolé, mais Jen a pleuré parce qu'elle avait lâché son soda… Quoi ?

En arrière-plan, une autre voix disait quelque chose.

— Mais je n'ai pas fini ! protesta Erin. Oh, bon, d'accord… Papa, je te passe Jen.

Il y eut un choc, un souffle trop proche du combiné, et le commentaire méprisant de la grande sœur à la petite :

— Bébé !

Luke fit un effort pour sourire.

— Papa ?

La voix de Jen était exubérante.

— C'est Jenny. J'ai fait tomber mon soda. Maman m'en a acheté un autre, et aussi une casquette avec un dauphin. Maintenant, on va aller au Royaume Magique. Je dirai bonjour à Peter Pan, comme tu avais dit.

Encore des bruits de fond. Puis les fillettes répétèrent en chœur :

— Salut, papa ! Salut, on t'aime !

Cette fois, Luke ne put retenir ses larmes.

— Voilà, on voulait te dire que tout se passait bien, Luke, reprit la voix de Kristin — sa voix de tous les jours, souriante et chaleureuse. Tu manques aux filles, mais elles s'amusent bien. Nous serons de retour samedi. Prends bien soin de toi.

Enfin, le déclic final.

Ecrasé par l'émotion, Luke se tassa sur le bureau. Sa femme et ses filles lui manquaient tellement ! Comment

29

pourrait-il continuer à vivre, maintenant qu'on lui avait arraché le cœur ?

— Monsieur Brennan ?

La main bandée de Sarah se posa sur son bras. Sa voix brisée était presque inaudible.

— Luke, qu'est-ce qui se passe ?

Il secoua la tête, essuya ses larmes. Perdue dans son immense T-shirt, elle le regardait avec inquiétude, les sourcils froncés.

— Dites-moi, demanda-t-elle encore.

— Mes petites filles, balbutia-t-il.

Il sentit sa main se resserrer sur son bras.

— Il leur est arrivé quelque chose ?

L'étau qui lui serrait le cœur se relâcha un peu ; il put respirer à fond.

— Non. Non, elles vont bien.

Il chercha un moyen de changer de sujet. Pourquoi lui parler de ses problèmes ? Pourquoi les ressasser une fois de plus ?

— Elles sont avec leur maman à Disney World, dit-il.

Spontanément, Sarah lui sourit. Puis elle fit la grimace parce que le seul fait de sourire lui faisait mal.

— Avec mon frère, ajouta-t-il.

Cette fois, elle eut l'air perplexe.

— Il a épousé Kristin samedi dernier, précisa Luke. C'est leur lune de miel.

Sur le visage expressif de la jeune femme, il lut d'abord la confusion, puis l'horreur. Elle laissa retomber sa main, puis recula d'un pas.

Luke se redressa en demandant :

— Vous voulez du café ?

En quelques gestes, il mit la machine en route, et le breuvage odorant se mit à couler goutte à goutte dans le pichet.

— Du lait ? Du sucre ?

Péniblement, Sarah s'installa sur une chaise en secouant la tête.

— Noir, merci. Luke…

Il l'interrompit en levant la main.

— Je suis désolé. J'aurais dû me taire. On oublie tout, d'accord ? J'ai apporté des beignets pour le petit déjeuner.

Sans faire un geste vers la boîte qu'il lui indiquait, elle continua de fixer sur lui son regard sérieux.

— Vous êtes divorcé ?

— Ouais, marmonna Luke en se retournant vers la machine à café.

— A cause de… lui ?

Avec des gestes précis, il sortit deux tasses d'un placard, puis referma la porte.

— Ouais, répéta-t-il.

— Je suis désolée.

Il laissa échapper un petit rire amer, tout en remplissant les tasses et en les apportant sur la table.

— Pour ça, personne n'est aussi désolé que moi ! Enfin, ce n'est pas tout à fait comme dans les journaux à scandales. Elle était d'abord fiancée à Matt, mais il a disparu pendant une mission militaire, et on nous a dit qu'il était mort. J'ai épousé Kristin, et nous avons eu deux filles. Et puis, au bout de cinq ans, il est revenu.

— Cinq ans !

— Il était prisonnier pendant tout ce temps. L'Armée prétendait ne rien savoir. Kristin n'avait jamais cessé de l'aimer, et… Voilà toute l'histoire.

Il saisit un beignet à la framboise, et croqua dedans avec voracité. Sarah, quant à elle, n'avait touché à rien.

— C'est très beau de votre part de lui avoir rendu sa liberté.

— Oui, c'est moi le chevalier blanc.

— Vos filles vivent avec vous ?

Cette fois, il ne trouva plus de commentaire léger.

— Pas à plein temps, non. Depuis que j'ai quitté la maison, l'an dernier, nous partageons la garde. Mais, maintenant qu'ils sont mariés…

Il n'osait même pas penser à ce que serait sa vie, désormais. Comment exprimer une telle angoisse ?

La jeune femme qui lui faisait face accepta son silence. Elle souleva maladroitement sa tasse entre ses mains bandées, et but une petite gorgée de café. Puis elle choisit un beignet et le mangea en silence.

— Je suppose que personne n'a rapporté mon sac au commissariat ? demanda-t-elle enfin.

Il la remercia silencieusement d'avoir changé de sujet. Il sentit qu'il respirait plus librement.

— Non. Pas encore.

Elle eut soudain l'air résigné.

— Je ne sais pas par où commencer, dit-elle. Toutes mes clés étaient dans mon sac. Je ne peux ni prendre ma voiture ni rentrer chez moi. La gardienne de l'immeuble est nouvelle : elle ne me reconnaîtra pas. Elle va me demander une pièce d'identité, et je n'ai plus aucun papier !

— Du calme, Sarah. Ne vous emballez pas. N'essayez pas de résoudre tous les problèmes en même temps. Y a-t-il un double de vos clés de voiture, dans l'appartement ?

Elle approuva de la tête.

— Très bien. Allons chez vous. Je convaincrai la gardienne de vous faire entrer.

— Comment ferez-vous ?

— Je suis flic. Elle sera bien obligée de me croire.

Elle lui adressa un petit sourire qu'il lui rendit aussitôt. Il se sentait mieux à l'idée de pouvoir s'attaquer à des problèmes pratiques.

— Quand nous serons chez vous, reprit-il, vous devrez téléphoner aux organismes qui vous ont délivré des cartes de crédit.

— Des cartes de crédit ?

— Sinon, vous risquez de vous retrouver avec de sacrées factures à payer !

Elle le contempla un instant, et secoua la tête.

— C'est... C'est tout à fait vrai. Je n'avais pas pensé aux cartes.

— Vous les ferez annuler et, ensuite, nous irons chercher votre voiture.

— Attendez, je ne sais plus où j'en suis. Pourquoi est-ce que vous... Enfin, vous devez bien... avoir autre chose à faire ?

— Bien sûr, répliqua Luke en essayant de rire. Mais vous avez besoin d'un coup de main, et j'ai du temps devant moi. Nous sommes faits pour nous entendre.

Elle posa sur lui son regard vert et or en quête de vérité. Gêné, il s'éclaircit la gorge, et avoua :

— Ecoutez, ce que ce type vous a fait, ça me met hors de moi. Si je ne peux pas l'arrêter tout de suite, je peux au moins vous aider à limiter les dégâts. Entre amis, c'est la moindre des choses. Et, je ne sais pas trop pourquoi, j'ai le sentiment que nous le sommes. Amis, je veux dire.

Voilà, il ne pouvait pas être plus sincère.

Cette fois, elle sourit. Son premier sourire depuis la veille au soir. Un sourire qui réchauffa Luke de la tête aux pieds.

— Moi aussi, j'ai cette impression, lui dit-elle. Et c'est vraiment bizarre parce que...

— Parce que je ne me souviens même pas de votre nom de famille.

— Randolph. Sarah Rose Randolph.

— Eh bien, Sarah Rose, vous êtes aussi habillée que la majorité des gens qui viennent ici l'été. Trouvez vos chaussures et allons recoller les morceaux de votre existence.

Ces derniers temps, elle avait tendance à ressasser les problèmes sans leur chercher de solutions. Aujourd'hui, cependant, tout lui semblait différent. Elle trouvait en un temps record les formulaires de ses cartes de crédit et tous les numéros dont elle avait besoin. Les gens qu'elle avait au téléphone lui paraissaient tous très compréhensifs. Etait-ce la présence de Luke qui avait sur elle cet effet apaisant ? Entre deux coups de fil, elle se retourna vers lui pour lui proposer :

— Je crois qu'il y a des jus de fruits dans le réfrigérateur. Servez-vous.

— Merci, je veux bien. Vous en voulez un ?

— Oui, s'il vous plaît.

Il trouva rapidement les verres, en choisit de très hauts et ajouta de la glace, comme elle l'aurait fait à sa place. C'était comme dans sa cuisine à lui, ce matin : elle avait su, d'instinct, où trouver chaque chose. Dans un sens, elle aurait dû se sentir inquiète à l'idée d'être aussi proche d'un inconnu. Mais elle se sentait surtout heureuse d'avoir trouvé un ami.

— C'était le dernier appel ? lui demanda-t-il quand elle raccrocha.

— Je crois, oui.

— Il y a eu de gros débits, entre hier soir et aujourd'hui ?

34

— Rien depuis plusieurs jours.

— Bien ! Il n'a pas eu le temps de se lancer.

Tout en parlant, il regardait le cadre posé sur la petite table au bout du canapé.

— C'est votre frère ? Votre petit ami ?

— C'est James Daley. Je… travaillais avec lui.

— Daley ? Le journaliste ?

— C'est ça.

— C'est un grand bonhomme. J'aime beaucoup ce qu'il écrit dans *Events*.

— Il écrivait toujours ce qu'il pensait.

— Vous parlez de lui… au passé ?

Elle récita les mots qu'elle s'était exercée à dire :

— Il a été tué par une balle perdue en Afghanistan, il y a sept mois.

— Vous y étiez ?

— J'étais son photographe.

Lentement, Luke remit le cadre à sa place.

— Alors, je devrais aussi connaître votre travail ?

— Pas obligatoirement. Mon nom se trouve généralement en toutes petites lettres à la fin de l'article.

— Mais alors, quand vous avez pris des photos de Jen et Erin… c'est vous qui nous faisiez une faveur. Moi qui croyais que vous cherchiez à gagner quelques dollars facilement…

En rougissant, il acheva :

— Je vous présente mes excuses.

— Pas de problème.

Elle vint s'asseoir près de lui sur le canapé en veillant à ne pas renverser son verre.

— Vous n'étiez pas au meilleur de votre forme, dit-elle.

— Tout de même…

— Quoiqu'il en soit, les photos sont très belles. Mais je ne les ai plus ; il les a prises aussi quand...

Un instant, elle sentit les gravillons lui déchirer les paumes, puis le genou de l'homme pesant sur son dos, ses mains brutales lui arrachant les photos... Elle lutta de toutes ses forces pour retenir ses larmes. Bientôt, elle sentit qu'on lui prenait son verre des mains, et les bras de Luke se refermèrent autour d'elle. Doucement, en veillant à ne pas lui faire de mal, il lui caressa les cheveux.

— C'est bon, Sarah, chuchota-t-il. Vous avez le droit de pleurer.

Elle posa la joue contre son torse, et respira son odeur masculine. Depuis combien de temps aucun homme ne l'avait prise dans ses bras ? Elle ne savait plus. Longtemps, en tout cas.

Malgré le talent et l'intelligence de James — ou peut-être à cause de ses dons exceptionnels —, sa présence n'était pas réconfortante. Il acceptait la réalité, la regardait en face et s'attendait à ce que les autres en fissent autant. Sarah avait mis un point d'honneur à répondre à cette attente... jusqu'à la mort de son équipier.

Ce jour-là, sa vie avait volé en éclats. Impossible de recoller les morceaux. Et plus personne ne tenait suffisamment à elle pour l'aider...

Elle resta immobile quelques minutes, en s'imprégnant de cette douceur qu'on lui offrait, puis, bien avant d'avoir envie d'y renoncer, elle se redressa et réussit à sourire.

— Merci, dit-elle en repoussant ses cheveux en arrière. Vous êtes un ami.

Les grandes mains de Luke s'attardèrent sur ses épaules.

— Ça va ?

Elle hocha la tête.

— Ça y est, le cap est passé. Je vais me changer et prendre les clés de la jeep. Je reviens dans une minute.

Il leva son verre comme s'il buvait à sa santé.

— Prenez votre temps.

Une fois dans sa chambre, elle se hâta, pourtant. Elle évitait autant que possible son reflet dans le miroir. Deux fois déjà, elle avait été agressée, dans des pays lointains, par des gens qui ne voulaient pas voir publier certains articles les concernant. Elle savait que la douleur physique passerait, que les bleus s'effaceraient. Refusant de tenir compte de ses côtes douloureuses, elle enfila un pantalon de lin chocolat et une tunique légère à manches longues pour cacher ses bras. Quand elle voulut se coiffer, un nouveau problème se présenta : elle était incapable de lever les bras et de tenir une brosse assez fermement pour démêler ses boucles. Oserait-elle...

Elle retourna dans la salle de séjour et trouva Luke plongé dans un exemplaire de *Events*. Il leva les yeux et lui sourit.

— Vous avez l'air nettement plus en forme.

— Je me sens beaucoup mieux, dit-elle avec une pointe de nervosité. J'ai encore un service à vous demander...

— Quoi donc ?

Très gênée, elle lui tendit la brosse.

— Vous voulez bien...

— Avec plaisir ! Asseyez-vous sur l'un de ces grands tabourets.

Elle obéit en silence, et il se planta derrière elle pour soulever sa chevelure à pleines mains.

— Vous avez une sacrée crinière.

Il se mit à lui brosser les cheveux avec une délicatesse surprenante, en faisant très attention à ses bosses et à ses pansements.

— D'habitude, je les tresse pour ne pas les avoir dans les yeux, murmura-t-elle. Ils ont dû se défaire, hier soir...

Les coups de brosse étaient apaisants, hypnotiques. Elle sentit que ses épaules commençaient à se détendre. Elle ferma les yeux, l'entendit demander :

— Vous voulez que je les tresse ?

— Vous sauriez le faire ?

— Je le fais tout le temps pour Erin et Jenny. C'est une qualification indispensable pour un papa.

— Parlez-moi de vos filles.

Il eut un petit rire.

— Erin, c'est l'aventurière. Elle est indépendante, butée ; elle sait ce qu'elle veut et elle fonce droit au but, quel que soit le risque. Elle aime l'océan, le vélo et les sciences naturelles.

— Elle tient tout ça de son père ?

Pendant un instant, il se figea, puis la brosse reprit son va-et-vient tranquille.

— Peut-être un peu. Jen est plus douce, moins bruyante, mais tout aussi têtue quand elle s'y met. Elle joue à la poupée, prend le thé avec ses copines, adore les contes de fées et veut toujours s'habiller comme une princesse.

Son vœu s'était réalisé, le jour du mariage de sa mère...

— Quel âge ont-elles ?

— Jen a quatre ans ; Erin en aura sept, cet été, répondit-il en posant la brosse sur le comptoir. Allons-y.

Avec délicatesse, il rassembla ses cheveux. Elle était si détendue qu'elle se crispa à peine quand il tira légèrement son pansement. Les mouvements de ses doigts dans ses cheveux provoquaient en elle des petites vagues de plaisir. Elle inspira profondément, puis expira longuement. Maintenant, elle savait pourquoi les femmes prenaient tant de plaisir à se faire coiffer. C'était si apaisant... si sensuel.

— Terminé, dit-il en passant le bout de sa tresse par-dessus son épaule. Vous avez quelque chose pour l'attacher ?

Elle lui tendit un élastique.

— Si jamais vous voulez vous reconvertir, vous saurez dans quelle branche vous lancer. Merci.

Quand elle se retourna vers lui, il avait reculé d'un pas, et ses mains étaient cachées dans ses poches.

— De rien, dit-il. Tout le plaisir était pour moi. Vous avez trouvé vos clés ?

Visiblement, il voulait s'en aller. L'intermède touchait déjà à sa fin.

— Elles sont ici, dans le tiroir.

Elle glissa de son tabouret, saisit le trousseau de clés, alla prendre un chapeau de paille accroché près de la porte.

— Voilà, je suis parée !

Ou, du moins, elle pouvait faire semblant...

3.

Dès qu'ils émergèrent de l'immeuble, Luke mit ses lunettes de soleil. Surtout pour se cacher. Car il avait pris beaucoup de plaisir à coiffer les cheveux de Sarah. Beaucoup trop. Ses boucles étaient si douces, comme de l'eau entre ses mains. Pendant qu'il les brossait, elle s'était détendue comme un chaton s'endort sous les caresses… et son propre corps avait réagi d'une façon tout à fait inattendue.

Depuis Kristin… depuis Kristin et Matt, il ne pensait plus au sexe. Le spectacle qu'offrait la nuque de Sarah, si vulnérable, sa peau lisse et bronzée, sa poitrine menue se soulevant quand elle respirait — tout cela avait opéré en lui une sorte de révolution. Pendant quelques instants, il avait désiré… une chose à laquelle il n'avait pas droit. Une fois de plus.

Il se secoua, et demanda :

— Où est votre voiture ?

— Garée derrière la Sawyer's Photo Shop. Tout près du poste de police.

Tout en parlant, elle frissonna et, sans réfléchir, il lui prit la main.

— Si jamais il est encore là, je ferai en sorte qu'il ne vous ennuie plus, ni vous ni qui que ce soit d'autre, pendant très longtemps. D'accord ?

Elle lui lança un sourire charmant.

— D'accord, répéta-t-elle.

Il l'accompagna d'abord à sa banque, et patienta pendant qu'elle faisait annuler son chéquier. Ensuite, ils s'occupèrent du permis de conduire.

Peu à peu, elle reprenait vie. Tandis qu'ils patientaient à un feu, elle alla jusqu'à lui demander :

— Vous avez les cheveux bien longs pour un policier de province. Le règlement aurait-il changé ?

Il lui lança un sourire amusé.

— J'étais en mission spéciale. Depuis un an à peu près, je traîne avec la faune de la plage pour surveiller leurs activités les moins... aquatiques.

— Un fondu du surf ?

— Le mot « fondu » ne se porte plus chez les vrais surfeurs. Ils sont très fiers de leur vie en marge de la société.

Elle hocha la tête d'un air sagace.

— Je m'en souviendrai. Ça doit être plaisant de faire du surf toute la journée.

— Surtout en janvier, dans une combinaison glaciale !

— Ah oui ! L'hiver, ça ne vous dit rien ?

— Je préfère de loin un feu de cheminée, un match à la télé et un saladier de *pop-corn*.

Il contempla un instant cette image créée par son esprit, puis compléta le tableau en y ajoutant Erin somnolant dans le grand fauteuil, et Kristin blottie contre lui sur le canapé, en train de donner le sein à Jen. Oui, il avait vraiment une existence idéale, *avant*.

— Luke ? Luke !

Il écrasa la pédale du frein, stoppant sa voiture à quelques centimètres de celle qui la précédait. Sarah le regardait, les yeux écarquillés.

— Elle a coupé la route juste devant vous, et j'ai eu l'impression que vous ne la voyiez pas.

Il passa la main sur son visage.

— Vous aviez raison. J'étais… ailleurs.

— C'est bien ce qu'il m'a semblé. En tout cas, vous avez de bons réflexes.

Un coup de klaxon derrière eux leur signala que le feu était passé au vert. Serrant les dents, Luke accéléra avec prudence, et ils atteignirent la Sawyer's Photo Shop sans autre incident.

Garées côte à côte, une jeep vert olive et une énorme Cadillac brillaient au soleil du matin.

Luke coupa le moteur, et la jeune femme accepta son aide pour descendre.

— Merci, inspecteur Brennan.

— Je ne suis que caporal.

Elle lui fit la grimace, et il retrouva son sourire. Tout en la suivant vers la jeep, il ajouta :

— J'ai passé un coup de fil à Hank Jordan, le collègue qui a pris votre déposition. Ils ont cherché des empreintes, sans résultat pour l'instant. C'est bizarre : ce type a vos clés mais il n'a pas pris la voiture. Pourtant, les jeeps valent cher sur le marché des voitures volées.

— Il trouvait peut-être la direction trop dure ?

Luke eut un petit rire, et répondit :

— En admettant qu'il n'en veuille pas, il connaît sûrement quelqu'un à qui faire plaisir.

Gênée par ses pansements, Sarah eut du mal à déverrouiller la voiture. Quand elle y fut enfin parvenue, une vague de chaleur leur sauta au visage.

— A mon avis, dit-elle, cette voiture n'a pas bougé d'ici depuis hier.

— Je me demande pourquoi…

Luke secouait la tête, perplexe. Ce comportement ne ressemblait à rien ; il n'y voyait aucune explication. Près de lui, Sarah contempla quelques instants l'intérieur du véhicule avant de se secouer.

— La vie continue ! Vous allez pouvoir rentrer chez vous et dormir un peu. Moi, je ferai d'autres tirages de vos photos. Heureusement, j'avais laissé les négatifs dans mes archives.

— Je crois que je vais plutôt aller me faire couper les cheveux, dit Luke. Je reprends les patrouilles normales mercredi soir.

— Plus de surf ?

— Je me mets au sec.

La jeune femme hocha la tête avec un sourire.

— J'apporterai les photos chez vous en milieu de semaine, d'accord ?

Le rebord de son chapeau de paille jetait de l'ombre sur ses bleus, ses pansements et ses éraflures ; son visage semblait presque normal : doux, serein et pourtant triste, comme Luke l'avait déjà remarqué sur la plage. Il n'avait aucune envie de la quitter comme ça, mais sa vie était trop compliquée, en ce moment, pour qu'il pût y inviter quelqu'un.

— Je suis généralement chez moi l'après-midi, dit-il en reculant d'un pas. Vous êtes sûre que vous pourrez conduire ? Vos mains doivent vous faire mal.

— C'est supportable, grâce aux analgésiques que m'a donnés le médecin. Et puis, j'ai une boîte automatique et la direction assistée.

Malgré l'assurance qu'elle affichait, elle semblait hésiter à monter en voiture. Il lui prit le coude pour l'aider.

— Je vous tiendrai au courant si on apprend quoi que ce soit sur votre agresseur, dit-il.

— Merci.

Un tour de clé, et le moteur gronda. Luke recula, et regarda la jeep se diriger lentement vers la sortie. Au moment de s'engager dans la rue, Sarah leva la main. Il lui fit signe à son tour, sans savoir si elle le voyait.

Resté seul, il se mit à examiner le sol du parking, au cas où Jordan aurait manqué un indice. Il ne trouva rien. Le gravier ne garde pas les traces, et d'autres personnes avaient dû passer par là, depuis la veille au soir. Comment en savoir plus ? Il n'avait aucune piste, aucune théorie, et une longue journée de canicule à remplir. Sans parler du reste de l'été... ni du reste de son existence.

— Un *daiquiri* à la fraise pour la demoiselle ?

A demi endormie, elle ouvrit les yeux, puis se redressa brusquement en retirant ses lunettes de soleil.

— C'est exactement ce qu'il me faut ! Comment as-tu deviné ?

Son mari s'assit près d'elle.

— Il fait chaud, nous sommes en Floride, et tu adores les fraises. Elémentaire, mon cher Watson.

— Mmm, murmura-t-elle en goûtant la boisson glacée. Je crois bien que je vais passer le reste de ma vie ici, à lire des romans d'amour, à profiter du soleil et à boire des *daiquiris*.

— L'hôtel te ferait sûrement un prix. Tu contribues grandement à améliorer le paysage.

Il avait posé sur sa cuisse brûlante une main large et fraîche. Elle se sentit frémir. Si seulement ils ne se trouvaient pas dans un lieu public... Faisant un effort pour rassembler ses idées, elle demanda :

— Et les filles ?

— Elles sont au club pour enfants, en train de peindre avec les doigts en écoutant la musique des films de Disney.

— J'espère qu'Erin ne va pas s'ennuyer.

Matt remonta doucement la main le long de sa cuisse. Elle se sentit fondre.

— Ils ont trois aquariums, murmura-t-il. Et plusieurs étagères de livres. Elle va s'éclater.

— Autrement dit, nous avons du temps… pour nous. Qu'allons-nous bien pouvoir en faire ?

— Je pensais à une sieste, dit-il à mi-voix, tandis que sa main remontait encore. Ou quelque chose d'approchant. Qu'en penses-tu ?

— Je n'en pense que du bien. Monte dans la chambre ; je te rejoins dans quelques minutes.

Elle vit ses sourcils se froncer très légèrement.

— Monte avec moi.

— Je veux me doucher : je suis couverte d'huile solaire.

Il déplaça légèrement sa main, et retrouva son sourire en l'entendant soupirer.

— Ça ne me dérange pas…

— Moi, ça me dérange. Je te retrouve tout de suite.

— Les femmes !

Il se leva en secouant la tête.

— Je t'attends là-haut.

Elle le regarda marcher à grands pas vers l'hôtel, le dos droit, les épaules carrées, l'allure militaire. Au moment d'entrer, il s'effaça et tint la porte à une femme accompagnée de trois enfants. C'était bien lui : la galanterie et le sens des responsabilités — le sens de l'honneur, aussi.

Il disparut derrière les vitres teintées, et elle se laissa aller au fond de sa chaise longue. Elle l'aimait tant, elle le désirait tellement… son idée du paradis était de se retrouver blottie contre lui dans une chambre tranquille. Et pourtant, elle restait allongée là, à hésiter. Pourquoi donc ? La réponse tenait en un mot : Luke. Elle aimait Matt de tout son cœur, mais elle se sentait si coupable d'avoir abandonné Luke…

Laissant derrière elle la piscine et le grand soleil, elle se doucha aux vestiaires, lava et sécha ses cheveux, puis se maquilla un peu, juste assez pour cacher les cernes sous ses yeux. Elle dormait mal, en ce moment, même après une journée passée à arpenter les parcs d'attractions avec les filles ou après une merveilleuse nuit d'amour avec Matt. Le visage de Luke la hantait jour et nuit. Elle pensait sans cesse à l'immense sacrifice qu'il avait fait pour elle et pour sa famille.

Huit années auparavant, elle avait trahi Matt en épousant son frère. Ensuite, elle avait renié le serment fait à Luke de rester avec lui « jusqu'à ce que la mort les sépare ». Et maintenant… Elle possédait tout ce qu'elle avait toujours désiré : l'homme qu'elle aimait depuis le collège, deux merveilleuses filles, la possibilité d'avoir d'autres enfants… elle avait tout, et Luke n'avait plus rien. Mais, d'un autre côté, comment aurait-elle pu refuser à Matt l'amour et la famille dont il rêvait ? C'était uniquement grâce à ce rêve qu'il avait tenu le coup pendant ses cinq années de détention.

A la porte de leur chambre, elle s'immobilisa un instant pour maîtriser un peu son émotion. Son mari ne devait rien deviner des regrets qui la tourmentaient.

La porte s'ouvrit. Matt l'attira aussitôt dans ses bras.

— J'ai cru que tu n'arriverais jamais.

Ses mains se promenaient sur ses épaules, glissaient sous les bretelles de son débardeur ; il posait des baisers sur ses paupières, sa gorge, ses oreilles… Elle trembla, soupira, saisit son visage entre ses paumes.

— Je ne te ferai plus attendre, Matt. Plus jamais.

L'attirant à elle, elle s'empara de sa bouche. Malgré la passion, elle garda les yeux ouverts... parce qu'elle redoutait de voir un autre visage se substituer à celui de Matt, si elle les fermait.

Un dîner solitaire, un film qu'il alla voir seul, et il prit son service de nuit, patrouillant les plages et les rues du centre. A minuit passé, les rues proches de la plage étaient encore très animées : c'était aussi le quartier des bars.

Il entendit la bagarre avant de la repérer : un fracas de verre brisé, des voix furieuses... il courait vers l'endroit d'où lui parvenait le bruit quand une bande jaillit du Blue Flamingo. Vite, il appela des renforts et s'avança vers le groupe d'hommes.

— Police ! En arrière ! lança-t-il en écartant deux curieux. La fête est finie : on rentre à la maison.

Saisissant un T-shirt au hasard, il tira son propriétaire en arrière.

Quand ses collègues arrivèrent, il avait déjà séparé les adversaires. Trop ivres pour protester, ils se laissèrent emmener au poste sans réagir.

— Vous vous prenez pour un super-flic ! dit l'un des gars.

C'était un tout jeune garçon, qui le regardait par en dessous avec l'expression vague d'un ivrogne. Visiblement, il n'avait pas l'âge légal pour consommer de l'alcool.

— Et toi, tu te prends pour un adulte ? Tes parents savent ce que tu fais ?

— Ouais, pas de problème ! lança le gamin d'un air désinvolte, tout en évitant son regard.

— Tu me montres tes papiers ?

— Je les ai perdus.

— Bien sûr ! Alors, donne-moi ton adresse.

— Oh, allez...

— C'est ça ou passer la nuit au poste. A toi de choisir.

Une heure plus tard, Luke quittait le domicile du garçon, après que sa mère lui eut expliqué longuement que tout le problème venait de son ex-mari. Elle n'avait sans doute pas complètement tort...

Le reste de la nuit se déroula tranquillement. Presque trop, car les temps morts lui permettaient de réfléchir, et ça ne lui réussissait guère. Il pensait au rôle du père. Le père avait une telle influence sur la vie de son enfant ! Quel genre d'avenir préparait-il à Erin et Jenny ?

Une clochette tinta quand il poussa la porte. Le magasin était très sombre. Murs et plafond peints en noir. Sur les étagères poussiéreuses, des cadres, des piles, des pellicules... et quelques photos encadrées.

Luke s'approchait pour voir si elles étaient de Sarah quand, derrière lui, il entendit un pas, le froissement d'une étoffe. Il se retourna, plein d'espoir... mais ce n'était pas Sarah. Un homme assez jeune, un peu trop rond, se planta derrière le comptoir, le toisant d'un air poli mais sans chaleur aucune.

— Que puis-je faire pour vous ?

— Ces photos sont extraordinaires, dit Luke en les montrant d'un geste.

Un grand sourire apparut alors sur le visage lunaire du garçon.

— Je vous remercie. Mon travail fait toute ma joie.

— Elles sont de vous ?

— Oui. Je suis Chuck Sawyer. Vous vouliez des pellicules ? Un appareil photo, peut-être ?

— Non merci. En fait, je cherche une personne qui travaille ici.

— Je suis seul à tenir le magasin.

— Mais Sarah Randolph développe bien ses photos ici ?

Le sourire de Chuck s'évanouit.

— Oui.

— Elle est ici, en ce moment ?

— Non. Elle a eu… un accident, la semaine dernière, et elle se repose chez elle.

Le ton de Chuck n'exprimait aucune compassion.

— Si vous avez besoin d'un photographe, je peux vous dépanner.

— Merci, non. Je suis Luke Brennan, l'officier de police qui l'a emmenée aux urgences, la semaine dernière. Je venais aux nouvelles.

Les yeux de Chuck se plissèrent.

— Vous êtes de la police ?

— Ça vous pose un problème ?

— Non. Pas du tout. Comme je vous le disais, je ne l'ai pas vue de la semaine.

— Vous lui avez parlé au téléphone ?

— Non.

— Vous ne vous inquiétez pas pour elle ?

— Pas vraiment, non, répondit Chuck avec un petit rire. Vous savez, Sarah est journaliste : c'est une dure à cuire.

Il réfléchit un instant, fit une petite moue, et ajouta :

— Enfin, elle l'était. Il y a quelques mois encore, elle travaillait pour l'hebdomadaire *Events*. Elle a craqué au milieu d'un reportage : il a fallu la rapatrier. Depuis son retour, je crois bien qu'elle n'a plus pris une seule photo valable…

« C'est là que tu te trompes », pensa Luke.

— Bon, merci, dit-il. Je finirai bien par avoir de ses nouvelles.

— Si je la vois, je lui dirai que vous êtes passé.

— Merci.

Il sortit, sans pouvoir s'empêcher de jeter derrière lui un regard hostile. Pour des raisons qu'il ignorait, la présence de Sarah posait un problème à Chuck Sawyer. Au point qu'il en arrivât à l'agresser ? Ce type était antipathique, mais pas forcément violent.

Bon, il fallait se renseigner. Dans la majorité des cas, les agressions étaient commises par une personne de l'entourage de la victime.

Si elle ne téléphonait pas ce soir, il la contacterait. Et si ses amis ressemblaient tous à ce Sawyer, elle avait grand besoin d'un soutien moral.

Sarah refusait de sortir. Si on lui avait demandé pourquoi, elle aurait expliqué qu'elle devait être là quand le serrurier viendrait, que le médecin lui avait recommandé de ne pas s'exposer au soleil tant qu'elle serait sous antibiotiques, ou encore que ses ecchymoses risquaient de traumatiser le voisinage. Mais elle n'était pas dupe de tous ces prétextes. En fait, elle n'avait pas assez d'énergie pour sortir.

Elle restait donc chez elle, en pyjama, à regarder les films qui se succédaient à la télévision, à dormir énormément. Cela ne semblait pas très important de manger ; elle grignota ses maigres réserves : des glaces, du *pop-corn*, un peu de pain grillé. C'était toujours plus que ce qu'elle mangeait en Afrique.

La gérante de l'immeuble envoya quelqu'un pour changer la serrure, et elle se sentit plus en sécurité. Elle aurait dû faire la même chose pour la jeep, mais ça nécessitait un déplacement chez le concessionnaire…

Le téléphone ne sonna pas une seule fois. Qui aurait pu l'appeler ? Pas son agent, puisque aucune négociation n'était en cours. Pas son rédacteur en chef qui n'avait rien à lui dire tant qu'elle ne serait pas en état de travailler. Une journaliste qui refuse de sortir de chez elle ne risque pas d'être débordée par les propositions de reportage. Luke Brennan peut-être ?

Bien sûr, elle n'attendait pas d'appel de sa part : c'était à elle de le joindre, d'apporter les photos chez lui. Et, pour développer ses photos, il faudrait aller au magasin, voir Chuck, supporter ses sous-entendus. Et ça, elle n'en avait pas le courage, même si ces photos constituaient son seul prétexte pour rendre visite à Luke.

Les glaces, le *pop-corn* et le pain finirent par s'épuiser, et Sarah comprit qu'elle allait devoir sortir de sa tanière.

La grande lumière du jour lui fit mal aux yeux, même derrière ses lunettes de soleil et sous le rebord de son grand chapeau. Après cinq jours de climatisation, elle trouva l'air lourd et moite. Les bruits ordinaires de la circulation, les tondeuses, les sirènes, et même les oiseaux lui semblèrent assourdissants. Elle hésita, faillit rebrousser chemin…

— Sarah ?

Stupéfaite, elle reconnut Luke Brennan, à califourchon sur une grosse Harley rangée à côté de sa jeep.

— Qu'est-ce que vous faites là ?

Son propre manque de courtoisie lui arracha une grimace.

— Je vois que vous vous êtes coupé les cheveux, reprit-elle, gênée. Ça vous va bien.

— Merci. J'étais sans nouvelles de vous, alors je suis passé voir si… si vous aviez fait ces tirages.

Il était magnifique dans son T-shirt blanc, son jean usé et ses bottes, assis sur son énorme moto noire. Sa nouvelle coupe mettait en valeur la beauté de son visage. Il ferait un poster extraordinaire. Torse nu, peut-être...

Stoppant net les dérives de ses pensées, elle répondit :

— Non. Non, pas encore. Je suis restée à la maison, cette semaine.

— Vous aviez besoin de repos. Votre voix est revenue.

— Oui, ça m'a fait du bien de ne pas parler.

— C'est ce que le médecin avait dit.

Il croisa les bras sur sa poitrine. La pose était très séduisante.

— Alors, quand pensez-vous pouvoir me montrer les photos ?

— Eh bien...

Gêné, tout à coup, il s'empressa de préciser :

— Je ne veux pas vous mettre la pression ! J'ai seulement hâte de les voir.

— Vous ne me mettez pas la pression.

En fait, il lui donnait une très bonne excuse pour ne pas retourner se terrer chez elle.

— Je peux y aller tout de suite. Venez donc avec moi, si vous avez un peu de temps devant vous.

— Ce serait avec plaisir, mais Jen et Erin rentrent de Floride cet après-midi.

Elle se sentit envahie par une déception tout à fait disproportionnée par rapport à la situation.

— Bon, je vous appellerai.

— Ou alors, dit-il en claquant des doigts, on pourrait se retrouver un peu plus tard ? Je passe voir les filles et je vous rejoins au magasin. Après, on ira manger un morceau. Qu'est-ce que vous en dites ?

Tentée, troublée, elle hésita un instant. Le sourire de Luke se fit enjôleur, un peu taquin, tout à fait irrésistible.

— Allez, Sarah Rose... Dites oui !

Il écarta les mains dans un geste ample.

— Un petit dîner entre amis : où est le mal ?

Quelquefois, maman sortait toute seule avec papa Matt. Ce n'était pas grave : à l'hôtel, il y avait des *baby-sitters*, plein de cassettes vidéo et de bonnes choses à manger. Jenny elle-même ne grognait pas parce qu'elle pouvait voir *Cendrillon* autant de fois qu'elle le voulait.

Il n'y avait donc aucune raison d'être triste ! En cet instant précis, elle se retrouvait assise dans un restaurant magnifique, vêtue d'une robe qu'elle avait choisie elle-même et qui ne grattait pas, et elle venait de terminer un plat énorme de très bons spaghettis. Bientôt, le serveur leur apporterait le dessert, dès que maman et papa Matt auraient fini de danser.

— Maman est jolie, dit Jenny. Comme une princesse.

— Une reine, corrigea Erin.

Dans ce cas, papa Matt serait le roi. Erin les regarda danser. La robe rouge de maman tourbillonnait autour d'elle. Ils se souriaient, les yeux dans les yeux. « Finalement, se dit la fillette, je n'ai plus faim pour le dessert. »

En les accompagnant dans leur chambre, maman souriait toujours en chantonnant l'air sur lequel elle avait dansé. Elle mit Jenny en pyjama, et prit le temps de leur lire une histoire. Comme d'habitude, Jenny s'endormit avant la fin. Erin resta éveillée, même après que maman fut repartie.

Dans l'autre pièce, elle l'entendait parler et rire avec papa Matt, puis il y eut de nouveau de la musique. Pas besoin de voir à travers les murs pour comprendre qu'ils s'étaient remis à danser.

Elle se retourna, et enfouit son visage dans l'oreiller — rien à faire, elle entendait toujours la musique dans sa tête. Les yeux fermés, elle voyait encore maman danser. Seulement, à ce moment-là, elle dansait avec le bon partenaire. Elle dansait avec papa.

Quand on a presque sept ans, on sait que les rêves se réalisent rarement, et on s'endort parfois en pleurant.

4.

L'avion des filles se posait à 15 h 30. Sachant que ses parents souhaiteraient passer un moment seuls avec les jeunes mariés et les petites, Luke prit le temps de faire des cookies avant de se rendre à la maison sur la grève.

En voyant le monospace vert de Kristin garé dans l'allée, il se détendit un peu : les filles étaient toujours là ; il ne les avait pas manquées. Restait à affronter la famille au grand complet. Il prit une profonde inspiration, coupa le contact et retira son casque. Il voulait seulement voir ses filles. On pouvait espérer que chacun réussirait à garder son calme, le temps d'une visite rapide !

Devant la porte, il hésita, puis préféra sonner. Une bonne décision, se dit-il lorsque sa mère lui ouvrit.

— Oh… Luke, bonjour. Nous ne t'attendions pas.

— Je voulais embrasser les filles.

Il y eut une cavalcade dans le couloir, et Jennifer se jeta dans ses bras en hurlant :

— Papaaaaaa ! On est rentrées !

— C'est bon de te voir, Jenny Penny, dit-il en la serrant contre lui.

Il avait fort à faire pour ne pas écraser le sachet de cookies, et aussi pour retenir ses larmes. D'autant plus que d'autres bras vinrent se nouer autour de sa taille.

— Papa, moi aussi ! Moi aussi !

Cette fois, les cookies étaient fichus.

— Toi aussi, l'Ourson, dit-il en se penchant pour soulever Erin. Alors, comment va Mickey ?

— Il est grand ! Grand comme ça ! cria Jen en ouvrant les bras. Moi, j'ai préféré Goofy.

Erin le contemplait, les sourcils froncés.

— Où sont passés tes cheveux, papa ?

— J'ai tout coupé, l'Ourson. Je reprends les patrouilles normales.

— Ça fait drôle.

— Oui, bien sûr, mais on s'habitue vite. Raconte-moi Disney World.

— J'ai eu ma photo avec Aladdin et le Génie, et Pinocchio et Hercule ! déclara la fillette en comptant sur ses doigts. Et aussi avec Donald.

— Super *cool*.

Luke constata que la porte d'entrée était refermée et que sa mère avait disparu. Il porta les filles dans le salon, et se laissa tomber sur le canapé, un enfant sur chaque genou.

— Et les attractions ? Qu'est-ce que vous avez préféré ?

La question déclencha un débat en profondeur. Tandis qu'elles comparaient leurs attractions favorites, il étudia leurs visages, un peu plus bronzés que la semaine dernière, et leurs vêtements qu'il ne connaissait pas.

Posant le doigt sur le pansement qui ornait le genou d'Erin, il demanda :

— Qu'est-ce qui t'est arrivé ?

La gamine éclata de rire.

— On est montés dans le manège des tasses de thé. Ça tournait ! En descendant, j'avais tellement le vertige que je suis rentrée dans un banc.

— Tu as pleuré, fit remarquer Jen.

— Juste un peu. Toi, tu as bien pleuré quand la baleine t'a éclaboussée.

— Et toi, tu as pleuré quand…

— Stop ! cria Luke. Je vois le tableau. Vous êtes montées dans le navire volant de Peter Pan ? C'était ton préféré quand on est allés au Royaume Magique, Erin.

— On était déjà allés à Disney World ?

— Oui, bien sûr ! Jen était encore un bébé mais elle est venue aussi. On a… on avait des photos, tu ne te souviens pas ? Toi et moi dans le bateau, prêts à s'envoler ?

Elle secoua sa tête blonde.

— Non, j'ai oublié. En tout cas, on l'a refait. Jen avait peur qu'on tombe.

— Tu n'étais pas rassurée non plus, la première fois, dit Luke avec un petit rire.

Satisfaite, la petite tira la langue à sa sœur.

— Jennifer ! s'écria Kristin, depuis le seuil de la pièce. C'est impoli et méchant. Fais des excuses à ta sœur.

— Pardon, marmonna Jen.

— Et toc ! lança la grande d'un air triomphant.

Luke lui tira doucement l'oreille, pour rire.

— On n'enfonce pas quelqu'un qui vous fait des excuses, Erin, tu le sais bien !

Ce fut son tour de baisser la tête.

— Oui, papa.

— Je suis venue vous dire que votre mamie était prête à servir le dîner, reprit fermement Kristin. Allez vous laver les mains.

— Ouais !

Le moment que Luke redoutait était arrivé. Il se leva lentement, et les filles s'engouffrèrent dans le couloir.

— Bonsoir, Luke, dit la jeune femme.

Le soleil avait doré sa peau.

Il s'éclaircit la gorge, et répondit avec effort :

— Bonsoir, Kristin.

— Tes cheveux sont bien comme ça.

— Merci. On dirait que tu as pris le soleil, en Floride.

— Il n'a pas plu une seule fois. Tu restes dîner ?

— Non, non. Je suis juste passé dire bonjour aux filles.

Gêné, il tendit son sachet de cookies en expliquant :

— J'avais apporté le dessert, mais il doit être en miettes.

Le beau sourire de Kristin apparut, puis s'éteignit très vite.

— Les miettes, c'est délicieux sur de la glace.

Il y eut un silence, puis elle s'éclaircit la gorge à son tour.

— Nous avons rapporté des photos. Tu viens les voir ?

Elle esquissa un geste, comme pour lui prendre la main, puis, en rougissant, elle tourna les talons et le précéda dans le couloir. La gorge serrée, il la suivit.

Matt et son père étaient ensemble dans le salon. Quand ils le virent, leur conversation s'arrêta net. Le Colonel lui sourit.

— Content de te voir, fils. Surtout avec une coiffure correcte. Comment va le gardien de la paix ?

Pour son père, les hommes, les vrais, entraient dans l'armée, et il ne faisait guère de différence entre un policier et un veilleur de nuit.

— Pas mal, merci, répondit-il. Et vous ? La semaine a été bonne ?

— Comme toujours.

— Tu as été très fatigué ! lança Elena Brennan, depuis la cuisine.

Le Colonel tira sur sa pipe, et le parfum de son tabac à la pomme se répandit autour de lui.

— C'était toute cette agitation autour du mariage…

Luke pouvait comprendre que l'on se sentît épuisé, après une telle cérémonie ! Tournant la tête, il croisa le regard de son frère.

— Bonjour, Matt.

— Bonjour.

Ce fut tout. Luke se dirigea vers la cuisine.

— Tu dînes avec nous, Luke ? lui demanda sa mère, qui mettait la dernière main à une rouelle de porc caramélisée.

— Non merci, maman.

Vite, avec l'impression de déranger, il s'assit près des filles, et réclama d'autres précisions sur le voyage. Kristin apporta les photos, et les petites se mirent à les commenter avec enthousiasme.

— Là, c'est moi et papa Matt sur le radeau de rondins.

— Là, c'est moi et maman avec Cendrillon.

— On a demandé à une dame de prendre cette photo-là. C'est *cool*, non ?

Il convint que c'était très *cool*, tout en se demandant jusqu'à quand il souffrirait en entendant ses filles appeler Matt « papa ». Sans doute éternellement.

Erin se retourna sur sa chaise.

— Maman, où est la grande photo ?

Elena répondit à la place de sa belle-fille :

— Je l'ai déjà accrochée au mur, ma chérie. Au-dessus de la télévision.

— Viens, papa, viens voir ! s'écria la petite en tirant Luke par la main.

— Elle est géniale, non ? On s'était tous fait beaux.

— Magnifique, dit Luke d'une voix rauque.

La nouvelle photo dominait toute la pièce. Les filles portaient de longues robes blanches avec de la dentelle ; Kristin était en rouge, un rouge qui éclairait ses cheveux et accentuait la couleur de ses yeux. Toutes trois étaient assises sur un canapé de velours à l'ancienne, et Matt, en costume — cravate, se tenait penché vers elles.

Les autres photos, celles d'avant où Luke apparaissait avec ses filles, avaient été déplacées : elles se trouvaient, désormais, tout en bas.

— A table ! lança sa mère.

Il se pencha vers Erin.

— Je vais vous laisser manger. Fais-moi un bisou.

Elle jeta les bras autour de son cou.

— Tu m'as manqué, papa !

— Toi aussi, Erin l'Ourson. Je suis content que vous soyez de retour.

— Quand est-ce qu'on peut venir chez toi ?

— Je vais téléphoner à ta maman pour qu'on organise quelque chose. Cette semaine, d'accord ?

— Demain ?

— Je ne sais pas. Bientôt, en tout cas : c'est promis.

Ensemble, ils retournèrent dans la cuisine. Erin serrait la main de son père de toutes ses forces.

Ils trouvèrent la famille assise autour de la table. Jen se trouvait tout au bout.

— Je te fais signe d'ici, Jenny Penny. A bientôt !

— Papa, attends ! cria la petite en esquissant un mouvement pour descendre de sa chaise.

— Non, reste assise, ma chérie, lui dit sa grand-mère en l'arrêtant d'un geste. Il n'y a pas assez de place.

Jen résolut le problème en passant sous la table.

— Ne t'en va pas, papa !

Luke la souleva dans ses bras, et la serra très fort.

— Je suis obligé, Jen. Il... il faut que j'aille travailler. Je te promets qu'on se verra très bientôt.

Du regard, il supplia Kristin de lui venir en aide. Elle contemplait son assiette en se mordant la lèvre inférieure. Il voulut poser Jen, mais la fillette s'accrocha à lui. Pas un mot, juste cette étreinte convulsive. Enfin, Kristin leva les yeux.

— Jenny, mon cœur, viens ici.

La petite fille secoua la tête.

Sa mère se leva, et vint la prendre par la taille. Dans son geste, elle effleura la poitrine de Luke, mais il réussit à ne pas sursauter.

— Lâche-le, Jenny ! dit-elle à l'oreille de sa fille.

Les petits bras de l'enfant relâchèrent leur étreinte, et Kristin recula.

— Merci, marmonna Luke sans regarder personne. A bientôt.

Il sortit, enfourcha sa moto, enfila posément ses gants, mit son casque, démarra... mais, dès le premier carrefour, il dut s'arrêter. Il ne respirait plus, ne voyait plus rien. Ses jambes tremblaient si violemment qu'il crut perdre l'équilibre. Pouvait-on mourir de ce genre de souffrance ? Et que serait sa vie s'il n'en mourait pas ?

— On ne laisse pas entrer n'importe qui.

— Et vous avez raison. Si vous voulez bien aller chercher Sarah, elle vous dira que je ne suis pas n'importe qui. Nous étions convenus de nous retrouver ici.

— Elle est dans la chambre noire. Il va falloir attendre qu'elle en sorte.

— Parfait. Je vais faire une petite inspection pour passer le temps. Je suis sûr que vos extincteurs sont conformes.

Ils entendirent un éclat de rire, et Sarah écarta le rideau.

— Je crois qu'il te tient, Chuck. Quand as-tu acheté un extincteur neuf pour la dernière fois ?

— Je ne m'en souviens pas, mais, dans ce domaine, permets-moi de te faire remarquer que tu n'as pas de leçon à me donner !

— C'est mon associé, expliqua Sarah en se retournant vers Luke. Il ne…

Elle s'interrompit net, et le regarda avec inquiétude :

— Qu'est-ce qui se passe ? Ça ne va pas ?

Il prit une longue inspiration tremblante.

— Si, si. Ça va très bien.

— Vous êtes allé voir vos filles, n'est-ce pas ? Il s'est passé quelque chose ?

— Rassurez-vous : je n'ai étranglé personne.

Elle ne demanda pas d'autre explication. Visiblement, il en avait assez enduré pour une seule soirée.

— Venez dans la cuisine. J'ai fait du thé glacé.

Elle souleva le battant du comptoir, puis écarta le rideau et le précéda dans l'arrière-boutique.

Luke avait une allure bizarre : contrairement à son habitude, il marchait maladroitement, comme s'il devait réfléchir avant de mettre un pied devant l'autre.

— Vous les avez développées ? demanda-t-il d'une voix lasse.

Elle hocha la tête. Chuck s'était enfermé dans son bureau. En silence, elle servit le thé glacé, et se tourna vers la chambre noire.

— Maintenant, venez me dire ce que vous en pensez.

Sur le seuil, il s'arrêta net avec une petite exclamation. Enchantée, elle sourit : c'était exactement la réaction qu'elle espérait. Comme dans un rêve, il alla se planter devant un agrandissement de Erin et Jennifer, penchées sur le seau d'appâts. La composition était parfaite, la lumière sur leurs robes vertes et roses semblait sortir tout droit d'une illustration de conte de fées. A l'instant précis où elle enfonçait le déclencheur, une petite brise avait gonflé leurs jupons de dentelles.

— C'est incroyable. Vous êtes très douée.

— J'ai surtout eu la chance de me trouver là.

— Je ne m'y connais pas assez pour vous contredire, mais… c'est hallucinant.

Il avançait lentement en étudiant chaque photo.

— J'aime beaucoup celle-ci, dit-il en indiquant un cliché qui les montrait tous les trois en train de rire. Ce serait possible de me faire un tirage ?

— Je vous tirerai un jeu complet. Et un autre pour votre famille.

— Oh, non ! dit-il avec un bref regard vers les photos sur lesquelles il apparaissait seul. Ce n'est pas la peine. Juste celles des filles et celle où nous sommes tous les trois pour moi.

Il avait un peu rougi. Surprise, elle insista :

— Mais, vos parents…

— Non, répéta-t-il en secouant la tête.

Il fit demi-tour, et alla examiner le premier tirage.

— C'est très impressionnant… Elles sont extraordinaires.

Nonchalamment appuyée au plan de travail, elle le laissa prendre tout son temps, et en profita pour admirer encore une fois la grâce et l'équilibre de son corps. Aux Beaux-Arts, elle avait vu des modèles bien moins beaux que lui. En tout cas, elle n'avait jamais soupiré en pensant à eux comme elle soupirait pour lui.

— Je ne vois pas comment je pourrais accepter ces photos sans vous les payer, dit-il tout à coup.

— Vous avez raison. J'accepte une invitation à dîner. Marché conclu ?

Il sourit, pour la première fois depuis son arrivée.

— Marché conclu. Allons-y.

— Vous voulez prendre votre voiture ? proposa-t-il. Ce serait plus confortable pour vous. Je vous laisserai même conduire, au cas où j'aurais encore une absence.

— Ce serait sans doute préférable, dit-elle en riant.

Elle s'approcha de la moto, et laissa courir sa main sur le siège de cuir, le guidon, le tableau de bord.

— Quelle superbe machine !

Il sourit, surpris. Kristin n'avait jamais compris sa fascination pour les motos.

— Vous êtes déjà montée sur un engin comme celui-ci ? demanda-t-il.

— Autrefois, oui. A dix-huit ans, j'ai traversé tout le pays, de Washington jusqu'en Californie sur l'Interstate 40.

— J'ai fait un peu le même voyage, sur la 10. Il y a eu un orage incroyable, près de La Nouvelle-Orléans. J'ai cru que j'allais me noyer.

— Il nous est arrivé la même chose, avec James, à Oklahoma City.

Un voyage à deux ? Ils avaient donc vécu une relation intime… Sarah continuait son histoire :

— Nous avons attendu sous un pont ; l'eau nous arrivait aux chevilles. J'ai eu peur, mais j'ai pris des photos magnifiques des éclairs.

— Je n'étais pas tranquille, moi non plus.

64

— En tout cas, on n'annonce pas de pluie pour aujourd'hui. On peut prendre la moto ?

Elle souriait comme une gamine. Enchanté, il sortit un deuxième casque de sa sacoche, et le lui tendit. Vite, elle noua ses cheveux, les fit disparaître sous le casque, et enfourcha souplement la moto. Elle se posa comme une plume, presque sans changer l'équilibre de la machine.

Quant à son propre équilibre... Luke ne pouvait pas en dire autant ! La présence de la jeune femme derrière lui le troublait profondément ; il avait une conscience aiguë de la proximité de leurs corps. Ses mains, débarrassées de leurs pansements mais encore à vif par endroits, vinrent se nouer autour de sa taille, et cette pression légère réchauffa sa peau comme le soleil de midi. Il n'avait plus l'habitude de se trouver aussi près d'une femme.

— Tenez bon ! lança-t-il.

Le moteur ronronna. Il embraya, sortit du parking, et vira en direction de la plage. Lentement, ils se frayèrent un chemin dans la circulation toujours dense en bord de mer. Des milliers de touristes déambulaient dans les rues.

Luke finit par se garer devant une petite échoppe qu'il connaissait, où l'on vendait des sandwichs superbes.

Après avoir glissé leur repas dans l'une des sacoches, ils purent enfin prendre la route.

Sur la longue ligne droite de la Highway 17, Luke lâcha la bride à sa monture. Le vent chaud de l'été les enveloppa ; les sons et les couleurs se fondirent dans un kaléidoscope joyeux. Cela faisait des mois que Luke ne s'était pas senti aussi libre, aussi jeune et heureux. Dix-huit mois exactement. Depuis le retour de Matt.

Ils dépassèrent la crique de Murrell's Inlet, puis l'île Pawley, très fréquentée par les touristes, et continuèrent vers le sud.

Grisé par cette course folle, Luke aurait volontiers roulé toute la nuit, mais son objectif était déjà en vue. Il changea de vitesse, et vira sous l'énorme statue représentant des chevaux cabrés, qui marquait l'entrée des Jardins de Brookgreen.

Sarah serra les bras autour de sa taille, et se pencha en avant.

— Les jardins sont ouverts le soir ?

Le grondement du moteur couvrait presque sa voix.

— Depuis quelques mois seulement ! lança-t-il par-dessus son épaule.

Au guichet, il montra sa carte d'abonnement, et on leur fit signe d'entrer. Remettant les gaz, il dit encore :

— J'ai pensé que ce serait un bon endroit pour pique-niquer.

Il n'entendit pas de réponse, mais les mains de la jeune femme remontèrent vers ses épaules et les serrèrent chaleureusement. C'était encore mieux que la sensation de la vitesse.

Il mit une bonne minute à se reprendre, le temps de remonter l'allée bordée d'azalées et de grands pins, de contourner la première fontaine avec son cavalier doré et d'atteindre le parking près du bâtiment principal. Là, il attendit que sa compagne eût mis pied à terre.

— Vous êtes une merveilleuse passagère. Je vous sentais à peine.

Enfin, c'était une façon de parler !

— Il y avait longtemps que je n'étais pas montée sur une moto.

Jetant un regard autour d'elle, elle huma avec gourmandise la douceur de l'air.

— Je suis très contente d'être ici.

Il tendit la main pour prendre son casque, le rangea avec le sien, et sortit le petit sac à dos contenant leur dîner.

Côte à côte, ils passèrent devant le magasin de souvenirs, s'arrêtèrent pour admirer un jardin aquatique, s'assirent sur le banc près d'une statue représentant un homme en train de lire son journal.

— J'ai toujours envie de tourner la page, dit Sarah en riant. Il doit s'ennuyer à lire toujours les mêmes articles.

— Ça doit être mortel. Où est la page des sports ?

Sarah éclata de rire, et l'entraîna dans l'une des galeries vitrées encadrant l'entrée du jardin.

— Voilà quelque chose qui va peut-être vous intéresser.

Il étudia la photo qu'elle lui montrait : une cabane branlante en pleine campagne. La porte moustiquaire ne tenait plus que par une charnière, la véranda était envahie par les mauvaises herbes, et des débris empilés encombraient les marches et les murs. Une image assez déprimante. Et pourtant, par une magie incompréhensible, cette première impression ne dura pas. Quelque chose poussa Luke à regarder mieux, à entrer dans la photo. Il se surprit alors à examiner les piles d'objets au rebut, tout en cherchant à y déchiffrer l'histoire de ceux qui les avaient abandonnés là. Autrefois, quelqu'un avait entretenu ce jardin avec amour. Le photographe avait su voir la vie secrète de cette cahute, et la capter sur sa pellicule.

— Stupéfiant, dit-il lentement. C'est vous qui avez pris cette photo ?

— Oh, non, c'est Felix Sawyer. Mon ancien professeur.

— Sawyer ? Comme le type du magasin ?

— Oui, Chuck est le neveu de Felix.

67

— Les photos qui sont sur les murs du magasin ressemblent beaucoup à celle-ci. Chuck m'a dit qu'elles étaient de lui.

— Ah bon ? murmura-t-elle, un peu absente. Le magasin est le domaine de Chuck. Moi, j'entre généralement par la porte de derrière. Je me sers juste de la chambre noire quand je suis en ville, ce qui n'arrive pas si fréquemment. J'ai dû passer deux fois par devant depuis la mort de Felix. Il faudra que je jette un coup d'œil à la décoration du magasin.

Cette perspective semblait la troubler.

— C'est donc Felix qui vous a appris le métier ? demanda Luke. Ça s'est fait comment ?

— Je l'ai rencontré sur la plage, l'été de mes douze ans ; j'étais en vacances chez ma grand-mère. Il a passé la journée à prendre des photos des dunes et des graminées, et je l'ai suivi partout en lui posant des questions. Le lendemain, nous nous sommes revus au même endroit, et il m'a tendu un appareil photo.

Elle poussa un petit soupir, et murmura :

— C'est lui qui m'a appris tout ce que je sais.

— Il devait être très fier de la carrière que vous avez faite.

— Je l'espère. On s'est un peu perdus de vue quand j'ai commencé à travailler à *Events*. J'étais toujours à l'étranger. Même quand il est mort.

— Je suis sûr qu'il a compris.

— Sans doute, oui. Mais si j'avais passé plus de temps avec lui, j'aurais davantage de souvenirs. Je pense que c'est pour ça que je suis venue ici, après...

Elle se tut un instant, et reprit :

— Je me sens plus proche de lui quand je travaille dans sa chambre noire. C'est un peu mon foyer.

— Et vos parents ? demanda Luke avec gentillesse.

— Ils sont morts dans un accident de voiture quand j'étais en terminale. Mon père était dans l'armée de l'air ; nous voyagions beaucoup, si bien que j'ai peu d'amis. Il me reste des photos, des souvenirs...

La tristesse de sa voix le renvoya à ses propres regrets.

— La vie n'est pas seulement faite de souvenirs, Sarah Rose.

Il lui pressa l'épaule, puis la lâcha très vite et décida d'alléger l'atmosphère.

— Vous voulez qu'on s'installe pour pique-niquer ou vous préférez grignoter en marchant ?

— En marchant.

— Quelle direction ?

— Le cadran solaire.

— C'est *cool*, comme dirait Erin.

Quand sa sculpture préférée apparut au détour de l'allée, elle fourra son sandwich dans les mains de Luke, et courut grimper sur les genoux du gigantesque ours de bronze.

— *Boucle d'Or* était mon histoire préférée, dit-elle, depuis son perchoir. Et vos filles ?

Il réfléchit un instant avant de répondre.

— Jen aime jouer à Rapunzel. Erin préfère *Hansel et Gretel*, surtout le moment où la sorcière est poussée dans le four.

— Votre fille est une dure à cuire !

— Seulement quand il s'agit de méchantes sorcières. Autrement, c'est un cœur tendre, surtout avec les animaux.

— Elle sera peut-être vétérinaire ?

Glissant des genoux de l'ours, elle reprit son sandwich et mordit dedans avec entrain. Cela faisait des mois, des années peut-être, qu'elle n'avait pas pris autant de plaisir à manger.

— Voilà le cadran solaire ! Vous croyez qu'on peut encore lire l'heure ?

Le cadran géant, au moins sept mètres de diamètre, ne fonctionnait plus au crépuscule. Perchés sur le muret, ils se montrèrent mutuellement les étoiles au fur et à mesure qu'elles leur apparaissaient, tout en partageant un sachet de chips. Puis ils reprirent leur promenade en se dirigeant vers les jardins à la française.

— J'ai apporté le dessert, dit Luke en tendant à la jeune femme le sachet de cookies. Dites-moi ce que vous en pensez.

Elle choisit un gâteau, le goûta, et poussa un gémissement de plaisir.

— J'en pense que je serais énorme si j'en trouvais d'aussi bons dans mon quartier.

C'était un mélange incroyable de chocolat noir et de noix de pécan, avec un soupçon de noix de coco, qui fondait sur la langue.

— Où avez-vous déniché ces merveilles ?

— Je les ai faites moi-même, répondit-il en riant.

— C'est vrai ? Vous faites ces cookies extraordinaires ?

— Je fais ces cookies extraordinaires.

— Ça, alors ! Moi, si j'allume le four, c'est uniquement pour faire réchauffer un plat que j'ai acheté chez le traiteur.

Elle prit un autre cookie et demanda, la bouche pleine :

— Erin et Jennifer ont hérité de vos talents ?

Il cessa de marcher. Un lourd silence s'abattit sur le jardin. Interdite, Sarah leva les yeux vers lui, et le considéra attentivement dans la pénombre.

— Qu'est-ce que j'ai dit ?

Sur son visage, il n'y avait plus trace de la gaieté qu'ils partageaient un instant plus tôt. Ses épaules s'étaient voûtées.

— Luke ? Qu'est-ce qui se passe ?

— Je crois que je ferais bien de tout vous expliquer, dit-il d'une voix âpre.

— Expliquer quoi ? demanda-t-elle sans comprendre.

— J'ai épousé Kristin parce que...

Il fronça les sourcils, et secoua la tête.

— Kristin était déjà enceinte quand nous nous sommes mariés.

Il la regardait toujours fixement. Elle devait avoir l'air perdue car il précisa :

— Erin n'est pas de moi.

— Oh !

— Elle l'ignore. Kristin et moi sommes seuls à le savoir. Enfin, avec vous, maintenant.

— Et le père ?

Luke eut un rire qui ressemblait à un cri de douleur.

— Le père est au courant, lui aussi, bien entendu. On cache difficilement ces choses à son mari.

Sarah comprit alors le reste de l'histoire.

— Matt ?

— Bravo, vous avez trouvé du premier coup. Le père... biologique d'Erin est mon frère Matt. Depuis le début, vous me plaignez, vous pensez que c'est moi la victime. Pas du tout ! Je lui ai pris sa femme et sa fille, pendant qu'il croupissait dans un camp de prisonniers.

Il tourna le dos à la jeune femme, et contempla l'étendue des jardins.

— Autrement dit, Matt méritait de les récupérer, et moi, je méritais de les perdre.

Il y eut un bref silence, puis il ajouta d'une voix à peine audible :

— Maintenant, vous savez qui vous fréquentez.

5.

Sarah passa un bras autour de son épaule, comme on réconforte un enfant malheureux.

— Je ne crois pas que l'histoire soit aussi simple, murmura-t-elle. Vous voulez bien me raconter ?

Il tourna vers elle un regard assombri par les tourments.

— Le bénéfice du doute ? Vous êtes trop généreuse.

— Et vous, trop dur envers vous-même. L'homme qui m'a remise sur les rails après mon agression n'a pas pu faire une chose vraiment mauvaise.

Son visage se ferma encore plus. Il se détourna, repoussant doucement le bras qui reposait toujours sur son épaule.

— C'est pour ça que vous êtes là ? Pour payer une dette ?

A grands pas, il s'éloigna vers le fond des jardins.

Fallait-il le suivre, s'expliquer ? Ou s'enfuir dans la direction opposée ? Cet homme l'écartelait ; l'attirance était trop forte, et elle avait l'impression de ne pas pouvoir lui donner ce dont il avait besoin. Pourtant, quand il disparut sous les arbres drapés de mousse, elle se lança à sa poursuite.

L'ombre était trop épaisse ; elle ne vit pas qu'il s'était arrêté, et le heurta de plein fouet. Il la prit dans ses bras pour la soutenir. Elle voyait à peine son visage dans la nuit.

— Doucement…

— Je suis ici parce que vous m'avez invitée, murmura-t-elle. Et parce que j'avais envie de venir.

Il desserra un peu son étreinte, et répliqua avec un petit rire :

— Vous êtes quelqu'un de spécial, Sarah Rose. Je ne sais pas du tout où j'en suis avec vous.

Elle avait posé les mains à plat sur sa poitrine.

— Ne vous sauvez pas !

— Franchement, ce n'est pas du tout ce que j'ai en tête.

Un rayon de lune éclaira ses yeux quand il inclina la tête. Ses lèvres étaient fermes et lisses. Il l'embrassa et l'enlaça avec douceur, l'entraînant pas à pas vers une découverte mutuelle. Elle se sentit fondre, se laissa guider… laissa son corps s'ajuster au sien comme un puzzle sensuel. Elle respirait le parfum de sa peau, une odeur de savon mêlée à une essence très masculine qui n'appartenait qu'à lui.

Quand il promena doucement la pointe de sa langue sur l'ourlet de ses lèvres, elle prit feu. La nuit tiède tourbillonna autour d'elle. Elle vit des éclairs de couleur et s'accrocha à son compagnon, exigeant davantage. Emportée par la passion, elle mordilla sa lèvre inférieure. Il l'écrasa alors contre lui avec une plainte sourde, les doigts plongés dans ses boucles soyeuses. Un désir insoutenable s'engouffra en elle ; son être tout entier se tendit vers lui.

Luke se sentait dévaler la pente. Les freins ne répondaient plus ; il ne cherchait même plus à diriger sa course folle. Il ne savait plus qu'une chose : la bouche de Sarah sous la sienne éteignait sa douleur. Pour la première fois en deux ans, il n'avait plus à lutter : il pouvait se contenter de savourer l'instant présent. C'était presque trop bon…

Elle reposait contre lui, si légère, si fine, si douce. Eperdu, il laissa courir ses paumes le long de son dos, caressa ses

74

hanches. Elle ronronnait presque. Emu, il la serra contre lui de toutes ses forces, sentit son sursaut, entendit son hoquet douloureux. Horrifié, il la lâcha en balbutiant :

— Oh, je suis désolé ! Je ne voulais pas… Ça va ?

Elle recula d'un pas. Comme c'était étrange de ne plus se toucher ! Il dut se retenir de tendre les mains vers elle… Il sentit la fraîcheur de la nuit l'envelopper, frissonna, et répéta sa question :

— Est-ce que ça va ?

Elle respira profondément, prudemment, et fit une petite grimace.

— Ça va, oui. Je… crois que mes côtes sont encore un peu fragiles.

Le retour à la réalité fut brutal. Il dut fermer les yeux pour encaisser le choc. Quand il les ouvrit, Sarah s'était détournée ; il ne la voyait presque plus dans la nuit. Quel crétin ! Quel monstrueux crétin il était, de lui faire des avances alors qu'elle avait tant souffert !

— Je crois que les moustiques sont en train de nous dévorer, dit-il d'une voix égale. On ferait peut-être bien de reprendre la route.

— Oui. C'est une bonne idée.

Elle tourna sur elle-même, hésita.

— Où est la sortie ?

— Par ici, je crois. Il y a une lumière.

— Allez-y, je vous suis.

Une fois de retour dans la partie éclairée des jardins, ils se dirigèrent sans parler vers la sortie. En chemin, ils passèrent devant des sculptures qu'il avait voulu admirer avec elle, mais ni l'un ni l'autre n'avait plus envie de s'attarder.

Sous un réverbère, il jeta un coup d'œil à sa montre. Presque 21 heures. Il reprenait son service dans deux heures.

Le trajet du retour fut une véritable torture. Les mains de Sarah autour de sa taille, son corps plaqué au sien… Si ce contact le troublait, tout à l'heure, maintenant, il le rendait fou. Serrant les dents, il poussa la moto à la limite de la vitesse autorisée.

Sur le parking du magasin de photo, il attendit qu'elle eût glissé de la selle. La sentant hésiter, il se retourna vers elle.

— C'est ridicule, murmura-t-elle d'une voix enrouée, mais je n'ai pas envie de monter dans la voiture. Je… Je ne veux pas descendre de la moto.

Il vit la frayeur dans ses yeux, et son cœur fondit de tendresse.

— Ce n'est pas ridicule du tout ! Il ne se passera rien, cette fois, je vous le garantis.

Il mit pied à terre, et lui tendit la main. Elle y glissa ses doigts, tout en soutenant son regard.

— D'accord. Je vous fais confiance.

Il lui prit les clés des mains, déverrouilla la jeep, jeta un coup d'œil à l'arrière, puis dans le coffre.

— Il n'y a personne. Vous pouvez monter.

Elle grimpa sur le siège avec plus d'aisance que la semaine précédente. Tout en bouclant sa ceinture, elle secoua la tête avec un sourire gêné.

— C'est passé. Désolée d'avoir fait tant d'histoires.

— Pas de problème. Je vous suis jusque chez vous.

— Ce n'est pas nécess…

Il l'interrompit en levant la main.

— Pas de discussion, Sarah Rose. Je veux m'assurer que vous rentrez chez vous sans problème.

Elle soupira, cessa de protester.

Un quart d'heure plus tard, ils se garaient tous les deux devant l'immeuble de la jeune femme. Luke descendit de moto, elle verrouilla la jeep, et ils grimpèrent ensemble l'escalier extérieur. Une fois la porte ouverte, la lumière allumée dans l'entrée, ils restèrent face à face, sans savoir que faire.

— Bon, tout va bien maintenant, dit-elle.

Il hocha la tête.

— Merci d'être venue, ce soir. J'ai passé une très bonne soirée.

C'était à la fois un mensonge et la vérité ; il ne s'y retrouvait plus lui-même. Elle lui sourit.

— Moi aussi. Je m'occupe de vos tirages et je vous les fais parvenir le plus vite possible.

Elle tenait déjà la poignée de la porte. C'était le moment pour lui de partir.

— Merci pour le dîner, ajouta-t-elle encore.

— Tout le plaisir était pour moi.

C'était absurde, toutes ces formules de politesse, il s'en rendait bien compte.

— Bonne nuit, Sarah Rose, dit-il enfin.

— Bonne nuit, caporal Brennan.

Il recula de deux pas, et elle referma la porte. Il entendit le bruit de la clé dans la serrure, et se sentit comme congédié.

Elle était en train d'étudier les photos qui ornaient les murs du magasin quand son associé entra.

— Tiens, te voilà ! Qu'est-ce que tu fais côté boutique ? lui demanda-t-il d'un air surpris.

— Luke Brennan a été impressionné par tes photos. Je voulais les voir. C'est du beau travail.

— Oh, grand merci ! minauda-t-il en époussetant le comptoir avec ostentation. Elles me rapportent une somme rondelette, de temps en temps.

— Tu en as vendu beaucoup ?

— Une vingtaine. J'ai mon public.

— C'est bien. Je suis contente pour toi.

Elle parlait sincèrement. Si Chuck réussissait à se faire une place, il serait moins jaloux de sa propre réussite. En supposant qu'elle se remît un jour au travail...

— Elles me font penser à Felix, mais il ne se servait pas de filtres colorés pour ses effets de lumière.

— C'est vrai ! J'ai pris ce que Felix m'avait enseigné, et j'ai continué sur la lancée. Ma carrière aura mis plus longtemps que la tienne à décoller, mais elle tient mieux la route.

Tout en lui lançant un sourire sournois, il proposa :

— Tu veux un café ?

— Non merci, répondit la jeune femme, luttant contre l'envie de le gifler. Je peux prendre la chambre noire ?

— Bien sûr : tu es chez toi ! Je suppose que c'est pour ça que Felix t'a légué la moitié du magasin. Il devait se douter que tu chercherais un emploi, un jour ou l'autre.

— J'en doute.

Elle n'avait pas l'énergie nécessaire pour entamer un nouveau round contre Chuck. Détournant la tête, elle passa derrière le comptoir. Sous prétexte de ranger les boîtes de pellicules sur leur présentoir, il ne s'effaça pas pour la laisser passer, et s'arrangea, au contraire, pour occuper tout le terrain.

Plus tard, quand elle ressortit de la chambre noire, il était rentré chez lui sans verrouiller la porte de derrière, ce qui signifiait que n'importe quel dingue, y compris son agresseur de l'autre soir, aurait pu entrer. La jeune femme poussa le verrou, prit un soda dans le frigo et se laissa tomber dans le vieux fauteuil de Felix. Elle avait besoin de réfléchir.

Luke. Elle sentait encore sa bouche sur la sienne ; elle entendait encore le grondement de plaisir vibrer dans sa poitrine. Elle n'avait pas une grande expérience des hommes : il y avait juste eu James. Personne d'autre. Et James s'intéressait à tant d'autres femmes…

Luke l'émouvait profondément… mais il ne se passerait rien entre eux. Il ne voyait pas en elle une amante. C'était le chagrin et la solitude qui le poussaient vers elle, le besoin de réconfort. Et elle, stupidement, elle ne mettait aucun obstacle entre eux : elle l'invitait quasiment à prendre tout ce qu'il voulait. S'il ne pouvait plus serrer dans ses bras la femme qu'il aimait, il pouvait toujours rêver à elle dans les bras d'une autre, n'est-ce pas ?

Cette idée lui fit affreusement mal. Elle se souvenait encore des femmes qui entouraient James : des beautés rencontrées dans des bars, des aventurières qui lui apportaient des informations et lui fournissaient des contacts. La première infidélité de James l'avait profondément blessée. A la troisième — au moment où ils avaient rompu —, elle avait appris à se protéger.

Elle sentait pourtant que Luke n'était pas comme James : loin de se servir des autres, il leur ouvrait son cœur, faisait des sacrifices pour eux. Sa situation actuelle en était un exemple : il avait épousé Kristin parce qu'elle était enceinte et que le père, qui se trouvait être son frère, était censé ne jamais revenir…

Comment refuser son cœur à un homme comme lui ?

En revanche, si elle allait trop loin, elle risquait de souffrir. Rien ne lui permettait de penser que Luke oublierait son ex-femme pour l'aimer, elle. Rien du tout.

Le mieux serait de lui poster ses photos, décida-t-elle. A lui de les distribuer à sa guise. De son côté, elle enverrait un jeu à son agent. Si quelqu'un faisait une offre, elle serait obligée de prendre contact avec Kristin et Matt pour leur demander de signer l'autorisation. Mais, d'ici là, à quoi bon s'inquiéter ?

— J'ai un reportage pour toi. Tu es prête à repartir ?

Elle chercha en elle un fond d'enthousiasme, mais ne trouva que de l'angoisse.

— Où ?

— En Amérique centrale. Il va y avoir une déclaration officielle au sujet d'un certain gouvernement militaire et du sort de bon nombre de citoyens disparus au cours des dix-huit dernières années. C'est un sujet en or : je veux tes photos.

— Qui fait le papier ?

— Len Markowitz. Tu en es ?

Elle se vit quitter Myrtle Beach, monter à bord d'un avion, débarquer dans l'atmosphère étouffante d'un pays du tiers-monde, son appareil photo à la main, prête à travailler. L'image la révulsa.

— Non, Oliver. Je suis désolée : je ne peux pas.

— Combien de temps est-ce que ça va durer, Sarah ? s'exclama-t-il. J'ai un hebdo à sortir ; nos lecteurs attendent tes photos. Sans parler des actionnaires.

Y avait-il un délai pour retrouver son courage ?

— Je ne sais pas combien de temps ça va durer, répondit-elle tristement. J'ai bien conscience du problème. Tu devrais peut-être embaucher quelqu'un d'autre.

— Peut-être.

Ce n'était pas une menace en l'air : Oliver disait toujours ce qu'il pensait. Elle ferma les yeux.

— Tu me tiens au courant, d'accord ? Une petite lettre de licenciement ?

— Sarah, je n'ai pas envie de faire ça, mais il me faut un photographe. Quel choix est-ce que tu me laisses ?

— Aucun, Oliver. Je comprends.

Il poussa un profond soupir.

— J'aimerais que tu prennes le dessus et que tu reviennes travailler. Tu n'en as pas envie ?

— Bien sûr que si ! Je fais de mon mieux pour m'en sortir.

Depuis sa soirée avec Luke à Brookgreen, elle passait le plus clair de son temps calfeutrée dans son appartement.

— Je t'appellerai dès que je me sentirai prête, dit-elle. Prends quelqu'un d'autre pour ce reportage.

— Si tu crois qu'on trouve des photographes de ton calibre à tous les coins de rue...

Il y eut un silence. Elle crut qu'il avait raccroché, mais il ajouta tout à coup :

— Au fait, il y a deux boîtes à ton nom, au courrier.

— Des dossiers ?

— Non, des lettres. Ils pensent qu'elles sont arrivées pendant que tu étais à l'étranger et qu'on les a mises de côté, sans penser à te les donner. Des lettres de Caroline du Sud.

Felix. Personne d'autre dans cet Etat n'avait de raison de lui écrire. Qu'avait-il pu lui envoyer ?

— Tu veux bien me les faire suivre ici ?

— Pas de problème.

S'éclaircissant la gorge, il reprit :

— Appelle-moi dès que tu auras décidé de revenir. Je vais prendre un photographe en *free lance*, en attendant.

— Merci. C'est très important pour moi que tu me fasses autant confiance.

— Tu le mérites.

Cette fois, il raccrocha.

Sarah resta longtemps assise, à contempler le téléphone muet. Et maintenant ? Oliver était adorable, mais, dans la presse, seuls les résultats comptaient. Les photographes traumatisés ou déprimés n'augmentaient pas le lectorat. On trouverait quelqu'un d'autre pour ce reportage, et si cette personne faisait du bon boulot, on finirait par l'engager fermement.

Si elle se retrouvait au chômage, l'argent ne poserait pas de problème immédiat. L'appartement et la jeep étaient payés. A force de passer le plus clair de son temps en voyage, tous frais payés, elle avait fait des économies. En revanche, sa vocation de photographe remplissait sa vie depuis qu'elle avait dix-huit ans. Sarah Randolph, photographe pour l'hebdomadaire *Events*, c'était son identité. Si elle la perdait, que lui resterait-il ? Qui serait-elle ? Où serait sa place ?

Vers qui se tourner, maintenant que ses parents, Felix, James étaient morts ? Il ne lui restait plus personne.

Qu'allait-elle faire ? Pour elle, désormais, le monde se résumait à ce point d'interrogation... et Luke Brennan ne pouvait pas être la solution.

— Désolé de vous avoir fait attendre, dit-il en passant la main dans ses cheveux. Vous avez quelque chose pour moi ?

— Un recommandé.

Elle était jeune, jolie, et elle lui souriait de façon charmante.

— Signez ici. Il fait chaud, hein ?

— Oui. Cette fois, l'été est bien arrivé.

82

Il lui rendit son calepin, et reçut, en échange, une grosse enveloppe rembourrée.

— Merci. Bonne journée !

Il fit de son mieux pour répondre à son sourire radieux. Sans un mot de plus, elle tourna les talons et rejoignit sa camionnette.

Tout en fermant la porte d'un coup d'épaule, il étudia l'enveloppe. Les photos, bien sûr ! Sarah les avait postées au lieu de les lui apporter. Affreusement déçu, il se laissa tomber sur le canapé. Il espérait tant la revoir !

Il finit par ouvrir l'enveloppe et, dès qu'il vit le premier cliché, il retrouva les sensations de ces quelques minutes passées sur la plage. La lumière, les sons, les odeurs… Alignées sur la table basse, les photos le narguaient.

Le droit de visite, entré en vigueur au moment du remariage de son ex-femme, ne lui accordait qu'une journée par semaine et un week-end sur trois. Une présence en pointillés dans la vie de ses filles. Avait-il seulement sa place dans cette famille reconstituée ? Entre leur maman et leur nouveau papa, Erin et Jenny avaient-elles encore besoin de lui ?

Ecartant momentanément cette question par trop cruelle, il réfléchit à la meilleure façon de faire parvenir les photos à Kristin.

En appelant son père, il apprit qu'un déjeuner de famille était prévu pour le dimanche suivant. L'aurait-on mis au courant s'il n'avait pas téléphoné ? Il ne posa pas la question, et se contenta de dire qu'il viendrait.

Il arriva à l'instant précis où la Cadillac de ses parents et le monospace de Kristin se rangeaient dans l'allée, au retour du temple. Son père leva la main pour le saluer ; sa mère hocha la tête et disparut, très affairée, par la porte de la cuisine. Matt et Kristin défaisaient les ceintures de sécurité des petites. Comme toujours, le véritable accueil vint des filles.

— Papa ! crièrent-elles en se précipitant vers lui.

Il souleva Jen dans ses bras, et serra Erin contre lui.

— Alors, les jolies ? C'était bien, le temple ?

Agrippée à lui, Erin répondit :

— On a parlé de Daniel dans la fosse aux lions ! Tu te rends compte qu'ils ne l'ont même pas dévoré ?

— J'ai dessiné une arche ! intervint Jennifer.

— Sauf qu'elle n'a mis que trois animaux ! Personne ne dessine une arche avec juste un ours, un canard et un zèbre.

— Les autres doivent être déjà à l'intérieur ! dit Luke.

— Ouais ! C'est justement ça ! fit Jennifer en lançant un coup de pied à sa sœur.

— Pas de coups ! lui dit Luke en la secouant doucement. On se met d'accord sans se taper, tu le sais bien !

Comme elle ne répondait pas, il insista :

— Tu te souviens ?

— Oui, je me souviens.

— Bonjour, Luke. Je suis contente de te voir.

C'était Kristin. Elle se tenait à deux pas de lui et, en même temps, elle paraissait complètement inaccessible.

Que pouvait-il lui répondre ? Il hocha la tête, et demanda platement :

— Tu retrouves tes marques après ce voyage ?

Elle regarda les filles courir après un goéland.

— Moi, ça va. Mais je crois que les filles ont un peu de mal à s'y retrouver.

— J'ai l'impression qu'elles ne sont pas faciles, en ce moment. Elles se disputent beaucoup ?

Lui aussi gardait les yeux fixés sur les enfants : c'était plus facile.

— Oui, elles se disputent sans arrêt.

— Il leur faut juste un peu de temps, trancha Matt qui venait de les rejoindre et posait déjà une main possessive sur l'épaule de sa femme.

— Bien sûr, répliqua Luke en soutenant son regard. On finit par s'habituer à tout, avec le temps. Les données sont plus faciles pour certains, mais à chacun son destin...

— Ne dis pas de conneries ! marmonna Matt.

— Ne sois donc pas aussi...

— Luke ! s'écria Kristin en lui saisissant le bras.

Par chance, la voix de Elena Brennan les interrompit. Plantée devant la porte d'entrée, elle appelait les filles. Luke s'écarta, et Kristin laissa retomber sa main.

— Allez-y, dit-il. Je prends quelque chose dans la voiture et je vous rejoins.

Il alla chercher l'enveloppe contenant les photos et, la serrant contre lui comme un talisman, il suivit ses filles, son ex-femme et son frère dans la fosse aux lions.

6.

Elena Brennan contempla les photos en silence. Puis elle poussa un profond soupir. Ses yeux bleus étaient très doux quand elle se tourna vers son mari.

— Elles sont belles. William, as-tu déjà vu des petites filles aussi belles ?

Luke se détendit un peu. Sa mère appréciait les photos, c'était déjà ça !

— Pas depuis...

Le Colonel s'éclaircit la gorge, et reprit :

— Pas depuis les photos de ta propre enfance, ma chérie.

Posant la main sur l'épaule de sa femme, il se pencha pour mieux voir.

— Il faudra trouver de jolis cadres, dit-il.

Kristin, qui était assise par terre avec Jenny, s'écria :

— Je n'arrive toujours pas à croire que tu sois sortie sur la plage dans cette robe, ma chérie ! Et si tu étais tombée à l'eau ?

Puis, en posant un baiser sur la tête blonde de sa fille, elle ajouta :

— En tout cas, elles sont magnifiques.

La mère de Luke leva les yeux vers elle.

— Vous avez beaucoup de chance d'avoir des filles, Kristin. La vie ne peut rien nous offrir de plus doux.

Pour une fois, sa voix tremblait un peu. Le Colonel eut un signe de tête vers Matt.

— Mais ce sont les fils qui perpétuent le nom ! Ce sont eux qui donnent à un homme sa place dans l'Histoire.

— C'est vrai, dit Elena, mais ces petits anges blonds… Je vais accrocher l'une de ces photos dans notre chambre. La grande. Et peut-être la petite dans la salle à manger ?

Elle prit l'un des clichés, et passa dans l'autre pièce pour chercher l'emplacement idéal. Erin s'accouda sur la table basse.

— Cette robe, elle tenait chaud. Et elle grattait ! J'ai failli mourir de suffocation.

Luke et Kristin éclatèrent de rire. Avec un léger temps de retard, Matt les imita.

— Tu as cru suffoquer, Erin l'Ourson ? demanda Luke. Mais, en fin de compte, tu as survécu !

— C'était tout juste.

La fillette prit une photo à son tour, et demanda :

— Je peux avoir celle-là pour ma chambre ?

— Bien sûr ! Tu peux…

Sa voix s'éteignit. Il venait de voir la photo qu'elle lui tendait : c'était celle où il était seul. Celle que Sarah n'aurait pas dû tirer.

— Fais voir ! dit Kristin.

Quand la petite tourna la photo vers elle, Luke vit qu'elle accusait le coup, elle aussi.

— C'est une… très jolie photo, Erin, dit-elle. On lui trouvera un cadre et on l'accrochera dans votre chambre pour que vous puissiez la voir tous les jours.

Luke risqua un coup d'œil vers Matt, assis dans un fauteuil, derrière Erin. Son visage était crispé.

Remettant Jenny sur ses pieds, Kristin se leva, impatiente de passer à autre chose.

— Nous allons ranger ces magnifiques clichés pour qu'il ne leur arrive rien pendant le repas.

Elle posa la main sur l'épaule de Matt, puis se tourna vers Luke.

— Tu déjeunes avec nous ?

Matt posa sur lui son regard bleu très dur. Luke se redressa.

— Pourquoi pas ? répondit-il en regardant son frère dans les yeux. Si ça ne dérange personne.

— Bien sûr que non ! s'écria Kristin, un peu trop vite. Qui veux-tu que ça dérange ?

— Elle était assise un peu plus haut sur la plage, expliquait Luke à ses filles. Elle avait un objectif spécial : c'est pour ça que vous avez l'air d'être prises de tout près.

Il la voyait encore telle qu'elle lui était apparue le premier jour : très mince, très bronzée, avec un chapeau de paille, le regard triste et lointain. Puis le tableau changea : il la retrouva dans le crépuscule d'un jardin parfumé. Ses cheveux châtains bouclaient encore davantage sous l'effet de la rosée… Elle avait des yeux rêveurs, juste avant qu'il l'embrassât.

— Votre père est ravi, déclara Elena, comme si cela réglait la question. Il a déjà emporté plusieurs photos dans la chambre.

Le Colonel avait quitté la table au milieu du repas, en prétendant qu'il se sentait fatigué.

Matt leva les yeux vers sa mère.

— Est-ce qu'il va bien ? Je le trouve plus fatigué que d'habitude.

Le front lisse d'Elena se plissa.

— Il ne veut pas l'admettre, bien sûr. Nous avons tout de même pris rendez-vous chez le médecin. Nous irons le mois prochain, après notre pique-nique de la fête de l'Indépendance. Vous serez tous là, bien sûr ?

Deux heures dans cette atmosphère, c'était déjà difficile. Luke se demanda comment il supporterait de passer l'après-midi et la soirée en famille, à faire comme si tout allait bien, comme s'il ne souffrait pas le martyre.

— Je peux apporter quelque chose ? Une salade composée, un dessert ?

Kristin proposait toujours sa contribution, et Elena trouvait systématiquement un prétexte pour refuser.

— Merci, non. Tout est déjà prévu.

Luke s'aperçut que lui aussi avait une question à poser.

— Ça ne vous ennuie pas si je viens avec une amie ?

Ils le regardèrent tous trois comme s'il venait de dire une incongruité.

— Tu parles de ton partenaire, Dominick ? lui demanda sa mère d'un air sceptique. Tu crois qu'il se sentirait à l'aise ?

Nick était à l'aise partout, mais les invités huppés de ses parents seraient sans doute un peu surpris par la présence de ce flic très terre à terre.

— Non, je pensais à Sarah Randolph. La photographe. Vous seriez probablement contents de la connaître.

— C'est une bonne idée, déclara Matt, le regard fixé sur son assiette. Je voudrais lui demander des copies de certaines photos, pour le bureau.

La décision finale revenait à la maîtresse de maison.

— Maman ?

— Eh bien, pourquoi pas ? Je suppose qu'elle est... présentable ?

— Tout à fait ! répondit Luke sans pouvoir retenir un sourire. Elle ne choquera personne, je peux vous l'assurer.

Il crut voir une étincelle d'humour dans les yeux de son frère, mais elle s'éteignit tout de suite et, dans le silence qui suivit, il comprit qu'il était temps pour lui de s'en aller.

— Bon, on se revoit le 4, dit-il. La même heure que d'habitude, maman ?

Elle lui présenta sa joue pour qu'il y déposât un baiser.

— A partir de 15 heures.

— Parfait. Nous y serons.

Il espérait de toutes ses forces que Sarah accepterait de l'accompagner.

— Je dis au revoir aux filles et je m'en vais. A bientôt, Kristin, Matt…

Kristin leva la main dans un geste plein de retenue, et Matt hocha la tête sans croiser son regard. C'était comme ça depuis un an et demi…

Erin et Jenny l'accompagnèrent jusqu'à la porte d'entrée. Il se mit à genoux, et les prit dans ses bras en murmurant :

— Je dois y aller, les jolies. Soyez sages.

Jenny se jeta à son cou.

— Quand est-ce que tu rentres à la maison, papa ?

Erin ouvrit la bouche pour lancer une réponse impatiente. Croisant son regard, Luke secoua légèrement la tête, et elle se tut.

— Je n'habite plus dans ta maison, maintenant, Jenny, murmura-t-il d'une voix rauque. Tu le sais bien !

— Mais je veux que tu reviennes.

— Je ne peux pas, mon cœur. C'est Matt qui habite avec ta maman, maintenant. Ils sont mariés.

La lèvre inférieure de la petite se mit à trembler.

— Mais j'aime mieux tes histoires à toi.

Il rit, malgré lui. Un petit rire étranglé.

— J'ai eu le temps de m'exercer. Donne du temps à Matt, et il sera aussi génial que moi. Peut-être même meilleur !

Matt avait toujours été plus doué que lui, dans tous les domaines... La fillette enfouit son visage dans son cou. Luke la serra doucement contre lui, et sentit la blessure de son cœur se rouvrir. Il éprouvait tant de tendresse pour sa petite fille !

Rassemblant son courage, il déclara :

— C'est l'heure de décoller, comme disent les poseurs de moquette.

Jenny releva la tête, perplexe.

— Comment ?

— C'est une plaisanterie ! fit Erin en levant les yeux au ciel.

— Mais c'est pas drôle.

— Si, quand on n'est pas un bébé de quatre ans.

— Je ne suis pas un bébé.

— Si !

— Stop ! Jenny, si tu allais choisir une photo, toi aussi ? Erin va m'accompagner à la voiture.

— Je veux venir aussi !

— Non. Mais je t'aime et je te dis à bientôt.

Il l'embrassa, la poussa doucement vers la cuisine, lui donna une petite tape pour jouer, et se tourna vers sa sœur.

— Tu es en train de compliquer les choses, Erin l'Ourson.

Luke se releva et, main dans la main, ils franchirent la porte et traversèrent le jardin en direction de la voiture.

— Pourquoi est-ce que tu es aussi dure avec elle ?

La petite haussa les épaules, et garda les yeux baissés.

— J'sais pas.

— Tu es sûre que tu ne sais pas ?

Elle secoua la tête. Elle était au bord des larmes. Luke s'accroupit, prit ses deux mains dans les siennes, et scruta son visage. Ses cheveux blonds et son teint de miel lui venaient de Kristin, mais comment ne pas reconnaître les yeux bleus de Matt ? Il trouvait stupéfiant que ni ses parents ni ceux de Kristin n'eussent remarqué la ressemblance. Ils ne devaient jamais la regarder vraiment !

En tout cas, il devait revenir à leur problème.

— Tu compliques la vie de ta maman, tu sais ? C'est difficile pour elle quand vous vous disputez.

Erin ne répondit pas, et garda la tête baissée.

— Tu veux bien faire quelque chose pour moi ?

— Quoi ?

— Tu veux bien être une grande fille et éviter de te fâcher avec Jen ? Elle fait de son mieux, mais elle est encore petite. Je ne peux compter que sur toi.

Il vit une larme glisser sur la joue d'Erin. Surpris et ému, il lui souleva le menton.

— Qu'est-ce qui se passe ? Je ne suis pas fâché contre toi ; je veux juste…

— Moi aussi, je veux que tu rentres à la maison !

Il prit une grande inspiration tremblante, et réussit à dire :

— Je vous ai déjà expliqué pourquoi c'est impossible. Tu m'as entendu, n'est-ce pas ?

— Mais je ne peux pas lui parler comme on parlait tous les deux. Il ne sait pas des trucs comme toi.

— Il sait des trucs différents, l'Ourson.

Il fouilla ses souvenirs.

— Quand on était gamins, Matt aimait les livres d'histoire. Les conquérants, les explorateurs, les grandes découvertes. Je parie qu'il te raconterait plein de choses là-dessus.

Pas de réponse. Juste un soupir.

— Et il joue très bien au base-ball. Bien mieux que moi. Demande-lui de t'apprendre le lancer : il sera content de le faire.

La tête blonde s'appuya contre son épaule.

— C'est trop dur. Ça ne me plaît pas. Pourquoi on ne peut pas rester comme on était ?

— Bientôt, ça ira mieux. Il faut juste qu'on fasse tous un peu attention les uns aux autres. Pendant un petit moment. C'est ce que je te demande. D'accord ?

En serrant son papa contre elle, elle marmonna :

— D'accord.

— C'est bien. C'est très bien. Maintenant, je vais m'en aller.

— Papa ?

Les yeux de la fillette étaient toujours humides. D'une toute petite voix, elle demanda :

— Tu veux bien m'appeler de temps en temps ? Je laisserai Jen te parler aussi.

Luke avait très envie de le lui promettre, mais il songea aux problèmes que cela risquait de créer.

— Tu sais quoi ? dit-il en s'accroupissant de nouveau pour être à sa hauteur. C'est toi qui vas m'appeler. Je suis chez moi presque tous les jours, jusqu'à l'heure où tu te couches. Si tu as envie de me parler, je pense que maman sera d'accord. Et à moi, ça me fera très plaisir.

La petite prit une profonde inspiration.

— D'accord. Mais j'appellerai peut-être pas tous les jours : papa Matt finirait par se vexer.

Luke dut faire un gros effort sur lui-même pour retenir ses propres larmes.

— Bien vu, Erin l'Ourson, dit-il dans un brouillard. Je savais que je pouvais compter sur toi. Un bisou !

Quelques secondes plus tard, la fillette s'éloignait au galop vers la maison. Quand elle fut hors de sa vue, Luke eut l'impression qu'on avait tranché net les fils qui le tenaient debout. Maladroitement, à tâtons, il monta dans sa voiture, démarra et resta assis, incapable de bouger, tandis que la climatisation l'enveloppait d'un air glacial.

Sarah, pensa-t-il tout à coup. Sarah allait l'aider ! Il se tiendrait correctement, et elle se sentirait en sécurité avec lui. Elle accepterait de le voir de temps en temps... Il se contrôlait, maintenant. Dès qu'il serait rentré, il lui passerait un coup de fil.

C'était la fête de l'Indépendance, et ils roulaient vers la maison du Colonel. Sarah écoutait son compagnon lui raconter ses expériences de policier.

— Violences physiques ? répéta-t-elle, bouche bée.

— Les affaires ne sont jamais arrivées jusqu'au tribunal. Les deux femmes ont quitté la ville.

— Qu'est-ce que ça veut dire ?

Luke gara la voiture, puis se tourna vers sa passagère, tout en posant le bras sur le dossier de la banquette.

— Ça veut dire, Sarah Rose, que vous devriez trouver un autre endroit pour développer vos photos. Ce type ne vous aime pas. Il pourrait très bien se révéler dangereux.

— Vous pensez que...

Elle se massa les tempes, essayant d'assimiler la terrible nouvelle.

— Je l'aurais tout de même reconnu, non ? Si c'était lui qui...

— Pas obligatoirement. Le type vous a surprise.

Il posa la main sur son épaule, et elle frémit.

— Je ne peux pas croire que Chuck soit capable de...
ça.

— Vous n'êtes pas obligée de le croire. Tout ce que je vous demande, c'est de ne pas retourner là-bas.

— Mais...

A la seule idée de ne jamais retourner au studio, Sarah sentait sa gorge se serrer.

— Toutes mes archives sont là-bas !

— Allez les chercher, un jour où il n'est pas là, et emportez toutes vos photos.

Elle regardait droit devant elle, les yeux brouillés de larmes.

— C'était le studio de Felix. J'y ai travaillé avec lui. Il m'a laissé la moitié du magasin. De *son* magasin. Comment pourrais-je m'en aller ?

— Vous devez le faire, tout simplement.

Avec beaucoup de douceur, il lui prit le menton et tourna son visage vers lui.

— Chuck risque de recommencer. En admettant que ce soit lui, bien sûr. Et, dans ce cas, ce sera peut-être pire que la première fois.

Il essuya une larme sur sa joue en murmurant :

— Je ne peux pas vous laisser prendre un tel risque.

Quelle intensité dans son regard ! Sarah résista à l'envie de presser sa joue au creux de sa paume. Il ne devait pas savoir à quel point elle désirait se rapprocher de lui.

— Vous avez parlé à Chuck ?

Comme elle s'écartait un peu, il laissa retomber sa main.

— Pas encore. J'ai préféré attendre que vous soyez hors de sa portée.

— Je...

Il avait sans doute raison, mais, depuis quelque temps, déjà, la raison n'avait plus beaucoup de prise sur elle.

— J'ai besoin de preuves pour bouleverser mon existence.

Il la regarda, surpris par sa véhémence.

— Comment savoir si ces accusations sont vraies ? s'exclama-t-elle. Les femmes dont vous parlez ont très bien pu raconter n'importe quoi.

— C'est possible, répondit-il patiemment, mais, en attendant d'en savoir plus, inutile de risquer votre vie.

— C'est moi qui ai été agressée, dit-elle avec toute la fermeté dont elle était capable. Felix m'a légué une responsabilité, et j'ai l'intention de l'assumer. Je lui dois bien ça. Je me le dois à moi-même.

Luke se détourna, et contempla en silence ses mains posées sur le volant. Elle cherchait une phrase plus conciliante quand il laissa sa tête retomber en arrière.

— Vous êtes majeure, Sarah Rose : je ne peux pas vous obliger à faire attention à vous, même si j'en ai très envie.

Avec un soupir, il ajouta :

— Maintenant que j'y pense, vous vous êtes retrouvée dans des situations encore plus dangereuses que moi, au cours de ma vie de flic.

Elle pensa à James, puis se hâta de repousser son image.

— C'est arrivé quelquefois, murmura-t-elle.

— Mais je ne renoncerai pas avant de savoir si, oui ou non, c'est Sawyer qui vous a attaquée. Quand j'aurai découvert quelque chose…

— Je vous écouterai, c'est promis.

— J'espère seulement qu'il ne sera pas trop tard.

Avant qu'elle ne pût répondre, il se redressa et lui demanda d'un ton léger :

— Alors, qu'en dites-vous ? Vous êtes d'humeur à fêter notre Indépendance ?

Bizarre. Cette femme ne correspondait pas du tout à l'image qu'elle s'en était faite. Sous son large chapeau entouré d'un foulard brun, elle était menue, presque fragile. Un fourreau de lin très simple la couvrait des épaules aux chevilles, ne laissant à nu que ses bras bronzés. L'impression globale était discrète, et même assez austère. Kristin s'attendait à quelqu'un de plus... voyant.

Sa propre réaction la surprit : un besoin presque physique de tout savoir de cette femme qui venait d'entrer dans la vie de Luke.

S'éclaircissant la gorge, elle s'avança à leur rencontre avec toute l'assurance dont elle était capable. Elle vit alors sur son visage un sourire comme il n'en avait pas eu depuis le retour de Matt...

— Luke, bonjour ! Tu nous amènes Mlle Randolph ?

— Tout juste ! Sarah, je vous présente Kristin Brennan.

— Je suis si contente de vous rencontrer ! dit Kristin, la main tendue. Les photos que vous avez prises des filles sont magnifiques. C'est très gentil d'avoir fait des tirages pour nous.

L'attitude de Sarah la surprit : elle se montra polie mais distante, et c'est à peine si elle lui rendit son sourire.

— Ce n'est rien, dit-elle calmement. Le tableau était trop beau : je ne pouvais pas le laisser passer.

Aucune chaleur non plus dans sa voix un peu enrouée.

— Vos filles sont très belles, ajouta-t-elle, néanmoins.

— Merci. C'est aussi notre avis.

— Où sont-elles ? demanda Luke en jetant un regard à la ronde.

— Elles se promènent sur la plage avec Matt.

Kristin hésita un instant, puis décida de prendre un risque.

— Va donc les chercher, Luke ! Pendant ce temps-là, je présenterai Sarah à tes parents, et je la soutiendrai pendant qu'ils lui réclameront une foule de nouveaux tirages.

Les yeux plissés, Luke contempla son ex-femme pendant quelques secondes, puis se retourna vers sa compagne.

— Et si vous veniez à la plage avec moi, Sarah ?

— Oh, non, allez-y tout seul ! lança la jeune femme, en souriant, cette fois.

Kristin hocha la tête, et se tourna vers son invitée.

— Entrez ! Nous allons vous trouver quelque chose à boire.

Les questions se bousculaient déjà dans sa tête. Comment s'assurer que son ex-mari n'était pas en train de commettre une nouvelle et terrible erreur ?

Ils échangèrent des saluts neutres, et se tournèrent vers les filles.

— Elles trouvent toujours à s'occuper, sur la plage, dit Luke.

— C'est un endroit magique, pour les enfants.

C'était triste de n'avoir que des lieux communs à échanger avec son frère. Mais, entre eux, tous les sujets étaient minés.

— Tu as amené ta photographe ?

Luke hocha affirmativement la tête. Le fracas des vagues, l'appel des goélands ponctuèrent le long silence qui suivit. Puis Erin se retourna.

— Papa !

Les deux filles remontèrent la plage au pas de charge, et dépassèrent Matt pour se jeter dans les bras de son frère.

— Bonjour ! s'écria Luke en les serrant contre lui. La fête se passe bien ?

Matt fourra les mains dans les poches de son short, et se retourna pour contempler le panorama. La plage, les rochers et, au loin, la silhouette brumeuse des hôtels du bord de mer. Derrière lui, Jenny et Erin parlaient à toute vitesse. En les écoutant, il apprit qu'elles étaient allées faire les magasins avec leur grand-mère, qu'elles avaient mangé des glaces, qu'elles étaient entrées dans une animalerie où il y avait des chiots adorables et qu'un jour, elles avaient trouvé un coquillage rare sur la plage. Un coquillage entier, sans un défaut... mais elles l'avaient perdu sur le chemin du retour. Autant d'événements dont elles ne lui avaient jamais parlé.

Serrant les dents, il ravala sa jalousie. Les changements importants ne se faisaient pas du jour au lendemain. Les filles apprendraient à l'aimer... avec le temps. Ce fichu temps ! Il en venait à se demander s'il y avait assez de temps sous le soleil pour régler les problèmes de cette famille. Pendant leur semaine en Floride, il avait eu l'impression de gagner du terrain. Il comprenait, maintenant, que la nouveauté du lieu, des repas au restaurant, des parcs d'attractions et de la pluie de dépenses avaient tout juste servi à masquer l'hostilité d'Erin et la perplexité de Jenny.

— Matt ?

Il se retourna vers le trio.

— On retourne à la maison. Tu viens ?

Les petites couraient déjà dans le sable meuble. Matt hocha la tête.

— Je vous rejoins dans cinq minutes.

Le temps de contrôler sa colère. Il savait trop bien à quel point Kris souffrait de la tension qui existait entre Luke et lui. Et les rapports difficiles qu'elle entretenait avec ses filles ne faisaient rien pour alléger l'atmosphère.

En fait, Kristin ressemblait de moins en moins à une mariée radieuse et de plus en plus à une femme minée par les soucis. Des soucis qu'elle ne lui confiait pas ! A une époque, ils étaient aussi proches qu'il est possible de l'être ; ils se comprenaient toujours à demi mot. Maintenant, il n'avait aucune idée de ce qui se passait dans sa tête. Aussi distante que les filles, elle ne lui disait rien de ses pensées. Il ne comprenait pas. Regrettait-elle d'avoir mis fin à son mariage avec Luke ? Ces cernes sous ses yeux, cette résignation...

Lentement, il remonta vers la maison de ses parents. Sa mère avait toujours compté sur lui lorsqu'elle donnait des réceptions : il devait parler à tous ses amis, les écouter attentivement, les mettre à l'aise. Son père l'encourageait à discuter politique avec les hommes, et à souligner discrètement sa supériorité en tant que soldat de la quatrième génération.

Depuis le bas des marches, il contempla la foule bruyante et gaie rassemblée autour de la piscine. Dans quelques heures, la plupart d'entre eux seraient légèrement ivres, et impatients d'exprimer leurs opinions à quiconque voudrait les entendre. Ce serait son boulot de les écouter.

Il ferait ce que ses parents attendaient de lui. Il se montrerait patient avec les filles, gagnerait leur affection à force de gentillesse et de disponibilité. Il continuerait à aimer Kris de toute son âme — pour cela, au moins, il n'aurait pas à se faire violence. Il ne lui mettrait pas la pression ; il attendrait qu'elle se décidât à lui confier ses pensées et ses espoirs.

Quant à lui… il lui restait à définir précisément ce qu'il attendait de cette nouvelle vie. Ce qu'il en attendait, et la manière dont il allait s'y prendre pour l'obtenir.

7.

Une délicieuse fraîcheur accueillit Sarah dès le seuil de la maison. Devant son sourire de bien-être, l'ex-femme de Luke lui sourit.

— Je ne comprendrai jamais comment on a pu vivre en Caroline du Sud avant la climatisation.

Un peu à contrecœur, Sarah répondit sur le même ton :

— Ma grand-mère l'a fait toute sa vie. Mais elle avait une toute petite maison, et ses fenêtres étaient toujours ouvertes.

Dans cette demeure imposante, par contre, on ne devait jamais ouvrir les fenêtres.

— Vous êtes originaire de Myrtle Beach ? lui demanda Kristin, tout en versant du thé glacé dans deux grands verres déjà garnis de rondelles de citron et de feuilles de menthe.

— Non, mais je venais la voir tous les étés, répondit Sarah en acceptant le verre que son hôtesse lui tendait. Je me souviens de l'air frais qui soufflait dans toutes les pièces.

Après avoir réfléchi un instant, elle ajouta :

— Ça me semblerait peut-être moins idyllique, aujourd'hui. J'étais très jeune.

— Nous avons tous été très jeunes !

Un homme très grand qui se tenait très droit venait de les rejoindre. Visiblement un ancien militaire.

— Qui est votre invitée, Kristin ? demanda-t-il cordialement.

La jeune femme fit les présentations et, pendant dix bonnes minutes, le colonel Brennan fit subir à Sarah un véritable interrogatoire. La carrière de son père dans l'armée de l'air, celle de sa mère dans l'enseignement, ses propres références, les biographies de ses grands-parents, tout y passa… Sarah répondit en s'efforçant de cacher son agacement, mais quand il s'interrompit enfin pour reprendre son souffle, elle se hâta de changer le sujet :

— Vous devez être fier de vos fils, Colonel.

— Effectivement !

Le vieil homme se mit à réciter l'impressionnant *curriculum vitæ* de Matt, et conclut par ces mots :

— Il ne tardera pas à demander son transfert dans une unité des forces spéciales.

Kristin pâlit brusquement. Mais le Colonel ne sembla pas remarquer sa détresse.

— Matt est un homme d'honneur pour qui l'essentiel est de servir son pays. Il nous en faudrait davantage comme lui.

— Nous avons également besoin d'hommes comme Luke, rétorqua Sarah, le plus posément qu'elle put. Je ne sais pas comment je m'en serais sortie sans lui, après mon agression.

— Comment ? Qu'est-ce qui s'est passé ? demanda Kristin, horrifiée.

Sarah raconta l'épisode brièvement, sans mentionner sa nuit chez Luke.

— Il m'a aidée à faire toutes les démarches nécessaires, le lendemain.

— Ça ne m'étonne pas de lui, dit Kristin d'une voix douce.

— Nous aurions moins besoin de protection policière si tous les jeunes faisaient leur service militaire, répliqua le Colonel. L'Armée ferait d'eux des hommes responsables.

A cet instant, la porte-fenêtre donnant sur la terrasse s'ouvrit, et Luke apparut, portant Jenny dans ses bras.

— Ah, vous voilà ! dit-il. Bonjour, papa. Vous avez fait la connaissance de Sarah ?

— Oui, oui, répondit le vieux monsieur qui n'avait d'yeux que pour sa petite-fille. Qui est là, c'est mademoiselle Jenny ? Tu viens voir ton pépé ?

La petite secoua la tête en resserrant son étreinte autour du cou de Luke.

— Bon, on se verra tout à l'heure ! lança le Colonel. Bienvenue, mademoiselle Randolph.

S'inclinant poliment, il les quitta et disparut dans les profondeurs de la maison.

— Vieille baderne, marmonna Luke.

Sarah faillit éclater de rire, mais Kristin braqua sur son ex-mari un regard sévère.

— Les enfants peuvent t'entendre !

— Désolé.

Gentiment, Luke présenta Sarah à sa fille.

— Jenny Penny, voilà la dame qui t'a prise en photo. Mlle Randolph.

— Je préfère que tu m'appelles Sarah, dit la jeune femme avec un sourire. Tu étais comme une princesse dans ta belle robe.

Jenny contempla Sarah, puis sa mère. Sans répondre, elle posa la tête sur l'épaule de son père.

— Luke ?

Sarah ne connaissait pas encore cette voix douce, cultivée, à l'accent délicat du Sud. Elle se retourna, et croisa le regard d'une femme grande et mince, aux cheveux blancs merveilleusement bien coupés.

— Luke, tu veux bien nous présenter ?

Son accent évoquait les gardénias et le froissement des crinolines, mais ses yeux bleu pâle semblaient vous jauger sans la moindre indulgence. Luke s'éclaircit la gorge.

— Maman, voici Sarah Randolph. Sarah, je vous présente ma mère, Elena Brennan.

Sarah tendit la main.

— Je suis heureuse de vous rencontrer, madame Brennan. C'est très aimable à vous de m'avoir invitée.

Une paume lisse effleura la sienne.

— Vous êtes la bienvenue…

Un instant plus tard, elle se tournait vers sa petite-fille, et son visage se trouva transfiguré par la tendresse.

— Jennifer chérie, je suis contente que tu aies mis la robe que je t'ai offerte !

Toute froideur envolée, elle souriait tout en caressant les cheveux de l'enfant. D'une secousse, Jenny enfouit sa tête plus profondément dans le cou de son père.

— Je crois que cette petite fille a besoin d'une sieste, dit Kristin en venant lui prendre la taille. Viens, mon cœur, on va lire une histoire.

— Non !

— Je te la lirai, moi, ton histoire. Viens avec ta mamie.

Par une manœuvre habile, Mme Brennan s'était interposée et tentait à son tour de prendre la petite dans ses bras.

— Non, non ! Je veux papa !

En entendant ce cri, quelques invités se retournèrent, surpris. Mme Brennan recula en serrant les lèvres. Luke lui lança un sourire d'excuse auquel elle ne répondit pas.

— D'accord, Jenny Penny, dit-il. Tu me veux, tu m'as. Sarah peut venir avec nous ?

La petite hésita, puis finit par approuver de la tête, sans regarder personne.

Ils montèrent au premier étage, et pénétrèrent dans une pièce remplie d'arcs-en-ciel et de comètes.

— Quelle jolie chambre ! s'écria Sarah en ouvrant le lit que lui indiquait Luke. Tu dois faire des rêves extraordinaires, ici !

Jenny se contenta de la regarder sans expression aucune, tout en suçant son pouce.

— Elle est très fatiguée…

Luke posa sa fille au creux de son lit, la couvrit, approcha un rocking-chair et fit signe à Sarah de s'y asseoir.

— Je parie qu'elle dormira avant le passage de la vieille dame qui dit « chut ».

La petite fille eut beau secouer la tête, son père avait raison. A la quatrième page du livre, ses yeux se fermèrent, et sa respiration prit le rythme lent du sommeil. Luke tira le drap sur ses épaules, passa un doigt sur sa joue.

Emue, Sarah murmura :

— C'est un ange.

— Oui, dit-il, le regard fixé sur sa fille. Nous ferions bien de rejoindre les invités…

Dans l'escalier, il passa le bras autour des épaules de Sarah.

— Je suis désolé que Jen n'ait pas été plus gentille. Elle est toujours grognon quand elle est fatiguée. Elle sera contente de vous parler, tout à l'heure.

Il se trompait. Vers 18 heures, Kristin ressortit sur la terrasse avec Jenny. Joyeuse, pas du tout intimidée par les groupes d'adultes qui l'entouraient, la petite s'installa devant une petite table sur laquelle trônaient un château, des princesses en robes diaphanes et un prince sur un blanc destrier.

Tandis que Luke rentrait chercher des glaçons à la demande de sa mère, Sarah alla s'asseoir près d'elle.

— Tu as un beau château. Tes poupées ont des noms ?

Sans répondre, Jenny se mit à changer la position des personnages.

— Ta sœur joue au château avec toi ?

— Sûrement pas ! C'est un jeu de bébé ! lança une voix dédaigneuse, tout près d'elles.

Sarah sourit et s'adressa à Erin.

— Ton papa m'a dit que tu aimais les animaux. Quel est celui que tu préfères ?

Visiblement, Erin n'avait pas envie de parler, elle non plus. Elle marmonna quelque chose, et s'éloigna dans la foule. Jenny jouait toujours en silence. Sarah attendit quelques minutes, puis fit encore quelques commentaires qui ne reçurent aucune réponse, et finit par s'éloigner.

Elle ne devait pas savoir parler aux enfants. Après tout, son expérience se limitait aux victimes des famines en Afrique, trop faibles et malades pour jouer, aux petits qui sautaient sur des mines en Asie, aux martyrs des guerres ethniques d'Europe centrale. Voilà les gosses qu'elle avait l'habitude de fréquenter. Des photos, prises autrefois, lui revinrent à l'esprit. Elle ferma les yeux et détourna la tête.

— Sarah ? Ça ne va pas ?

La paume tiède de Luke vint se poser sur sa joue.

Elle se reprit, et revint au moment présent : à cette fête au sein de la bonne société de Caroline du Sud.

— Si, tout va bien.

— A quoi pensez-vous ?

— Euh… rien dont j'aie envie de parler en ce moment.

Elle lui sourit, vit ses yeux gris s'éclairer, et ajouta :

— En revanche, je prendrais bien un autre verre.

— Enfin un problème que je suis capable de régler !

Cette Sarah croyait peut-être qu'elle jouait aux mêmes jeux que Jenny ? Elle ne savait donc pas que les filles pouvaient jouer à autre chose qu'à la poupée ? Assise sur la dernière marche de l'escalier donnant sur la plage, Erin enfonça ses pieds dans le sable en se demandant si cette fête allait durer toute la nuit.

Derrière elle, quelqu'un descendit les marches. Elle ne releva pas la tête, même quand cette Sarah s'assit sur la marche juste au-dessus d'elle.

— A quoi penses-tu ?

— A rien.

— C'est un rien plutôt triste, alors.

La fillette haussa les épaules en enfouissant les pieds plus profondément dans le sable.

— Si on partait d'ici en bateau, dit lentement la dame, comme si elle réfléchissait tout haut, et qu'on voguait tout droit, où crois-tu qu'on arriverait ?

Erin connaissait la réponse ; elle en avait souvent parlé avec son papa.

— En Afrique.

— Tu as sûrement raison. Qu'est-ce qu'on verrait, là-bas ?

— La jungle. Les animaux.

— Quel animal aimerais-tu voir en premier ?

Cela méritait réflexion. Erin prit son temps avant de répondre :

— Des lions, peut-être.

— Les lions sont magnifiques. Un jour, j'en ai vu tout un groupe qui dormait à l'ombre d'un arbre. Ils avaient l'air très doux ; on serait presque allés les toucher.

Cette fois, Erin se retourna.

— Tu es allée là-bas ?

Puis elle se rappela que cette dame ne lui plaisait pas, et se remit à contempler l'océan. Sarah ne se formalisa pas pour autant.

— J'ai passé un certain temps en Afrique à prendre des photos, dit-elle.

— Tu veux dire : comme un safari-photo ?

— En général, ce sont surtout les gens que je photographie, mais j'ai aussi fait un ou deux safaris-photos.

— Tu as dormi dans les arbres ?

Sarah se mit à rire. Elle avait un rire agréable.

— J'aurais bien aimé, mais les guides avaient apporté des tentes.

— Les lions ont attaqué votre campement ?

— Non, jamais.

Déçue, Erin posa son menton sur ses genoux.

— Par contre, un jour, un rhinocéros a attaqué notre camionnette.

— C'est vrai ? Tu as eu peur ?

— J'étais terrorisée.

Fascinée, Erin oublia qu'elle ne voulait pas regarder cette Sarah en face. Et elle dut admettre que ses yeux aussi étaient agréables. Ils souriaient.

— J'ai pris photo sur photo, en espérant que quelqu'un ferait démarrer la camionnette avant que le rhinocéros ait tout défoncé.

— C'est *cool* !

— Qu'est-ce qui est *cool* ?

Luke dévala les marches, vint s'asseoir à côté d'Erin, et tendit un verre à Sarah en lui disant :

— Voilà pour vous.

Puis il ébouriffa les cheveux d'Erin.

— De quoi est-ce que vous parlez, toutes les deux ?

Comme Sarah ne répondait pas, la fillette expliqua :

— Un rhinocéros a attaqué sa voiture, un jour. C'est génial, hein ?

— Je crois que j'aurais eu très peur, à sa place.

— J'ai aussi vu le désert. Des montagnes de sable, dit Sarah en se penchant pour en prendre une poignée qu'elle laissa filer entre ses doigts. Rien que du sable pendant des centaines de kilomètres.

— Vous aviez un chameau ? demanda papa.

— Une journée à dos de chameau à l'aller, une journée pour le retour. Pas d'eau, pas d'ombre… Si vous saviez comme j'étais contente de revoir les dattiers !

Elle fit une grimace, mima un frisson d'horreur. Elle était drôle, quand elle voulait !

Au-dessus, sur la terrasse, la voix de papa Matt couvrit le brouhaha des invités. Heurtant les outils du barbecue l'un contre l'autre comme une cloche fêlée, il criait :

— Les steaks sont prêts ! Venez vous servir !

Papa se releva, et tendit la main à Sarah. Erin fronça les sourcils, mais dès que la dame fut sur pied, il la lâcha et demanda.

— Tu as faim, Erin l'Ourson ?

Sarah grimpait déjà les marches sans les attendre. Soulagée, Erin glissa la main dans celle de son père en soufflant :

— Je peux manger avec toi, papa ?

— Ah, te voilà ! s'écria maman, du haut des marches. Je me demandais où tu étais passée. Je t'ai préparé une assiette et je t'ai gardé une place à côté de Jenny. Viens manger.

— Mais… protesta-t-elle en levant les yeux vers son père.

— Ne t'en fais pas, ma grande, dit-il. On se retrouve après le dîner, d'accord ?

Il préférait manger avec la dame ! Erin se mit à bouder. Dès qu'ils arrivèrent sur la terrasse, elle lui lâcha la main, passa de force entre sa mère et Sarah sans même dire pardon, et alla s'installer près de Jenny. Maman la suivit et s'assit avec ses deux filles. Jenny et elle bavardèrent pendant tout le repas, mais Erin ne prononça pas un mot. Elle n'avait rien à dire à personne.

— Votre frère fait des steaks fantastiques, dit Sarah. Ça fait des années que je n'ai rien mangé d'aussi délicieux.

— Avant, mon père se chargeait toujours du barbecue. Depuis le retour de Matt, il a laissé sa place… C'est vrai qu'ils sont bons.

— Votre famille reçoit beaucoup ?

Il s'installa plus confortablement sur sa chaise. C'était bon de pouvoir enfin se détendre.

— Plus tellement. Quand j'étais petit, il y avait très souvent du monde. Ça fait partie de la vie militaire.

— Mes parents aussi invitaient souvent des amis ou des relations. On me demandait généralement de rester dans ma chambre.

— Pourquoi ?

— Parce que je faisais toujours une gaffe épouvantable. C'était comme une fatalité.

— Comment ? Vous aussi ?

Enchanté, il but une gorgée de soda, et secoua la tête.

— Matt était capable de rester planté là pendant des heures, droit comme un I, à dire « oui, monsieur », « non, madame », les vêtements propres, les chaussures bien cirées. Moi, il fallait aller me repêcher dans le bassin des poissons rouges.

— Un soir, j'ai renversé dix litres de punch aux fraises sur les uniformes et les robes d'été.

111

Elle avait un rire adorable ! Comme il voulait l'entendre encore, il raconta :

— Un jour, les chiens m'ont échappé : ils sont passés à travers les jets du système d'arrosage, sur les plates-bandes fraîchement retournées, et se sont précipités sur un groupe de dames qui prenaient le thé.

— Oh, non ! J'ai fait la même chose avec des chats. Et les chats, ça griffe, surtout quand ils ont peur ! Il y en avait même un perché sur le chapeau d'une dame particulièrement élégante !

— Sarah Rose, je crois bien que vous me battez. A moins que… vous vous êtes déjà cassé le bras au beau milieu d'un dîner de douze personnes ?

Enchantée, elle se pencha en avant, les coudes sur la table.

— Racontez.

Il lui confia l'histoire de sa pire humiliation — la pire de son enfance, en tout cas.

Il égrenait encore ses souvenirs quand sa mère apporta solennellement son gâteau de fête, couronné de fraises, de mûres et de bâtonnets lanceurs d'étincelles. Son père fit son discours habituel, puis les invités chantèrent en chœur quelques couplets patriotiques.

Luke suivait vaguement cette cérémonie informelle ; il était surtout attentif à la façon dont les bougies éclairaient le visage et les cheveux de Sarah. En trois semaines, les traces de son agression avaient presque disparu. Cette lumière douce et changeante lui faisait comme une auréole dorée, chaleureuse. Il eut envie de réclamer une part de cette chaleur, esquissa même un geste pour couvrir sa main de la sienne… A cet instant, dans un grand remue-ménage de chaises et un brouhaha d'exclamations, les invités descendirent sur la plage pour assister au feu d'artifice municipal. Sarah se leva.

— Je vais demander à votre mère si je peux l'aider à débarrasser.

Luke fit une petite grimace, et voulut l'arrêter. Mais elle se dirigeait déjà vers les portes-fenêtres. Il la rattrapa juste à temps pour entendre la réponse de sa mère.

— Merci, non. J'ai mes habitudes : vous ne feriez que m'embrouiller.

— Oh ! murmura Sarah, stupéfaite et confuse. Alors, je me contenterai de vous remercier encore pour cette journée.

Elena inclina la tête.

— De rien. Maintenant, si vous voulez bien m'excuser, j'ai beaucoup de travail.

Sarah recula, et se heurta à la poitrine de Luke. Instinctivement, il lui prit les épaules. Quand ses paumes touchèrent sa peau lisse et nue, il se sentit parcouru par une décharge électrique.

— Venez voir le feu d'artifice, dit-il.

La petite foule s'était rassemblée sur la plage. Du haut des marches, Sarah jeta un regard furtif vers la maison.

— C'est à cause de moi ou votre mère tient vraiment à faire tout toute seule ? demanda-t-elle.

— Elle ne laisse pas Kristin faire grand-chose non plus, si ça peut vous rassurer.

Cette fois, Sarah se laissa entraîner sur la plage. Le sable était encore tiède, mais une brise se levait. Elle frissonna.

— Vous avez froid ?

— Un peu.

— C'est mieux comme ça ? lui demanda-t-il en passant un bras autour de ses épaules.

Il s'attendait un peu à être rabroué, mais elle ne se raidit même pas. Au contraire, il sentit qu'elle se rapprochait un peu de lui.

— Bien mieux, merci.

Ils atteignaient le bord de l'eau quand les premières fusées jaillirent dans un bruit d'explosion. Sarah leva la tête vers son compagnon, et lui adressa un sourire.

— J'adore les feux d'artifice.

— Alors, celui-ci est pour vous. Je vous le dédie.

A quelques mètres, elle vit Erin et Jenny avec leur mère et Matt. Erin se tenait bien plantée sur ses jambes, les mains croisées dans le dos, la tête levée dans l'attente du prochain bouquet de lumière, mais Jenny, blottie dans les bras de sa mère, cachait son visage et sursautait à chaque explosion. Bientôt, Kristin glissa un mot à l'oreille de son mari, et retourna vers la maison. Sans doute pensait-elle que la petite avait eu sa dose d'émotion.

Au moment où elles atteignaient les marches, le feu d'artifice s'intensifia. Le ciel s'emplit de toupies aveuglantes, le bruit devint assourdissant. Quand les détonations s'apaisèrent Sarah entendit une plainte aiguë. Jenny se débattait de toutes ses forces en cherchant à échapper aux bras de sa mère.

— Papa ! hurlait-elle. Je veux mon papa !

Luke se précipita… et s'arrêta net au bout de quelques pas. Car Matt aussi avait répondu à l'appel, et il était arrivé le premier. Il prit Jenny dans ses bras et s'efforça de la calmer, mais elle se débattit de plus belle, le repoussant de toutes ses forces, pleurant à gros sanglots. Presque malgré lui, Luke fit encore quelques pas… Kristin avait repris sa fille dans ses bras, et elle grimpait déjà les marches en direction de la maison.

Les deux frères se retrouvèrent face à face. Sarah pressa ses mains sur sa bouche. Qu'allaient-ils se dire ? Que *pouvaient-ils* se dire ?

Puis Matt haussa les épaules et s'éloigna dans la foule. Luke resta seul.

— Je ne crois pas que nous ayons été présentés. Je suis Matt Brennan, le frère de Luke.

— Sarah Randolph.

— C'est vous qui avez pris les photos des filles. J'apprécie énormément que vous ayez fait ces tirages pour nous. Ils seront encore plus précieux quand elles auront grandi.

Elle lui sourit.

— Je suis contente d'avoir été sur place au bon moment.

Se retournant vers le large, Matt s'accouda à la balustrade.

— Kristin dit que mon frère vous a rendu service. Vous avez été agressée ?

— Oui. Il m'a emmenée à l'hôpital et m'a aidée à faire toutes les démarches. Je n'avais plus de clés : je ne pouvais même pas rentrer chez moi.

— Il faut toujours qu'il vole au secours de quelqu'un !

Et parfois, ces sauvetages tournaient très mal. Matt s'éclaircit la gorge, chercha ses mots.

— Je ne sais pas si vous êtes au courant, mais…

— Kristin était mariée à Luke quand vous êtes rentré d'Afrique.

— Il vous en a parlé ? s'écria Matt, interdit.

— Bien sûr ! Nous sommes amis.

Il n'aurait rien dû dire de plus, il le sentait bien… mais il ne pouvait pas s'arrêter là.

115

— Je voulais juste vous prévenir… Luke vient de vivre deux années assez rudes. Il n'est pas à même d'entamer une relation sérieuse.

— Oh !

— Je ne veux pas le voir souffrir, ajouta Matt assez sèchement. La situation est déjà assez difficile : il ne sait ni où il en est ni ce qu'il veut vraiment.

— Je n'ai aucune intention de faire du mal à Luke, dit la jeune femme.

Le calme avec lequel elle lui avait répondu l'impressionna malgré lui. Il hésita un peu, et reprit finalement :

— Nous non plus. Mais les bonnes intentions ne suffisent pas toujours.

— C'est vrai…

Elle contempla l'océan un instant, puis se retourna vers Matt.

— Le souci que vous vous faites pour votre frère est tout à fait remarquable, mais je trouverais encore bien plus admirable que vous teniez compte de ses sentiments au lieu de prendre le risque de démolir sa vie. Bonne nuit.

Sur ces mots, elle le planta là, et quitta la maison.

Matt laissa tomber sa tête entre ses mains. « Un point pour elle ! », se dit-il.

— Ouf ! Quelle soirée !

— Jenny va bien ?

— Kristin l'a calmée. Ensuite, je lui ai lu une histoire et elle s'est endormie. Demain matin, elle n'y pensera plus.

Il s'étira en prenant appui sur le volant.

— C'était la première fois qu'elle voyait un feu d'artifice. Je… ils auraient dû se douter qu'elle aurait peur.

Spontanément, Sarah posa la main sur la sienne.

— Vous faites de votre mieux, Luke.

Il ne répondit rien. L'émotion que provoquait en lui le contact de cette main le privait de toute énergie. Il prit une longue inspiration… qui ne l'apaisa pas car il respira son parfum. Non pas un parfum artificiel mais l'essence même de Sarah Rose. S'il la regardait, ou si elle s'approchait encore d'un centimètre, il oublierait toutes ses bonnes résolutions. Il avait tellement envie d'elle ! Par chance, ou par malheur, elle s'écarta avant qu'il n'ait fait un geste qu'il aurait pu regretter.

— La journée a été longue. Vous êtes vraiment obligé d'aller travailler ?

Il soupira, et hocha la tête.

— La nuit va être difficile ?

Ça avait déjà bien démarré… Sans répondre, il ouvrit sa portière.

— Je vous accompagne jusqu'à votre porte.

Ils grimpèrent l'escalier sans parler. Arrivée devant chez elle, elle se retourna vers Luke.

— Merci, lui dit-elle. J'ai été contente de revoir Erin et Jenny.

— C'est moi qui vous remercie. Sans vous, je ne sais pas si je serais resté.

— Bonne nuit ?

— Bonne nuit.

Spontanément, il posa la main sur sa joue. Ses yeux s'élargirent un instant, mais elle ne s'écarta pas. Il aurait tant aimé se perdre au plus profond de cette femme qui donnait tant, si librement. Elle pourrait le guérir si seulement elle le voulait…

Mais pourquoi le voudrait-elle ? Elle pouvait difficilement trouver pire que lui.

Il déposa un baiser sur le bout de son nez, puis recula en fourrant les mains dans ses poches.

— Dormez bien, Sarah Rose.

Il eut l'impression qu'elle voulait lui dire quelque chose d'important, mais elle parut y renoncer, et se contenta de répondre :

— Vous aussi. Enfin... quand vous dormirez, demain matin.

— Je peux vous appeler un de ces jours ?

Voyant qu'elle hésitait, il chercha un prétexte acceptable.

— Juste pour m'assurer que tout se passe bien entre vous et Sawyer.

— Oh ! Oui, d'accord.

Elle recula d'un pas. Elle était déjà hors de sa portée.

— Si je ne réponds pas, laissez un message.

— Entendu.

Il leva la main dans un geste d'adieu. Elle l'imita et ferma la porte sans bruit, le laissant seul dans le noir. Une fois de plus.

8.

Le dimanche après-midi, couverte de boue, en sueur et de très mauvaise humeur, Sarah freina brutalement sur le parking du magasin de photo. Sous ses chaussures de toile détrempées, l'asphalte était brûlant. Elle poussa la porte et s'arrêta dans la pénombre trop fraîche où seule brillait une petite lampe.

— Chuck ? Tu es là ?

Il ne répondit pas. Ce qui ne voulait rien dire car il adorait ce genre de blagues. Parfois, il se garait ailleurs pour qu'elle le crût parti, et il arrivait sans bruit derrière elle pendant qu'elle se concentrait sur un tirage. Tout de même, il n'irait pas jusqu'à... Pour quoi faire ? Qu'aurait-il à gagner ?

« Sans toi, il aurait le magasin entièrement pour lui », songea-t-elle.

A cette seule idée, elle frissonna.

Après avoir posé à terre sa lourde sacoche remplie de matériel-photo, elle retira ses chaussures. Ça ne tenait pas debout ! En réalité, Chuck avait tous les avantages : il gérait le magasin à sa guise, sans qu'elle n'intervînt jamais dans ses décisions et, en même temps, il avait quelqu'un pour partager les frais.

Mais aucun raisonnement n'aurait pu atténuer le malaise de Sarah. Luke avait-il raison ? Etait-il imprudent de rester ?

L'aspect le plus frustrant, le plus horripilant de ce dilemme était de ne pas parvenir à se décider. James se serait attendu à ce qu'elle prît tous les risques, Luke voulait la mettre en sécurité, et elle était elle-même d'accord avec ces deux points de vue...

Pendant une éternité, elle resta paralysée, le cœur battant. Puis, tout à coup, elle se mit en colère. Chuck serait trop content de la voir tapie là comme un lapin, à l'affût du moindre son ! Puisqu'il ne se montrait pas, elle allait rester.

Il lui suffit de quelques minutes en tête à tête avec le matériel de Felix, à répéter les gestes rituels si souvent effectués avec lui, pour lui faire oublier son angoisse. L'éternelle recherche du meilleur équilibre entre l'ombre et la lumière absorba toute son attention. Au bout de trois heures, pourtant, l'agacement la gagna. Elle avait passé la matinée dans les marais à photographier les animaux et les plantes, l'eau et le ciel, et elle n'avait rapporté que des images d'amateur. Il manquait un élément vital. Une grue perchée sur un chêne mort, c'était joli, mais quel sens cela avait-il ?

Elle y verrait peut-être plus clair après avoir mangé quelque chose. Elle avait aussi très soif. Avec un soupir, elle mit ses clichés à l'abri de la lumière, puis ouvrit la porte... et se trouva nez à nez avec une ombre massive. Elle laissa échapper un cri étouffé.

Un instant plus tard, elle reconnut Chuck, mais sa terreur ne s'apaisa pas.

— Je ne savais pas que tu étais là, dit-il en s'avançant.

Elle dut reculer pour le laisser passer. Il examina les tirages qui étaient en train de sécher, puis se retourna vers elle.

— Des cartes postales ? demanda-t-il avec un mince sourire.

Elle serra les dents.

— Non. J'expérimente.

— Pas très réussie, l'expérience !

— Non. Pas très.

Le laissant savourer sa joie mauvaise, elle alla se verser un verre de thé glacé. Il la suivit.

— Tu as peut-être besoin de corps morts ou mutilés pour générer une émotion réelle.

Elle s'interdit de se retourner, se força à boire le contenu de son verre avant de répondre :

— C'est horrible de dire une chose pareille ! Comme si je me défoulais en faisant ces reportages !

— Je lance juste une hypothèse, fit-il en haussant les épaules. C'est peut-être la mort qui t'excite. Ça expliquerait aussi pourquoi tu traînes avec un flic.

Cette fois, elle se retourna d'un bloc :

— Qu'est-ce que tu racontes ?

— Je parle de ce type qui est venu me harceler : Brennan. Flic, ce n'est pas un boulot sûr, de nos jours. Moi, je crois que tu te shootes au danger. Tu pourrais coucher avec lui ce soir… et apprendre sa mort demain.

Elle eut une vision subite de James glissant le long du rocher, un trou dans la poitrine. Puis ce fut Luke qui tombait comme un pantin désarticulé… Elle eut l'impression que le plancher basculait sous ses pieds, et dut s'adosser au placard de la kitchenette, les yeux fermés, cramponnée des deux mains à son verre glacé.

— Quel est ton problème, Chuck ? chuchota-t-elle, la gorge serrée. Tu me détestes à ce point ?

— Moi, te détester ? Pas du tout, dit-il avec un petit rire flûté. Tu me fournis beaucoup de distractions.

Sans rien ajouter, il s'éloigna d'un pas lourd.

Quelques secondes plus tard, le moteur de la Cadillac vrombit, puis s'évanouit dans le lointain.

Sarah posa son verre avec précaution, fit couler de l'eau sur ses poignets, puis se tamponna le visage et la nuque. Luke avait en partie raison : Chuck était dangereux. Mais il se servait de paroles plutôt que de ses poings. Cela dit, le résultat était payant : elle avait mis six mois à dompter ces souvenirs et, en une phrase vicieuse, Chuck venait de balayer toutes ses défenses. Elle se retrouvait au cœur de la scène : le vent glacé de l'hiver lui enfonçait dans la gorge les odeurs âcres de la poudre, du bois calciné et des cadavres. Elle entendait les enfants pleurer, les femmes gémir, les hommes jurer… et elle voyait James figé dans la mort.

Les ténèbres se refermaient sur elle quand la sonnerie du téléphone éclata à ses oreilles.

Convulsivement, elle plaqua les mains sur sa bouche, retint un cri de terreur. Au bout de deux sonneries, le répondeur se mit en marche. Elle entendit d'abord le message mutin de Chuck, puis *sa* voix :

— Luke Brennan à l'appareil. J'essaie de joindre…

Maladroite, fébrile, elle décrocha le combiné.

— Allô ? Allô ?

— Sarah, c'est Luke. Vous allez bien ?

Le soulagement lui donna un nouvel accès de vertige.

— Pas vraiment, non, chuchota-t-elle.

— Qu'est-ce qui se passe ? Sawyer est là ? Il vous a fait du mal ?

Elle en eut les larmes aux yeux. Une chaleur fluide naquit au plus profond de son corps. Elle se demanda laquelle des deux réactions devait l'inquiéter le plus.

— Je viens de me disputer avec Chuck. Juste des mots, précisa-t-elle en entendant Luke jurer furieusement. En fait, je crois que je suis surtout très fatiguée.

Le monde reprenait peu à peu sa place autour d'elle. Elle eut alors envie d'alléger l'atmosphère.

— Je ne veux plus penser à lui. Vous avez revu Erin et Jenny, depuis la fête ?

— Elles sont venues chez moi mercredi après-midi. On a passé un bon moment sur la plage, et puis on s'est fait des *hamburgers* au barbecue pour le dîner. Ensuite, je les ai ramenées… là-bas, à l'heure du coucher.

— Une bonne journée, alors ?

— Oui. On va se revoir mercredi prochain.

Il y eut un bref silence, puis il proposa :

— Vous auriez envie de venir nous rejoindre ?

— Je…

— Je ne sais pas encore ce que nous allons faire, mais je… nous serions contents de vous avoir avec nous.

Cette invitation la précipita de nouveau au cœur du conflit. Elle n'avait pas l'habitude que l'on se soucie autant d'elle… Face à l'horreur de ses souvenirs, Luke et ses filles lui offraient un rempart fait de tendresse familiale, de jeux et de rires. Et pourtant, elle hésitait à accepter car, si elle le revoyait, elle ne serait sans doute pas capable de rester dans le registre d'une simple amitié. Elle s'attacherait à lui, et son fragile équilibre volerait en éclats. Sans parler de celui de Luke. Elle n'avait pas oublié les paroles de son frère.

— Je suis désolée, dit-elle, la gorge serrée. Mercredi, j'ai déjà prévu quelque chose. Une autre fois, peut-être ?

— Bien sûr. Un samedi, ce serait peut-être mieux. Je vais demander à Kristin de me laisser les filles le week-end prochain, puisque je suis de repos.

— C'est une bonne idée.

Il y eut un silence, puis Luke s'éclaircit la gorge.

— Au revoir, Sarah Rose. Prenez bien soin de vous.

— C'est promis !

Elle se hâta de raccrocher avant de changer d'avis. Elle avait fait le bon choix : c'était bien de prendre une décision logique et de s'y tenir... mais pourquoi cela faisait-il aussi mal ?

Surprise, Kristin leva les yeux vers Matt. Elle recousait le short préféré d'Erin. Il était installé près d'elle avec son journal.

— Comment ?

— Je me demandais si ce ne serait pas une bonne idée de contacter Sarah Randolph, répéta-t-il. Tu sais bien, Luke l'a emmenée à la fête, la semaine dernière...

— Je me souviens d'elle, bien sûr ! Je voulais dire : pourquoi ?

Il replia soigneusement la page des sports.

— J'ai eu le sentiment qu'ils s'intéressaient l'un à l'autre. Il me semble qu'une petite mise en garde serait judicieuse.

— Qu'est-ce que tu veux dire, exactement ?

Il lui adressa un regard patient.

— Il est encore sous le choc. Il ne peut rien offrir à une femme avant de s'être remis... de votre séparation.

S'interdisant de réagir avec trop de véhémence, Kristin se pencha sur son ouvrage.

— C'est leur affaire, non ? Elle m'a paru très intelligente, très fine : elle doit savoir où elle met les pieds.

— Ça, je n'en suis pas sûr. J'ai bien essayé de l'avertir, mais...

— Tu l'as *avertie* ? s'écria Kristin, outrée. Qu'est-ce que tu lui as dit exactement ?

— Ce que je viens de te dire à toi. Qu'il venait d'avoir un gros choc et qu'il n'était pas vraiment prêt pour une relation.

Kristin ferma les yeux, luttant contre la colère. Matt n'avait que de bonnes intentions, mais...

124

— Comment as-tu pu faire une chose pareille ? lui demanda-t-elle d'une voix lasse.

— Mais qu'est-ce que j'ai fait ?

— Tu es intervenu dans la vie privé de ton frère. Tu as parlé de lui derrière son dos, comme s'il était une sorte... d'incompétent.

Un éclair de colère s'alluma dans les yeux très bleus de Matt.

— Je cherche à éviter qu'il fasse encore des dégâts, voilà tout.

— Il ne fait pas de dégâts.

Matt la regarda, le visage fermé. Elle s'entêta :

— Il ne m'a pas épousée pour te faire du mal. Je pensais que tu l'avais compris.

Il secoua son journal, se replongea dans sa lecture.

— J'ai vécu avec lui plus longtemps que toi. J'ai plus d'expérience de ce qu'il fait et de ce qu'il ne fait pas.

— Et tu as peut-être...

— Maman ! Maamannnn !

La voix de Jenny venait du jardin. Elle paraissait terrifiée. Lâchant sa couture, Kristin se précipita vers la porte.

— Qu'est-ce qui se passe ?

— Erin est tombée de la balançoire !

En voyant sa fille allongée sous le portique, Kristin crut que son cœur s'arrêtait de battre. Elle tomba à genoux, notant vaguement que Matt écartait la balançoire pour lui faire de la place.

— Erin ? Erin, tu m'entends ?

La fillette ouvrit les yeux, mais les garda fixés dans le vide. Il ne se passa rien pendant plusieurs secondes, puis, avec une toux et une forte respiration rauque, elle se redressa. Les larmes aux yeux, Kristin la soutint.

— Mon cœur, tu vas bien ?

La gamine hocha la tête.

— C'était… bizarre, dit-elle d'une voix enrouée. Je ne pouvais plus respirer.

Kristin la palpa, fit jouer tous ses membres, et l'aida à se relever. Tout semblait bien fonctionner.

— Qu'est-ce que tu faisais quand tu es tombée ?

— Elle est montée tout en haut du portique, cria Jenny en montrant la barre transversale qui soutenait les jeux.

— Cafteuse ! lâcha sa sœur avec un regard désabusé.

Jenny lui tira la langue. Kristin soupira. Visiblement, tout rentrait dans l'ordre.

— Venez, on va rentrer dans la maison. Il fait chaud, et vous avez besoin de boire quelque chose.

Sentant que Matt ne les suivait pas, elle se retourna vers lui… et découvrit son visage livide.

— Qu'est-ce qu'elle fichait là-haut ? lança-t-il. Elle aurait pu se tuer !

Kristin rebroussa chemin, et alla lui prendre la main. Automatiquement, il passa le bras autour de sa taille.

— Tout s'est bien terminé, dit-elle doucement. Les enfants tombent souvent ; ils se font mal. On ne peut pas tout contrôler. On ne peut pas les protéger de tout.

Il inspira profondément, l'attira contre lui.

— C'est un véritable métier d'être parent.

Elle hocha la tête, la joue pressée contre sa poitrine.

— C'est plus facile quand on commence par le commencement, mais tu trouveras les bons réflexes. Je te promets.

Elle lui tendit sa bouche, il l'embrassa très tendrement, et ils rentrèrent en se tenant par la main. Pourtant, Kristin se demandait combien de temps ils parviendraient encore à éviter le désastre. Avec les filles et avec Matt.

— Bonsoir !

— Euh… bonsoir.

La lumière du couchant l'enveloppait d'un halo doré. Ses yeux verts, en revanche, semblaient illuminés de l'intérieur. Elle souriait. Quand il vit ce sourire, il faillit lui ouvrir les bras… et se réfugia, in extremis, dans les bonnes manières.

— Comment allez-vous ? demanda-t-il.

— Très bien. Je suis désolée de passer sans prévenir, mais j'ai de bonnes nouvelles, et j'avais envie de les partager avec vous.

— C'est vrai ? Entrez vite !

Il ferma la porte derrière elle en admirant discrètement son dos mince et droit, son épaisse tresse si douce.

— Alors, quelles sont ces bonnes nouvelles ?

Elle se retourna vers lui, rayonnante.

— Mon agent a téléphoné. Nous avons une offre pour les photos.

— Les photos des filles ?

Elle hocha la tête avec enthousiasme.

— C'est une revue très haut de gamme spécialisée dans les voyages. Ils font un article sur le charme des plages du Sud. Les photos des filles entrent parfaitement dans leur thème.

Il la contemplait, enchanté de la voir si joyeuse.

— C'est fantastique, Sarah Rose. Je ne sais pas comment ça se passe… Ils vont vous payer ?

— Et comment ! s'écria-t-elle avec un nouveau sourire. Très bien, même. Ça fait partie des bonnes nouvelles.

— De mieux en mieux ! J'ai une bonne bouteille : vous voulez bien que je l'ouvre pour fêter ça ?

L'invitation lui était venue spontanément, mais il la regretta tout de suite. Pourquoi accepterait-elle, après s'être montrée si distante au téléphone, la semaine passée ? Il fut stupéfait de la voir hocher la tête avec entrain.

— Bonne idée !

La pizza arriva alors qu'il servait le vin. Ils emportèrent tout sur la petite véranda à l'arrière de la maison, face aux plates-bandes fleuries qu'il binait avec les filles, quand ils en avaient le temps.

Intéressée et amusée à la fois, Sarah admira son petit jardin.

— Vous faites pousser des tomates ?

— C'est l'un des grands plaisirs de l'été : des tomates bien mûres qu'on cueille soi-même.

— Ma grand-mère en mettait dans tout.

— Moi aussi. Il y a quelques années, j'ai appris à faire un gaspacho de derrière les fagots.

— Mmm ! J'adore le gaspacho, dit-elle en s'installant sur la balancelle. Que faites-vous d'autre, à part ça et des cookies à faire damner un saint ?

Se penchant vers elle, il fit tinter son verre contre le sien.

— Avant tout, portons un toast. A mes petites filles et à votre talent. Une combinaison fameuse !

Elle eut un petit rire heureux. Tout en buvant une gorgée de vin, il captura son regard. Les ombres de ses yeux étaient presque effacées, remplacées par cette lumière qui semblait briller pour lui et pour lui seul. S'il se laissait aller, s'il lui montrait son attirance, risquait-il d'éteindre ce rayonnement ?

S'appuyant de l'épaule contre le mur, il brisa délibérément l'enchantement.

— Comment les choses vont-elles se passer ? Vous avez tous les détails ?

— L'article paraîtra en septembre. C'est un numéro spécial intitulé : « Adieu à l'été ». Ils me demandent de faire signer des autorisations à toutes les personnes concernées par ces photos.

— Je ne peux pas parler pour Kristin, mais je ne vois pas pourquoi elle refuserait.

— Est-ce que ce sera mieux si vous êtes là quand je lui poserai la question ?

— Peut-être. Quand devez-vous leur donner une réponse ?

— D'ici huit jours.

— Kristin doit être débordée, cette semaine : elle prépare la fête d'anniversaire d'Erin. Elle attache beaucoup d'importance aux anniversaires.

— Les filles doivent adorer ça.

— C'est vrai. En fait...

Il hésita un instant, puis décida de prendre le risque :

— Le meilleur moyen de voir Kristin cette semaine, ce serait de venir à la fête, vendredi après-midi. Vous voulez bien ?

— Il faudrait que tout le monde soit d'accord.

— Je ne vois pas qui pourrait s'opposer à votre présence.

— Mais, Erin...

— Ecoutez, si vous voulez, je lui poserai la question. A mon avis, elle dira que plus on est de fous, plus on rit.

— D'accord.

Cette fois, ce fut elle qui se pencha en avant pour faire tinter son verre contre le sien.

— A l'anniversaire d'Erin !

— A Erin. Vous ne pensez pas qu'on devrait manger cette pizza avant qu'elle soit tout à fait froide ?

— Et vous, vous ne trouvez pas qu'on pourrait se tutoyer ?

Une fois de plus, Jen secoua la tête.

— Tu sais, quand ta maman est partie pour cette soirée chez sa cousine, elle m'a fait promettre que tu te laverais les dents avant de te coucher. Je dois tenir ma promesse.

Pas de réponse.

— Tu te laveras les dents si je te raconte une deuxième histoire ?

Toujours rien.

Vaincu, Matt rinça la brosse à dents et la remit dans le verre en plastique.

— Tu as gagné, Jen. Au lit.

Quand il la souleva, elle resta toute raide et droite. Quand c'était Kristin ou Luke qui la mettait au lit, elle se blottissait dans leurs bras. « Il faut encore un peu de temps », se dit-il.

Il la déposait dans son lit quand Erin entra dans la pièce.

— Il faut que je parle à mon papa.

Matt ravala un mot assez courant dans l'armée mais peu usité dans les chambres de petites filles. Car *son papa* se trouvait dans la chambre avec elle, mais elle ne le savait pas.

— Euh… demain, Erin. Votre maman a dit que vous deviez être au lit à 21 heures.

— Je ne pourrai pas dormir si je ne parle pas à mon papa.

— Moi aussi ! s'écria Jenny en se redressant. Moi aussi, je veux parler à mon papa.

Il comprit qu'il n'aurait pas gain de cause.

— Bon, d'accord. On va téléphoner à votre… papa. Ensuite, on lira une histoire et vous vous endormirez. Nous sommes bien d'accord ?

— Oh, super ! cria Jenny en battant des mains. Je vais parler à papa !

Serrant les dents, Matt passa dans la chambre qu'il partageait avec Kristin, saisit le téléphone sans fil, et appuya sur la touche numéro 1 : celle qui correspondait au numéro de Luke. Qui d'autre aurait pu figurer en première place sur le téléphone de Kristin, sinon son ex-mari ?

— Quand je suis loin, j'oublie toujours la magie des nuits du Sud.

— Moi, je serai sans doute parti depuis longtemps, s'il n'y avait pas les filles et si je n'aimais pas tant ce coin.

— Tu sais, les voyages, ce n'est pas forcément la solution. Je n'ai pas dû passer plus de deux mois au même endroit au cours des huit dernières années.

— Il faut trouver un équilibre.

— Je le pense aussi.

L'équilibre ? Elle avait du mal à saisir le concept, ce soir, auprès de Luke… Ses cheveux, mouillés quand il lui avait ouvert la porte, retombaient sur son front en boucles douces qu'elle mourait d'envie de toucher. Son T-shirt aussi avait séché sur lui, mais elle se rappelait encore la façon dont le coton humide révélait les muscles de sa poitrine.

Elle avala sa salive avec difficulté. Elle ferait bien de s'en aller avant de…

— Je ferais bien de m'en aller.

— Bon…

131

Du bout de son pied nu, il stoppa le lent balancement de leur siège, se leva et lui tendit la main.

— Je suis vraiment content que tu sois passée.

Elle leva la tête vers lui, vit l'éclair de lune posé sur ses cheveux noirs, sentit la chaleur des doigts solides qui tenaient les siens.

— Moi aussi, je suis contente.

— Sarah, je…

Il détourna la tête, et haussa vaguement les épaules. Mi-déçue, mi-soulagée, elle s'apprêtait à partir quand il plongea de nouveau son regard dans le sien. Sans l'avoir vraiment décidé, dans un glissement irrésistible, ils s'unirent dans un baiser qui semblait ne jamais devoir finir.

Enfin, enfin elle pouvait laisser courir ses mains dans ses cheveux, palper leur texture si douce ! Sa nuque était tiède et lisse, la peau de ses épaules ferme et encore plus douce. Elle aurait volontiers passé sa vie à le toucher et à savourer ses caresses ! Les mains de Luke enfouies sous son corsage faisaient courir des éclairs sur sa peau. Elle se souleva vers lui, grisée de plaisir. Leur baiser s'approfondit encore.

Quand la paume de son compagnon recouvrit son sein nu, elle comprit que les plaintes qu'elle entendait venaient d'elle. Quelle importance ? Seul comptait ce moment incroyable, ce besoin de l'attirer encore plus près, de le sentir contre elle : sa bouche sur ses épaules, sa gorge. Elle voulait…

A l'intérieur de la maison, le téléphone sonna.

9.

Ils sursautèrent, s'écartèrent d'un bond. Passant une main tremblante dans ses cheveux, Luke se détourna, puis revint vers elle.

— Il faut répondre, chuchota-t-elle.

Il disparut dans la maison. Restée seule, elle pressa ses mains sur ses yeux et attendit que ses genoux cessent de trembler.

— Oui, Erin, je crois que la fête va être super *cool*… De la pluie ? Jamais de la vie ! Bien sûr, je t'ai acheté un cadeau !… Non, je ne te dirai pas ce que c'est : tu dois attendre encore trois jours.

Quand Sarah passa devant lui, il leva les yeux vers elle avec une mimique comique.

— Dis donc, Erin l'Ourson, ça te plairait que j'amène mon amie Sarah à ta fête ? Elle pourrait peut-être prendre des photos de ton anniversaire ?… Attends, je lui demande.

Il haussa les sourcils d'un air interrogateur, et la jeune femme acquiesça avec un sourire. Puis elle disparut dans la cuisine en emportant leurs deux verres. Voilà, elle allait encore passer une journée avec Luke. Une occasion supplémentaire d'aggraver sa situation. Elle ne savait pas si elle devait rire ou pleurer.

A côté, il y eut un bref silence, puis Luke reprit, d'une voix très différente :

— Bien sûr, passe-le moi.

Sarah se mit à laver les verres, et la conversation fut brouillée par le bruit de l'eau. Quand elle ferma le robinet, Luke parlait avec une dureté qu'elle ne lui connaissait pas :

— Je sais que c'est un vrai problème pour toi, mais est-ce que tu veux qu'elle s'endorme ce soir ou non ?... Alors, laisse-moi lui raconter une histoire. On essaiera d'y voir clair une autre fois.

Il y eut un long silence, puis il retrouva sa voix normale.

— Salut, Jenny Penny. Tu es au lit ?... Je parie que je peux te raconter l'une de tes histoires préférées sans même regarder le livre.... Bien sûr que je peux : écoute.

Le cœur serré, Sarah l'écouta, elle aussi, raconter une histoire à sa fille au téléphone. Il y avait en lui tant de douceur, et aussi tant de passion ! Elle n'aurait jamais cru qu'un homme pourrait l'attirer de cette façon. Pourtant, elle ne cessait de se le répéter : il n'y avait pas de place pour une femme dans la vie de Luke. Ses filles avaient besoin de tout son amour, de toute son attention, de toute son énergie.

Quant à elle, quelle place pourrait-elle faire dans sa vie à cet homme et à ces deux adorables fillettes ? Un jour ou l'autre, elle reprendrait le fil de sa carrière et la seule existence qu'elle eût jamais connue. Alors, elle les abandonnerait et ne leur rendrait visite que de loin en loin. Ce serait trop injuste ! Luke avait déjà tant perdu. Un amour en pointillés, c'est ce qui pourrait lui arriver de pire.

La meilleure chose à faire serait de battre en retraite. Chacun d'entre eux portait déjà plus que sa part de souffrance.

Tout en prenant ses clés de voiture sur la table, elle capta le regard de Luke, et murmura :

— Bonne nuit.

Puis elle se dirigea vers la porte.

Sans cesser de parler à Jenny, Luke sauta sur ses pieds, la main levée pour tenter de la retenir.

Elle ne s'arrêta pas. Souriante, elle lui fit un signe de la main, puis sortit et s'engouffra dans sa jeep.

Le comportement bizarre de cet automobiliste justifiait un alcootest.

Luke alluma son gyrophare, puis vint se placer à la hauteur de la voiture, et fit signe au chauffeur de se ranger. Comme s'il n'avait rien remarqué, celui-ci poursuivit son chemin, toujours aussi lentement. Apparemment, il se demandait s'il allait ou non bifurquer vers l'océan. Luke donna un petit coup de sirène, puis alluma son projecteur. Toujours pas de réaction. La Volvo ne s'arrêta pas, n'accéléra pas, se contenta de rouler très lentement dans la nuit.

Luke finit par déboîter, et doubler la Volvo, sirène hurlante. Cette fois, la voiture se rangea sur le bas-côté, et la vitre du chauffeur s'ouvrit. Le type avait l'air mal en point : très pâle, les yeux vitreux. L'intérieur de l'habitacle était un fouillis innommable : sachets de *fast-food*, cannettes de bières, journaux et revues.

— Je peux voir votre permis et les papiers du véhicule ?

Sans paraître alarmé le moins du monde, l'homme sortit son portefeuille, et tendit ses papiers. Tout en étudiant son permis, Luke demanda :

— Vous avez bu quelque chose, ce soir ?

— Une bière. Vers 18 heures. Si vous voulez, je peux vous montrer que je marche droit.

135

Les ivrognes proposaient souvent de montrer ce dont ils étaient capables.

— Attendez un petit moment dans la voiture, monsieur. Je reviens tout de suite.

L'ordinateur ne lui apprit rien : le chauffeur n'avait pas de casier, aucune infraction préalable. Il revint vers la Volvo... et trouva l'inconnu en larmes. Surpris, il lui rendit ses papiers en disant :

— Monsieur Craven, écoutez-moi. C'est dangereux de conduire quand on est bouleversé. Vous devriez rentrer chez vous et dormir un peu.

— Je ne peux pas, bredouilla l'homme.

Luke devinait aisément le reste. Des problèmes à la maison, une dispute conjugale.

— Alors, prenez une chambre quelque part.

— Elle s'en va. Ma femme veut me quitter.

Luke réprima une grimace.

— Je suis désolé, monsieur, mais vous êtes un danger pour vous-même et pour les autres. Roulez derrière moi : je vais vous emmener...

— Je savais qu'elle n'était pas heureuse. Je travaille trop, j'ai toujours trop travaillé. C'est le seul moyen de rester dans la course. On voulait que les gosses puissent faire des études.

— Monsieur Craven...

— Je croyais qu'on pourrait régler nos problèmes une fois que les gamins seraient partis. Le plus jeune vient de s'installer à Washington pour son travail, et maintenant...

Maladroitement, il fourra le permis dans son portefeuille, puis le portefeuille dans sa poche. Cette fois, son mouvement délogea un objet qui tomba sur le plancher de la voiture avec un choc mat.

— Qu'est-ce que je peux faire ? Comment la garder si elle ne veut pas rester ?

Luke connaissait trop bien la réponse à cette question. Il se pencha, et posa la main sur l'épaule de l'homme.

— Vous ne pouvez rien régler ce soir, monsieur Craven. Surtout pas tout seul. Laissez-moi vous emmener…

Il vit alors l'objet qui était tombé aux pieds de l'homme. A demi caché par la pédale du frein, le canon d'une arme à feu luisait sourdement dans la pénombre.

— Monsieur Craven, vous avez un permis pour cette arme ?

Sans aucune expression, Craven se retourna à demi pour regarder le policier, puis écarta son genou, et contempla le revolver.

— Euh… je dois avoir ça quelque part.

— Vous ne le portez pas sur vous ?

— Non.

— Donnez-moi cette arme, monsieur Craven. La crosse en avant.

— Non.

Pour la première fois, l'homme se redressait, apparemment lucide et conscient de ce qu'il disait.

— Non, je ne suis pas obligé de le faire.

— Si, monsieur, vous êtes obligé. Je vous demande de me donner cette arme tout de suite, répéta Luke en tendant la main.

Craven resta immobile, les mains bien en vue sur le volant. Luke attendit longtemps. Plusieurs automobilistes passèrent sans se douter de rien.

— Ecoutez, monsieur Craven, reprit Luke en s'accoudant au toit de la voiture, je ne suis pas thérapeute, mais… je suis passé par là. C'est l'enfer, je sais, mais on peut survivre.

Après un silence interminable, l'homme demanda tout à coup :

— Qu'est-ce que je vais faire sans elle ?

— D'abord, vous allez avoir mal. Très mal. Mais la douleur ne vous tuera pas.

L'homme jeta un bref regard à son arme.

— Et pourquoi pas ?

Cette question, Luke se l'était posée bien des fois.

— Vous dites que vous avez des enfants ?

— Ils sont grands, maintenant. Ils n'ont plus besoin de moi.

— Si. Toujours. Et leurs propres gosses auront besoin de leur grand-père. Pensez à tout ce que vos petits-enfants rateront si vous… renoncez.

Craven réfléchit en silence. Luke resta parfaitement immobile ; il redoutait de faire basculer la situation par un geste intempestif. Il pensait à Erin et Jen. Avaient-elles encore besoin de lui ? Et Sarah Rose ? C'était lui qui commençait à avoir terriblement besoin d'elle…

Enfin, l'homme se baissa lentement, le bras tendu. Luke se crispa, prêt à bondir. Quand Craven se redressa, il tenait le pistolet par le canon, et le lui tendait.

— Tenez. Prenez ça, que je ne le voie plus.

Une demi-heure plus tard, l'homme avait pris une chambre dans un motel voisin.

Quand, enfin, Luke remonta dans sa voiture, il laissa tomber sa tête dans ses mains, comme l'avait fait Craven, un peu plus tôt. L'heure qui venait de s'écouler l'avait épuisé plus qu'une nuit entière de patrouille. Il espérait que Craven s'en sortirait. Quelquefois, on se sentait mieux après avoir pu exprimer sa souffrance. Luke était bien placé pour le savoir : le fait de tout raconter à Sarah avait changé sa vie ; elle était devenue son guide dans les ténèbres. La seule idée de devoir attendre dix heures avant de la revoir le démoralisait.

Le reste de la nuit se passa sans autre incident. A la fin de son service, Luke se changeait au vestiaire quand Hank Jordan vint le trouver.

— Hé, Brennan, j'ai pensé que ça t'intéresserait : on a un rapport sur une agression qui ressemble beaucoup à celle dont Sarah Randolph a été victime. C'est arrivé lundi soir.

Tout en faisant passer sa chemise par-dessus sa tête, Luke demanda :

— Où ça ?

— Dans le parking d'un centre commercial, en banlieue. La femme a voulu reprendre sa voiture, on l'a attaquée par-derrière et tabassée. Son agresseur lui a pris ses clés et son sac mais pas la voiture. Et tiens-toi bien : c'était encore une jeep.

— Et il ne s'est pas fait prendre, bien sûr ?

Jordan secoua la tête.

— Eh non ! Enfin, on augmente les patrouilles autour des centres commerciaux. On finira bien par le cravater. Il nous faut juste un coup de chance.

Il ressortit en sifflotant.

Luke secoua lentement la tête. Dépendre de la chance, cela ne lui plaisait guère, mais ce type était malin : il ne laissait aucune trace derrière lui. Tant qu'il ne commettrait pas d'erreur, on aurait du mal à le pincer.

En refermant la porte de son casier, Luke se demanda où pouvait bien se trouver Chuck Sawyer au moment de la deuxième agression.

— Désolé d'être en retard ! Je n'ai pas entendu mon réveil.

— Pas de problème : je prends un chapeau et j'arrive.

Elle souriait, mais il eut l'impression qu'elle se forçait.

Quand il fut seul, il jeta un regard à la ronde, et aperçut des photos posées sur la table : des échassiers, des cerfs, une grenouille acrobate accrochée à un jonc… Il sourit.

— Ne regarde pas ça ! lui dit Sarah en revenant, coiffée d'un chapeau de paille à larges bords. La nature n'a jamais été ma spécialité.

Elle saisit ses clés et ouvrit la porte. On aurait dit qu'elle se préparait à affronter une épreuve.

— En tout cas, lui dit Luke, tu photographies les gens de façon extraordinaire. Je suis allé à la bibliothèque consulter des anciens numéros de *Events*…

Elle verrouillait soigneusement sa porte, sans le regarder et sans même paraître l'entendre.

— J'ai bien regardé les photos, reprit-il. Tu as couvert les endroits les plus chauds de la planète.

Elle resta silencieuse encore un instant, puis répondit :

— La plupart d'entre eux, oui.

En descendant l'escalier derrière elle, Luke s'aperçut que le chapeau ne lui plaisait pas. Il lui cachait le visage : impossible de voir ses réactions. Avec prudence, il reprit :

— Les flics, surtout dans les grandes villes comme Los Angeles ou New York, sont confrontés à tant de violence qu'il leur arrive souvent de craquer. En regardant tes photos, je me suis demandé si les journalistes avaient le même problème. Les journalistes ou les photographes.

Ils montèrent dans la voiture de Luke, et il démarra.

La réponse de Sarah arriva enfin :

— Pas James, dit-elle. Il ne ralentissait jamais ; il ne perdait jamais le cap. Jusqu'à la toute dernière seconde.

— Il ne devait pas être facile à suivre…

Luke était légèrement inquiet d'avoir touché un sujet aussi sensible. En s'arrêtant à un feu rouge, il jeta un bref coup d'œil à sa passagère. Ce fichu chapeau l'empêchait de voir son regard.

— Ça faisait partie du boulot, dit-elle d'une voix brève.

Il décida de ne pas tenir compte de l'avertissement.

— Tu dois avoir des histoires incroyables à raconter.

— Ce qui semblait excitant, sur le moment, a souvent l'air stupide, avec le recul. James serait encore en vie s'il n'avait pas pris un risque exagéré.

— Vous étiez... proches, tous les deux ?

Il n'aurait pas dû poser cette question, mais il avait tellement envie de connaître la réponse !

Elle eut un petit rire triste.

— James et moi, nous sommes passés par toutes les facettes des relations humaines : nous avons été amis, amants, puis ennemis.

Luke sentit la jalousie se glisser en lui. La jalousie et l'angoisse.

— Où en étiez-vous, à la fin ? demanda-t-il avec toute la légèreté dont il était capable.

Une fois de plus, la jeune femme mit très longtemps à répondre.

— Pas amants, en tout cas. J'avais rompu depuis longtemps : quand j'avais compris qu'il ne serait jamais fidèle.

Luke s'aperçut qu'il retenait son souffle, et le relâcha dans un long soupir silencieux.

— Pas ennemis non plus. J'aurais eu beaucoup de mal à détester James... Mais notre amitié n'était plus très solide : j'en avais assez de ses manipulations et de son besoin d'être toujours le premier en tout. Pourtant, j'admirais sa façon d'écrire, et la passion avec laquelle il s'investissait dans ses reportages.

Un nouveau silence, puis elle dit :

— Et maintenant… Je me demande si je vais pouvoir retourner sur le terrain.

Elle parlait d'une voix basse et torturée.

Après avoir garé la voiture devant la maison de Kristin, Luke se tourna vers sa compagne, et lui retira doucement son chapeau. Puis, du bout des doigts, il essuya ses joues mouillées de larmes.

— Je suis désolé, Sarah Rose. Je sais que cela te fait mal.

Elle secoua la tête énergiquement.

— Ce n'est pas… Je veux dire… C'est horrible de penser que James est mort.

— Il ne voudrait pas que tu souffres à cause de lui, dit Luke avec douceur. Il préférerait que tu gardes le cap, que tu continues ta vie et ta carrière. Pour toi comme pour lui.

— C'est bien le problème, dit-elle d'une voix tremblante. J'ai essayé de continuer. J'y suis à peu près parvenue pendant une semaine. Et puis, un jour… je n'ai… plus pu…

— Tout le monde peut avoir besoin d'une coupure.

— Pas une coupure : une rupture complète. Je ne pouvais plus penser ni conduire ni trouver un hôtel ni décider où je voulais aller… Des copains journalistes, qui étaient là-bas avec moi, m'ont mise dans un avion pour New York, et mon rédacteur en chef m'a trouvé un thérapeute… Je me suis plus ou moins remise sur pied. Aujourd'hui, je me débrouille avec les détails du quotidien, mais…

Quand elle leva la tête vers lui, il vit que, dans ses yeux, les ombres avaient entièrement conquis la lumière.

— Les photos de tes filles… c'était la première fois que je me servais d'un appareil, depuis… ce jour-là. Ma carrière est probablement finie. Je ne peux même pas envisager de repartir. Dès que j'y pense, je craque.

Elle jeta un coup d'œil par la vitre de la voiture. Erin traversait la pelouse comme une flèche pour courir droit vers eux.

Posant la main sur la poignée de sa portière, Sarah réussit à offrir à Luke un sourire tremblant :

— Ne t'en fais pas, je ne suis pas dangereuse. Seulement…

Son sourire s'éteignit, et elle conclut à voix basse :

— Seulement bonne à rien.

En contrebas, dans l'herbe, dix petites filles étaient alignées, prêtes pour faire la course. Chacune d'elles portait un œuf dans une cuillère.

Matt repéra Erin en tête de la file. Elle avait consenti à se faire belle, aujourd'hui, et il était content de la voir aussi rayonnante, elle qui semblait parfois écrasée sous le poids de sa propre vie. Bien sûr, son existence était un peu plus compliquée que celle de la plupart des fillettes de son âge. Avoir deux papas, c'était déjà difficile, mais quand ils étaient frères…

Une jalousie brûlante s'empara de lui. C'était Luke qui avait vu naître Erin, Luke qui l'avait tenue dans ses bras, toute petite. Luke avait accompagné ses premiers pas, lui avait appris l'alphabet. Pendant ce temps— pendant cinq ans —, Matt ne savait même pas qu'il avait une fille. Kristin s'était enfin décidée à le lui dire après que Luke eut déménagé. L'aurait-il jamais su, si elle n'était pas revenue vers lui ? Certains jours, il se posait la question.

— Matthew ! Je me demandais où tu étais.

S'approchant de lui, sa mère lui tendit la joue. Il se pencha pour l'embrasser, en prenant soin de ne pas froisser sa tenue ni déranger sa coiffure.

— Bonjour, maman, dit-il. Je crois que la fête se passe bien.

— Oui. Je trouve tout de même ces courses trop turbulentes pour des petites filles.

— Les gosses ont besoin de se dépenser…

Il chercha son père des yeux, et le repéra bientôt : il était installé dans une chaise de jardin, sous un arbre.

— Comment va papa ?

— Il est constamment fatigué, répondit Elena d'une voix soucieuse. Je suis un peu inquiète.

— Il est bien allé voir le médecin, cette semaine ? Vous avez appris quelque chose de nouveau ?

— Ton père m'a dit qu'il avait juste été question d'un régime sain, d'exercice et de repos.

— Ça me paraît un peu léger.

— A moi aussi. J'ai rappelé le médecin ; je lui ai parlé de cette fatigue perpétuelle, mais il m'a répété les mêmes choses.

— Le prochain rendez-vous, c'est pour quand ?

— Au mois d'août.

— Entre-temps, tu vas prendre soin de lui. Il ne pourrait pas avoir de meilleure infirmière.

Elle ne répondit pas. Suivant son regard, il vit approcher Luke en compagnie de Sarah Randolph. Il tenait Jenny dans ses bras.

— Pas d'inquiétude, maman, murmura-t-il. Nous saurons nous comporter comme des adultes, pour le bien de papa.

Etait-ce sa mère qu'il cherchait à rassurer, ou lui-même ?

— Je l'espère, dit Elena, les yeux fixés sur Luke.

*
**

144

— Il n'est pas question de vendre quoi que ce soit. Ce n'est pas de la publicité. Juste un reportage sur Myrtle Beach.

Six paires d'yeux étaient braquées sur Sarah. Pendant un temps qui lui sembla très long, personne ne dit un mot. Puis Elena intervint :

— Quel genre de publicité trouve-t-on dans cette revue ? demanda-t-elle. De l'alcool, des cigarettes ? Je ne voudrais pas que les filles se prêtent à ça !

— Maman, Sarah t'a dit que ces photos n'étaient pas destinées à la publicité.

— Je sais, Kristy, mais le fait de figurer dans une revue qui fait la promotion de ces produits…

Sa voix s'éteignit. En face d'elle, Matt secouait la tête.

— Moi non plus, l'idée ne me plaît guère. Les filles n'ont pas à être exhibées de cette façon. Les pervers ne lisent peut-être pas ce genre de revue, mais les producteurs ou les agents, sans doute. Nous n'avons pas envie d'être harcelés.

L'air amusé, Luke répondit :

— A mon avis, vous avez peu de chance de voir des agences de mannequins ou des producteurs de Hollywood faire la queue devant votre porte.

Il n'y avait aucun humour dans le regard que Matt lui lança en retour.

— C'est une question de principes, Luke. De principes.

— Je crois que la décision revient aux parents, trancha Elena.

La mère de Kristin hocha la tête d'un air convaincu.

— Parfait, dit Matt.

— Bonne idée ! ajouta Luke. Kristin et moi, nous allons en discuter, et nous vous ferons part de notre décision.

Sarah réussit à contrôler sa réaction. Tous les regards étaient braqués sur Kristin. Quant à celui de Matt, il était rempli de haine.

Kristin se leva enfin, et reprit le contrôle de la situation.

— C'est ça, dit-elle. Matt, Luke et moi, nous déciderons ensemble. Sarah, ça ira si on vous donne une réponse lundi ou mardi ?

— Ce sera parfait. Passez-moi un coup de fil, répondit la jeune femme en réprimant un soupir de soulagement.

Kristin avait sauvé la situation avec un brio qui forçait l'admiration. Elle avait du cœur et du courage, Sarah devait bien l'admettre, même si elle lui en voulait d'avoir fait tant de mal à Luke. Mais peut-être n'avait-elle pas eu le choix ? Sarah commençait à comprendre que Kristin était, tout autant que Luke, victime des circonstances.

La fête continua. Sarah prit une foule de photos, saisissant au vol des moments cocasses ou charmants, la tendresse palpable entre les parents Brennan, l'amour qu'ils portaient à leurs petites-filles.

La jeune femme commençait à apprécier l'ambiance joyeuse et détendue quand un échange entre Matt et Luke vint tout gâcher pour elle. A travers son objectif, elle vit les deux hommes dressés l'un en face de l'autre dans une attitude hostile. Puis Luke prononça quelques mots, tourna les talons et s'éloigna. Matt le suivit du regard avec une expression haineuse.

Sarah oublia un instant son appareil pour jeter un regard à la ronde. Elle s'aperçut alors que Kristin avait, elle aussi, assisté à la scène. Leurs regards se croisèrent. Kristin lui offrit un sourire las, et haussa les épaules. Sarah se surprit elle-même en hochant la tête d'un air encourageant.

Le moment des cadeaux était arrivé. Luke vint s'accouder à la balustrade de la terrasse, à côté de son ex-femme. Sarah, qui se trouvait de l'autre côté, appareil photo en main, se demanda si elle ne devrait pas se glisser entre eux, par mesure de sécurité. Avant qu'elle ne pût faire un geste, Matt vint se planter près de Kristin. Son regard était fixé sur les enfants, mais ce fut à elle qu'il s'adressa :

— Je vois que vous avez beaucoup de choses à vous dire, tous les deux.

Kristin ouvrit la bouche pour répondre, mais Luke la devança :

— Il faut que tu assumes, Matt. Kristin et moi, nous avons des enfants.

— Une enfant. Une seule.

Il y eut un silence de plomb. Ce fut Kristin qui se reprit la première.

— Matt, je t'en prie. Tu sais bien que c'est plus compliqué que ça.

— En fait, je ne sais rien du tout, répliqua-t-il aussitôt. Je sais seulement que la situation n'a aucune chance de se simplifier tant que nous ne dirons pas la vérité.

— Tu as accepté d'attendre, lui rappela Luke.

Sa voix tendue et très basse tranchait avec le bavardage des fillettes.

— Et toi, tu as laissé à Kristin le soin de décider à quel moment il conviendrait de parler aux filles. Elle a promis de le faire le plus tôt possible. Il eut un rire ironique. J'attends encore de voir ce que vaut cette promesse.

— Matt ! s'exclama Kristin, outrée.

— Papa, maman, regardez !

Erin sautait de joie au centre de son petit groupe d'amies.

— Un aquarium !

Avec un regard de reproche qui englobait les deux frères, Kristin se hâta de la rejoindre.

— C'est merveilleux, mon cœur ! Qui te l'a offert ?

Tâtant bruyamment dans l'amas de papier qui entourait la boîte, la petite trouva une enveloppe et en sortit une carte qu'elle lut tout haut :

— Pour l'anniversaire d'une petite fille pas comme les autres. Beaucoup d'amour. Papa...

Elle releva la tête et conclut :

— Papa Matt.

C'était terrible de voir ainsi retomber son excitation.

— Bon anniversaire, Erin, dit Matt avec effort. Je me suis dit qu'on irait choisir des poissons ensemble, quand on aurait tout installé.

— Ce sera *cool*.

La petite regarda sa mère, puis se retourna vers Matt.

— Merci, papa Matt. Il me plaît beaucoup.

Matt hocha la tête, et s'appuya de la hanche à la balustrade. Les bras croisés sur sa poitrine, il semblait dresser une barrière invisible entre lui et le reste du monde. Quant à Luke, son visage était un masque parfaitement inexpressif.

— Ça va ? lui glissa Sarah en posant la main sur son bras.

Lentement, il émergea de sa prison intérieure.

— Ça va. Je suis désolé que tu aies assisté à ça.

— Vous êtes tous dans une situation intenable.

Elle laissa glisser sa main le long de son bras nu, et noua ses doigts aux siens.

— Chacun fait de son mieux.

— Généreuse Sarah Rose, murmura-t-il.

Erin ouvrit le cadeau de Luke en dernier.

— Oh là là, papa !

Emerveillée, elle faisait tourbillonner le globe terrestre multicolore.

— Et toute une collection de livres sur les animaux !

Elle courut se jeter dans les bras de Luke.

— Merci ! Je t'aime !

Luke serra la fillette contre lui.

— De rien, Erin l'Ourson. Bon anniversaire !

Du coin de l'œil, Sarah capta un mouvement au bord de la terrasse. Elle tourna la tête, juste à temps pour voir Matt dévaler les marches, traverser la pelouse et disparaître à l'angle de la maison.

10.

Un à un, les parents vinrent chercher leurs enfants. Kristin dut attendre qu'ils fussent tous partis pour aller à la recherche de Matt. Laissant Erin et Jenny sur la terrasse avec une douzaine de jouets neufs et six adultes pour les surveiller, elle se mit en quête de son mari, et le trouva à l'étage, dans leur chambre. Assis dans un fauteuil, il regardait fixement les stores baissés.

La jeune femme s'éclaircit la gorge.

— Tous les invités sont partis. On s'est dit que l'on mangerait bien des *hamburgers* pour le dîner, mais on ne trouvait pas le cuisinier en chef.

— J'arrive, dit-il sans tourner la tête.

Elle s'accroupit près de lui, posa la main sur sa cuisse.

— Matt... Tu sais que je ne te mens pas. Nous allons tout expliquer à Erin.

— Oui.

Il mit sa main dans celle de sa femme.

— Je suis désolé de m'être mis en colère, dit-il. Il faut que je sois plus patient. Nous faisons tous de notre mieux...

Il serra sa main, se leva, et l'aida à se relever. Enfin, il la regardait en face.

— Viens, on va faire un vrai dîner, après tous ces amuse-gueules.

150

A la porte, voyant qu'elle ne le suivait pas, il se retourna vers elle et lui demanda en souriant :

— Tu comptes me laisser faire tout le travail seul ?

Il semblait presque redevenu lui-même, mais elle ne s'y trompait pas. Et son chagrin lui brisait le cœur.

— C'est tentant, répondit-elle en lui souriant à son tour. Non, je viens. Je me recoiffe et j'arrive.

Il hocha la tête, puis sortit. Restée seule, Kristin contempla leur chambre, le lieu de leur intimité. Tout semblait à sa place, et pourtant... quelque chose d'intangible mais de tout à fait essentiel venait de mourir entre eux.

Juste avant la nuit, Sarah rangea son appareil photo et vint s'asseoir sur l'herbe, près de Luke, tandis qu'Erin galopait vers la maison.

— Elle m'a épuisée ! s'écria-t-elle en repoussant ses boucles en arrière. Où trouve-t-elle toute cette énergie ?

— Je crois qu'elle prend des vitamines au petit déjeuner.

Il changea de position, et Jenny suivit le mouvement, nichée contre lui, son pouce posé sur sa lèvre inférieure. Sarah la regarda avec un sourire.

— Elle est mignonne...

Il sourit aussi, d'un air heureux.

— Je me demande toujours comment un type comme moi a pu faire une gamine aussi craquante.

Elle allait répondre quand, sur la terrasse, le groupe se dispersa. Les parents Jennings embrassèrent leur fille et son mari, échangèrent quelques mots avec les parents de Matt, et disparurent dans la maison, suivis de Kristin et Erin.

— Ils n'ont pas dit au revoir, murmura Sarah, abasourdie. Pas même un signe de la main !

— De leur point de vue, murmura-t-il en faisant tomber un insecte de l'épaule de Jenny, j'ai profité de Kristin à un moment où elle était trop vulnérable pour se défendre. Une fois que Matt est revenu, j'ai disparu de leur horizon.

Sarah le regarda en fronçant les sourcils.

— Comment peuvent-ils se tromper autant sur ton compte ?

Cette réaction réchauffa le cœur de Luke, mais il voulut quand même lui donner davantage d'explications.

— Matt met la barre très haut, dit-il. Dès son retour, j'ai compris que je ne serais pas à la hauteur, et je suis allé un peu loin dans l'autre sens, pour bien faire comprendre à tout le monde que je ne comptais pas m'interposer.

— Mais…

Ils se turent en voyant une silhouette se diriger vers eux. Le Colonel descendait les marches de la terrasse, lourdement appuyé sur la rampe. Les lumières de la maison faisaient ressortir sa position voûtée. Luke se redressa à demi, inquiet, et tendit Jenny à Sarah.

— Tu veux bien la prendre ?

Le mouvement ne réveilla pas la petite. Sautant sur ses pieds, Luke s'avança à la rencontre de son père.

— Vous partez ? lui demanda-t-il.

— Ta mère pense qu'il est temps pour moi d'aller au lit.

Le Colonel voulut rire, mais il se mit à tousser.

— Elle s'inquiète trop ! grommela-t-il.

Son visage était livide. Luke chercha fiévreusement un prétexte pour lui prendre le bras.

— On dit que c'est le bon côté de la retraite, dit-il d'un ton léger. Couché avec les poules, levé avec le soleil.

Il hocha la tête d'un air de doute, puis leva la main pour saluer Sarah, assise sous un arbre avec Jenny.

— Content de vous avoir revue, mademoiselle Randolph.

Luke rebroussa chemin avec son père. Au bas de l'escalier, le vieil homme s'immobilisa comme pour rassembler ses forces, et gravit la première marche, puis deux autres… à la quatrième, il s'arrêta avec un hoquet. Luke passa un bras autour de la taille mince.

— Papa ? Vous vous sentez bien ?

Le Colonel ne répondit pas, et s'affaissa un peu plus contre son fils. Levant la tête, Luke cria :

— Matt ! Tu veux bien venir une minute ?

Sa mère parut à la porte-fenêtre, vit le tableau et appela à son tour :

— Matt !

L'aîné arriva au pas de course, et se plaça de l'autre côté de son père.

— Laissez-vous faire, papa. Détendez-vous.

Ensemble, les deux hommes le soulevèrent, puis le portèrent à l'intérieur et l'allongèrent sur le canapé du salon. Puis Luke retourna à grands pas vers la cuisine.

— J'appelle un médecin.

— Pas question !

Même affaibli, son père savait encore donner des ordres. A contrecœur, Luke revint vers lui et voulut discuter. Le Colonel se souleva sur un coude.

— Je n'ai pas besoin d'un fichu médecin.

— Bien sûr que si ! lança Elena en s'asseyant près de lui pour lui prendre la main. Tu n'es pas bien du tout.

— Mais si !

Il lâcha la main de sa femme, se redressa, et se mit doucement sur pied. Il était redevenu lui-même, bien que son visage demeurât livide.

— Nous allons rentrer, maintenant, dit-il. Vous dînez avec nous demain, n'est-ce pas ?

D'un geste de la main, il invita sa femme à le précéder.

— Papy ? dit une petite voix. Papy, est-ce que ça va ?

Personne n'avait remarqué la présence d'Erin. S'arrêtant devant elle, le Colonel se pencha lentement pour se mettre à sa hauteur.

— Très bien, ma chérie. Juste un peu fatigué. J'ai beaucoup aimé ta fête d'anniversaire. Donne-moi un baiser.

La petite fille s'exécuta, et le couple entra lentement dans la maison.

Quand la porte se referma derrière eux, Luke, Kristin et Matt échangèrent un long regard. Ce fut Erin qui rompit le silence.

— Où est Jenny ?

— Ici !

Luke se retourna. Sarah sortait de la cuisine avec une petite grimace comique, tenant par la main une Jenny très grognon.

— Elle n'était pas contente de se réveiller dehors, avec moi pour toute compagnie !

— Maman ! cria la petite en tendant les bras vers Kristin.

La jeune femme se hâta de la rejoindre.

— Tout va bien, mon cœur. Je crois que c'est l'heure du bain pour mes deux grandes filles. Erin, embrasse ton papa… et aussi ton papa Matt.

Erin courut vers Luke.

— Tu veux bien me lire une histoire avant de partir, papa ?

Il lui pinça le nez en riant.

— Il est trop tard, Erin l'Ourson. Un autre soir, d'accord ?

La fillette se détourna d'un air boudeur, puis jeta un regard à Matt, et lui demanda :

— Et toi, tu veux bien ?

Evidemment, Matt n'hésita pas.

— Bien sûr ! Va choisir un livre : je viens te rejoindre dès que tu seras au lit.

Luke attendit d'être sûr qu'Erin était montée dans sa chambre pour murmurer :

— Voilà un bon moyen de marquer des points, frangin.

— Ce n'est pas un jeu, Luke. Il n'y a aucune raison pour que je ne lui lise pas une histoire.

— Sauf que je venais de lui dire non. Sauf qu'il est tard et qu'elle a besoin de dormir.

— Et alors ? Elle s'endormira pendant l'histoire. Où est le problème ?

— Nous nous étions mis d'accord pour collaborer, pas pour tirer la couverture à soi.

— C'est pour ça que tu te mets entre nous en permanence ? Pour collaborer ?

Derrière lui, Sarah poussa une petite exclamation désolée. Serrant les poings et les dents, il répondit :

— Je m'occupe de mes enfants.

— Ce sont *mes* enfants, maintenant. Et *ma* femme.

A ces mots, Luke cessa de se contrôler : il se précipita vers Matt, le prit par le col de sa chemise, et lui lança au visage, d'une voix menaçante :

— Seulement parce que je me suis retiré de la compétition, mon frère. N'oublie jamais ça ! Penses-y pendant que tu joues avec tes enfants, pendant que tu fais l'amour à ta femme. Je t'ai laissé la place. Si je ne l'avais pas fait, tu n'aurais rien du tout.

Il commença à secouer Matt, mais celui-ci ne recula pas. Finalement, il le lâcha, lui tourna le dos, et découvrit Sarah, figée, les doigts pressés sur ses lèvres.

— Je suis désolé, Sarah Rose. Je crois qu'il est temps de partir.

Il l'entraîna énergiquement, et sentit sa main trembler dans la sienne. A moins que ce ne fût la vibration de son propre corps ?

Ils roulèrent en silence jusque chez la jeune femme. Cette fois, elle ne discuta pas quand il lui proposa de l'accompagner jusqu'à sa porte.

Après avoir ouvert, elle lui dit simplement :

— Entre.

Infiniment soulagé, il la remercia d'un signe de tête.

Assis côte à côte sur le canapé, ils sirotèrent plusieurs verres sans dire un mot. Enfin, Luke laissa reposer sa tête sur les coussins.

— Je regrette, tu sais ? Tu n'aurais pas dû assister à ça.

— Ne t'en fais pas pour moi. Ce sont les filles qui souffrent de cette situation.

Il ferma les yeux, secoua la tête.

— Je sais. Ça leur fait du mal. Je ne vois qu'une solution… et je ne peux pas aller jusqu'au bout.

Elle lui prit son verre des mains, le posa sur la table basse avec le sien.

— Quelle solution ? demanda-t-elle.

— Je pourrais m'en aller, répondit-il d'une voix étranglée.

— Luke…

— Les tensions s'apaiseraient si je mettais de la distance entre nous. Si les filles me voyaient moins souvent.

— Tu leur manquerais terriblement.

— Elles s'habitueraient à Matt. Kristin et lui vivraient plus tranquillement : je ne serais plus là pour leur rappeler le passé en permanence.

Elle posa une main légère sur son bras.

— Pourquoi est-ce toi qui devrais partir ? Ils pourraient déménager, eux aussi. Matt pourrait demander une mutation.

— Mais alors, les filles seraient privées de leurs grands-parents, de leurs copines ; elles devraient changer d'école. Moi, je n'ai de liens nulle part. Je pourrais vivre n'importe où.

— Tu as envie de partir ?

— Pas du tout ! Je deviens fou si je reste une semaine sans les voir. Je passerais mon temps à me torturer en pensant à tout ce qui peut leur arriver. Et puis, il y a mon père. Il ne va pas bien du tout, c'est évident. Quand j'avais onze ans, il a fait une crise cardiaque. C'est à ce moment-là qu'il a pris sa retraite de l'armée, et qu'il s'est installé à Myrtle Beach. S'il est malade, je préfère être près de lui.

Sarah hocha la tête, et ils se turent de nouveau. Luke ne s'était pas rendu compte qu'il avait froid avant de sentir la chaleur de sa paume sur son bras. Il se cramponna à cette sensation tellement réconfortante.

— Tu es une amie, Sarah Rose. Une véritable amie. Merci de me supporter.

Il vit qu'elle rougissait.

— J'aime bien être ton amie, murmura-t-elle.

Elle leva la tête vers lui. La lumière douce se refléta dans ses yeux mouillés.

— Ne pleure pas ! supplia-t-il. Je ne veux pas te faire pleurer.

Elle cligna des yeux, et une larme roula sur sa joue, s'attarda au coin de sa bouche. Luke tendit la main, et l'essuya doucement. Sa peau était douce comme du velours. Du bout des doigts, il dessina le contour de son visage. Elle pencha la tête comme pour savourer ce contact, puis murmura son nom dans un soupir…

Sans qu'ils sachent qui avait fait le premier geste, leurs bouches se rejoignirent.

Aussitôt, Luke s'émerveilla de la sentir si menue entre ses bras. Elle leva les bras pour les nouer autour de son cou, plongea les doigts dans ses cheveux, les glissa sous sa chemise… elle le foudroyait de désir. Le désir sans le désespoir !

Il avait presque oublié le bonheur d'être désiré. Sarah disait son désir avec chacune des plaintes étouffées qui lui échappaient. Quel merveilleux cadeau ! Il avait renoncé à tout, et voilà que cette femme surgissait dans sa vie…

Les baisers de Luke lui coupaient le souffle. Ses mains lui communiquaient une véritable fièvre de désir, et pourtant, pourtant… elle en aurait pleuré, mais il restait encore une contrainte entre eux. Il demandait si peu, se donnait tout entier à ceux qu'il aimait… quelqu'un devait enfin répondre à sa générosité, sans réserve et sans arrière-pensée. Sans tabler sur l'avenir ni se souvenir du passé.

Tout à coup, elle sentit ses mains s'immobiliser. Il prit une respiration tremblante, et dit d'une voix rauque :

— Sarah, je n'ai rien. Aucune protection.

Elle se nicha contre lui.

— Moi non plus, je n'ai rien.

— Alors, je vais aller…

Elle secoua la tête en pressant son visage contre lui.

— Non, ne t'en va pas !

— Il le faut ! dit-il avec un petit rire. Je vais aller acheter ce qu'il nous faut. Ou alors, ajouta-t-il en lui caressant les cheveux, je peux rentrer chez moi.

Elle se figea. Il lui offrait une chance de faire machine arrière…

Elle s'écarta, juste assez pour croiser son regard gris, étincelant de passion.

— Reviens vite, chuchota-t-elle. Je t'attends.

Le sourire heureux de Luke fut sa récompense.

— Te voilà, murmura-t-elle.

Il lança la petite boîte de préservatifs sur le lit, et marcha droit sur elle.

— Tu es belle.

Elle avait défait sa tresse, peigné ses longs cheveux et enfilé une tunique blanche et douce qui effleurait la pointe de ses seins, le renflement de ses hanches.

— Tellement belle…

Plongeant les doigts dans cette merveilleuse chevelure, il attira sa bouche vers la sienne. Avec un petit gémissement, elle glissa les mains sous sa chemise. Il retint son souffle et l'embrassa de toute son âme.

— Pas de regrets ? demanda-t-il au bout d'un moment.

Elle secoua la tête, lui mordit le cou. Il ne put retenir une plainte. Elle frémit en entendant sa voix vibrante de désir, en sentant ses doigts jouer avec la bretelle de sa tunique. Il allait prendre tout son temps, elle le sentait. Et elle qui mourait d'impatience !

Il prit, en effet, le temps de découvrir chaque courbe, chaque secret de son corps. Jamais elle n'avait été aimée de cette façon, jamais on ne l'avait emportée aussi loin hors d'elle-même.

Ils tremblaient tous les deux.

Bientôt, les mains de Luke se firent plus impatientes. Il lui retira sa tunique, et elle partit, à son tour, à la découverte de son corps.

Enfin, il s'abandonna complètement entre ses bras, sa peau chaude et lisse contre la sienne, leurs souffles mêlés. Elle l'accueillit en elle, se donnant tout entière pour le bonheur fou de l'entendre crier son nom.

A la place de la crispation douloureuse et si familière, il ressentait un apaisement. Une aisance et une légèreté toutes neuves. Enfin, une journée qu'il ne redoutait pas, une journée qu'il n'aurait pas à endurer en attendant de pouvoir se réfugier dans le sommeil ! Aujourd'hui, il y aurait Sarah.

Il tourna la tête. Elle dormait, blottie contre lui. Tandis qu'il la contemplait, ses cils battirent, ses paupières se soulevèrent un instant.

— J'adore ce genre de rêve, murmura-t-elle en refermant les yeux.

— Quel genre ?

Elle s'étira, se rapprocha encore de lui.

— Le rêve où je me réveille auprès d'un homme adorable. Quand on fait l'amour, toi et moi, il y a un échange si fort que je le sens encore en me réveillant.

Cette voix enrouée, délicieusement langoureuse...

Il sentit son cœur s'emballer, et enfouit la bouche au creux de son cou, là où battait son pouls. Elle renversa la tête en arrière, et poussa un long soupir.

Le dimanche soir, ils reprenaient leur souffle, mêlés l'un à l'autre, quand le téléphone sonna. Sarah fit un geste pour s'écarter, mais Luke la retint contre lui tout en décrochant.

— Allô ?

Sa voix était encore plus sensuelle, plus moelleuse après l'amour. Elle sourit en l'entendant vibrer à son oreille, dans les profondeurs de sa poitrine.

Mais, soudain, il se raidit.

— Bonsoir, Kristin.

Cette fois, quand Sarah s'écarta, il la lâcha et se redressa à son tour.

— Pourquoi m'appelles-tu ?

L'air de la chambre se refroidit comme si une trappe s'était ouverte quelque part. Luke se détourna complètement, offrant au regard de Sarah la ligne élégante de son dos.

Tout en s'habillant, elle entendit, malgré elle, une partie de la discussion.

— Bon, je trouve ça raisonnable. Je préviendrai Sarah. Pas de problème. Les filles vont bien ?... Des glaces ? Sa cote va monter en flèche... Oui, je sais : il fait des efforts. Je te rappelle que moi aussi.

Il se tut quelques secondes.

— Tu es bien la seule. Oui, tu as raison. On a tous besoin de temps. C'est ça. A bientôt.

Il raccrocha, resta quelques instants immobile au bord du lit, puis, avec un soupir, il tendit la main vers sa chemise.

Une fois habillé, il se tourna vers Sarah.

— Kristin a convaincu Matt de signer l'autorisation. Tu vas pouvoir faire publier tes photos, Sarah Rose.

Il lui sourit, mais elle sentit l'effort qu'il faisait. La tension était de retour dans ses yeux, autour de sa bouche. Elle eut du mal à lui rendre son sourire.

— Parfait. Je vous fais parvenir les papiers dans un jour ou deux.

La présence de Kristin se dressait entre eux. Pour la première fois depuis vendredi soir, Sarah se sentait coupée de son amant, gênée par son regard.

— Euh... j'ai faim, dit-elle gaiement. J'irais bien manger des fruits de mer quelque part !

Il lisait en elle, devinait ce qu'elle ressentait. Son regard d'excuse lui serra le cœur.

— C'est une excellente idée !

Pendant tout le repas, ils évitèrent avec soin les sujets de conversation importants. Quand Luke ramena la jeune femme chez elle, elle hésita. Devait-elle lui proposer d'entrer ? Elle ne savait plus ce qu'il souhaitait ni même ce qu'elle souhaitait elle-même.

— Qu'est-ce que tu dirais d'une bonne nuit de sommeil ? demanda-t-il en glissant la main dans la sienne.

Cherchait-il à prendre ses distances ? Troublée, elle protesta :

— J'ai très bien dormi, ces derniers temps !

— Ce n'est pas le souvenir que j'en garde. Tu as envie d'une nuit tranquille ? Je ne veux pas prendre toute la place.

— Tu as pris juste la place qu'il fallait.

Voulait-il dire qu'il avait besoin d'un peu de temps à lui ?

— Cela dit, j'avoue que j'ai des petites choses à faire, ajouta-t-elle. Des factures à payer, par exemple. Ce serait le moment de rattraper mon retard.

Il approuva de la tête, descendit de voiture et vint lui ouvrir sa portière.

— D'accord. Je t'appelle demain matin ?

Douze longues heures de solitude...

— Très bien !

Il l'accompagna jusqu'à sa porte, et ils se dirent au revoir sur le seuil. Elle se sentait affreusement triste. Luke se penchait pour l'embrasser quand deux gosses surgirent. Luke entraîna la jeune femme à l'intérieur, et repoussa la porte derrière lui.

— Je n'aime pas me donner en spectacle.

Ses bras se refermèrent sur elle, sa bouche s'empara de la sienne… elle se sentit fondre. Elle ne voulait pas le laisser partir ; elle ne voulait pas passer cette nuit toute seule. Saurait-elle le convaincre de rester ?

— Sarah, murmura-t-il, tu ne me facilites pas la tâche.

— Tant mieux ! chuchota-t-elle. C'est bien le but.

Elle glissa les mains à l'intérieur de sa chemise, se réchauffa les paumes à la peau lisse de son dos nu.

Il eut un petit rire heureux.

— Dans ce cas…

A tâtons, il verrouilla la porte, et s'attaqua au premier bouton de son corsage.

Les yeux ouverts dans la nuit, Sarah tenait doucement sur sa poitrine la tête de Luke endormi. Physiquement, ils n'auraient pas pu être plus proches. Leur passion ne faisait que grandir chaque fois qu'ils faisaient l'amour. Mais le lien entre eux était brisé. Ou, tout au moins, effiloché. Kristin occupait de nouveau le territoire… à supposer qu'elle l'eût jamais libéré.

Sarah savait bien, pourtant, avant de faire l'amour avec Luke pour la première fois, que son cœur appartenait à son ex-femme et à ses filles. Elle avait cru pouvoir accepter le risque, et maintenant… maintenant qu'il était trop tard pour revenir en arrière, elle découvrait que le fait d'être prévenue ne faisait rien pour adoucir son chagrin.

11.

En ouvrant la porte à son ex-mari, Kristin sentit tout de suite que quelque chose avait changé. Pendant plusieurs secondes, elle scruta son visage, puis se ressaisit et l'accueillit normalement.

— Entre, lui dit-elle. Les filles terminent leur repas.

— Merci. Le dîner de dimanche s'est bien passé ?

Il passa devant elle et, dans ses mouvements, elle discerna une liberté et une aisance qu'elle ne lui connaissait plus.

— Bien. Très bien.

Elle n'osa pas lui demander pourquoi il n'était pas venu.

— Et papa, il se sentait bien ?

Tout en le précédant vers la cuisine, elle secoua la tête.

— Il n'a rien dit, bien sûr, mais... il a un autre rendez-vous chez le médecin, la semaine prochaine. Ta mère a insisté.

— Elle a bien fait.

Dès qu'ils entrèrent dans la cuisine, Jenny glissa de sa chaise et se rua dans les bras de son père.

— On peut jouer au golf ? Dis, on peut ?

Erin imita sa sœur, et renchérit :

—Ça fait très longtemps qu'on n'a plus fait le circuit du dragon, papa !

Luke éclata de rire. Un rire libre et joyeux.

— Pourquoi pas ? On fera aussi un tour en bateau, pendant qu'on y est. Prenez vos chapeaux : on file !

Les petites se précipitèrent à l'étage, laissant leurs parents en tête à tête. Curieusement, leur gêne semblait s'être dissipée. S'appuyant de l'épaule au chambranle de la porte, Luke annonça :

— Sarah va apporter des copies de l'autorisation de publication, cet après-midi. Tu pourras signer quand je ramènerai les filles.

En l'entendant prononcer le nom de Sarah, elle comprit tout. Le timbre de sa voix, la douceur de ses yeux, cette détente de tout son corps… Luke et Sarah Randolph avaient fait l'amour, elle en était certaine. Après cinq années de vie commune, elle savait lire en lui.

Kristin se sentit submergée par une foule d'émotions : sentiment d'abandon, soulagement, deuil et joie.

— Sarah vous accompagne, aujourd'hui ?

— Oui. Je voudrais que les filles apprennent à mieux la connaître. Et vice versa.

— C'est quelqu'un de bien. Et une merveilleuse photographe.

— Oui, c'est vrai.

Elle entendit de nouveau cette richesse particulière dans sa voix. Dimanche soir, au téléphone, elle l'avait déjà notée sans en deviner la raison… Ce souvenir la fit rougir. Tournant le dos à Luke et à ses propres pensées, elle se mit à essuyer le plan de travail immaculé.

Erin et Jenny revinrent au grand galop, casquettes de base-ball de travers, les yeux brillants d'excitation.

— On y va, papa ! cria Erin en lui saisissant la main.

— On y va ! répéta Jenny. Au revoir, maman.

Sans même un baiser, elle courut vers la porte. Erin la suivit, tirant Luke par la main.

— Je te les ramène avant 20 heures, promit Luke. Profites-en pour te reposer... ou pour t'amuser !

Sur ces mots, et pour la première fois depuis un an, il posa la main sur son épaule.

Elle essayait encore de se reprendre quand il rejoignit les filles qui trépignaient d'impatience.

— On y va, les jolies !

La voiture s'éloigna. Les filles agitaient furieusement les mains par les vitres ouvertes. Kristin leur fit signe à son tour, puis referma la porte et s'adossa contre le battant en écoutant le silence qui régnait dans la maison.

Luke avait repris sa liberté. Entre l'anniversaire d'Erin et aujourd'hui, il s'était remis à vivre. Une autre femme était entrée dans son existence, un nouvel amour allait remplacer la relation tendre qu'ils avaient bâtie avec tant de soin. Elle avait envie de pleurer et, en même temps, elle se sentait heureuse pour lui. Sincèrement heureuse. Luke était sauvé.

Mais était-il encore temps de sauver la relation entre les deux frères ? Et sa propre relation avec son mari ?

Elle l'ignorait.

— Salut ! Il paraît qu'on va jouer au golf miniature ?

Jenny fourra son pouce dans sa bouche. Sur un ton glacé, Erin demanda :

— Tu viens avec nous ?

— C'est extra, non ? lança papa. Sarah ne sait même pas jouer. J'ai pensé que vous pourriez lui apprendre.

— Mais...

Erin se tut, abasourdie par cette trahison. Comme elle ne disait plus rien, son père la regarda dans le rétroviseur.

— Oui, Erin l'Ourson ?

— Rien.

Il fronça les sourcils sans insister.

Erin donna un coup de poing contre le dossier de son siège, et braqua son regard furieux sur le plafond. Elle commençait à en avoir assez ! D'abord, il y avait eu papa Matt. Au début, il n'était que tonton Matt. Il était parti pendant très longtemps et, quand il était revenu, tout le monde s'était mis à pleurer, même papy Brennan. Ensuite, tout avait commencé à aller de travers. Maman pleurait — pas comme quand on lui apportait le petit déjeuner au lit pour la Fête des Mères : elle pleurait de tristesse, et ça faisait très peur.

Papa ne disait plus rien. Ils ne parlaient plus ensemble, papa et maman, sauf tard le soir, quand ils pensaient qu'elle dormait. Elle les entendait, de temps en temps, et ce qu'ils disaient lui donnait mal au ventre.

Puis il y avait eu le jour où ils s'étaient assis tous les quatre à la table de la cuisine, avec un grand plat des cookies spéciaux de papa. Maman s'était mise à parler la première, pour expliquer que les gens mariés ne réussissaient pas toujours à vivre ensemble. Il pouvait arriver des choses, et ils devaient réfléchir à ce qu'ils voulaient faire. Ensuite, papa avait dit que c'était arrivé à lui et à maman. Ensuite…

Erin ferma les yeux de toutes ses forces. Elle détestait se souvenir de la suite. Ensuite, papa était parti. Il avait emballé ses affaires pour s'installer dans la petite maison où il habitait maintenant. C'était déjà assez dur, mais après, tonton Matt avait commencé à venir chez eux. Il les emmenait au cinéma, à la plage, aux parcs d'attractions. Quelquefois, il sortait avec maman, et papa venait les chercher, Jen et elle. D'autres fois, elles restaient à la maison, et une jeune fille venait les garder.

Le 13 janvier, une semaine après l'anniversaire de Jenny, maman avait dit qu'elle allait épouser tonton Matt. C'était le pire souvenir de tous. Et maintenant, papa voulait emmener cette espèce de Sarah avec lui pour leurs sorties ? Est-ce qu'il allait l'épouser, lui aussi ? Elles n'allaient tout de même pas avoir deux papas et deux mamans !

Comment pouvaient-ils leur faire ça ? Ils ne voyaient pas que c'était trop difficile à comprendre ? A sept ans, on pouvait supporter pas mal de choses, mais Jenny était encore un bébé : elle ne comprenait rien à ce qui se passait. Ce n'était pas juste ! Pourquoi est-ce que tout ne pouvait pas redevenir comme avant ?

— On y est ! s'écria papa. Je vois déjà le grand dragon au-dessus de l'entrée.

Il arrêta la voiture, puis délivra Jenny de son siège auto. Sarah tendit la main à Erin pour l'aider à descendre, mais la fillette fit comme si elle ne l'avait pas vue. On tient la main des gens qu'on aime. Elle était obligée de tenir la main de papa Matt parce qu'il était le mari de maman, mais ça suffisait comme ça. Pas question de le faire avec les autres, et surtout pas avec cette Sarah !

Munie de ses autorisations de publier, Sarah accompagna Luke quand il ramena les enfants. Dès qu'il freina devant la maison, elles filèrent vers la porte sans les attendre.

Kristin apparut, embrassa ses filles, s'agenouilla pour tenter de démêler le sens de leur torrent de paroles. Lorsque Sarah s'approcha, elle leva la tête en riant, un peu rougissante.

— On dirait que l'après-midi s'est bien passé. Bonjour, Sarah. Entrez.

Elle les précéda dans la salle à manger où les attendait Matt. Il ouvrit de grands yeux en les voyant entrer.

— Dis, Erin, qu'est-ce que tu as là ?

— C'est un dragon.

Elle brandit sa peluche, sans s'approcher pour autant.

— J'en ai un aussi ! s'écria Jenny. Le mien est violet.

— Je vois ça, dit Matt en souriant. Qu'est-ce que tu vas faire avec un dragon violet ?

— Je vais dormir avec lui.

— Dormir avec un dragon ? répéta-t-il avec un long sifflement, l'air impressionné. Tu es plus courageuse que moi.

Jenny pouffa, mais Erin s'accrocha au bras de sa mère.

— Je peux prendre quelque chose à boire, maman ?

— Bien sûr. Il y a des jus de fruits au frigo.

— Moi aussi ! Moi aussi !

Jenny se précipita à la suite de sa sœur, laissant les adultes en tête à tête.

Ce fut Kristin qui parla la première :

— Vous avez apporté les autorisations, Sarah ? Je vais chercher un stylo.

Lorsqu'elle quitta la pièce, la température sembla encore chuter de plusieurs degrés. Sarah décida d'ignorer l'hostilité ambiante.

— Vous travaillez au bureau de recrutement, Matt ? Vous avez beaucoup de candidats ?

Il lui sourit, comme s'il appréciait l'effort qu'elle faisait pour briser la glace.

— Surtout l'été, à la fin de l'année scolaire. Et puis de nouveau à l'automne, quand certains jeunes abandonnent la fac.

— Quelle est la proportion de femmes qui veulent entrer dans l'armée ?

— Par ici, c'est minime. En un an, j'ai dû voir une dizaine de candidates, mais il y en a beaucoup plus dans d'autres régions.

— Voilà un stylo ! lança Kristin en revenant dans la pièce. J'ai eu du mal à trouver : les filles font main basse sur tout ce qui permet de dessiner.

Son regard inquiet passa de Matt à Luke, et elle s'avança entre eux en demandant gaiement :

— Où est-ce que je signe ?

Sarah lui montra l'emplacement. Luke avait déjà apposé son nom de son écriture fine et nette ; Kristin inscrivit le sien au-dessus, en grandes lettres rondes et généreuses. Il ne resta à Matt qu'une petite place en bas. Les lèvres serrées, il signa d'une façon qui ressemblait beaucoup à celle de son frère.

— Parfait, dit Sarah, soulagée à l'idée que cette journée si difficile serait bientôt terminée. Quand le numéro paraîtra, j'essaierai de vous en obtenir plusieurs exemplaires. Je suis vraiment contente que vous ayez accepté…

— Ça me fait plaisir à moi aussi, dit Kristin avec un nouveau regard vers son mari.

Sarah comprit qu'elle l'encourageait à se montrer plus cordial. Elle aussi avait envie de secouer Luke pour l'arracher à son silence buté. Ce fut seulement quand Kristin leur ouvrit la porte, au moment du départ, qu'il desserra les dents.

— Il faut que je dise au revoir aux filles. Je reviens tout de suite.

Voyant son frère se diriger vers la cuisine, Matt se leva en lançant :

— Je vous dis bonsoir. J'ai du travail.

— Merci encore, lui dit Sarah.

Il hocha la tête sans sourire, et disparut. Avec un gros soupir, Kristin ferma les yeux et appuya son front contre la porte.

— Ça ne marche pas, dit-elle à voix très basse.

Elle semblait parler toute seule. Sarah se demanda si elle devait répondre. Avant qu'elle ne parvînt à se décider, Kristin reprit :

170

— Je comprends le comportement des enfants, mais je pensais que Matt et Luke...

— Ils vous aiment tous les deux, dit Sarah à contrecœur.

Les yeux bruns de Kristin s'emplirent de larmes.

— Et je les aime aussi, mais pas de la même façon. C'est tout de même incroyable, avec tout cet amour, que nous soyons si malheureux. J'ai pris ce que j'ai voulu, et j'ai gâché la vie de tout le monde.

Sarah lui tendait la main en cherchant une réponse quand Luke reparut.

— Elles sont déjà à moitié endormies. Tu n'auras aucun mal à les coucher, ce soir.

Kristin se redressa.

— Ce sera une grande première. J'espère qu'elles garderont les yeux ouverts assez longtemps pour prendre leur bain.

— Ce ne serait pas un drame de sauter le bain, pour une fois.

— Nous avons déjà eu cette discussion. Le bain est obligatoire.

Amusé, il leva les mains pour montrer qu'il capitulait.

— D'accord, d'accord ! Bon courage, et bonne nuit.

Une fois dans la voiture, son sourire disparut.

— Je suis désolé, Sarah Rose. La journée ne s'est pas du tout passée comme je l'espérais.

— Ce n'est pas grave, dit-elle.

— J'aurais dû me mettre d'accord avec les filles avant de t'inviter. Je crois que, depuis quelques jours, je ne pense plus comme un papa.

Il lui lança un clin d'œil, et elle ne put réprimer un sourire.

— Pas de problème. Chacun essaie encore de s'y retrouver.

— Je suppose que, tôt ou tard, Matt et moi, nous cesserons de nous comporter comme des enfants gâtés.

— Ah, tu t'en rends compte ?

— Oh, oui ! Et lui aussi. Un jour, nous irons même jusqu'à nous l'avouer… mais j'ai bien peur que ce ne soit pas pour demain.

— Ce serait pourtant mieux pour tout le monde. Et surtout pour Kristin.

— Elle a l'air fatiguée, dit-il d'une voix douce. Stressée.

Sarah avala sa salive avec effort.

— Elle se trouve dans une situation intenable. Et elle tient à toi.

— Ouais…

Il démarra doucement en poussant un soupir.

Ils ne se dirent rien de plus, mais Luke prit la main de sa passagère, et mêla ses doigts aux siens. Le plaisir, la souffrance de ce simple contact faillit la faire pleurer.

Après s'être garé devant son immeuble, Luke se retourna vers elle, sans lâcher sa main.

— Je prends mon service dans deux heures. Tu vas encore avoir une bonne nuit de sommeil.

— Pas toi.

— Je dormirai demain matin. Je peux t'appeler, dans l'après-midi ? Je n'ai rien prévu de précis, mais…

Elle n'eut pas la sagesse de chercher à se protéger.

— On trouvera bien quelque chose…

A la lueur du réverbère, elle vit une étincelle s'allumer dans ses yeux.

— Je le pense aussi, murmura-t-il en s'approchant.

Elle sentit son souffle, ses lèvres sur sa peau, faillit se pencher vers lui pour obtenir au moins un baiser. Au dernier instant, elle préféra lui retirer sa main.

— Quittons-nous ici, d'accord ? A demain.

Il soupira, sans chercher à la retenir.

Sarah rentra chez elle, agita la main par la fenêtre, et regarda la voiture quitter le parking. Puis elle éteignit la lampe qu'elle venait d'allumer, et se laissa tomber sur le canapé, le regard fixé sur le vide. Elle pensait à Kristin, au désespoir dans les yeux de Matt, à la tension de Luke, à la confusion sur le visage des deux petites filles. Elle avait peur pour les Brennan, et aussi pour elle-même. Elle avait besoin de tellement plus que ce que Luke pouvait lui donner ! Désirer à ce point ce que l'on ne pouvait obtenir, c'était le meilleur moyen d'avoir le cœur brisé.

— Sarah, tu dois bien être prête à reprendre le collier, depuis le temps ! Le problème des réfugiés est un sujet crucial : tu es la seule à pouvoir faire les photos qu'il me faut.

Après la nuit presque blanche qu'elle venait de passer, elle réagit sans aucune diplomatie.

— Je ne peux pas.

Pas d'explications, pas un mot d'excuse. Il y eut un silence sur la ligne, puis Oliver reprit :

— D'accord. Tu ne peux pas. Je regrette, parce que tu es la meilleure photographe que j'aie jamais eue, mais je ne peux pas te garder si tu ne travailles pas. Je vais demander à quelqu'un d'emballer tes affaires.

Sarah ferma les yeux, se prit la tête dans les mains, et murmura :

— D'accord.

— Appelle-moi un de ces jours.

Il raccrocha sans lui dire au revoir.

*
**

— Désolé, je ne me suis réveillé qu'à 15 heures.

— C'est bien. Tu avais besoin de repos.

Sa voix était morne, découragée. Inquiet, il s'écria :

— Qu'est-ce qui ne va pas ?

— Je viens d'être virée.

— Du journal ? Pourquoi ?

— Parce que j'ai refusé de couvrir un reportage.

— Tu n'as pas voulu parce que...

Il vit tout à coup les choses très clairement. Le jour où elle accepterait un reportage important, Sarah quitterait Myrtle Beach. Cette seule idée lui glaçait le sang.

— Ils ne peuvent pas te donner encore un peu de temps ?

— Mon rédacteur en chef me couvre depuis plus de six mois. Il peut difficilement faire plus. On ne verse pas indéfiniment un salaire à quelqu'un qui ne fait rien.

— Je suis vraiment désolé.

Il disait ça mais, en fait, tout au fond de lui, il était soulagé.

— Tu veux qu'on aille se promener sur la plage ? Ou qu'on mange un morceau tous les deux ?

Il y eut un nouveau silence, puis un nouveau soupir.

— Tu es gentil, mais je ne suis pas de très bonne humeur. On pourrait faire ça demain ?

Il cacha sa déception, s'interdit d'insister.

— Bon. Je t'appelle. Prends bien soin de toi.

— Merci. Toi aussi.

— Je prends toujours soin de moi.

Cette nuit-là, vers 1 heure du matin, il s'arrêta devant un *fast-food* pour prendre un café à emporter. Personne ne prit sa commande. Après avoir patienté plusieurs minutes, il roula jusqu'au guichet suivant, celui des livraisons. La lucarne était vide. Pourtant, l'intérieur de l'établissement était éclairé, et il sentait les arômes qui venaient du gril.

Il avança encore légèrement, de façon à pouvoir jeter un coup d'œil à l'intérieur du restaurant proprement dit. Un seul client se tenait au comptoir, cachant à demi un employé. Luke ne voyait personne d'autre, ni dans la cuisine ni derrière les comptoirs. Un tableau inquiétant.

Il fit marche arrière, alla se garer derrière l'établissement, et appela les renforts par radio.

En les attendant, il réfléchit à toute vitesse : la porte de derrière devait être verrouillée de l'intérieur ; les flics ne pourraient donc pas entrer par là. Mais, en même temps, c'était la sortie la plus logique pour le braqueur.

Retirant le cran de sécurité de son arme, il s'accroupit derrière sa portière ouverte, et patienta.

Comme il l'espérait, aux premières sirènes, la porte du restaurant s'ouvrit à la volée, et un homme sortit en courant.

Aussitôt, il sauta sur ses pieds.

— Police ! Restez où vous êtes !

Des yeux remplis de panique se tournèrent vers lui.

— Allez vous faire… hurla le type en levant son arme.

Une balle vrombit à l'oreille de Luke. Il se tassa sur lui-même, vit l'homme détaler, et se lança à sa poursuite en criant de nouveau :

— Stop ! Police !

L'homme tourna à l'angle d'une rue, et disparut.

Luke s'immobilisa.

— Ecoutez, cria-t-il, vous n'irez nulle part : vous êtes cerné par la police. Laissez tomber avant qu'il n'y ait des victimes. Pour l'instant, on ne peut vous inculper que pour le braquage… Vous voulez vraiment que ça aille plus loin ?

Rangeant son arme sans bruit, il s'accroupit tout contre le mur. Pendant dix bonnes secondes, il ne se passa rien, puis le type sortit de l'ombre, et tira à l'aveuglette.

Aussitôt, Luke se jeta sur ses jambes en pesant de tout son poids. L'arme tomba avec un bruit métallique, et ils roulèrent tous les deux sur le bitume. Luke cherchait furieusement une prise, mais ses mains glissaient sur les vêtements de son adversaire et sur sa peau trempée de sueur. A un moment, il se retrouva au-dessus de lui, mais un coup de poing bien asséné lui coupa le souffle. Il se roula en boule un court instant, puis réussit de nouveau à s'accrocher.

Bon sang, où étaient les renforts ?

Un poids de cent kilos lui écrasait la poitrine et des mains énormes lui serraient le cou quand le déclic sec d'un pistolet que l'on arme retourna la situation.

— Relève-toi, les mains en l'air ! Tout de suite !

Luke songea vaguement que Nick était très impressionnant dans ce rôle de justicier.

Les doigts autour de sa gorge se relâchèrent, ainsi que la pression sur sa poitrine. Il cligna des paupières pour chasser les points noirs qui l'aveuglaient, et vit le canon d'une arme à feu pressé contre l'oreille de son braqueur.

Il s'accorda quelques secondes supplémentaires avant de se redresser, histoire de reprendre son souffle. Nick passa les menottes au malfrat, puis revint se pencher sur son ami.

— Ça va, Brennan ?

— Ouais. Juste un peu essoufflé.

Il se releva, pressa les mains sur ses yeux pour lutter contre une nausée subite.

— Il a blessé quelqu'un, à l'intérieur ? marmonna-t-il.

— Personne. Il leur a fait peur, c'est tout. Allez, va te faire examiner : il y a un médecin dans l'ambulance.

Nick parlait avec désinvolture, mais il lui prit tout de même le coude, et l'aida discrètement à se relever.

— Tu as du sang des deux côtés de la tête, dit-il.

Pendant que l'équipe médicale soignait ses éraflures au front, aux coudes, aux mains et au-dessus de l'oreille où la balle l'avait atteint, il dicta à Nick un rapport sur l'incident. Quand son capitaine lui ordonna de rentrer chez lui, il commença par protester. Avec douceur, Nick le poussa vers sa voiture.

— Va dormir un peu. On peut se débrouiller sans toi pour une nuit.

— Tu crois ça ? Pourtant, regarde : c'est moi qui suis couvert de pansements !

— Oui, tu veux toujours jouer les vedettes. Le seul moyen d'y échapper, c'est de te mettre en arrêt maladie. Et, ce soir, c'est l'occasion ou jamais.

Ces piques amicales le réconfortèrent beaucoup. Il retrouva son sourire.

— Si vous vous décidiez à travailler un peu, bande de flemmards...

— Tu vois, tu peux monter en voiture !

Jenny se contenta de le regarder en suçant son pouce.

— Viens, on va retrouver ta sœur.

Poussant son Caddie, il sillonna les travées... il ne voyait Erin nulle part. Son cœur se mit à battre plus fort. Il arrivait que des gosses disparaissent dans les supermarchés, et qu'on ne les revoie jamais...

Il la trouva, comme il aurait dû s'y attendre, à la librairie. En le voyant, elle sursauta et rangea bien vite le livre qu'elle tenait à la main. Matt respira à fond. Inutile de faire toute une histoire. Un jour ou l'autre, elle aurait confiance.

— Qu'est-ce que tu lisais ?

— Juste un livre pour dresser les chiens.

— Tu aimes les chiens ?

Elle fit oui de la tête.

— Tu en as déjà eu un ?

— Non. Maman dit qu'on n'est pas assez grandes.

— Eh bien… on pourrait peut-être en reparler. Moi, ça me manque de ne pas avoir de chien.

Pour une fois, sa fille le regarda droit dans les yeux.

— C'est vrai ?

— Vrai de vrai, répondit-il avec un large sourire.

Elle faillit sourire en retour.

— Ce serait *cool* !

Reprenant son Caddie, il se dirigea vers le bout de la travée.

— Alors, dépêchons-nous de finir les courses. Plus vite on rentrera, plus vite on pourra en parler avec maman.

Ils mirent aussitôt leurs forces en commun : Matt lisait la liste de Kristin, Erin prenait les produits sur les étagères, et Jenny grignotait des biscuits.

En chargeant les sacs à l'arrière du monospace, Matt était plutôt satisfait…

Au lieu de se reposer comme il le lui avait conseillé, Kristin avait profité de l'absence des filles pour faire la lessive, laver les sols et nettoyer le four.

Laissant les filles monter dans leurs chambres, il se mit à ranger les provisions.

— Tu travailles trop, madame Brennan, dit-il. Tu étais censée faire la sieste.

Elle avait tant besoin de se reposer ! La nuit ne lui apportait aucun répit ; s'il se réveillait, il la trouvait généralement assise dans la cuisine devant une tisane. S'il l'interrogeait, elle disait seulement : « Je réfléchis ».

— Je me suis reposée, je t'assure, dit-elle.

— Cinq minutes ?

— Au moins dix !

Jenny redescendit bruyamment de l'étage.

— Maman ! Erin ne veut pas me montrer son nouveau livre.

— Quel nouveau livre, mon cœur ?

— Celui qu'elle a eu au magasin.

Kristin lança à Matt un regard interrogateur.

— Je n'ai acheté aucun livre, affirma-t-il. Sinon, je leur en aurai pris un à chacune.

Elle approuva de la tête, et prit la main de Jenny.

— Allons voir ce livre.

Matt les suivit. Ils trouvèrent Erin assise sur son lit, plongée dans un grand livre sur les océans. Kristin s'assit près d'elle.

— Jenny dit que tu as un livre neuf ?

La gamine secoua la tête sans regarder sa mère.

— Il est à moi, maman. Tu te souviens ? Tu me l'as acheté au Monde de la Mer.

— Je m'en souviens, oui.

Se tournant vers la plus petite, elle demanda :

— C'est ce livre que tu as vu, Jenny ?

Butée, la cadette fit la moue.

— Non. C'était un livre avec des chiens : je voulais voir les images et elle ne voulait pas.

Matt, qui s'était appuyé au chambranle de la porte, se redressa, interdit. Avant qu'il ne pût intervenir, Kristin posa la main sur le genou de sa fille aînée.

— Erin, tu as un nouveau livre sur les chiens ?

— Cafteuse ! lança-t-elle à sa sœur en lui tirant la langue.

Puis elle glissa la main sous son oreiller, et en tira le livre en question.

— Où as-tu eu ce livre, Erin ? demanda Matt.

Kristin lui lança un regard d'avertissement, qu'il décida d'ignorer.

— C'est le livre dont nous avons parlé au supermarché, dit-il. Comment est-il arrivé ici ?

— Matt...

La réponse était évidente. Kristin ne voulait pas qu'il s'en mêlât, mais Erin était sa fille, et il irait jusqu'au bout.

— Dis-nous comment tu as eu ce livre, Erin.

Elle le jeta sur le lit.

— Je l'ai pris, d'accord ?

— Erin ! s'écria Kristin, abasourdie. Tu as pris ce livre sans le payer ?

— Tu sais comment ça s'appelle ? demanda Matt.

— Voler, répondit la petite, les yeux baissés.

Puis elle se redressa brusquement, l'air furieux.

— Bon, j'ai volé ce livre, avoua-t-elle. Et alors ?

12.

Médusée, Kristin dévisagea sa fille. Des mensonges ?
De l'insolence ? Du chapardage ?

— Erin, reste dans ta chambre, dit Matt. Ta maman et
moi, nous devons parler. Donne-moi le livre.

Erin le lui lança, puis se jeta en travers du lit.

— Viens, Kris, dit Matt en prenant la main de sa femme.
Jenny, sois gentille, va jouer dans ta chambre un petit
moment.

— Je veux rester avec Erin.

— Je ne crois pas que ce soit une bonne idée.

Devançant les objections de Kristin, Matt prit Jenny dans
ses bras, et sortit avec elle. La petite se mit à pleurer. Sans
fléchir, il la déposa sur son lit, puis il entraîna Kristin dans
leur propre chambre.

— Qu'est-ce qu'on fait, maintenant ? demanda-t-il en
s'adossant contre la porte close. Elle a déjà fait quelque
chose de ce genre ?

— Bien sûr que non ! s'exclama Kristin en se laissant
tomber dans un fauteuil. Je n'arrive pas à y croire. Tu es
bien sûr que tu n'as pas acheté ce livre ?

— J'en suis sûr, Kris. Elle l'avait remis en rayon. Elle a
dû le reprendre dès que j'ai eu le dos tourné. Nous n'avons
pas payé ce livre.

— Eh bien, il va falloir que je lui parle très sérieusement. Il faut qu'elle comprenne.

— Je vais m'en charger.

— Pourquoi ?

— Je suis son père.

— Mais…

Kristin avait très peur du résultat.

— Je sais que tes intentions sont bonnes, Matt, mais la situation est tellement compliquée ! Si tu estimes que je suis trop indulgente avec Erin, peut-être… peut-être que Luke…

Violemment, Matt heurta le panneau de la porte du plat de la main.

— Je le savais ! Je savais que tu allais dire ça.

— Il connaît Erin mieux que quiconque. Il saura lui parler.

— Il n'y a pas de place dans cette famille pour deux pères… ou deux maris. Tu vas devoir te décider…

Il se tut, et se passa les mains sur le visage.

— Nous sommes mariés depuis deux mois, lui dit Kristin, et tu parles de partir ?

— Parce que tu me pousses dehors !

Elle le regarda droit dans les yeux. Il soutint son regard. Ses yeux très bleus, si semblables à ceux d'Erin, jetaient des éclairs de défi, brûlaient de chagrin. Le souffle coupé, Kristin ravala tout ce qu'elle aurait aimé dire, toutes les protestations, les argumentations, les accusations… Elle avait gâché son premier mariage : elle ne pouvait pas détruire aussi le second.

— Je suis désolée, dit-elle. Tu as raison : c'est à toi de parler à Erin. Elle a fait ça alors qu'elle était avec toi.

Il la regarda avec une certaine méfiance.

— C'est rapide, comme volte-face.

— Je me trompais.

Elle traversa la pièce, vint se planter devant lui, et posa ses mains tremblantes sur sa poitrine.

— C'est toi mon mari ; c'est toi le chef de famille.

Il referma les bras autour d'elle, et elle sentit sa poitrine se soulever dans un énorme soupir. Il était là, en chair et en os ; il avait survécu pour revenir vers elle et l'enfant qu'il ne connaissait pas. Que demander de plus ?

Ce cadeau qui lui était fait, elle le mériterait. Matt ne douterait plus jamais de son amour. Ils étaient faits pour vivre ensemble ; les filles finiraient bien par le comprendre. Elle les y aiderait. La santé et la force de leur mariage, l'équilibre de toute la famille dépendait d'elle. Elle ne laisserait plus rien ni personne le menacer.

Luke ne cessait de penser à Sarah, qui avait perdu son job parce qu'elle ne voulait pas repartir. Avait-il une part de responsabilité dans cette décision ? Ils n'avaient fait aucun projet, n'avaient jamais mis de mots sur ce qui se passait entre eux. Luke aurait été bien en peine de le définir. Tout ce qu'il savait, c'est qu'avec Sarah, la vie valait la peine d'être vécue. Elle était sa raison de continuer. Rien ne comptait plus que cela.

Il retourna ce raisonnement dans sa tête, tout en s'habillant et en avalant une tasse de café. Puis il l'appela chez elle. Il tomba sur le répondeur, mais ne laissa pas de message.

Sur une impulsion subite, il composa le numéro de Kristin.

— Quoi de neuf avec les petites Brennan, aujourd'hui ?

Elle hésita.

— Euh… pas grand-chose. J'emmènerai peut-être Jenny à la bibliothèque, après sa sieste.

183

— Et Erin, qu'est-ce qu'elle fait ? demanda-t-il, surpris.

— Erin est privée de sorties. Depuis vendredi.

— Tu as privé de sorties une gamine de sept ans ? Pourquoi ?

Médusé, il écouta les explications de son ex-femme.

— Erin a volé un livre ? Mais pourquoi ?

— Elle refuse de le dire. Je crois qu'elle est en colère. Contre tout le monde.

— Nous avons pourtant répété aux filles qu'elles pouvaient tout nous dire, qu'elles n'avaient aucune raison de redouter notre réaction...

— C'était avant... avant le retour de Matt. Je ne crois pas qu'Erin soit très à l'aise pour parler avec lui.

— Et dire que je n'étais pas là !

— Ce n'est pas ta faute : tu le sais bien !

— Alors, tu lui as démontré les conséquences de sa bêtise ? Ça me semble raisonnable.

— En fait, Luke...

Il sentit qu'elle rassemblait son courage pour continuer.

— En fait, Matt a géré toute la situation. Erin a pris le livre pendant qu'elle était avec lui, sous sa responsabilité. J'ai trouvé plus juste que la punition vienne de lui.

Le premier réflexe de Luke fut de protester avec véhémence — puis il ravala son orgueil.

— Je suppose... que c'est logique. Elle a le droit de parler au téléphone ?

— Seulement à toi. Je vais la chercher.

Il n'eut que quelques secondes à attendre.

— Papa ?

— Salut, Erin l'Ourson. Il paraît qu'il s'en passe de belles ?

Elle ne répondit pas.

— Tu sais que c'est mal de voler, n'est-ce pas ?

— Il m'a obligée.

— Qui t'a obligée ?

— Papa Matt.

Luke faillit éclater de rire, mais se contrôla de justesse.

— Comment ça ?

— Si tu habitais avec nous, tout serait normal.

— Erin, si j'habitais avec vous, je t'obligerais à ranger ta chambre et à être gentille avec ta petite sœur. Rien n'est parfait, ma chérie. Et tu sais que je t'aime, quoi qu'il arrive. Tu le sais bien ?

Il entendit un reniflement, puis un sanglot. Ce fut difficile, mais il réussit à la calmer. Longuement, il lui expliqua qu'elle était en droit d'être furieuse contre lui, contre sa mère, contre Matt, contre le monde entier, mais que le fait de voler dans les magasins n'arrangerait rien. Il parlait d'expérience : des bêtises, il en avait fait plus que sa part.

Il raccrocha sur des mots de tendresse… pour se retrouver confronté à ses propres problèmes.

Entre un homme et une femme, il savait ce qui comptait : un engagement, un mariage, une famille — tout ce qu'il croyait avoir construit avec sa femme.

Mais, aujourd'hui, Kristin cessait d'être pour lui une source de souffrance. Sarah Rose lui avait apporté la joie et le réconfort. Et lui, qu'était-il pour elle ? L'inquiétude ne cessait de grandir en lui, car il ne savait pas ce qu'elle faisait ni à quoi elle pensait. Elle avait téléphoné vendredi, alors qu'il dormait encore. Dans son message, elle disait seulement qu'elle reprendrait bientôt contact mais qu'elle devait d'abord réfléchir un peu. Que voulait-elle dire par là ? Avait-elle changé d'avis à son sujet ? Lui était-il impossible de renoncer à sa carrière ? Elle ne serait tout de même pas partie faire un reportage à l'autre bout du monde, sans même lui dire au revoir ! Que ferait-il, si jamais elle partait ?

Le lundi matin, Sarah décida d'aller faire un tour sur le front de mer, du côté des magasins de souvenirs, des cafés bondés et colorés où se retrouvaient les touristes et les gens du cru, les uns pour s'amuser, les autres pour travailler.

Comme une vacancière, elle emporta son appareil photo, et fit quelques portraits : des enfants, des surfeurs, de jeunes beautés accoudées à la rambarde de la promenade, un vieux couple marchant bras dessus, bras dessous… Les deux rouleaux de pellicule qu'elle avait emportés furent terminés en un temps record.

De retour chez elle, elle grimpa l'escalier en sifflotant. Du haut des marches, elle jeta un coup d'œil vers sa porte… et vit le gros colis posé sur le seuil.

Elle ralentit, s'arrêta à bonne distance. Quelqu'un lui avait envoyé un cadeau ? Mais qui ? Dans certains endroits du globe, un colis abandonné représentait un danger mortel ; elle avait fait un reportage sur le sujet. La matinée ensoleillée lui sembla tout à coup très froide. Etait-il possible que ce fût une bombe ? Devait-elle soupçonner le fou qui l'avait déjà agressée ? Fallait-il appeler la police ?

Pendant un temps qui lui sembla interminable, elle resta paralysée. Puis, derrière elle, quelqu'un grimpa les marches. Elle se retourna d'un bond en étouffant un cri.

— Sarah, je suis désolé, dit Luke. Je sais que tu voulais du temps pour te retourner, mais… il fallait que je sache.

Elle leva la main pour l'arrêter.

— Ne bouge plus. Il y a un…

Il avait déjà vu le paquet. Les sourcils froncés, il se rapprocha d'elle et posa sur son bras une main tiède, réconfortante.

— Tu sais d'où ça vient ?

Elle fit non de la tête, se pencha légèrement vers l'objet de ses craintes, et reconnut le logo qui figurait sur le papier d'emballage. Un E majuscule par-dessus un cercle représentant le monde. Le bureau de la rédaction de *Events*, à New York. A la fois gênée et soulagée, la jeune femme s'adossa au mur avec un soupir.

— C'est mon journal. Le rédacteur en chef. J'avais oublié qu'il devait m'envoyer... du courrier qu'il gardait pour moi.

— Ouf !

— Autrefois, on était toujours content de recevoir un colis. Maintenant, à moins de savoir qui l'a envoyé, ça fait froid dans le dos !

Elle regardait le paquet avec l'impression de le voir pour la première fois.

— A propos de choses qui font froid dans le dos, reprit-elle, qu'est-ce qui t'est arrivé ?

Luke haussa les épaules, réprima une grimace.

— J'ai eu des difficultés avec un type qui braquait un *fast-food*. Les risques du métier...

Elle s'approcha pour mieux examiner les dégâts : un pansement en travers du front, un autre au-dessus de l'oreille. Les marques de doigt sur son cou lui arrachèrent un frisson douloureux. Sans avertissement, les images se remirent à défiler dans sa tête : James pendant les cinq dernières secondes de sa vie, lancé à la poursuite d'un jeune homme qui lui avait promis des informations et s'était ensuite ravisé. Une rafale, le corps de James qui se cabre... son propre cri strident.

— Sarah ?

Luke avait posé les mains sur ses épaules. Il la guidait vers sa porte. Sa voix lui parvint, déformée et lointaine. Repoussant le colis du pied, il lui prit sa clé des mains, ouvrit la porte, l'entraîna vers le canapé.

— Je vais bien, dit-elle en se dégageant doucement. C'est juste…

Elle se tut, incapable d'expliquer ce qui lui arrivait.

— Très bien. Disons que moi, j'ai besoin de m'asseoir.

Il passa devant elle, se laissa tomber sur le canapé avec un soupir, puis tapota le coussin près de lui.

— Tu viens me tenir compagnie ?

— Dans une minute. J'ai passé toute la matinée au soleil, et je meurs de soif. Tu veux un jus de fruits ?

— Avec plaisir. Où es-tu allée ?

Consciente de son regard qui suivait tous ses gestes, elle lui apporta son verre, retourna prendre le sien, et resta accoudée au plan de travail. Elle l'évitait, elle le savait et elle s'en voulait. Mais comment faire autrement ?

— Sur la promenade, répondit-elle enfin. J'ai pris deux rouleaux de pellicule. Je ne sais pas du tout ce que ça va donner.

Ses yeux gris braqués sur elle exigeaient la vérité.

— Quel est le problème, Sarah Rose ? Qu'est-ce que j'ai fait ?

— Rien du tout !

En fait, elle ne pouvait se défaire d'une idée nouvelle : la vie que menait Luke n'était pas si différente de celle de James. Elle était aussi dangereuse, en tout cas…

— Alors, qu'est-ce qui te tourmente ?

— Je…

Elle posa son verre, et pressa ses doigts contre ses yeux.

— Je ne m'attendais pas… Tu as l'air vraiment…

— Ce ne sont que des éraflures !

— Et ça t'arrive souvent ? demanda-t-elle sans le regarder.

— D'avoir des éraflures ?

— Qu'on te batte, qu'on cherche à t'étrangler.

— Je suis flic, Sarah Rose. Mon boulot comporte quelques risques.

Elle leva la tête vers lui, et il consentit à lui répondre :

— Une fois par an, à peu près. Peut-être moins. Je ne note pas les dates. En fait, je passe le plus clair de mon temps à donner des contraventions et à retrouver les gamins égarés.

Sarah fut incapable de lui rendre son sourire.

— Et James était censé prendre des notes et écrire des articles.

Le regard de Luke se fit plus aigu.

— C'est à ça que tu penses ? Tu as peur que je finisse comme lui ?

— Non… Je ne sais pas. Je crois que j'ai surtout peur de ne pas pouvoir surmonter mon angoisse à l'idée de ce qui pourrait t'arriver.

Au moment où il se levait pour venir la prendre dans ses bras, le téléphone sonna, et elle alla répondre.

— Bonjour, Kristin. Oui, vous tombez bien : il est là. Une minute, je vous le passe.

— Ne te sauve pas ! dit-il en prenant le combiné.

Puis il s'adressa à son ex-femme.

— Bonjour, Kristin ! Tout va bien ?

La réponse prit un certain temps. Sarah le regardait en silence.

— Bien, dit-il enfin. Je serai là dans quelques minutes. Tiens bon.

Il contempla d'un air hébété le combiné qu'il tenait à la main. Sarah le secoua doucement.

— Luke ? Dis-moi.

— C'est mon père... Il s'est levé, tout à l'heure, après sa sieste... et il a fait une crise cardiaque.

— Comment va-t-il ? Quelles sont les nouvelles ?

Comme Luke serrait sa main dans la sienne, Sarah se trouva entraînée dans le cercle de famille, malgré ses efforts pour rester en retrait. Mme Brennan ne leva pas la tête ; ce fut Matt qui répondit à son frère :

— Pas de nouvelles. On ne sait rien encore.

— Ça fait combien de temps qu'il est ici ?

— Près de deux heures.

— Vous avez cherché à parler à un médecin ?

Exceptionnellement, les deux hommes se regardèrent en face.

— Aux urgences, il faut attendre. Tu crois que tu peux faire mieux ? demanda Matt.

Sarah sentit la tension de Luke monter d'un cran.

— Non, sans doute pas, répondit-il. Je posais juste la question.

Légèrement en retrait, Kristin examinait son ex-mari.

— Qu'est-ce qui t'est arrivé ? Encore cette moto ?

Son ton était taquin, mais il y avait dans sa voix une inquiétude sincère. Voyant que Luke ne s'expliquait pas, Sarah le fit à sa place :

— Il a arrêté un braqueur, il y a quelques jours.

— Oh ! Tu vas bien ? murmura Kristin, interdite.

— Ouais. Des bleus, des éraflures.

190

— La dernière fois que c'est arrivé, tu avais des côtes fêlées et tu n'as pas voulu te soigner. Pendant trois semaines ! Tu as failli finir à l'hôpital.

Risquant un coup d'œil vers Matt, Sarah vit ses lèvres se pincer, ses yeux s'assombrir. Luke, quant à lui, ne remarqua rien. D'un geste, il balaya l'inquiétude de Kristin.

— C'est une vieille histoire.

— Trois ans.

— Je suis plus malin, maintenant.

— C'est ce que je vois !

— Madame Brennan ?

Ils se retournèrent. Un homme en blouse blanche venait d'entrer. Les yeux fatigués, un sourire plein de gentillesse, il scrutait les visages de ceux qui patientaient là. Elena se leva, et s'avança vers lui.

— Oui, c'est moi. Comment va mon mari ?

Elle faisait un tel effort pour se contrôler que sa voix n'avait aucune inflexion.

— Son état est stabilisé. Il se repose. Mais je suis un peu inquiet pour la suite.

Elena recula comme s'il l'avait frappée. Matt la rejoignit, lui prit discrètement le bras.

— Je peux le voir ? demanda-t-elle d'une voix blanche.

— Bien sûr.

Sans un regard pour eux, elle suivit le médecin.

Ils restèrent pensifs plusieurs instants, puis Kristin fit signe à Luke de prendre le siège libre.

— Assieds-toi : tu tiens à peine debout.

— Tu es là depuis plus longtemps que moi.

— Il faut que j'appelle ma mère. Je lui ai amené les filles en catastrophe, sans expliquer grand-chose…

— Je viens avec toi ! lança Matt.

Le message était clair. Il était de nouveau sur la défensive. Enfin, il défendait son territoire. Un bras autour de la taille de sa femme, il l'aida à fendre la foule. Quant à Luke, il ne les regardait même pas. Lorsque Sarah se retourna, elle s'aperçut qu'il avait les yeux fixés sur elle.

— Tu n'as qu'à t'asseoir, toi, lui proposa-t-il.

— Pas question. Tu prends cette chaise ou nous la proposons à quelqu'un d'autre.

A sa grande surprise, il céda. Mais, tout en s'asseyant, il garda sa main entre les siennes et l'attira sur ses genoux.

— Voilà, tu es contente ?

— Oui, dit-elle en cédant à l'envie de repousser ses cheveux noirs de son front. On dirait que, pour l'instant, ton père est hors de danger ?

— Oui.

Avec un long soupir, il laissa retomber sa tête contre le mur, derrière lui.

— La famille n'avait pas besoin d'une complication supplémentaire.

— Vous êtes solides. Vous vous en sortirez.

— C'est bien le problème. Chacun d'entre nous est solide individuellement, mais en tant que famille...

Il soupira encore, profondément.

— En tant que famille, nous sommes sur la mauvaise pente. Et il semble que je ne sache que mettre de l'huile sur le feu.

— Non, ce n'est pas vrai !

Ce cri du cœur valut à Sarah des regards surpris de la part de ses voisins. Jetant un coup d'œil à la ronde, elle s'accroupit devant Luke, et serra ses mains entre les siennes.

— Ce n'est pas ta faute, lui dit-elle en baissant la voix. Pas plus que celle de Matt, de Kristin ou de ta mère.

— Pourtant, tout serait plus simple si je m'en allais.

Elle ouvrait la bouche pour protester quand Mme Brennan refit son apparition, pâle, les lèvres serrées ; elle semblait sur le point de tomber d'épuisement.

— Où est Matt ?

Luke aida Sarah à se remettre sur pied, puis se leva à son tour.

— Il a accompagné Kristin qui voulait téléphoner à sa mère, répondit-il. Tout va bien ?

Elle le regarda comme s'il avait perdu la raison.

— Ton père vient de faire une crise cardiaque. Non, tout ne va pas bien.

Sarah se raidit, choquée par la dureté de cette réponse. Près d'elle, Luke prit une profonde inspiration.

— Je sais, maman. Je voulais dire : est-ce que je peux faire quelque chose ? Vous conduire quelque part ?

Le regard de Mme Brennan passa de Luke à Sarah, puis revint vers son fils. Sa voix vacilla, faillit s'éteindre.

— Je dois repasser à la maison chercher des affaires pour ton père.

— Nous pouvons vous emmener, et vous ramener ici, proposa Sarah.

Les lèvres serrées, Elena approuva d'un geste sec du menton.

— Je vais chercher la voiture, dit Luke, et je vous prends toutes les deux à l'entrée principale. Donnez-moi dix minutes.

Il s'éloigna le long du couloir, la tête haute, d'une démarche énergique. Comme si le fait de pouvoir rendre service à sa mère était pour lui une grande joie et une source de fierté.

Mme Brennan se tourna vers la porte ; Sarah la suivit en silence.

Dans le couloir, ils rencontrèrent Matt et Kristin. Quand Matt fut au courant de la situation, il proposa à son tour d'accompagner Elena chez elle.

— C'est sur notre chemin, dit-il, puisque nous allons chercher les filles.

Sarah en eut mal pour Luke.

— Si Luke est déjà parti chercher sa voiture, laissons-le faire, intervint Kristin. Les filles risqueraient de s'énerver pendant que vous faites la valise du Colonel. Personne n'a besoin d'entendre gémir Jenny, aujourd'hui.

Matt et sa mère toisèrent Kristin avec des expressions d'agacement presque identiques, mais Sarah l'aurait volontiers embrassée.

— Tu as sûrement raison, dit enfin Matt. On vous attend ici.

— D'accord, mon fils.

Elle s'appuya à son bras pour gagner l'ascenseur, laissant Sarah et Kristin marcher derrière. Les laissant prendre un peu d'avance, Sarah murmura :

— Vous avez été formidable.

— J'ai toujours eu l'impression de marcher sur la corde raide, à force de vouloir contenter tout le monde. Maintenant, c'est pire que jamais !

— La corde est au-dessus de la fosse aux lions ?

— C'est à peu près ça !

Elles souriaient encore en rejoignant Matt et sa mère dans l'ascenseur. Même le regard peu amène de Mme Brennan n'y fit rien.

Luke les attendait à la porte. Vite, Sarah se glissa à l'arrière, et Matt aida sa mère à s'installer à l'avant.

— Papa s'en tirera très bien, dit-il en serrant ses mains dans les siennes. Essayez de ne pas trop vous inquiéter.

— Bien sûr, murmura Elena, lointaine.

Elle n'ajouta pas un mot pendant tout le trajet. Luke ne chercha pas à lui parler, et Sarah n'osa rien dire.

Une fois arrivés à destination, Luke se hâta de déverrouiller la porte, et s'effaça pour laisser passer les deux femmes. Mme Brennan resta un instant immobile dans l'entrée, regardant autour d'elle comme si elle avait besoin de s'orienter dans sa propre maison. Doucement, Luke lui demanda :

— Vous avez besoin d'aide pour la valise ? Il y a quelque chose que nous pouvons faire ?

Sa mère redressa les épaules et releva le menton.

— Rien. J'aurai terminé dans quelques minutes.

— Nous vous attendrons sur la terrasse.

D'un pas ferme, elle se dirigea vers l'arrière de la maison. Son fils la suivit des yeux, et Sarah l'entendit soupirer.

Une fois dehors, Luke resta muet si longtemps qu'elle crut qu'il s'était endormi sur sa chaise longue. Elle tourna la tête pour l'étudier. Il était si beau, malgré les égratignures visibles sur son visage ! Et ses pauvres mains enflées et éraflées, comme elle aimait leur douceur ! Quant à son cœur, c'était le plus généreux qu'elle eût jamais connu.

Il tourna la tête vers elle, ouvrit les yeux.

— Bonjour, toi.

Elle ne put retenir un sourire.

— Bonjour toi-même.

— A quoi penses-tu ?

— A pas grand-chose, murmura-t-elle en rougissant. Et toi ?

Il tendit la main ; elle y posa la sienne.

— Je pensais encore à cette histoire de départ.

— Et ta conclusion ?

— Elle est très simple : ce serait beaucoup plus facile si tu venais avec moi.

13.

Sarah éprouva d'abord une joie immense, mais son enthousiasme retomba très vite.

— Je ne crois pas, commença-t-elle faiblement.

Il se redressa d'une détente, se pencha vers elle.

— On irait où tu voudrais. Les montagnes de l'Est, les plages de Californie... Je peux me faire muter sans difficulté : on a besoin de flics partout.

Son métier ! C'était bien là le problème. Quelle compagne ferait-elle pour un homme qui risquait régulièrement sa vie ? Depuis la mort de James, elle manquait sérieusement de courage.

Un peu anxieux devant son silence, Luke lui demanda :

— Il y a peut-être un endroit qui serait mieux pour toi, pour ta carrière. New York ? Los Angeles ?

Deuxième problème. Avec un sourire triste, elle répliqua :

— Je n'ai plus de carrière, tu le sais bien.

Il la secoua tendrement.

— Ne dis pas ça ! Ton métier fait partie de toi. Tant que tu prendras des photos...

— C'est justement le problème !

Voyant ses yeux s'élargir sous le coup de la surprise, elle se hâta de baisser la voix.

— Je ne prends plus de photos.

— Mais, ce matin, tu disais que…

— C'était… insignifiant. De jolies images, mais aucune véritable photographie.

— Et qu'est-ce que c'est, une *véritable* photographie ?

Retirant sa main de celle de Luke, elle se leva nerveusement, et se dirigea vers la balustrade de la terrasse.

— La vraie photographie a du cœur, de l'âme, une valeur artistique. Comme les photos de Felix. Comme les photos que vend Chuck dans son magasin. Une photo doit dire quelque chose. Avoir un sens. Raconter une histoire.

Il vint se planter derrière elle, sans la toucher.

— Pourquoi as-tu perdu la foi en toi-même ? Tes photos des filles étaient comme des miroirs.

Elle sentit des larmes lui piquer les yeux.

— Ce jour-là, c'était exceptionnel. Il y a eu… un déclic en moi. Un instinct. Comme avant. Mes meilleures photos n'ont jamais été posées ou composées ; elles se sont… faites toutes seules. Je savais toujours quand je tenais un bon cliché ; je n'avais pas à réfléchir.

— Et maintenant ?

— Maintenant, je dois réfléchir. Seulement… je ne peux pas. Quand j'essaie de composer, d'analyser… je n'obtiens rien du tout. Ou alors des photos banales. J'ai perdu mon instinct et, sans lui, je ne suis plus photographe.

Dans le long silence qui suivit, elle regarda pour la première fois son désespoir en face.

— Eh bien, tu feras autre chose ! dit Luke. Tu enseigneras. Tu feras de la mécanique. Tu seras P.-D.G. d'une grande société.

Regardant par-dessus son épaule, elle croisa ses yeux rieurs, remplis de chaleur, sans ironie aucune.

— Tu es capable de réussir tout ce que tu tenteras, n'importe où... du moment que c'est avec moi.

Ses bras vinrent s'enrouler autour d'elle ; il l'enveloppa de sa chaleur, promena ses lèvres sur sa tempe.

— Toi et moi... on possède un trésor quand on est ensemble. Pour la première fois depuis deux ans, je suis content de me réveiller le matin. Je suis redevenu un être humain, grâce à toi. J'ai besoin de toi dans ma vie.

Troisième problème. Il ne disait pas « je t'aime », mais « j'ai besoin de toi ». Il ne lui demandait pas d'amour ; il ne lui en offrait pas non plus. Près d'elle, il se sentait bien, et ça lui suffisait... Quelques jours plus tôt, elle aurait pu s'en contenter, et accepter ce projet absurde de quitter la ville avec lui. Mais, maintenant... elle était tombée profondément amoureuse.

— Je pense qu'il est trop tôt pour prendre une décision pareille, murmura-t-elle. Nous nous connaissons depuis si peu de temps.

— Nous nous sommes connus dès le premier instant.

Sans le regarder, elle secoua la tête.

— Matt a dit... Enfin, tu viens de rompre avec ta femme, tu es privé de tes filles... Ce n'est peut-être pas le moment de te précipiter dans une autre... aventure.

Il n'avait rien entendu après le premier mot.

— Qu'est-ce que Matt vient faire là-dedans ?

— Il a suggéré...

Doucement, irrésistiblement, il la fit pivoter vers lui.

— Il t'a parlé, à toi ?

— Oui.

— Qu'il aille... Il n'avait aucun droit de te parler de moi.

— Luke ? lança la voix d'Elena, depuis l'intérieur de la maison. Je suis prête, allons-y !

— J'arrive, maman !

Il se mordit la lèvre, voulut dire quelque chose à Sarah... mais elle se dirigeait déjà vers la porte.

Ce second trajet fut aussi silencieux que le premier. A l'hôpital, Matt et Kristin les attendaient devant la porte de la chambre.

— Il va mieux ; il se repose. Il veut vous voir, maman.

— J'y vais.

Elle passa les doigts dans ses cheveux pour se recoiffer à la va-vite, redressa les épaules, et entra dans la chambre : une pièce blanche baignant dans une lumière tamisée.

— Nous ramènerons maman chez elle, dit Kristin. Allez manger quelque chose : vous avez l'air épuisé, tous les deux.

Sarah lui sourit.

— D'accord, dit Luke, mais je veux d'abord parler avec Matt. Tête à tête.

A cet étage, ce n'était plus le chaos des urgences. Les deux frères s'isolèrent dans la pièce voisine qui était vide.

Kristin et Sarah échangèrent un regard anxieux, puis s'approchèrent de la porte, presque malgré elles, pour écouter la discussion. Après quelques phrases inintelligibles, elles entendirent un fracas de meubles renversés. Elles se précipitèrent. Dans la petite pièce, trois chaises étaient couchées, une table basse avait perdu un pied. Face à face, haletants, les pieds déchirant les revues éparpillées, les deux frères se faisaient face. Tous deux portaient des marques de coups, mais Luke semblait nettement plus mal en point.

La situation se dégrada encore quand une nouvelle voix s'exclama :

— Au nom du ciel, qu'est-ce qui se passe ici ?

Luke se retourna, vit sa mère plantée sur le seuil et chuchota un juron.

Matt l'avait déjà rejointe.

— Rien d'important, maman. Vous êtes prête à rentrer ?

Elle se dégagea.

— Vous vous êtes battus ? Alors que votre père est si malade ?

Haletante d'indignation, elle leva la tête vers Matt.

— Tu n'as rien ?

— Non.

Elle se tourna vers Luke.

— Tu trouves que je n'ai pas assez de soucis ?

Il se dit qu'il devait être comme anesthésié car la question de sa mère ne lui fit presque pas mal.

— Je suis désolé, maman. J'espère que papa n'a pas été dérangé.

— Heureusement, ton père dormait quand j'ai quitté sa chambre. Je ne veux même pas penser à sa réaction s'il savait...

Elle s'interrompit, secoua la tête.

— Si c'est pour te comporter de cette façon, attends qu'il soit rétabli avant de revenir nous voir.

Luke n'avait jamais été mis à la porte, jusqu'ici. Du moins, pas officiellement...

— Très bien, dit-il. Si c'est ce que vous voulez...

Il se tourna vers Sarah qui assistait à la scène, et lui demanda :

— Tu es prête ?

Puis, sans attendre sa réponse, il sortit dans le couloir et se dirigea vers l'ascenseur, muet, le regard braqué droit devant lui. L'effort qu'il faisait pour marcher normalement lui demandait toute sa concentration. Ses côtes et sa hanche lui faisaient un mal de chien, sans parler de sa mâchoire.

Sarah le rejoignit dans la cabine. Les portes se refermèrent, et il s'appuya à la paroi, épuisé.

— Ça va ? On redescend aux urgences ? proposa la jeune femme à mi-voix.

Il secoua la tête, vacilla un peu, et ne répondit pas.

Quand ils eurent regagné la voiture, elle lança d'une voix brève :

— Je vais conduire. Donne-moi les clés.

Il ne protesta pas. Il ne lui restait plus de mots.

Kristin prit le volant, elle aussi, car Matt n'était pas en état de conduire.

— Tu es furieuse parce qu'on s'est battus ? lui demanda son mari. Il a cogné en premier, je te jure, Kris !

— Tu ne t'es pas fait prier pour lui rendre ses coups.

Matt ne répondit rien, elle se concentra sur sa conduite. Un peu plus tard, elle reprit d'une voix neutre :

— Je n'ai jamais compris pourquoi votre mère était si dure avec Luke.

Pendant un long moment, Matt la regarda en silence.

— Je ne suis pas sûr qu'elle le sache elle-même, répondit-il enfin. Luke a toujours été difficile. Je l'entends encore pleurer, quand il était bébé : ça n'arrêtait jamais. Mon père était en Asie du Sud-Est. Maman a embauché une nounou spécialement pour lui : elle ne pouvait pas s'occuper de nous deux.

— Luke était aussi son fils.

— Ouais. Mais il était différent. Elle n'a jamais compris ce qu'il voulait.

— Et toi ?

Kristin faisait un effort surhumain pour parler d'une voix normale, pour ne pas avoir l'air de parti pris.

— Moi non plus. Je ne comprenais pas pourquoi il avait des notes aussi moyennes alors qu'il estintelligent. Je ne comprenais pas pourquoi on le convoquait tout le temps chez le proviseur. Et je n'ai jamais compris ce qu'il voulait faire de sa vie.

Kristin se gara dans leur allée, coupa le moteur et se tourna vers son mari.

— Tu devrais peut-être parler à ta mère. Elle ne peut tout de même pas empêcher Luke de voir son père !

Matt secoua la tête.

— Rien de ce que je pourrai dire ne la fera changer d'avis.

Elle ne bougea pas, scrutant son visage dans la pénombre.

— Tu pourrais quand même essayer de défendre ton frère !

Il eut un rire bref, assez dur.

— Je ne suis pas franchement dans son camp, Kris. Il vient ici le plus souvent possible, pour bien s'assurer que ma fille continue à voir en moi un ennemi : celui qui a pris la place de son papa. Pour être franc, je trouve que ma mère n'a pas tout à fait tort.

Kristin mourait d'envie de défendre Luke… mais cela comportait un gros risque. Si elle allait trop loin, elle y laisserait son mariage. Si elle devait perdre Matt une deuxième fois, elle en mourrait. Elle l'aimait tant ! Et les filles avaient déjà tant enduré…

Poussant un soupir, elle retira la clé de contact.

— Il va falloir régler le problème, ne serait-ce que pour les filles. Elles ne vont pas comprendre pourquoi Luke ne peut plus venir chez leur mamie.

Ensemble, ils descendirent de voiture, et rentrèrent chez eux.

— Maman va céder, tôt ou tard. Elle l'a toujours fait. Quand papa se sentira mieux, tout se règlera naturellement.

Kristin sentit qu'il glissait le bras autour de sa taille. Puis il l'attira contre lui dans l'ombre de la véranda.

— En attendant, j'ai droit à un baiser ?

Il parlait d'un ton léger, mais elle devinait sa tension. Elle fit un effort pour lui sourire.

— Un seul ? demanda-t-elle.

Son regard bleu étincela de désir, tandis qu'il se penchait vers elle.

— Un seul pour commencer...

— Je n'ai pas beaucoup de provisions...

— Sur ce point, au moins, nous nous ressemblons : chez moi, il n'y a généralement que du *pop-corn* et du jus d'orange.

— Si on vivait ensemble, on se nourrirait peut-être mieux ?

Elle leva les yeux. Etait-il en train de plaisanter ? Voyant qu'elle ne réagissait pas, il secoua la tête et eut un geste résigné.

— Je ne dis plus rien. Pas besoin d'un marteau pour me faire entrer les choses dans le crâne. Quoiqu'en pense mon frère.

Tout en se laissant tomber sur une chaise, il contempla les sandwichs sans avoir le courage de tendre la main pour en prendre un.

— Ta mère va changer d'avis, n'est-ce pas ? lui demanda Sarah.

Il haussa les épaules.

— Qui sait ? Elle s'est déjà mise en colère, mais c'est la première fois qu'elle m'exclut carrément de la famille.

Il réfléchit un instant.

— Qu'est-ce que je raconte ? En fait, je n'ai jamais fait partie de la famille ! Une fois que tu m'auras mis dehors à ton tour, tout sera réglé.

— Tu as le droit d'être amer, dit la jeune femme en repoussant son assiette, mais je ne suis pas en train de te mettre à la porte.

— On ne peut pas dire que tu me laisses vraiment entrer dans ta vie ! En réalité, on était plus proches l'un de l'autre avant de faire l'amour.

— Je fais de mon mieux.

— Je ne vois pas ce qu'il y a à faire. Ou bien tu veux être avec moi, ou bien tu n'en as aucune envie. En tout cas, tu ne dois pas me supporter par pitié ni pour me protéger de ma famille ni parce que tu as l'impression que tu me dois quelque chose. Je voudrais que tu sois là parce que tu le veux. Tout simplement.

« Ce serait si simple, s'il m'aimait ! », songea Sarah.

— Jusqu'ici, lui dit-elle, je n'ai rien fait à contrecœur. Je n'ai pas pitié de toi, je ne te dois rien, et je sais que je ne peux pas te protéger. C'était peut-être une erreur de nous… impliquer autant. On aurait dû attendre de savoir où on allait.

— Ou plutôt où on n'allait pas ! rectifia-t-il avec un petit rire sans joie. Moi, en tout cas, je n'aurais pas renoncé à ce moment magique avec toi, même si j'avais su à l'avance à quel point ça ferait mal.

— Je n'ai pas ma voiture, dit-elle en changeant brusquement de sujet. On est partis de chez moi avec la tienne.

— Voilà qui répond à la question suivante, dit-il en se levant lentement. Je te ramène.

Allongé dans le noir, Luke attendait le sommeil. A son chevet, la radio jouait de la musique en sourdine, pour couvrir le brouhaha de ses pensées qui le ramenaient toujours vers Sarah, vers son corps mince et ardent accroché au sien, vers cet avant-goût du paradis. Il préférait penser à Kristin, puisqu'il pouvait, désormais, évoquer son image sans souffrir. Grâce à Sarah. Kristin avait été à la fois son amie, son amante, son épouse — mais Sarah représentait davantage encore, sur tous les plans. En tant qu'amie, elle le comprenait mieux que personne. En tant qu'amante, elle était l'autre moitié de lui-même, l'âme qu'il pouvait rencontrer face à face, sans se cacher ou se protéger.

Il avait pensé… en fait, il n'avait pensé à rien du tout avant de lui proposer de partir avec lui.

Elle venait de traverser une période terrible ; il savait à quel point elle était fragile. Mais elle tenait à lui, il l'aurait juré. Il lui avait offert tout ce qu'il pouvait offrir, mais, apparemment, ce n'était pas suffisant…

Comme la musique ne parvenait pas à l'endormir, il changea de station, et tomba sur un bulletin météo.

—… l'ouragan Daniel se trouve à 460 milles au sud-est des Bermudes ; il se déplace nord-nord-ouest à 55 km/h, avec des vents qui atteindront leur maximum demain, en fin de journée.

Un ouragan ? Il ne manquait plus que ça ! Les derniers à passer par là avaient tous fini par se diriger vers la Caroline du Sud ; celui-ci en ferait sans doute autant.

D'une certaine façon, ce serait assez commode d'être tué par un ouragan. Au moins, personne ne pourrait dire que c'était sa faute.

— Bonjour à toi aussi, Chuck, dit Sarah en entrant dans l'arrière-boutique. Quelle chaleur !

— Patience : l'ouragan va nous apporter un peu de fraîcheur.

— Quel ouragan ?

— L'ouragan Daniel ! Il se dirige droit sur nous.

Pour la première fois, il leva la tête de son livre.

— Tu ne savais pas ? Tu vis sur quelle planète ?

— Je n'ai pas écouté la météo, voilà tout.

Elle avait passé les trois derniers jours enfermée dans son appartement, à se demander pourquoi elle n'acceptait pas tout simplement ce que Luke lui proposait : une relation intime, excitante, avec un homme bien, le meilleur ami et le meilleur amant qu'elle eût jamais eus. Pourquoi cela ne lui suffisait-il pas ?

— Tu as pris des photos, ces derniers temps ?

— Quelques-unes. Je viens les développer. Il fait trop chaud pour aller sur la plage.

Chuck hocha la tête, tourna une page.

— J'ai mis de côté tes derniers tirages : ceux du marais.

— Merci, c'est gentil.

Elle passa dans la chambre noire, alluma la lumière, décrocha sa sacoche de son épaule et la posa sur une chaise. Puis elle sortit les deux pellicules de l'autre jour, et se tourna vers le plan de travail, choisissant déjà mentalement ses filtres et ses cadrages. Ses dernières photos étaient empilées à l'extrémité du plan de travail. Au-dessus, sur l'étagère, une bouteille de produit chimique était couchée sur le flanc dans une flaque à l'odeur âcre. Le reste du produit avait goutté sur les tirages… et sur l'enveloppe contenant les négatifs, placée au sommet de la pile.

— Nom d'un chien, Chuck ! Qu'est-ce que tu as fichu ?

Son associé entra au petit trot.

— Quoi ? De quoi parles-tu ?

Elle lui tendit la pile de photos.

— Comment est-ce que ça a pu arriver ?

Les mains dans les poches, il s'approcha.

— Je pense que le bouchon n'était pas bien vissé et que la bouteille a été renversée.

— Comme ça ? Par l'opération du Saint-Esprit ?

Elle avait le visage brûlant, les mains glacées. Cela faisait des années qu'elle n'avait pas ressenti une telle colère.

— Je ne me suis pas servi de ce produit depuis une éternité ! affirma Chuck.

— Et il est tombé tout seul ?

— Peut-être. Si la porte a claqué, si un avion est passé trop bas... qui sait ? Si tu prenais soin de ton matériel, il n'y aurait pas de problème.

Tout en ajoutant quelques mots inintelligibles, il se détourna pour sortir.

— Qu'est-ce que tu viens de dire ?

— Seulement que ces photos n'avaient rien d'extraordinaire. Tu l'as dit toi-même. Pourquoi faire tant d'histoires ?

Pourquoi, effectivement... Quelle importance avaient ces photos médiocres ?

Avec un soupir, Sarah enfila de gros gants de caoutchouc, traîna la poubelle près du plan de travail, y poussa les clichés irrécupérables.

Elle ramassait la bouteille d'acide pour la jeter, elle aussi, quand elle fut surprise par son poids. Ou plutôt par son absence de poids ! Quand elle l'inclina vers la poubelle, il n'en sortit pas une goutte. Une bouteille tombée sur le flanc ne se vide pas entièrement ! Celle-ci avait été vidée, délibérément.

Elle la laissa tomber dans la poubelle, lava le plan de travail et le sol, sécha les surfaces avec des serviettes en papier, puis les lava de nouveau.

Après avoir remis la poubelle à sa place, elle rangea dans sa sacoche ses deux rouleaux de pellicule, s'assura que les négatifs d'Erin et de Jenny étaient intacts. Par chance, elle avait laissé ses appareils chez elle, et sa sacoche presque vide pourrait accueillir la plus grande partie des photos et négatifs entreposés au fil des ans dans les tiroirs que Felix lui avait attribués. Elle prit tout, même l'étiquette à son nom calligraphiée par lui, et émergea de la chambre noire, portant sa sacoche en bandoulière et quelques dossiers supplémentaires à bout de bras.

Chuck la regarda passer, bouche bée. Le front plissé, il demanda :

— Qu'est-ce que c'est que ça ?

— Mes photos. Je les emporte avec moi.

— Ah ? Bon.

— Je ne viendrai plus travailler ici, Chuck. Tu as délibérément versé de l'acide sur mes photos.

Et si Luke avait raison ? se demanda-t-elle tout à coup. S'il l'avait aussi agressée ?

— Tu deviens paranoïaque, en plus d'être dépressive ? Pourquoi j'aurais fait une chose pareille ?

Il s'était levé de son fauteuil. Sa silhouette replète faisait facilement oublier sa haute taille. Peut-être sous-estimait-elle sa force ? Elle était si furieuse qu'il n'y avait plus en elle de place pour la peur.

— Je n'en ai aucune idée, dit-elle. J'ai renoncé depuis longtemps à comprendre ce qui se passe dans ta tête. En tout cas, je ne prendrai plus le risque de voir mon travail détruit.

— Pour ce qu'il vaut !

Elle l'aurait peut-être giflé si elle avait eu les mains libres… et si les avertissements de Luke ne lui étaient pas revenus à l'esprit.

Elle prit une profonde inspiration, et lutta pour se calmer.

— A l'avenir, tu n'auras qu'à envoyer ma part de bénéfices à ma boîte postale. Si je ne vois rien venir, j'enverrai un avocat te demander pourquoi.

Les bras croisés sur la poitrine, il sourit. Un sourire satisfait, victorieux.

— Fais-toi une bonne vie, dit-il.

Elle lui jeta un regard de mépris, et partit sans ajouter un mot.

14.

Dès que Luke arriva au commissariat, ce soir-là, le sergent lui fit signe de venir le voir, et lui tendit un rapport.

— Encore une agression ! dit-il d'un air fataliste. Même tableau, même dingue.

— Fantastique ! Il va finir par tuer quelqu'un pour avoir vraiment l'impression qu'on s'intéresse à lui !

Son chef se mit à rire.

— Du calme, fils ! La Criminelle est en train de préparer un piège à son intention. Des femmes flics avec des jeeps, qui tourneront sur différents parkings. On l'attend au tournant.

Luke revit le visage de Sarah, le soir de son agression — puis le sourire mauvais de Chuck Sawyer.

— J'espère seulement que je serai de service, marmonna-t-il. J'adorerais être là pour faire tomber ce fumier.

— Ton père est sorti de l'hôpital !

Il soupira, soulagé.

— Voilà une bonne nouvelle. Comment est-il ?

— Plutôt en forme, je trouve. Il a récupéré plus vite que le médecin ne s'y attendait. Ils l'ont renvoyé chez lui en lui prescrivant un régime sévère, de l'exercice et l'arrêt total du tabac. Tu imagines sa réaction !

— Oh, oui !

Kristin hésita un instant, puis passa au motif réel de son coup de fil.

— Il m'a demandé de t'appeler et de te demander de passer le voir.

— Maman risque de mal le prendre.

— Dimanche matin, elle sera au temple. Il voudrait que tu viennes vers 10 heures.

— J'y serai. Merci d'avoir joué les intermédiaires. J'espère que tu ne te feras pas prendre.

— Ta mère changera bientôt d'avis. Elle est stressée à cause de tous ces soucis...

— Ne te fais pas trop d'illusions ! Elle serait plutôt soulagée si elle ne me revoyait jamais. D'ailleurs, je pense sérieusement à partir.

— Pardon ? A quoi est-ce que tu penses !

— Matt a sans doute raison : je devrais vous laisser tranquilles, tous les quatre.

— Luke, les filles seraient effondrées si elles te perdaient !

— Elles s'en remettraient. D'autant plus vite que Matt se débrouillerait beaucoup mieux si je n'étais plus là.

— Je t'en prie, réfléchis encore ! Je ne crois pas...

Elle ravala ses objections. Elle avait gâché sa vie ; de quel droit l'empêcherait-elle de partir, à présent ?

— Je... Je ne sais pas si je pourrais supporter l'idée de t'avoir chassé...

La voix de Luke était très douce quand il répondit :

— Kristin, tu ne chasses personne, et surtout pas moi. J'essaie seulement de prendre la meilleure décision pour nous tous : toi, Jen, Erin, Matt et moi... sans parler de maman. Je vais encore réfléchir, mais c'est de ce côté que penche la balance.

Elle hésita encore, puis demanda :

— Et Sarah ?

— Quoi, Sarah ? demanda-t-il d'une voix lasse.

— Elle… partirait avec toi ?

Il mit un certain temps à répondre.

— Je ne crois pas, non.

— Elle est attachée à toi.

— Oh, tu sais…

— Et tu es attaché à elle. Elle me plaît beaucoup. Je t'en prie, ne l'écarte pas trop facilement.

Il se mit à rire.

— Tu ne trouves pas ça bizarre de chercher à orchestrer la vie sentimentale de ton ex-mari ?

— Pas s'il est mon meilleur ami.

— Kristin…

Il s'éclaircit la gorge, puis osa demander :

— Est-ce que ça se passe bien, entre toi et Matt ?

— Ça va bien se passer. Je ferai tout pour le rendre heureux.

— Et toi ?

Elle lui donna la bonne réponse, la seule dont elle fût vraiment sûre.

— S'il est heureux, je serai heureuse.

— Ça fait plaisir de te voir, fils. Entre.

Luke vint s'asseoir sur le bras du fauteuil qui faisait face à celui du Colonel.

— Vous avez l'air en forme, papa. Comment vous sentez-vous ?

212

— Beaucoup mieux. Grâce aux miracles de la médecine moderne.

Il tendit la main, tâta machinalement la petite table qui les séparait, et soupira :

— A part pour ma fichue pipe. Un homme ne devrait pas être obligé de renoncer à sa pipe.

— Même si c'est le tabac ou la vie ?

Le commentaire lui valut un regard froid. Sans se laisser démonter, il demanda :

— Vous vouliez me voir ?

— Oui, dit le Colonel. Va dans mon bureau, ouvre le tiroir en bas à droite de la table de travail, et rapporte-moi le livre que tu y trouveras.

Il lui tendit une petite clé de bronze :

— Il faut d'abord déverrouiller le tiroir du milieu...

Le tiroir du bas, conçu pour accueillir des dossiers suspendus, ne contenait qu'un gros volume. En le prenant, Luke comprit qu'il s'agissait d'un album photo — sans doute des photos de bébé, si l'on se fiait à la couverture. Après avoir refermé la porte du bureau, il le rapporta à son père.

— Assieds-toi, ordonna celui-ci.

Luke obéit, de plus en plus déconcerté.

— Papa, qu'est-ce qui se passe ?

— Regarde les photos.

Le cœur serré, il ouvrit l'album, et se mit à étudier les premières photos.

— Là, c'est Matt ?

Son père approuva de la tête.

— Et maman ?

— Oui.

Elena était blonde, à l'époque. Blond cendré, comme Jennifer. Près d'elle, un bambin joufflu soufflait ses bougies d'anniversaire. Derrière lui, on distinguait un cheval à bascule avec lequel Luke se rappelait avoir joué, lui aussi. Pourquoi son père l'invitait-il à se plonger dans le passé ?

— Quel âge a Matt ? demanda-t-il. Trois ans ?

— Deux ans. Regarde mieux.

De plus en plus inquiet, Luke se pencha de nouveau sur les photos. Matt portait un chapeau de cow-boy blanc, des bottes et une chemise à carreaux. Un vrai petit chérubin. Elena Brennan, en long corsage orange sans manches et short à carreaux, était une maman typique du début des années 60 : bronzée, sportive et... enceinte. Ce n'était pas une grossesse très avancée, mais elle n'échappa pas au regard de Luke. Il tourna alors la tête vers son père.

— Tu m'as dit que Matt avait quel âge sur ces photos ?

Pour toute réponse, le Colonel conseilla :

— Tourne la page.

Encore des photos. Matt à Halloween, planté près d'une citrouille grimaçante. Matt et sa mère à un dîner de Thanksgiving, avec toute la famille.

— Vous étiez outre-mer, cette année-là ? demanda-t-il sans relever les yeux.

— Je suis rentré pour le nouvel an.

Des photos de Noël. Matt, solidement planté sur ses jambes, une figurine entre les mains.

— G.I. Joe, marmonna Luke avec un brin d'ironie.

Sur toutes les photos, sa mère rayonnait. Belle, pleine d'assurance, gracieuse même dans les dernières semaines de sa grossesse.

— Maman était absolument superbe, dit-il.

— Elle l'est toujours, répliqua William Brennan d'une voix austère. Continue.

Le bébé était arrivé pendant l'hiver. Son petit visage fripé, sur les photos prises à la maternité, rappelaient Erin et Jen. Un cliché montrait Elena sur le perron d'une maisonnette de l'armée entourée de neige. Matt se tenait à côté d'elle, engoncé dans une combinaison de ski, et elle portait dans les bras un paquet de couvertures : sans doute le nouveau-né. Deux pages de photos prises à l'intérieur de la même maison montraient un petit ange vêtu de rose pour la Saint-Valentin. La petite tête chauve se couvrait de boucles sombres, de grands yeux noirs contemplaient le monde avec gravité. Du rose ?

Luke jeta un nouveau coup d'œil à son père, puis tourna la page. Les photos s'arrêtaient à la Saint-Valentin. Le reste de l'album était vide.

Revenant à la dernière photo, Luke remarqua la date imprimée dans la marge. 1965. Trois ans avant sa propre naissance.

— Matt est là, dit-il en désignant le visage rond de son frère. Mais qui... qui est l'autre enfant ?

Cette fois, il regarda son père en face. Le regard du vieil homme le bouleversa. Jamais il n'y avait lu ce chagrin, cette tendresse.

— Melody, murmura le Colonel. Ta sœur, Melody Ann.

— Il faut qu'on parle.

Matt recula d'un pas pour laisser entrer son frère. Luke passa tout droit dans le living, puis se retourna pour lui dire :

— J'ai passé un moment avec papa, ce matin.

— Maman avait pourtant dit...

— Il m'a demandé de venir.

— Bon, fit Matt en restant sur le seuil de la pièce, les bras croisés sur la poitrine. Alors ?

— Il m'a appris ce que tout le monde avait omis de mentionner pendant toutes ces années.

— C'est-à-dire ?

— Que je suis leur troisième enfant, pas le deuxième.

Matt eut l'impression d'encaisser un coup au plexus.

— Qu'est-ce que tu racontes ?

Luke hocha vigoureusement la tête.

— Il y a eu une petite fille entre toi et moi. Elle est née en janvier 1965. Et elle est morte.

— Attends une seconde ! Papa t'a dit ça ?

— Il y a un album, avec des photos. Pourquoi est-ce que tu n'as jamais rien dit ?

— Parce que je n'étais pas au courant !

— Tu t'imagines que je vais te croire ?

— Tu sais, je n'avais pas plus de deux ans ! J'ai dû oublier...

Il secoua la tête.

— Tu dis que c'était une petite fille ?

— Melody Ann.

— Qu'est-ce qui s'est passé ?

— Maman est entrée dans sa chambre, un matin, pour la réveiller, et elle ne respirait plus.

— Mon Dieu ! Ça a dû être effroyable.

— D'après papa, elle a été très déprimée pendant plus d'un an. Incapable d'assumer le quotidien. Tu avais une nounou.

Matt faillit secouer de nouveau la tête, mais il s'interrompit. Un visage venait de se présenter devant ses yeux : une femme aux cheveux sombres, qui sentait bon les épices.

— Où est-ce qu'on habitait ?

— A Fort Campbell.

Il essaya de visualiser la maison.

— Je ne me souviens pas. De toute façon, qu'est-ce que ça change ? Trente-cinq ans, ça fait un paquet d'années.

— C'est bien mon avis, riposta Luke. Papa essayait de m'expliquer pourquoi j'avais toujours endossé le rôle de bouc émissaire dans la famille.

Matt se cabra, refusant ce rapprochement qui ne lui plaisait guère.

— Un bébé est mort, c'est très triste. Mais quel rapport avec toi ?

— Maman voulait une fille ; c'était important pour elle. Quand je suis né, elle est retombée dans sa dépression. Moi aussi, j'ai eu une nounou.

— Oh, arrête ! Maman est quelqu'un de rationnel. Elle ne… Elle ne chercherait pas à te faire payer le fait que tu sois un garçon.

— D'après papa, c'est exactement ce qu'elle a fait. Tu as une autre explication ?

— Je ne sais pas, moi !

Matt s'était souvent posé cette question quand il essayait de comprendre sa famille, à l'époque où il habitait encore chez ses parents. Puis il s'était rendu à l'évidence.

— Tu étais perpétuellement puni, toujours en train de te bagarrer, avec moi ou avec un autre. Ça devait être difficile pour elle de supporter les soucis que tu lui créais. Surtout après avoir perdu un bébé.

— Ça fait un certain temps que je n'ai pas créé de problème majeur dans sa vie. L'explication tient toujours, à ton avis ?

— Tu plaisantes ? Tu n'as jamais arrêté ! Tu as laissé tomber la fac pour traverser le pays en moto, tu es devenu flic alors que les parents rêvaient de te voir entrer dans l'armée. Tu as épousé ma fiancée, tu as eu des bébés avec elle — pas un mais deux, pour autant que maman le sache. Tu n'as pas arrêté de créer des problèmes depuis mon retour ! Moi, je vois des raisons pour qu'elle t'en veuille.

Après un très, très long silence, Luke réussit à reprendre son souffle.

— Tu es vraiment un fumier, tu sais ? Un petit fumier égoïste et étriqué.

— Luke ! s'exclama Kristin.

Passant devant elle, Matt ouvrit la porte à la volée et se retourna en foudroyant son frère du regard.

— Dehors ! Tout de suite. Tu es peut-être le bienvenu dans la maison de papa, mais n'essaie pas de revenir dans la mienne.

— Matt, dit Kristin très bas, en tendant la main vers son ex-mari.

Luke se contenta de rire.

— Raté, grand frère. On a passé un accord pour le droit de visite, ratifié par Mme le juge. Tu ne peux pas m'empêcher de voir mes filles.

— Je me fiche de tes accords. Dehors !

Luke jeta un bref coup d'œil à Kristin.

— Désolé. Je ne suis pas venu pour me disputer avec lui. Prends bien soin de toi et des filles.

Il sortit sans un regard pour son frère. Matt claqua la porte derrière lui.

— Maman ?

Erin se tenait sur la dernière marche de l'escalier, et Jenny sur la troisième.

— Qui a claqué la porte ?

Avec un regard d'avertissement à l'adresse de Matt, Kristin se dirigea vers ses filles.

— C'était le vent, mon cœur. Juste le vent.

*
* *

— J'ai besoin de votre aide, dit Kristin d'une voix basse et tremblante.

— Qu'est-ce qui se passe ?

— Luke…

Sarah crut que son cœur allait s'arrêter.

— Il va bien ? souffla-t-elle.

— Je crois. Il faut que vous le trouviez.

— Pourquoi ? C'est son père ?

— Dans un sens, oui. Le Colonel a parlé à Luke, aujourd'hui, et ce qu'il lui a dit l'a complètement bouleversé. Il est venu directement trouver Matt.

— Ils se sont encore battus ?

— Seulement avec des mots. Mais il avait l'air si… blessé, Sarah ! Je sais qu'il tient énormément à vous… Luke mérite de trouver enfin une femme qui tienne à lui, qui le fasse passer en premier. On ne lui a jamais donné ça de toute sa vie.

Sarah ferma les yeux, bouleversée.

— Je ne sais pas si vous l'aimez de cette façon, mais il a besoin de vous, en ce moment, reprit Kristin.

En quelques mots, elle lui relata la dispute qui avait eu lieu entre les deux frères.

— Il faut qu'il parle à quelqu'un !

— Je ne sais pas si je suis la mieux placée… chuchota Sarah.

— Je crois que vous êtes la seule. Je vous en prie, essayez !

Comment refuser, si Luke avait mal ?

— D'accord. Je ferai de mon mieux.

Agenouillé près d'un plant de tomates, il posait avec précaution des fruits rutilants dans un panier. Entendant sans doute le froissement de ses sandales dans l'herbe, il leva la tête et s'assit sur ses talons.

— Bonjour.

Maintenant qu'elle le voyait, elle comprenait l'inquiétude de Kristin. Son visage était pâle et complètement ravagé.

— Bonjour, Luke.

Il baissa les yeux sur son panier.

— Tu veux une tomate ?

— Tu me ferais un sandwich ?

Il hésita un peu avant de répondre :

— Pas de problème. Entre.

Ils confectionnèrent leurs sandwichs en silence. Sarah attendit que Luke eût terminé le sien avant de parler.

— Kristin m'a téléphoné.

Il ne broncha pas.

— Ça a dû être une grosse surprise pour toi, reprit-elle. Toujours pas de réponse.

— Quel dommage que ta mère n'ait pas pu réagir autrement !

— Perdre un enfant, il y a de quoi vous rendre fou.

— Tu étais un enfant, toi aussi. Un bébé.

Il haussa les épaules.

— Luke…, murmura-t-elle.

Il versa du thé glacé dans leurs verres et, sans lever les yeux, il lança :

— Il n'y a rien à dire. On va continuer comme avant. Matt me dit que c'est la solution la plus adulte.

— Matt a beaucoup à perdre dans l'histoire. Il était sous le choc, comme toi.

— Matt récupère vite.

— Il fait semblant.

Luke haussa de nouveau les épaules,et se concentra sur son second sandwich.

— Et toi, qu'est-ce que tu comptes faire ? demanda-t-elle.

— Je vais partir.

Elle sentit un grand vide dans son cœur et dans son corps.

— Tu t'enfuis ?

— On peut dire ça comme ça, répondit-il en découpant soigneusement une rondelle de tomate.

— Et de quelle autre manière pourrait-on le dire, d'après toi ?

— J'essaie de m'en sortir en un seul morceau.

— Tu n'es déjà plus en un seul morceau.

Il lui lança un regard très bref, rempli de colère et de souffrance.

— Tu as fait ce qu'il fallait pour ça ! répliqua-t-il.

Elle ne chercha pas à se défendre. Enfin, elle lui avait arraché un éclair d'émotion vraie.

— Donc, tu me fuis, moi aussi ?

— J'ai plutôt l'impression qu'on me demande de partir.

Ce fut comme si on lui retirait brusquement le bandeau qu'elle avait sur les yeux. Dans une sorte de révélation, elle comprit le fonctionnement qu'il répétait sans cesse.

— Eh bien, moi, j'ai l'impression que si les choses ne se passent pas comme tu l'as décidé, tu ne vois qu'une solution : disparaître.

Il leva brusquement la tête, laissant son sandwich retomber sur son assiette.

— On peut dire que tu es douée pour les coups de couteau !

Encore une fois, elle s'interdit de relever.

— Luke, tu as décidé d'emblée que tu ne pouvais pas te mesurer à Matt. Du coup, tu es allé le plus loin possible dans la direction opposée.

Le crépuscule assombrissait la pièce, mais elle vit tout de même la colère dans ses yeux. Elle attendit sa riposte, mais il se contenta d'aller se planter devant la fenêtre. Elle reprit, néanmoins, la parole.

— Quand ton frère est revenu d'Afrique, tu as décidé que tu ne ferais pas le poids. Est-ce que tu as seulement laissé la possibilité à Kristin de décider avec lequel de vous deux elle voulait vivre ? Non, tu as simplement déclaré forfait, abandonné le terrain. Et maintenant, au lieu de chercher à régler la situation avec les filles, avec tes parents, avec moi, tu décides de t'en aller. Une fois de plus.

Il posa les mains de part et d'autre de la fenêtre.

— Je suis un lâche, c'est ça ?

— Tu es un type qui ne supporte pas l'idée de l'échec.

Elle vit les muscles de son dos se crisper.

— J'ai essayé avec tout le monde. J'ai essayé avec toi.

— Qu'est-ce que tu as essayé avec moi ? s'exclama-t-elle soudain. Quel risque as-tu pris ? Est-ce que tu as joué ton cœur, tes émotions ? Est-ce que tu as laissé tomber ton orgueil une seule fois ?

— Je t'ai demandé…

— De partir avec toi, oui, mais pourquoi ? Parce qu'on est amis ? Parce qu'on fait bien l'amour, tous les deux ? Parce que j'aime ta Harley ? Pourquoi, Luke ? Pourquoi ?

Il savait ce qu'elle lui demandait. Il lui aurait suffi de dire : « Je t'aime, Sarah Rose ». Mais il ne le ferait pas, parce qu'elle avait raison : dès qu'il s'agissait de sentiments, il était un lâche et un imbécile. Jamais il n'aurait dû s'autoriser à aller aussi loin. Pour leur bien à tous les deux. Mieux valait toujours garder ses sentiments et ses désirs pour soi.

— Parce que, dit-il enfin, parce que je croyais qu'il existait un lien entre nous. Je croyais que nous voulions les mêmes choses. Apparemment, je me suis trompé.

222

Quand il se retourna, elle le regardait, pâle, les yeux élargis comme sous l'effet d'un choc ou d'un chagrin... elle le regardait comme si quelqu'un venait de mourir.

— Oui, tu as dû te tromper, murmura-t-elle.

— Ce ne serait pas la première fois, dit-il en se redressant. Alors, on n'a qu'à se dire au revoir. Envoie-moi une carte postale, un jour, de quelque part.

— C'est toi qui pars ! Comment saurais-je où tu es ?

— Tu as raison. Laisse tomber, dit-il en essayant de rire.

Comme quand on vient de prendre une balle dans la peau, il ne sentait pas encore la blessure.

— J'ouvrirai l'œil, pour tes photos.

Elle secoua la tête.

— Ne te donne pas cette peine. Je doute qu'il en paraisse d'autres.

Elle tourna les talons, et marcha vers la porte de la cuisine.

— Bonne chance, Luke.

— A toi aussi, Sarah Rose.

Il ne se retourna pas pour la voir sortir, et répéta seulement :

— A toi aussi...

Erin se retourna d'un bond dans son lit, le cœur battant à tout rompre... Non, c'était stupide de faire des souhaits : rien n'allait changer ; maman resterait mariée à papa Matt.

Et ce ne serait... pas si épouvantable que ça. Il était *cool*, des fois. Bien sûr, il l'avait obligée à rapporter ce livre nul au magasin, et à le rendre au gérant en lui faisant des excuses. Elle aurait voulu disparaître sous terre. Ensuite, ils étaient allés à l'aquarium, rien que tous les deux. Ils avaient regardé les poissons et discuté de ceux qu'elle aimerait avoir. Il l'avait aidée à installer son aquarium d'anniversaire, et à choisir trois poissons. Papa Matt savait beaucoup de choses sur les poissons. Pour ça, il était *cool*.

Si papa Matt restait, papa ne pourrait pas revenir vivre à la maison. Ce n'était pas très juste envers papa de trouver papa Matt gentil — mais si elle ne l'aimait pas, maman serait malheureuse. Papa Matt aussi. Il ne disait rien, mais ça se voyait dans ses yeux.

Elle bâilla, frotta ses yeux fatigués. Même à sept ans, il y avait des jours où on n'arrivait pas à décider de ce qu'il fallait faire. C'est sûrement pour ça qu'il y avait des parents : pour aider les enfants à régler les questions vraiment difficiles. Dans un sens, elle était presque contente d'avoir deux papas. Elle avait besoin de toute l'aide possible !

15

Sarah s'éveilla tard, le lendemain matin, le cerveau engourdi, sans aucune envie d'émerger du brouillard. Face à un présent aussi désastreux, elle préféra se réfugier dans le passé.

Le colis envoyé par Oliver contenait une liasse de lettres, certaines datant de plus de deux ans. Le service du courrier les avait fourrées dans une boîte, sans jamais penser à les lui remettre lors de ses brefs passages au journal. Elle les ouvrit une à une, et lut les minces feuilles de papier couvertes de l'écriture pointue de Felix. Ce n'était souvent que de petits mots, et pourtant, ils restituaient son ton inimitable.

« Les touristes chassent les gens du cru ; ils n'ont pas compris qu'il ne restera plus personne pour les dorloter quand nous serons tous partis. » Dans cette lettre, elle trouva deux photos : des pélicans colorisés sur fond de ciel jaune. « Je n'aime pas ces fichus ordinateurs. Restons dans la chambre noire ! »

Un commentaire sur Chuck attira son regard : « Ce garçon ne fera jamais rien. Il restera toujours à la case départ ». La formule lui arracha une grimace. Elle aussi était retournée à la case départ…

Dans une autre lettre, elle trouva des photos splendides. Felix était alors au mieux de sa forme ; il travaillait dans un réalisme total qui transformait l'image en commentaire. Un cliché en particulier attira l'attention de la jeune femme : une juxtaposition de cannettes et de bouteilles de bière sur une de ces plaques fleuries qu'on place sur le bas-côté des routes pour commémorer un accident mortel. Cette photo, il lui semblait l'avoir déjà vue quelque part.

Quelques lettres plus tard, elle trouva une autre image familière, puis une autre. Quand la boîte fut vide, elle en avait reconnu douze, sans pouvoir se rappeler où elle les avait vues, auparavant. Chuck dirait sans doute qu'elle perdait la tête, mais... Chuck dirait... ? Une idée fugace lui traversa l'esprit, mais, avant qu'elle ne pût la saisir, on sonna à la porte. Elle se leva d'une détente en s'efforçant de ne pas penser à Luke. Non, ça ne pouvait pas être lui. Pas après leurs adieux d'hier soir. Des adieux pleins de rancune.

En effet, le visage qu'elle découvrit en ouvrant la porte n'était pas celui de Luke mais celui de Kristin.

— Entrez, dit-elle. Ne faites pas attention au désordre : je triais du courrier.

— Bien sûr, murmura vaguement Kristin. Vous avez... trouvé Luke ?

— Oui.

— Vous lui avez parlé ?

— Nous avons parlé, mais ça n'a pas servi à grand-chose. Il était encore bouleversé quand je suis partie.

— Au moins, vous gardez le contact ?

— En fait, nous nous sommes dit au revoir, hier soir.

Elle débarrassa un fauteuil des journaux qui l'encombraient, tout en expliquant :

— De toute façon, je pense que je partirai bientôt. Mon... travail ici ne débouche sur rien.

— Ah ?

Kristin resserra les mains sur son sac.

— Dans ce cas, j'ai un service… un très gros service à vous demander.

— Asseyez-vous.

Sans l'écouter, Kristin enchaîna :

— Les autorités nous ont conseillé d'évacuer la ville avant demain à midi. Matt et Luke vont rester pour participer aux secours, mais moi, je pars demain matin avec les filles et les parents de Matt. Nous allons à Fayetteville. Est-ce que vous voulez bien… venir avec nous ?

— Mais pourquoi ? demanda Sarah, stupéfaite.

— J'ai… j'ai besoin d'aide.

Désemparée, la jeune femme se percha sur le bord du fauteuil.

— Mme Brennan est épuisée et très inquiète pour le Colonel. Elle adore les filles, mais elles sont trop remuantes pour elle, en ce moment : elle ne supporte aucune agitation. Je ne peux pas m'occuper de tout le monde en même temps.

Sarah essayait d'imaginer une cohabitation avec les parents de Luke. Impensable ! D'un autre côté, comment refuser ?

— Mais… votre famille, vos amis…

Kristin secoua la tête.

— Mes parents vont rester : ils sont volontaires pour travailler avec la Croix-Rouge. Mes amis s'occupent de leur propre famille. J'ai passé je ne sais combien de coups de fil pour trouver une infirmière, une *baby-sitter*…mais personne n'est disponible. Je dois prendre soin des parents de Matt, Erin et Jenny ont besoin de moi… Vous êtes mon dernier recours.

Sarah se sentait faiblir. Luke l'avait aidée à un moment où elle ne savait vers qui se tourner. Même si elle ne devait jamais le revoir, elle pouvait faire ce geste envers ses filles.

— D'accord, dit-elle. A quelle heure voulez-vous qu'on se retrouve ?

Elles fixèrent un rendez-vous, discutèrent des détails. Enfin, Kristin adressa à celle qui avait accepté d'être son amie un sourire lumineux et triste à la fois.

— J'apprécie énormément que vous fassiez cela pour nous. Je ne sais pas comment vous remercier.

— C'est moi qui paie une dette. A demain, 10 heures. Oh... Kristin ? Ne dites pas à Luke que je viens avec vous.

— Mais...

— S'il vous plaît !

— Très bien, si c'est ce que vous voulez. A demain !

Sarah referma la porte derrière elle. Ce départ lui donnait une énergie nouvelle ; il l'obligeait à réfléchir, à s'organiser. Voyons, elle devait emporter des vêtements, de l'argent, ses appareils photo. Il faudrait fixer de l'adhésif à toutes les fenêtres, peut-être couvrir les meubles de bâches en plastique... D'autres détails lui vinrent à l'esprit, et elle s'aperçut avec surprise qu'elle ne craquait pas, qu'elle ne tournait pas en rond, qu'elle ne fuyait pas la situation. Elle gérait sa vie ! Peut-être saurait-elle, après cela, prendre d'autres décisions, mettre en œuvre de nouveaux projets. Mais, tout d'abord...

Tout d'abord, elle devait rendre une dernière visite à Chuck Sawyer. Elle avait des questions à lui poser.

— J'arrive, j'arrive !

Un appel d'air gonfla le rideau noir, et Chuck parut.

— Que puis-je... Ah, c'est toi !

Son sourire pâle s'était instantanément effacé.

— Qu'est-ce qui me vaut le plaisir de ta visite ?

Elle eut un instant de frayeur en se rappelant les soupçons de Luke, puis sa colère reprit le dessus.

— Escroc ! lança-t-elle.

— Pardon ?

— Ces photos, Chuck ! Tu vends les photos de Felix en prétendant que ce sont les tiennes.

— C'est absurde. J'ai les négatifs dans mes archives ; je peux prouver que je les ai prises.

— Et j'ai des lettres vieilles de deux ans qui accompagnent les mêmes photos. Des lettres écrites par Felix, dans lesquelles il me raconte comment il a pris ces clichés et de quelle manière il a fait ses réglages.

— Et alors ?

Il essayait de faire bonne figure, mais ses paupières battaient rapidement, et ses doigts tapotaient le comptoir.

— Felix ne peut plus dépenser l'argent, reprit-il. Moi, je peux.

— Tu es son héritier : tu pouvais gagner de l'argent en les vendant sous son nom. Probablement beaucoup plus d'argent, puisqu'il est célèbre. Tu y as pensé ?

— Et tout partager avec toi ? s'écria Chuck, hors de lui. Il t'a donné la moitié du magasin, il ne s'est occupé que de toi. Je suis son neveu ! Et tu voudrais que je partage les bénéfices ? Merci bien !

Elle serra les poings.

— Tu dois cesser de vendre ces tirages sous ton nom. Ce n'est pas honnête envers lui.

— Il n'a pas été honnête envers moi !

Sarah leva les yeux vers les photos de Felix, puis réfléchit un instant, et se retourna vers son prétendu associé.

— Je vais partir. Je ne reviendrai sans doute jamais. Je veux bien te vendre ma moitié de l'affaire.

— Comme si j'avais de quoi l'acheter ! A lui seul, le terrain doit valoir au moins cent mille dollars.

— Je me fiche de l'argent, Chuck. Je te vends tout pour un dollar, plus les négatifs de Felix et tous les tirages que tu en as fait.

— C'est ça ! Pour que tu puisses les vendre et t'enrichir sur mon dos. Pas question !

— Je ferai peut-être une exposition, mais je ne les vendrai pas. Dès que l'ouragan sera passé, j'irai trouver un avocat, et je lui demanderai de rédiger un accord destiné à protéger nos intérêts à tous les deux.

Il la contempla un long moment, puis lâcha du bout des lèvres :

— D'accord. Marché conclu.

— Bien. Tu peux me donner les négatifs et les tirages tout de suite.

— Désolé, ma chère, répondit-il en retrouvant son plus vilain sourire. Ils sont dans mon coffre, à Chuckton. Je dois attendre que l'ouragan soit passé pour y aller.

— D'accord. Mais n'oublie pas que j'ai les lettres de Felix. Si tu essaies de te défiler, je transmets tout à la police.

— Pas de problème. Il y avait autre chose ?

Son visage était parfaitement inexpressif. Au point qu'il en devenait inquiétant.

— Je prends ces tirages avec moi, déclara-t-elle en les décrochant du mur. Je t'appellerai dès que je serai de retour en ville. On s'occupera de l'accord.

— C'est ça.

Il lui tourna le dos, ouvrit le rideau noir, et la regarda par-dessus son épaule.

— Tu sais, si tu étais simplement partie quand tu t'es fait agresser, tout aurait été plus simple pour nous deux.

Il disparut.

Elle quitta le magasin, sachant qu'elle n'en franchirait plus jamais le seuil. Elle avait l'impression de perdre Felix une deuxième fois. Après l'ouragan, où irait-elle ? Elle n'aurait qu'à monter dans sa jeep et rouler au hasard. Au fond, la destination n'avait pas beaucoup d'importance.

Dans le courant de l'après-midi, le ciel bleu vif devint gris terne, et le vent lourd, humide et salé. La circulation était épouvantable : les touristes rentraient chez eux en toute hâte, et les gens du cru se dirigeaient vers l'intérieur des terres. Assoiffée d'air pur, Sarah remonta le flot à contre-courant et alla s'accouder à la rambarde surplombant la plage. Les vagues tourmentées se précipitaient sur le sable ; quelques surfeurs ignoraient les consignes de la police…

Des surfeurs, la police… Luke ! Elle allait devoir lui laisser un message pour le prévenir qu'elle se mettait en sécurité, sinon il s'inquiéterait, et perdrait peut-être du temps à tenter de la retrouver. Il était comme ça.

Tôt ou tard, il saurait où elle était allée et avec qui. Sans doute par les filles ! S'il cherchait à la remercier, elle serait peut-être obligée de le revoir…

Elle sembla hésiter. Il attendit la suite, mais le message s'arrêtait là. Elle lui avait dit qu'elle partirait, et elle l'avait fait, pensa-t-il en frottant ses yeux douloureux. Une femme de parole. Et il n'avait pas prononcé le seul mot qui aurait pu la convaincre de rester.

Après avoir téléphoné pour s'assurer que Matt ne serait pas là, il passa voir les filles, tôt dans la matinée, avant leur départ.

— On part en vacances avec papy et mamie, expliqua Erin. On sera dans un hôtel avec une piscine et des jeux.

— Encore des vacances ! s'écria Luke en s'asseyant sur le lit.

Jenny grimpa sur ses genoux.

— Tu n'as qu'à venir avec nous, papa !

— J'aimerais bien, mais je dois rester ici pour aider les gens qui auront des problèmes pendant l'ouragan. Tout le monde ne part pas, tu sais ?

— Alors, pourquoi on part, nous ? demanda Erin d'un air boudeur.

— Vous partez pour vous mettre à l'abri. Comme ça, je n'aurai pas à m'inquiéter pour vous. C'est difficile de travailler quand on s'inquiète pour quelqu'un. En fait, vous me rendez un grand service.

Jenny soupira en posant la tête sur son épaule. Erin, quant à elle, se remit à fourrer des livres dans son sac de voyage, en expliquant la raison de chacun de ses choix.

Luke se sentait attendri. Il mesura, une fois de plus, à quel point il aimait ses petites filles.

— Matt reste à Myrtle Beach, lui dit Kristin alors qu'il repartait. Il va condamner les fenêtres ici et chez ses parents, puis se porter volontaire auprès des pompiers, je crois.

— Ils auront besoin de toutes les bonnes volontés.

— Tu veux bien… ?

Elle se mordit la lèvre, leva la tête vers lui :

— Tu voudras bien garder un œil sur lui, quand tu auras un moment ? T'assurer qu'il va bien ?

Luke hésita entre éclater de rire, se mettre en colère, faire de l'ironie… Finalement, il réussit à contrôler toutes ces réactions. Kristin avait confiance en lui, et il devait faire ce qu'elle lui demandait.

— O.K. Dis-moi où je peux vous joindre à Fayetteville, et je vous passerai un coup de fil chaque fois que je le pourrai.

— Merci, Luke. Tu es… extraordinaire.

Il lui ouvrit les bras, la serra un instant contre lui.

— Tu n'es pas mal non plus. Prenez bien soin de vous.

— Toi aussi.

Il remonta dans sa voiture, le cœur un peu plus léger. Leurs rapports étaient redevenus amicaux. C'était une bonne chose.

— Pourquoi est-ce que tu viens ? lui demanda Erin avec méfiance. Mon père a dit qu'il restait ici.

— Ta maman m'a demandé de lui donner un coup de main. Elle a beaucoup à faire pour s'occuper de vos grands-parents et de vous deux.

— Mais c'est nous qui l'aide ! piailla Jenny. Elle dit toujours qu'on l'aide.

— Je sais bien, mais, cette fois, elle a aussi besoin de l'aide d'une plus grande. Comme votre père et… Matt… sont occupés avec l'ouragan, c'est moi qui viens.

Poussée par un vent d'est, la pluie se mit à tomber avec violence. Sarah poussa la manette de dégivrage à fond.

— Tu ne fais pas partie de la famille, marmonna Erin.

— Non. Mais je suis tout de même une amie.

— Tu sais raconter des histoires ? demanda Jenny.

— En fait, je ne sais pas du tout. Je n'ai jamais eu l'occasion de m'exercer.

— Racontes-en une tout de suite. Comme ça, on verra.

— Hmm, murmura Sarah en s'efforçant de se souvenir d'un conte de fées. Il était une fois…

Le chuchotement perçant de Jenny l'interrompit :

— Tu vois, elle commence comme il faut, soufflait-elle à sa sœur.

— C'est la fin qui compte, répliqua Erin sur le même ton.

— Il était une fois un ours énorme. Un ours vraiment gigantesque, avec une longue fourrure brune, de longues griffes et de grosses dents pointues.

— Dans les histoires, il faut qu'il y ait des gens, dit Erin.

— Chut ! souffla sa sœur.

— L'ours vivait dans une grotte sombre…

Elle parla pendant le reste du trajet, racontant l'histoire de Zander, beau prince condamné par un enchantement à rester ours jusqu'à ce qu'il eût sauvé trois vies, et de Persis, la belle perdue dans la forêt, qu'il faillit dévorer.

— Ça y est, il lui a sauvé la vie, annonça Erin. Plus que deux et il peut redevenir un prince.

— Qui d'autre est-ce qu'il a sauvé, Sarah ? Qui ?

— Si tu te taisais, elle pourrait nous le dire.

Devant elle, Sarah vit s'allumer le clignotant du monospace.

— On le saura plus tard. Pour l'instant, je crois que nous sommes arrivées.

— Oh, non ! protestèrent les gamines. Pas maintenant !

La pluie commença à tomber au moment où il se mettait au travail. En quelques minutes, son blouson fut trempé. Deux heures plus tard, le vent se leva. Perché sur son échelle métallique si glissante, heurté par les rafales, il pensa avec nostalgie à l'échelle de bois dont il se servait autrefois.

Luke et lui avaient assisté à des ouragans spectaculaires, les premières années, alors qu'ils venaient de s'installer sur la côte. Luke étudiait la météo et les marées, et ses prévisions étaient souvent justes. Quand l'œil du cyclone était sur eux, sans écouter les protestations de leur mère, ils sortaient tous les deux regarder le ciel et évaluer les dégâts. Où était passée cette vieille connivence ? A quel moment leurs chemins s'étaient-ils séparés ?

Perdu dans ses souvenirs, Matt chargea son échelle et ses outils sur le plateau de son pick-up, et roula jusque chez lui. C'était bon de se mettre à l'abri dans la voiture, même pour quelques minutes. Voyant les rues déjà jonchées de branches, il rentra le véhicule dans le garage, et referma la porte pour ne pas laisser entrer la pluie.

Il ferait nuit très tôt sous ce ciel d'encre. Levant la tête, il soupira en mesurant le travail qui l'attendait. Cette maison avait vraiment trop de fenêtres !

Quand il remonta, l'échelle se balançait sous la force du vent, les éclairs crépitaient dans toutes les directions, le tonnerre faisait vibrer les vitres. L'air était chaud, mais la pluie le glaçait. Il allait perdre un temps fou si le froid le rendait maladroit.

Il garda pour la fin les fenêtres orientées à l'ouest : à l'abri du vent, elles seraient les plus faciles à couvrir quand il commencerait vraiment à sentir la fatigue. Au moment de transporter son échelle de ce côté, il se demanda si ça en valait la peine. Il avait mal aux pieds, à force de rester en équilibre sur un étroit barreau de métal, et ses mains étaient couvertes d'ampoules sous ses gants mouillés. Il n'avait qu'à laisser ce côté ouvert ! Non, il ne pouvait pas, parce que c'était la chambre de Jenny et la salle de bains qu'elle partageait avec Erin. Il devait faire en sorte que leurs peluches restent au sec. Plus que trois fenêtres. Plus que trois.

Soulevant une nouvelle feuille de contreplaqué, il grimpa lourdement l'échelle. Deux fois, il glissa ; la seconde, il se heurta violemment le genou. Sifflant de douleur, il reprit très lentement son ascension, lutta contre le vent pour placer le contreplaqué sur la fenêtre, glissa quelques clous entre ses dents, et tira le marteau de sa ceinture.

Il ne lui restait qu'un côté à clouer quand le vent le poussa dans le vide. Il se raccrocha des deux mains à l'échelle, la sentit glisser, s'immobiliser. Le cœur battant, le souffle coupé, il resta figé de longues secondes... pour s'apercevoir enfin qu'il avait laissé tomber son marteau.

Tout en jurant, il redescendit. La pluie l'aveuglait ; il dut se mettre à quatre pattes pour chercher son outil à tâtons.

— Je te tiens, saleté ! s'écria-t-il enfin.

Il rampa jusqu'au marteau, le saisit par le manche, et se remit à genoux sous l'échelle, le corps endolori, luttant pour reprendre son souffle.

Devant lui, à l'angle de la maison, la foudre déchira un grand pin. Un jaillissement de lumière, un coup de boutoir à vous crever les tympans ! Cloué sur place, il regarda le tronc se fendre en deux parties égales. Des aiguilles en feu tournoyèrent, emportées par le vent, suivies de branches flambant comme des torches, malgré la pluie. Lentement, les deux moitiés du tronc commencèrent à basculer.

Il voulut sauter sur ses pieds, glissa sur l'herbe détrempée, la boue et les aiguilles de pin. Dans un craquement sonore, l'arbre se brisa à la base, les deux moitiés se détachèrent... Matt fonça dans la seule direction possible : vers le portillon du jardin.

Il était à un mètre de la délivrance quand son pied se prit dans un tuyau d'arrosage. Il tomba violemment, s'arracha à la boue, se retrouva à quatre pattes... Poussée de côté par la chute de l'arbre, l'échelle le heurta violemment. Tout autour de lui, des bouts de branches brisées s'enfoncèrent dans le sol meuble. Le tronc de l'arbre le heurta, et il s'abattit face contre terre.

16.

Luke passa la nuit de l'ouragan à courir d'urgence en urgence, jusqu'à ce que la chute des câbles téléphoniques mette un terme aux appels. Ensuite, il patrouilla dans sa voiture de police, repérant les immeubles endommagés et cherchant des victimes. Les quartiers les plus proches de la plage étaient totalement évacués ; on avait emmené aux abris les dernières petites mamies ainsi que leurs chats qu'elles refusaient de laisser derrière elles.

Dans un monospace gisant sur le côté dans un fossé rempli d'eau, il trouva une mère qui avait tenté, un peu tard, de mettre sa famille à l'abri. Il sortit cinq gosses du véhicule, trois d'entre eux encore dans des sièges de bébé. Dieu merci, les autres avaient mis leur ceinture ! Blottie au milieu de sa couvée sur la banquette arrière, la maman éclata en sanglots.

— Mon mari travaille à la compagnie électrique, balbutia-t-elle en acceptant le mouchoir en papier que Luke lui tendait. Tous les employés sont de service. Je pensais pouvoir rester à la maison sans lui, mais le vent faisait tant de bruit, les arbres tombaient... J'ai eu peur pour les enfants.

— Je vais vous emmener à l'abri. Je laisserai un message à votre mari pour lui dire où vous êtes.

Elle lui sourit avec reconnaissance.

— Il se fait du souci…

— On s'en fait tous, marmonna Luke en démarrant.

L'œil du cyclone passa au-dessus de la ville à 4 heures du matin. Curieusement, le silence subit était presque plus impressionnant que le vacarme de fin du monde qui l'avait précédé. Les nuages s'écartèrent ; on put voir les étoiles. Luke trouva un sans-abri blotti dans un coin de parking, et l'emmena en sécurité. Il voyait tant d'arbres abattus, tant de maisons au toit crevé par leur chute qu'il limita ses rapports aux situations les plus critiques— lorsqu'il voyait des câbles électriques rompus jeter des étincelles, ou de grosses branches à demi arrachées battre l'air.

Puis le vent revint avec la pluie, et les vagues envahirent les rues, charriant des tonnes de sable. La grande artère du centre-ville ressemblait à un torrent. Cherchant un itinéraire praticable pour revenir au commissariat, Luke passa devant une maison totalement détruite. Quatre arbres s'étaient abattus sur elle de quatre directions différentes. Un chien terrifié hurlait, dressé contre la barrière.

Luke freina, sortit encore une fois dans la tourmente, et fit le tour complet de la maison, de l'eau jusqu'aux mollets, projetant le faisceau de sa lampe torche par les fenêtres brisées.

— Il y a quelqu'un ?

Des pièces vides, pas de voiture dans l'allée. Les habitants s'étaient enfuis en laissant leur chien attaché à la barrière.

Ce n'était qu'un chiot, constata Luke en s'approchant de lui. Très jeune, très grand — et qui promettait de grandir encore, vu la taille de ses pattes.

— Salut, Buster !

La pauvre bête lécha avec enthousiasme la main qu'il lui tendait, frétillant de tout son corps malgré les tremblements convulsifs qui l'agitaient.

— Pauvre petit père ! Viens, on va te détacher.

Le nœud était serré, la grosse ficelle mouillée. La pluie le giflait. Il renonça vite, et enroula la corde autour de sa main pour la trancher avec son couteau. Le chien poussa un jappement, et bondit, manquant lui arracher le bras.

— Du calme, mon gros ! Par là, dans la voiture.

Sans se faire prier, l'animal se précipita sur la banquette arrière. Luke eut une pensée fugitive pour son siège, puis il haussa les épaules et emmena Buster à l'abri organisé pour les animaux. De là, il n'était pas très loin de chez Kristin. Il fit le détour, et vit que Matt était passé : les portes et fenêtres étaient couvertes de grandes feuilles de contreplaqué. A l'angle du jardin, le grand arbre était tombé, abattu par la foudre. Il distinguait un grand amas de débris noircis, mais, par chance, une moitié était tombée en travers de la pelouse, sans rien abîmer, et l'autre gisait le long du mur. Il suffirait d'une heure avec une tronçonneuse pour tout remettre en ordre.

Sa radio crépita, annonçant que le vent soufflait à 150 km/h et qu'il accélérait encore, et ordonnant à toutes les patrouilles de se mettre à l'abri.

Luke retourna au commissariat.

A 9 heures du matin, l'ouragan Daniel quitta Myrtle Beach, emportant les nuages vers l'ouest, laissant derrière lui une matinée chaude et moite. Des silhouettes isolées parurent dans les rues et se mirent à examiner les dégâts : arbres couchés, voitures écrasées, rues et fenêtres défoncées.

Il s'agissait maintenant de prévenir les pillages, de tenir les curieux à distance des câbles électriques arrachés. A midi, quand il termina son service, Luke était éreinté. Il venait juste de s'asseoir quand le téléphone sonna.

— Brennan.

— Luke, c'est ton père à l'appareil.

Il se redressa, inquiet.

— Tout va bien ? Vous êtes tous arrivés sans problème ? Les filles…

— Nous allons tous bien. Il y a eu du vent et de la pluie, mais le courant n'a même pas été coupé.

Le Colonel hésita un instant, puis demanda :

— Tu as parlé à Matt ?

Luke fit une grimace.

— Non. Et vous ?

— Non plus. Il avait prévu de contacter Kristin, mais…

— S'il a été aussi débordé que moi, il n'a pas eu un moment pour le faire. La tempête vient juste de se terminer.

En arrière-plan, il entendit la voix de sa mère — sans distinguer les paroles, mais le ton était suffisamment éloquent. Le Colonel s'éclaircit la voix.

— Retrouve-le, tu veux ? Nous sommes assez inquiets, Kristin s'attendait vraiment à avoir des nouvelles plus tôt.

— Je téléphone à son responsable et je vous rappelle dès que je sais quelque chose. Ça peut prendre un certain temps : une heure, peut-être. Surtout, ne paniquez pas.

— Nous attendons ton appel.

Il y eut un déclic, puis la tonalité. Luke raccrocha en murmurant :

— Oui, je vais bien, papa. Merci de t'en être inquiété.

A cet instant, tout le poids de la fatigue s'abattit sur lui. Il s'accorda une deuxième tasse de café, et composa le numéro du poste de pompiers auprès duquel Matt s'était porté volontaire. Par chance, on lui passa rapidement le capitaine.

— Je cherche à joindre le lieutenant-colonel Matt Brennan. Il faisait partie de votre équipe de volontaires.

— Oui, on aurait eu du travail pour lui, dit une voix aussi lasse que la sienne.

— Vous auriez eu… ? Qu'est-ce que ça veut dire ?

— Simplement que je ne l'ai pas revu depuis avant-hier.

Quand le Colonel rapporta ces paroles au reste de la famille, le visage déjà pâle de Kristin devint livide. Jetant un coup d'œil aux filles qui regardaient la télévision dans la pièce voisine, Sarah tira la porte de communication avant de demander :

— Luke va bien ?

— Il a eu beaucoup à faire. Il nous recontactera dès qu'il aura du nouveau.

Installé dans l'unique fauteuil de la pièce, le Colonel avait l'air très fatigué.

— Mais est-ce qu'il va bien ? répéta Sarah.

Le vieil homme fronça les sourcils.

— Je pensais surtout à Matt… je n'ai pas demandé. Il avait l'air bien. Sinon, il me l'aurait dit !

Sarah échangea un regard avec Kristin.

— Vous croyez ? demanda cette dernière assez sèchement, en s'adressant à son beau-père.

— Kristin, vous faites des histoires, coupa Mme Brennan. Si Luke avait eu un problème, il l'aurait dit… William, c'est l'heure de ton médicament.

Quand son mari eut avalé ses cachets, sentant sans doute le regard de Sarah peser sur elle, elle reprit :

— Je me suis peut-être montrée un peu dure avec Luke, ces temps derniers. Je le reconnais volontiers, mais… c'est de Matt que nous sommes sans nouvelles, aujourd'hui. C'est plutôt de lui que nous devons nous inquiéter.

Elle promena à la ronde son regard bleu, sûre de ne rencontrer aucune contradiction.

— Vous devez avoir besoin de vous reposer, dit Kristin. Nous allons vous laisser.

— Vous nous préviendrez, n'est-ce pas, quand Luke rappellera ? ajouta Sarah avant de refermer la porte.

Jusque-là, Kristin s'était contrôlée. Mais, une fois à l'abri du regard de ses beaux-parents, Sarah craignit de la voir craquer. Aussi, sans réfléchir plus longtemps, elle passa à l'action.

— Les filles, vous voulez la suite de l'ours Zander ?

— Oui !

— Alors, éteignez la télévision, et suivez-moi sur le terrain de jeux. On racontera l'histoire sur les balançoires.

Kristin lui lança un regard reconnaissant.

Le terrain de jeux était aménagé à l'ombre d'un bouquet de pins. Erin prit une balançoire et Jenny l'autre. Sarah se chargea de pousser la benjamine.

— Raconte, raconte ! suppliait la petite.

Sarah reprit le fil de l'histoire et arriva au moment où le bébé jaguar est sauvé alors qu'il se cramponne au bord de la falaise.

— C'est le deuxième ! cria Erin d'un air triomphant. Il en a sauvé deux !

S'écartant un peu, Sarah sortit discrètement son appareil photo.

— Ça vous ennuie si je prends quelques clichés ? Votre papa sera content de voir où nous étions.

Les deux gamines prirent instantanément des poses absurdes. Puis elles oublièrent l'appareil, se remirent à s'amuser, et la jeune femme obtint quelques images superbes. Elle décida de les envoyer à Luke ; ce serait une sorte de message pour exprimer tout ce qu'elle ne pouvait dire avec des mots.

Il se fraya un chemin à travers les branches brisées jusqu'à la porte d'entrée, sonna, frappa en vain. Le pick-up de Matt n'était pas garé dans l'allée. Impossible de vérifier si il se trouvait au garage : il n'y avait pas de fenêtre, et il ne connaissait pas le code de la porte. D'ailleurs, cela ne lui aurait rien appris de plus, car il était inconcevable que Matt se fût terré ici pour attendre la fin de l'ouragan. Ce n'était pas son genre.

Où pouvait-il être ?

Le portique du jardin était renversé mais semblait intact. Un auvent métallique, arraché à une autre maison, s'était abattu sur la terrasse, mais, grâce au contreplaqué qui condamnait les portes-fenêtres, rien ne semblait brisé. Le grand pin abattu avait écrasé une partie de la clôture ; des débris de planches de cèdre se mêlaient aux branches.

Luke s'approcha pour examiner les dégâts… et vit briller les barreaux métalliques d'une échelle à travers la verdure.

Seigneur… pas ça !

— Matt ?

Il dut s'éclaircir la gorge pour retrouver sa voix.

— Matt, tu es là ?

Il n'y eut pas de réponse, mais il crut voir trembler une branche.

— Matt !

Toujours pas de réponse. Et il lui était impossible de s'approcher suffisamment de ce côté pour voir le tronc. Glissant sur l'herbe mouillée, il fit le tour de la maison en courant, se précipita vers l'arbre.

— Matt ?

Cette fois, il entendit une plainte, vit remuer les aiguilles de pin.

— Tiens bon, frangin. Je vais voir ce que je peux faire.

Il ne pouvait pas faire grand-chose ! Il tenta de soulever le tronc, mais n'arriva à rien. L'échelle était coincée : impossible de s'en servir comme levier.

— Matt, il faut que je demande de l'aide. Si le portable fonctionne, j'appellerai d'ici. Sinon, il faudra que j'aille chercher quelqu'un. Je reviendrai le plus vite possible. Tiens bon, d'accord ? Je reviendrai vite et on te sortira de là.

La réponse lui parvint sous la forme d'un grognement.

Bien entendu, le portable ne fonctionnait pas. Le vent avait dû détruire les émetteurs à des kilomètres à la ronde. Lentement, Luke se fraya un chemin dans les rues inondées jusqu'à la caserne de pompiers la plus proche. Il expliqua la situation de son frère, mais il y avait tant de monde à secourir qu'il pourrait encore se passer des heures avant qu'une équipe ne se penchât sur son cas…

Il revint donc près de Matt, se mit à plat ventre et tenta de se frayer un chemin dans le fouillis de branches.

— Tu es là-dedans, Matt ? Tu peux me parler ?

Il avançait peu à peu, sans rien voir.

— Ce serait vraiment bien d'entendre un mot ou deux.

— Le moment est… mal choisi pour discuter, dit enfin Matt d'une voix rauque et épuisée, quelque part dans la verdure.

Serrant les dents pour contrôler son émotion, Luke répondit :

— Pourquoi ? Pour une fois que je te tiens à ma merci, je pourrai peut-être marquer quelques points.

— Dans tes… rêves.

— Fais-moi un rapport, alors.

— J'ai la figure dans l'herbe et un arbre sur le dos.

— Sois plus précis, s'il te plaît, dit Luke en riant malgré lui. Tu as mal ?

— Et comment !

— Tu saignes ?

— Je ne crois pas.

— Tu peux bouger tes mains, tes pieds ?

Le silence qui suivit cette question le terrifia.

— Oui, souffla enfin Matt d'une voix faible. Ma main gauche me fait un mal de chien. Je crois qu'elle est cassée.

— S'il n'y a que cela, on s'en sort bien.

Il avança encore un peu, forçant un passage entre les branches odorantes et collantes de sève. Quelque part tout près de lui, Matt s'éclaircit la gorge.

— Qu'est-ce qui t'a amené ici ? demanda-t-il.

— Un coup de fil du Colonel, bien sûr ! Tu n'as pas donné signe de vie, alors ils m'ont envoyé aux nouvelles.

Enfin ! Il voyait un pantalon kaki sous les aiguilles. Avec des précautions infinies, il brisa et écarta plusieurs branches pour se frayer un chemin vers la tête de Matt.

— Une… bonne chose…

— Autrement, tu aurais pu attendre longtemps.

— J'ai attendu longtemps.

— C'est arrivé quand ?

— Avant la nuit.

— Tu as toujours aimé dormir à la belle étoile.

— Pas… sous un ouragan. Pas sous un arbre.

Maintenant, Luke voyait un pan de chemise à carreaux. Ecartant une nouvelle branche, il trouva le bras gauche de son frère, visiblement brisé. Il empoigna une grosse branche, recula comme un crabe pour la manœuvrer hors de son chemin, et découvrit l'arrière de la tête de Matt. Son souffle, qu'il retenait sans s'en apercevoir, s'échappa dans un long sifflement étouffé.

— Te voilà. Tu peux ouvrir les yeux ?

Il n'y eut rien pendant un instant, puis Matt tourna péniblement la tête, et Luke vit son œil bleu.

— Je ne peux pas… rester comme ça, souffla le blessé.

— C'est bon, mets-toi comme tu veux. Je ne tiens pas tant que ça à te contempler. Dis donc, j'ai un Thermos dans la voiture. Tu veux boire quelque chose ?

La tête de Matt reprit sa position première.

— J'ai eu… toute l'eau nécessaire, merci.

Luke se dit qu'il faudrait une grue pour régler le problème. Si on attaquait l'arbre à la tronçonneuse, tout le poids s'abattrait sur Matt. Posé en appui sur ses branches brisées, retenu par l'échelle et la barrière, l'arbre avait miraculeusement trouvé un équilibre qui ménageait un petit espace entre le tronc et le sol… mais ces grosses branches fichées dans le sol faisaient à la fois office de béquilles et de barreaux, empêchant Matt de sortir de sa cage. On ne pouvait pas les scier sans prévoir d'autres soutiens.

Posant deux doigts sur le cou de son frère, Luke tâta son pouls : il le trouva ferme et régulier, mais un peu rapide.

— Les secours sont prévenus : il n'y a plus qu'à les attendre.

— Au point où j'en suis !

— Ta maison s'en est tirée sans dommage. Kristin sera contente.

— C'est bien.

Luke s'installa aussi confortablement qu'il le put dans son nid d'aiguilles, et se prépara à attendre.

— Ils sont tous arrivés à Fayetteville sans problème. Papa avait l'air en forme quand il a téléphoné.

— Bien.

— Tu as froid ? Je peux aller chercher des couvertures dans la maison, si tu veux.

— Non, ça va.

Luke tendit l'oreille. Il avait cru entendre la sirène des pompiers... Mais ce n'était pas ça. Alors, il dit la première chose qui lui vint à l'esprit :

— Je vais quitter Myrtle Beach.

— Pour aller... où ?

— Je ne sais pas exactement. Dans un premier temps, je ne m'éloignerai pas trop. Et puis, quand les filles seront... habituées, on verra.

— Ne cherche pas à me rendre service.

— Je le fais pour Kristin. Et aussi pour Erin et Jenny. Je me suis trop... accroché à elles.

Matt ne dit rien pendant un long moment. Inquiet, Luke se redressa à demi.

— Tu es toujours là ?

Matt ne répondit pas directement à la question, mais il déclara :

— Partir... ce n'est pas une bonne idée.

L'effort qu'il devait faire pour parler arracha une grimace à Luke. Pourquoi avait-il abordé ce sujet ?

— On en reparlera demain.

— Tout de suite. Quoi qu'on ait... raté, on peut... réparer. Je ne peux pas parler pour... maman...

Une respiration rauque et laborieuse, puis :

—... mais on est une famille. Pas besoin de... se faire la guerre.

Ne sachant que répondre, Luke balbutia :

— O.K., frangin... C'est toi le patron.

— Du moment que tu ne l'oublies pas, souffla Matt avec un petit rire.

Pendant deux heures, ils parlèrent sporadiquement. Le soleil atteignit son zénith, amorça sa descente vers l'ouest. Par moments, Luke somnolait, puis il se réveillait dès que sa tête basculait en avant.

— Matt ?

— Tu… ronfles.

— Toi aussi. Je me souviens, quand on était partis camper…

A 16 heures, Luke décida que si rien ne se passait dans l'heure suivait, il retournerait chercher de l'aide.

Le capitaine des pompiers évita ses foudres de justesse en arrivant dix minutes avant la limite. Le premier commentaire du spécialiste fut brutal et concis :

— Ça va être une saloperie.

A bout de patience, Luke émergea du fouillis d'aiguilles en criant :

— Raison de plus pour commencer le plus vite possible !

Il fallut une éternité pour fixer les câbles. Luke se joignit à l'équipe trop réduite, luttant avec les lourdes chaînes, les glissant avec prudence sous le tronc, creusant parfois le sol pour ménager un passage.

— Désolé pour ta pelouse, dit-il dans un grognement d'effort. Tu vas avoir du boulot pour la récupérer.

— Je verrai… ça… plus tard.

La voix de Matt faiblissait. Il était couché là dans l'herbe mouillée depuis près de vingt-quatre heures : il ne tiendrait pas le coup indéfiniment !

— Bon, lança le chef de l'équipe en examinant son installation. On va soulever un peu et scier quelques branches. Faites en sorte que ce fichu tronc ne parte pas en vrille.

— Prépare-toi à être sauvé ! lança Luke, agenouillé près de son frère.

— C'est quand vous voudrez, répliqua Matt avec un rire épuisé.

Luke recula. Le moteur du treuil vrombit, les chaînes se tendirent bruyamment et mordirent l'écorce. Dans une plainte déchirante, l'arbre se souleva enfin.

L'envie de se précipiter, de traîner Matt en sécurité était presque insupportable, mais Luke resta à sa place. Un plan avait été élaboré : il aurait risqué de tout gâcher par une initiative intempestive. Trépignant d'impatience, il s'aperçut que le treuil tournait au ralenti et que les chaînes ne bougeaient plus. Plantés de part et d'autre de l'arbre, les trois pompiers discutaient sombrement. Il les rejoignit juste à temps pour entendre la mauvaise nouvelle.

— La grosse branche est déjà fendue. On ne peut pas scier si près de lui. Si on soulève trop, elle va se détacher et lui défoncer la tête.

Luke voyait la même chose qu'eux. L'une des branches les plus grosses et les plus longues avait été brisée. Si on soulevait l'arbre, elle se retrouverait suspendue dans le vide, et on voyait déjà les fibres éclatées se rompre une à une sous son poids. S'ils ne se hâtaient pas, elle allait tomber.

— Il vous faut un étai, dit Luke. Quelque chose pour soutenir cette branche pendant que le treuil soulève le reste.

— L'étai tombera dès qu'on soulèvera l'arbre.

— Il vous en faut un qui s'ajuste au fur et à mesure.

— Ça existe, ça ?

— Oui. C'est moi.

17.

Le plus difficile fut de se glisser sous le tronc.

Luke plongea dans le labyrinthe de verdure froissée, rampa, lutta, et finit par s'allonger sur le dos dans l'herbe détrempée, l'énorme masse de l'arbre suspendue devant son visage. Désormais, tout dépendait de lui.

Le tronc suspendu oscilla légèrement. Quelque part, une branche craqua — pourvu que ce ne fût pas la sienne ! Se propulsant sur les coudes et les talons, il reprit son avancée en suivant le tronc. Des brindilles l'égratignaient, la sève le barbouillait, l'étouffant de son odeur pénétrante. Il parvint enfin à la hauteur des jambes de Matt.

— C'est moi, dit-il en le palpant rapidement, à la recherche de fractures.

— Kristin ne... sera pas contente... si l'arbre... nous écrase tous les deux.

— Ça n'arrivera pas, vieux. On en a pour une minute.

Sur ces mots, il se mit en position sous la branche brisée. Quand il fut en place, elle reposait sur sa poitrine. Calant ses coudes sur le sol, il empoigna l'écorce poisseuse et souleva légèrement. Elle ne tenait plus à rien.

— C'est bon ! cria-t-il. J'y suis !

— Ça marche !

Le moteur du treuil rugit. Au-dessus de Luke, l'arbre trembla, se balança. Pendant un instant, la branche dans ses mains se fit plus lourde. Puis, peu à peu, le fouillis d'aiguilles se souleva de son visage. Aspirant une énorme bouffée d'air frais, il étendit progressivement les bras pour soutenir son fardeau qui se soulevait à son tour. Le tronc monta encore de quelques centimètres et, avec une explosion comparable à un coup de fusil, la branche se détacha d'un coup : un énorme poids mort sur ses bras tendus. Le choc lui arracha une exclamation ; il se sentit écrasé, enfoncé dans le sol. Les dents serrées, il haleta d'effort, cherchant la force de tenir.

— Luke ? cria la voix de Matt toute proche. Ça va ?

Impossible de répondre, impossible de desserrer les dents pour former des mots. Tout autour de lui, il entendait des froissements dans les branches.

— On vous sort de là, Matt ! cria un homme. Détendez-vous. Je soulève cette échelle, et mes collègues vous feront glisser. Surtout, laissez-vous faire : n'essayez pas de nous aider.

Les yeux fermés, Luke entendit des talons traîner dans l'herbe, puis un hoquet épuisé, un soupir.

— Pauvre type ! dit un pompier. Il a fini par s'évanouir. Bon, et vous, maintenant ? Luke ? Vous êtes prêt à lâcher ou vous comptez rester comme ça toute la nuit ?

Avec des gestes rapides malgré leur décontraction apparente, les pompiers dégageaient le tronc, passaient les chaînes autour de la branche qui emprisonnait Luke, la soulevaient à l'aide du treuil. Cela lui fit un mal de chien. Quand le poids se retira, ses épaules étaient des boules de feu. Ses deux bras retombèrent, inertes.

— Ça va aller, vieux ?

Il leva les yeux, vit un pompier penché sur lui. Sa tête se découpait sur un merveilleux ciel rempli d'étoiles.

— Ça va aller, murmura-t-il d'une voix qui ressemblait à celle de Matt. Il faudra peut-être m'aider à me relever.

Une fois sur pied, il partit à la recherche de son frère, et le trouva allongé sur un brancard près de l'ambulance. Epuisé, raide et endolori, il alla se pencher sur lui.

— La prochaine fois, attaque-toi à un lilas, dit-il. Ils sont plus faciles à déplacer.

Les yeux bleus s'ouvrirent. Matt le contempla un instant, puis souleva sa main droite.

— Merci, Luke, dit-il. Merci beaucoup.

Malgré la douleur, Luke referma la main sur la sienne. Il aurait aimé dire quelque chose, mais il ne trouvait pas les mots.

— On va t'emmener, maintenant. Je serai juste derrière vous, dans la voiture. On se retrouve à l'hôpital.

— Ce n'est pas tout à fait ça, dit l'interne. Il y a un autre brancard pour vous.

— Moi, ça va ! affirma Luke. Il faut que je…

— Ne discutez pas : couchez-vous.

Maintenant qu'il y pensait, il avait un peu le vertige. Il devait absolument appeler Kristin, mais, ensuite, ce serait bien de s'allonger.

— Ecoutez, je me ferai examiner tout à l'heure. Il faut que je passe un coup de fil.

— Si vous ne vous allongez pas de vous-même, je vais…

La voix diminua brutalement dans le lointain, couverte par le grondement qui s'enflait à ses oreilles. La nuit autour de lui vira au blanc. Il s'appuya de la hanche contre le brancard en bredouillant :

— En fait, je crois bien que je vais m'asseoir.

Ce furent les dernières paroles qu'il prononça, cette nuit-là.

— Kristin ?
— Non, c'est Sarah. Matt ?
— Ouais...

Il semblait totalement épuisé.

La porte entre les deux chambres s'ouvrit, et le Colonel parut. Sarah tendit le combiné à Kristin qui s'agenouillait sur le lit, tremblante.

— Matt ! répéta-t-elle.

Quand elle entendit sa voix, ses yeux se fermèrent, les larmes roulèrent sur ses joues.

— Tu vas bien ? Luke va bien ?

Se retournant vers Sarah avec un sourire radieux, elle hocha la tête, et murmura :

— Ils vont bien. Ils seront ici vers midi.

Ravalant ses propres larmes, Sarah emmena Erin et Jenny au café de l'hôtel manger des *pancakes* pour le petit déjeuner. Les filles n'avaient aucune idée de ce qui se tramait, et la jeune femme voulait que les adultes puissent savourer la bonne nouvelle en paix.

Ils arrivèrent à midi exactement. Elena poussa un petit cri, puis fondit en larmes. Bondissant du lit où elle jouait avec les filles, Sarah rejoignit Kristin à la porte de communication.

Matt avait un bras dans le plâtre, l'autre autour des épaules de sa mère qui sanglotait sur sa poitrine.

— Il ne fallait pas vous inquiéter, disait-il. J'ai été... retardé.

A côté d'elle, Kristin vacilla, s'affaissa sur elle-même. Sarah la soutint de son mieux. Matt se précipita.

— Kris, mon amour, tout va bien. Je sais que tu as eu peur. Mais je t'avais bien dit que je ne me perdrais plus...

Murmurant dans ses cheveux, la portant à demi, il l'entraîna dans l'autre pièce... au moment où les deux petites filles en jaillissaient comme un ouragan miniature.

— Papa, papa !

Sarah osait à peine regarder à la porte. Quand, enfin, elle tourna les yeux, elle vit Luke entrer à son tour.

— Salut, Erin l'Ourson. Salut, Jenny Penny.

Péniblement, il se baissa, serra ses filles dans ses bras.

— Vous vous amusez bien à Fayetteville ?

Puis il leva les yeux... et la vit. Son visage changea sous le coup d'une émotion qu'elle n'osa pas nommer.

Luke poussa un long soupir. Quand il la regarda de nouveau, il souriait.

— C'était ici que tu projetais de t'enfuir, Sarah Rose ?

— Kristin... m'a demandé un coup de main.

Il hocha la tête avec précaution.

— Merci.

Ce n'était pas de la gratitude qu'elle attendait de lui, mais c'était déjà ça.

Une voix cassante lança alors :

— J'aimerais que quelqu'un me dise exactement pourquoi nous sommes restés vingt-quatre heures sans nouvelles. Nous étions fous d'inquiétude.

Se redressant, Luke se dirigea à petits pas vers le lit le plus proche, et s'assit, une fille sur chaque genou.

— Matt était coincé sous un arbre. On n'a pu le sortir qu'hier, dans la soirée.

— Et, une fois qu'il a été sorti, tu ne pouvais pas appeler ?

Matt revint dans la pièce, l'air sévère... mais Sarah fut stupéfaite de voir que ce n'était pas Luke qu'il foudroyait du regard, mais sa mère.

— Calmez-vous, maman, s'il vous plaît ! Nous avons passé la nuit à l'hôpital, tous les deux. Nous n'étions pas en état de passer des coups de fil.

Sarah le regarda poser un baiser sur le visage éperdu que sa femme levait vers lui. L'expression de Luke ne changea pas. Etait-il trop éreinté pour réagir au spectacle de leur intimité ? Pour la première fois, le Colonel prit la parole :

— Tu aurais dû me dire que tu étais blessé quand nous nous sommes parlés au téléphone, fils.

— Je ne l'étais pas. Je ne le suis pas. Juste un peu raide...

— Enfin, Luke, ton père est resté éveillé toute la nuit : ce n'est pas recommandé pour un homme qui vient d'être gravement malade.

— Ça suffit !

La voix de Matt ressemblait à celle de son père.

— Arrêtez de vous acharner sur Luke, maman. Ouvrez les yeux et regardez la réalité en face, pour une fois !

— Je ne te comprends pas, Matthew. Ton frère...

— Votre fils, maman. Votre autre fils, qui n'était pas la fille que vous désiriez mais qui ne mérite pas pour autant d'être... écarté.

Abasourdie, Elena tourna les yeux vers son mari.

— Tu lui as *dit* ?

— Une crise cardiaque, ça fait réfléchir, Elena. Toi et moi, nous avons commis de sérieuses erreurs avec nos garçons. J'espère seulement qu'il est encore temps de les rattraper.

Se tournant vers Matt, il ordonna :

— Dis-nous ce qui s'est passé.

Luke voulut protester, mais la voix de Matt couvrit la sienne. Il raconta par le menu le sauvetage de la veille, terminant par ces mots :

— Sans lui, je ne serais plus là. A mon avis, il a pensé à tout le monde sauf à lui-même, et ce n'est pas la première fois.

Mme Brennan contemplait Luke d'un air abasourdi.

— Merci, fils, dit le Colonel en tendant la main au héros du jour.

Luke prit cette main qu'on lui offrait.

— Et, en plus, reprit Matt, il m'a offert un chien.

— Un chien ? répétèrent les deux filles à l'unisson.

— Un chien ? murmura Kristin.

— Un pauvre chiot que quelqu'un avait laissé attaché à une clôture, en plein ouragan, expliqua Luke. Je l'ai emmené à l'abri, mais il a eu l'air tellement catastrophé en me voyant repartir que j'ai dit au responsable que je reviendrais le chercher. Il s'appelle Buster.

Matt vint s'accroupir devant les filles.

— J'ai raconté à Luke qu'on avait parlé, tous les trois, de prendre un chien. Je crois que Buster tombe à pic, non ?

— Oh, *cool* !

Spontanément, Erin lança les bras autour du cou de Matt... puis se retourna vers Luke.

— Tu serais d'accord, papa ? C'est ton chien, c'est toi qui l'as trouvé.

— Je serais très content que vous vous occupiez de Buster, oui.

— Je ne sais pas pourquoi, dit Kristin, mais j'ai l'impression que cette tâche va plutôt me revenir.

Les deux frères se retournèrent vers elle d'un même mouvement. Il y avait entre eux une réelle ressemblance, malgré toutes leurs différences.

— Quelle idée ! lança Matt, les yeux remplis d'amour.

— Oui, vraiment, quel pessimisme ! renchérit Luke en souriant à son tour.

Et cette ressemblance provenait aussi de leurs expressions identiques, à la fois épuisées et apaisées.

— Bien, lança Matt avec entrain. Si on s'organisait ? Les abords de la plage sont toujours inondés : vous ne pourrez pas atteindre votre maison, papa. Venez vous installer chez nous. Nous sommes passés, ce matin, pour vérifier : il n'y a pas eu de dégâts majeurs.

— Bonne idée, dit le Colonel en se remettant sur pied. Je serai content de partir d'ici.

— Moi aussi ! cria Jenny en battant des mains.

Erin résuma l'opinion générale en déclarant :

— On rentre à la maison et on va chercher Buster !

— Alors, vous avez fait quoi pendant ces deux jours ? Erin, tu as lu tous tes livres ?

Il se retourna à demi, et le mouvement lui arracha une grimace involontaire.

— Tous ! Et on est allés à la piscine…

— On a fait de la balançoire !

— Sarah a pris des photos !

Il jeta un coup d'œil à la jeune femme, qui évitait son regard depuis le début du trajet.

— J'ai hâte de les voir…

— On a joué au golf. J'ai gagné !

— Tu gagnes toujours, Erin l'Ourson.

— Et Sarah nous a raconté *Zander et Persis*.

— *Zander et Persis* ?

Tout en se coupant constamment et en s'interrompant pour donner des explications supplémentaires, les filles se lancèrent dans l'histoire de l'ours et de la belle, jusqu'au dénouement :

— Un jour, un autre prince traverse la forêt en chassant, et Zander le voit. Il a drôlement faim, parce que c'est l'hiver. Alors, il se dit que ce prince suffira peut-être à le nourrir pendant qu'il hiberne, expliqua Erin, volubile. Les ours hibernent, tu le savais ?

Jenny écoutait en silence, reprise par l'histoire.

— Oui, je le savais. Continue, dit Luke.

— Alors, Zander se précipite sur le prince. Mais, au dernier moment, Persis apparaît. « Non, Zander, arrête ! »

La voix enfantine prit des accents de tragédie.

— Zander a très faim, seulement il s'arrête quand même. Mais le prince a son arc : il se met à tirer sur Zander. Persis l'arrête aussi. Et là, le sortilège est rompu, et Zander se retransforme en prince.

— Et Persis et lui se marient et vivent heureux jusqu'à la fin de leurs jours, conclut Jenny.

— C'est une histoire géniale, dit Luke en gardant son regard fixé sur les filles et en suppliant mentalement Sarah de l'écouter. Mais moi, je connais une fin un peu différente.

Pour la première fois, Sarah tourna les yeux vers lui.

— Comment, papa ? demanda Jenny, très excitée. Ça finissait comment ?

— Eh bien, moi, on m'a dit que quand Zander est redevenu prince, Persis a dû faire un choix. Le prince qu'elle avait sauvé, qui s'appelait, euh… Kurin, était tombé amoureux d'elle en voyant avec quel courage elle l'avait sauvé de l'ours.

— Mais Zander aussi l'aimait.

Luke approuva de la tête.

— Je sais bien ! Alors, Persis a dû décider lequel des deux princes elle voulait épouser. Et, même si elle était très attachée à Zander, elle aimait le prince Kurin depuis très, très longtemps. Bien qu'il soit en terre étrangère.

— Très loin, traduisit Erin à l'intention de sa sœur.

— Persis a donc épousé Kurin, et ils ont vécu heureux jusqu'à la fin de leurs jours.

— Et Zander, alors ?

— Justement ! Zander est retourné dans son royaume et, là, il a rencontré une jeune fille ravissante, très courageuse et très bonne. Il l'a tant aimée qu'il était prêt à renoncer à sa couronne et à tous ses trésors si seulement elle voulait bien l'épouser.

Jenny le contemplait, subjuguée.

— Comment est-ce qu'elle s'appelait, papa ?

Il réfléchit un instant.

— Solara. Parce qu'elle était comme un soleil.

— Et qu'est-ce qui est arrivé à Zander et Solara ?

— A ton avis ?

— Un dragon arrive en volant, décida Erin. Il emmène Solara dans son repaire dans les montagnes. Et le prince Zander doit réussir plein d'épreuves pour la sauver. Mais quand il arrive là-haut…

— Non, ce n'était pas comme ça ! clama Jenny en rebondissant comme une balle. Je veux que Zander et Sol-Solara se marient. J'aime mieux parce que, comme ça, tout le monde peut être heureux.

— Moi aussi, Jenny Penny. C'est comme ça que toutes les bonnes histoires devraient se terminer.

L'expression de Sarah était très familière. Erin avait vu la même sur le visage de maman quand elle regardait papa Matt, et chez mamie quand elle regardait papy. D'habitude, maman ou mamie souriaient, mais quand Sarah se remit à conduire, elle s'essuya les joues du bout des doigts.

Erin referma les yeux pour réfléchir. Cette expression, c'était l'amour. Sarah aimait papa. Papa était-il amoureux d'elle ? Elle n'en était pas sûre : les papas ne montrent pas ce qu'ils ressentent, comme les mamans. Avec Sarah, il souriait beaucoup ; c'était pour cela que Sarah n'avait pas plu à Erin, au début. Avant, il n'y avait que Erin et Jenny à pouvoir faire sourire leur papa.

Si Sarah rendait papa heureux, alors elle devait rester. Elle racontait bien les histoires et elle aimait aller très haut sur la balançoire. Elle pourrait peut-être lui apprendre à prendre des photos, et alors, un jour, ils iraient tous en Afrique faire des photos d'animaux... Elle sombra doucement dans un rêve.

Luke trouva sa mère dans le salon, plantée devant une photo des filles sur la plage. Quand il s'immobilisa sur le seuil, elle se détourna vivement en s'essuyant les yeux.

— Maman... Ça va ? Je peux faire quelque chose ?

Comme elle ne disait rien, elle crut qu'il l'importunait. Il se détournait pour sortir quand elle le rappela.

— Entre, Luke, je te prie. Et ferme la porte.

Le cœur battant, il obéit et s'avança un peu dans la pièce. Après un nouveau silence, sa mère soupira :

— Je... Il me semble que tu dois le savoir : ce n'est pas seulement le fait que tu n'aies pas été... une petite fille.

— Inutile de revenir là-dessus, maman. C'était normal...

Elle leva la main pour l'interrompre.

— Non. Rien n'a jamais été normal. Pas depuis que... le bébé est mort. Elle me manquait, chaque minute de chaque jour. Elle me manque encore, à la fois la petite fille et la jeune femme qu'elle serait devenue.

— Ça a dû être terrible.

— Tu comprends, j'ai grandi entre deux frères. Ma mère est morte quand j'avais cinq ans. Je ne rêvais que d'une chose : avoir une fille à mon tour pour pouvoir lui offrir tous les merveilleux moments entre mère et fille dont j'avais été privée.

Luke en eut le cœur serré. Il connaissait son histoire, bien sûr, sans jamais avoir deviné ce que cela pouvait signifier pour la petite Elena Calhoun.

Elena Brennan, aujourd'hui une vieille femme, se tourna vers lui, les mains serrées devant elle, les yeux baissés.

— J'étais heureuse quand j'ai été de nouveau enceinte. J'étais certaine que le bébé serait une fille.

Elle leva la tête et soutint son regard.

— C'est vrai aussi que j'ai été déçue en apprenant que j'avais un deuxième garçon. La naissance avait été… difficile, avec une anesthésie générale, une opération. Je ne pouvais plus avoir d'autre enfant. Seulement mes deux fils.

— Je suis désolé.

Elle hocha vaguement la tête, tout entière à son histoire.

— Ce qui s'est passé ensuite est plus compliqué. J'ai toujours fait mon devoir et assumé mes responsabilités. Je voulais être une bonne mère pour toi.

— Je ne vous ai pas facilité la tâche.

— C'est vrai.

Tout à coup, elle sembla rapetisser et vieillir sous les yeux de Luke. D'une voix rapide et plaintive, elle souffla :

— Chaque fois que tu t'endormais, j'avais peur. Je passais des heures debout près de ton berceau, à te regarder respirer. Je vivais dans l'angoisse que tu me… quittes à ton tour.

Elle semblait au bord des larmes.

— Je ne pouvais pas supporter cette angoisse perpétuelle. Je ne mangeais plus, je ne dormais plus. Je ne pouvais plus rien faire.

— Maman… murmura Luke, atterré.

— En fin de compte, j'ai décidé qu'il n'y avait qu'une solution. Si je me détournais de toi, je souffrirais moins à l'idée de te perdre. C'était si simple ! Je pouvais gérer le reste de ma vie sans difficulté, tant que je ne m'autorisais pas à… t'aimer.

Ils se regardèrent longuement sans rien dire. Enfin, Elena prit une profonde inspiration.

— Je ne peux pas changer le passé. Pas même transformer le présent d'un seul coup. Je te suis reconnaissante d'avoir été là pour Matt, hier. Et… et je vais m'efforcer de changer d'attitude. J'aimerais que nous soyons… amis.

— Moi aussi, j'aimerais, maman, murmura Luke en s'approchant un peu. Merci de m'avoir dit tout ça. Je me doute que ce n'était pas facile. Ça va aller mieux, maintenant, n'est-ce pas ?

— Je le crois, Lu… fils.

Elle le prit par les épaules, l'attira plus près et lui, et l'embrassa sur la joue.

Quand elle recula, elle avait retrouvé toute son assurance.

— Je ferais bien de me mettre à la recherche de ton père. C'est l'heure de son médicament.

Fourrant les mains dans ses poches, Luke la regarda se diriger vers la porte, digne et très droite comme à l'accoutumée. La main sur la poignée, elle se retourna vers lui.

— Je suppose que nous serons encore ici dimanche. Nous te verrons au déjeuner ?

Il lui lança un large sourire.

— J'y serai, maman. Merci.

262

***

— C'est horrible, dit Kristin dans un frisson. Il a vraiment passé la nuit là-dessous ? Une nuit d'ouragan !

— Il n'a pas renoncé un seul instant. Il voulait te retrouver, quoi qu'il arrive.

— Tu es vraiment guéri, n'est-ce pas ? murmura-t-elle.

Luke se sentait mieux que guéri : l'espoir brûlait en lui comme une grande flamme. Pourquoi le nier ?

— Je crois, oui.

— Je suis contente.

— Moi aussi, je suis content pour toi, dit-il en lui effleurant le menton du bout des doigts.

Matt et Sarah émergèrent de l'angle de la maison.

— Eh bien, au revoir, dit la jeune femme.

Elle s'arrêta devant l'arbre couché, et murmura :

— Quelle horreur !

— C'est terminé, lui dit Kristin en la serrant dans ses bras. Oh, je ne sais pas ce que j'aurais fait sans vous ! On s'appelle, d'accord ? On pourrait peut-être déjeuner ensemble, aller voir un film ?

— Ça me ferait plaisir...

Un peu timidement, elle sourit à son amie, et se tourna vers Matt.

— Prenez bien soin de vous.

— Promis. Merci d'avoir pris soin de ma famille.

Gravement, il se pencha pour poser un baiser sur sa joue. Elle se tourna vers Luke, sans le regarder en face.

— Toi aussi, Luke. Prends soin de toi.

Avec un dernier sourire à la ronde, elle quitta la maison. Luke la suivit sans un mot. Se glissant derrière son volant, elle se retourna vers lui avec un peu d'impatience ; elle aurait aimé partir plus simplement, sans qu'il se sentît obligé de dire quoi que ce fût.

— Je suis contente que tout semble s'arranger, dit-elle. Vous êtes en train de renouer des liens familiaux. Peut-être, si tu décides finalement de rester ici…

— Sarah Rose ?

Elle se tut, sans le regarder pour autant.

— Il faut qu'on parle, dit-il en posant sa main sur la sienne.

— Je… non, nous… Je veux dire…

— Il faut qu'on parle, répéta-t-il. Tout de suite, s'il te plaît.

— Non !

Il la vit rougir, retint sa main alors qu'elle cherchait à se dégager.

— Il me faut du temps, Luke. Il s'est passé tant de choses ; ma vie n'a plus de… Je dois y voir plus clair, prendre quelques décisions.

Elle leva ses grands yeux vers lui, et il eut l'impression de basculer dans leurs profondeurs.

— Je t'appelle, d'accord ? balbutia-t-elle.

Il ouvrit la bouche pour protester, s'interrompit, recula pour la laisser partir.

Avec un sourire forcé, elle démarra.

— J'attendrai ton appel, dit-il. Sarah ?

Quand elle se tourna vers lui, il avait un visage calme et confiant, et parlait avec une conviction absolue.

— N'oublie pas, Sarah Rose. Je t'attends.

18.

Les organismes fédéraux réagirent très vite pour réparer les dégâts provoqués par l'ouragan Daniel. Bientôt, les commerces du front de mer rouvrirent, les touristes revinrent, ainsi que les habitants des quartiers sinistrés — certains pour découvrir qu'ils n'avaient plus de foyer. Les parents Brennan furent parmi les plus chanceux : ils n'avaient plus ni terrasse ni piscine, mais leur maison était toujours debout.

Deux semaines passèrent, et Sarah ne téléphona pas. Luke ne tenta pas de la joindre. Cette fois, il lui laisserait le temps. Et puis, il voulait lui parler face à face, voir son regard quand il lui proposerait de bâtir une vie à deux. Il patienta donc.

En revanche, un autre de ses vœux se réalisa : le filet tendu pour attraper l'agresseur en série fonctionna. Un soir, il s'attaqua à une femme policier qui s'apprêtait à rejoindre sa jeep... Luke était de service quand l'appel leur parvint, et il arriva à temps pour lui passer les menottes. Il fut presque déçu de constater qu'il ne s'agissait pas de Chuck Sawyer.

— Ce sont des tueuses ! criait l'homme en se débattant comme un fou, tandis que deux collègues l'entraînaient vers une voiture de police. Toutes des tueuses ! Il faut les arrêter !

Perplexe, Luke interrogea son sergent du regard.

— On vient juste d'interroger l'ordinateur, répondit celui-ci. La femme et les trois gosses de ce type ont été tués dans un accident il y six a mois. La responsable de la collision conduisait une jeep couleur olive. Il a dû décider qu'il devait prendre leurs clés à toutes les conductrices de jeeps vertes, pour protéger la population...

La rage qu'il ressentait contre l'agresseur de Sarah s'évapora d'un coup.

— J'espère qu'ils pourront faire quelque chose pour lui, marmonna-t-il.

— Moi aussi, dit le sergent en suivant la voiture des yeux.

Lentement, il roula vers la plage. Sans qu'il sût pourquoi, le fait que le magasin de photos eût été détruit par l'ouragan balayait toutes ses certitudes. Et si, en fin de compte, Sarah était partie sans rien dire ? Et si elle se sentait incapable de le revoir, même pour lui dire adieu ? Les lèvres pincées, il roula très vite jusqu'à son immeuble. La jeep n'était pas sur le parking. Que pouvait-il faire de plus ? Longtemps, il resta accroché à son volant, anéanti. Puis le flic en lui trouva l'étape suivante : se renseigner auprès de la gérante de l'immeuble. Quinze minutes plus tard, grâce à une utilisation peu réglementaire de son insigne de policier, il apprenait que Sarah Randolph n'avait annoncé son départ à personne et qu'elle n'avait pas mis son appartement en location. Bon, elle n'était pas partie... mais avait-elle le projet de le revoir bientôt ?

Il se mit à marcher dans la rue. C'était l'heure du dîner. Les foules de touristes avaient disparu dans les restaurants ; la marée basse révélait une immense étendue de sable. Il marcha vers le sud, laissant derrière lui les cafés et les forains, cherchant un peu de silence et de nature. Il cessa de voir les grands hôtels, resta seul avec l'océan et ses questions.

Quand il se retrouva entouré d'eau de toutes parts, il émergea enfin de ses pensées en se demandant où il avait échoué. Il lui fallut quelques secondes pour reconnaître le petit bras de mer encerclant la dune devant le Sandspur Country Club. L'endroit précis où il avait rencontré Sarah pour la première fois. Quelle ironie !

— Luke ?

Tournant la tête, il la vit marcher vers lui sur le sable, mince et gracieuse dans son maillot de bain cuivré — une sorte de paréo transparent autour des hanches — avec son grand chapeau de paille sur la tête. Sarah !

La première question qu'elle lui posa fut la dernière qu'il attendait :

— Tu as eu mon message ?

— Quel message ? demanda-t-il stupidement.

Elle avait changé, au cours de ces quelques jours. Son visage mince s'était un peu arrondi ; les ombres de ses yeux s'étaient transformées en lumière.

— J'ai laissé un message sur ton répondeur, cet après-midi. Pour te dire que je t'attendrais ici.

Ses yeux dorés s'élargirent, et elle murmura :

— Ce n'est pas pour ça que tu es venu ?

— Je ne suis pas rentré chez moi depuis midi.

— J'ai appelé vers 13 heures.

Ils restèrent debout côte à côte. Sarah contemplait le large, Luke l'intérieur des terres. Ils étaient l'un et l'autre incapables de dire un mot de plus.

Après un long moment, Luke finit par trouver une question intelligente :

— Que voulais-tu me dire ?

— Pourquoi es-tu venu ? demanda Sarah au même moment.

Ils se détendirent un peu, se sourirent.

— Toi d'abord, dit-il.

Elle faillit protester, puis rassembla son courage.

— J'étais sûre de dominer la situation, mais, maintenant que tu es là… Tu es passé au magasin ?

— Oui. Enfin, devant les ruines. Que s'est-il passé ?

— C'est compliqué. J'ai découvert que Chuck vendait des photos de Felix en prétendant qu'elles étaient de lui.

Elle parla des lettres et des tirages qui les accompagnaient.

— J'ai proposé de lui vendre ma part de l'affaire en échange des négatifs.

— Il a marché ?

— Il a dit qu'il marcherait, mais que les négatifs étaient dans son coffre à la banque et qu'il ne pouvait pas les prendre tout de suite. Puis l'ouragan est arrivé, et il a laissé le magasin sans prendre la moindre précaution. Tu as vu le résultat.

— Mais pourquoi ? Puisque l'affaire tout entière allait lui revenir…

— C'est une bonne question. Je suis allée à Georgetown la poser à sa mère, la sœur de Felix. A son avis, Chuck a l'intention de disparaître avec les négatifs.

— Et de continuer à faire passer ces photos pour les siennes ?

Elle poussa un petit soupir.

— J'ai porté plainte et contacté un avocat spécialisé. Il m'a recommandé de faire circuler l'information dans le milieu de la photo et dans les musées.

Dire qu'elle était là, tout près ! Il avait tellement envie de la toucher qu'il dut enfoncer ses mains dans ses poches.

— J'ai quand même une bonne nouvelle, dit-il. Nous avons attrapé ton agresseur.

— C'est vrai ? Qui est-ce ?

Il lui raconta toute l'histoire.

— Le pauvre ! murmura-t-elle. Il va aller en prison ?

— Plutôt à l'hôpital. J'espère que les médecins trouveront un moyen de l'aider.

— Oui.

Elle se remit à contempler le large. Il attendit en silence et, enfin, elle sembla secouer sa tristesse. Quand il revit son sourire, il éprouva un plaisir qui ressemblait curieusement à une souffrance.

— En fait de reconstruction, j'ai mes propres projets, dit-elle.

Une boucle folle vola sur sa joue. Luke faillit la repousser tendrement, mais il se l'interdit.

— Le contrat de copropriété nous donnait à tous deux le droit d'agir au nom de l'autre, expliqua Sarah. Puisqu'il est parti, je peux prendre des décisions. J'ai décidé de vendre le magasin.

— Tu vas être riche.

— Oui, pendant dix bonnes minutes. Dès que la vente sera signée, j'achèterai un autre magasin, près du Hard Rock Café. L'un des meilleurs emplacements de Myrtle Beach !

Luke sentit sa gorge se serrer.

— Un magasin pour vendre quoi ?

— Viens, je te montre.

Paralysé par un émerveillement de matin de Noël, comme si une chose qu'il désirait de tout son cœur se trouvait tout à coup à portée de sa main, il ne put la suivre tout de suite. Elle dut revenir sur ses pas et lui saisir le poignet pour l'entraîner.

— Viens !

Le contact de ses doigts sur sa peau le ramena à la vie. Il gravit la dune, et découvrit, au sommet, une couverture, deux chaises basses, un parasol.

— Tu veux un jus de fruits ? lui demanda-t-elle en signe de bienvenue.

Il se laissa tomber sur une chaise, et retira ses sandales. Le sable était chaud sous ses pieds. S'installant à son tour, elle tira à elle une sacoche de toile, et en sortit un mince dossier.

— Dis-moi ce que tu en penses.

Il ouvrit la chemise, et vit un grand portrait de Jenny, accroupie, en train d'examiner une chenille. Le blond cendré de ses cheveux, le rose de ses joues rondes, sa concentration absolue, cette position que prennent les toutes petites filles… C'était si criant de vérité qu'il eut le sentiment d'entrer lui-même dans la photo.

— Fantastique, murmura-t-il. Je peux avoir un exemplaire ?

— Elles sont toutes pour toi.

Il leva les yeux vers elle, puis passa à la deuxième photo. Elle représentait Erin, la tête renversée en arrière, presque horizontale sur sa balançoire. Sa vitalité, son bonheur éblouirent Luke ; il ne trouva pas de mots pour décrire ce qu'il ressentait.

Il ne connaissait pas l'enfant qui figurait sur la photo suivante : un petit garçon en équilibre sur sa planche de surf, résolu, les sourcils froncés, prêt à enfourcher la vague qui arrivait vers lui.

Toutes les photos représentaient des enfants, et chacun d'entre eux personnifiait l'enfance. Luke avait envie de les encadrer toutes, pour les voir chaque jour. Et Sarah, qui guettait ses réactions, penchée sur l'accoudoir de son siège… elle aussi, il voulait la voir chaque jour.

— Je ne sais pas quoi dire. Elles sont fantastiques...
Chacune de ces photos est fantastique.

La jeune femme hocha vigoureusement la tête, les yeux
lumineux.

— C'est revenu.

— C'est... ?

Un instant de perplexité, puis il crut comprendre :

— Tu veux dire : ton instinct de photographe ?

— Je l'ai retrouvé avec Erin et Jenny. Il fonctionne aussi
avec d'autres gosses. Je peux de nouveau prendre des photos
pleines de vitalité et de joie.

Les mains de Luke tremblaient un peu lorsqu'il referma
la chemise.

— Alors, tu vas ouvrir un studio spécialisé dans les
photos d'enfants ?

— Oui. Sans en faire une exclusivité. J'aimerais aussi
photographier des adultes. Je vendrai des pellicules, bien
entendu, et des appareils jetables. Je développerai les photos
de mes clients...

Jamais il ne lui avait vu ce visage heureux, ces joues roses,
ce sourire rayonnant. Elle lui coupait le souffle.

— Alors... tu restes ici ?

— Oui !

Le moment de vérité était arrivé. Seuls sur cette plage
déserte, ils auraient pu être les seuls habitants de la planète.
Elle demanda :

— Et toi... tu restes ?

— Ça dépend.

— De quoi ?

— De toi.

Sarah entendit ces mots qu'elle avait tant attendu dans un
éclair de terreur pure — ou peut-être de bonheur terrible,
bouleversant.

Luke se pencha en avant pour glisser le dossier dans sa sacoche. Quand il s'écarta, elle lui saisit la main, la serra entre les siennes, soutint le regard gris qu'il levait vers elle. Elle y lut une question, répondit par une autre :

— Et Kristin ?

Son front se plissa un instant, mais elle ne perçut aucune trace de regret dans sa voix quand il dit :

— Nous avons une petite fille ensemble : c'est un lien qui ne se défait pas. Mais, pour le reste...

Il la tira doucement à lui, et elle quitta sa chaise pour s'agenouiller sur la couverture.

— Mais ?

Du bout des doigts, il lui retira son chapeau, et le laissa tomber dans le sable.

— Kristin et moi, ça n'avait rien à voir avec... Elle a eu besoin d'aide, j'étais là, mais elle n'a jamais été amoureuse de moi.

Il referma tendrement les mains sur ses épaules, l'attirant encore plus près de lui.

— Et moi, je n'ai jamais été amoureux d'elle. J'étais très ému qu'on ait besoin de moi. J'adorais faire partie d'une famille qui fonctionnait... mais je ne l'ai jamais aimée comme on aime une femme qui nous éblouit, qui nous habite et nous complète...

Avec une passion retenue, il prit son visage entre ses mains.

— Je n'avais jamais aimé de cette façon, Sarah, avant de te rencontrer.

— Oh, Luke...

Elle se pencha vers lui, et il la happa dans ses bras.

— Je t'aime, Sarah. Je t'aime tellement !

Leur baiser fut sensuel et fiévreux. Quand elle redescendit sur terre, elle chuchota :

272

— Quelqu'un va nous voir !

— Quelle importance ?

Pourtant, après un dernier et long baiser, il la laissa s'échapper. En silence, ils replièrent les chaises, le parasol et la couverture. Quand tout fut rangé, Sarah se tourna vers le large.

— Je n'ai jamais envie de partir à cette heure-ci. C'est tellement beau !

Il vint juste derrière elle, et noua les bras autour de sa taille.

— Tu pourras revenir chaque soir de ta vie. Je t'accompagnerai, si tu veux.

Elle se raidit un peu.

— C'est... Tu parles de toute une vie ?

— Un mariage, c'est censé être pour toute la vie.

— Oh, Luke ! Je ne pensais pas que tu voudrais te marier.

— Je t'aime, alors je veux tout. Avec toi.

Elle hésita un instant, bouleversée, puis demanda timidement :

— Même des bébés ?

— Bien sûr que je veux des bébés !

Elle se détourna légèrement, et resta silencieuse si longtemps qu'il crut l'avoir heurtée. Inquiet, il chercha son regard, et vit son visage baigné de larmes.

— Sarah ! Oh, Sarah, si tu ne...

Elle posa les doigts sur ses lèvres.

— Chut... C'est juste... Je croyais que je n'aurais jamais... de bébés à moi.

— A nous, corrigea-t-il en embrassant sa main.

Elle ferma les yeux avec un sourire de bonheur.

— A nous, répéta-t-elle.

Puis elle sursauta, et leva vers lui de grands yeux inquiets.

— Mais… Erin et Jenny, qu'est-ce qu'elles vont dire ? Et tes parents ?

— Les filles s'adapteront : nous les aiderons, dit-il en l'attirant contre lui. Mes parents… là, nous aurons du travail, mais j'ai parlé avec ma mère, récemment, et je pense que nos rapports devraient s'adoucir un peu. Quand j'ai mentionné ton nom, maman a répondu que tu étais une jeune femme présentable.

Il eut un petit rire, et conclut :

— Bref, il y a de l'espoir. Au moins, Matt et Kristin viendront au mariage.

— Ton frère, ton ex-femme et tes filles qui sont aussi les leurs. Un entourage assez spécial pour la cérémonie !

Secouant la tête, elle se mit à rire à son tour.

— Pense aux photos ! dit-il. Celles-là raconteront toute une histoire !

Épilogue

Au moins, la robe d'Erin ne grattait pas. Sarah l'avait laissée choisir la couleur vert mousse et l'étoffe, qui flottait quand elle tournait sur elle-même. La robe de Jen était rose, et elle avait un chapeau. Erin ne voulait pas de chapeau, et Sarah avait dit qu'elle n'était pas obligée d'en porter un. En l'entendant, mamie Brennan avait pris son air sévère.

Erin était juste à côté de papa et Sarah quand ils se marièrent sous une arche de fleurs, dans un grand jardin rempli de sculptures. Sa préférée était celle d'un homme qui lisait son journal, mais Jenny aimait mieux le gros ours. Sarah les prit en photo, perchées sur les statues.

La fête après la cérémonie se passa aussi dans les jardins. Le soleil brillait, les nappes des tables claquaient au vent… le chapeau de Jenny s'envola.

Erin s'exerça à marcher en équilibre sur tous les petits murets entre les pelouses et les plates-bandes. C'était nouveau de s'amuser à un mariage.

Papa aussi s'amusait beaucoup. Depuis que Sarah avait dit qu'elle voulait bien l'épouser, il souriait souvent, et aujourd'hui encore plus que d'habitude. Il était très beau dans son costume. Papa Matt aussi était beau, et maman magnifique dans sa robe verte, plus sombre que celle d'Erin mais tout aussi douce.

Quant à Sarah… Sarah était comme une princesse avec ses boucles sur les épaules. Elle avait un voile sur la tête et une robe qui faisait penser aux contes de fées.

Maintenant, ils faisaient tous partie de la même famille, avec tout en double : les mamans, les papas, les grands-parents. Sarah avait dit qu'on pouvait l'appeler par son prénom, et c'était vraiment mieux, parce que « maman Sarah », ça faisait bête. Il faudrait demander à Matt si on pouvait faire la même chose avec lui.

— Erin ?

La fillette leva la tête, et Sarah la prit en photo.

— Tu fais la photographe à ton propre mariage ? demanda papa en s'approchant à son tour. J'aime ton sens de l'économie.

— Au moins, je suis sûre d'avoir les bons clichés. Erin, tu veux bien nous prendre en photo tous les deux ?

Erin ouvrit des yeux ronds.

— Moi ? Avec ton appareil ?

— Viens, je te montre.

Accroupie dans l'herbe, elle lui mit l'appareil dans les mains en disant :

— Tu regardes à travers cette fenêtre, tu essaies de nous placer bien au centre et… « clic ! » : tu as une photo.

Regardant par la petite fenêtre, Erin vit papa soulever Jenny dans ses bras, la jeter très haut en l'air. Retenant son souffle, elle appuya sur le bouton. Clic !

— Très bien !

Sarah reprit l'appareil et lui fit faire un bruit différent.

— J'avance la pellicule. Maintenant, on est prêts pour la suivante.

Elle courut se planter près de papa et Jenny.

— Souriez, tout le monde !

Erin retint de nouveau son souffle, plaça Jenny au centre de l'image, et prit la photo.

— C'est trop *cool* !

— Maintenant, il en faut une de tous les quatre ensemble, dit papa Matt qui venait de les rejoindre. Je vais la prendre.

— Fais attention ! lui dit Erin en lui tendant l'appareil. C'est très fragile.

Papa Matt aussi souriait plus souvent, depuis quelque temps. Pas autant que papa, mais c'était quelqu'un de plus sérieux. Tout le monde a le droit d'être différent.

Erin courut rejoindre les mariés. Papa Matt regarda dans l'objectif, puis il fit quelque chose avec les ronds qui étaient devant.

— Pas mal du tout ! Tout le monde est prêt ?

Il prit une photo, puis une autre. Papa souleva Erin dans ses bras.

— Qu'est-ce que tu en dis, l'Ourson. Tu es contente ?

Elle réfléchit un instant, puis expliqua :

— En gros, oui. Sauf que je n'aime pas le calcul à l'école.

Il éclata de rire, puis posa la même question à Jenny qui refusa de répondre.

— Et vous, madame Brennan ? demanda-t-il enfin en entourant Sarah de son bras libre.

Maintenant, ils étaient tous les quatre serrés dans un gros câlin général. Sarah ferma les yeux avec un énorme sourire.

— C'est le plus beau jour de toute ma vie. Et vous, monsieur Brennan ?

— Moui, pas mal, répondit papa en haussant les épaules.

Outrée, Erin lui lança un coup de poing dans l'épaule.

— Papa ! Sois poli !

Il se remit à rire.

— J'ai les bras pleins de bonheur. Les meilleures petites filles de tout l'univers, l'amie et l'amour de ma vie... Qu'est-ce que je pourrais demander de plus ?

Voilà qu'ils s'embrassaient de nouveau. Erin patienta aussi longtemps qu'elle put, puis finit tout de même par les interrompre.

— Une part de gâteau, papa ! s'écria-t-elle en se tortillant pour descendre. Voilà ce qui te manque : une part de gâteau de mariage. Et moi aussi, j'en veux une !

Chère lectrice,

Vous nous êtes fidèle depuis longtemps?
Vous venez de faire notre connaissance?

C'est pour votre plaisir que nous avons
imaginé un rendez-vous chaque mois
avec vos auteurs préférés, vos
AUTEURS VEDETTE dans les
collections Azur et Horizon.

Les AUTEURS VEDETTE vous
donneront rendez-vous pour de
nouveaux livres vedette.

Pour les reconnaître, cherchez
l'étoile... Elle vous guidera!

Éditions Harlequin

HARLEQUIN

LE FORUM DES LECTEURS ET LECTRICES

CHERS(ES) LECTEURS ET LECTRICES,

VOUS NOUS ETES FIDÈLES DEPUIS LONGTEMPS?

VOUS VENEZ DE FAIRE NOTRE CONNAISSANCE?

SI VOUS AVEZ DES COMMENTAIRES, DES CRITIQUES À FORMULER, DES SUGGESTIONS À OFFRIR, N'HÉSITEZ PAS… ÉCRIVEZ-NOUS À:

LES ENTERPRISES HARLEQUIN LTÉE.
498 RUE ODILE
FABREVILLE, LAVAL, QUÉBEC.
H7R 5X1

C'EST AVEC VOS PRÉCIEUX COMMENTAIRES QUE NOUS ALLONS POUVOIR MIEUX VOUS SERVIR.

DE PLUS, SI VOUS DÉSIREZ RECEVOIR UNE OU PLUSIEURS DE VOS SÉRIES HARLEQUIN PRÉFÉRÉE(S) À VOTRE DOMICILE, NE TARDEZ PAS À CONTACTER LE SERVICE D'ABONNEMENT; EN APPELANT AU (514) 875-4444 (RÉGION DE MONTRÉAL) OU 1-800-667-4444 (EXTÉRIEUR DE MONTRÉAL) OU TÉLÉCOPIEUR (514) 523-4444 OU COURRIER ELECTRONIQUE: AQCOURRIER@ABONNEMENT.QC.CA OU EN ÉCRIVANT À:

ABONNEMENT QUÉBEC
525 RUE LOUIS-PASTEUR
BOUCHERVILLE, QUÉBEC
J4B 8E7

MERCI, À L'AVANCE, DE VOTRE COOPÉRATION.

BONNE LECTURE.

HARLEQUIN.

VOTRE PASSEPORT POUR LE MONDE DE L'AMOUR.

ROUGE PASSION

De fiévreuses histoires d'amour sensuelles!

De provocantes histoires d'amour passionnées et romantiques qu'on lit d'une seule traite. Aventureuses, parfois humoristiques, et sensuelles, elles mettent en vedette des hommes et des femmes d'aujourd'hui.

ROUGE PASSION... quatre nouveaux titres chaque mois.

COLLECTION HORIZON

Des histoires d'amour romantiques qui vous mènent au bout du monde!

Découvrez la passion et les vives émotions qu'apportent à la Collection Horizon des auteurs de renommée internationale!

Captivantes, voire irrésistibles, ces histoires d'amour vous iront assurément droit au coeur.

Surveillez nos quatre nouveaux titres chaque mois!

La COLLECTION AZUR

Offre une lecture rapide et

- ☑ stimulante
- ☑ poignante
- ☑ exotique
- ☑ contemporaine
- ☑ romantique
- ☑ passionnée
- ☑ sensationnelle!

COLLECTION AZUR … des histoires
d'amour traditionnelles qui vous
mènent au bout du monde!
Six nouveaux titres chaque mois.

L'ASTROLOGIE EN DIRECT
TOUT AU LONG
DE L'ANNÉE.

(France métropolitaine uniquement)
Par téléphone 08.36.68.41.01
0,34 € la minute (Serveur SCESI).

Composé et édité
PAR LES ÉDITIONS HARLEQUIN
Achevé d'imprimer en août 2003

BUSSIÈRE
GROUPE CPI

à Saint-Amand-Montrond (Cher)
Dépôt légal : septembre 2003
N° d'imprimeur : 34163 — N° d'éditeur : 10077

Imprimé en France